NAAMAH'S BLESSING

Also by Jacqueline Carey from Gollancz:

Naamah's Kiss
Naamah's Curse

JACQUELINE CAREY

NAAMAH'S BLESSING

GOLLANCZ

LONDON

The right of Jacqueline Carey to be identified as the author
of this work has been asserted by her in accordance with the
Copyright, Designs and Patents Act 1988.

First published in Great Britain in 2011 by
Gollancz
An imprint of the Orion Publishing Group
Orion House, 5 Upper St Martin's Lane,
London WC2H 9EA
An Hachette UK Company

A CIP catalogue record for this book
is available from the British Library

ISBN 978 0 575 09364 5 (Cased)
ISBN 978 0 575 09366 9 (Trade Paperback)

1 3 5 7 9 10 8 6 4 2

Printed and bound in the UK by
CPI Mackays, Chatham, Kent

The Orion Publishing Group's policy is to use papers
that are natural, renewable and recyclable products and
made from wood grown in sustainable forests. The logging
and manufacturing processes are expected to conform to
the environmental regulations of the country of origin.

www.jacquelinecarey.com
www.orionbooks.co.uk

NUHUATL
EMPIRE

• Tenochtitlan
•Orgullo del Sol

TAWANTINSUYO

• Vilcabamba

•Qusqu

ONE

Unable to sleep, I stood in the stern of the ship, watching the past fall farther behind me. The moon was bright and full, turning the ship's wake into a wide, silvery path on the dark water behind us. A handful of seagulls winged across the night sky, following us, their presence lending credence to the captain's claim that we would make port in Marsilikos on the morrow.

A thousand thoughts and memories crowded my mind.

I tried to still them as Master Lo Feng had taught me, breathing the Five Styles and emptying my mind.

Tonight, it didn't work.

Four years. By my best guess, that was how long it had been since I stepped onto a Ch'in greatship in the harbor of Marsilikos, and sailed off in pursuit of my everlasting destiny.

Now that same destiny was leading me back to Terre d'Ange, land of my father's birth, where my patron-goddess Naamah held sway, worshipped as one of Blessed Elua's Companions.

Naamah, goddess of desire; the bright lady. And Anael the Good Steward, the man with the seedling cupped in his hand, who had given me a gift for coaxing plants to grow.

The thought prompted a memory of marigolds exploding from the earth in a field in Bhaktipur, a riot of orange, saffron, and yellow, blooming in glorious profusion, all out of season. That, and the look of wonder on the Rani Amrita's lovely face.

It made me smile wistfully. Bhaktipur was far, far behind me now. So were Amrita and her clever son, Ravindra, and the *tulku* Laysa, one of the reborn Enlightened Ones, who had told me I had oceans yet to cross.

So much lay behind me.

Villains and heroes, the kindness of ordinary folk—aye, and the pettiness and cruelty, too. Battles and intrigue, long, grueling journeys. Epic tales come to life, dire futures glimpsed and averted.

I leaned on the railing, remembering.

Beneath the moonlight, the ship sailed smoothly across the face of the sea. Its sounds had grown familiar; the creaking of timber and rope, the snap and flutter of the sail, the sleepy murmur of sailors on night-watch.

After a time, I sensed Bao's approach, the divided half of my *diadh-anam* drawing nearer to me.

Bao, my husband.

Despite the long months that had passed since we were wed, I wasn't accustomed to the word.

He came to stand beside me, gazing out at the silvery wake, his forearms braced on the railing and his shoulder brushing mine in a companionable manner. "Did you dream of her?" he asked in a low voice. "The White Queen?"

I shook my head. "Just restless."

"Ah. With Terre d'Ange so close, I thought maybe..."

"I did, too." I took a deep breath. "But no."

Bao nodded, and said nothing. In the silence, his *diadh-anam* entwined with mine, a sensation as intimate as a caress.

Until I was a woman grown, I had not fully understood that most folk do not carry their *diadh-anams* within them. Although I was half-D'Angeline, Naamah's child on my father's side, I was born in Alba to the folk of the Maghuin Dhonn, the Great Bear Herself, who planted a spark of Her soul in each of Her children, a flickering inner light to guide us through our lives.

Never, ever had I heard of a *diadh-anam* being divided—but mine had been.

It had restored Bao to life.

The deed lay behind us in distant Ch'in, Bao's homeland, farther in the receding past than Bhaktipur, where we had saved an empire and freed a dragon, where a sorcerer had slain Bao with a poisoned dart.

And Master Lo Feng, in his grief and sorrow, had used his arts and my magic to give his life and half my divine soul-spark to bring Bao back from the dead, inextricably linking our destinies.

Master Lo couldn't have known that it would send his stubborn magpie of an assistant, a reformed prince of thugs, into headlong flight from a destiny he hadn't chosen; nor that I would be compelled by my *diadh-anam* to follow him.

On the Tatar steppe at last we admitted to ourselves and each other that it was love, as well as Master Lo's art, that bound us together. But as soon as we began to truly explore our bond, we were betrayed—me into the hands of a Yeshuite fanatic in northern Vralia, wrapped in chains that stifled my very soul-spark, while Bao was sent on a fruitless quest in the opposite direction to rescue me.

Still, in the end, we had found one another again. In the valley kingdom of Bhaktipur, we were wed.

Of course, our union was complicated by the fact that on the eve of our wedding, I was visited in my dreams by the ghost of Jehanne de la Courcel, the impossibly beautiful and highly mercurial D'Angeline queen I had loved so very much; and that Jehanne had told me I had unfinished business with a man both of us had loved, and would need her aid before it was over.

I stole a glance at Bao. His face was calm in the moonlight. Shadowed eyes; high, wide cheekbones; full lips. Moonlight silvered his unruly shock of black hair, glinted on the gold hoops in his earlobes and the bands of iron reinforcing the bamboo staff he wore lashed across his back.

He caught me looking, and raised his brows. "Like what you see, huh?" he asked in a teasing tone.

I tugged on one ear-hoop hard enough to make him wince. "Mayhap."

Bao grinned. "You do."

I slid one hand around the back of his neck and kissed him. "I do."

He kissed me back, then pulled away, his expression turning serious. "It's going to be hard for you, Moirin. Coming home."

"Home." The word escaped me in a sigh. "Terre d'Ange isn't home, not really."

"Alba?"

"Aye." I gazed into the distance. "But…"

"Raphael de Mereliot." Bao finished my unspoken thought for me. His mouth twisted. "That idiot Lord Lion Mane."

I said nothing.

Raphael de Mereliot was the man that Jehanne and I had both loved—her favorite courtier, the man I had believed held my destiny for a time. Tall, tawny-haired Raphael de Mereliot with his healer's hands. I'd let him use me, use my small gift of magic to augment his healing arts.

Together we had saved lives, including my father's.

But I had let Raphael use me for other purposes, summoning fallen spirits filled with trickery. It had nearly killed me.

I had been very young, and very foolish.

Jehanne…

Ah, gods!

She had saved me from Raphael's ambition, saved me from *myself*, claiming me for her own. And I had let her, gladly. She'd had a bower filled with plants made for me, granting me a safe haven. She had made me her royal companion. She had trusted me to be there for her when she honored her promise to her husband, King Daniel de la Courcel, setting aside Raphael de Mereliot and praying to Eisheth to open the gates of her womb, that she might bear the King a child.

But I had left her.

And while I was on the far side of the world, pursuing my everlasting destiny, Jehanne had died in childbirth.

If I had been there, we could have saved her, Raphael and I.

I wept.

Bao's arms encircled me. He spoke no words of false comfort, only breathed the Breath of Ocean's Rolling Waves, drawn in through the nostrils into the pit of the belly, expelled through the mouth.

Slowly, slowly, as I had done so many times before, I matched my breathing to his, my thoughts growing calm.

The ship swayed and creaked beneath us. The past continued to draw farther and farther away, the shining trail of wake etched in the moonlight, ever fading behind us and drawn anew.

I wiped my eyes. "Thank you."

Bao nodded. "I am here, Moirin."

My breath caught in my throat. Those were words I had spoken to Jehanne many times—and they had always been true, until they were not. I turned in Bao's arms, studying his face, wondering if he knew. "You are, aren't you?"

A wry smile lingered on his lips. "Try getting rid of me."

"Oh…" I reached up to tweak his ear-hoops again, then tugged his head down for another kiss. "I'd rather not."

Bao laughed softly.

The ship sailed onward, rendering the past a series of memories, carrying us toward a new destiny.

I prayed that for once, the gods would be merciful.

But I doubted it.

TWO

Come daybreak, we saw the distant harbor.

Marsilikos.

The golden dome of the palace of the Lady of Marsilikos gleamed in the early autumn sunlight, a beacon to sailors everywhere. I'd been there once, and it wasn't a good memory. Raphael de Mereliot's sister Eleanore ruled Marsilikos, and she'd had me summoned to upbraid me for ruining her brother's reputation. I'd lost my temper and shouted at her, telling her some unpleasant truths about her brother.

I wasn't looking forward to a repeat encounter.

It was early afternoon when we made port. I hoped we would be able to disembark without fanfare. The ship was a Bhodistani trade-ship, our passage having been arranged by the Rani Amrita's family in the coastal city of Galanka. I'd thought Bao and I might slip out of the harbor unnoticed among the sailors and traders; but it was not to be. No sooner had we arrived on the quay, surrounded by our trunks carried by Captain Ramchandra's able sailors, than a horde of sharp-eyed, half-grown youths descended on us, shouting offers.

"Hey, messire, hey, messire! Best price porter, best guide! Best lodging for you and the noble lady!"

Bao caught my eye and grinned. "I told you not to wear so much jewelry."

I spared a glance at the bangles that adorned my wrist: the jade bangle the color of a reflecting pool that had been a gift from our

Ch'in princess Snow Tiger, the many gold bangles Amrita had insisted on gifting me. "True."

The young mercenaries pressed closer, clamoring. With one fluid motion, Bao whipped his bamboo staff loose over his back, twirling it before him so fast it was a blur that made the air sing.

Our would-be porters and guides yelped with alarm and delight, jumping backward and falling silent.

Bao's grin widened. "So!" He planted the butt of his staff on the quay with a resounding thud. "I am the best at what *I* do. Which of you is the best at what *you* do?"

A copper-haired youth with eyes almost as green as mine stepped forward without hesitating. "Me, messire!" He jerked his head, and four more youths fell in behind him. "You want the best of everything for you and the beautiful lady? Best guide, best lodging?" With a smile that managed to be at once sly, reverent, and wise beyond his years, he kissed his fingertips. "Best pleasure-houses for a noble foreign couple? Oh, yes! Let Leo be your guide."

I hid a smile of my own. Only in Terre d'Ange would a stripling street-lad offer to escort an apparently high-born couple to a pleasure-house within seconds of their arrival. "Lodging first," I said firmly. "Anyplace with a nice bathing-chamber."

The lad Leo blinked in surprise at my near-flawless D'Angeline accent. It wasn't my mother-tongue, but I'd learned to speak it at an early age, and Bao and I had been practicing on the ship to improve his fluency. Leo gave me an appraising look, seeing past the foreign bangles and jewelry, past the bright orange and gold-trimmed silks I wore wrapped and draped in the Bhodistani fashion, past my honey-colored skin and black hair, registering my half-D'Angeline features. His brow furrowed in confusion. "You speak awfully good for a foreigner, madame."

"She's not a foreigner," a new voice said behind us. "Not exactly."

I turned to see the harbor-master, a stern-faced fellow I vaguely recognized from four years ago.

He inclined his head to me. "Lady Moirin mac Fainche, I believe. Welcome home."

"Thank you, messire." I raised my brows at the coolness of his tone. "You do not come bearing another summons, I hope? I do not wish to trouble the Lady of Marsilikos with my presence."

"No." A shadow of sorrow crossed his features. "I fear the Duchese Eleanore de Mereliot succumbed to a grave illness these two years gone by."

"Oh!" My breath caught in my throat. "I'm sorry," I said sincerely. "Did Raphael inherit—" Belatedly, I remembered that Marsilikos was always ruled by a woman, and the question died on my lips.

The harbor-master shook his head. "No. Her Grace the Duchese Laurentine de Mereliot, a near kinswoman, rules in Marsilikos now."

Despite everything, my heart ached a little for Raphael. He had lost so very, very much in his lifetime. "I'm sorry," I repeated inadequately. "So he's...he's not here, is he?"

Beside me, Bao shifted slightly. He disliked Raphael de Mereliot, and for good reason, but I had to ask. Whatever the unfinished business between us was, I'd as soon see it swiftly concluded.

"You hadn't heard?" The harbor-master looked surprised for a moment. "No, but of course, you've been away, or you'd have known about the Lady. Forgive me, I wasn't thinking. After his sister's death, Lord Raphael joined the Dauphin's expedition to Terra Nova."

Ah, gods! My heart sank, and Bao gave me a stricken glance. The vast lands of Terra Nova, only discovered within my lifetime, lay on the far side of the world.

But the harbor-master was still speaking. "...expedition is due to return in the spring."

I breathed a sigh of relief. "Gods be thanked! That's good news, then."

"Indeed." The man looked uncomfortable. Based on my unfortunate history with House Mereliot, he might not have been kindly disposed to me, but he wasn't heartless. "Lady Moirin, Terre d'Ange has suffered other losses in your absence. Were you aware that Queen Jehanne...?" Like me earlier, he let the sentence dangle unfinished.

"Aye," I murmured. "That, I heard."

He straightened his shoulders. "Well, then. I would not be remiss in my duty to a descendant of House Courcel." He gestured at young Leo and his crew of street-lads, listening and gaping silently. "Shall I disperse this ragtag rabble for you? I can assign a cadre of guards to assist you with your needs."

I hesitated.

"Oh, that won't be necessary," Bao interjected, slinging one arm over Leo's shoulders, causing the lad's eyes to brighten. "We like... how do you say it? Ragtag rabble."

The harbor-master bowed formally. "As you wish."

After he took his leave, we said our thanks and farewells to Captain Ramchandra, who had escorted us safely to these shores. He bowed to us in the Bhodistani manner, his palms pressed together.

"It has been my very great honor!" he said. "I give thanks to you for restoring Kamadeva's diamond to its proper place."

Bao glanced sidelong at me, amused.

I cleared my throat. "It was our honor to do so."

We had done that, Bao and I. The Rani Amrita had charged us with the task of returning Kamadeva's diamond, a black jewel forged from the ashes of the Bhodistani god of desire, to the temple from which it had been stolen by Jagrati, a woman reckoned by her own people to be *untouchable*. I had carried it in a locked coffer for leagues upon leagues, fearful of its temptations.

All too well, I knew its power.

So did Bao, better than I did.

But we had carried it willingly for the sake of our lady Amrita; she who had withstood its allure when Jagrati the Spider Queen bore it; she who had had the strength to surrender it. In the temple where it had resided for many, many hundreds of years, we watched the priests break open the coffer, daring with trembling hands to transfer the diamond with its fiery heart filled with dark, shifting hues into the cupped and open hands of the god Shiva's effigy.

There, it resided—a blessing ready to be invoked by all who sought it, and not a weapon to be wielded by any one soul.

The bright lady had approved.

"Hey, lady!" young Leo called breathlessly, trotting beneath the weight of one of our trunks. "I know who you are! I remember!"

"Oh, you do, do you?" I glanced at him. He couldn't have been more than nine or ten when I'd left Terre d'Ange, but there was no underestimating the D'Angeline capacity for gossip.

"Oh, aye!" His face was flushed, but his eyes shone. "It was when the biggest ship in the world was in the harbor! D'ye remember, Michel?" he asked one of his companions. The other lad grunted in assent. "We went to look at it every day! From Ch'in, they said. You look like one of their sailors," he added to Bao.

"Was he uncommonly handsome?" Bao inquired cheerfully.

"No!" Leo's flush deepened. "I mean, not like one particular fellow. You look like all of them."

Bao raised his brows at me.

"Uncommonly handsome," I assured him.

"Anyway," Leo continued heedlessly, "I remember! We went to watch the ship set sail, too. It was like watching a floating palace set out to sea! And everyone said that half-breed"—he lowered his voice—"*bear-witch* who summoned demons and ruined Lord Raphael and seduced the Queen was being sent away on the ship! That was you, wasn't it?"

I sighed. "First of all, they were fallen spirits, not demons—"

He interrupted me. "What's the difference?"

"Ah . . . I'm not sure," I admitted. "At any rate, *I* didn't summon them, I just . . . helped."

"Those idiots couldn't have done a thing without you," Bao scoffed. "Your magic opened the doorway that let the demon through."

"You're not helping," I informed him.

"So you really *can* do magic?" one of the other lads asked, wide-eyed. He stumbled over a cobblestone, and would have dropped the trunk he was carrying if Bao hadn't caught it. "Can you turn into a *bear*?" He looked excited and horrified at the thought.

"No," I said gently. "The Maghuin Dhonn Herself took that gift away from us long before I was born. Do you know the story of Prince

Imriel?" All of them nodded; it was one of the great tales of Terre d'Ange. "Well, that's why She took it away. Now all my people have left is a small gift for magic meant to conceal and protect us."

"But it can be used for other things, too," Bao added. "Good and bad. Moirin was very foolish to use it to help summon demons, but it was not her idea. It was your Lord Raphael's idea. And she was not sent away. She left to accompany me and my wise mentor, Master Lo Feng, to save a princess and rescue a dragon in faraway Ch'in." He gave me an inquiring look. "Better?"

"Better," I agreed.

The lads looked skeptical. "There's no such thing as a dragon," Leo said.

"Oh, there is!" Bao grinned. "Maybe not here, but in Ch'in. We have ridden in one's claw as he soared through the sky and called the thunderstorms."

"Also, I did not *seduce* the Queen," I put in stubbornly. They blinked at me, having forgotten the initial topic in the talk of dragons and faraway lands. "Queen Jehanne," I reminded them. "Tell me, does her daughter thrive?"

Leo nodded vigorously. "Oh yes, madame! They call her the Little Pearl. She is much beloved in the City of Elua."

"And his majesty King Daniel?"

He hesitated. "It is said he is ... sad. He grieves deeply for the loss of the Queen, and he quarreled bitterly with the Dauphin when Prince Thierry insisted on leading an expedition to Terra Nova."

I fell silent, thinking and remembering while Leo pressed Bao for more talk of dragons and cursed princesses.

I hadn't known Daniel de la Courcel well, but I had liked him. Even before Jehanne's death, sorrow at the loss of his first wife, Prince Thierry's mother, had marked him. He was a grave and honorable man whose only fault, if it could be called one, was that he was overly cautious. While other countries had launched explorations into Terra Nova, and Thierry had pressed for the right to do the same, King Daniel had refused to allow it

Not until Jehanne conceived had Daniel relented, promising to let his firstborn son and heir sail off in pursuit of glory if a second child was born hale, securing the line of succession.

Knowing of him what I did, I could well imagine Daniel would have had a change of heart upon Jehanne's death. He had loved and lost two women; I did not think he had it in him to risk losing a third. He would have refused to remarry and he would have wanted to keep both his heirs close and safe.

But it seemed Thierry had held his father to his word, and now he was in Terra Nova—and Raphael with him.

"Moirin?" Bao's voice broke my reverie. "We have reached the inn. Do you find it acceptable, or do you wish to inspect the bathing-chamber?"

Meeting his gaze, I saw the sincere concern behind his jesting, and summoned a smile. "I'm sure it's fine."

He nodded. "I told you this homecoming would be hard."

"Aye." I took a deep breath. "So you did."

THREE

The inn was fine; more than fine.

An hour after our arrival, I sank into the depths of a generous marble tub, submerging my entire body. I scrubbed months' worth of shipboard grime from my skin and washed my salt-stiffened hair. Servants of the inn brought bucket after bucket of freshly heated water to replace the dirty water, until the chamber was filled with steam.

The third time they entered, Bao followed.

"Come to join me?" I inquired.

He flashed a grin at me. "Uh-huh. Think there's room?"

I smiled. "Aye, I do."

The attendants left, giggling as Bao began to strip off the embroidered Bhodistani tunic and breeches he wore, revealing his lean-muscled fighter's body. He paused, gazing at me with half-lidded eyes. "You look like something out of those stories sailors tell. What is the word in D'Angeline?"

I stirred the water. "Mermaid?"

"That's it." He climbed into the opposite end of the marble tub, dunking his whole head, coming up streaming water. "Soap?"

"Here." I handed the ball of soap to him and watched him wash, taking pleasure in the sight. The black zig-zag tattoos he had acquired in Kurugiri stood out in stark contrast against the brown skin of his corded forearms, marking the way up and down a secret passage through a mountainous labyrinth, at the top of which the Spider

Queen Jagrati and her husband the Falconer made their lair. Or at least they had, until we overthrew them with the help of the Rani Amrita and her army.

We had lived through a lot together, Bao and I.

"Do you ever think of her?" I asked him.

He followed my gaze, lifting one arm and letting it drop. "Jagrati? Sometimes, yes. I try not to. Why?"

I shrugged. Bao had spent long months under her thrall, bound by Kamadeva's diamond and opium. Believing me dead, he had been content to wallow in darkness. "I just wondered."

Bao leaned against the back of the tub. "Your presence keeps the memories away, Moirin," he said in a serious manner; and then his grin returned. "Leo asked me if I was a prince in my own land. I told him that I was, but I gave up my kingdom to be with you."

I raised my brows. "That is stretching the truth, my magpie."

"Only a little," he said in an unrepentant tone. "I'm sure the Great Khan would have gifted me with a territory of my own if I had remained wed to his daughter."

"It's possible," I admitted.

"Anyway, Leo thought it was a very admirable story." Bao nudged me with one foot. "Am I royalty now that I'm wed to you?"

"Does it matter?" I asked.

His dark eyes gleamed. "No, of course not. I only wondered if I was entitled to be called *Lord* Bao."

I shook my head. "I don't think so."

"Oh, well." Bao gave a good-natured shrug. "Still, pretty good for a bastard peasant-boy with no family name."

"I've no lands to my name, you know," I commented. "None of the Maghuin Dhonn do. We are allowed to dwell in the wild places of Alba in the terms of a sacred trust forged by Alais the Wise many years ago, but we do not own them. I have no title. Lady Moirin is just an honorific acknowledging my heritage."

"I am only teasing, Moirin." Bao leaned forward, tugging me so that I slid to straddle his waist. Water slopped over the edges of the tub. Intensity heated his gaze. "I love you, and I would choose to be with you whether in a slum or a cave or a palace. All right?"

I cupped his face and kissed him. "Aye."

His callused hands slid over my slippery skin, creating a glorious friction. I rubbed myself against him, feeling his arousal.

One of the inn's servants opened the door to the bathing-chamber, then closed it with a soft laugh.

Bao reached down into the bath-water, grasping his taut phallus, fitting the swollen head between my nether-lips. "You see?" His other hand slid around the nape of my neck, pulling me down for a kiss as he pushed himself into me. "For you, I will even learn to be more like a D'Angeline." His hips thrust upward. "Depraved and scandalous."

I drew a long, shuddering breath as he filled me, my fingers digging into his shoulders. "Indeed."

He smiled. "I have always been a clever student."

Laughing, the bright lady agreed.

In the morning, with young Leo's eager aid, we set about procuring passage overland to the City of Elua.

After the close quarters I had endured on the ship, I could not bear the thought of being cloistered in a carriage for days. Mercifully, Bao understood, knowing that there was a part of me that chafed at being confined, all the more so since the ordeal I had undergone in Vralia.

So it was that we bartered with a horse-trader that Leo assured us was reputable for a pair of saddle-horses and a pair of pack-horses. Bao watched with considerable amusement as I introduced myself to all four, cupping their velvety, whiskery muzzles and breathing into their nostrils, touching their placid equine thoughts with my own, leaning my brow against the bony plates of theirs.

"Does she really *talk* to them?" Leo asked in a loud whisper.

"I'm not sure," Bao whispered in reply.

One of the saddle-horses gave a dignified whicker. I patted his withers. "Well said, my friend."

The trader, testing the purity of our Bhodistani coinage bite by bite, widened his eyes

I smiled sweetly at him. "We will take them."

He coughed and nodded.

There was scant hope in outpacing gossip anywhere in the world, and least of all in Terre d'Ange. I did not try. Within a day of our arrival, word had gone out ahead of us that Moirin mac Fainche had returned to D'Angeline shores.

I hadn't expected otherwise. Still, it galled me a little. Only because my reputation had sunk so low in Marsilikos, where I was reckoned to have seduced Jehanne and ruined Raphael. And now, thanks to Bao's creative reinvention of history, it was rumored I had seduced a prince of faraway Ch'in to my own ends.

It made Bao laugh.

I scowled at him. "I did *not* seduce you! Stone and sea! You *chose* this!"

He shrugged with amusement. "No, Moirin. I was helpless before your charms. Haven't you heard?"

I eyed him. "I wish!"

"But I am," he said guilelessly, fluttering his lashes at me.

"I should have left you to Jagrati," I muttered.

At that, Bao caught me by the shoulders, giving me a shake. "Not that," he said fiercely. "Not ever! Don't say it, Moirin. Don't even think it."

I nodded. "Don't jest, then."

Bao took a deep breath. "I am sorry. It is only that my mistakes lie behind me, while yours..." He shrugged again. "They're still awaiting us, aren't they?"

Raphael...

Jehanne. Jehanne had not been a mistake. Never, ever would I believe it. She had saved me from myself.

"Aye," I said firmly. "And I will deal with them, husband of mine. *We* will deal with them, one by one as they come. Agreed?"

Bao nodded. "Agreed."

Two days after our arrival, we left the city of Marsilikos behind us.

I was not sorry to see the last of it; but if I thought my reputation would be restored as we grew closer to the City of Elua, I was mistaken.

Contrary to gossip in Marsilikos, I hadn't left Terre d'Ange in disgrace, but I *had* left under a cloud of scandal. There was a kernel of truth to Leo's accusation. Raphael de Mereliot and a group of scholars calling themselves the Circle of Shalomon had been involved in the arcane pursuit of summoning fallen spirits, rumored to possess the ability to bestow fabulous gifts on their summoners.

And I had helped them; at first because I foolishly believed myself in love with Raphael, and in the end, because he extracted a promise from me in exchange for helping to save my father's life.

With my aid, the Circle of Shalomon had succeeded—at least in summoning spirits.

Spirits who tricked them, over and over. The only gift ever bestowed on the members of the Circle of Shalomon was the ability to speak the language of ants. Still, they kept trying.

Focalor, a Grand Duke of the Fallen, was the last spirit summoned, the price for saving my father's life. He had found a flaw in the chains that bound him and broken free, attempting to take possession of Raphael's body and killing a woman in the process.

If it hadn't been for Bao and Master Lo coming to the rescue, Focalor would have succeeded. With their aid, I'd managed to force him back through the gateway my gift had opened.

The next day, I'd left the City of Elua, bound for Ch'in, called to destiny by my *diadh-anam*.

I remembered how Jehanne had insisted on giving me a royal escort to the gates of the City. She had made a production of bidding me farewell so that everyone would know I wasn't leaving in disgrace, had kissed me, and given me a bottle of her perfume to remember her by.

I had it still.

And if Jehanne had lived, it might have been enough. Despite whatever cloud of rumor hung over me when I departed, I would be returning in triumph to a royal favorite's welcome. But I had left, and Jehanne had died.

It was enough to make folks eye me with resentment and suspicion; and to be honest, I couldn't blame them for it. It might not be fair, but I blamed myself, too.

"You could disguise yourself," Bao suggested at the end of our second day on the road. "Dress like a respectable matron."

I stroked the edge of the green silk sari I wore, another gift from our lady Amrita. The border was a handspan deep with gold embroidery. "Do you think it would help?"

"No," he said honestly. "Not really. You couldn't look respectable if you tried, Moirin."

I sighed.

"Moirin." Bao pulled me close. "You are Emperor Zhu's jade-eyed witch, who freed a dragon and saved an empire. You are the Rani Amrita's *dakini*, who helped conquer Kurugiri and rescue Kamadeva's diamond." He kissed me, then looked serious. "Do not forget these things are true."

I ran my fingers through his thick, unruly hair. "Remind me again?"

He lowered his head to kiss me again. "Anytime, my disreputable wife."

Despite everything, it made me laugh.

FOUR

Some days later, we presented ourselves at the southern gate of the City of Elua.

"Lady Moirin mac Fainche." The guard said my name slowly, looking me up and down. His expression was unreadable. "So it's true. You have returned to the City of Elua, my lady?"

"I have." There was a chill in the autumn air. I fought the urge to grip my Bhaktipuran coat of colorful squares of padded silk more tightly closed against it, holding the guard's gaze instead.

His gaze slid sideways away from mine, settling on Bao. "And...?"

My peasant-boy turned Tatar prince sat on his horse with careless grace, easy in the saddle, his bamboo staff strapped across his back. Gold hoops glinted in his ears, and his tattooed forearms showed beneath the wide cuffs of his embroidered tunic. He looked very, very foreign in this setting. "Bao."

"Bao," the guard repeated in an uncertain tone. "You must be—"

"My husband," I supplied helpfully.

"Just... Bao?"

I glanced at Bao, who shrugged and raised his brows. "I have had other names," he admitted, affecting a look of innocent candor. "But that is the one my mother called me. Is it not good enough?"

It flustered the guard. "Of course, my lord...messire...Bao." Opening the gates, he waved us through. "Ah...my lord, my lady, be welcome in the City of Elua."

Behind the gleaming white walls surrounding the city, all was as I remembered it; and yet it was different, too.

I was different.

I had come to this place young and naïve, overwhelmed by its splendor; a child of the Maghuin Dhonn who had scarce known more than the cave and the wilderness in which I was raised. Now I was not so easily impressed. And yet I found myself longing for the familiar.

I wished Jehanne were here. And I missed my mother.

"Moirin?" Bao asked gently.

I wiped my eyes surreptitiously. "This way." I nudged my mount. "Let's see if my father's in residence."

Leading our pack-horses, we made our way to the Temple of Star-Crossed Lovers, drawing stares and murmurs all the way. A part of me wished I had taken Bao's suggestion and purchased attire for both of us that would let us blend more smoothly into a crowd.

But then I thought about the simple delight Amrita had taken in showering gifts on us. I remembered Bao's reminder and rode with my head held high.

Even so, I was profoundly grateful to see a familiar face when the priestess Noémie d'Etoile opened the temple door.

"Do you seek sanctuary—?" she began the traditional greeting, then halted, her breath catching in her throat. "Oh, child!" Noémie swept me into an unhesitating embrace. Beneath the crimson silk robes, her body was warm and comforting, and I returned her embrace gladly. She drew back, holding my shoulders and studying me with warm hazel eyes. "I'm so pleased the rumors were true! You've come a long, long way, haven't you?"

"Aye." I swallowed against the lump in my throat. Noémie was as gracious and lovely as ever, but visibly older. I'd been gone long enough that her hair had turned completely grey. "Is my father here, my lady?"

"Not at the temple, no," she said. "You'll find Brother Phanuel at the Palace more often than not these days."

I blinked. "The Palace?"

"You've not heard?" she asked. I shook my head. Noémie pursed her lips, glancing past me to take in the sight of Bao holding the reins of all four horses in the street behind me. "Is that your Ch'in prince?"

I smiled. "I suppose so."

Noémie was too polite to comment on the ambiguity of my answer. "He's quite the exotic young man, isn't he? Moirin... if you wish to go straightaway to the Palace to seek out your father, I will understand. But I would be pleased to offer you and your prince lodging here, and send word to Brother Phanuel."

"I would like that," I said honestly. "And...whatever you may have heard, my lady, Bao is here of his own will."

"I would never for an instant have thought otherwise." She smiled and gave me the kiss of greeting; and there was enough of a mother's tenderness in it that my eyes stung. "Welcome home, Moirin."

As soon as the young priest serving as an ostler had come to tend to our horses, Noémie extended the same greeting to Bao, kissing him warmly.

"Well met, your highness," she said to him. "In Naamah's name, be welcome here."

Bao cleared his throat. "Ah...I am not exactly a prince."

Her brows rose. "No?"

"No." He shook his head. "Not exactly."

Noémie regarded him with bemusement. "Well, you are welcome here nonetheless."

He bowed to her in the Ch'in manner, hand over fist. "For that, and for your kindness to Moirin, I am grateful."

Inside the temple, an air of quiet grace prevailed. Priests and priestesses in flowing robes of red silk glanced at us with gentle curiosity as they went about their duties, curiosity tempered by a long habit of patience.

This was Naamah's place, and all lovers were under her protection. I felt a tightness inside me begin to ease.

"Tell me, my lady," I said to Noémie over a light meal of honeycakes and sweetened tea. "How does it come to pass that my father spends his days at the Palace? I thought him more the wandering type."

"So he was." She rested her chin in her hand. "But since the Duc de Barthelme was appointed Lord Minister of the realm, he has wished to keep the companion of his youth close by him."

I frowned. "The Duc de Barthelme?"

"Rogier Courcel," she clarified. "Another descendant of House Courcel, and a close kinsman of the King. Your father served as his royal companion."

"Aye, I remember." I did, although it was a vague memory. I'd met the man but briefly, distracted by the woeful tangle of affairs in which I'd gotten myself enmeshed and the enormity of meeting my long-lost father. "What does it mean that he was appointed Lord Minister?"

Again, Noémie studied me. "You heard of Queen Jehanne's death?" she asked gently.

I nodded.

Her kind gaze was troubled. "Since that time, King Daniel has been . . . disengaged from the affairs of the realm. Recognizing his failings, he appointed his grace the Duc de Barthelme to administer to matters of importance."

"You don't think he should have done that, do you?" Bao asked.

Noémie d'Etoile looked mortified. "I did not say that!"

His lean-muscled shoulders rose and fell. "You didn't need to."

She was silent a moment. "I think it sets a dangerous precedent," she admitted at length. "But mayhap a necessary one. I will be glad when Prince Thierry returns from Terra Nova to help his father bear the burden of rule."

"Thought so," Bao confirmed, helping himself to another honey-cake. "At least this Duc has the sense to seek out Moirin's father's counsel. So that's good, huh?"

Noémie sighed. "It is."

Intrigue.

Politics.

To be sure, I had returned to Terre d'Ange. I sighed too, already feeling weary. "My lady," I said to Noémie. "Might I visit the temple proper, and pay my respects to the goddess and my ancestress?"

She stood with alacrity. "Of course, child!"

It was a powerful thing to see the image of my great-great-grandmother posing for the likeness of Naamah. The first time I had beheld it was the first time I'd felt myself truly connected to the rich history of Terre d'Ange. Her head was tilted to one side, regarding the pair of doves held nestled in her cupped hands. She looked so very, very serene.

I sank to my knees, gazing at her.

Bao sat cross-legged beside me. "So she's your ancestress, huh?"

"Aye." I smiled a little. "Well, it was my great-great-grandmother who posed for the effigy. She was a priestess of Naamah, and the first royal companion."

He cocked his head, contemplating the image. "Something in her face reminds me of the *tulku* Laysa. Not a likeness, but a calmness."

My smile turned rueful. "I suppose I'm not at all like her, am I?"

"Oh, I don't know," Bao said, surprising me. "You can be. You're different with women than you are with men."

"I am?"

"You hadn't noticed?" He looked amused. "Yes, Moirin. I heard the stories when you were with your Queen Jehanne. You soothed her temper. And although it was a different matter, I saw how you were with the princess in Ch'in. You were always patient and kind." Bao shrugged, and made an eloquent gesture with one hand. "With women, you are like water, flowing and yielding. With men..." He grinned, banging his fists together. "Sparks."

"Hmm." Thinking on it, I realized there was a measure of truth to Bao's words. "I don't intend it."

"It's not good or bad," Bao said philosophically. "It's who you are." He nudged me with one knee. "Anyway, I like sparks."

"Lucky for us both." When I leaned over to give him a fleeting kiss, he uncoiled smoothly and pulled me down atop him, startling a laugh from me. "You're becoming more D'Angeline than D'Angelines," I said breathlessly.

Bao slid one arm around my waist, cupped the back of my head, and kissed me. "I do not think your ancestress will mind, nor will Naamah," he said. "After all, she did bless our wedding."

I smiled at the memory of Naamah's blessing unfolding like a burst of golden warmth over the Rani's garden, the looks of wonder on the faces of all assembled. "So she did," I agreed, returning his kiss.

There was the sound of soft laughter.

Extricating myself from Bao's arms, I rose to see my father standing in the doorway, his green eyes sparkling with affection and mirth. Sunlight from the oculus above us gleamed on his long hair the color of oak-leaves and illuminated his crimson priest's robes until they glowed. His smile widened as a joyful cry escaped my lips, and I flung myself on him. "You're here!"

"I've been here all along, Moirin." My father held me close. "You're the one who's been gone, and I give thanks to Blessed Elua for your safe return." Like Noémie, he drew back to look at me. "Your mother will be so very, very glad."

My heart leapt into my throat. "You've had word from her? She's well?"

He nodded gravely. "Oh, yes. I sent word of your departure to Clunderry Castle as you asked. Since then, once or twice a year, we've exchanged letters."

I rubbed my eyes. "I wonder who writes them for her. Or reads them, for that matter."

"Aislinn mac Tiernan, I believe," my father said.

"Oh."

"Who is Aislinn mac Tiernan?" Bao inquired. "Another of your royal ladies?"

"Royal, but not mine." I gathered my scattered thoughts, smiling through my tears. "Father, this is Bao, my husband."

"Indeed, so I heard. Naamah's blessing on your union." My father executed a graceful Ch'in bow. "Master Lo Feng's apprentice, I believe?"

Bao blinked at him. "You remember?"

My father's eyes crinkled. "A day of breathing lessons, yes. And then you and your mentor spirited my daughter to the far side of the world. It is not the sort of thing one forgets."

Bao looked guilt-stricken. "Ah...we did not mean to take her from you." Without thinking, he touched his chest where the spark of our shared *diadh-anam* flickered deep inside. "Moirin was following her destiny."

My father laid one hand on Bao's shoulder. "I know," he said somberly. "And I am grateful to you for bringing her safely home." His gaze settled on me. "Did you find it?"

"I did." I took a deep breath. "Although...I do not think it is finished."

For a moment, I saw the weight of worry and years age my father's face; then he squared his shoulders, and it passed. "Will you be leaving again, then?"

Bao and I exchanged a glance. Since arriving in Terre d'Ange, neither of us had felt the imperative drive of destiny; only a sense that it was lying in wait.

"No," I said. "Not right away, I don't think. I don't know. I've unfinished business here, too." I rubbed my eyes again. "I'd like to see my mother, but 'tis late in the season to set out for Alba, isn't it?"

"It is," my father said in a gentle tone. "Already the Straits grow dangerous. You might send word through a swift courier, but I'd advise against travel."

"Spring," Bao said firmly. "After the expedition to Terra Nova returns, and that idiot Lord Lion Mane with it. You will finish your business with him, Moirin, and we will go to Alba."

"Aye?"

He gave a decisive nod. "I dream of a cave in the hollow hills, and a stone doorway. I dream of a bear unlike any mortal bear. We will go there."

My father glanced from one of us to the other. "You've stories to tell, haven't you?"

I thought of the long history that unfurled behind the shining wake of the ship that had brought us to these shores; of the bronze cannons of the Divine Thunder booming on the battlefield, our princess Snow Tiger dancing on the precipice of a cliff with an arrow in each hand, brave Tortoise blown into a smoking crater.

Of the dragon in flight, summoning the thunderstorms; of the vast blue sky unfolding above the Tatar steppe.

Of Vralia and chains, scrubbing the endless tiles of the floor of a Yeshuite temple. The Patriarch of Riva's creamy smile, and my sweet boy Aleksei's reluctant heroism, until he became a hero in truth.

Of Bao tossing and turning in sweat-soaked sheets in the Rani's palace, purging the poppy-sickness from every pore and orifice.

Of Jagrati seated in the throne-room of Kurugiri, the black fire of Kamadeva's diamond at her throat, glaring at me through the twilight while the Rani Amrita stood between us, her hands raised in a warding *mudra*.

"Oh yes, we've stories to tell," I murmured to my father. "And I daresay you'll not believe half of them."

He inclined his head to me. "I will try."

FIVE

To his everlasting credit, my father *did* try to believe and understand.

I could not blame him for struggling with it.

Even to me, who had lived through it, the tale Bao and I told
seemed like a child's fable.

"Enough," I said at length. "There will be time aplenty to tell the
whole of it. Tell me, Father, what passes here in Terre d'Ange? I was
surprised to learn you've become involved in politics."

He gave a graceful shrug and spread his hands. "Not involved, not
really. Rogier asked me to provide a shoulder on which to lean, a willing ear to listen without judgment. As I think you came to know, it
is one of the most important aspects of serving as a royal companion.
You would have done the same for Jehanne if she'd asked it."

I was silent.

"Ah, gods!" My father looked stricken. "Forgive me, Moirin. That
was uncommonly thoughtless of me."

"No, it's all right." I fidgeted with my bangles. "Do people...does
everyone blame me for her death?"

"Of course not!" His reply was swift. "Why would you even
think it?"

"Moirin blames herself," Bao murmured.

I shook my head. "It's not that simple. I couldn't have chosen otherwise. But I cannot escape the knowledge that Raphael and I could have saved her if I had stayed. And . . . folk look askance at me. They must know it, too."

My father steepled his fingers, touching them to his lips. "Moirin, I'll not pretend there wasn't a good deal of speculation surrounding your departure," he said slowly. "And there's bound to be the same surrounding your return. You're a child of the Maghuin Dhonn. That alone is cause for suspicion. It always was. Given the history of our people, it cannot be helped."

I looked away. "I know."

My mother's folk were wild and reclusive, and all that was known of them in Terre d'Ange was that the bear-witches of the Maghuin Dhonn possessed dire magic, even if it was no longer true.

"If you had stayed, it would be different," my father said gently. "Those who came to know you came to love you. And they will again. Give them time to acquaint themselves with you once more, time to forget tales of summoning demons, and remember that you were the one who coaxed Jehanne de la Courcel into going forty days without making a chambermaid weep." He smiled. "Do you suppose you could manage to avoid causing a scandal for a month or so?"

I gave a reluctant smile in reply. "I'll try." Taking a deep breath, I confronted another prospect I didn't relish. "I should pay my respects to King Daniel on the morrow, shouldn't I?"

He nodded. "It would be the proper thing to do."

The three of us talked long into the evening, and then my father departed to return to the Palace, with a promise that we might seek him out there on the morrow.

That night, I lay restless in bed. The chamber that Noémie had given us was small, but pleasant. It had a window that overlooked an inner courtyard, so I would be less inclined to the stifling sensation that sometimes overcame me in man-made spaces, and the bed-linens were soft and scented with lavender. It should have been a peaceful place for repose, but my mind was too full for sleep.

"What is it?" Bao asked drowsily. "Are you fretting over meeting the King? I thought you liked him."

"I do," I said. "I don't know if I can bear to face his grief."

Bao propped himself on one elbow. "His or yours?"

"Both," I admitted.

He stroked my cheek with his free hand. "Moirin, it is part of the price of being alive. Of loving."

"I know," I murmured. "It hurts, that's all."

"I know," he echoed, tugging me into the curve of his body and breathing the Breath of Ocean's Rolling Waves until I began to relax. "So tell me," he whispered against the back of my neck. "Who is Aislinn mac Tiernan if not one of your many royal ladies?"

It made me smile in the darkness, although there was sorrow in it. "Cillian's sister."

Bao went still. "He was your first love?"

Unseen, I nodded. "Aislinn was kind to me. She was the only one in her family who didn't blame me for Cillian's death."

He released his breath. "I had forgotten. No wonder it grieves you so to think to be blamed for Jehanne's."

"That, and being accused of having seduced and ensorceled her," I said. "Or you, or anyone. Stone and sea! The only time I *tried* to seduce someone, I failed miserably."

Bao stifled a yawn. "Your spineless Yeshuite boy?"

I rolled over in his arms. "Aleksei wasn't spineless."

His eyes glinted. "Oh, he was! But he ended up in your bed anyway, didn't he? So I suppose you succeeded after all."

"That was Naamah's blessing, and an altogether different matter," I informed him.

"If you say so."

"I do." It was a familiar argument between us. I realized that Bao had succeeded in breaking the endless chain of thought I'd been chasing, which had likely been his intention all along. For that, I kissed him. "Good night and thank you, my Tatar prince."

He gave me a sleepy smile. "You're welcome."

In the morning, aided by a night's sleep, I was calmer than I would have reckoned. My apprehension had settled into a deep place inside of me. This was going to be painful, but it was necessary.

Bao and I rode to the Palace, where the royal steward greeted us both with a sincere bow.

"Lady Moirin mac Fainche," he said in a respectful tone. "Messire...Bao, is it? Welcome. Brother Phanuel indicated that you would visit today."

"Is his majesty King Daniel receiving?" I inquired.

The steward hesitated. "His majesty is enjoying a concerto." He lowered his voice. "Music is one of the only things in which he yet takes pleasure. But I think, my lady, that he would wish to be interrupted by you."

My stomach tightened. "You're sure?"

He nodded. "I do believe so. Come, permit me to escort you and your...husband."

It felt strange, so strange, to walk the marbled halls of the Palace with its gilded columns and ornate frescos. We passed the Hall of Games, where Prince Thierry had taught me to play games of chance. I remembered Jehanne carelessly wagering a love-token that Raphael had given her as an apology for some offense, a choker of pale blue topaz that matched her eyes. She'd demonstrated her annoyance with him by putting it around her silken-haired lap-dog's neck as a collar, and then tossing it upon the gaming table as though it meant less than nothing to her.

She'd won her wager, though.

I remembered the cool touch of her fingertips on my face, her complicated expression, and her barbed warning. *You oughtn't play games you're bound to lose.*

I had; and I hadn't.

I'd never stood the least chance of winning Raphael de Mereliot's affections away from Jehanne. That, I'd come to understand at last. But never, ever had I imagined that I would win a portion of hers instead; that tempestuous Jehanne would take it upon herself to rescue me, that I would offer my loyalty to her, and she would come to love and trust me.

That I would find a place in her heart.

Tears blurred my eyes.

"Moirin?" Bao touched my arm.

I blinked away tears. "Memories."

He nodded, understanding.

After a discreet pause, the royal steward led us onward. We passed the great, winding staircase that led to the upper stories of the Palace, where Jehanne had ordered a suite filled with green, growing things, an enchanted bower made just for me.

I'd awoken there to find Bao keeping watch over me. I saw him glance at the staircase, remembering. Gods, we hadn't even *liked* one another then. It had been a long, long journey that had led me back to this place.

It was in that enchanted bower that Master Lo Feng had lectured me against letting my gift be used in unnatural ways—ways that had nonetheless saved lives, including my father's.

Ways that could have saved Jehanne's life.

I breathed the Breath of Earth's Pulse, grounding myself. I remembered Jehanne naked and shameless in my bower, the green shadows of ferns decorating her alabaster skin.

Her blue-grey eyes sparkling at me the first time she had visited during my convalescence. *Are you wondering if I mean to kiss you before I leave?*

I had laughed. *I am now.*

She had.

She had ducked beneath the immense fern fronds and kissed me; and she had stayed when I begged her to stay, winding my arms around her neck. She had stayed, and she had loved me. And she had known, all along, that I would not stay, could not stay. She had not asked, nor had she held any part of herself back from me.

And King Daniel . . . he had *known* her. Known and loved Jehanne in a way few folk could understand, even in Terre d'Ange where love was reckoned an art. Raphael de Mereliot was her storm; Daniel de la Courcel was her anchor.

"My lady?" The steward stood with his hand poised on the door to the Salon of Eisheth's Harp.

I nodded. "Aye."

Inclining his head, he opened the door. Music spilled into the hallway. I took one step beyond the threshold. A bow screeched across the strings of a violoncello, and the music went silent. In the arranged chairs, heads turned.

A tall figure rose.

"Moirin." Daniel de la Courcel, King of Terre d'Ange, said my name quietly. Our gazes locked.

Ah, gods! There was a world of sorrow in his, as much as I had feared and more. Lines of grief etched his handsome face.

A terrible memory surfaced behind his dark blue eyes, and I *saw*. I saw Jehanne on her death-bed, her fair skin deathly white from loss of blood—white as lilies, white as paper. I saw her pale lips move, shaping a word.

Desirée, her daughter's name.

Somewhere in the King's memory, Raphael was still trying, still plying his physician's arts, still trying to stanch the endless flow of blood that spilled from her and sopped the bed-linens with crimson, still raging, still exhorting Jehanne to stay with him, to be strong and live.

But Daniel had known it was already too late.

I saw the light in her sparkling eyes, her eyes like stars, flicker and die. I saw them stare blindly, her head going slack on her pillow, her perfect lips parted.

"I'm sorry!" I fell to my knees in the aisle, borne down by the weight of his grief; tear-blinded, limp as a cut-string puppet. I buried my face in my hands. "Oh, my lord! I'm so very, very sorry. I should have been there."

"No." His hands descended onto my shoulders, and his deep voice was firm. "Moirin, no."

I peered up at him between my fingers.

"You could not have known," Daniel said. "You loved her. It was enough."

"But it wasn't," I whispered. "It *wasn't*."

Gently, inexorably, he raised me to my feet. "It was." The King's arms enfolded me, and I clung to him. "Against all odds, you were one of the better things in her life. It was enough."

His words, and the tenderness with which he held me, broke open a dam of grief and guilt inside me. Only the King, who had loved Jehanne more than anyone, had the right to absolve me. I accepted it and wept unabashedly, my tears dampening the front of his velvet doublet.

When at last Daniel released me, there were tears on his cheeks, too. A soft sigh ran through the salon, and I could feel the mood of the D'Angeline people shift toward me. In one compassionate stroke, the King's absolution had changed me from a figure of suspicion to one of tragic romance.

A discreet attendant handed Daniel a silk kerchief. He blotted his tears, summoning the ghost of a weary smile. "A poor greeting, I fear. Come, cousin, introduce me to this husband you have brought from afar."

Stepping beside me, Bao bowed deeply in the Ch'in manner. "We have met, your majesty," he said. "Years ago. I served as Master Lo Feng's apprentice."

"Ah, yes." The King nodded. "A very wise man, your master. Does he prosper?" His tired smile turned wistful. "Did the Camaeline snowdrop bulbs I gave him survive the long journey?"

Bao hesitated. "I fear Master Lo is no longer with us."

King Daniel's faint smile vanished, the weight of grief returning to his features. "I am sorry to hear it."

"Your gift survived the journey, my lord," I said softly. "I kept them alive. And on the slope of White Jade Mountain, where no mortal foot had trod before, I planted three snowdrop bulbs. It is a sacred place. There, I have been promised that the snowdrops will thrive, until mayhap one day they will play a role in someone else's story."

The King's deep gaze settled on me. "Then you found the destiny your gods ordained for you?"

I nodded. "I did."

He exhaled a long breath. "Was it worth the cost?"

I thought of the future I had glimpsed on the battlefield where the bronze cannons of the Divine Thunder boomed, a future written in blood and fire, where there were no bear-witches or dragons. I thought of the thousands upon thousands more men who would have died had the dragon not called the rain and lightning, drowning the dreadful cannons.

I thought of Jehanne, too.

"How can one measure such a thing, my lord?" I asked. "All I can tell you is that if I had to make the choice over, knowing what would come to pass, in sorrow and grief, I would choose as I did."

Wordlessly, the King bent to kiss my brow, then straightened. "Would it please you to meet her?" he asked. "Jehanne's daughter?"

"Aye, my lord. Very much so."

The King's gaze drifted onto the distance. "I do not see her as often as I ought," he murmured, half to himself. "I should. But it is . . . painful." I waited in silence, not knowing what to say, until his gaze returned, and he beckoned to the royal steward. "Messire Lambert will escort you to the nursery. It is what Jehanne would have wished. Later, mayhap, we will talk."

I curtsied in the D'Angeline manner. "My thanks, my lord."

"Moirin." After I thought myself dismissed and had turned to follow the steward, the King's deep voice called me back. With considerable effort, he summoned another weary smile. "I am glad you are here."

My eyes stung, and my *diadh-anam* gave an unexpected flicker of agreement hinting at the presence of destiny's call. "So am I."

SIX

What do you suppose it means?" Bao asked as we followed Messire Lambert, the royal steward.

I didn't have to ask what he meant; Bao had felt the spark of our shared *diadh-anam* quicken as surely as I had. "I don't know."

"Do you ever?" he asked.

"Seldom precisely." I smiled ruefully. "The Maghuin Dhonn Herself may guide us in certain directions, but She leaves us to make our own choices. Especially the difficult ones."

"I don't see a choice here," Bao remarked. "Difficult or otherwise."

"Not yet," I agreed.

We climbed the wide, winding staircase to the second floor and followed the steward down the hall. Outside the door of a corner chamber, Messire Lambert hesitated. Beyond the door came the sound of women's voices raised in frantic pleading.

"Wait here, please," the steward said to us before knocking.

The door opened a crack, and a woman with a pretty, harried face peered out, her eyes widening at the sight of the steward in the livery of House Courcel. "Oh, messire! Tell me his majesty's not sent for her!"

"No, no," he assured her. "But his majesty sends visitors. Lady Moirin mac Fainche, and Messire . . . Bao."

Her eyes widened further, showing the whites. "Jehanne's *witch*?"

The steward cleared his throat. "As I said, Lady Moirin and her husband."

The young woman shuddered. "Elua have mercy! All right, all right, messire. Give us a moment."

She closed the door behind her. Sounds of a heated argument interspersed with urgent pleas ensued. Bao raised his brows at me. I shrugged in reply. The royal steward looked profoundly uncomfortable.

"Oh, let them in!" a second woman's voice said in frustration, loud enough to be heard clearly through the door. "If the Queen's witch can lay a spell on the child before she breaks her stubborn neck, so much the better!"

"Fine!"

The door was flung open wide. The young woman dropped a curtsy, her face flushed. "Welcome, my lady, my lord." She made a sweeping gesture. "Forgive us. Her young highness is as you find her."

I entered the nursery chamber, and caught my breath.

It was a pleasant, sunlit chamber with a canopied bed set into the near wall. Against the far wall stood an array of ornately painted cubes filled with cunningly made toys and dolls. Atop a dangerous perch on the highest cube sat a girl of some three years of age, kicking her heels and giggling.

Jehanne's daughter.

Belatedly, it struck me that that was what King Daniel had called her—Jehanne's daughter, as though she were not his own, too.

Gazing at her, I understood why. Desirée de la Courcel was her mother in miniature, a picture of gossamer beauty. A thin white shift adorned her small figure, leaving her arms and legs bare, skin so fair the pale blue tracery of her veins showed through it. Her pink lips formed a perfect bow. Her white-blonde hair curled in soft ringlets, haloing her head. Her eyes were Jehanne's eyes, an ethereal blue-grey.

And ah, gods! How they sparkled.

It wasn't just the resemblance; it was Jehanne's mercurial spirit that shone forth from her, delighting so shamelessly in her own misbehavior that one could not help but be charmed by it. At least, I couldn't.

My heart contracted sharply. Beside me, Bao chuckled.

Desirée stopped giggling and contemplated us.

I bowed to her in the Bhodistani fashion, my palms pressed together. "Well met, young highness."

"Who are you?" Her childish voice was high and clear.

I shifted my hands into a calming *mudra* that Amrita had taught me, steepling my middle fingers. "Come down and find out."

"No." Considering it, she shook her head. "I don't want to."

"Well, then, you will have to wonder," I said.

Behind us, the nursemaids whispered while the steward questioned them in a frantic hiss, wondering how the child had gotten up there in the first place. It seemed she had climbed the staggered blocks one by one, and refused to come down.

"She's uncommonly agile for her age!" the older nursemaid said in an aggrieved tone. "And uncommonly precocious!"

I ignored them.

Bao whistled through his teeth, inspecting the toys stored in the hollow cubes. "Look at this, Moirin," he said cheerfully, showing me a miniature carriage. "The doors open, and the wheels turn."

"That's *mine*!" Desirée said with a flash of temper.

He glanced up at her. "But you're not playing with it."

"It's *mine*!" Her perfect pink lips formed a pout. Bao shrugged and put the toy back.

"Your mother used to pout when she didn't get her way," I informed her. "But even she admitted that it was tiresome."

Her fair brows knit. "You knew my mother?"

I nodded. "Very well."

"I'm coming down," Desirée announced, beginning a precarious descent.

Both nursemaids rushed forward to aid her.

"Don't," I murmured under my breath. "She's Jehanne's daughter; she thrives on drama of her own creation. Don't encourage her. It's all right. Bao will catch her if she falls."

She didn't.

Once she reached the floor safely, her nursemaids descended on her, chastising her, hastening to get her clothed in a miniature satin gown stiff with elaborate beadwork. Desirée bore it with surprising patience, all the while keeping her eye on Bao and me.

"I am being good now," she said when her nursemaids had finished with her. "Now you have to tell me."

"Moirin." I knelt to sit on my heels opposite her. "That is my name, young highness."

She tilted her head. "And him?"

Bao threw a standing somersault, drawing startled squeals from the nursemaids, landing and settling to sit cross-legged in one fluid movement. "Bao."

"Bao?" Desirée mimicked his inflection exactly, capturing the rising and falling tone with a child's careless ease.

He grinned. "Uh-huh."

She studied him. "Why do your eyes look so funny?"

"Mine?" Bao touched the outer corners of his almond-shaped eyes. "I am from Ch'in, young highness. This is how we look. There, *you* would be funny-looking." Dragging down his underlids, he widened his eyes. "Round eyes!" Making a beak with forefinger and thumb, he touched his nose. "A big nose, like a bird." Stretching out one arm, he compared his tawny-brown skin to hers. "And so pale! In Ch'in they would ask, what happened? Did someone leave you in the bath too long, so all your color faded away?"

Desirée giggled. "That's silly!"

"I suppose it is," he agreed gravely.

I could sense the royal steward hovering behind us, and turned to him. "Please, do not wait on us, Messire Lambert. I know my way around the Palace. Tell his majesty I am at his disposal whenever he pleases. We'll be some while making her young highness' acquaintance. If that's all right?" I added with an inquiring glance at her nursemaids.

The younger glanced at the older, who shrugged. "After you coaxed her down from yon perch? Take all the time you like, my lady! I don't care if it *is* magic."

I smiled. "No magic. She's got her mother's temperament. I knew it well, once."

The royal steward departed with a relieved bow, and the younger nursemaid left to bid the princess' tutor to delay the morning's lesson.

"Do you like your tutor?" I asked the child. "What do you study together?"

"Manners and counting and singing," she answered obediently. "And I am learning my letters. Nurse says I am too little for letters, but mademoiselle says she could read whole books by the time she was four." She considered. "Most of the time, she is nice."

"Only most?"

Desirée looked down, plucking at the beaded hem of her gown. "Not when I am naughty." She looked back up at me, her expression achingly candid and woeful. "My mother was naughty, wasn't she?"

"Oh, dear heart!" I suppressed the urge to hug her, knowing I was far too much a stranger still. "Your mother was a great many things. Sometimes, yes, she was naughty. But she was kind and generous and brave, too."

"She was?"

"She was," Bao confirmed. "I did not know her so well as Moirin, but I know this is true."

"How?" Desirée demanded.

"When you are older, I will tell you the whole story," I said. "It is a story for grown-ups. But I will tell you this. I was there when your mother learned she was going to have a baby. You." I laid one hand on my belly. "And she was happy, so very happy. That is why she named you Desirée, so you would always know that she loved you and longed for you."

She looked down again. "Is my father coming to see me today?"

I glanced at the nurse, who shook her head. "Not today, your highness. You know the King is a very, very busy man."

"*You* told the steward my father could see you when he wanted." Desirée gave me an accusatory look.

I had no doubt that Jehanne had been as precocious as her daughter; I wondered if she'd been as observant, too. "So I did," I replied calmly. "Bao and I have come from very far away, and we have much news of foreign lands to tell him."

She shook her head, silver-gilt ringlets dancing. "He never wants to see me." Her fingers plucked at the beadwork of her gown again. Two seed pearls came loose and rolled across the floor, accompanied by an indrawn breath of dismay from her nurse. Desirée flashed her a look at once guilty and defiant. "I don't care! I don't like this gown anyway! It prickles!"

"It's all right, young highness." The nurse sounded resigned.

"It's because I'm naughty, isn't it?" Desirée patted the hem, trying to smooth it. "That's why he doesn't come."

It had the sound of a punishment she'd heard voiced many times before. I glanced at the nurse again, and saw her flush with guilt and resentment; and then at Bao, who shook his head.

"I am good at entertaining with tricks and jests, Moirin," he murmured. "This is beyond me."

Settling back onto my heels, I let my hands fall into a contemplative *mudra* and breathed slowly, thinking. "Your father loved your mother very, very much, young highness. He loved all the things that were good in her—and even the things that were naughty, too. Every day, he misses her, and it makes him sad. When he sees those things in you..." I touched my chest. "It makes his heart hurt more. It does not mean he doesn't love you."

It was a difficult concept for a child to grasp, and a heavy burden to bear. I watched her wrestle with it, praying that I'd not overstepped my bounds or overburdened the child.

At length, Desirée cocked her head. "Why do you do this?" she asked, doing her best to emulate the *mudra* I had taken. "Is it a game?"

"Ah." I smiled. "You might call it a thinking-game, young highness. Each shape you make with your hands is a thought, or...or a wish, or a prayer."

"What kind of prayer?"

I folded my hands together, steepling my fingers. "A prayer for peace." I shifted my hands, one above the other, forming an open circle. I could not achieve the gestures with the grace with which

Amrita had taught me, but I did my best. "For wisdom." I fanned my hands before me, interlocking my thumbs. "A prayer that the gods might speak clearly to me."

She looked interested. "It's a funny kind of game."

"It's a thinking-game," I said. "Not the kind you win or lose. It helps you to think and wish and pray better, that's all."

Her small fingers fumbled through an approximation of the poses I'd shown her. "Will you teach it to me?"

I inclined my head to her. "It would be my honor, young highness."

During a long winter on the Tatar steppe, where I had first begun to learn patience, I'd learned, too, that young children relished games of hands and words and thoughts. For another hour, with Bao's helpful aid, I taught the *mudras* I had learned from my lady Amrita to my lady Jehanne's daughter. The three of us sat cross-legged on the floor of the nursery, arranging our hands and fingers in contemplative poses and gravely discussing their meaning.

When I sensed that the elder nursemaid, whose name was Nathalie Simon, was growing restless at the interruption in the princess' daily routine, I rose to bid Desirée farewell.

"I fear your tutor has been kept waiting overlong, your highness," I said apologetically. "'Tis best Bao and I leave for now."

"Thank you for coming to see me." There was a formal, rote quality to the words; a seriousness of purpose that was the first I'd seen of Daniel de la Courcel in the child. "It was very nice."

"We'll come again if you like," Bao offered.

Her face brightened, blue-grey eyes sparkling to life. "*Will* you?"

"Uh-huh." He grinned at her and nudged me. "Won't we, Moirin?"

"We will," I confirmed. "I promise."

The senior nursemaid Nathalie ushered us into the hallway, closing the door behind us. "My lord, my lady...as you have seen, she's a precocious and complicated child." Her expression was stony. "By her standards, she behaved well enough for you today. If there was truly no magic in it, it is only because the two of you presented her with a novelty. Do not presume to understand the difficulties of raising her day in and day out. Do not presume to tell me my business."

"I don't," I murmured.

"I think you do." Nathalie's gaze was sharp. "I know who you are, and what you were to Queen Jehanne for a brief time." She lowered her voice. "Just because you shared her bed gives you no special insight into her daughter."

I held her hard gaze. "Does the gown prickle?"

The nursemaid blinked. "I beg your pardon?"

"It is a simple question," I said. "Children's skin is more tender than ours, especially when they are young. It seems to me that if the underside of the embroidery pricks her skin, it might be enough to goad her into misbehaving. Have you felt it?"

"She is a King's daughter, and a Princess of the Blood. Jewels are her birthright." Her expression hardened further, challenging me. "Name of Elua! Would you have the child dressed in rags?"

"No," I said. "Of course not. But have you felt it?"

Gritting her teeth, Desirée's senior nurse drew herself upright. "No, my lady, I have not. I will do so."

"Good," Bao said simply.

Her glare followed us down the hallway.

SEVEN

N ot long afterward, we met Rogier Courcel—the Duc de Barthelme, Lord Minister of the realm, and the companion of my father's youth.

"I trust we're meeting under happier circumstances, Lady Moirin." The smile he summoned was tired, but not so deeply tired as the King's. It held the weariness of a man overburdened by duty. "As I recall, you were rather distraught on the previous occasion."

I flushed, remembering.

The Duc de Barthelme and my father had ridden out to meet the royal hunting party I had accompanied, and I had been in a rare state of anguish, conflicted over my feelings for both Raphael and Jehanne, and feeling as though I'd not a friend in the world. Upon meeting my father for the first time, I'd flung myself into his arms and wept on his shoulder.

"Indeed, your grace," I murmured. "Forgive me my rudeness. I was young and foolish."

My father chuckled, and the Duc glanced sidelong at him. Rogier Courcel was a handsome fellow with thick, curling black hair, the strong brows of House Courcel, and grey-green eyes. I liked the easy manner he and my father had with each other, which spoke of their long familiarity. "You did manage to generate a considerable amount of scandal in a short time," he agreed. His gaze shifted to Bao. "I take it those days are behind you?"

Bao bowed. "I would not count on it, my lord."

The Duc's smile deepened. "Ah, well! The City of Elua can always use a measure of scandal. Moirin, Phanuel tells me you wish to send a message to your mother in Alba. I've a courier leaving on the morrow with a packet for the Cruarch, and he's likely to be the last of the season. Would you care to add a letter?"

"Very much so, your grace." I smiled back at him. "Thank you for your kindness."

He waved a dismissive hand. " 'Tis nothing. Please, call me Rogier. After all, we're near-kin."

"Rogier," I echoed.

"You're lodging at the Temple of Naamah in the Tsingani quarter?" he inquired. "If you wish, I'd be pleased to grant you and your husband a suite of rooms in the Palace."

I hesitated. "My thanks. But ... I think we will wait awhile. There are too many memories here, at least for me."

"Of course." Rogier shifted a stack of papers on his desk, which bore a considerable amount of clutter. "I do have a favor to ask in turn. If I understand rightly what Phanuel has told me, among other things, you were involved in an unpleasant business in Vralia which could have political repercussions for Terre d'Ange. I'd like to hear about it in detail."

"Certainly," I said. "His majesty also indicated he might wish to speak with me."

"About *Vralia*?" The Duc looked startled.

"Ah ... no." I frowned, realizing it was unlikely that King Daniel knew aught of my misadventures yet. "He did not say."

My father and Rogier Courcel exchanged a glance. The latter folded his hands on his desk. "Moirin, I have nothing but respect for my kinsman," he said quietly. "But I fear Daniel de la Courcel's days of taking an active hand in steering the realm are over. He has no heart for it. Until the Dauphin's return, that burden falls to me, and I have accepted it. Does that make you uncomfortable?"

"No, of course not," I protested; although in truth, I wasn't sure if it did.

"It should." Rogier smiled ruefully. "It makes *me* uncomfortable, and a number of the members of Parliament, too."

"You've done a fine job," my father murmured. "Parliament has no cause for concern."

The Duc raked a hand through his hair. "Even so, I will be grateful when Prince Thierry returns, and I can rejoin my wife and children in Barthelme."

"Why do they not join you here?" Bao inquired. "Surely, there is room."

"My wife, Claudine, maintains an…extensive…household," Rogier replied in a dry tone. "'Tis not worth the toil and effort of moving it for two seasons' time. And my boys are happy in Barthelme, where they can run wild."

My father chuckled again. "Your eldest might feel otherwise if he were sixteen and old enough to gain admission to the Night Court."

"He might," Rogier admitted. "But Tristan's two years shy of that gilded threshold."

"Speaking of children," I began. Both of them turned their attention to me, and I paused, trying to frame the matter politely. "In Marsilikos, we were told that the young princess Desirée was known as the Little Pearl, and was much beloved in the City of Elua. But Bao and I met with her this morning, and she seemed to me to be a rather lonely little thing."

"To say the least," Bao muttered.

"I'm sorry to hear it." Rogier Courcel paused, too. "In the spring, on the occasion of her highness' third natality, Daniel was persuaded to hold a procession throughout the City in celebration, so that the people might have a glimpse of young Desirée. It was a touching sight, the widowed King with his beautiful young daughter in his arms. To be sure, it charmed the populace."

My father nodded. "That was when they began calling her the Little Pearl." He gave me a quiet smile. "The City of Elua has not forgotten Jehanne de la Courcel nor the endless delight they took in gossiping about her. They took her daughter quickly to heart. But I fear it was the last time his majesty appeared in public with her."

"A pity," I said.

The Duc raised his brows. "Is the child being mistreated?"

"No," I said slowly. "I would not go so far as to say that. But it was my sense that she feels unloved."

Rogier sighed. "Your concern is admirable, Moirin. However, I must tread a fine path here. Daniel has ceded the duties of state to me during this interim. He has not abdicated the throne, nor has he given me authority over his private affairs." His mouth twisted. "It would be different if he had seen fit to appoint..." He let the thought go unfinished, shrugging. "I fear that if I were to intervene in the matter, Parliament would rebel and declare I had overstepped my authority."

"Mayhap you should speak to the King about your concerns," my father suggested.

I blinked. "Me? Ah, gods! I'd rather not intrude further on his grief."

He regarded me somberly. "You may be the only person in the world who can do so with impunity, Moirin. I heard about this morning's display."

"I'll think on it."

"Do," the Duc agreed, rising from his chair. "Now, if you'll forgive me, I've a great deal to do, and I believe you've a letter to write."

"Oh, yes." I rose, too. "Thank you again, my lord."

"Rogier," he repeated with a pleasant smile. "When I've more time, I'll ask you for the whole of your Vralian tale. Were you there, too?" he asked Bao.

Bao stretched out his arms, contemplating the zig-zag tattoos that marked them. "No," he said darkly. "I wish I had been. But no."

My father shuddered. "You'll want to hear the whole of their tale someday," he said to Rogier Courcel. "Trust me, it's one to daunt the poets."

The Lord Minister of the realm inclined his head toward us. "I look forward to it."

With that, we were dismissed.

Since there was no word from King Daniel, Bao and I returned to the Temple of Naamah. This journey through the streets of the City of Elua was markedly different. Word of the King's absolution and embrace of me had spread, and the gazes that followed us were more curious than suspicious. I felt all the more grateful for his generosity, and all the more uneasy at the notion of presuming to tell him how his daughter ought to be raised.

"Why?" Bao asked when I voiced my reluctance. "Don't you think he might be glad of it?"

"I don't know," I said. "He's just so terribly *sad*. I hate to add to his burden."

He shook his head. "If he's a man, he will bear it. You heard him this morning. He knows he's neglected the child. If you ask me, he was very nearly begging for your assistance."

"Do you think so?"

Bao gave me one of his rare, utterly sincere smiles. "Yes, Moirin. I do. I think the King recognizes that you have a very, very large heart, and that he hopes you will make a place for his little stormcloud of a daughter in it."

"You, too," I said. "You liked her, didn't you?"

"I did," he admitted.

At the temple, I begged paper, ink, and a pen of Noémie d'Etoile, who granted my request readily and showed me to the study, which was filled with texts dedicated to the arts of love and pleasure.

There, I did my best to concentrate on writing a letter to my mother, while Bao perused the shelves and cubbies. Although he could not yet read the western alphabet, many of the volumes were illustrated. There were at least a dozen different versions of the *Trois Milles Joies* alone.

"Have you ever read this?" Bao demanded.

"Aye, I have." With a twinge of sorrow, I remembered how Jehanne had sent a volume to me after our first liaison at Cereus House.

"Look at this." He showed me a print titled *The Wheel-Barrow*. "Have you ever tried it?"

"No."

He studied it from all angles. "We should."

"Bao, I'm writing to my *mother*!"

He flashed me an unapologetic grin. "All right, all right! Later, huh?"

I plucked the tome from his hands. "Later, yes."

In the end, after long hours of agonizing, I made my letter a simple one. I wrote that I had returned to Terre d'Ange well and safe. I wrote that I had many adventures to tell, and that the Maghuin Dhonn Herself had done right in sending Her child so very, very far away. I wrote that I hoped to return to Alba in the spring, after Prince Thierry's expedition came home.

I wrote that I loved her.

No matter how far I went, mother mine, I never ceased to think of you and miss you. I hope you are well, and Oengus and Mabon and all our kin, too.

I wept a bit.

Bao looked over my shoulder. "Did you tell her about me?"

"I did." I traced a line of text with my finger, reading the words aloud. "It may surprise you to learn I have wed. I will bring my husband, Bao, when I come. He is exceedingly insolent, boastful, and arrogant, and I love him very much. I think you will like him."

He pursed his lips. "You think so?"

I laughed through my tears. "I do."

I folded my letter carefully, placing it in a vellum envelope. I addressed it to my mother in care of the Lady of Clunderry, as she had bade me so very, very long ago. I lit a taper, and sealed it with a careful blot of wax, pressing the signet ring my mother had given me into the hot wax.

A young, obliging priest offered to carry it to the Palace for me.

Off it went.

Bao cocked his head at me, waiting.

"Oh, fine," I said. "Let's try it."

EIGHT

The Wheel-Barrow was a vigorous position, requiring a certain athleticism on the part of both participants. I wasn't sure if I cared to repeat it, but it was an interesting experiment, and it tired me enough so that I slept soundly and late.

I awoke to find that the King's absolution of me had further repercussions. Noémie d'Etoile presented Bao and me with a stack of engraved cards printed on thick, expensive paper.

"What are these?" I asked in bewilderment.

"Calling cards," Noémie said. "It's become quite the fashion in the past few years. These were left by all the people who came to pay you a visit this morning."

I flipped through the cards, glancing at the names engraved on them. "But I don't even know these people!"

She smiled. "Well, it seems they wish to make your acquaintance."

"Do I have to meet *all* of them?" I asked in dismay.

" 'Tis your choice," Noémie said. "No doubt most of them seek to curry favor since the King's embraced you and your father has a certain amount of influence with the Lord Minister. Are there none you would call a friend from your time here in the City before?"

"Prince Thierry was the closest thing to a friend I had here," I said absently. "And he's on the far side of the world."

"Didn't you bed him?" Bao commented.

"Only the once! And we made our peace with it. There's no one—" I turned over another card. "Oh."

"Someone you know?"

"Aye." I gazed at Lianne Tremaine's name, surrounded by a printed wreath of delicate blossoms. "She was the King's Poet once—the youngest ever appointed. And she was a member of the Circle of Shalomon."

"The demon-summoners?" Bao asked.

I nodded, glancing at Noémie. "You must have known."

"I did." Her expression remained serene. "People make mistakes, Moirin. Sometimes they learn from them. I believe Lianne Tremaine has done so. She's fallen far from her days of glory." Leaning over, she tapped the card. "Those are eglantine blossoms. Since the King dismissed her from her post, she's taken a position at Eglantine House."

It surprised me. "As a Servant of Naamah?"

"No, no." Noémie shook her head. "As a tutor to their young poets, although it's also true that many patrons commission her to write poems on their behalf. Whatever else may be true, her talent is undeniable."

Bao examined the card. "You should see her, Moirin."

"Why?" My memories of Lianne Tremaine weren't particularly fond ones.

He gave me one of his shrewd looks. "You and she, you made the same mistake."

"I didn't *want* to!" I protested.

Bao shrugged. "But you did it. Maybe you can learn from each other. Maybe she knows something about that idiot Lord Raphael that can help you figure out what unfinished business you have together."

"You have an irksome habit of being right," I observed. "My lady Noémie, was there any word from his majesty?"

"No," she said. "Were you expecting it?"

"I'm not sure what I expected," I admitted.

"Let's go call on the little princess," Bao suggested. "Afterward, you can decide what you want to do about this." He flicked Lianne Tremaine's card with one finger. "*And* the King."

"Do you think we should return so soon?" I asked.

He nodded. "We promised her. Soon never comes soon enough to a young child. And I think that one has been disappointed many, many times before. Let her see that we mean to keep our promise."

I smiled at him. "You're uncommonly sensitive when it comes to children, my bad boy. All right, then. Let's go."

Once again, Bao was right.

Upon presenting ourselves at the royal nursery, we were confronted by the stony-faced nursemaid Nathalie Simon. "You're interrupting her highness' morning lesson," she informed us.

"Do you mean to forbid us entry?" I inquired.

Bao favored her with one of his most charming smiles. "We'll be only a minute, my lady."

Grudgingly, she admitted us.

Desirée and her tutor were seated in undersized chairs in a sunlit corner of the chamber, heads bowed over a slate of sliding alphabet blocks. I paused, listening to the sound of her childish voice chanting the alphabet.

"Ah...Bay...Cey..."

"You've guests, young highness," Nathalie announced in a hard tone.

Desirée's silver-gilt head lifted, and a dazzling smile dawned on her face. "You came!"

"Of course!" Bao scoffed. "Did you think we wouldn't?" With careless grace, he crossed the room and sank to sit cross-legged beside her, peering at the slate of blocks. "So these are D'Angeline letters, huh? Maybe you can teach them to me."

Her fair brow furrowed. "Are you mocking?"

Bao shook his head. "No. In Ch'in, we write differently."

"Why?"

"I don't know," he admitted. "We just do."

Watching them, I couldn't help but smile. Desirée's tutor rose, her expression caught somewhere between respect and defiance.

"Lady Moirin, I believe?" She made a reluctant curtsy, bobbing her head. "I'd heard you'd taken an interest in the child."

"So I have," I said calmly.

"She's bright, very bright." Her chin rose. "I'll not apologize for teaching her beyond her years."

"Nor should you," I agreed. "What's your name?"

"Aimée Girard."

A thought came to me as I watched Desirée earnestly teaching the alphabet to Bao. "Do you suppose you might take on a second pupil, my lady?"

"You're serious?"

I nodded. "Bao, what do you think of the notion?"

He glanced up. "I think I would like to read the names written on these calling cards we are receiving." A grin crossed his face. "Not to mention what is written in the very interesting books in the temple's library."

Aimée Girard flushed. "Ah...well. You understand we will be reading only very, very simple texts?"

"Yes, of course." With one finger, Bao pushed blocks around on the slate. "Would you like me to study with you, your highness?"

Desirée's expression was dubious. "You're *not* mocking?"

"No." His voice was solemn. "I promise."

"Then I would like it very much," she said decisively. "Can Bao stay, mademoiselle?"

"Will you be on your best behavior if I say yes?" her tutor inquired. The child nodded vigorously. "Very well, then." She smiled. "Messire Bao, it seems we have an arrangement."

I smiled, too. "Then I will leave you to it, and return in a while."

Desirée rose and gave me an unexpected hug, her small arms tight around my legs. "Thank you for coming," she said in a muffled tone, loosing me as unexpectedly as she'd embraced me. "And for bringing Bao."

"Of course, dear heart." I bowed to her in the Bhodistani manner. With a giggle, she returned the bow, and then sat back down on her little chair, arranging her hands in a contemplative *mudra*. "See! I remember."

"So you do!" I clapped. "Very well done, your highness."

The nursemaid Nathalie escorted me to the door, every line of her body expressing disapproval. "Do you imagine his majesty will be pleased to hear you're teaching the child heathen prayers, and now setting strange foreigners to study with her?" she asked in a low voice.

"I imagine he'll be pleased to know his royal daughter is learning about other cultures," I said evenly. "Ancient, venerable cultures. And I would thank you not to speak of my husband as a strange foreigner."

"It's unsuitable!" Her face hardened. "He made a jest about reading texts from the Temple of Naamah in her very presence!"

"That was ill advised," I agreed. "But it was a jest the child is too young to grasp. I'll speak to him about it."

It didn't placate her. With a look of unmitigated disgust, she flung the nursery door open, startling a young page in House Courcel's blue livery, who was lounging in the hallway.

"Lady Moirin!" He sketched a hasty bow as I exited the nursery. "Forgive me, I wasn't expecting you so soon. His majesty wishes to see you."

"By all means," I agreed. Nathalie sniffed and closed the door firmly behind me. Eyeing the closed door, I hoped very much that the King's summons boded good rather than ill.

King Daniel de la Courcel was in the Hall of Portraits. Approaching, I would have expected to find him contemplating Jehanne's portrait, or the portrait of his first wife, Seraphine, whom he had also loved deeply. To my surprise, I was wrong. The page coughed discreetly to announce our arrival, and the King shifted slightly to acknowledge it. For several minutes, we waited in silence, not wishing to intrude on his reverie.

At length, he turned. "Thank you, Richard. You may go." The page bowed and took his leave. "Do you know who she is?" his majesty asked me, indicating the portrait of a beautiful dark-haired woman

with strong brows, candid blue eyes, and a mouth that promised firmness and compassion alike.

"Aye, my lord," I said. Prince Thierry had taken me to see the Hall
of Portraits on my first visit to the Palace. "Anielle de la Courcel. She
would have been your grandmother, yes?"

"Yes." Daniel touched the gilded frame with reverent fingers. "She
was the last great ruler Terre d'Ange has known. Did you know they
called her reign the Years of Joy?" His mouth twisted. "I wonder what
they will call *mine*."

I said nothing.

"You're no courtier to feed me smooth lies," he observed. "Nor a
false friend to give me words of false comfort. I appreciate it."

"Your majesty—"

King Daniel raised one hand to silence me. "I meant my words.
Moirin, there's a matter I wish to discuss with you in private. Come,
we'll speak in my study."

I inclined my head. "Of course, my lord."

As I followed him, I couldn't help but hesitate in front of Jehanne's
portrait, newly hung since last I had visited the Hall of Portraits. The
King paused, his expression pained. "That was done the first year of
our marriage," he said quietly. "She sat for it in the costume she wore
for the Longest Night."

I gazed at it without speaking. It was beautiful, of course—it was
Jehanne. The artist had done a good job of capturing the sparkle of
her eyes, the translucence of her skin. Her pale hair was piled in a coronet, and she wore a high collar of delicate silver filigree from which
diamonds spilled like droplets of ice, hundreds of scintillating points
of light. Her wicked little smile looked like it belonged to a woman
keeping a delightful secret—and knowing Jehanne, she probably was.

"It's very beautiful," I murmured.

Daniel turned away. "I know."

His study was as I remembered it, a warm, masculine room with
a great deal of polished wood. It was tidier, though. There were no

papers cluttering his gleaming desk, as there had been in the Lord Minister's study.

At his majesty's urging, I took one of the high-backed chairs before the fireplace. He stirred the coals with a poker. "You paid a second visit to the princess. I thought you would stay longer."

"She was at her studies," I said. "Bao stayed. Unless you disapprove, he will learn to read alongside her."

The King looked startled. "He will?"

"Unless you disapprove," I repeated. "It is not that he cannot *read*," I added. "The Ch'in use a very, very different form of writing." The memory of my Ch'in princess Snow Tiger tracing characters on my bare skin with the end of her braid and laughing at my struggles came to me, and I cleared my throat. "It is actually quite difficult to learn."

"Ah...yes." Daniel blinked. "I recall seeing Master Lo Feng's poetry. Lovely, but incomprehensible. Tell me, Moirin...how do you find my daughter?"

I met his gaze. "Much like her mother, my lord. Willful, with moods that switch like the wind. Charming, despite her temper. Clever and quick-witted."

"Is that all?"

His gaze was steady. I drew a deep breath. "No, my lord. I find her lonely and neglected."

"Ah."

"Desirée is a tempestuous child," I said. "But she *is* a child nonetheless. If you are asking, your majesty, I think she would be better served by nursemaids more inclined to patience and tolerance of a child's foibles." I frowned in thought. "I am not sure, yet, about her tutor. That is one of the reasons I suggested Bao stay and study with her. He will be able to provide a better gauge."

The King raised his brows. "Was that your true purpose in suggesting such an unorthodox arrangement, then?"

I shrugged. "It was a convenient confluence of purposes."

"I see."

"Do I overstep my bounds, my lord?" I asked him honestly.

"No more than I had hoped." Daniel de la Courcel poked at the fire a second time, then settled into the chair opposite me, gazing into the shifting embers in the grate. "Moirin, do you know of the Montrèvan Oath?"

I shook my head. "No, my lord."

He gave a faint smile. "It began when Anafiel Delaunay de Montrève...Have you heard of him?" I nodded. "Ah, good. When Anafiel Delaunay, for he was disinherited at the time, swore an oath to Rolande de la Courcel"—the King counted on his fingers—"my thrice-times great-grandfather...swore an oath to protect the interests of Rolande's infant daughter Ysandre."

"I know the story," I murmured.

He nodded. "That oath was sworn in secret. But it formed the basis for a new tradition begun by Sidonie and Imriel de la Courcel, who openly invited their kinsman Barquiel L'Envers to be the oath-sworn protector of their firstborn child."

"Your grandmother Anielle?"

"Even so." Daniel de la Courcel sighed. "And if I read the histories rightly, it was meant to acknowledge the healing of a rift between House Courcel and House L'Envers. Since then, it has become something of a political prize to be won."

"Oh?" I inquired.

The King leveled his gaze at me. "When Thierry was born, I appointed my kinsman Rogier Courcel, the Duc de Barthelme, to be the oath-sworn protector of my firstborn son. This charge, he accepted with grace and gratitude. He swore the Montrèvan Oath."

"Do you doubt him?" I asked softly.

"No." He leaned forward, hands braced on his knees. "Not his loyalty, no. I would never have appointed him Lord Minister if I did. But my daughter, Jehanne's daughter..." His fingers clenched, bunching the fabric of his breeches. His voice broke. "She should have an oath-sworn protector who *cares* for her happiness. Someone like you, Moirin."

I saw the picture he was painting.

"My lord!" I said in protest. "Oh, my lord! It is a great honor you offer, but I cannot promise to stay with her. My home lies in Alba, and I mean to return there in the spring, at least for a time. And…" I touched my chest. "There is the matter of my inconvenient destiny, which I do not think is finished with me. What if it calls me away from her side…as it did—as it did from her mother's?"

King Daniel de la Courcel's gaze was unwavering. "And yet it brought you back, too. I am not asking you to *stay* with her, Moirin. I am asking you to *love* her. Will you?"

I sighed. "How can I do otherwise?"

He leaned back in his chair. "Before you accept, hear me out in full. I fear this will not be a popular decision. You're a descendant of House Courcel, but you're a young woman without land or a title. You're only half-D'Angeline—"

"And the other half Maghuin Dhonn," I said wryly. "Believe me, my lord, I know the regard in which my mother's folk are held."

Daniel nodded. "Many will claim I chose you out of sentimental folly. It's likely to cause a scandal, and I daresay you've had your fill of those. That's why I make this offer in private. If you wish to decline, I will understand. No one else need ever know this conversation took place."

"Are you sure it's *not* sentimental folly?" I asked him.

"No." His expression was candid. "Not entirely. But sentimental folly lies at the heart of all that is good in Terre d'Ange."

"Love as thou wilt," I murmured.

"Yes." He fixed me with his unblinking gaze. "So, Moirin. Do you accept or decline?"

My *diadh-anam* flickered, but it gave no guidance, merely warned me that this was a decision of moment, and my own to make. "If I accept, does it grant me the authority to replace the head nursemaid?"

He gave me his faint smile. "And the tutor, too, if you deem her unsuitable."

It occurred to me that I should talk to Bao before making such a grave decision; and then I thought twice, and knew what he would say. For all his teasing ways, Bao had a hero's romantic heart. He wouldn't hesitate. "I accept."

The King inclined his head. "I will make the announcement, and see that a date is set for the ceremony."

NINE

While I waited for the princess' lesson to finish, I sought to distract myself in the Hall of Games, where I encountered a pair of young noblemen I had known years ago, members of Thierry's circle of friends.

"Lady Moirin!" Marc de Thibideau greeted me with ebullience. "I'd heard you returned. Surely that means my luck's changed."

I smiled. "I'd thought to find you gone with Prince Thierry. How is your leg? Does it trouble you?"

"Only when it's dire cold." He rubbed his thigh. It had been badly broken years ago, and I'd used my gift to help Raphael heal it. "But I'm still grateful to you, my lady. If not for you, I'd have lost the leg for sure."

The second nobleman slung an arm over Marc's shoulder. "And his father's still so shaken by nearly having a crippled son, he begged Marc not to join the expedition." He gave his friend a squeeze. "You're a good son, aren't you?"

Marc flushed. "Are you calling me a coward?"

"Not for a minute." Balthasar Shahrizai smiled lazily. "I'm praising your sense of filial duty. Me, I *am* an avowed coward. I never had the slightest interest in sailing with Thierry. Lady Moirin, welcome back. Come, join us at the dicing table. As I recall, you used to enjoy a friendly game of chance."

"I've no coin on me," I protested.

"You're wearing a queen's ransom in gold." He pointed at the bangles adorning my wrists. "Wager one of those."

I opened my mouth to decline, and then thought in an odd way it would be a fitting tribute to my memories of Jehanne. "All right, I will."

For the better part of an hour, I wagered at the dicing table, retaining possession of all my bangles and earning a small purse of coin in the bargain. Marc was an easy companion. Balthasar wasn't, but his barbed wit and the predatory light behind his eyes no longer disconcerted me as they had long ago. Gods knew, I'd faced worse.

All in all, it was a pleasant enough way to while away an hour. I realized I'd lost track of time when I sensed Bao's *diadh-anam* moving toward me, navigating the maze of the Palace to find me in the Hall of Games.

"Ah." Balthasar gazed intently across the chamber. "That must be the infamous Ch'in husband."

I glanced at Bao. "Infamous, is he?"

"Well, I confess myself confused," Balthasar said. "Is he an ensorceled prince, or a humble physician's assistant? I've heard different accounts."

I laughed. "Ask him yourself."

He looked under his lashes at me. "Oh, to be sure, I'll ask him *something*."

When Bao reached us, I made the introductions.

"I think...I think I remember you," Marc de Thibideau said uncertainly. "The day that Moirin healed my leg...you were there, you and that elderly Ch'in physician that Raphael de Mereliot thought of so highly." He gestured at the bamboo staff strapped across Bao's back. "You brought a cauldron of vile soup dangling from that thing, didn't you?"

"Bone soup," Bao agreed. "Very healthful."

Balthasar Shahrizai cocked his head, myriad blue-black braids rustling. "That's a *very* long staff. Do you know how to use it?"

Bao smiled serenely at him. "Do you want to find out?"

Balthasar laughed. "I might!"

"You do realize he's not talking about fighting?" I asked Bao.

"Yes, Moirin. I know." He gave me an amused sidelong look. "I did not think to find you here gambling. Did I not hear that his majesty the King sent for you?"

"He did." I fiddled with my bangles.

"Ah." Bao misread my unease. "We will speak of it later."

"No. No, no, it's all right." I took a deep breath, preparing to deliver the news. Everyone in the City of Elua would learn of it soon enough, and I had to start facing it somewhere. It might as well be here. "King Daniel offered me a very great honor," I said, striving for the dignity the announcement deserved. "He asked me to stand as the oath-sworn protector of his daughter, Desirée."

Bao's dark eyes gleamed. "You said yes, didn't you?"

"He did *what*?" Marc de Thibideau's voice cracked on the word. "Name of Elua! You can't be serious."

"Why ever not?" Balthasar inquired lightly.

Marc gave him a startled look. "Because...because...Gods, man!" He gestured at me. "Everything!"

"Ah, yes." Balthasar tapped one elegant forefinger against his lower lip. "Because one of her ancestors did somewhat terrible, once. Therefore, all of his descendants should be held in suspicion, eh?"

Once again, Marc flushed—more deeply this time. "We're not speaking of House Shahrizai, Balthasar!"

"No." The other settled a surprisingly grave gaze on me. "We are speaking of Moirin mac Fainche of the Maghuin Dhonn, whose folk have been reviled worse than House Shahrizai for the past hundred years and more. And yet, as I do recall, one of her first public acts in Terre d'Ange involved saving a man's life. Lord Luchese, was it not?" he asked me.

I nodded. "I believe so. I did not know the fellow."

"Then there was your leg, if I am not mistaken, Marc," Balthasar continued in a judicious tone. "And after that...oh! There was the hunting party. You weren't there for that, were you?"

"What hunting party?" Marc de Thibideau demanded.

Balthasar Shahrizai smiled, enjoying himself. "The one where Thierry was thrown from his horse and nearly bitten by a viper. So he would have been, if Moirin had not lifted her bow, the rustic ill-hewn bow we had all mocked, and pinned the deadly creature to earth with a single well-placed arrow." He mimed the act, hissing between his teeth. "Just like that!"

"I had not heard that story," Bao commented.

"Oh . . ." I shrugged. "Viper bites are not always fatal."

"Forgive me, my lady," Marc said to me. "I don't mean to insult you. It's just that the role is a significant one, meant to be awarded to a peer of the realm capable of wielding political influence at need."

"Moirin has the King's favor," Balthasar observed. "You don't consider *that* political influence?"

Their argument was beginning to draw a crowd, and the process of rumor and hearsay was already under way. I wished I'd kept my mouth shut.

"No." Marc de Thibideau lowered his voice. "No, I don't, and you know why! He's ceded the right to political power. He's a figurehead, nothing more."

Balthasar glanced around. "You don't want to have this conversation here, Marc."

"You're right, I don't." He swept his stake from the table, shoving the coins in a purse. "In fact, I wish I weren't having it at all." He shot me an apologetic look. "Again, it's nothing personal, Moirin. It's just that there's a great deal you don't understand about politics."

Balthasar watched him go. "He really should have disobeyed his father and sailed with Prince Thierry," he said in a mild tone. "He's been out of sorts ever since. Lady Moirin, Messire Bao, would you care to walk with me in the garden? I'd have a further word with you if you're willing."

Although I'd never been particularly fond of Balthasar Shahrizai, his unexpected support had surprised me. I glanced at Bao, who nodded. "Yes, of course."

It was chilly enough outdoors that no one else was taking in the Palace gardens. The gnarled branches of trees in the decorative orchard were barren of leaves, the trees dreaming of spring to come. Here and there were banks of late-blooming autumn flowers like chrysanthemums, but most of the flowerbeds were covered with mulch. Even the greensward looked listless. Only the evergreens were bright and lively, the brisk sap crackling in their veins; the tall cypresses standing like sentinels in a line, the pine trees shaped like umbrellas.

We strolled along a promenade dotted here and there with marble benches meant for enjoying the view.

"D'Angelines do love a scandal," Balthasar said presently. "And you do seem to enjoy providing them, Moirin."

"The King is aware that his choice will be controversial," I said. "He reckoned it worth the risk."

"As did you?"

"She's Jehanne's daughter," I said simply.

He blew on his fingers to warm them. "Beastly cold! So you and his majesty made a choice of the heart rather than the head."

"Is that not the D'Angeline way?" Bao inquired with deceptive innocence.

Balthasar gave him an astute glance. "Ideally, yes. In practice, love and politics often make bad bedfellows."

"There have been great political love-matches in the history of Terre d'Ange," I said.

He nodded. "So there have. And each and every one of them has been accompanied by controversy. If you would hear my counsel, I will tell you this. Many members of the Great Houses will be angered by this appointment, having hoped the honor would fall to one of their own."

"I am not a fool, my lord," I said dryly. "The Lord Minister hinted at as much yesterday."

"So you know your potential enemies," Balthasar said shrewdly. "But do you know who your potential allies are?"

I shook my head. "To be sure, I didn't expect you to be one."

At that, he laughed. "We Shahrizai often surprise! From time to time, it is in a good way."

"I like this fellow," Bao remarked to me.

"You would," I commented.

Balthasar smiled sideways at both of us. "The priesthoods," he said, ticking off the point on his fingers. "And by extension, the Servants of Naamah. They will always err on the side of love. If you gain *their* support, it will fire the imagination of the commonfolk, who will raise their voices on your behalf. Your father's a Priest of Naamah, that will help. Have you any ties to the Night Court?"

"No—" I remembered Lianne Tremaine's calling card. "Ah, well. Mayhap."

"Eglantine House," Bao supplied helpfully.

"The poetess?"

I nodded.

"Good, very good." Balthasar blew on his fingers again, then shivered and wrapped his fur-lined cloak around him. "Never underestimate the power of a poet, even a disgraced one. After all, Anafiel Delaunay's verses were banned once upon a time. Use whatever resources are available to you, Moirin."

"Why are you aiding me?" I asked him.

"I'm not sure," he said in a thoughtful manner. "Except that we do share one thing in common."

"Reviled ancestors?"

"Yes." He touched my cheek briefly with cold, cold fingertips. "I wish you luck, Moirin."

With that, he took his leave of us.

"So!" Bao put his arm over my shoulders and breathed the Breath of Embers Glowing, generating heat throughout his body. Fire had always been the element he favored most. I leaned in to his strength and warmth. "Eglantine House?"

"Aye," I agreed. "Eglantine House."

TEN

E glantine House.
It sat midway upon the slope of Mont Nuit, where the Thirteen Houses of the Court of Night-Blooming Flowers, commonly known as the Night Court, was situated. I had only ever visited one of them before—Cereus House, oldest of the thirteen, renowned for celebrating the ephemeral nature of beauty.

It was where Jehanne had been born and raised, trained to become the foremost courtesan of her age—and also where she had first seduced me. It was an elegant, gracious place.

Eglantine House was different, very different. There they celebrated artistic genius in all its forms, and even the architecture itself reflected the nature of the House. It was an exuberant mixture of styles, with soaring arches and cunningly wrought turrets, built with stone of subtly contrasting hues that somehow managed to achieve a pleasing and harmonious whole.

A handsome young adept with red-gold hair and a dancer's slim muscles opened the door. The sound of music spilled out, and somewhere a lone woman's voice rose above it in an exquisite cadence.

The adept took one look at us, and grinned. "Lady Moirin mac Fainche, and Messire . . . Bao, is it?"

I smiled at the welcome. "It is."

"Come in, come in!" He gave us both the kiss of greeting, ushering us inside. "Welcome to Eglantine House! How may we delight you today? Song? Poetry? Tumbling?"

"Tumbling?" Bao looked interested.

"Oh, yes!" The adept nodded enthusiastically. "The finest acrobats in Terre d'Ange are trained here. Are you an afficionado?"

"Ah..."

"Are you fond of it," I clarified for Bao's sake, adding to the young fellow, "Bao was trained as an acrobat."

"In Ch'in?" The adept widened his hazel eyes.

"It was a long time ago," Bao said in an offhand manner. "But we are not here to see tumbling. We are here to see the lady poetess."

"Oh." He seemed disappointed. "I will send for Mademoiselle Tremaine, of course." He beckoned, and two charming attendants who couldn't have been more than thirteen or fourteen hurried over. "Wine for our guests, and a summons to Mademoiselle Tremaine."

"I would not *mind* seeing the tumblers," Bao said to me. "Later, of course."

I shrugged. "Why not?"

"I can arrange a performance," the adept said eagerly. "Or, or... Messire Bao, if you are interested, mayhap we could learn from one another. No one has ever seen a tumbler from Ch'in." He sketched an apologetic bow. "I do not mean to presume, but it would be a pleasure. By the way, I am Antoine nó Eglantine, the Dowayne's second. And if there is anything I may offer you to enhance your visit, please do not hesitate to inquire."

"My thanks," I said to him.

Antoine bowed again, more extravagantly. "Of course, my lady!"

One of the little attendants returned with two glasses of wine on a silver tray, offering them with a pretty curtsy.

"Terre d'Ange is more pleasant than I remembered it," Bao remarked, sipping his wine.

"*You* are more pleasant, my magpie," I informed him. "It took me weeks to coax a smile from you. All it took Balthasar Shahrizai was one flirtatious comment."

Bao gave me a serene look. "Jealous?"

"A little," I admitted.

He laughed.

We sat on a cushioned bench in the foyer, drinking our wine and listening to the lovely songs coming from a nearby salon. It wasn't long before Lianne Tremaine appeared.

I stood without thinking.

She halted a few paces away, regarding me uncertainly. The last time we had seen each other, a woman had died—poor Claire Fourcay, enamored of Raphael de Mereliot. Focalor, Grand Duke of the Fallen, had inhaled her life's essence and breathed it into my lungs, forcing me to remain alive to keep the doorway between our world and the spirit world open.

And then he had very nearly taken possession of Raphael, before Bao and Master Lo swept into the chamber, holding the fallen spirit at bay with a whirling staff, fire-powder, and mirrors, allowing me to thrust Focalor back into his world and close the door I had opened.

Lianne Tremaine looked as I remembered her, with light brown hair, topaz eyes, and sharp, intelligent features that put me in mind of a fox. But the uncertainty in her gaze was new.

"I wasn't sure you'd see me," she said in a low voice.

"Neither was I."

She took a deep breath, her chest rising and falling. "May we speak in private?"

I nodded. "I think it's best."

After being formally introduced to Bao, she escorted us to her chamber, a generous room at the top of one of the turrets. It had windows that looked out over the whole of Mont Nuit, autumn sunlight streaming in to illuminate the space. The walls were lined with shelves and cubbyholes, holding a small fortune in books and scrolls.

"Please, sit," Lianne said. With a nervous gesture, she indicated a cozy arrangement of four upholstered chairs around a low table. "Shall I send for wine? Tea and pastries?"

I remembered that she had been the first formal visitor I had entertained in Terre d'Ange, when I had been a guest in Raphael's home. Raphael's maid had had to prompt me to offer the niceties of hospitality.

It seemed like a long, long time ago.

"Thank you, no," I said politely.

The former King's Poet twined her hands together before her. "Lady Moirin... words are my métier. I use them to puncture the inflated sensibilities of pompous souls who hold themselves in high regard. I use them to soothe the tender spirits of offended lovers. I use them to build edifices to raise up and celebrate the achievements of worthy heroes, past and present. I use them to charm, to cajole, to sway. But I confess, I do not know how to use my words to frame the apology you deserve."

"Maybe you should stop trying so hard to make it sound pretty and just say it," Bao suggested

A brief flare of irritation came and went in her eyes. "You're right. I should." Lianne Tremaine met my gaze. "I did wrong by you, Moirin, and I am sorry for it. Can you forgive me?"

"I'm not sure yet," I said honestly.

She sighed, and took her seat. "I cannot fault you for it. Those of us in the Circle of Shalomon, we knew what we were doing was dangerous. We knew Raphael was putting undue pressure on you to aid us. We saw the terrible toll that the summonings took on you. And yet we persisted."

"You were stupid," Bao said bluntly.

Lianne spread her hands. "I do not argue the point, Messire Bao. But to come so close to succeeding in our long quest... it was more heady and intoxicating than *joie* on the Longest Night. Compulsion gripped us like madness, ever driving us to make just one more attempt, just one more." She shook her head. "I do not seek to justify it, only to explain."

Bao was silent.

Having tended him through the ravages of opium-sickness, I suspected that he understood her explanation better than he wished. "You've made no further attempts?" I inquired.

"No." Her tone was adamant. "None. I swear it."

"Good."

She looked steadily at me. "Moirin, I confess it; I resented you. All of us did. It seemed unfair that we, who had studied for so long and worked so hard, were dependent on a backwoods Alban half-breed blessed with a gift of undeserved magic for our success."

I raised my brows at her.

"But I was wrong to do so," Lianne admitted. "I have a poet's trained memory. I have lived and relived those moments over a thousand times, and I have come to realize that the voice of protest you raised was a wise one. And to conclude that mayhap there are forms of wisdom that owe nothing to diligence, ambition, and intellect; and that mayhap the gods in their own wisdom bestow their gifts accordingly."

Her expression was sincere, and as close to humble as I suspected it ever came. I toyed with the bangles on one wrist, thinking. "I asked you why you did it, once. Do you remember what you told me?"

Lianne tilted her head, the sunlight making her golden-brown eyes glow. "Of course."

"You told me that there are always further thresholds to cross," I said slowly. "That despite the skills you already possessed, you sought words of such surpassing beauty that they would melt the hardest heart of stone."

She nodded. "Yes."

I looked northward. "I thought of those words in a country far, far away. In Vralia, where I was held captive in chains that bound my magic, by a man whose beliefs were as rigid as stone. I tried and tried to tell him truths his faith would not allow him to hear. I would have paid any price to succeed."

It piqued her poet's ear. "I would hear that story."

"It's a terrible story," Bao muttered. "I hate that story."

I ignored him. "I will tell it to you if you like; that, and others, too. And I will grant you my forgiveness . . . for a price."

Lianne Tremaine smiled wryly. "You're not exactly the naïve backwoods soul you were, are you?"

"His majesty Daniel de la Courcel means to appoint me his daughter Desirée's oath-sworn protector," I informed her.

Her lips parted. "That's...awkward."

"It is," I agreed. "It will be unpopular in certain circles. But I have accepted the offer for the child's sake."

There was a shrewd look on her face. "You want my aid."

"I do."

"It's a good story." Lianne drummed her fingertips against the arms of her chair. "A story that gets to the heart of all that Terre d'Ange holds sacred. A love-match, an unlikely love-match...no, not one. Two, three...ah, Elua! You're a descendant of Ysandre de la Courcel and Drustan mab Necthana. Alais the Wise and her Dalriadan harper-boy. Then there is your mother's liaison with a Priest of Naamah. It may not have been a love-match, but it was certainly unprecedented." There was compassion in her gaze as it settled on me. "And you and Jehanne de la Courcel—the courtesan queen and her unlikely companion." She paused. "You did love her, didn't you?"

My throat tightened. "Stone and sea! Aye, I did."

She met my gaze evenly. "I can work with this."

"*Will* you?" I asked.

"Yes." Lianne's expression was candid. "Have I not made myself clear, Moirin? I crossed the will of the gods, and I have paid a price for it. I do but seek to regain their favor."

"This is not only a means of redemption," Bao warned her. "A child's happiness is at stake. She should not suffer for the cause of politics."

She gave him a brisk nod. "That is exactly what I shall seek to ensure."

ELEVEN

It was a good meeting, and we parted on good terms, with a promise of more meetings to come. I wanted to speak further with her about the Circle of Shalomon, and most especially about Raphael de Mereliot in the aftermath of the fatal summoning and his near-possession by the spirit Focalor, but there was time. We had the long winter months ahead of us before the Dauphin's expedition returned in the spring, and the matter of the Montrèvan Oath was more pressing.

One of Eglantine House's young attendants was waiting for us at the foot of the stair.

"Lady Moirin, Messire Bao." She curtsied. "Messire Antoine asks if you would like to watch the tumblers at practice."

"I suspect we would," I said, glancing at Bao.

"We would," he confirmed.

She escorted us through the halls of Eglantine House. It seemed a joyful establishment, filled with music and laughter. We passed a salon where a group of patrons and adepts were engaged in a game of poetic word-play, each seeking to outdo the other in extending a clever metaphor.

"This *is* a . . . a place of whores, is it not?" Bao asked me in a low voice.

Not so low that the attendant did not hear him. "Oh yes, Messire Bao!" She glanced over her shoulder. "Like all of the Houses of the

Night Court, Eglantine House is dedicated to Naamah's Service. But we celebrate all the arts, not only the arts of pleasure."

"Forgive me," he said to her. "I did not mean to use an impolite term. I am still learning your tongue."

"You speak it very well, messire," she assured him.

Bao switched to the scholar's tongue of Shuntian. "Do they begin so young, Moirin? That one cannot be more than twelve."

"No." I replied in the same language. "Only as attendants. They are not allowed to take their vows until they are sixteen."

He looked relieved. "I am pleased to hear it."

"Were you thinking of the past?" I asked.

Bao nodded. "It has been a long time since I have seen tumblers perform. Just the thought stirs memories."

I touched his arm. "We don't have to do this."

"No." He shook his head. "It has been *too* long. And I am curious. I was very good once, you know."

"I know." I smiled. "I've seen it."

Bao scoffed. "You've seen me perform tricks to amuse children, Moirin. Not *art*."

"It is not the art you chose to pursue, my magpie," I said mildly.

"True," he admitted. "But I was good at it."

I did not doubt it, having never known Bao to boast in vain. At the age of three, his family had sold him to a travelling circus, where he trained and performed as an acrobat. At the age of thirteen, he decided he wanted to learn the art of stick-fighting instead. It was a matter of desire and pride—and there was a girl involved, too.

He had asked Brother Thunder, the troupe's best stick-fighter, to teach him. And Brother Thunder had agreed ... for a price.

I remembered Bao telling me about it on the greatship to Ch'in, naked in the bed we had just shared, his arms folded behind his head.

So I ask and he say, you be my peach-bottom boy, I teach you.

Bao had agreed.

He'd spent two years as Brother Thunder's reluctant catamite, learning to fight. At the end of two years, he defeated his mentor. The fellow's daughter, the girl in question, was angry at him for besting her father. She refused to honor her promise to run away with Bao.

So he ran away alone, all the way to Shuntian, where he fought his way to becoming the leader of an unscrupulous group of thugs—until a young lad came asking to be taught.

Bao had offered him the same bargain.

The boy had agreed.

And Bao had walked away from the bargain he had struck, walked away from the life he had built for himself. He had accepted an offer he had mocked only days before, and became Master Lo Feng's magpie, setting him on the wandering course across the world that had brought us together.

"Here we are!" our little attendant said cheerfully, opening the door onto the rear entrance of a theater. Beyond the door, one could hear the thuds and grunts and shouted comments of tumblers at practice.

"You're sure?" I asked.

"Yes, Moirin." Bao gave me an affectionate look. "I am sure, and I am grateful for your concern."

It was a vast space, filled with the various apparatuses of the tumblers' art. There were trapezes hung from the rafters, and a high rope stretched across the vaulted ceiling. The floor was covered with mats of coarse fabric stuffed with chaff, dotted here and there with springboards.

"Messire Bao!" Antoine nó Eglantine dropped from a hanging trapeze with a flip and a flourish. He bowed, his face flushed. "Lady Moirin! Congratulations. We heard the news."

"Already?" I asked in dismay.

"His majesty issued a proclamation at noon," he informed me.

"Ah."

There must have been a dozen lithe adepts at practice, swinging from the trapezes, flinging themselves into space and catching one another; springing from the boards to deliver intricate flips and somersaults, forming human pyramids, walking the high rope, toeing the line, and putting one careful foot in front of the next.

Antoine ran a hand through his sweat-dampened hair. "So, messire! What do you think?"

"They're very skilled," Bao said, watching them with a practiced eye.

"I am glad you think so." Antoine offered a polite bow. "Do you suppose you have aught to teach us? Exotic secrets from faraway Ch'in?"

"I might." He glanced around the stage, taking stock of the equipment and props. "I don't see any balancing poles."

"Gervaise is using one now," Antoine said with a bewildered look, nodding at an adept crossing the high rope, holding a supple staff before him to aid in keeping his balance.

Bao shook his head. "Not that kind. The kind you balance *on.*" He held his hands apart, then widened them. "So high to so high, with a small platform on one end."

The adept looked no less confused. "How does one use them?"

"I will try to show you." Bao unlashed his staff from across his back. "This is not right for it," he said. "Too high, no platform. And I have not done it for a long time. But I will try to show you what I mean." Planting the butt end of his staff at an angle, he grasped the top and vaulted into the air. How he did it, I couldn't say, but he managed to stop the vault at its apex.

The staff stood upright, wavering and bending. With careful precision, Bao kept his right hand atop it, extending his other limbs in a graceful pose in mid-air.

A soft murmur of interest ran through the theater.

After the space of a few heartbeats, he overbalanced and dropped back to the floor. "Like so. If you had a proper pole, you could do this." Setting down his staff, he went into a handstand, then assumed the same pose as before. From there, Bao levered himself to a horizontal position, still balancing on one hand.

The adepts applauded.

"It is to show strength and grace." He got to his feet, dusting chaff from his hands. "A slower kind of art, I think."

"I like it," Antoine said. "What other kinds of tumbling artistry do you not see practiced here, messire?"

Bao smiled at him. "I am not sure I should give away all my secrets for free."

The second of Eglantine House returned his smile. "Mayhap we might come to an . . . arrangement."

"Oh, indeed." Bao tilted his head. "I think the young princess Desirée would very much enjoy seeing tumblers. Mayhap Eglantine House's troupe could arrange a special performance in honor of the occasion the King announced today?"

Antoine raised his brows. "Thus implying our support?"

Bao shrugged. "I am a stranger here. Is it customary for a troupe to question an invitation to perform for royalty?"

"No." The other laughed. "No, it is not. Can you guarantee this royal invitation? I'm not aware that his majesty has a fondness for the art."

"I can," I said promptly. "I cannot promise that his majesty himself will attend it, but I am sure he will issue the invitation if I ask him."

"It would have to be a performance appropriate for the occasion," Antoine nó Eglantine mused. "No japes, no foolery. It would be an interesting challenge." He glanced around at his tumblers, who had abandoned their practice and gathered close to overhear the conversation. "What do you say?" he asked them. "Should Eglantine House stage a performance to celebrate Lady Moirin's appointment as Princess Desirée's oath-sworn protector?"

There were nods all around.

"Who better, Antoine?" a blond fellow demanded. "This is Jehanne de la Courcel's daughter we're speaking of! The Night Court should be represented at the ceremony."

"You're right," he said thoughtfully. "We should be there."

"Do we have a bargain?" Bao inquired.

Antoine grinned and thrust out one slender, callused hand. "I will have to confirm it with my Dowayne," he said. "But if you can teach us further novelties, and Lady Moirin can deliver a royal invitation, I say we have a bargain, messire."

Bao clasped his hand. "Then we do."

TWELVE

Tumblers." Daniel de la Courcel looked blank and uncomprehending.

"Aye, my lord." I cleared my throat. "It will be a delightful spectacle. I am confident it will please your daughter."

"It's...undignified."

"She's not yet four years old," I murmured.

He drummed his fingers on the arms of his chair. "*This* is how you
would mark a solemn occasion?"

"A joyous occasion," I reminded him.

Daniel shook his head, dubious. "Moirin—"

"My lord." I leaned forward, nervous sweat prickling my skin.
Mayhap I had boasted too quickly of my ability to deliver a royal invitation. "Believe me, I take my oath very, very seriously. If you know
aught of the history of the Maghuin Dhonn, you must know we do
not swear oaths lightly or in vain."

"'Tis not a question of doubting your oath, Moirin," the King
said. "'Tis a question of propriety."

"Eglantine House is mindful of the need for propriety." I breathed
slowly and evenly to settle my nerves. "And Bao is teaching them
Ch'in tumbling arts based on strength and grace."

"He is?" He sounded startled. "I thought he was Master Lo's
apprentice, not a tumbler."

"Bao has been many things." My hands fell into a reassuring

mudra. "My lord, I am not sure your choice can provoke any more controversy than it has. I have been advised that at such times, it is the Priests and Servants of Naamah and the commonfolk who will side with love's cause. That is who I seek to woo, who I seek to charm with this gesture."

Daniel de la Courcel's brow furrowed. "I did not realize there was such considered thought behind the notion," he admitted. "And there is merit to the idea of a performance celebrating your accomplishments in Ch'in."

With an effort, I kept my voice serene. "Will you countenance the performance, my lord?"

He picked up a piece of stationery emblazoned with the insignia of House Courcel. "With reservations, yes. I suppose I must trust you, having made my choice."

I watched him dip a pen in ink and write. "It is not too late to change your mind, my lord."

"My heart tells me I have chosen rightly." His pen skated across the page. "And...mayhap *you* are right, too. This should be a joyous occasion." Pausing, the King glanced at me, making an effort to smile through the deep wells of sorrow in his eyes. "Jehanne wouldn't have hesitated to hire the tumblers of Eglantine House for such an occasion, would she? She would have delighted in the scandal it provoked."

"Aye, she would," I said softly.

"So be it." He inked the royal seal and stamped the page. "I will have the invitation sent forthwith."

Relief flooded me. If the King had refused, my standing with the Night Court would surely have fallen. "My thanks, your majesty."

"You are welcome." Daniel wiped the seal with a clean cloth. "I fear...I fear my grief has been an anchor weighing down the entire realm. It is good to be reminded that there is cause for joy in the world."

Reaching across the desk, I laid my hand over his. "I know."

He squeezed my hand in reply. "I daresay you do."

Dismissed from the King's presence, I made my way through the Palace to the nursery, where Bao was concluding his second lesson with the young princess. I made it a point to meet the gaze of everyone I passed, smiling pleasantly and inclining my head in greeting. Some smiled broadly and openly in response—most notably the vast array of Palace servants and guards.

The response from peers was mixed.

Some smiled with mask-like politeness; some did not. A few offered genuine smiles.

Some looked away, snubbing me pointedly.

It had taken only a day for the news to spread throughout the City of Elua and for the City to become divided over it. A part of me yearned to flee from the scrutiny, back to the Alban wilderness of my childhood, or even the wide-open expanses of the Tatar steppe. To the valley kingdom of Bhaktipur, where my golden lady, the Rani Amrita, ruled with a gentle hand, presiding over an adoring populace.

None of these things were possible; and there was a child's happiness at stake.

Jehanne's daughter.

In the nursery, I greeted her brightly. "So, dear heart! Did you and Bao study well today?"

"Moirin!" Desirée flung herself toward me, and I scooped her into my arms, hoisting her onto one hip. "Yes, we did."

"They did," her tutor agreed.

The senior nursemaid Nathalie Simon gave a huff of disapproval.

I ignored her, inhaling the scent of the child's hair. She smelled of lavender soap and innocence. "Well done."

Bao rose from his cross-legged pose. "Did his majesty approve?"

I nodded. "He did."

"We should ask her highness before we proceed," he said gravely. "My lady Desirée, you understand that Moirin will take a sacred oath to protect you?"

"Yes, Bao." She squirmed impatiently in my arms, and I set her down. "That means *you* will, too. Doesn't it?"

"It does." He smiled, the corners of his eyes crinkling. "Would you like to have tumblers at the ceremony?" Bouncing on the balls of his feet, he turned a flip. "Performing tricks?"

Her blue-grey eyes grew wide. "Oh, yes!"

"It will be a very serious occasion," Bao cautioned her. "Mayhap a bit frightening. Tell me, highness. Do you fear loud noises? Thunder?"

Desirée looked indignant. "I am not a baby!"

"Do you fear . . . dragons?" Dropping to a squat and hunkering on his thighs, Bao glared at her and uttered a menacing roar. "There may be dragons there."

She let loose a peal of screaming laughter, the sound high and piercing enough that I winced. The tutor Aimée Girard glanced at me in sympathy as Bao and the young princess roared at one another.

"Fly me, Bao!" Desirée extended her arms to him. "Fly me like a dragon!"

He obliged, plucking her up under the arms and tossing her skyward, catching her effortlessly.

I daresay her shrieks of delight rattled the rafters of the Palace. "Bao . . ."

"Enough." The word fell like a hammer. The senior nursemaid drew herself up with dignity. "It is clear to me that his majesty is deranged with grief, to allow such persons to attend his daughter," she said grimly. "For that, I am sorry. But I will not be party to it. As of this moment, I resign my post." Her gimlet gaze settled on me. "I daresay my days were numbered anyway."

I made no reply, letting her sweep out of the chamber.

In the silence, Bao lowered the princess to her feet.

Aimée Girard sighed.

"Who will take care of me if Nurse is gone?" Desirée asked in a plaintive voice, promptly bursting into wailing tears of abandonment.

Bao shot me a helpless look.

"Hush, dear heart." I sank to the floor on my knees, taking her into my arms again. "You have Paulette still, and we will find a new nurse."

It was to no avail. She wriggled out of my embrace and hurled herself into a full-blown tantrum, red-faced and squalling, beating her fists and heels on the floor and sobbing for her nurse. The harried junior nursemaid, Paulette, tried in vain to comfort her.

"You see how it is, my lady," she said to me, weariness and defeat in her tone. "Madame Nathalie was stern with the child, but I fear she needs a firm hand."

I shook my head. "It's not her fault. Bao overexcited her, and all children find sudden change to be upsetting." I remembered Jehanne hurling things around my chamber and weeping in a fit of temper. "She's too far gone for comforting. Ignore her, and it will pass."

It wasn't long before the storm passed, sobs abating to sniffles. Like her mother, Desirée was contrite in the aftermath of anger. "I'm sorry, Moirin," she whispered while I wiped her tear-stained face with a kerchief. "Will Nurse come back now?"

"No, I don't think so."

"Because I was bad?" Her earnest eyes were the hue of rain-washed lilacs.

"No!" I stroked her hair. "No, dear heart. It's not your fault at all." I chose my words carefully, mindful that she was a precocious child, but a very young one, too. I wanted to be truthful with her, but I didn't want to teach her acrimony, either. "It's frightening when things change all of a sudden, isn't it?"

She nodded.

"Well, it is the same for grown-ups. We're scared, too. Change can be a good thing, a happy thing. But sometimes when we're scared, we don't wait long enough to find out." I handed her the kerchief. "Here, blow your nose."

She obeyed. "Why was Nurse scared?"

"Because you are growing older, and there have been changes in *your* life, which means changes in *her* life, too."

"She didn't want Bao to study with me," Desirée said. "She didn't like him. Or you."

"Perceptive child," the tutor Aimée murmured.

I silenced her with a look. "Now, that's not true. Nurse didn't wait long enough to know for sure if she liked us or not. That's why it's important to be patient. Sometimes we think we know things about people that turn out to be all wrong. Did I tell you about the winter I spent with the Tatars?"

She shook her head.

I spun a tale of that long winter; how I had ventured into Tatar territory believing them to be a ferocious and dangerous folk; how I had avoided them until a blizzard drove me to seek sanctuary among them; how I found them to be kind and generous, defying all my expectations. I described the felt huts called *gers*, the warm, salty tea we drank, the layers and layers of thick clothing we wore, the numbers and rhyming game the children taught me.

Worn out by her tantrum, Desirée fell asleep in my lap, listening to the sound of my voice. Her tutor took the opportunity to steal quietly from the nursery with a hushed promise to return on the morrow.

"You've a knack with the child," Paulette said softly. "Do you want me to take her? I daresay she'll nap for a time."

"Aye, my thanks." Rising, I shifted my burden into her arms.

Clinging to her nursemaid, Desirée roused sleepily. "Bao?" she asked. "Where were you when Moirin was with the Tatars?"

"Oh..." He met my eyes. "Well, you might say I was hiding, young highness. A big change, a very big change, happened in my life. I was scared, and I ran away from it. But in the end, I learned it was one of the best things that ever happened to me. I would not be here if it hadn't."

"I'm glad you are, even if Nurse doesn't like you. *I* do." She hesitated. "Can I still have tumblers?"

"Oh, yes!" Bao grinned. "I will make sure of it."

THIRTEEN

As one might expect, the City of Elua was also divided over the matter of Eglantine House's invitation to perform at the ceremony, which was scheduled to take place in a month's time.

The announcement was made in the grand salon of Eglantine House in the evening of the day the invitation was received, and it was accompanied by Lianne Tremaine declaiming a poem she had composed for the occasion.

By the next day, the poem was on everyone's lips.

The former King's Poet hadn't held back. The poem lauded the King's decision as a return to the true origins of the Montrèvan Oath, the oath that Anafiel Delaunay had sworn to his beloved, Rolande de la Courcel, to protect his infant daughter Ysandre. Lianne Tremaine made the bold claim that this was the first time in generations that the honor had been bestowed in keeping with the spirit of that oath, making much of my having returned from great tribulation to accept the role.

"Thus was the sorrowful spirit of the lamented Queen at long last appeased/For knowing her eldritch lover would stand guard over the child, her grieving heart was eased," Lianne quoted with a shudder. "Dreadful pap, but I had to work quickly. 'Tis the sentiment that matters. Does it meet your needs?"

I'd gone to pay her a visit while Bao had his morning's lesson with Desirée. "It's...a bit excessive," I said carefully.

"Poetry glories in excess," she said. "When it's not extolling the virtues of austerity. Do you think I went too far in comparing you to Anafiel Delaunay de Montrève? After all, you did say you loved Jehanne."

"Aye," I murmured. "But I left her."

Lianne cocked her head. "Why *did* you leave?"

Long ago, before I'd known about the Circle of Shalomon, I had tried to explain my *diadh-anam* and the prompting of destiny to Lianne Tremaine, who was still the King's Poet at the time. Unlike most D'Angelines, she had at least some familiarity with the notion from her extensive reading. Now I reminded her of that conversation, telling her how the same prompting had driven me to Ch'in. She listened quietly, seeming to understand it better than most. "Jehanne knew," I said when I was done. "She always knew I would leave. It's just that neither of us thought it would be so soon. If I had been able to stay longer..." I couldn't finish the thought. "When I told her, she said it was as well she was an adept of Cereus House, and taught to revere the transience of beauty, for this had been a fleeting and precious thing." My eyes stung. "And when I left... when I left, I asked her how one could find beauty in somewhat that hurt so much."

"What did she say?" Lianne asked quietly.

I rubbed my eyes. "Jehanne said that it would always be like this. That I would always be young and beautiful in her memory, and she in mine. That I would never grow resentful, never be tempted to betray her. That she would never grow restless and fickle, and seek to replace me." I smiled through my tears. "So you see, not exactly the sentiments of a great and terrible love affair."

"Oh, but it is." There was sorrow in Lianne's gaze. "If Jehanne had lived, mayhap it would have been otherwise. Mayhap you would have returned to find yourselves both too changed to resume the liaison. But Jehanne died, and it will ever be what it was, exactly as she said. Fixed in time, like a portrait of a delicate blossom cut too soon immortalized in paint." Steepling her fingers, she touched her lips in thought. "That's not a bad image."

"Mayhap you can work it into your next poem," I murmured.

Lianne grimaced. "Forgive me, I didn't mean to make light of your grief. But I do know what I'm doing, Moirin. No one will accuse you of comparing yourself to Anafiel Delaunay. They will blame *me*. That is the risk poets take when we exaggerate for the sake of effect, which is what we do. And believe me, there are many who agree with the sentiment."

"I'm sorry," I apologized. "I didn't mean to question your knowledge of your craft. I'm grateful for your aid."

She lifted her chin. "And you owe me for it. Tell me the tale of your ordeal in Vralia. No . . . wait. That's not where it begins, does it?"

I shook my head. "No."

"Begin at the beginning," she demanded. "Begin with the Ch'in expedition that came in search of that physician. What was it they were after? What was so urgent that the Emperor of Ch'in would send well nigh an entire army to fetch one lone man?"

I told her.

Not all of it; there were a few parts I left out. I did not tell her what had passed between the Emperor's dragon-possessed daughter and me at our first encounter, when the dragon had chosen me for her mate; and I did not tell her what had passed between us at the end, when Snow Tiger had asked me to invoke Naamah's blessing on her behalf. That, no one knew; nor was it anyone's business but Naamah's.

I did not tell her about the aftermath of the battle that had nearly torn Ch'in apart, when I had served as Emperor Zhu's swallower-of-memories, using the gift of the Maghuin Dhonn Herself to take into myself the memories of every soldier, engineer, and alchemist with knowledge of the workings of the Divine Thunder. D'Angelines already had enough cause to fear the folk of the Maghuin Dhonn, and I did not need to give them one more reason.

But I did tell Lianne Tremaine one thing I'd told no one else. "There is a part of the tale I left out. Do you remember the spirit Marbas?"

"Of course." There was an edge to her tone. We had not spoken of the summonings yet. "He took the form of a lion."

I nodded. "And you could not compel him to speak, because you could not compel him to take human form."

"I remember." Her fox-like gaze was sharp.

"He spoke to me in the twilight," I said slowly. "All of the fallen spirits did. But Marbas offered me a gift. He offered to teach me the art of shape-shifting, the art my mother's folk lost."

Lianne's breath hissed between her teeth. "Name of Elua!"

"I refused it," I hastened to add. "I will own, I was tempted, but the Maghuin Dhonn Herself took that gift away from us, and it is Hers, and Hers alone, to restore. But Marbas... Marbas said that for that, he would give me a gift unasked. And he did." I took a deep breath. "The charm to reveal hidden things. He roared, and placed it in my thoughts like a jewel. He said the words would be there if I needed them."

Her expression was unreadable. "Have you?"

"Aye," I said. "In the reflecting lake on White Jade Mountain. When the princess and I jumped into its depths, nothing happened except that she began to drown, and take me down with her. It came to me that the dragon's spirit was surely a hidden thing—and then the words of the charm were there, and I spoke them. That is when the dragon's spirit emerged from the princess."

"You never told any of us that the spirit Marbas had given you a gift," Lianne said in a flat tone.

"No," I said. "I didn't."

Lianne Tremaine rose from her chair and paced her tower chamber restlessly. "Elua have mercy! All that time we were haggling for gifts, and the spirits were showering you with them unasked."

"Just the one," I murmured. "And I suspect it was because it *was* unasked. I do not think bargains with them ever end well, my lady. How do you like the one gift you bargained for?"

She gave me a strange look, her nostrils flaring. "The language of ants? Let us say there is a reason I begged a chamber high above-ground, and that I am grateful for winter's dormancy."

"Even so."

"You tried to tell us." Lianne raked both hands through her hair. "From the first time when we summoned the spirit Valac; it was a trick, it was always going to be a trick. And none of us listened. Gods! We were fools."

I watched her pace. "And yet if you had not done it, my Ch'in princess would have died in that lake," I said. "And the dragon with her. The Emperor would have been overthrown, Ch'in conquered from within, and the weapons of the Divine Thunder loosed upon the world. So mayhap there was some greater purpose in it after all."

The poetess laughed, but it was a harsh, bitter sound. "Ah, gods! There is a part of me that hopes it is true, Moirin mac Fainche, for it redeems our folly in some measure."

"And there is a part of you that resents the notion," I observed.

She shrugged. "That all of us in the Circle of Shalomon were but unwitting bit players in a drama meant to be played out on a stage far, far away? Yes, of course. I cannot help it."

"I know."

Lianne gave me a wry smile. "And we have not even gotten to Vralia yet."

"No," I said. "Nor to Raphael de Mereliot, of whom I would speak."

Her brows rose. "You care for him yet?"

I frowned. "I have a sense that there are matters yet unsettled between us," I said, choosing not to elaborate. "But it can wait longer. There are more pressing matters at hand."

"Yes, there are." Lianne resumed her seat, regarding me with a critical eye. "And I've a few thoughts on them, starting with your attire."

I ran a fold of my gold-embroidered orange sari through my fingers. "Too exotic?"

"Too foreign," she said bluntly. "To be sure, I suspect we'll see the influence emerge in the next season's fashions, but in the meanwhile, you ought to pay a visit to the couturiere."

I nodded in understanding. "I've not had time, that's all."

"Make time, you and your husband both. And this business of

your living at the Temple of Naamah..." Lianne shook her head. "It's not good. It suggests you're merely seeking sanctuary along the way. Folk in the City need to have the sense that your presence here is more permanent. I understand that your...your *diadh-anam* may send you elsewhere, but you can't afford to maintain the appearance of some pair of romantic vagabonds."

"The Royal Minister offered us a suite at the Palace," I noted.

"I suggest you accept the offer."

"All right." It would evoke painful memories, but it was a small sacrifice to make if it rendered this process more acceptable, and kept any hint of the politics involved far, far from Desirée's notice. "What else?"

Her topaz eyes glinted. "Antoine nó Eglantine promises that the performance will be a great spectacle. The royal theater holds only so many seats, and every peer in the City will be clamoring for one whether they support you or not. I'd advise his majesty to reserve a block of seats to be allotted to the commonfolk, awarded by lottery. They'll adore the gesture."

"That's a good thought," I said.

"I've a cunning mind," Lianne said unapologetically. "Be grateful I'm putting it at your service."

"I am." I glanced at the window. "I should leave; the morning's passing. Thank you for your counsel."

"Thank you for your candor." She paused. "The tale you told me, your adventure in Ch'in, the princess and the dragon, the Divine Thunder...Moirin, tell me. How much of it was true?"

I rose. "All of it."

Her mouth twisted. "I feared as much."

"Feared?" I echoed curiously.

"I'm envious." She gave another shrug. "'Tis a poet's curse to live in placid times."

"Do you think so?" I asked. "The Ch'in have a saying that speaks to it. That it is better to be a dog during peacetime than a man during a time of chaos." I gazed at her clever, sharp-featured face, feeling a memory not my own surface in my thoughts: a young Lianne Tremaine, no more than a child of nine or ten years, huddled over a rough-hewn plank by the light of a single guttering candle, scrawling urgently on it with a hunk of charcoal while an unseen woman's voice harangued her. I felt the yearning in the child—a yearning for greatness, for an opportunity for glory beyond what her meager life afforded her.

Lianne turned away. "Don't *do* that!"

"I'm sorry," I whispered. "Truly, my lady! I cannot help it. It comes upon me unbidden."

When she glanced back at me, unshed tears glittered in her eyes, and I understood that despite her penitence, Lianne Tremaine would always hunger, always yearn. And that she would always hate me a little bit for having lived through events she longed to have witnessed.

If she had, I thought, she would feel differently.

It was one thing to hear tell of the weapons of Divine Thunder. It was another thing to have ridden across that battlefield, to see our brave, good-hearted comrade Tortoise jouncing in the saddle, one hand clinging to the pommel, the other clutching his reins, his face terrified but determined as he rode to the aid of the dragon-maddened princess.

To hear the weapons cough and boom, to feel the acrid wind pass overhead...

To see the smoking crater where Tortoise had been...

What Lianne saw in my face, I could not say. "I don't—" She broke off her thought, clearing her throat. "You should go, Moirin. We've work to do, you and I. Best we get to it. I've poems to write—better poems, gods willing. And you've much to do in a month's time."

I bowed in the Ch'in manner, hand over fist. "Aye, my lady. I'm sorry."

She scowled at me. "For what?"

I didn't answer.

"Oh, go!" Lianne's scowl deepened. "Go! Don't stand there being all polite and obsequious and...and gods-sodding *understanding*.

I can't bear it. Go!" She flapped one hand at me. "Go, go! Take my counsel and put it to use. We'll meet again later as matters progress."

I bowed again, and made to take my leave.

"Moirin?" Her voice called me back. I paused and turned, seeing a rare vulnerability in her expression. "Thank you."

I inclined my head. "And you."

FOURTEEN

—————✦—————

That afternoon, I met alone with Rogier Courcel, the Duc de Bar-thelme and Royal Minister of the realm.

I had requested an audience thinking it might be some days before he had time to grant it; but to my surprise, the royal steward ushered me into his presence in his study straightaway.

My father was not there. I wished he was.

"Moirin." The Duc tapped his pen on his desk. "I'm pleased you've come. As I said, I wanted to speak to you regarding the Vralian matter. Please, sit."

I sat, sinking into one of the padded leather chairs opposite his desk, tracing the rivets in the armrests with my fingertips.

"So?" He arched his strongly etched Courcel brows. "Do I under-stand that you contend that Vralia has committed an act of aggression against Terre d'Ange?"

I shook my head. "Not exactly, my lord."

He looked curious. "What, then? I am unclear on the details."

I told the tale in brief. How I had been betrayed by the Great Khan Naram, whose daughter Bao had wed, and been delivered in chains to Pyotr Rostov, the Patriarch of Riva. How the Patriarch rep-resented an extreme faction of a schism within the Church of Yeshua in Vralia, and how he fervently believed that a holy war against the licentious D'Angelines and all they represented, as well as rooting out the blasphemous bear-witches of the Maghuin Dhonn, would lead to the return of Yeshua ben Yosef. How I had escaped with the aid of Rostov's sister and nephew.

The Royal Minister listened, sketching occasional notes. It reminded me uncomfortably of being forced to confess my sins to the Patriarch, and I tried not to squirm in my seat. "You're right," he said when I had finished. "We cannot exactly hold Vralia to account for one man's actions. Still, it is troubling."

I nodded. "Pyotr Rostov was acting in his capacity as the spiritual leader of Riva. But he had the support of the Duke of Vralsturm, who was acting in a political capacity. When the Patriarch ordered me stoned to death, I begged him to aid me as a descendant of House Courcel. He refused."

He tapped his pen again. "I will inquire into the matter."

"Oh...well, you should probably know that I tried to kill the Patriarch," I said reluctantly.

"*What?*" Rogier Courcel's face froze in shock.

"He and the Duke of Vralsturm and his men caught up with Aleksei and me in the city of Udinsk, my lord," I said. "If I hadn't resisted, they *would* have stoned us to death." Remembering the future of endless war and bloodshed that would have ensued, I shuddered. "And believe me, it would have stoked the fires of their cause."

"I...how? The two of you, alone?"

I spread my hands. "Yes and no, my lord. Aleksei and I were alone at the time. The Patriarch gave the order to take us, and I...well, I had my bow drawn and an arrow trained on him. I warned him," I added. "It was a fair warning. I did not shoot until he gave the order."

He stared at me. "But you *didn't* kill him."

"No." I shook my head. "Aleksei threw himself at me, knocked me from my horse and spoiled my aim. As a result, I only wounded his uncle. But make no mistake, I meant to kill him. And then that is when Vachir's tribe rode into the city center and intervened."

A soundless breath escaped the Royal Minister. "Vachir's tribe?"

"Tatars," I said. "They were in Udinsk to trade. They felt strongly that the Great Khan had violated the laws of hospitality in betraying me, so they came to my aid to set matters right."

Rogier Courcel was silent for a time. "My thanks, Moirin," he said at length. "I think mayhap...mayhap I'll let discretion prevail, and not inquire into the specifics of the matter. It's over and done with, and there's no need to provoke a diplomatic crisis. But this business of a schism and anti-D'Angeline fanaticism concerns me."

I noted that he expressed no concern for the Maghuin Dhonn, but I held my tongue on the thought. "So it should, my lord."

His pen tapped. "How was it called again? The church of faith your Patriarch espoused?"

"The Church of Yeshua Ascendant." I watched him write down the words, his pen scratching over the paper, adding further notes to those he had already taken. "My lord?"

"Hmm?" He glanced up as though surprised to see me there. "Oh, my pardon. You may go."

"Thank you, my lord," I said politely. "But I had another purpose in requesting an audience. Begging your kindness, I would accept your offer of a suite of rooms at the Palace."

"Ah." A look of dismay settled over his features. "Elua, forgive me, Moirin! The Comte de Rochambeau decided at the last minute to winter in the City instead of the country. He is an old friend, and I offered him lodging at the Palace." The Duc de Barthelme gave a helpless shrug. "Messire Lambert has advised me it was the last unoccupied suite in the Palace."

I eyed him without speaking.

"I did not think you would have a change of heart so soon," Rogier Courcel apologized—but I detected a note of smoothness beneath the seeming sincerity of his tone. He had practiced this exchange in his thoughts. "Of course, I can order the Comte and his family evicted."

"I do not think that gesture would be well received," I said slowly. "Do you?"

He frowned with regret. "Likely not."

My skin prickled, and I thought to myself, I have made an enemy of this man all unwitting. The Royal Minister, his majesty's chosen appointee; my father's lover, the companion of his youth. Unlike the former King's Poet, he harbors ambitions he is only just beginning to realize.

I met his dark blue gaze.

He held mine steadily, blinking only a little bit. "I *am* so very sorry, Lady Moirin."

I rose. "Think nothing of it, my lord."

It wasn't until evening that I had a chance to discuss the day's events with Bao, who had spent the afternoon at Eglantine House, coaching their tumblers on Ch'in techniques and meeting with the mistress of wardrobe and the master of props to advise them. He was in good spirits, filled with excitement over planning for the coming spectacle.

"Tomorrow I will meet with the master of percussion," he informed me. "Antoine does not think he has such drums as I described, but he agrees that it would be a very fine effect."

I smiled, glad to see Bao in such a cheerful mood. "Oh, he does, does he?"

"Oh, yes. It is only a question of getting them made in time." He folded his arms behind his head. "Also, there have been a dozen applicants for the post of Desirée's nurse. It will take time to speak with all of them and find the right one. We have a lot to do, huh?"

"That we do, my magpie." I leaned over to kiss him. "Lianne Tremaine has advised me that we had best find ourselves a more permanent residence within the City, so that we do not appear a pair of romantic vagabonds."

Bao yawned. "Well, that minister fellow offered us rooms at the Palace."

"So he did," I agreed. "But it seems that within a day's time, he's given them to someone else, and there are no other quarters available."

"That seems…sudden," Bao said slowly.

"I thought so, too." Sitting cross-legged on the bed, I ran a boar-bristle brush through my hair. "I fear we may have made ourselves an enemy."

Frowning in thought, Bao sat up and took the brush from me. "Here, I'll do it." He knelt behind me and I let him take over, luxuriating in the sensation. "Maybe you are reading too much import into it."

I shook my head without thinking. "I could be, but I don't think so."

Bao untangled the brush without comment, resuming his long, steady strokes. "How dangerous an enemy?"

"I don't know," I admitted.

"It's a petty gesture," he said. "Maybe he will be satisfied with it."

"I hope so," I said. "But at any rate, we'll need to find suitable quarters to rent. Oh, and to visit a couturiere. It seems our clothing is too foreign."

His hands slid beneath the silk folds of my sari to find the bare skin of my waist, the brush forgotten. "I *like* your Bhodistani clothing," he whispered in my ear. "I do not want you wearing D'Angeline gowns that prick your skin."

I leaned against Bao's chest, feeling the strange yet familiar intimacy of our *diadh-anams* entwining at the contact. "Well, then, we will have to commission clothing that does not prick."

Bao's hands slid higher, over the fine linen undershirt I wore beneath the sari, callused palms gliding over my breasts. The combination of gentleness and coarseness was tantalizing and exquisite, my nipples growing tight and aching under his touch. "I like you best in no clothing at all."

I laughed breathlessly. "I do not think that would go over well at Court!"

"Why ever not?" One hand dipped beneath the silk folds pinned around my waist, stroking my thigh. He kissed the side of my throat, and I let my head fall back on his shoulder. "You are very, very beautiful, Moirin." His hand slid between my thighs, one finger parting my nether-lips and slipping inside me, the heel of his palm rubbing against Naamah's Pearl. "And very, very wet."

Holding me effortlessly in place with one arm, Bao kissed my throat, teased and fingered me to a gasping climax.

Afterward, he unpinned my sari, unwinding the complicated folds with care. "I will miss these, after all."

"So it seems." I regarded him languorously, hooking my fingers in the drawstring waist of his loose Bhodistani breeches. I could feel his taut phallus straining beneath the fabric and blew softly on it, then looked up beneath my lashes at him, and licked my lips. "Shall I bid farewell to your attire?"

He grinned. "You need to ask?"

FIFTEEN

G ods, there was so much to be done!

In the days that followed, Bao and I had a series of unsatisfying interviews with applicants for the post of royal nursemaid. All of them came with excellent credentials, having served in similar posts in one or more of the Great Houses of Terre d'Ange. Most of them struck me as competent; none of them struck me as possessing the combination of steady patience, discipline, and compassion necessary for coping with a willful, neglected child. Far too many of them seemed to possess a sense of entitlement based on the patronage of the families they had served in the past.

With reluctance, I declined them all and continued the search, praying that the harried junior nursemaid Paulette wouldn't reach her wits' end.

Bao continued his studies with Desirée and her tutor in the mornings, spending his afternoons at Eglantine House.

I paid a visit to Bryony Associates, the banking-house where I had deposited a letter of credit over four years ago. I was pleased to find that Caroline nó Bryony, who had issued the original letter at their establishment in Bryn Gorrydum in Alba, had been transferred to the City of Elua, and was happy to serve as my personal factor.

Unfortunately, she informed me that while a substantial balance remained, it was insufficient to purchase a suitable house in the City.

"You've plenty of funds to see you through the winter," Caroline assured me. "You can rent quarters at one of the finest inns in the City. Come spring, if you're still looking to establish a household, we'll send to Bryn Gorrydum to issue a new letter of credit."

I toyed with the signet ring my mother had given me, the ring bearing the twin crests of the Black Boar of the Cullach Gorrym and the swan of House Courcel. The ring marked me as a descendant of Alais the Wise, permitting me to draw on the trust my ancestress had created generations ago for her errant offspring who had fled civilization to live in the wilderness among the Maghuin Dhonn. "I had hoped it might be done sooner."

"I can imagine." Caroline nó Bryony gave me a look at once shrewd and sympathetic. "Moirin, if you were the only descendant, I would gladly advance you funds against the trust. But there are others. I dare not, without knowing for sure none of the others have made claims. And that I cannot determine until spring when the Straits are calm enough to pass."

"It's not likely."

"No." She sighed. "It's highly *unlikely*. But there are rules governing such matters, and Bryony Associates are strict about such matters."

"I understand," I said.

Caroline wrote out a letter of introduction in her graceful hand. "Present this at the Sauvillon Inn if you wish. I promise, it's a very elegant establishment."

"I'm sure it is." I didn't doubt it; but I also didn't doubt that taking lodgings at an inn, no matter how fine, failed to create an air of permanence that would reassure wary D'Angelines. "Thank you for your kindness."

Rising to bid me farewell, she gave me a rueful smile. "I wish I could do more. You're a long way from the half-wild young Maghuin Dhonn savage who appeared in my quarters all those years ago, ill at ease indoors, planning to live on *taisgaidh* land in the City of Elua."

Hearing a word of my mother-tongue spoken made me catch my breath and brought unexpected tears to my eyes.

"Or mayhap not so far after all?" Caroline asked gently, touching my cheek.

"No." I laid my hand over hers, smiling through my tears. "In some ways, aye. Not in others."

"I'm glad." She gave me a warm embrace. "I quite liked that half-wild young savage."

Although the encounter brought me no closer to resolving the issue of lodging, it heartened me to remember that there were D'Angelines who had lived in Alba and knew its folk, D'Angelines for whom the term Maghuin Dhonn did not automatically evoke shades of oath-breaking, babe-slaughtering bear-witches.

I also paid a visit to Atelier Favrielle to request an appointment with the famed couturier Benoit Vallon, who had accepted a commission to design a wardrobe for me when I had first come to the City.

There, I was dismissed summarily by the attendant on duty, who was mortified to learn that I did not possess a calling card.

"Good day, my lady," he said in a voice dripping with contempt, ushering me out the door. "If you must return, I pray you do so when you are prepared to observe the proper social protocol."

When I complained about the incident to Bao, he merely laughed.

"That is the exact kind of insufferable fellow that made me dislike D'Angelines the first time," he said cheerfully. "Luckily, I have found some I like better this time. Look, Moirin." He showed me a calling card that had arrived for us at the temple, engraved with an insignia of three ornate, interlocking keys. "This is from that nice fellow who was so helpful, isn't it? I was able to make out the name myself," he added with pride.

I glanced at it. "Balthasar Shahrizai?"

Bao nodded. "There's a note written on the back. I haven't quite made out that part yet."

"He's inviting us to dine at a supper-club with a few friends two nights from now," I said.

"That should be pleasant." Bao caught my expression and sobered.

"Moirin, I know we've a great deal to do. Don't worry. We've been through far worse. All this is just…politics." He lowered his voice. "Have you spoken to your father yet about the Royal Minister?"

I shook my head. "No. What if I'm wrong, Bao? I don't want to drive a wedge between them."

"Yes, better your father should serve as a bridge, maybe," he said philosophically. "Today's news was bad."

"What news?"

"You hadn't heard?" Bao winced. "I heard it at Eglantine House. They say gossip flows swiftly to the Night Court."

"What?" I demanded.

"The Lady of Marsilikos has made a formal complaint protesting your appointment as Desirée's oath-sworn protector." He met my gaze. "I'm sorry, I thought you would have heard."

"It seems you're keeping company in more well-informed circles than I these days," I said wryly. "On what grounds?"

Bao took a deep breath. "On the grounds that it's a grave offense against House Mereliot."

"Because I ruined Raphael's reputation?"

"That, and because Raphael de Mereliot was Jehanne's other true, great love," he said. "Not you. And that if anyone deserved the role, it should have been him. That the appointment should have been given him at Desirée's birth."

I was silent.

"Moirin?"

"Jehanne *did* love him," I said slowly. "Very much. Mayhap as much as the King—likely more than me. But that is not what she chose. She chose the future she wanted for herself and her child—to be a good queen, to be a good mother. I was there when she confessed her fears and wept. I was there when she honored her promise to King Daniel and lit a candle to Eisheth, beseeching her to open the gates of her womb. I was the first to see the spark of the child's life within her."

"I know." Bao took my hands in his. "And you are here, now, for her."

"But that's not why we came," I whispered.

He took one hand away, laid it on my chest. My *diadh-anam* pulsed beneath it, flickering in time with his. "Are you sure?"

"Not entirely."

"You are here doing what you have always done, Moirin." Bao's tone was firm. "Obeying the call of destiny, no matter how vague. If you are here, it is because you are meant to be here."

I exhaled in frustration. "Gods! I want to believe it. But we cannot even find a suitable nursemaid."

"We will." Leaning forward, Bao kissed me. "And a suitable place to live, and a suitable couturier—or at least a suitable printer, so that we might have suitable calling cards made. And if *that* fails, I am quite certain that the couturieres of Eglantine House would be more than happy to design suitable attire for us. Until then..." He plucked at the hem of my sari. "I am quite content to continue bidding farewell to these garments, over and over."

I wound my arms around his neck. "Are *you* sure?"

His eyes gleamed. "I have been to hell and back with you, Moirin. I am very, very sure."

Come morning, the entire City was abuzz with the news of the Lady of Marsilikos' complaint.

It seemed there were a handful of other signatories, mostly minor Eisandine lords, but a few members of the Great Houses as well, including the Duc de Somerville, who wielded considerable clout in L'Agnace province.

A young, upstart poet based in Night's Doorstep and sponsored by persons unknown had written a satire mocking my relationship with Jehanne, calling it a liaison of convenience fabricated for the sole purpose of provoking Raphael de Mereliot. The tide of public opinion was turning against me.

I didn't care.

I didn't care, because Bao and I found our nursemaid.

It surprised me to find an applicant who was no servant of a royal house, but instead a Priestess of Eisheth, goddess of healing, clad in the flowing sea-blue robes of her order.

"Lady Moirin." She greeted me with a shy smile. "It's been a long time. I daresay you don't remember me."

I blinked, trying to recall. "I *almost* remember."

Her chin lifted. "Gemma, my lady. Gemma Tristault. I was an acolyte of Eisheth's Order at the time. I came to you and Lord Raphael on behalf of our Head Priestess, Sister Marianne Prichard."

"Oh, aye!" I said. "She was bitten by a rat, and the wound had poisoned her blood."

Gemma nodded. "It festered, and she hid it too long, trying to tend it herself." She smiled affectionately. "Stubborn old woman. We would have lost her if not for you and Lord Raphael."

"Is she well?" I asked.

"She is," the priestess said. "She sends her regards, as well as this letter of commendation." She extended a neatly rolled scroll.

I unrolled it and skimmed the contents, Bao peering over my shoulder and sounding out the letters to himself. "Forgive me, Sister Gemma," I said. "But... I confess myself perplexed. Why is a Priestess of Eisheth applying for the post of royal nursemaid?"

"Why not?" she asked in a reasonable tone. "A hundred and some years ago, the head of Naamah's Order had the notion of assigning young acolytes to serve as royal companions. Who better than one of Eisheth's servants to nurture royal peers in their youth?" She gestured at the scroll. "As Sister Marianne indicated, since I took my vows, it's been my task to care for children brought to the sanctuary to seek healing."

I was intrigued. "The young princess needs a nursemaid, not a physician."

"Although it would not be a bad thing to have a nursemaid with a physician's skills," Bao noted.

The priestess folded her hands in the arms of her robes. "Many of the children brought to us, especially the very young ones, are fright-

ened and confused. Part of my duty is to soothe and comfort them."
She hesitated. "I do not wish to sound presumptuous, my lady. But
since resigning her post, Nathalie Simon has been spreading tales
about her young highness, claiming that she is an unmanageable child
growing worse under your influence."

"Ah...that would be me," Bao admitted. "But I have learned better
than to overexcite her."

Gemma smiled at him. "Be that as it may, Messire Bao, I do not
believe there is such a thing as an unmanageable child. Only frightened or angry children, and caretakers who lack the patience to manage them."

I steepled my fingers in a contemplative *mudra*. "I trust you
and Sister Marianne are aware that there is a political aspect to this
appointment?"

Her blue eyes were grave. "Very much so, Lady Moirin. Sister
Marianne was most distressed to hear of the Lady of Marsilikos' complaint. House Mereliot is one of Eisheth's most ancient and venerated
lines; and Eisheth's business is healing, not causing strife."

"Would your appointment further this strife?" I inquired.

She inclined her head. "It is a valid question, and one I cannot
answer with certainty. The High Priestess does not believe so. She
believes it would deliver a necessary reminder to Eisandine peers."

"How so?" Bao asked.

Again, Gemma hesitated. "I do not wish to be presumptuous—"

"Presume," I said.

"It is no secret that his majesty avoids the child," she said softly.
"That it pains him to see Queen Jehanne in her. Even young children
sense such things. Surely, it has hurt the princess in turn. So if I *may*
presume, I would say that his majesty's decision to assign you a significant role in the princess' life represents his best effort at mending
the damage. You can see the mother reflected in the child, and love
her for it as his majesty is unable to do. There are wounds of the spirit
as grave as wounds of the flesh, and they, too, need healing. This is the
reminder that Eisheth's Order would offer the peers of the realm."

Bao turned to me. "Hire her."

I ignored him for the moment. "How can you be sure?" I asked the priestess. "I might be seeking the role for political purposes."

"You, Lady Moirin?" Gemma laughed, but nicely. "No, I do not think so. Nor do I think you would be going to such trouble on her highness' behalf if you did not care for her."

A smile tugged at my lips. "Would you like to meet her?"

"It would be my honor."

We found Desirée fitful and restless, having refused her afternoon nap; and the nursemaid Paulette near tears.

Within a quarter of an hour, the young princess was half-asleep in the priestess' lap, her head nodding while Gemma sang low, rhythmic songs to her in a remarkably soothing voice.

"Elua have mercy!" Paulette breathed. "'Tis a miracle."

"No miracle." The priestess smiled. "Music is Eisheth's other gift to mankind, and there's healing in it, too."

"Do you truly desire the post, my lady priestess?" I asked her.

Gemma stroked Desirée's flaxen hair, trailed one fingertip over the curve of the child's fair cheek, touched the perfect bow of her pink, parted lips. As her gaze lifted to meet mine, I fought a surge of irrational jealousy. "I do, my lady Moirin."

I bowed to her. "It is yours."

SIXTEEN

Almost immediately, Desirée flourished under Sister Gemma's care. She became calmer, happier, eager to please for the sake of the pleasure that came of behaving kindly toward others.

I was glad.

And a little bit jealous, still.

"It's for the best," Bao consoled me, his arms wrapped around me. "You do know that, don't you, Moirin?"

"Of course I do."

His arms tightened. "We'll have babes of our own one day," he predicted. "Remember? I told you so a long time ago."

I laughed and kissed him. "Aye, I do. Fat, happy babies."

"Exactly."

The tides of public opinion continued to sway back and forth. For a mercy, they began to swing in our direction. The appointment of Sister Gemma, and the support of Eisheth's Order that accompanied it, were the first stroke of good fortune.

The second stroke came the following day, or more precisely, very early in the morning of the following day, when Bao and I were awakened by an urgent summons from one of the young acolytes in the temple.

"Forgive me," she apologized as we gazed sleepily at her. "But it's Messire Benoit Vallon from Atelier Favrielle to see you, and he's in a considerable state of irritation."

I yawned and tried to shake the cobwebs from my thoughts. "Oh, is he?"

Her lips quirked. "Considerable."

I clambered out of bed and splashed water on my face, fumbling for clothing. "Best send him in, then."

Benoit Vallon swept into our bedchamber with a satchel in one hand and a scowl on his face. He was a tall, lanky fellow who moved with loose-limbed grace, and every line of his long body expressed his considerable irritation.

"Well met, Messire—" I began.

His scowl deepened. "Yes, yes! It's my fault for hiring my idiot nephew. He should never have turned you away." He made an impatient gesture. "Come now, my lady! It's less than a month's time until the oath-taking ceremony, with the Longest Night hard on its heels. Strip!"

"Ah . . . is that customary, Moirin?" Bao inquired.

"It's all right." I began removing the sari I'd hastily pinned in place. "Messire Vallon needs to take measurements." I glanced at the couturier. "You *are* here to accept a commission?"

Benoit Vallon favored me with a saturnine smile. "I'm not letting it fall to Eglantine House, that's for certain. Atelier Favrielle has a reputation to maintain, and you're surely one of the more interesting creatures I've dressed over the years." He plucked up the sari I'd let fall, stretching out the unwieldy length of embroidered, sequined silk. "This is gorgeous fabric. It's been a while since I've seen Bhodistani work so fine. Have you more?"

"Aye, but—"

"But what?" He shot me an impatient look. "It's gorgeous, yes, but you cannot run around the City of Elua in midwinter looking like you've escaped from some pasha's harem, Lady Moirin. So show me what you have, and let me find a way to incorporate it, hmm?"

I nodded reluctantly. "All right. But not *all* of it."

"Fine." Benoit began taking my measurements with a cloth tape, jotting down figures. When he was satisfied, he turned his attention to Bao. "So this is the infamous juggling physician-prince husband?"

"Tumbling," Bao supplied.

"Tumbling." The couturier repeated his impatient gesture. "Strip."

Bao blinked. "Me?"

With a sigh, Benoit Vallon indicated Bao's loose-fitting Bhodistani tunic and breeches. "Must I repeat myself, messire? All *you* need is a turban to play the part of the pasha from whose harem your wife escaped. Now strip, please."

"We talked about this," I reminded Bao, pinning my sari back in place and opening one of our trunks. Ironically, it contained the crimson turban Bao had worn at our wedding.

"You did not tell me it involved stripping for strangers," he complained, but he obeyed, shucking his clothing.

"Hmm." Benoit circled him, gazing intently. "Very nice. Lean, yet muscular. An excellent physique for well-tailored attire. No more baggy, ill-fitting atrocities for you, messire." He took in the gold earhoops, the tattoos marking Bao's forearms like streaks of jagged, black lightning. "Very...piratical." He pointed at the latter. "Are those some sort of tribal markings?"

"No." Bao didn't elaborate.

"There's a certain brooding darkness about you," Benoit said shrewdly. "A roguish glamour, one might say...but it's somewhat more, too." He hoisted his measuring tape. "May I?"

I rummaged through our trunks, putting to one side those saris with which I did not want to part, like the crimson one I'd worn at our wedding and the mustard-yellow one that had been Amrita's first gift to me, keeping half an eye on Bao as he suffered himself to be measured.

There *was* a faint aura of darkness that clung to him, and there had been ever since he had died and been restored to life. I could see it more clearly in the twilight, but I could see it in daylight, too.

I'd never known anyone else to remark on it.

Finished with his measurements, Benoit Vallon gestured for Bao to clothe himself once more. "Very good. Do you remember what I told you at our first consultation, my lady?"

I smiled. "I do, messire. You advised me that autumn hues would flatter me best, and that if I must wear color, to avoid bright hues in favor of deep jewel tones. Oh, and that I should never wear stark white, but ivory instead."

"So I did. Well done, child." He picked through the piles of fabric I'd heaped on the bed. "I'll take this, and this..." A pair of squares of embroidered silk I'd set to the side caught his eye, and he picked them up to study them. "Interesting. These were never Bhodistani work, were they?"

"No," I said. "Ch'in."

There were two squares, one embroidered with a pattern of flowering bamboo, the other with a pattern of black-and-white magpies. I had purchased them both in a Ch'in village called Tonghe. The first had been embroidered by Bao's half-sister; the second, by his mother.

Benoit glanced up at me. "They're lovely."

"They are," I agreed. "But I fear they're not available."

"Why not, Moirin?" Bao asked softly. I looked at him in surprise. "Such things were meant to be used," he said. "To be worn, to be enjoyed and admired. It is what my mother would have intended." He smiled at me. "Even though you are apt to hoard your treasures like a dragon with his pearl, it is what she would have wished. And I would wish to honor her; and my sister, too."

"These were made with love, then." Benoit Vallon spread one long-fingered hand over the squares, the expression on his face somber. "If you allow me to take them, I will do justice to them."

Bao and I looked at one another.

I nodded. "Take them."

For the balance of the day, Bao and I went our separate ways. He kept his standing appointment with Desirée and her tutor, improving his grasp on the western alphabet, before meeting with the tumblers of Eglantine House to counsel them further on the spectacle they were planning.

I met with Lianne Tremaine, who served me fragrant tea and unveiled her latest poem pushing back against the narrative the unknown poet in

Night's Doorstep had advanced, accusing the Lady of Marsilikos of taking advantage of the controversy to promote House Mereliot's influence.

I studied the rough draft, sketched on foolscap. "You're holding back."

"Do you think I should have been more aggressive in challenging the notion of Jehanne and Raphael as star-crossed lovers?" she asked dryly. "Moirin, the problem is that they *did* carry on a very long, very infamous affair, and everyone in the City of Elua and I daresay the entire realm knows it. You even said so yourself. To argue against it would be...un-D'Angeline. And I cannot assail Raphael's character on the grounds it deserves without dragging you into the fray by implication."

"You, too," I noted.

"Precisely." Lianne tapped the foolscap. "So, as you say, I'm holding back. Sometimes discretion is the better part of valor."

"I understand." I took a deep breath. "About Raphael...tell me, how did he seem to you after the...incident?"

She was silent a moment. "We didn't have much contact with one another for a long time afterward," she said at length. "None of us did. Knowing Raphael, and knowing how I felt, I can only guess." She gave me a fleeting glance. "Mainly, horrified. Horrified by the results of our failure, horrified at what befell Claire Fourcay." A shudder ran over her. "Horrified at how much worse it might have been. And as to how Raphael felt about *that*, I cannot even begin to guess." She shuddered again. "He had that, that thing's essence *inside* him."

"That thing had a name," I said. "Focalor, Grand Duke of the Fallen."

"I know that!" Lianne Tremaine snapped at me. "Name of Elua! Do you imagine I could ever forget it?"

"No." I did not say what I was thinking, which was that the fallen spirits were no better than things to the Circle of Shalomon, useful tools they hoped to wield. If they knew the spirits' names, it was only for the purpose of binding them. Still, the memory was a heavy burden to carry. "No, I do not."

Both of us were silent, remembering. I didn't know if the poetess had seen what I'd seen in the fallen spirit's incandescent eyes: staved hulls and storm-tossed seas beneath a raging sky; hundreds, mayhap thousands, drowning; mayhem and destruction for the sheer joy of it. Whatever she had seen, it was enough to horrify her.

I thought, too, of the last glimpse I'd had of Raphael de Mereliot; of the faint spark of Focalor's lightning I thought I'd seen in Raphael's eyes. To this day, I didn't know if I'd imagined it or not. "Lianne... did you ever have cause to suspect there was aught of Focalor's essence that lingered in him?"

Her face turned white. "No! Gods, no! Do you think it did? Is that even possible?"

"I don't know," I admitted. "But I would not have thought it possible for my *diadh-anam* to be divided."

Lianne gave another violent shudder and made an old-fashioned gesture to avert ill luck. "I didn't see Raphael until after..." She hesitated. "After Jehanne's death. And he was well nigh as broken as his majesty. She'd refused to see him, you know. After the summoning."

"No," I murmured. "I didn't know."

She nodded. "Jehanne was furious at him—truly furious, not like one of their usual spats." There was sympathy in her gaze. "She blamed him for nearly getting you killed."

"It was my choice," I said. "And Claire Fourcay *was* killed."

Lianne shook her head. "Claire took the risk willingly; we all did. Not you. Raphael blackmailed you into it."

"I know." That final summoning had been the price of saving my father's life; but it was still my choice. "So Raphael never saw Jehanne again until...?" It was still hard to say the words.

"On her death-bed." Lianne supplied them gently. "The King sent for him before the end. He tried to save her."

I knew; I'd seen his majesty's memory. But I hadn't known it was the only time Raphael had seen Jehanne since I'd left. "Stone and sea!" My voice shook a bit. "That's hard."

"It is," the poetess agreed. "So you can see why I'm reluctant to assail their tragic affair." She cocked her head. "Moirin, if I may ask, why do you care? Why such an interest in Raphael de Mereliot?" She lowered her voice, eyes widening. "Do you really think a part of Focalor resides in him?"

I traced the rim of the tea-cup that sat on the table before me. "Truly, I don't know. I only know that Jehanne came to me in my dreams and told me that I have unfinished business with him." I glanced up at Lianne. "Does that sound too absurd for belief?"

"From you?" She smiled wryly. "Hardly."

I sighed. "My lady Jehanne says she doesn't know *why*, only that it's so. And she cannot pass on to the Terre d'Ange-that-lies-beyond or to rebirth until it's done. She says I'll need her before the end."

"Did she bid you serve as Desirée's protector?" Lianne asked. "That would add a fine twist to the tale."

"No." I shook my head. "I've not dreamt of her since before leaving Bhaktipur. She asked me only to promise that I would tell her daughter good things about her mother, things no one else knew, things no one else would tell her."

Her mouth twisted. "Like the fact that Jehanne tried to protect you from being killed by Raphael and the Circle of Shalomon's ambition?"

"Aye."

"And she did, didn't she?" Lianne mused. "She sent aid because you left a note for her that day telling her what we were about."

I nodded. "Raphael had made me swear not to *speak* of the matter, so I didn't. It took me a while to find the loophole."

Lianne eyed me. "Most sensible folk would simply have broken their oath."

"I swore by the sacred oath of the Maghuin Dhonn," I said simply. I touched my chest. "If I had broken it, my *diadh-anam* would have been extinguished forever, and I would no longer be Her child."

"You and your bear-goddess," she said, but the words were uttered in an amiable enough tone. "Well, assuming your dreams are indeed true ones, I suppose you'll find out what unfinished business lies between you and Raphael when Prince Thierry's party returns in the spring."

"I was surprised to learn that he went," I said. "Raphael lost both his parents in a boating accident. I wouldn't have thought he'd embark on such a long, dangerous sea voyage."

Lianne shrugged. "I told you, he was a broken man after Jehanne's death. When his sister Eleanore succumbed to illness a year later, I suspect it was the final straw. Raphael de Mereliot didn't care if he lived or died. As I heard it, when Prince Thierry asked him to accompany the expedition as their official physician, he accepted it without hesitating."

"Anything to flee his sorrow," I murmured.

"I suspect so."

We sat a while longer in silence together with our memories. "I don't want to hurt him," I said eventually. "Raphael's been hurt too much already. He's made mistakes, aye, but fate's dealt him cruel blows in turn. I wish I knew what this was about."

The former King's Poet met my gaze, a furrow of concern etched between her brows. "If it *is* a piece of Focalor's spirit inside him... Moirin, what in the name of Blessed Elua and his Companions will you do?"

I lifted my tea-cup and drained the dregs, peering at the leaves plastered to the bottom of the cup, turning it this way and that, and finding no answers there. "Truly? I haven't the faintest idea."

She gave another wry smile. "Well, that's comforting."

SEVENTEEN

That night, Bao and I dined with the Shahrizai.

It seemed that for Balthasar Shahrizai, a few friends meant a few members of his notorious and notoriously close-knit family.

There was his uncle, Gamaliel, a laconic fellow with a predator's hooded gaze; and his oh-so-quiet wife, Mariette. There was his cousin, their daughter Josephine, high-spirited and flirtatious, although it was the kind of flirting that carried a sharply honed edge. Somewhat about her put me in mind of Jagrati, only it was a Jagrati filled with playful malice instead of banked rage.

And then there was Balthasar's great-aunt Celestine, the matriarch of House Shahrizai in the City of Elua, with her long silver hair confined in an elaborate chignon, ivory skin like wrinkled parchment stretched over elegant bones, and dark blue, blue eyes that missed absolutely nothing.

She smiled with genuine pleasure upon being introduced to Bao. "Oh, you're an interesting one, aren't you?"

Bao smiled back at her, his expression serene. "Am I?"

Celestine Shahrizai patted his cheek. "You're not afraid of much, are you?"

He raised his brows. "Should I be?"

"Most people are," Josephine remarked, approaching to give him the kiss of greeting, drawing back and flicking her tongue over her lips as though to evaluate the taste of him. "It's always...interesting...to meet someone who isn't."

"Told you so," Balthasar offered.

She glanced at him under her lashes. "So you did, cousin mine."

I cleared my throat.

"Lady Moirin," Gamaliel Shahrizai said smoothly, offering me a courtly bow before giving me the kiss of greeting. "We've heard so much about you. 'Tis a pleasure to meet you at last."

"I'm honored, my lord," I said politely. "I wasn't aware I'd been the topic of so much discussion."

He looked amused. "Certainly of late."

We sat to dine. I had been assured by both Lianne Tremaine and Noémie d'Etoile that the supper-club to which Balthasar Shahrizai had invited us was a very fine, very exclusive establishment.

By all appearances, it lived up to its reputation. The dining room had an enormous crystal chandelier hanging in the center of the room, lit with fresh tapers, and there was a matching candelabra on each of the four tables. Cloths of rich silk damask in muted golden hues and intricate patterns covered each table, and the tables were placed so that all the diners could see one another, but far enough away that one could speak without being readily overheard. Even so, folk spoke in low tones, the atmosphere well nigh as solemn and hushed as a temple.

I was seated between Balthasar and Gamaliel, who made desultory small talk as the first course of pigeons baked in pastry was served, pointing out various peers among the other diners. "That's the Marquise de Perigord," Balthasar said with a discreet nod at an attractive blonde woman in a complicated gown, surrounded by admiring suitors. "A recent widow, and a wealthy one. Since her husband's death, she's become quite a figure in society."

I recognized Marc de Thibideau among her suitors. He caught my eye, and quickly glanced away. "Are you saying she's someone we should court as an ally?"

Gamaliel Shahrizai wagged a finger at me. "Ah, now, Lady Moirin! We try not to be so...obvious...with our counsel. You've been away for some years. We merely point out persons of interest."

The crust on the pastry was exquisitely light and flaky. I let a forkful melt on my tongue, digging up a bite of the meat below. It was tender and savory beyond belief. I wondered what game House Shahrizai was playing with us. Whatever it was, Bao seemed to be enjoying himself. I watched him banter blithely with Josephine under the matriarch Celestine's keen gaze.

"You're suspicious," Balthasar observed.

I laughed. "Wouldn't you be?"

"Quite." He grinned. "I promise you, our motives may not be pure, but they're not bad, either. Enjoy yourself." He gave another discreet nod. "The gentleman in the blue doublet at the far table? Mercer Trevalion, Comte de Fourcay. Not one you ought to seek to engage. Claire Fourcay was his niece."

"Duly noted."

As the night wore on, dish after dish was served to us by attendants in spotless white linen aprons. Each one was truly delicious. There was a rich, dense venison broth, followed by a haunch of venison, ground mustard seed, roasted pheasants, a variety of pates and terrines, fine white bread to sop up the meat juices. There were dishes of bitter winter greens that reminded me of home in their simplicity, and sauces so complex I couldn't begin to guess what I tasted in them. All of it was washed down with copious amounts of wine.

It was pleasant...and strange. The Shahrizai were at ease with one another, but I felt a prickly quality to their company. They were descendants of Kushiel, and his gift carried sharp edges.

Once, it had made me nervous. Although I wasn't easy with it, I wasn't troubled by it anymore, either. But I did wonder what they were after, and what I'd gotten myself into. The other diners were curious, too, most especially, the Marquise de Perigord's table.

"Everyone is looking at us," Gamaliel murmured in my ear, leaning in closer than I liked.

"Do you enjoy that?" I inquired.

He chuckled. "I suppose I do."

"Do you, my lady?" I asked, looking past him at his wife. Mariette Shahrizai flushed, and did not answer.

Gamaliel laid a possessive hand over his wife's. "She enjoys it for my sake, don't you, love?"

Her flush deepened. "As you say, my lord."

I glanced at Bao, who shrugged.

At last, the dessert courses were served: apple tarts spiced with clove, a creamy flan custard, sweet jams, and tart cheeses, accompanied by perry brandy. One by one, the other tables began to depart. The last to leave save ours was that of the Marquise de Perigord. She approached our table, trailing her retinue of suitors.

"Balthasar Shahrizai!" she said in a light, teasing tone. "You've been keeping secrets. Do introduce us, will you?"

"But of course, lovely one." Balthasar rose, bowing to her. "You know my uncle and aunt, of course; my cousin Josephine, and my great-aunt Celestine. I am pleased to present Lady Moirin mac Fainche and Messire Bao."

All of us rose and exchanged polite greetings.

"How very…interesting," the Marquise said thoughtfully. "You Shahrizai do like to defy expectations, don't you?"

"It seems we do," Balthasar agreed with a lazy smile. "But we always have our reasons for it."

"And the rest of us can but wonder at them, you gorgeous, secretive creature," she said in turn, kissing his cheek. "Anon, then!" I watched her sweep out of the supper-club, suitors in tow. Marc de Thibideau cast an uncertain look over his shoulder at me as they went.

It left our table alone in the dining room.

"Mayhap we should depart, too," I suggested. "The hour must be passing late, and the servants weary."

The members of House Shahrizai glanced at one another; and then at their matriarch, Celestine.

She gave a decisive nod. "I like them." She patted Bao's hand. "Especially this one."

"So be it," Balthasar agreed. Fishing in a velvet purse at his waist, he drew forth an ornate iron key, placing it on the damask-covered table before me. "Here. This is for you."

I stared at the key, uncomprehending. "I don't understand."

He took a deep breath. "Not so long ago, we spoke of ancestors, reviled ancestors, did we not? This is the key to the front gates of a modest domicile on the outskirts of the City of Elua that once belonged to *our* most reviled ancestress." He glanced around the table, receiving reassuring nods. "We understand that you are in need of suitable lodgings. We would offer this to you as a gift, if you are willing to accept it. For so long as you wish to remain in residence, it is yours."

"Why?" Bao asked succinctly.

"We are not ungrateful," I added. "But . . . aye. *Why?*"

Celestine Shahrizai beckoned impatiently to the hovering servants. "Come, come! Let us have the final course."

I rubbed my overfull belly. "I am not sure it is necessary, my lady."

She bent her gimlet gaze on me. "Trust me, child, you will find it worthwhile."

The white-aproned attendants brought forth silver trays containing goblets and various accoutrements. They poured boiling water into the goblets, frothing the contents with whisks, judiciously adding honey and spices, grating a sprinkling of cinnamon into each cup, and then scraping out the tiny seeds of a long, slender pod I didn't recognize. One by one, a frothy, foaming goblet was set before each of us.

I tasted mine.

Heaven.

Ah, gods help me! It was heaven in a cup. It sang on my tongue, all at once bitter and sweet. Dark and divine; light and scrumptious and filled with promise. The spices in it warmed my belly, and set Naamah's gift to stirring within me.

I made an involuntary sound.

"*Chocolatl*," Balthasar said. "It's made from a bean that comes from Terra Nova. It's good, isn't it?"

"Gods!" Bao uttered in a reverent whisper. "It's *very* good!"

"And very, very costly." Gamaliel steepled his fingers. "We went to considerable lengths to purchase *chocolatl* beans from Aragonia."

"But oh, so worthwhile," Josephine said in a sultry tone. "We Shahrizai do savor life's rarest pleasures."

I lifted my goblet to her. "I cannot disagree on this count. But I fail to see what it has to do with giving Bao and me a house."

"Nothing, really." Balthasar smiled. "But it was a good excuse to serve *chocolatl*, and set the stage for sharing our thoughts." He dismissed the attendants before continuing. "You're aware that Prince Thierry hopes to establish a direct line of trade between Terra Nova and Terre d'Ange?"

I took another sip. "Yes, of course."

"And that his majesty was reluctant to allow him to lead the expedition after Jehanne's death?" His tone was surprisingly gentle. I nodded. "Well, Thierry held his father to his word. While the King eventually agreed to issue a letter of decree authorizing the mission, he refused to fund it from the royal treasury."

"That, I didn't know."

"It was kept quiet," Gamaliel said. "Neither wanted the realm to know how acrimonious their dispute had become. Thierry was forced to seek funds for the expedition elsewhere—discreetly, of course."

"House Shahrizai is one of the major backers of the venture," Balthasar informed me.

"Along with a few lesser investors to spread the blame around should the venture fail," his uncle added.

I inhaled the aroma of the *chocolatl* and took another sip, letting it linger on my tongue. "I trust it was more than a love of *chocolatl* that motivated you."

"It might be enough," Bao commented, his nose deep in his goblet.

Balthasar laughed. "Oh, there's more! More exotic foods and spices; jade, feathers, gold. If Thierry can succeed in breaking the Aragonian monopoly on trade with the Nahuatl Empire, there's a world of profit to be made."

"But House Shahrizai is already wealthy," I said, thinking out loud. "And I still cannot see what this has to do with giving us a house, which is a gesture quite contrary to acquiring profit."

He shrugged. "As I said, it's a modest house. It was used for private entertainment."

"They're courting the prince's favor, Moirin," Bao said, lifting his head from his goblet and glancing around the table. "*That's* why you backed the venture in the first place, isn't it? And you haven't forgotten that the prince was more than passing fond of Moirin. You think he's likely to side with his father's choice of her, and that he will look kindly on you for having supported her."

Celestine Shahrizai gave him a look of approval. "Now, see? There's a clever young man."

"What is it you want from Prince Thierry?" I asked.

"It's a small matter." Balthasar made a dismissive gesture. "Merely politics. But for hundreds of years, despite the considerable influence House Shahrizai has wielded, the Duchy de Morbhan has been the sovereign duchy in Kusheth. We would see that changed."

"Why?" I asked him.

It was Celestine who answered, steel in her voice. "Because Kushiel's line throws truer in House Shahrizai than any other! The right of sovereignty in Kusheth province should be *ours*."

The air seemed to shiver at her words. I toyed with the iron key. "You do not even know for a surety that Thierry *will* side with his father's choice. And I cannot promise to advance your cause if he does. I know far, far too little of the politics involved."

"Nor are we asking you to do so, Moirin." Balthasar smiled at me. "This is a gamble, nothing more."

"You set no conditions on your gift?" Bao inquired.

"None." Balthasar shook his head.

"There is, of course, the risk involved with accepting the support of the notorious House Shahrizai," Josephine added in a silken voice. "But as my cousin notes, you come from notorious stock yourself. And…" She gestured idly around the empty dining room. "As you have seen tonight, we are not without our admirers."

I ignored the latter comment. "Your infamous kinswoman Melisande Shahrizai's blood runs in the veins of House Courcel, does it not?"

"It does indeed," Balthasar agreed. "But while they are quick to claim her son Imriel de la Courcel as an ancestor, they are not so eager to acknowledge his maternal parentage." His expression was serious. "History casts a shadow over the Shahrizai name as surely as it does the Maghuin Dhonn. But I know Thierry de la Courcel well, and loyalty counts for a great deal with him."

"Bao?" I asked.

"Hmm?" His head came up; I'd lost him to the *chocolatl* again. He wiped froth from his upper lip. "I think they are being honest, and it is a gamble. Do what you think best, Moirin."

"What do *you* think, my lady?" I asked Gamaliel's wife.

"Me?" Mariette Shahrizai looked startled.

I nodded. "You."

Once again, she flushed; but she held my gaze without flinching. "I am not entirely sure what you are asking me, Lady Moirin," she said slowly. "But I will tell you what I know of House Shahrizai. They are Kushiel's faithful scions, and they serve him with honor and integrity. That may mean nothing to one such as you, touched only by Naamah's bright grace. But it means the world to me." She hesitated. "Will that answer serve, my lady?"

I didn't understand; not wholly. But I felt a sense of rightness. "I do believe it will."

"Then you will accept our gift?" Celestine demanded, sitting very straight and upright in her chair.

I smiled at the matriarch of House Shahrizai. "Aye, it does. I will accept it with thanks, my lady."

This time, I won a look of approval from her. "A wise choice."

I took another deep drink of *chocolatl*, and hoped it was true.

EIGHTEEN

—◆—

The house was perfect.

As Balthasar had said, it was situated on the outskirts of the City of Elua—a modest dwelling surrounded by trees, many of them evergreens. I strolled the grounds, inhaling deeply.

Bao regarded me fondly. "Have you been missing your wilderness?"

"I have," I admitted, resting one hand on the rough bark of a graceful cypress tree. "But this helps."

Once inside, I was surprised to find that the house came equipped with elegant furnishings, as well as a staff that was modest by D'Angeline standards, but extravagant by mine—a steward, a cook, two maidservants, a footman, and a groom.

"We are here to serve at a moment's notice should any of the House wish to entertain here." The steward, Guillaume Norbert, was a grave fellow with silver-grey hair tied back in a severe braid, but he unbent enough to offer a faint smile. "Now we are here to serve at your pleasure, madame."

I hoped I had sufficient funds to pay their wages.

As though reading my mind, the steward gave a discreet cough. "Of course, Lady Celestine has ordered all relevant details of our service to be directed to her factor."

"That's . . . very generous," I said.

There was quiet pride in his face, in the faces of all the household staff. "I am pleased that you think so."

"Moirin?" Bao's voice came from another room. He sounded strange.

"Aye?"

"Come see."

Guillaume Norbert arched his brows. "I believe messire has found the seraglio."

I found Bao in a sumptuous room beyond the far doors of the dining hall, covered with Akkadian carpets, strewn with cushions, and outfitted with many of the accoutrements of violent love-play the Shahrizai favored, including a tall, glass-fronted case that displayed an array of whips and paddles, and a tall wooden wheel equipped with four leather manacles.

Bao spun the wheel. "Huh."

"Does messire desire a demonstration?" the steward inquired with perfect equanimity, beckoning to the younger of the two maidservants. She stepped forward willingly.

"No!" Bao backed away from the wheel. "No, messire does not." He eyed me uncertainly. "Does he?"

"No." I reached out to halt the wheel's spinning. "I think not."

The steward Guillaume inclined his head. "Shall I have these items removed, madame?"

"No." I gazed at the weathered wood and the leather manacles, wondering who had worn them and what pleasures they had found in it. "Let them stay for now. It is a part of the house's history."

"As you will."

There was one item I *did* ask to have removed—an iron hook that hung on a chain from the highest rafter of the master bedchamber. What it had been used for, I could not even begin to guess, but I felt better for having it gone.

After that, Bao and I settled quite comfortably into our new lodgings. As expected, the news of House Shahrizai's patronage caused ripples in the City of Elua; but overall the tide of fortune continued to turn in our favor.

First and foremost came a message of support from the Cruarch of Alba.

I had never met Faolan mab Sibeal, the Cruarch of Alba. But he had a name for being a strong, just ruler; and he was a kinsman, a descendant of Alais the Wise. His message was brief but succinct, thanking and congratulating King Daniel for making a choice that acknowledged the shared heritage and long-standing history that lay between Alba and Terre d'Ange.

"How?" I asked when I heard the news, glad but bewildered. "I thought the Straits were impassable in the winter!"

"They are for ships." Bao's eyes glinted. "But Naamah's temples use doves to carry messages. You didn't know?"

I shook my head. "I did not."

"They say at Eglantine House that the monarchs of both realms have tried to duplicate the feat," Bao offered. "Without success. The doves fly only for priests of Naamah's Order."

My father confirmed it when I met with him the following day.

"Oh, yes," he said. "'Tis an art honed over the centuries. We thought the Cruarch ought to know."

He looked tired to me, more tired than he ought. "We?" I asked.

"Naamah's Order, yes." My father gave me a faint smile. There were dark smudges beneath his green, green eyes. "I had the honor of playing a part in the decision."

"That must not have sat well with his grace the Royal Minister," I said softly.

My father didn't deny it. "My lord Rogier is...concerned... that the orders of the priesthood have involved themselves in politics. First Eisheth's Order, and now Naamah's." He knuckled his eyes and yawned. "But we discussed it into the small hours of the night, and I believe he understands that this is a courtesy we felt compelled to extend to the Cruarch, not some nefarious plot to undermine his influence."

I touched his crimson sleeve. "I'm sorry. I never meant to put you in an awkward situation."

His gaze cleared. "Nor did you, Moirin. It's nothing, I promise." He changed the subject. "So tell me, how are the plans for Eglantine

House's spectacle progressing? Everyone in the City is perishing of curiosity."

I laughed. "I've no idea. Bao's taken to being almighty secretive about the entire thing. All I know is that he's consulting with the master of props to devise somewhat he claims has never been seen in Terre d'Ange. And if Bao's boasting, like as not he'll make good on his claim."

My father smiled. "I rather like that young man."

"He rather likes you," I said. "I think you may have been the first D'Angeline he *did* like. I certainly wasn't."

He laughed, too. "Well, he's more than changed his mind on that score. You've done well together, the two of you." His expression turned serious. "I'm very proud of the way you've dealt with this business, Moirin. You've handled it with grace and thoughtfulness."

I kissed his cheek. "Thank you. It means a good deal to me to know you think so."

"I do," he affirmed.

Plans continued apace, secretive and otherwise.

Benoit Vallon summoned Bao and me to Atelier Favrielle for a fitting. Like all his work, the wardrobe he had created for Bao was elegant in its simplicity: close-fitting black breeches that tucked into boots, and creamy white shirts that lay open at the neck, with a bare minimum of ruffle at the cuff. He'd sewn the black-and-white magpie square onto the back of a black velvet coat that fell to knee-length, also fitted, but loose enough to permit freedom of movement. It looked D'Angeline, but it spoke of Ch'in, too.

"I like it," Bao said decisively, examining himself in the mirror and adjusting his cuffs. "I like it very much. Moirin?"

"You look splendid," I assured him.

He preened. "I do, don't I?"

For me, the couturier had created a series of gowns in deep jewel-toned hues: emerald, ruby, amethyst. He had used the sari fabric as subtle accents to complement the gowns, hints of their ornate richness revealed in the borders and linings. I had to own, it was a clever usage, though I was glad I'd kept a few back.

"*This* is what you will wear to the oath-swearing ceremony, my lady," Benoit announced, a gown of pale gold brocade fabric over his arm.

It was the piece on which he had used the square of embroidered bamboo, cutting it apart and reassembling it as a high collar that framed my face. The green and gold silk harmonized surprisingly well with the gold brocade.

"Very nice." Benoit fussed with the collar. "You see the effect it creates? As though you are rising from a bamboo grove like some... some exotic young goddess." He scowled uncertainly at my reflection. "Are you angry that I did not keep the square intact?"

It was the first time I'd ever heard him sound nervous. "No, Messire Vallon," I said. "It's beautiful."

His scowl vanished. "Ah, good! My thought was to use both pieces in a symbolic manner." He laid one hand on Bao's shoulder. "The magpie square represents the love of your distant mother, spread across your shoulders like a protective cloak. And this..." He traced the line of my bamboo-embroidered collar. "This represents the embrace of your distant sister, placing her arms around your neck."

My breath caught in my throat as I thought of Bao's mother and sister; so far away, so briefly met. It was unlikely we'd ever see them again. "Oh, that's lovely! Thank you, Messire Vallon."

Bao nodded, his eyes bright with unshed tears. "Very lovely. Thank you for honoring them."

Benoit Vallon's scowl returned. "Oh, now! If you want to *thank* me, you'll grant me an invitation to the ceremony." He gave a loud sniff. "I'd rather not have to take my chances on the lottery like the common rabble."

I smiled at him. "I will see that an invitation is delivered on the morrow, Messire Vallon."

He gave another resounding sniff. "Good."

NINETEEN

A week before the oath-swearing ceremony, a lottery was held for the commonfolk of the City. By the excitement it generated, I daresay it was one of the better ideas Lianne Tremaine had given me.

The royal theater in which the ceremony and ensuing celebratory spectacle was to take place had seats for two hundred, with standing room for another fifty or so. While the seats were reserved for peers of the realm, King Daniel had agreed that invitations for the standing spaces should be allotted to ordinary folk and determined by lottery.

One had gone to Benoit Vallon. No doubt he would have preferred a seat in one of the boxes, but my influence extended only so far.

Forty-nine would be drawn from a great urn in Elua's Square.

Notices had been posted on broadsheets about the City. The day dawned bright and cold, cold enough that one's breath frosted the air, but the cold did nothing to deter D'Angelines eager for a spectacle. By mid-day when the lots were to be drawn, Elua's Square was filled with a throng of people.

Young Princess Desirée had begged to be allowed to attend, but the King had refused, citing the difficulty of protecting a small child amidst a crowd. Gazing at the throng, I had to agree.

"This is fun, isn't it?" Beneath the leafless crown of Elua's Oak where a dais had been erected, Bao nudged me. He cut a striking figure in his black-and-white magpie coat.

I smiled. "Aye, it is."

Tradesmen, shopkeepers, and housewives called out good-natured pleas for a chance at the lottery, promising all manner of extravagant bribes. The squadron of royal guardsmen dispatched to maintain order attempted to shout them down in an equally good-natured manner, keeping rough track of who had arrived first, thus deserving the first crack at the lottery.

The urn itself was a massive thing, dark blue enamel etched in silver with the swan insignia of House Courcel. It rested in a stand atop the dais, canted toward the crowd. It had a narrow opening, but its large, rounded belly contained some five hundred porcelain tiles stamped with the royal seal, forty-nine of which were gilded and could be presented to admit the bearer to the ceremony.

As the sun climbed toward its zenith, the crowd grew louder and louder; but it was a joyous sound, and I was glad of it.

There were a handful of others on the dais with us, including the Secretary of the Presence representing the King's authority, and a priest or priestess representing each of the orders of Blessed Elua and his Companions. My father was there for Naamah's Order, smiling with quiet pride. But it was Bao and I who were presiding over the event, and it was toward us that the eager, hopeful citizens directed their shouts and pleas.

A great cheer arose as distant bells sounded the hour. The Captain of the Royal Guard offered me a courtly bow. "Are you ready, my lady?"

"I am, my lord captain." Raising my voice, I called, "Let the lottery begin!"

The crowd cheered again.

With a smile, the captain ushered the first aspirant forward. A burly fellow with a blacksmith's knotted muscles stuck his meaty hand into the mouth of the urn, fishing around inside it. He had a difficult time drawing his clenched fist out, prompting laughter and cat-calls from the crowd.

"Maybe we need to send for some goose-grease, Moirin?" Bao suggested cheerfully.

"No, no! Not yet!" Easing his hand out of the aperture, the smith opened it to show us a white porcelain tile. "No luck today, eh?"

"I'm sorry, messire," I offered with sympathy.

He lifted his wide shoulders in a shrug. "Still, it's something to tell the grandchildren, eh? Thank you for the chance, lady," he added. "Not many folk would have thought of it."

"Nor did I," I said honestly. As much as I would have liked to take credit for the notion, it seemed unworthy—especially with my father and assorted priests and priestesses in attendance. "I must confess, the idea was another's."

The smith laughed deep in his chest. "Ah, gods! It took a bear-witch to make an honest peer!" He thrust out one big hand. "I like you better for it, lady. You keep that young princess safe now, mind?"

I leaned down and clasped his hand, squeezing it warmly. "I swear I will do my utmost."

The crowd liked that, too.

One by one they came to take their chances at the urn, escorted by the solicitous guardsmen. None of the first dozen had the good fortune to draw a gilded tile, but they bore their failures in good spirits. Many of them took the opportunity to beg blessings of one or more of the priests on the dais.

Many of them thanked me, too, waving aside any protestations on my part.

I had entered D'Angeline society as Raphael de Mereliot's unlikely protégée, and I had left it as Jehanne de la Courcel's unlikely companion. But that day, on the dais beneath Elua's Oak, surrounded by ordinary citizens of the realm, was the first time I truly felt myself to be part of Terre d'Ange and its folk. When an elderly woman supported by a pair of strapping grandsons drew the first gilded tile and opened her trembling fist to show it to me, her eyes damp with gratitude, I cheered as loudly as anyone.

Bao whooped and did a careless handspring, pleasing the crowd further.

I laughed for sheer gladness.

So it went throughout the day. It took several hours. I commiserated and congratulated until the urn was empty, and the royal guardsmen had to disperse the lingering crowd.

My father embraced me. "That," he said, "was exceedingly well done, daughter of mine."

I gave him a tired smile. "Was it?"

"It was," he said firmly.

Elua's priestess stepped forward, clad in sky-blue robes. "You did well, Lady Moirin," she affirmed. "Very well. Have you given thanks to the gods?"

I shook my head.

"You should." She kissed my cheek. "Think on it."

I prayed in my own way that day, laying my hands on the trunk of Elua's Oak and communing with it.

Once again, I felt its age. It *remembered*. It had been planted by Blessed Elua himself long centuries ago when there was no City, only a tiny village in a river valley. Elua had held an acorn cupped in his hands, and his Companion Anael the Good Steward had blown on it, coaxing it to grow. Together, Elua and Anael had planted it here, and the City had grown around it.

My father was descended from Anael's line as well as Naamah's, and it seemed I had inherited that gift, sparked to life by the inherent magic of the Maghuin Dhonn.

I still wondered what it meant.

In Bhaktipur, I had coaxed a field of marigolds to bloom out of season, spending my strength to breathe summer into winter, creating a miracle that lent the appearance of divine approval to the sweeping change the Rani Amrita was implementing. Ordinary folk had celebrated that day, too, weeping and laughing and rejoicing; most especially the folk of the lowest caste, those reckoned unclean and untouchable.

Mayhap it was enough. It ought to be, but I wasn't sure.

Elua's Oak held no answers, only memories and the sleepy thoughts of impending winter. I took my hands away to find the guards waiting patiently, and Bao regarding me with fond bemusement.

"If you are done talking to the tree, Moirin, I think the priestess' suggestion is a good one," he said. "I have not visited any of the temples of the gods of Terre d'Ange but Naamah's."

"And I have not visited them since Jehanne was trying to get with child and had little time for me," I said softly, remembering. "It would be good to visit them again, to thank the gods for their gifts and offer prayers on Desirée's behalf."

Bao nodded. "It seems fitting."

In the days leading up to the ceremony, we made a pilgrimage of the City's temples, beginning with the Temple of Eisheth where the feisty Sister Marianne Prichard presided.

She gave me a firm hug in welcome, unexpectedly strong for her age. "Have you come to light a candle to Eisheth, Lady Moirin?"

"No." I smiled. "Not yet."

Sister Marianne cast a dubious eye on me. "Don't wait too long, child! How old are you now?"

I hazarded a guess. "Twenty...one?"

"We've come to give thanks and make an offering on the young princess' behalf," Bao interjected. "Later, perhaps, I can persuade Moirin to beseech Eisheth to open the gate of her womb."

The elderly priestess chuckled. "You do that, lad! Spring's a good time, when all the world is fertile."

"Fat babies," Bao reminded me. "Round as dumplings."

My *diadh-anam* flickered, telling me it was not time yet; and I knew Bao felt it, too. "We will see, my magpie."

There was a garden in the inner sanctum of Eisheth's temple where a spring burbled through the rocks to feed a natural pool. An effigy of the goddess knelt beside it, her cupped hands extended over the healing waters. Having paid our tithes, Bao and I made our offerings, pouring incense of hyssop and cedar gum into Eisheth's hands and kindling the incense with wax tapers.

Fragrant smoke rose.

The marble effigy knelt, streaked with traces of green moss, her head bowed in modesty.

We knelt, too.

I breathed through a cycle of the Five Styles, clearing my mind. I gave thanks to Eisheth for her gifts of healing and music, and for the kindness she had shown us in sending one of her priestesses to tend to my lady Jehanne's daughter. I prayed that Eisheth would ever grant good health to Desirée. When we had finished, both Bao and I dipped our hands in the sacred pool and drank the healing waters with their acrid tang of minerals.

It felt good and right.

At the temple of martial Camael, I meditated on the battles I had seen, gave thanks for having survived them, and prayed that Desirée would ever be spared the horrors of war.

I felt myself humble at the Temple of Shemhazai, the greatest scholar among Elua's Companions. I thanked him for his gifts, and prayed that he would grace Desirée with wisdom.

Bao gazed for a long time at the effigy of Azza, whose gift to the D'Angeline folk was pride and knowledge. Azza held a sextant with which to explore the world in one hand, the other raised in warning.

"What are you thinking?" I asked Bao.

"I am thinking that pride is a dangerous gift," he murmured. "But betimes a necessary one."

I prayed that Desirée would find pride in good measure.

At Anael's temple, I gave thanks for the gift that the Good Steward had given me. I prayed that I might be worthy of it, whatever its ultimate purpose, and that the young princess might grow up to understand the worth of tending to the world with loving care.

We visited the great Temple of Naamah in the City, releasing doves beneath the dome of the temple and laughing, confident in the bright lady's love. I thanked her for the gifts, so many gifts, that she had given me; and for allowing me to serve as the vessel for her blessing.

I prayed that Desirée would know it, too.

And I understood Kushiel's worship far better than I had the first time when we visited *his* temple.

Expiation.

The penitents who sought out Kushiel's untender mercies had cause. I gazed at the bronze-faced effigy with his rod and flail crossed on his breast, remembering the penance that the Patriarch of Riva had laid upon me. I had not found expiation in it, but nor had I believed myself guilty of sin. Valentina, who had freed me, told me she *had* found comfort in performing penance for her own sins; and I understood that it was a gift for those in need.

By the expression on his face, Bao was thinking similar thoughts. "I punished myself in Kurugiri," he said somberly. "This way is better."

"It is," I agreed.

There, I prayed that Desirée would never be in need of such penance; but that if she did, she would find comfort in Kushiel's mercy.

Lastly, on the eve of the ceremony, we paid a visit to the great Temple of Elua.

It was the oldest temple in the City. In the antechamber, a priest and priestess welcomed us with the kiss of greeting and accepted our tithes. A graceful acolyte knelt and removed our shoes and stockings that we might walk unshod in the presence of Blessed Elua, and gave us garlands of dried anemone flowers for our offering.

The ground was cold and hard beneath our bare feet, the autumn grass damp and yellow. Blessed Elua's marble effigy towered atop an altar beneath the open sky, flanked by four roofless pillars and oak trees almost as ancient as Elua's Oak in the square of the City.

The statue of Elua smiled down upon us, one hand extended in offering, the other cupped to reveal the mark of the wound he had inflicted upon himself in reply to the One God's messenger.

My grandfather's Heaven is bloodless, and I am not.

Without thinking, I summoned the twilight for the first time in many weeks, drawing it deep into my lungs and breathing it out, spinning it around Bao and myself like a cloak.

Bao uttered a startled sound.

In the soft, muted hues of the twilight, Elua's effigy glimmered, shadows in the creases of his smile. I laid my garland of dried flowers on the altar, and stooped to press my lips to Elua's marble foot. In my heart, I thanked him for the many gifts of love that had graced my life.

And ah, gods! I *had* been blessed.

From the stalwart love of my mother in Alba to the discovery of my father in Terre d'Ange; from Cillian's youthful ardor and friendship to the mercurial affections of my lady Jehanne, whose daughter I would vow to protect on the morrow. Noble Master Lo Feng. My proud, reserved princess, Snow Tiger; my treasured friend, the celestial dragon whose spirit she had harbored within her mortal flesh. My sweet boy Aleksei, and my golden, laughing Rani Amrita. All the myriad folk I'd met along the way who had shown me kindness and generosity.

Bao.

He, too, laid his garland on the altar. Our eyes met in the twilight. "I am grateful for the gift of you, Moirin."

I nodded. "And I, you."

Beneath the twilit shadow of Elua's effigy, Bao kissed me, the shared spark of our *diadh-anam* entwining.

I wound my arms around his neck and returned his kiss; and I prayed with all my heart that Blessed Elua would be as kind and gracious to the young princess Desirée as he had been to me.

Elua smiled.

TWENTY

The oath-swearing ceremony was a solemn affair, as it should be.

It took place in the throne room of the Palace. There was not the large crowd that would be present later at the royal theater for the celebratory performance, but there were still some thirty or forty peers in attendance, including the royal minister, Rogier Courcel, Duc de Barthelme.

For a mercy, none dared show disapproval in the King's presence, although I knew full well many of them felt it. Duc Rogier wore a look of studied neutrality that spoke volumes, and I could sense tension between him and my father, who couldn't conceal his pride.

I breathed slowly and deeply to settle my nerves, holding Desirée's hand in mine. Earlier, she had been high-strung and excited, but the solemnity of the occasion had made an impression on her, and she was behaving herself impeccably.

His majesty greeted his young daughter with quiet dignity, doing his best to mask the pain the sight of her caused him. Clad in a white satin gown, her fair hair caught in a gilded mesh net studded with pearls, Desirée looked more than ever like a miniature version of Jehanne.

I stood beside her as the senior priest from the Temple of Elua gave an invocation, citing the bonds of love and loyalty in which the tradition was rooted.

"The gods in their wisdom answer our prayers as they see fit, not as we ask." The priest fixed me with a deep-set gaze. "Love and courage are often found in unlikely places, and there is no nation on earth that knows this better than Terre d'Ange, no nation better suited to honor this truth. Moirin mac Fainche, is it your will to accept this duty offered you today?"

"It is," I said in a firm tone.

The priest inclined his head. "May Elua's blessing be on your undertaking."

King Daniel beckoned for Desirée and me to approach the throne, summoning his daughter to the dais beside him, while I stood before them. Together they made an achingly poignant picture: the dark, melancholy King with lines of sorrow etched on his face, his gossamer-pale daughter with hair like spun moonlight. A soft sigh went around the room. Whether they agreed with the King's choice or not, no one could fail to be moved by the sight.

"Moirin mac Fainche," the King said in his deep, resonant voice. "Do you pledge yourself this day to be her highness Desirée de la Courcel's oath-sworn protector?"

"I do."

"Will you regard her interests as your own, seek to defend her from every danger, and hold her happiness as a matter of sacred trust?"

"I will."

His majesty extended his right hand, the signet ring of House Courcel on his forefinger. "Then in the presence of all assembled here, I bid you give your oath."

There was a weight to the moment. I felt it pressing down on me, felt my *diadh-anam* flicker in response to it.

The folk of the Maghuin Dhonn did not swear oaths lightly. I had prayed to the gods of Terre d'Ange; now I prayed to the Great Bear Herself to give me the strength to carry out this duty.

"On the blood of Blessed Elua, I swear it." Raising my voice, I added the ancient oath of the Maghuin Dhonn. "By stone and sea and sky, and all that they encompass, by the sacred troth that binds me to my *diadh-anam*, I swear it!"

The words rang in the quiet throne room, followed by a startled murmur. But King Daniel met my eyes with grave approval, understanding what it meant to one of the Maghuin Dhonn. I knelt and pressed my lips to his signet ring. "So be it," he murmured, laying his hand on my head in benediction. "May you serve my daughter as faithfully and truly as you served her mother."

My eyes stung. "I will do my best, your majesty."

He smiled sadly. "I know."

"Thank you, Moirin!" Desirée flung her arms around my neck, hugging me hard. "Can we see the tumblers now?"

I kissed her soft cheek. "I do believe we can, dear heart."

She gave her royal father an unwontedly shy look. "Will you come, Father? To see the tumblers?"

The King hesitated.

"It is a day for joy," I reminded him. "A day to be celebrated. And I have just sworn an oath to hold your daughter's happiness as a sacred trust. Would you have me forsworn already?"

His mouth quirked. "Yes, child," he said gently to Desirée. "I will come see the tumblers."

Of all the gifts I could have given the young princess, I daresay that was the best one. She glowed in her father's presence, basking in his rare affection.

Every seat in the Palace theater was filled to capacity, and there were ordinary D'Angeline citizens who had drawn gilded tiles in the lottery standing shoulder to shoulder on the floor, gazing up at the stage in eager anticipation. We sat in the royal box, directly overlooking the stage.

"Will there be dragons, Bao?" Desirée asked, her blue-grey eyes sparkling at him. "Truly?"

He nodded. "Oh, yes. Only one, but truly."

She shivered with delight. "Did you hear, Father?"

"I heard." King Daniel spared Bao a rueful glance. "I hope this spectacle of yours does not disappoint."

"It won't," Bao said confidently.

It didn't.

It was a gorgeous, glorious affair. Antoine nó Eglantine began by taking the stage and announcing that the day's performance was a tribute to my adventures in the faraway, exotic empire of Ch'in.

That, I hadn't known.

I looked sideways at Bao, who grinned. "Just watch, Moirin."

There were tumblers performing slow, measured feats of strength, grace, and balance atop high poles; and somehow it reminded me of learning the Five Styles of Breathing from Master Lo.

There was a sequence with trapezes that somehow managed to evoke the feel of a long sea-voyage.

Then came war.

It began with drums—gods, so many drums! There must have been two dozen of them, deep-bellied and resonant. At first, the drummers beat softly on them, but the percussive chorus rose steadily. Tumblers on one side of the stage shot mock arrows from mock bows, trailing glittering strands of gilded fabric. On the other side, tumblers tossed round balls trailing broad crimson ribbons. Back and forth they went, filling the air between them.

The drums grew louder.

In the background, a pair of women mounted a scaffold, climbing ever higher and higher.

When they reached the apex, they jumped, silken robes billowing around them.

The drumming reached a crescendo, and halted. All the tumblers onstage fell down, exiting the stage with backward somersaults.

Somewhere, bronze sheets rattled, evoking thunder and lightning.

And then the dragon appeared, eliciting a shriek of pure joy from Desirée and gasps of awe from the crowd.

It was immense, long silvery coils shimmering in the lamplight as it flowed sinuously over the stage, winding like a river. The long-jowled whiskered features were so familiar, my heart ached at the memory.

"How in the world...?" my father whispered in bemusement.

"Look." The King leaned forward. "The tumblers are underneath it, holding it up on poles."

Desirée gazed raptly at it.

I stole a glance at Bao. "Well done, my magpie."

He gave me a quiet smile. "It looks a lot like him, doesn't it?"

I nodded. "Very like."

Onstage, the dragon continued its graceful, flowing dance, accompanied by the sound of flutes. And somehow it truly did manage to convey the beautiful and terrible majesty of the dragon in flight as he rose from the peaks of White Jade Mountain and descended onto the battlefield.

All too soon, the performance ended. The tumblers hoisted their poles, revealing themselves beneath the silvery segments of the dragon's carapace.

The applause was thunderous.

Antoine nó Eglantine strode onstage and bowed in all directions, beginning and ending with a deep bow in the direction of the royal box.

"May I throw the flowers, Moirin?" Desirée looked at me with shining eyes. "May I?"

I handed her a bouquet of white roses grown out of season beneath the warmth of the glass pavilion. "Indeed, you may, young highness."

"'Tis a long way to the stage." Daniel de la Courcel took his daughter's hand as she leaned over the balustrade, his voice gentle. "May I help?"

She nodded, wordless.

All around us, peers of the realm in their boxes watched. Below us, fifty faces were raised in wonderment as the King helped his daughter toss a bouquet onto the stage of the royal theater.

It landed at Antoine nó Eglantine's feet.

He accepted it with a bow and a flourish. "Long life and good health to her highness, the princess Desirée!" he called. "Elua's blessing on her and her oath-sworn protector!"

More cheers.

More applause.

I was glad. Glad for Bao and the tumblers of Eglantine House, who had worked so hard to make this occasion a worthy spectacle. Glad for myself that it had exceeded the considerable expectations it had raised. Most of all, I was glad to see his majesty allowing himself to love his tempestuous young daughter, at least in this moment.

My father laid one hand on my shoulder. "You've done a good thing here, Moirin."

I smiled at him. "I have, haven't I?"

There was no doubt in his voice. "Indeed."

TWENTY-ONE

W inter in Terre d'Ange.
        It was long, and it was cold. Even so, it was a good time. Thanks to good counsel, a considerable measure of hard work, and the support of the priestly orders, Bao and I had won the battle in the court of public opinion. We were well liked by many, and with the deed done and my oath sworn, those who had spoken against it ceased their grumbling.

Desirée continued to flourish under the firm, tender care of Sister Gemma and the tutelage of Aimée Girard. Bao continued to study with her on a daily basis. King Daniel paid more attention to his daughter, making a point of visiting her at least twice a week.

Thanks to the largesse of House Shahrizai, we settled into a comfortable routine in our borrowed home, and began to entertain visitors like Balthasar Shahrizai, whose company Bao enjoyed, and Lianne Tremaine, for whom I had come to feel a certain prickly fondness.

It was a good time.

The Longest Night drew nigh. Benoit Vallon devised costumes for Bao and me, deciding that we should attend the Midwinter Masque in the guise of Hades, the Hellene god of the dead, and his bride Persephone.

"I'm not usually so literal, but it seems apt," he said, framing Bao with his hands. "I'm not sure why."

As with everything the couturier did, the costumes were lovely.

Bao made a grave Hellene deity in robes adorned with sparkling jet, a wreath of iron laurels on his head. My gown was green and gilt for spring, and my hair was crowned with a wreath of gold.

We attended the royal masque with her young highness, who was dressed as a winter sprite in a frothy white gown with a pair of charming gauze wings.

I had to own, the taste of *joie* and the sight of the great hall filled with massive pine trees shimmering with glass icicles evoked memories that made my heart ache. "Did you know it was your mother who first thought to decorate the hall with trees on the Longest Night?" I asked Desirée.

She shook her head, gazing up at a towering specimen. "Truly?"

"Oh, yes." I brushed the fragrant green needles with one finger. "She did it just to please me."

"What did she wear?" she inquired.

I smiled. "White, just like you. She was dressed as the Snow Queen, with a white cloak trimmed with ermine. And after the pageant when the lights were rekindled, tumblers from Eglantine House came and begged her to come to the Night Court. Every year, they would come, and every year, your mother refused. But that year your father told her she should go, and take me with her, since I'd never seen the Night Court's masque.

There was a yearning to hear more in her gaze. "Did you go?"

"We did," I said. "And when the night was over, we went up to the rooftop terrace to watch dawn break, your mother and I and all the beautiful adepts of the Night Court, none of whom were as beautiful as she was. It was cold, very cold, and your mother wrapped her ermine cloak around me to keep me warm."

"I bet that's not all she did," Bao commented in the Ch'in scholar's tongue. I chose to ignore him.

"I wish I could have known her," Desirée said in a wistful tone.

"I know, dear heart." I stroked her fair hair. "She wished it, too. Do you know what we did the very next day?"

"What?"

"We rode in a carriage to a Temple of Eisheth called the Sanctuary of the Womb," I told her. "There's a hot-spring pool with water as warm as a bath, and as white as milk. And there, your mother waded into the pool and lit a candle to Eisheth, praying that the goddess would send her a child. You."

Desirée slid her hand into mine. "I'm glad you were there, Moirin."

I gave her hand a gentle squeeze. "So am I."

She searched the bright hall. "My father isn't here tonight, is he?"

"No." I shook my head. "His grace the Duc de Barthelme, the Royal Minister, is here in his stead."

"Because it makes my father sad to remember?" she asked.

"Aye." I swallowed against a sudden lump in my throat. "I'm afraid so. But there is joy in remembering, too. That's why I shared my memories with you tonight, so that you might share my gladness."

Together, we watched the peers of the realm in their gorgeous, glittering costumes mingle and dance. Sister Gemma hovered in the background, ready to intervene if Desirée grew tired and fretful.

The Duc de Barthelme came to pay his respects to the princess. "Joy to you on the Longest Night, young highness," the Royal Minister said, offering her a formal bow. "Is the ranking member of the royal family here in attendance enjoying herself?"

Somewhat about his choice of words made my skin prickle, and I caught Bao frowning.

"Oh, yes!" Desirée said politely. "Thank you."

He inclined his head to me. "I see you take your duties seriously, Lady Moirin."

"I do," I said, laying a hand on Desirée's shoulder. "But it is also a pleasure to see the Longest Night through fresh, unspoiled eyes." I held his gaze. "I recall Prince Thierry saying much the same thing to me."

The Royal Minister's eyelids flickered briefly, and I thought to myself that Duc Rogier did not care to be reminded that I had the favor of more than one member of the royal family; and one who would be returning to a position of influence come spring. Still, his expression remained pleasant. "No doubt." He turned back to Desirée. "Do you plan to stay all the way until the pageant, young highness? It will be quite late, you know."

She nodded vigorously. "Oh, yes! I had a very long nap."

He smiled. "Well, then, I will be sure you have a chance to meet the Sun Prince himself. Would you enjoy that?"

She nodded again, eyes sparkling with excitement. "Yes, thank you!"

"The pleasure is mine." Duc Rogier gave her another bow and a wink. "I think you will like him. *I* certainly do."

It was an odd exchange. We did not speak of it in Desirée's presence, but it weighed on my thoughts as we plundered the banquet table heaped high with delicacies. I didn't know what this business with the Sun Prince was about, and it seemed strange that Duc Rogier had made such a deliberate point of noting Desirée's rank. I had assumed that his resentment of my appointment as her oath-sworn protector had to do with the fact that it was an honor of which he felt me unworthy, and one he had desired for himself, but mayhap there was more to it.

Desirée de la Courcel was a Princess of the Blood, and in Thierry's absence, her father's heir. Whoever wielded influence over the choices she made in life might one day affect the course of the realm.

That, I'd never considered. Stone and sea, I just wanted the poor child to have a measure of happiness.

Although her eyelids were growing heavy, the young princess did indeed manage to stay awake and alert through the pageant. We all cried out when the horologist called the hour, the Winter Queen in her crone guise hobbled into the center of the room, and almost every lamp and candle in the great hall was extinguished, plunging the hall into darkness.

Then came the pounding on the doors, and the Sun Prince in his chariot drawn by a pair of matched white horses rode into the hall, gleaming in his gilded armor and sunburst mask. Servants with lit tapers waited poised next to intricate series of braided wicks.

The Sun Prince leapt from his chariot with a lithe twist, pointing his gilded spear at the crone.

Everyone cheered as she threw off her ragged robes and crone mask to reveal herself as a young, beautiful maiden. The servants lit the wicks, and light was restored to the world. The royal pair mounted the chariot, wherein it was evident that she overtopped him by a head.

"He's kind of puny for a Sun Prince," Bao whispered to me. I hushed him, although I was thinking the same thing.

The chariot made a circuit of the hall, stopping before us. The Sun Prince leapt down once more, going to one knee before Desirée.

"Joy to her highness on the Longest Night!" he cried, taking her small hand and pressing his lips to it.

Overwhelmed, she tried in vain to stifle a giggle.

"And here we are," Duc Rogier announced with pride, coming alongside them. The Sun Prince raised his gilded mask, revealing a handsome, youthful face. He couldn't have been much more than thirteen or fourteen years old. "Your highness, may I present my eldest son, Tristan."

The lad rose and bowed, smiling at her. "Well met, my lady. I hope we will see more of each other, but for now, I fear duty beckons."

With that, the shining Sun Prince returned to his chariot and his rather irritated-looking Winter Queen. They exited the hall to cheers, with an underlying murmur of speculation. Desirée gazed after them in awe.

I looked at the Royal Minister. "I thought your family preferred to remain in Barthelme, my lord."

He gave a graceful shrug. "I changed my mind. I thought it was time Tristan began learning the ways of the Court, so I sent for him to winter here. Besides, it will be good for her highness to have some younger folk here at the Palace, don't you think? I hear she's quite precocious, and her tutor is very skilled. Mayhap they can take lessons together."

"Your son is at least ten years older than her," Bao said in a flat tone.

"And you considerably more, Messire Bao," the Duc observed. "Yet you appear to benefit from it. Young highness, would *you* like Tristan to study with you?"

Her cheeks were pink with pleasure. "Yes, my lord!"

"Well, then." Rogier Courcel smiled at all of us. "It seems the matter is settled."

I smiled back at him. "So it does."

TWENTY-TWO

I don't like it," Bao fretted.

Neither did I, but there was nothing I could do about the situation. On the face of the matter, it was a perfectly logical thing for the Royal Minister to do; and a thoughtful gesture in the balance. And so young Tristan began spending time with Desirée during her studies.

He was a pretty lad with golden hair and vivid blue eyes, and he was unfailingly charming to the princess. In the manner of young children being flattered by older children everywhere, she delighted in the attention.

My father assured me there was nothing untoward in the matter.

Lianne Tremaine was less sanguine. "He's courting her."

"She's a child!" I protested.

The former King's Poet shrugged. "It's common practice in Aragonia to arrange betrothals between children in royal families. And it's been known to happen here, too."

"But would it not violate Blessed Elua's precept here in Terre d'Ange?" I asked. "Love as thou wilt?"

"That's why he's courting her," Lianne said cynically. "Oh, please! The dashing young Sun Prince in his gilded armor bending a knee to her? What better manner to plant a seed of girlish infatuation in her heart? I couldn't have crafted a better storyline myself. And there's a long history of politicking surrounding the pageant on the Longest

Night. Now all this attention? Please. What fourteen-year-old boy willingly devotes himself to a girl her age? He's courting her."

"She's a *child*!" I was repeating myself. "She's four years old!"

"And when I was five years old, I informed my mother I meant to marry the baker's boy." She shook her head. "If she dotes on the lad, and squeals with delight when Duc Rogier proposes a betrothal, no one will speak against it. Not if the King gives his consent to the union. Do you think he would?"

"I don't know," I said. "But as Desirée's oath-sworn protector, I would argue against it. No one knows their heart at that age."

"Mayhap you should speak to his majesty," Bao suggested.

"I wouldn't," Lianne countered. "Not yet. Your father's right, there's nothing untoward in the situation...yet. You run the risk of looking vindictive and overly suspicious."

"Aye," I said slowly. "But if I wait for them to show their hand, it may be too late." I made up my mind. "I'll speak to him."

The next day, I begged an appointment with King Daniel, who heard me out patiently. When I had finished, he folded his hands on his desk. "Moirin, I have no intention of arranging a betrothal for Desirée before she comes of age."

A wave of relief washed over me. "You don't?"

"I don't," he said in a firm tone. "However, when that day comes, I would certainly find Tristan de Barthelme an acceptable candidate should my daughter find his suit pleasing, and I do not begrudge Duc Rogier the opportunity to allow his eldest to befriend her. Indeed, I would have thought it would please you."

I bit the inside of my cheek. "I am pleased to see Desirée happy, your majesty. But—"

The King sighed. "But you suspect their motives. Ah, Moirin! This is Court; no one's motives are entirely devoid of self-interest." He summoned his faint smile. "Except mayhap yours, which is another reason I appointed you. Desirée is a child, let her have her happiness and bask in the boy's attention. She's D'Angeline, and her mother's daughter." His smile turned sorrowful. "When she does come of age, she's like to fall in love ten times over before she settles."

I laughed ruefully. "True."

He rose. "I give you my word, I'll not see her betrothed young. And if Duc Rogier does propose it..." He hesitated. "Let us say he is not the man I took him to be, and I will feel my trust misplaced."

I rose, too. "I hope I am wrong, my lord."

"I suspect you are." Daniel de la Courcel clasped my hand. "Nonetheless, I appreciate your concern. But I think it best you keep it to yourself rather than spread further ill will in the realm. Do not forget, all of this will change when Thierry returns in the spring."

My *diadh-anam* flared, reminding me that Prince Thierry's return also meant the return of Raphael de Mereliot. Hopefully, whatever unfinished business lay between us would at last be concluded, and I would be freed from my everlasting destiny. "I look forward to it."

"So do I," the King said quietly. "So do I."

I left the King's presence comforted by his promise, but still uneasy with the situation. Mayhap I was being overly suspicious, my thoughts poisoned by Lianne Tremaine's cunning mind. Mayhap I was overly naïve in the intricate ways that courtship and politics intertwined in Terre d'Ange; or mayhap simply overprotective of Jehanne's daughter.

I wished Jehanne would appear in my dreams once more to give me guidance, but she didn't.

Short winter days wore on to long winter weeks, winding slowly toward spring. I debated sharing my fears with Sister Gemma or the tutor Aimée Girard and decided against it, based on the King's warning. During their studies together, Bao kept watch over Tristan's dealings with Desirée.

"He's patient with her," he said. "*Too* patient, at least for a boy his age. The poetess is right. It's unnatural."

"And Desirée?"

"She adores him," Bao confirmed. "But, Moirin...what do you suppose he's like when he's *not* with her?"

I was intrigued. "I could find out, couldn't I?"

Bao grinned. "None better!"

Summoning the twilight, I wrapped myself in its cloak and spent a day stalking Tristan Courcel de Barthelme through the halls of the Palace.

It wasn't easy.

'Twas a tricky business at best to exist between the mortal realm and the spirit realm, rendered trickier by having to navigate the crowded Palace. But I managed, following pretty golden-haired Tristan and dodging peers, guards, and servants in the hallways as he departed the nursery and caught up with friends, twin sons of the Comte de Rochambeau, whose household was alleged to have taken the last available suite in the Palace.

For the most part, I found that young Tristan was a perfectly normal adolescent boy. He was far less polite with friends his age, given to bragging about unlikely exploits, but that was normal.

By the time he abandoned his friends to return to his father's quarters in the Palace, I was in two minds as to whether or not to follow him. It was more risky to be trapped in a private space than roaming a public one, and I'd not learned anything useful of the lad thus far. On the other hand, if the Duc was in residence, mayhap they would speak openly of their intentions.

Deciding that the latter possibility was worth the risk, I slipped into their quarters behind Tristan.

Unfortunately, the only other person there was an attractive little maidservant in the process of dusting. She startled at the sight of the lad. "Oh! Forgive me, my lord! I'll be on my way."

"No, no, don't go." Tristan caught her wrist. "Sylvie, isn't it?"

"Aye, my lord." She tugged in vain. "I should be going."

His voice took on a wheedling tone. "Just one kiss."

Reluctantly, the maid gave him a quick peck on the cheek. Tristan took the opportunity to put his arms around her and pull her close, nuzzling her neck. She struggled. "Please, my lord!"

"What's the matter?" He tightened his grip on her. I daresay

I could have broken it easily enough, but she was a slight wisp of a thing. "Don't you like me, sweet Sylvie? You said I was a lovely boy."

There were tears in her eyes, glimmering in the twilight. "So you are, but I'm newly wed and faithful to my husband."

"I know." Tristan traced the curve of her shoulder. "Which is why you'll not speak of this, will you?"

She shook her head. "Don't, my lord! It's heresy."

"Not if you're willing." He tried to kiss her lips, grabbing her chin when she sought to evade him. "Come, come, sweet Sylvie! It's just a kiss." The wheedling tone in his voice gave way to a threatening one. "Don't you know I could have you dismissed from your post? Now give me a proper kiss."

I'd heard enough—and I had an idea.

Grabbing a handful of his thick, golden hair, I gave it a firm yank, then took him by the scruff of his neck and shook him. Tristan's entire body went rigid. I didn't know firsthand what it felt like when I touched someone in the twilight, but Bao said it was like being touched by a ghost.

To be sure, the lad found it profoundly unnerving.

Lowering my voice, I willed him, and him alone, to hear me. "Tristan de Barthelme, make no mistake! The path you tread is one of heresy," I intoned in his ear. "Let the girl go, and trouble her no more."

He released her as quickly as though her touch scalded him, backing away so fast I had to spin out of his way and nearly lost my grip on the twilight. "I'm sorry!" he said to her, his eyes as wide as saucers. "Just...go!"

The maid fled without hesitation, still clutching her feather duster. I had to hurry to slip out the door behind her.

When I told Bao what I'd done, he laughed until he wept. "Ah gods, Moirin! Why didn't you tell him to leave Desirée alone while you were at it?"

"I didn't think of it," I admitted. "Mayhap I should go back?"

"No, best not to." He wiped his eyes. "Too many folk know about your gift. The lad's likely to figure it if you push your luck too far."

"Well, at least we know he's a lout," I said.

Bao shrugged. "He's a boy trying to steal a kiss from a pretty maid. I was no different at his age."

"No." I shook my head. "It's not *that*. That, I understand. It's that he didn't care that she was unwilling, that he'd thought through the reasons she wouldn't dare speak of it." I shuddered. "And he was quick to threaten her. I don't like him, Bao. And I don't want his majesty thinking he's a fit suitor for Desirée, now or ever."

He sobered. "No, you're right. You should speak to him again."

I did; or at least I tried to.

King Daniel willingly granted me an audience, but he held up one hand when I sat opposite him in his study, forestalling my tale. The lines of sorrow etched on his face were deeper than ever.

"You were right, Moirin," he said heavily. "Duc Rogier approached me yesterday with a proposal that we arrange a betrothal."

I swallowed the words I'd meant to speak. "I'm so sorry, my lord."

"I'd thought better of him," he mused. "Truly, I did. Why? Was it not enough that I appointed him to administer the affairs of the realm?"

As ever, his grief made my heart ache. "Ambition is a dangerous thing," I murmured. "One can harbor it unknowing, only to find it sparked into life when the opportunity presents itself." I thought about the offer that the fallen spirit Marbas had made me, and about how I'd been tempted by Kamadeva's diamond. "No one is immune to it, my lord. I know that I myself am not."

He sighed. "Would that I had been born a simple shepherd!"

I met his gaze. "We do not choose our destinies, my lord. I am sorry, but it is true. What will you do?"

His shoulders rose and fell. "I have denied his proposal. Now I suppose I must appoint someone else to serve in his stead."

"*Your* stead," I reminded him.

It was a piece of insolence, and a part of me hoped that his majesty would rally against it, chastising me. Instead, he bowed his head, dark locks of hair spilling over his brow, his eyes in shadow.

"My stead," he agreed softly. "At least until Thierry returns. I plan to abdicate the throne to him, you know."

I nodded. "I suspected you might."

But in less than a week's time, everything changed.

TWENTY-THREE

A s though the fates were conspiring to grant the King's wishes, the very day after my meeting with his majesty word came that the Dauphin's flagship had reached the harbor at Pellasus and was making its way up the Aviline River toward the City of Elua.

The City rejoiced; and I breathed a sigh of relief.

Spared from the necessity of having to appoint a new Royal Minister, I daresay the King was relieved, too. Couriers tracked the ship's progress along the river. His majesty arranged for a royal reception to greet his returning son, and on a bright spring afternoon, we gathered at the wharf.

Flying the silver swan of House Courcel beneath the lily-and-stars pennant of Terre d'Ange, the ship made dock.

I was there with Bao and Desirée, alongside his majesty and his Royal Minister, presenting a seemingly united front to the realm. Whatever discord seethed beneath the surface was hidden. My father was there, and Tristan de Barthelme beside his own father, the sun glinting on his golden curls. He was on his best behavior.

Desirée squirmed with impatience as we waited for the gang-plank to be lowered, eager to meet the older brother of whom she had heard so much and knew so little. I held her hand, praying that Thierry's return would suffice to make up for the loss of Tristan's attention likely to come. I would urge Prince Thierry to be kind to her, I thought. He had a good heart, and he would listen to me. I hoped so, anyway. During the time that I had served as Jehanne's companion, we had come to form an odd bond of kinship, Thierry and I.

At last, the gangplank was lowered, and a lone figure descended it. The crew remained on the ship, watching in unusual silence for sailors come to port after a long journey. A soft hiss ran through the gathered crowd.

"Moirin?" Bao inquired. "That's not the prince, is it?"

My throat felt tight. "No."

It was someone I knew, though—Denis de Toluard. He had been one of Raphael's closest friends, and a member of the Circle of Shalomon.

It appeared he was fighting tears.

For once in Terre d'Ange, truth had outstripped rumor. There on the wharf, Denis de Toluard made his way to King Daniel's presence and fell to his knees. He gazed upward, his eyes filled with tears and his mouth working.

"Your majesty," he said in a husky voice. "I'm sorry! I'm so sorry! I wanted you to be the first to hear it."

"Tell me." The words dropped like two stones from the King's lips. Desirée had gone still, and her hand felt slippery in mine, although I daresay it was mine that sweated.

Denis bowed his head. "The Dauphin is gone."

Although he spoke softly, the words carried in the stillness; and where they did not carry, they were passed from mouth to ear. A great outcry of shared grief arose, a spontaneous ululating. The only thing that kept me from joining it was the pressure of the young princess' hand in mine.

"Moirin?" she whispered.

"I'm sorry, dear heart," I whispered in reply, my own heart breaking. "Ah, gods! I wish it had been otherwise."

Later, we would learn more details about how the Dauphin's expedition had found favor with the Nahuatl Emperor by virtue of Raphael de Mereliot's skills as a physician. It seemed that along with foreign elements such as horses and steel, the Aragonian explorers who established a base of trade with the Nahuatl unwittingly introduced foreign diseases that ravaged the native folk, rendering them helpless before its onslaught.

The killing pox.

It was Raphael who found a way to ameliorate the effects of the pox, persuading the Nahuatl Emperor to allow him to inoculate him and his extensive family with a lesser strain of the disease.

When it proved effective, the Emperor rewarded him with knowledge, knowledge of another empire on the far side of the sea, rich in gold. But that day on the docks, we learned only that Thierry had set out on a secondary expedition that vanished into the jungles of Terra Nova.

"I was sick myself," Denis de Toluard murmured, still kneeling. "Dysentery. I was too weak to travel. I agreed to stay behind and wait. I waited and waited, your majesty. Months past the appointed time." He lifted his face, screwed up with grief. "But he never came. Prince Thierry never came back. None of them did. He made me promise that if anything befell him, I'd tell you myself. So I took charge of the flagship, and set sail."

The King laid one hand on his head. "It wasn't your fault. You did the right thing."

"It wasn't enough!"

"No." The King smiled sadly. "It never is, is it?"

I swallowed my grief as best I could.

Ah, gods! *Thierry*, good-natured Prince Thierry, who had forgiven me all my transgressions.

Gone...

It seemed impossible—and yet it was so. Of course, it had *always* been a possibility. In my head, I knew this. Ships foundered, men died. Seafaring and exploring was a dangerous business. But in my heart, I simply hadn't thought the gods would be cruel enough to deal one more crushing blow to a man who had experienced so much grief in his life.

King Daniel turned away and began walking toward the royal

carriage like a blind man, his face gone utterly blank. Guards and spectators moved out of his way uncertainly.

Trusting Desirée to Bao's care, I ran after his majesty. "My lord!" I wasn't sure what to say. "You . . . you should not be alone."

He looked at me as though I were a stranger for a moment. "Moirin. Oh. The child." His blank gaze shifted to Desirée, holding Bao's hand, tears streaking her face. "See that she's safely returned to the Palace."

"You should not be alone right now," I said stubbornly.

My father came alongside me. "My daughter is right, your majesty."

"Thank you for your concern," Daniel de la Courcel said with gentle firmness. "You are dismissed."

We could not ignore a royal command, could do nothing but watch as he climbed into the carriage and gave the order to depart.

I stole a glance at Duc Rogier. He was standing with one hand on his son Tristan's shoulder. I thought the look of sorrow on his face was genuine, but behind it, calculating wheels were turning. It struck me that Desirée had just become the heir to the throne of Terre d'Ange in earnest.

Beneath the bright spring sunshine, I shivered.

Obeying the King's order, Bao and I saw the young Dauphine returned to the nursery, where she wept herself into a state of profound exhaustion. Not even Sister Gemma's most soothing cradlesongs could comfort her for the loss of her absent brother. I wondered if she sensed the burden that had settled on her shoulders that day. At last, wrung as limp as a dishrag, Desirée fell asleep with her thumb in her mouth. I stroked her damp hair, plastered to her cheeks. Her tear-spiked lashes were like fans.

"You should go," Sister Gemma said wearily. "She'll sleep for hours now."

"I know."

Our eyes met. "It was a bad day," the priestess said. "A very bad day."

I nodded. "One of the worst."

Bao leaned over the bed, coaxing Desirée's thumb out of her mouth and crooning to her in the Ch'in dialect of his youth. "Tomorrow will be better," he said with a confidence none of us felt. "It will, won't it?"

My eyes stung. "Gods, I hope so!"

It wasn't.

Worn out by my own grief, I slept hard that night. I woke from a dream of a great bell tolling for all the world's sorrows to find Bao shaking me, and every bell in the City of Elua tolling loudly.

"What is it?" I asked sleepily.

"I don't know." Bao's expression was alert and grim. "But I think we ought to find out."

Outside, we found commonfolk roaming the streets of the City, and rumor running wild. We followed the course of the rumors to a promenade along the banks of the Aviline River, close to the Palace, where guardsmen in the livery of House Courcel raced frantically back and forth, torches streaking the night with flame, firelight glinting off the waters of the river. All the while, the bells continued their urgent summons.

"Here, here!"

"No, *here*!"

"There he is!" one shouted, pointing at the river. "There, there!"

I covered my mouth with one hand. "Oh, gods! No!"

Guards plunged into the river.

Bao put his arm over my shoulders, pressed his lips to my hair. "Moirin, don't look."

But I did, because I had to. I looked. I watched as members of the Royal Guard swam and gasped in the benighted waters of the Aviline River, sodden in their livery, towing their burden ashore.

King Daniel.

For once, he looked at peace. His pale, grave face was at peace with death, his dark hair strewn about him in wet tendrils.

There was more shouting.

There were physicians—to no avail. They breathed into his mouth, but he did not respond. His body lay still and lifeless. Daniel de la Courcel, the King of Terre d'Ange, was dead.

Later, we would learn that the King had begged his Captain of the Guard for solitude, and a chance to walk alone along the banks of the river. That his guards had trailed him at a respectful distance, leaving him to his grief. In the darkness, they'd lost sight of him from time to time.

No one knew when he'd slipped over the embankment and waded into the river. All they knew was that he'd done it a-purpose, for he hadn't made a sound and there were stones in his pockets, weighting him down.

I wept.

Bao held me.

Everything had changed.

Everything.

TWENTY-FOUR

Terre d'Ange mourned.

Everywhere in the City of Elua, swags of black crepe were draped over doorways. The trunk of Elua's Oak was swathed in it. Folk gathered in taverns and wineshops, in each other's homes, offering comfort to one another. No one wanted to be alone.

Bao and I spent a great deal of time with Desirée. If the news of her brother's death had sent her into paroxysms of grief, her father's suicide had an even worse effect. Somewhat inside her shut down, and she was near as lifeless as a doll.

I asked my father what was to become of the realm.

"Parliament will convene after the funeral to appoint a regent until the princess gains her majority," he said soberly. "Since Duc Rogier's done a fine job as Royal Minister, odds are they'll select him."

It was what I feared. "Father, they can't!"

He stared at me. "Why ever not?"

"Because the King was going to replace him." I told him what I knew. When I had finished, he closed his eyes for a long time. "I'm sorry!" I whispered in anguish. "I know you care for him."

"I do," he murmured. "But if what you're telling me is true...it should at least be taken into account."

"What do we do?" I asked him.

My father sighed. "You'll have to petition to address Parliament,

Moirin. And I warn you, they will not want to hear what you have to say, and you'll earn his grace's enmity in the bargain." He ran a hand over his face. "Think well on it. Rogier may be more ambitious than I reckoned, but he's a good man at heart."

"Is his son?" I asked. "Because *that's* who he's aiming to put on the throne. *That's* who he'd see betrothed to Desirée."

He fell silent for a time. "I don't know. Just... think on it."

My *diadh-anam* flickered. "I will," I said. "But I may not have a choice. I'm oath-bound."

"I know." He took my hand. "And I will stand by you, no matter what you decide."

Three days after the King's death, a joint funeral service for Daniel and Thierry de la Courcel was held at the great Temple of Elua. Bao and I rode in the royal carriage with Desirée, Duc Rogier, and his son.

All throughout the streets of the City, folk turned out to share their grief, weeping openly and calling out blessings on the young princess. Desirée stared straight ahead without responding, clad in a black gown that made her translucent skin look ghostly pale. A delicate crown of gold filigree sat atop her fair hair. I held her hand and whispered words of comfort to her.

Duc Rogier acknowledged the mourners with solemn nods. Young Tristan looked grave and noble, bending forward from time to time to pat Desirée's other hand. She gazed at him with listless eyes.

I remembered how she had sparkled at the tumblers' performance the day of the oath-swearing ceremony, how his majesty had reached out to her and helped her throw the bouquet at Antoine nó Eglantine's feet, and I wanted to weep.

For Desirée's sake, I didn't.

Bao gave me a miserable glance over the top of her crowned head, understanding.

At the temple, we removed our shoes and stockings in the vestibule and proceeded into the garden sanctum. Directed by priests and priestesses, we took our place at the base of the plinth on which the effigy of Blessed Elua stood. A seemingly endless throng of mourning peers followed us, jostling for position. Exchanging complicit nods with the royal guardsmen in attendance, Bao took a protective stance beside Desirée, leaning on his bamboo staff. Somehow, they'd gotten word of his prowess.

Once the sanctum was full and the doors to the temple had been barred, the senior Priest of Elua who had presided over the oath-swearing ceremony gave the invocation. It was earnest and heart-felt, reminding the crowd of all the tragic losses House Courcel had suffered over the years, and it reduced well nigh the entire crowd to tears—including me. Although I managed to keep from sobbing aloud, this time I couldn't stop the tears from falling.

I couldn't help it.

When he was done, Duc Rogier spoke. "They were kin," he said simply. "And I loved them both very much. Prince Thierry for his unfailing good nature, his boundless spirit of adventure. King Daniel for his vast, gentle heart, and his gracious manner. And today I am angry at the gods for allowing their best qualities to destroy them."

A murmur ran through the crowd.

The priest raised one hand for silence. "The gods understand."

"I hope they do." Duc Rogier Courcel de Barthelme turned to glance at Blessed Elua's effigy. "While I am not a member of House Courcel proper, I am descended from it. I bear the Courcel name, as do all the members of House Barthelme." He bowed in Desirée's direction. There were tears in his eyes, but the line of his jaw was set and firm. "I was your brother's oath-sworn protector, young majesty, not yours. But I swear to you today, I will do all in my power to keep further sorrow from touching House Courcel."

"As will I!" Tristan called in a ringing voice. "I promise, Desirée!"

It was well received—and it made me angry.

The worst part of it was that I *didn't* doubt the Duc's grief was sincere. But it was still a piece of theater. He was willing to use his grief and the plight of a royal orphan to further his own ends.

At least it dried my tears.

"Moirin, don't glower," Bao murmured to me. "You can't afford to lose sympathy."

I gritted my teeth. "I am trying!"

Desirée tugged at my hand. "What's wrong, Moirin? Are you angry at the gods, too?"

It was the first spark of life I'd seen from her since her father's death. I knelt and hugged her. She felt oh, so very fragile in my arms. "Today, yes, dear heart. Today I am hurt and angry. But it's all right. It's all right to feel such things. Everyone does. You heard the priest, didn't you? The gods understand sorrow—and anger, too."

She put her arms around my neck, nestling her face against my throat. "Why do they send so much of it?"

"I don't know," I admitted.

Bao crouched beside us. "It is their way of teaching us to be strong," he said to her. "It is a hard way, but it is the only way. And you *are* strong, aren't you?"

The young princess gave him a faint smile. "Strong like a dragon?"

He nodded. "Exactly."

After the funeral service was concluded, there was another procession through the streets of the City of Elua, ending in a reception at the Palace. Sister Gemma reclaimed Desirée and restored her to the nursery. I watched the politicking that took place, feeling uneasy at it.

Life ended, but politics continued.

When the delegation from House Shahrizai approached us, I felt chagrin added to my grief. They, too, would suffer from the way the politics of this tragedy played out. "I'm so sorry, my lady," I said to Celestine Shahrizai. My voice sounded hollow. "I fear your generosity toward us proved a bad investment."

The matriarch of the House gave my elbow a hard squeeze—hard enough to hurt, yet strangely bracing for it. "Do not blame yourself for the vagaries of fate, young one, nor fear our generosity will be withdrawn. We knew the risk we took."

"It's not your fault," Balthasar added. With his blue-black hair and ivory skin, he looked well in mourning garb, but his eyes were rimmed with red and there were dark shadows beneath them. His mouth twisted bitterly. "I should have been there. I should have gone with Thierry."

"There's nothing you could have done," his cousin Josephine murmured.

Balthasar turned his grief-haunted gaze on her. "We'll never know, will we?" His gaze shifted onto Rogier Courcel, deep in conference with the Comte de Thibideau, with a handful of other peers respectfully waiting their turn to speak with him. "And gods damn Daniel de la Courcel for putting us in this situation!"

The other Shahrizai hushed him hastily. I glanced around, but it didn't seem anyone had noticed.

"I'm going to go get drunk," Balthasar announced. "Who's with me?"

Bao and I declined. I had to address the Parliament tomorrow, my petition to do so having been reluctantly granted, and I would need my wits about me. As the reception thinned, we took our leave, returning home through the somber, silent streets of the City of Elua. Our house steward, Guillaume Norbert, greeted us with weary gravity and asked if there was aught that we required.

All I wanted was to sleep, and wake to find this was all a terrible dream. I thanked him for his kindness and retired to the bedchamber. I undressed and crawled into bed. Bao moved around the chamber quietly, snuffing the lamps.

"It will get better, Moirin," he murmured, joining me in our bed. "Day by day, bit by bit. It will get easier to bear."

"It's just so *unfair*!" My voice broke on the last word.

"I know." Bao held me and breathed the Breath of Ocean's Rolling Waves, deep and soothing. "I know."

Comforted by his warmth and worn out by sorrow, I fell into

sleep as though it were a bottomless pit from which I never wished to emerge.

I slept, and dreamed.

I dreamed I was back in the Palace, standing in the hallway outside the door to the enchanted bower Jehanne had had made for me.

I took a deep breath before I opened the door.

Jehanne was there, seated on the edge of my bed beneath the green fronds of the great fern. As ever, the fern-shadows painted delicate traceries on her fair skin; but this time, she was fully clothed. She lifted her head as I entered the room, and her blue-grey eyes were bright with tears.

She knew.

A choked sound escaped me. I crossed the room and fell to my knees before her, burying my face in her lap. My shoulders shook with sobs, the sobs of profound grief that I'd not yet loosed. Jehanne held me, stroking my hair until the worst of the storm had passed. It was a long time before I could look up at her.

"I'm so sorry," I whispered.

"I know," she said sadly. There was a depth of knowledge and wisdom in her beautiful face that she'd only begun to acquire in life. "So am I. And I am angry, too, my beautiful girl. But Daniel had borne all that he could, and I forgive him for it." She stroked my cheeks, wiping away the tracks of my tears. "This was one blow too many."

I repeated what I knew was a child's futile protest. "It's not *fair*!"

"No, it's not," Jehanne agreed. "But that doesn't mean there isn't a purpose in it." Her hand lingered against my cheek, cupping it with affection. The sorrow in her star-bright eyes reminded me of the sorrow in the gaze of the Maghuin Dhonn Herself when She had laid a destiny on me. "It's coming time, Moirin."

Even in a dream, I felt cold. "Time for what?"

"You."

I swallowed hard. "What do you mean?"

Jehanne bent her silver-gilt head toward me as though she meant to kiss me or whisper a secret in my ear. I could smell her glorious, intoxicating scent wrapped around me, feel her soft breath on my cheek.

"Thierry is alive," she said to me.

TWENTY-FIVE

Thierry is alive.

For the second time in my life, I jerked away from my lady Jehanne's touch. I found myself on my feet without knowing how I'd gotten there. She sat without moving on the edge of the bed. I stared at her, aghast.

"Why didn't you tell me before?" I shouted at her. "Gods, Jehanne! I could have kept your husband from killing himself! I could have kept your daughter from becoming an orphaned political pawn!"

She shook her head with regret. "I couldn't."

"Why?" I demanded.

"There are rules, Moirin," Jehanne said in a gentle tone. "I don't always understand them, but there are. I wasn't allowed to know until now. It was his fate. Desirée's depends on you now."

I paced the room in a fury. "Thierry's alive? You're sure? You're *sure?*" She nodded. I fetched up before her, flinging my arms wide. "So what am *I* to do about it?"

"You're to cross the sea to Terra Nova, find Thierry, and bring him back," Jehanne said simply.

Tears of frustration stung my eyes. "That's all?"

"Yes and no." Her exquisite face was grave. "I don't know, Moirin. Not all of it. Only what I'm allowed to. But this business with Raphael . . . that's where it's meant to be concluded."

That caught me up short, my *diadh-anam* blazing like a bonfire in my chest.

Raphael de Mereliot.

He had vanished along with Prince Thierry and the rest of the expedition, and my destiny was bound up with his. It always had been, and it remained unfinished. Of course he was alive, too. In my grief, I hadn't even thought of it. I sighed and sat beside Jehanne on the bed. "I swore an oath to protect your daughter, my lady," I murmured. "Would you have me forsworn?"

"Never." Jehanne laced her fingers with mine, raising one hand to kiss it. "But you can't do it from here."

"I can try!" I protested. "Better here than afar!"

"You'll fail," she said with candor. "Moirin, you're a bear-witch of the Maghuin Dhonn. You've done well, so very well, to court favor among certain quarters of Terre d'Ange." She hugged my hand to her breast. "But it's not going to be enough. There are too many forces arrayed against you, too many folk eager to resent you. If you stay, you will try and fail, and Desirée..." Her voice faltered. "You saw how she's been since her father's death? With the spark of life crushed out in her?"

I nodded.

"*That* will be her fate, if you do not bring her brother home."

I sighed.

I paced the room.

"I'm scared," I admitted at last. "Oh, Jehanne! I've already gone so very far, far from home."

"I know." She stood and wrapped her arms around me, leaned her brow against mine. "Gone and returned, my beautiful girl. Can you not do it once more?"

The memory of the Maghuin Dhonn Herself turning Her face away came to me, Her vast muzzle blotting out the stars. Behind Her oceans beckoned to me through the stone doorway, a multitude of sparkling oceans to cross.

"I will try," I promised.

Jehanne kissed me tenderly, her lips soft and lingering on mine. "That is all I can ask of you."

All too soon, I awoke with a gasp, cast out of my dream and into the grey dawn of reality. My *diadh-anam* continued to blaze within me. Bao was awake, staring at me with wide eyes and parted lips, and I knew he felt it, too.

"Moirin?" he said. "What passes here?"

"Thierry's alive," I whispered.

"How . . . ?" Bao ran one hand over his disheveled hair, which stuck out in every direction. "Jehanne." I nodded. He cast an unerring glance toward the west. "And we're meant to go and fetch him, I suppose."

I swallowed hard, fighting tears. "So it seems."

"Gods, Moirin!" he grumbled, clambering out of bed with a yawn. "Could your destiny possibly be any more burdensome? And what is it with D'Angeline princes going missing? Didn't you tell me a long story about another one who couldn't manage to stay put?"

It made me laugh through my tears. "Bao . . ."

"It's all right." He pulled on a pair of breeches and came over to kiss me, strong hands gripping my shoulders. "Moirin, if it is what must be done, it is what we will do. But we can only take one step at a time, and today you're addressing the members of Parliament."

"What's the point?" I said dully. "Jehanne told me I'm bound to fail."

"Does Jehanne know everything?" he asked. "Did she tell you exactly *where* to find Prince Thierry, and why in the world he and his party never returned?"

"No," I admitted. "She said there are rules. That she only knows what she's allowed to know."

"Well, then." Bao gave me a little shake. "Even if you do fail, it may be that the attempt is important. And anyway, you have to try. It's in Desirée's best interest, and you're oath-bound."

My *diadh-anam* flickered in agreement. I smiled ruefully at Bao.

"Now you're developing the sensibilities of the Maghuin Dhonn, my magpie."

He let go of me and touched his bare chest with a somber look. "I have to. What would become of me if you broke your oath, Moirin?"

I didn't answer; we both knew. The spark of my divided *diadh-anam* had restored Bao to life. I'd sworn the sacred oath of the Maghuin Dhonn. If I broke it, that spark would be extinguished in me. I would live, albeit in a hellish state of separation from all that was sacred to my people, stripped of the gifts of the Maghuin Dhonn Herself, barred forever from Her presence.

But Bao... Bao would die.

The reminder gave me the strength to rise and wash and dress, to break my fast and prepare to face the members of Parliament.

I spent the morning going over what I meant to say to them. There were two branches of Parliament in Terre d'Ange, the High and Low Councils. The High Council was composed of seventy hereditary seats among the Great Houses, ten for each province in the realm, plus a vote for the monarch and his or her heir; or in the absence of an heir of age, two votes for the sitting monarch. Since Terre d'Ange lacked a monarch, there would be only seventy votes cast by the High Council.

Naturally, Duc Rogier de Barthelme's would be one of them.

The Low Council was composed of fourteen seats from the Lesser Houses of Terre d'Ange. These too were hereditary, held by descendants of the minor lords and ladies who had formed a shadow Parliament under the aegis of Alais de la Courcel, the Queen's younger daughter, in a desperate attempt to restore order during a time when most of the Great Houses had been driven mad by dire magic and the realm torn asunder by the threat of civil war.

If I had any allies, it would likely be in the Low Council. It was a pity there were only fourteen members.

The Hall of Parliament was an imposing chamber, a vast space of unadorned marble with a high, vaulted ceiling. The members sat in tiered rows in a gallery that curved around the room, looking down on the speaker's floor.

I'd been allotted a mere quarter hour in the early afternoon to address them. When I arrived, the atmosphere was calm, and I had the feeling that a consensus had already been reached. It made what I was about to do harder. Bao and my father both accompanied me, but they had to remain in the background while I walked onto the center of the speaker's floor alone. Faces peered down from the gallery, some neutral, some curious. Only Celestine Shahrizai met my gaze with sympathy. Duc Rogier's expression was unreadable.

"My lords and ladies..." My voice shook. I cleared my throat and took a few deep breaths. "You know me as Moirin mac Fainche of the Maghuin Dhonn, but as I stand here before you, I would remind you that I, too, am a descendant of House Courcel—a direct descendant of Alais de la Courcel. There are fourteen of you sitting here today who would not be here were it not for my great-great-grandmother's strength and courage."

There were nods of agreement all along the upper tiers of the gallery, where members of the Low Council sat.

It heartened me. "In Alba, her counsel is credited with ensuring peace among all her folk," I continued. "There, she is remembered as Alais the Wise. And I stand before you in the spirit of my great-great-grandmother, who never quailed in the face of terrible truths."

Murmurs ran around the chamber. Rogier de Barthelme frowned. It was not a tack he had expected me to take.

I took another deep breath. "It is a difficult truth I must ask you to hear today. As you know, I also stand before you as Desirée de la Courcel's oath-sworn protector, chosen by King Daniel himself. What you do not know is that his majesty planned to replace Duc Rogier de Barthelme as the Royal Minister."

In the shocked silence that followed, his face flushed with anger.

"Is it true?" someone from the upper tiers called.

"No," Duc Rogier said shortly. "It's not."

"His grace was unaware of this turn of events." I met his gaze. "The day after his majesty made his decision, he received news of Prince Thierry's return, rendering his decision moot. After that..." I spread my hands. "To our everlasting sorrow, we all know what transpired."

There were a few moments of shouting and pandemonium before the Parliamentary adjudicator banged his gavel and called for order. "Your grace, do you wish to rebut the accusation?" he inquired.

"I don't deem it worthy of a rebuttal," the Duc retorted in a scathing tone. "But I would ask Lady Moirin on what grounds she bases this ridiculous accusation. Why would the King replace me?"

"Because he grew wary of your ambitions when you proposed a betrothal between your eldest son and his four-year-old daughter," I said.

Duc Rogier laughed. "Because I proposed strengthening the alliance between our houses based on the fact that the young princess dotes on my boy? Why in the world would Daniel take offense?"

I raised my voice. "Because she's *four years old*!"

He shrugged. "And if she were to come of age and have a change of heart, the betrothal would be annulled. This is Terre d'Ange, after all."

It was a lie, but it was an effective one. In the gallery, even in the upper tiers where the Low Council sat, heads nodded. I'd had them— and I'd lost them.

Even so, I shook my head. "By then it would be too late. You've coached your son to manipulate her, to engage her affections by false means. You arranged that whole business with the Sun Prince—"

"*Enough.*" The Duc de Barthelme slammed his hand down on the marble railing in front of him. "This is serious business we're about here, Moirin mac Fainche of the Maghuin Dhonn." His eyes blazed with righteous fury. "King Daniel indulged you long enough in memory of the inexplicable favor his late wife bestowed on you. But I think we have had enough, and more than enough, of your fanciful tales, your dragons and tumblers and blind princesses and the like; and now these absurd accusations. Your presence here has sown nothing but scandal, gossip, and discord from the day you arrived. Go home to Alba, and spin tales for your own folk. Go back to the land Alais de la Courcel chose to make her home. Leave the governance of Terre d'Ange to D'Angelines."

The lower galleries roared in approval, clapping their hands and stamping their feet. The upper galleries were silent.

I felt my shoulders slump in defeat.

"Are you calling my daughter a liar, Rogier?" my father asked from the back of the chamber in a clear, carrying voice. Unbidden, he came onto the speaker's floor to join me, elegant and graceful in his crimson robes. The guards let him pass unimpeded, reluctant to lay hands on a Priest of Naamah. "Because I will not have it."

"This isn't Naamah's business, Phanuel," Duc Rogier said curtly. "Stay out of it."

My father ignored his command. "Do you say Moirin lies?"

The Duc locked gazes with him. "I do."

"Well, then." My father inclined his head. "I fear this concludes the long friendship between us."

Duc Rogier's jaw tightened visibly. "You would do that, Phanuel?" There was genuine pain mixed with the anger in his voice. "You would throw away our history, everything we have been to one another, for the sake of a daughter you barely know?" He gestured at me. "A daughter gotten on a single night's pleasure with a half-wild Alban bear-witch?"

"You don't need to do this," I whispered.

My father turned to me, gazing at me with his green eyes so very like my own. "I do." He turned back to face the gallery. "Yes, Rogier, I would. Because I didn't need to know Moirin long to come to love her. Because I know that she did not lie here today. And I would remind you, and all here assembled, that it was Naamah herself that called me to Moirin's mother."

There was a hushed silence in the chamber.

Spreading his arms, my father continued. "You say it is not Naamah's business you do here; but who are you to say? Can you discern the will of the gods? As surely as Naamah called me to Moirin's mother, it was Naamah who led Moirin to Queen Jehanne, whose daughter she seeks to protect here today, in obedience to her oath. So, my lords and ladies, I bid you think on *that* as you make your decision."

All eighty-four voices of the members of Parliament spoke at once, repeating and discussing my father's words.

Belatedly, the adjudicator banged his gavel and called the proceedings to order. "My lords, my ladies!" He gave me a stony look. "Lady Moirin, your allotted time has come to an end. Have you any final words?"

I did not think I could surpass my father's comments. "No, messire. I do not."

The adjudicator banged his gavel again. "Then you are dismissed."

TWENTY-SIX

The debate I had sparked in Parliament, fueled by my father's words, raged on for two more days.

In the end, it was closer than it might have been, but not close enough. When at last the two branches agreed to vote on the confirmation of Duc Rogier de Barthelme as the Regent of Terre d'Ange, almost a full third of the members voted against it.

Almost.

All fourteen members of the Low Council voted against it; and seventeen members of the High Council joined them. But it wasn't enough. By a quorum of two-thirds of his peers, Rogier de Barthelme was appointed Regent.

"You did your best," Bao consoled me. "And your father was splendid."

I sighed. "Aye, but now we've a new dilemma."

Bao glanced westward. "Terra Nova?"

I nodded. "It's not as though there's a ship on which we can book passage. I don't have the first idea about how to get one to take us there. Do you?"

"No," he admitted. "But I know who does. And I think he will be very interested in what you have to say."

"Do you think he'll believe it?" I asked. "Because apparently, my credibility is questionable."

Bao shrugged. "We can but try, Moirin."

Somewhat to my surprise, Balthasar Shahrizai *did* believe me. He heard me out as I told of Jehanne's appearances in my dreams, and the last one in which she had revealed that Prince Thierry was alive. When I had finished, he paced our parlor like a captive panther, lean and restless, his blue-black braids swinging. "You're sure?" he asked, echoing my question to Jehanne. "You're *sure*?"

My *diadh-anam* flared. "Quite sure, my lord."

"I know it may seem strange," Bao added. "But I would willingly wager my life on it."

Balthasar paused and tapped his lips in thought. "Money's no object," he said absently. "House Shahrizai is swimming in it. I've no doubt I can persuade my great-aunt Celestine to back a second expedition, and I daresay there are others who would be willing to support it, especially on the rumor that Thierry lives. But it would require a letter of decree from our blasted Regent to authorize it." He gave me a deep look. "I suspect it best if you stay far, far away from that process, Moirin."

I shuddered. "Gladly."

"We need more information," he said in a decisive tone. "We need to talk to Denis de Toluard and find out everything he knows. What made him so certain that Thierry was dead? And if he's not, what in the seven hells happened to him?"

"Good questions," Bao agreed, slinging his staff over his shoulder. "Let's go find him."

As it happened, that was easier said than done. At Denis de Toluard's townhouse, his steward informed us that his lordship had gone to Night's Doorstep to drink himself into a stupor after the funeral, with strict orders that he was to be left to his own devices until he was good and ready to return.

"But that was two days ago," the steward added, a worried look on his face. "I'd be grateful if you'd find him and bring him back. I haven't seen him in such a state since—" He gave me a sidelong glance and didn't finish.

I knew what he was thinking. Other than that day on the docks,

the last time I'd seen Denis de Toluard was the day the Circle of Shalomon summoned Focalor, and Claire Fourcay had been killed.

The steward wrung his hands. "Just bring him home safely, will
you? I'd never forgive myself if he followed in his majesty's footsteps."

"We'll find him," Balthasar promised.

We spent the day searching every tavern and wineshop in Night's
Doorstep, where no one had seen Denis since the night before. At last,
a worn-looking young woman in a threadbare gown, pretty enough
to serve Naamah, but not pretty enough to serve in one of the Houses
of the Night Court, told us that she'd seen him staggering toward the
wharf around dawn.

"I recognized him," she said. "So I followed him for a time. I was
afraid he might…" She hesitated.

"Follow in his majesty's footsteps?" I asked gently.

The young woman nodded. "He didn't, though. He turned into
the first tavern he came to. So I went home."

"You're a good girl," Balthasar said in approval, fishing in the purse
at his belt. "What's your name?"

She curtsied. "Caterine, my lord."

He pressed several coins into her hand, closing her fingers over
them. "A token of thanks for your concern. Buy yourself a new gown,
my love."

Caterine peered into her hand and gaped. A good deal of gold
glinted in her palm. "My lord!"

Balthasar patted her on the head. "Or a dozen gowns, or a pony.
Whatever you like. Come, let's on to the wharf."

"See, I told you he was a good fellow, Moirin," Bao said to me as
we set out to follow him in the direction of the river, the girl Caterine
staring after us.

"So it seems," I agreed. "Despite appearances."

"Keep it to yourselves," Balthasar said with an ironic glance over
his shoulder. "I wouldn't want to ruin my hard-won reputation."

The taverns along the wharf were rough places, catering to the
sailors and boatmen who frequented them. These were not establish-

ments where one went to enjoy the conviviality and slightly disreputable thrill of Night's Doorstep. They were places where men went to drown their sorrows and brawl. To be sure, I received some strange looks as we searched for Denis de Toluard in them, and Bao unslung his staff after our first unsuccessful foray, holding it in a casual defensive pose, his dark eyes glinting in warning.

The sun was beginning to set in the west, slanting rays gilding the Aviline River, when at last we found our quarry. It was in the fourth tavern or fifth tavern we tried along the docks; a fusty little place with rough-hewn walls streaked with the soot of decades' worth of candle and lamp-smoke.

"Him?" The innkeeper nodded at Balthasar's inquiry, jerking his thumb toward the back of the room. "Oh, aye. I reckon that's who you're after."

Denis de Toluard was a wreck.

When I'd first met him, I'd reckoned him a pretty enough fellow with a handsome face, brown curls, and bright blue eyes. Now his face was haggard and lined beyond his years, his hair was greasy and matted, and his bleary, red-rimmed eyes could barely focus on us as we approached him where he slumped over a table, surrounded by half a dozen drunken sailors.

"Balthasar?" he slurred.

Balthasar Shahrizai folded his arms over the chest of his elegant velvet doublet. "Time to go home, Denis."

"Nuh-uh. Nuh-uh." He wrapped his hands protectively around a leather tankard, giving me a blurry look. "Moirin?"

"Hello, Denis," I said softly. I had lingering cause to be angry with him, but I couldn't be cruel. Not here, not now. "Balthasar is right. It's time to go home."

"No!" His hands tightened, denting the leather tankard. "I don' wanna!"

"You're coming with us," Balthasar said mildly, exchanging a glance with Bao. "Willing or no."

"I'm not goin' anywhere with you. You didn' even have the ballocks to come with us. These are my friends, my only real friends." Denis de Toluard gestured around him with drunken dignity. "Sailed with 'em to Terra Nova and alla way back. Damn bloody Nahuatl, damn bloody place. Thierry, Raphael, alla them...Gone, all gone. And we did nothing. Nothing, I tell you! Don' know what we could, but we didn't." He rubbed at his eyes. "They unnerstand, they do. So lemme be."

One of the sailors rose unsteadily, looming over the table. "You heard 'is lordship. Let 'im be."

"Sit down." Bao tapped him smartly in the center of his chest with the butt end of his staff. The sailor fell back into his chair and looked surprised. Others rose with menacing intentions. Bao grinned and twirled his staff until it was a blur, making the air sing. "It's been too long since I had a good fight," he said cheerfully. "Go ahead."

Two of them lunged at him at once. Bao's staff whipped left and right, and both sailors fell back, clutching their heads and groaning. He jabbed a third in the belly, and the fellow doubled over with a grunt of pain.

"Bao, wait." I tugged on his black-and-white magpie coat. "My lord Denis, listen. We need to talk to you. I have reason to believe Thierry is alive."

Denis de Toluard stared at me with bleary eyes.

"Raphael, too," I added.

He held up one hand to forestall the sailors, who were all too glad to comply, then leaned over and vomited a copious quantity of ale onto the tavern floor.

"Oh, gods!" Balthasar Shahrizai exclaimed in disgust. Bao leaned on his staff without comment.

"Do you mean to torture me, Moirin?" Denis lurched upright in his chair, wiping his mouth with the back of his hand. At least he sounded marginally less incoherent after having spewed the contents of his belly. "Is that it? Is this repayment for the way the Circle of Shalomon used you?" His mouth twisted bitterly. "A trick, like the tricks the spirits we summoned taught you to play? That would be a fine jest."

"No." I stooped beside his chair, taking care to keep my skirts out of the puddle of vomit, and looked him in the eyes. "I swear to you by stone and sea and sky, and all that they encompass, by the sacred troth that binds me to my *diadh-anam*, it is no trick."

All the sailors were silent.

Denis de Toluard held my gaze for a moment, reading the truth of my words written there; and then buried his face in his hands. "Elua!" he gasped in a muffled tone. "Take me home, please."

TWENTY-SEVEN

---·✦·---

Much like finding him, the task of escorting Denis de Toluard home was easier said than done.

He was still very, very drunk.

We got him upright, although he was unsteady on his feet. Balthasar Shahrizai settled his tab with the innkeeper, who shrugged stoically, pocketed the coin, and poured sawdust from a bucket over the puddle of vomited ale.

"Dark days," was the innkeeper's only comment.

Bao and Balthasar slung Denis' arms over their shoulders and set about the chore of helping him out of the tavern.

One of the sailors staggered after us. "Lady!" he called. "Hey, lady! Did you mean it?"

I inclined my head. "I did."

There were tears in his eyes. "If there's a chance Prince Thierry's alive, if you're bent on getting his highness back, I'll sail with you, lady. We all will, every last one of us, even if it means going back to that godforsaken place."

"Was it truly that terrible?" I asked with sympathy and genuine curiosity. "Terra Nova?"

He nodded. "It's bad."

"We'll see," I promised him.

Among the three of us, we maneuvered Denis de Toluard back to his townhouse, Balthasar alternating between grumbling that we should have taken a carriage and making insinuating comments in praise of Bao's prowess with his staff. I rather thought Bao enjoyed the latter. Slung between them, Denis kept his head down and concentrated on putting one wavering foot in front of the other, the toes of his boots catching on the cobbled streets from time to time as the two men half assisted, half dragged him homeward.

"Sorry," he mumbled, over and over. "Sorry, sorry."

"Don't worry." Bao patted his back encouragingly. "You're doing well. Under the circumstances, who could blame you?"

"Sorry to be a problem, not sorry I'm drunk." Denis swung his head from side to side. "Can't help it, don't regret it. Only thing kept me sane. But you, Moirin. I owe you an apology, don't I, my lady? A big, big apology."

"Mayhap," I murmured. "But now's not the time to speak of it."

Ignoring my words, he coughed and hiccupped, releasing a waft of stale ale and bile on the night air. "You tried to tell us, but we were so damn *sure*. Raphael most of all. He thought you were sent by the gods to aid us. Him."

"So did I for a time," I admitted. "But not that way."

Denis hiccupped again. "It all went wrong, Moirin. So very, very wrong. All of it. That's where it all began. We should never have attempted to summon Focalor."

"I know," I said quietly.

"You always did," he said. "But we were too goddamned proud to listen to you. Well, I'm listening now."

By the time we got Denis de Toluard home, he was nearly able to walk on his own. His steward thanked us profusely, taking custody of his drunken lord.

"Get a good night's sleep and sober up," Balthasar advised Denis, adding a pointed sniff. "And have a good, long bath. We'll call on you on the morrow."

That was our plan, at any rate; but we had not reckoned on the very public nature of our retrieval of Denis de Toluard, and the inevitable gossip it spawned. D'Angeline sailors are a garrulous lot, especially drunken ones. By morning, my claim that Prince Thierry was alive was all over the City of Elua, and Bao and I found ourselves summoned to appear before the newly appointed Regent.

Duc Rogier was in a state of white-hot fury. His anger in the Hall of Parliament was mostly theatrics. This, this was genuine rage.

"*What*"—he gritted out the word, and had to pause to collect himself with a violent shudder before continuing—"what in the name of all that's holy do you mean by spreading such a rumor? Moirin, I understand you're unhappy at being thwarted. But this…" He shook his head in disbelief. "This is beyond the pale. It's irresponsible, childish, and downright *cruel*."

"It's not a ploy, my lord," I murmured. I couldn't blame him for thinking otherwise. "I had…a vision."

The Duc picked up a paperweight of colorful Serenissiman glass, squeezing it so hard his knuckles whitened. Bao eased his staff surreptitiously out of its harness, but the Duc was merely trying to contain his fury. "You had a vision," he repeated in a flat voice. "A vision."

"Moirin's folk are known for such gifts," Bao offered.

"I know what Moirin's folk are known for!" Duc Rogier shouted at him. "Do you think to tell a descendant of House Courcel what comes of the Maghuin Dhonn meddling with visions?"

"It wasn't that kind of vision." While the Duc and Bao were glaring at one another, I took a deep breath and summoned the twilight, wrapping it around all three of us and plunging the study into dimness.

In the soft blue gloaming, Duc Rogier startled, the whites of his eyes showing. "What threat is this?" he demanded. "Guards!"

"They can't hear you," I informed him. "And this is no threat, my lord." I let the twilight fade away. "It is a way of taking half a step into the spirit world. I wanted you to see, so that you might understand better. It is a gift that has allowed me, from time to time, to do things others cannot. I believe it is why this…vision…was given to me." I met his gaze without flinching. Balthasar had told me to stay well away from discussing an expedition with the Duc, but I reckoned it was a moot point now. "As Denis de Toluard can attest, I have already sworn on the sacred oath of the Maghuin Dhonn that this is no trick. I believe Prince Thierry is alive. So let us lay our cards on the table, my lord. I mean to gather an expedition to Terra Nova and attempt to bring him back. Do you mean to oppose me?"

He looked at me, his rage slowly ebbing and turning to wonder. "You really do believe this, don't you?"

I had a feeling I'd be answering a version of that question many times before this was over. "Aye," I said. "I do."

Duc Rogier's death-grip on the glass paperweight eased. He tossed it in the air and caught it as he contemplated his response. "Do I mean to oppose you?" he mused. "I'd like to, Moirin. Even assuming you *are* telling the truth, it's a foolhardy notion with little chance of success, and I suspect more men will die for your precious vision."

"I fear it, too," I said honestly.

He gave me a sharp glance. "But you've done a fair job of setting a third of my Parliament against me. What will they say if I oppose you?"

"They will say that you were afraid that Moirin would succeed in restoring the rightful heir to the throne," Bao said in a calm tone. "And they will meet again, and vote to strip you of your appointment and replace you. And then the new Regent will grant us a letter of decree, and we will sail anyway."

Duc Rogier was silent, his lips pressed tight. At length, he dismissed us with a curt gesture. "Go. Get out of my sight."

Outside the door to his study, I let out a breath I hadn't realized I'd been holding.

"That went reasonably well," Bao observed. "He can't afford to oppose us. See, Moirin? I told you there was a reason for you to address the Parliament."

I took his arm. "So you did, my magpie."

"Lady Moirin?" one of a pair of royal guardsmen stationed outside the Regent's study addressed me in a deferential manner. "We heard your witchcraft tells you his highness Prince Thierry and his company yet live. Is it true?"

"I believe it to be true," I said. "Although I fear I can offer no proof."

"And you mean to try to rescue them?" the second guard inquired.

"We do," Bao confirmed.

The guards exchanged a glance. "I've heard tales of Terra Nova," the one who'd spoken first said. " 'Tis a dangerous place. You'll need good steel by your side—sharp swords, and strong arms to wield them." He lowered his voice. "You'll find no shortage of volunteers amidst the Royal Guard, my lady. Prince Thierry was a great favorite in the Palace, always quick with a kind word and a jest."

"My thanks," I said to him, my eyes stinging. "I will remember it."

He nodded. "You do that."

Ah, gods! Last night, the sailor; today, the guards. It was almost too much to bear, for I knew in my heart that Rogier de Barthelme was right. If we undertook this quest, whether we succeeded or failed, men would die.

It was as simple as that.

And their blood would be on *my* hands.

"It's not your fault, Moirin," Bao said quietly to me on the carriage-ride to Denis de Toluard's home. "You didn't choose your destiny, burdensome as it is."

"No." I wiped my eyes. "But this time I am the one setting this thing in motion, Bao. That means *I* am responsible for it. And I cannot help but think..." I paused, and he waited patiently. "I cannot help but think Denis de Toluard is right," I said at last. "Somehow, everything goes back to the Circle of Shalomon. That's where it all began to go wrong. My lady Jehanne even said I'm meant to finish my business with Raphael in Terra Nova. I don't know how, but it's all tied together, and Thierry is caught up in it through no fault of his own." I shook my head. "I should never, ever have aided them. And that, too, is my responsibility."

Bao shrugged. "And you are facing it."

"Aye," I said. "But so are *you*. And others! Stone and sea, so many!"

"I chose this," he reminded me. "I chose you, Moirin. And I found a way to do it on my own terms." Bao put his hands on my shoulders and gave me a hard kiss, firm and anchoring. "Everyone makes their own choices. Let them, eh?"

I laughed ruefully. "I'll try."

"Good." As the carriage-driver drew rein outside the de Toluard townhouse, Bao kissed me again, hard and long and deep, his tongue delving into my mouth, his *diadh-anam* intertwining with mine until I felt myself melting against him.

Naamah, the bright lady, smiled. Her enduring grace showered down upon us like a hail of golden sparks.

I made an inarticulate sound of protest when he pulled away. "Bao!"

He gave me a serene smile. "Let us finish Naamah's business later, Moirin. Now let us go see if Denis de Toluard is sufficiently sober to tell us what might have befallen your Prince Thierry, and why Terra Nova is such a terrible place." He adjusted the sleeves of his black-and-white magpie coat, affording me a glimpse of the stark zig-zag tattoos on his corded forearms and reminding me of all we had endured together. "After all, it can't be worse than Kurugiri, can it?"

"Surely not," I agreed.

As it transpired, it could.

TWENTY-EIGHT

I t's a bloody place," Denis de Toluard said bluntly.

"How so?" I inquired.

He sighed and scrubbed at his face with both hands. He looked better, much better, but still ages older than he ought. "They're a bloody folk, the Nahuatl. And I mean it quite literally. It's not just that they built an empire by conquering damn nigh everything in sight. They practice human sacrifice."

"Oh." I felt a bit sick. "Gods! Why?"

"They believe it's their duty," Denis said. "They believe it's necessary for the world to continue. That the gods sacrificed parts of themselves to create the world, and that ongoing sacrifice is necessary to sustain it. They believe that without it, the sun will not rise and the rain will not fall." He gave us a grim smile. "According to Diego Ortiz y Ramos, the commander of the Aragonian garrison, it's a great deal better than it used to be. When they first arrived in Tenochtitlan, the Nahuatl would sacrifice hundreds, even thousands, of victims at a single festival. The steps of the temples would run red with blood."

"But no longer?" I asked hopefully.

Denis shrugged. "The Aragonians have been working to convert the Nahuatl to the worship of Mithras, and they've had some success. But the practice continues on a lesser scale. I've seen it," he added with a shudder. "And it's horrible."

Balthasar Shahrizai looked unwontedly pale. "Exactly where do they find all these victims to sacrifice?"

"Prisoners of war, for the most part," Denis said. "They actually fight to maim and injure rather than kill in order to take prisoners to sacrifice to their gods. Warriors gain status that way. But there are also those who go willing to the altar, and reckon it an honor. Apparently, it's one of two ways to ascend immediately to the highest heaven, bypassing some rather unpleasant stages of the afterlife."

"What's the other?" Bao asked.

Denis gave him a jaundiced look. "A noble death on the battlefield."

I glanced at Bao. Upon dying a hero's death, he had been granted a reprieve from the more unpleasant aspects of the Ch'in afterlife. By aiding Master Lo in trading his life for Bao's, I had stolen that from him all unwitting. Bao caught my not-so-stealthy glance and returned a level gaze, reminding me without words that he *had* found a way to choose this fate for himself.

I cleared my throat. "So it's a bloody place, and the Nahuatl are a bloody folk. Do you suppose Thierry ran afoul of them?"

"No." Denis shook his head. "That's the thing. I *don't*. If we ran afoul of anyone, it was the Aragonians. They treated us civilly enough, but they weren't happy about Terre d'Ange encroaching on their territory. And they weren't happy that Raphael rose so high in the Emperor's regard."

"Do you suspect this commander...what was his name? Diego Ortiz y Ramos? Of being somehow complicit?" Balthasar inquired delicately.

"No. No, I don't think so." Denis hesitated. "Ah, gods! What do I know? I was shitting myself half to death with dysentery at the time. Here's what I *do* know." He unrolled a scroll on a low table between us. "This is a copy of the map the Emperor Achcuatli gave to Raphael, that he and Thierry might seek out the empire of Tawantinsuyo." His finger traced a course. "Here is the isthmus overland." He tapped the map. "Here the jungle begins; and here is the river on which they were meant to travel."

I peered at the map. "My lord Denis, forgive me, but…why were you so sure Thierry died?"

He raised his voice. "Because he didn't come back!"

"Aye, but—"

"Thierry's word is his bond," Denis said, and Balthasar Shahrizai nodded in agreement. "He'd no sooner break it than you would break your people's oath, Moirin. He promised his father he would do everything in his power to return in two years' time. He gave *me* his word the secondary expedition would return within a year's time no matter what they found; and made me promise to sail without him if they didn't. I waited for almost a year and a half. There's a reason even the Nahuatl haven't sought to conquer Tawantinsuyo. Do you know how many ways there are to die in the jungles of Terra Nova?"

I shook my head humbly.

Denis de Toluard regaled us with a litany of horrors ranging from hostile natives, raging rivers, poisonous snakes, strangling snakes, maddening insects, ravenous ants, hideous diseases, suppurating wounds, and razor-teethed fish that could strip a man's flesh from his body in a matter of minutes. "That's where you mean to go," he said when he had finished. "*That's* what you're bound for."

Everyone was silent for a moment.

"Well," Bao said presently. "But people live there, don't they? So it must have some merits."

"They say it's beautiful," Denis murmured. "Beautiful and terrible. That there are flowers of surpassing beauty that bloom there and nowhere else in the world. That you can go for days and days without seeing the sky, only an endless roof of green leaves high overhead. It can drive a man mad."

"In the Tatar lands, nothing blooms, there is only sky overhead, and you can ride for days and days without seeing a tree," I observed. "I think I would like this better."

"You really mean to go? You, yourself?" Denis asked. "Elua have mercy, Moirin! It's no place for a woman."

I shrugged. "I have to."

"You and your bear-goddess," he said in a mild tone that intended no offense. "All right. All right, then." He took a deep breath. "I'm coming with you."

"Are you sure?" Given our history, I didn't like him well enough to relish the prospect.

Denis met my gaze and smiled bitterly. "If you're right, Thierry's alive and I abandoned him. All of them. I could have begged the Aragonians to mount a search for them, promising a vast reward, promising we would abandon efforts to infringe on their trade rights. I could have begged Emperor Achcuatli, promising him horses and steel weapons. I could have done *something*, and I didn't. I gathered our crew, turned tail, and sailed for home, in time to deliver the news that drove the King to take his own life."

To that, I said nothing.

"If I stay here, I'll just drink myself to death," he said. "Besides, I can be useful to you. I've met the Emperor, and I'm on fair terms with Commander Ortiz y Ramos. I learned quite a bit of the Nahuatl tongue."

"He's right, Moirin," Bao observed.

"So be it," I agreed.

"What about you?" Denis asked Balthasar Shahrizai, an edge of scorn creeping into his voice. "As I recall, you're a fair hand with a sword. But I don't suppose you've any intention of risking your pretty neck this time, either."

"You wound me, Denis." Balthasar studied his fingernails, which were neatly trimmed and buffed. "Actually, yes. I have every intention of joining the expedition."

It surprised me. "You do?"

He glanced up at me. "Let's just say I've a fancy to see these flowers of surpassing beauty that bloom nowhere else in the world, shall we?"

I found myself unexpectedly touched. "You needn't risk yourself, my lord Balthasar. You're already doing a great deal. This expedition wouldn't be possible without the support of House Shahrizai."

"All the more reason to keep an eye on our investment." He shot a needling look at Denis de Toluard. "It didn't turn out so well the first time, did it?"

Denis flushed with anger, but held his tongue.

"Well, I think it's a fine idea," Bao said cheerfully. "It will certainly make the voyage more interesting."

Of that, I was certain.

By the time we left the de Toluard household, the City of Elua was abuzz with the news; and predictably, opinion was torn as to whether there was genuine cause for hope, or I was a lying charlatan bent on exacting revenge on the Duc de Barthelme by embarking on a fool's errand bound to have a terrible cost.

My father came to pay us a visit, and I had no doubt what he thought. From the beginning, he had believed in me. He embraced me without a word and I clung to him, finding myself in tears again.

"My mother..." I whispered, the realization only just dawning on me. "Ah, gods! By this time, I'd hoped to be bound for Alba."

"I know," he said. "That's why I mean to go in your stead, Moirin."

I blinked away tears. "You do?"

"I do," my father said firmly. "I'll gladly carry a letter for her, but this news should be delivered in person. Twenty-some years ago, we made a child together. I mean to find Fainche, and tell her what manner of woman you've grown into since you left her side, and of the adventures that have befallen you." He glanced at Bao with a faint smile. "I will assure her that I very much like your unusual husband, and that if anyone can keep you safe, he can. I will tell her that our very disparate gods brought us together for a purpose." He took my hand. "And I will kneel beside her, and we will pray to our disparate gods, to the Maghuin Dhonn Herself, to Blessed Elua and Naamah and all the Companions, and any other gods that might be listening, that you will return safely home."

"Thank you," I said. "Just...thank you."

Bao nodded in agreement. "You are a very kindhearted man, Brother Phanuel," he said in a respectful tone. "Moirin is fortunate to have such a father."

My father dismissed our thanks with a graceful gesture. "It is the least I can do. To be sure, my lord Rogier has no more use for me or my counsel." His expression turned somber. "Have you spoken to the young princess about your plans yet?"

Bao and I exchanged a glance. "No," I admitted. "Frankly, I'm rather dreading it, and if you have counsel, *I* would be grateful for it. Desirée's been abandoned so many times, I fear she may take this as another."

"It's possible," my father acknowledged, his gaze gentle. "And that cannot be helped. Be honest with the child. Be hopeful, but make her no promises you cannot be sure of keeping. Do not speak of any strife between you and Duc Rogier, nor attempt to warn her of your suspicions. Any such words you might speak would only be twisted and turned against you in your absence."

"I wouldn't!" I protested. "I would not put a child in such a position."

He inclined his head. "You've been very careful to shield the young princess from the politics at stake here."

I sighed. "I hate this."

"I hate it, too." The sorrow in my father's green eyes made my heart ache. "Believe me, Moirin, I am more than a little angry at the gods myself today. They have already asked so much of you."

"Don't be." I shook my head. "I fear I brought this on myself. Whatever happened in Terra Nova, I believe it is somehow connected to the summonings I helped the Circle of Shalomon perform."

"I don't see how it could be," he said.

"Neither do I." I touched my chest, feeling my *diadh-anam* flicker inside me. "And yet I am sure of it. If I had not been such a love-struck idiot, this would not have happened. Like my ancestors, I believed what I wished to believe. I failed to discern the will of the Maghuin

Dhonn Herself." I smiled ruefully. "And attempting to set matters right is the price I must pay for my mistake."

" 'Tis a steep one," my father murmured.

"It was a pretty big mistake," Bao said, shrugging at the surprised look my father gave him. "Well, it was! They nearly set loose a demon that wanted to wreak havoc on the world and slaughter as many people as possible."

"But that catastrophe was averted, was it not?"

Bao shrugged again. "Thanks to me and Master Lo."

"We set *something* loose." Once again, I remembered the faint lightning flash I'd last glimpsed in Raphael de Mereliot's stormy grey eyes, and gave myself a little shake. "I don't know. Honestly, I don't see what possible connection there is between the events; but then, we've no idea what happened in Terra Nova. Mayhap I'm wrong. After all, I was wrong before. Even so, I would still have to go. I swore an oath, and my lady Jehanne tells me this is the only way to keep it."

My father didn't argue. "Don't wait overlong to discuss it with the young princess," he said instead. "Someone's bound to slip and gossip in front of her. Best she hear it from your own lips."

"If someone hasn't already told her," Bao muttered.

"I suspect my lord Rogier would do his best to prevent it," my father said. "For his own reasons."

"Why?" I asked.

"He thinks you're bound to fail," he said simply. "That way, when her highness Desirée's hopes are dashed, it will be the two of you, and no one else, who raised them; and she will blame you for it accordingly."

"Then why would you urge us to—?" I began, puzzled. "Oh!"

Bao grinned. "He doesn't think we'll fail."

My father smiled his quiet smile. " 'Tis a considerable test of faith, especially when one is angry at the gods. But that gets to the very heart of faith, does it not? Here and in Alba, I will pray, and I will have faith that the gods are merciful and will answer my prayers. Wherever your fate takes you, whatever you find in Terra Nova, know that I will be here, keeping the flame of faith alight, believing that you will succeed."

"Don't cry, Moirin," Bao warned me. "You've cried enough."

"Oh, shut up." I returned my father's smile through tears. "Thank you. Surely, that will give me courage in dark times."

He kissed my brow. "I am glad."

TWENTY-NINE

On the morrow, Bao and I broke the news to Desirée.

It was difficult.

In the first place, Tristan de Barthelme was there in the nursery when we arrived, and insisted on remaining present for the conversation, refusing our polite request for privacy. "The Regency of House Barthelme is responsible for her highness' well-being," he informed us with fourteen-year-old hauteur. "I am here at my father's wishes." He turned to Desirée and held out his hand to her, his voice turning soft and coaxing. "Besides, you want me here, don't you, ducky?"

She nodded, taking his hand.

Swallowing my ire, I knelt before her. "Do you remember how I've spoken of your mother, dear heart?"

Desirée nodded again, her blue-grey eyes wide as she listened.

I took a deep breath. "Well, your mother came to me in my dreams, and she told me something very, very important. She told me that your elder brother Prince Thierry is alive, and that Bao and I must go to Terra Nova to find him."

Her cheeks turned pink. "He's alive? My brother is alive?"

"I believe so," I said carefully. "I believe it was a true dream. But it means we will be gone a long time finding him."

She searched my face. "I don't want you to go! Why can't someone *else* go?"

Ah, gods! I couldn't explain the Circle of Shalomon and my foolish behavior to a child; and I couldn't tell her about her mother Jehanne's warning, not in front of the smirking young Tristan de Barthelme. Not at all according to my father's wise counsel, with which I agreed. It left me not knowing what to say.

Bao rescued me. "Because heroes and heroines always get the hard jobs, young highness," he said in a matter-of-fact tone. "It's what we do. That's why the gods choose us for the task."

Desirée pitched a tantrum anyway.

It was a full-blown tantrum of epic proportions, filled with wailing and flailing, fists and heels pounding on the nursery floor. And gods help me, I was almost glad of it, for it meant the spark of quicksilver joy and temper in her that had guttered so low after her father's death was yet alive and well. Also, it drove Tristan de Barthelme from the nursery in a sullen adolescent retreat, for which I was grateful.

Sister Gemma hummed a soothing song, doing her considerable best to comfort the child.

In time, the storm passed.

"I don't *want* you to go," Desirée repeated, weary and fretful.

I stroked her hair. "I know, dear heart."

She ground her rosy knuckles into her eyes. "You'll come back, won't you? Promise it!"

I hesitated. "Dear heart, I know you're still a little girl, but you're a very clever one, so I'm going to tell you a very grown-up thing. Will you hear it?"

Her tear-stained face was grave. "Yes, Moirin."

"I will not make you a promise I cannot be sure of keeping," I said gently. "And I will not lie to you. Terra Nova is a dangerous place. But I promise that Bao and I will do our very, very best to find your brother and bring everyone home safe. You can help us by trying to be brave. Do you understand?"

Desirée bowed her head, loose ringlets of silvery-blonde hair curtaining her face. "Yes, Moirin," she murmured. "I will try."

"Good girl." I kissed the top of her head. "I have a present for you."

At that, she looked up. "What is it?"

Reaching into the purse at my waist, I withdrew a small, stoppered bottle of cut crystal with an inch or so of liquid in it. Sunlight slanting through the windows caught its facets, decorating the nursery with rainbow prisms. "Your mother gave this to me," I said to Jehanne's daughter, handing her the bottle. "So that I might never forget her. But I think she would want you to have it now."

"It's pretty." Desirée tilted the bottle, then gave me a perplexed look. "Thank you, Moirin. What is it?"

"Perfume." I pulled out the stopper for her, and a heady, intoxicating scent filled the air. "It's a very special blend. Your father had it made for your mother when he was courting her. No one else was allowed to wear it and the Head of the Perfumers' Guild swore he would never, ever tell anyone the formula."

She sniffed the bottle. "It's *beautiful*."

I smiled, hiding a pang of sorrow. "Aye, it is. Like your mother, and like you. And it's a gift given twice in love now." Carefully, I guided her hands in replacing the stopper. "So any time you're feeling frightened or lonely, I want you to smell this, and remember that your mother loved you. That *I* love you."

"Me, too," Bao added. "Although I do not smell as nice as your mother or Moirin."

Desirée turned the bottle in her hands, regarding its sparkling facets. "Moirin . . . why doesn't my mother visit *me* in my dreams?" She gave me a plaintive look. "Did she love you better?"

"Oh, dear heart, no!" I hadn't thought of that. "No, no, no. You know that my own mother's folk are not D'Angeline?"

She nodded. "You're a bear-witch. That's what Tristan says."

"Aye," I said softly. "And because of it, I have a small gift for magic. That, and that alone, is the reason your mother, Jehanne, can speak to me in my dreams." I touched her cheek. "If she could choose between us, she would choose you."

"Truly?"

"Truly." I folded her fingers over the bottle. "Never, ever forget it."

So it was done. Desirée hugged us both fiercely in parting, her arms clinging around our necks, making us promise we would see her before we left for Terra Nova. That, at least, was a promise I could make gladly.

Sister Gemma escorted us to the door of the nursery. "That was well done, my lady," she murmured in a low tone. "I fear for the child in your absence. Duc Rogier's son—"

"I know."

Her pretty face hardened. "I'll do my best to protect her highness. But the Duc has made it clear to me that my position here is tenuous. My status as a member of Eisheth's Order is the only thing that keeps me here, and he's hinted that it may not suffice. I dare not speak against the lad lest I lose it."

I drew a sharp breath. "He'd dare?"

Gemma nodded. "Oh, yes. His grace would see the young princess isolated from those who care for her. I suspect he'll seek to replace me with a peer of the realm chosen from amongst his allies, one whose stature he can claim will serve to better honor the princess than a mere priestess."

Bao muttered an unintelligible curse.

I glanced over the priestess' shoulder to see Desirée sitting on the floor of the nursery, absorbed in counting the facets of the crystal bottle. "You are no mere priestess, my lady. I thank Eisheth and Sister Marianne for sending you. And I know you will do your best. It's all any of us can do."

Unexpectedly, Gemma took my hand and kissed it. "Eisheth's blessing on you, Lady Moirin; and you, too, Messire Bao," she said, tears in her eyes. "I will pray for your success and safe return."

This time, I managed not to cry. "Thank you," I said to her. "We are grateful for it."

In the days that followed, our expedition began to take shape. The majority of the planning was handled by House Shahrizai, for which I was grateful since I had no experience in such matters.

The captain and nearly two-thirds of the crew of Prince Thierry's flagship volunteered for the return voyage. The ship itself was named *Naamah's Dove*, which I thought was a hopeful omen. Balthasar Shahrizai set about recruiting trained warriors for the search party. Scores of young noblemen, especially from the Lesser Houses, applied for positions, along with dozens of members of the Royal Guard and a handful of mercenaries. After testing their skills on the practice field, where he did indeed prove surprisingly handy with a sword, Balthasar settled on a hand-picked group of forty men.

On the advice of Denis de Toluard, a shipment of trade goods was assembled. It seemed that while Terra Nova was rich in numerous resources, iron was not one of them, and much coveted by the Nahuatl.

"They'd love to get their hands on weapons and armor," he said grimly. "But they'll settle for tools."

Accordingly, our manifest included a variety of useful implements: hoes and plows and awls and the like. It also included many strings of translucent, colorful glass beads and bright, shimmering mirrors, other items unknown in Terra Nova.

While our plans proceeded apace, the Duc de Barthelme's plans marched alongside them.

To considerable fanfare, the Regent of Terre d'Ange moved his entire household from the duchy of Barthelme to the City of Elua, including his wife, Claudine, and his younger son, Aristide. As Duc Rogier had indicated to me long ago—or what felt like long ago—his wife maintained an extensive household. The train of heavily laden wagons approaching the City seemed half a mile long. Claudine de Barthelme presided over the entry like a Queen, riding a white palfrey, her chin held high. Her younger son, Aristide, rode beside her on a coal-black gelding.

They were met at the gates of the City by Duc Rogier with his elder son, Tristan, and young Desirée in attendance. The Duchese Claudine made a show of dismounting and curtsying gracefully to Desirée, who handed her a posy of spring flowers. Smiling, Claudine stooped and kissed her cheek.

It made a pretty picture, the orphaned princess embraced by her new family, and I daresay many of the cheers that greeted it were genuine. Desirée was all smiles, her eyes sparkling.

Despite the insistent warning of my *diadh-anam*, I couldn't help but wonder if I was wrong. After all, I'd misread it before; and a part of me wished I *was* mistaken. I wouldn't mind if it meant Desirée's happiness.

But then Duc Rogier introduced me to his wife in my capacity as Desirée's oath-sworn protector.

Claudine de Barthelme was an attractive woman, with the golden hair and blue eyes her eldest son had inherited; but there was a calculating coolness behind those eyes and a falseness to her smile.

"Ah yes, Lady Moirin." She pressed my hand between hers. "I've heard so much about you." Her brows rose. "But I understand you mean to leave us soon? Undertaking a dangerous quest to Terra Nova?"

"I fear it's true," I said.

Her lips pursed. "It seems a strange way of honoring your oath."

"Does it?" I asked. "I can think of no better way than restoring her young highness' brother and the rightful heir to the throne."

Something flickered in her calculating gaze. "Of course," she said smoothly, reaching down to lay one manicured hand on Desirée's head. "I hope you will rest assured knowing that her highness will receive the best of care in your absence." She glanced down with another benevolent smile. "The poor lass has been motherless for too long."

I inclined my head. "I can only hope that you come to love her as I do, my lady."

Claudine's smile didn't waver. "I'm sure I shall."

Bao and I watched the procession make its way toward the Palace, the handsome royal family followed by a long line of wagons snaking its way through the City, cheers following in their wake. "That woman is the goad that drives the Duc's ambitions," he remarked. "Count on it."

"I think so, too." I sighed. "Would that we could be in two places at once! I don't like leaving Desirée at their mercy."

Bao gave me a worried look. "Do you think she's in danger?"

I gazed after them. "I don't think they'd dare *harm* her. It would raise too much suspicion."

"There are a lot of ways of harming a child," Bao said darkly.

"I know." Sister Gemma's words haunted me. "Believe me, I do." I could see Desirée's future unfolding step by step. At first, the Duc de Barthelme and his wife, Claudine, would embrace her, giving her the semblance of family she had never known. And then they would begin to isolate her, replacing her unconventional nurse with an ambitious peer looking to curry favor, replacing the clever tutor who sought to feed her eager young mind with someone more placid and malleable.

And at every turn, they would assure her it was for her own good.

They would chide her for her temper. They would play on her child's sense of guilt, subtly blaming her for the tragedies that had befallen her.

In the end, they would crush her spirit.

I had a vision of Desirée at sixteen, anxious, overly thin, and as hollow-eyed as a doll, holding the loathsome Tristan's hand in the Temple of Elua, reciting her wedding vows while the young man smirked, his father watched with pride, his brother with envy, and his mother smiled a beatific smile.

I gritted my teeth. "*That* will not happen."

"Moirin?" Bao inquired.

I shook my head, dispelling the vision. "Come, my hero. We've a good deal of work yet to do."

THIRTY

Two weeks later, all was in readiness.

The ship *Naamah's Dove* was laden, the captain and crew assembled. Balthasar Shahrizai's hand picked party of fighting men were ready to board at a moment's notice. I'd written yet another letter of explanation and apology to my mother, entrusting it to my father's care.

I had one last meeting with Lianne Tremaine, the former King's Poet.

"What can I tell you, Moirin?" she said with a shrug. "I've done my best to shape opinion and foster the notion that this is a noble quest. But after the losses Terre d'Ange has suffered, a lot of folk long for stability, not more pointless tragedy. Seeing House Barthelme embrace the young princess has soothed their nerves. Almost half the realm fears you're mad to undertake this."

"Do you?" I asked her.

"No." Her mouth twisted. "But I was there when the Circle of Shalomon had its ill-advised successes. I saw what you're capable of doing and what your damnable gift can achieve."

We sat together in silence a moment.

"If I were more brave, I would ask to come with you," Lianne said presently. "It's what I always wanted, isn't it?"

"The prospect of an epic tale to tell," I agreed. "You'd be welcome. I'd be glad of your company."

She shuddered. "I can't. I'm afraid."

I couldn't blame her for it. I was afraid, too. Ah, gods! I was afraid of so much. Of the journey to come, of Terra Nova and what awaited us there. Of leaving Desirée behind and what might befall her here. Of never seeing Alba again, of never seeing my beloved mother again.

The Duc de Barthelme hosted a farewell supper for us, inviting the principal organizers of the expedition, members of the Great Houses, and a selection of the fighting noblemen from the Lesser Houses who would be accompanying us.

It was an extravagant, glittering affair held in the great hall of the Palace. While the cooks labored in the kitchen to prepare the endless stream of dishes that would strain the long tables, servants in immaculate livery circulated with trays of food and drink to tantalize our palates.

Duc Rogier and his wife, Claudine, were unfailingly gracious, their sons, Tristan and Aristide, handsome and charming. Desirée, permitted to attend the reception prior to the dinner, was glowing, the excitement of the occasion overshadowing the fact that it was meant to celebrate our departure.

"I have a secret, Moirin," she whispered to me.

"Oh? What is it, dear heart?"

She giggled and shook her head. "I can't tell you. I promised Papa Rogier. He wants to tell you himself."

I raised my brows. "Papa Rogier, is it?"

Desirée nodded. "He said it was all right to call him that, him and Maman Claudine. It is, isn't it?"

I made myself smile at her. "Yes, of course, if he said so."

Before we were seated to dine, the royal steward rang a silver bell, summoning us to attention. "My lords and ladies!" he called. "His excellence, Duc Rogier Courcel de Barthelme, Regent of Terre d'Ange, begs your indulgence for an announcement of joyful tidings!"

"Uh-oh," Bao muttered.

"He wouldn't dare," I said under my breath. "Not here, not tonight. Would he? Is he *that* confident?"

Gathering his family, including Desirée, at the head of the hall,

Duc Rogier smiled beneficently at the murmuring crowd. "My thanks to all of you for gathering together on this momentous eve!" he said in a carrying voice. "In a moment, we will sit and break bread together, sharing our hopes and prayers for our valiant explorers as they prepare to embark on a quest of imminent danger. Before we do, I am pleased to share news of a joyous nature!"

Tristan de Barthelme reached down to take Desirée's hand. She held his gladly, gazing up at him in adoration.

"He *is*," I said in disbelief.

But instead of making the announcement I dreaded, Duc Rogier gestured toward the back of the hall. Attendants opened the doors and ushered in a fair-haired couple who looked to be in their mid-fifties or later. She possessed a delicate, ephemeral beauty that had turned brittle with age, harsh lines bracketing her lips. He had greying silver-gilt hair caught back in a long braid, and blue-grey eyes whose sparkle had dimmed. Although I'd never seen either of them before, they looked familiar nonetheless.

I caught my breath, suspicion rising.

Together, they approached the head of the hall, exchanging greetings with Desirée, who had clearly met them already and been delighted by the revelation. Duc Rogier's smile broadened.

"My lords and ladies, I present to you the Comte and Comtesse de Maillet, her highness' maternal grandparents," he said. "With their blessing, I am pleased to announce that the ties between House Courcel and their descendants in House Barthelme will be strengthened even further with the betrothal of her highness Desirée de la Courcel to my eldest son, Tristan Courcel de Barthelme."

If Desirée hadn't looked so gods bedamned happy, mayhap there wouldn't have been as many cheers; but she did. Happiness radiated from her every pore as she stood clutching the hand of her betrothed Sun Prince, the hands of her newly found grandmother resting on her shoulders, her newly found grandfather with an arm around his wife's waist, Papa Rogier and Maman Claudine gazing on with approval. No one could begrudge the orphaned Little Pearl her joy.

It was a brilliant move.

"Queen Jehanne's *parents*?" Bao asked me.

I nodded. "She couldn't abide them, or at least not her mother. They had a dreadful relationship."

He eyed them. "Why would they be a party to this?"

"I don't know," I said. "Except that according to my lady Jehanne, her mother ever resented her. Jehanne convinced his majesty to gift them with a modest title and send them into virtual exile in the provinces. Mayhap this is her chance at last to eclipse her daughter's star, or exact petty vengeance for being banished from her life."

Across the hall, Duc Rogier caught my eye. He lifted his chin a fraction, daring me to speak out against this.

I glanced around the hall. I had allies here, allies amongst House Shahrizai, amongst the Lesser Houses. Amongst the guardsmen and attendants, who were not greeting the news with cheers.

Not enough.

You'll fail, Jehanne's voice murmured in my memory; and I saw the truth of it unfurl before me. I may have been Desirée's oath-sworn protector, appointed by King Daniel himself, but his majesty was dead and I was a bear-witch of the Maghuin Dhonn. In Terre d'Ange, I would always be suspect. If I spoke out now, all I would do was further alienate those who thought I was mad, and jeopardize the goodwill of those who believed in me enough to risk the voyage to Terra Nova.

I inclined my head to Duc Rogier, ceding this battle.

He smiled, glancing sidelong at his wife, Claudine. She smiled, too.

The balance of the evening was like a dream best forgotten. For Desirée's sake, I put the best face I could on it. Breathless with excitement, she was permitted to introduce Bao and me to her newly found grandparents.

I greeted them politely. Behind the reciprocal politeness of the Comtesse de Maillet, I saw only dislike born of a lingering resentment. I had loved her daughter, therefore, she opposed me. It was as simple as that. Jehanne's father was another matter.

"I understand my daughter found comfort and kindness in your companionship," he said to me in a low voice. "I was glad to hear it."

"And I to provide it," I said honestly. "My lord, if I might have a word in private regarding this betrothal—"

Averting his gaze, the Comte de Maillet turned away from me. "I beg you, do not speak to me of politics. I have no stomach for controversy. We do but seek what is best for our granddaughter, and it seems to me that this alliance will serve her well."

"It won't," Bao interjected in a blunt tone. "And you ought to know it."

Shaking his head in denial, the Comte withdrew further, demurring and deferring to his wife.

I sighed.

"Well!" A heavy hand settled on my shoulder. "Looks like you've been outflanked, eh?"

"Oh, aye?" I glanced up at the owner of the hand, finding a pair of bright blue eyes in a face homely by D'Angeline standards, topped with a thatch of copper-red hair. "And who might you be, my lord?"

He laughed. "You don't know?"

Bao shifted uneasily, reaching for his staff.

"Peace, peace!" The redheaded fellow unhanded me, backing away, his blue eyes bright with mirth. "I mean no harm. I'm your captain, you idiots. I've been to Terra Nova and back. And I come from a line of naval commanders foolish enough to believe that the gods choose unlikely vessels." He bowed with surprising grace. "Lord Septimus Rousse, at your service."

Balthasar Shahrizai drifted alongside us. "Oh, good!" he said in a languid voice. "You've met." He nodded toward the Comte and Comtesse de Maillet. "Quite the masterstroke, eh, digging up dear old Grandmother and Grandfather to lend their blessing to the whole affair? I nearly thought I'd hear you denounce it."

"I wanted to," I admitted. "But it wouldn't have done any good."

"You're learning." He continued to gaze toward the royal family, eyes narrowing in thought. "Fourteen years."

I blinked. "I beg your pardon?"

"That's how long the Regent would be in power until Desirée is old enough to take the throne," Bao said. "That's what you meant, isn't it?"

"Exactly." Balthasar gave a precise nod. "Fourteen years to rule the realm, fourteen years to train his successor. If we fail, that child will never be anything more than a figurehead."

"Then we'd best not fail," I murmured.

"I'll hold up my end of the bargain," Septimus Rousse said in a steady tone. "And that's a promise."

It made me feel a little better.

But only a little.

THIRTY-ONE

When the royal steward rang the bell summoning us to the dinner table, it was time for Desirée to return to the nursery, and time for us to say our final farewells. Now came the realization that this occasion marked the separation to come, and the inevitable tears and protestations.

The assembled peers watched the scene uncomfortably, and Claudine de Barthelme gave Sister Gemma a discreet order to remove the princess forthwith.

I shook my head at her. "Wait, please."

Although it earned her a none-too-subtle glare from Maman Claudine, the priestess obeyed.

I knelt before Desirée, Bao crouching on his heels beside me. "Dear heart, it's time to say good-bye for now. Remember how we talked about being brave?"

She nodded.

"Remember this?" I shifted my hands into a reassuring *mudra*, and then a *mudra* of concentration. "And this?"

The effort of concentrating on emulating my gestures distracted Desirée from her tears. "I remember, Moirin. It's a way to make prayers."

"Good girl." I kissed the top of her head. "When you think of Bao and me while we are gone, mayhap you will pray for us, and for your brother, Thierry, and all the men with him, and everyone travelling with us. All the way across the ocean, it will gladden our hearts, and it will help you to be brave, too."

She gazed at me with a child's wide-eyed willingness to believe. "Truly?"

"Truly," I said firmly. "Now, give us both a good-bye hug."

"A really, really good one," Bao added. "As hard as you can, so we'll feel it for days and days!"

With a sound halfway between a laugh and a sob, Desirée obliged, wrapping her slender arms around my neck and squeezing me with fierce strength, burying her face against the curve of my throat. "I love you," she whispered in a muffled tone. "I do! And I will pray every day, I promise!"

I returned her embrace, pressing one last kiss against her fine, silken hair. "I love you too, dear heart," I whispered in reply. "And I thank you for your prayers."

When I released her reluctantly, she hugged Bao with equal fervor. He whispered somewhat in her ear, and rose to his feet holding her. When she unwound her arms from around his neck, Bao tossed her a foot or so into the air, then caught her effortlessly, eliciting a faint, sorrow-tinged giggle from her. After one more hug, he kissed her cheek and set her on her feet.

A soft murmur ran through the hall.

It may not have been as poignant a sight as the tableau Duc Rogier had staged, but it came close—and it was genuine. Not a few peers dabbed at their eyes with handkerchiefs as Sister Gemma escorted the young princess from the hall, Desirée glancing tearfully over her shoulder until the doors closed behind her.

I closed my eyes and took a deep breath.

When I opened my eyes, the Comtesse de Maillet was staring at me with a disdain she could barely conceal. "My granddaughter lacks manners," she said in a stiff voice. "I must confess that I am sorry to see that behavior that would not be tolerated in the Night Court is encouraged in the Palace. That, I assure you, will change."

Without thinking, I summoned the twilight.

It could not hide me from a gaze already upon me, but I knew it manifested nonetheless as a visible sparkling in the air around me, a sign that a gate partway into the spirit world had been opened.

A few folk cheered; some whistled in awe. Others raised their hands in an ancient sign to avert evil. Bao gave a low chuckle.

Jehanne's mother took a step backward.

"Your granddaughter lacks affection," I said in a precise tone. "Somewhat I am given to understand House Barthelme seeks to provide her. Since you have seen fit to insert yourself into her life, I hope that you will aid them."

She opened her mouth to reply, but no words emerged.

"Yes, yes, of course!" Duc Rogier came forward, putting his arms around Desirée's newly found grandparents, steering the whole of the royal family toward the waiting tables, beckoning to all of us. "We are all concerned for her young highness' well-being. It is a concern you voiced to me long ago, Lady Moirin, and I am doing my best to rectify the lack." The Duc permitted himself a faint smile. "How fortunate we are that the child's own grandmother, appointed a peer of the realm by King Daniel himself, has consented to serve as the Royal Governess in the days to come! I am only sorry I did not act sooner." He met my gaze. "Shall we dine, and toast to the success of your endeavor?"

Holding his gaze, I let the twilight fade. "By all means, my lord."

We dined.

It was an awkward meal. I daresay a good many of the folk present didn't appreciate the stakes at play, but I knew.

Duc Rogier made many toasts in honor of the expedition, speaking of it in fulsome terms, giving it his every blessing, praying for our success. *I* knew he was lying through his teeth. And by the cynical expressions on the faces of our allies like Balthasar Shahrizai and Septimus Rousse, they knew it, too.

But others didn't—not the members of the Great Houses, and surely not the impoverished young noblemen of the Lesser Houses who had pledged themselves to our quest. With every toast, they cheered and stamped their feet.

"To Thierry!" they cried. "Prince Thierry!"

"*King* Thierry! Long may he live!"

It brought me a certain grim pleasure to see Duc Rogier's face harden at the reminder that Thierry de la Courcel, if he was indeed alive, was in fact the rightful King of Terre d'Ange. Mostly, though, I wanted this charade of an evening to end. For the first time since my lady Jehanne had come to me in my dream, I was looking forward to getting this venture under way.

And although it seemed that it never would end, at last the evening did. The only thing left to endure was the Duc's final farewell. There, before all the assembled peers, he clasped Bao's hands in a respectful manner, and then embraced me warmly and wished us well on our quest.

"All of Terre d'Ange will pray for your success and safe return," he said in a solemn voice.

I smiled sweetly at him. "Your excellence, I am perfectly well aware that you consider this quest a monumental folly without a chance in the world of succeeding, and that you are only backing it because to do otherwise would lay your grasping ambition bare for all the realm to see." Pressing my palms together, I bowed to him in the Bhodistani manner. "I will do my best to prove you wrong."

Rogier de Barthelme gaped at me.

Without giving him a chance to reply, I turned and made my exit from the great hall, Bao beside me.

Outdoors, I felt limp with relief that the ordeal was over. Bao was chuckling over my parting comments.

"I knew you wouldn't be able to hold your tongue all night long," he said. "Did you see the look on his face?"

"It was foolish of me," I muttered.

"No, I don't think so." Bao shook his head. "You're right. If you'd faced him down earlier, all it would have done was cause strife and weaken our hand. But this, everyone will remember. You had the final word."

"Finding Thierry and bringing him safely home will be the final word, my magpie," I reminded him.

"True," he agreed.

As endless as the evening had seemed, out of consideration for the morrow's dawn departure the fête had begun early by D'Angeline standards, and the first stars were only just beginning to emerge when Bao and I returned to our borrowed house. I stood outside for a long moment, breathing in the scent of the cypress trees and the spring-damp soil, listening to the plants in the garden rustle and grow.

After tomorrow, it would be a long, long time before I saw dry land again.

Inside, we confirmed that all was in readiness for our departure, our trunks packed with attire suitable for travel. I strung my faithful yew-wood bow that my uncle Mabon had made for me and tested its draw, finding it as resilient as ever, and then unstrung it and wrapped it in oilcloth for the journey.

At my request, our steward Guillaume Norbert assembled the entire household staff. Bao and I thanked them for their gracious service, presenting each one with a small purse as a token of gratitude.

Each and every one of them tried to refuse it, but I insisted. "You've all been very kind," I said. "And I know ours is hardly the sort of household in which any of you dreamed of serving."

For the first time since we'd met, Guillaume laughed. "No," he admitted. "It isn't. In the long history of House Shahrizai, the door to the seraglio has never been closed for so long. Nonetheless, it's been a privilege, my lady." He bowed. "It is a valiant quest you undertake. We will pray, all of us, for your success and your safe return."

I was grateful to hear the words spoken with sincerity. "My thanks."

He bowed again. "Of course. I'll see that you and Messire Bao are awoken in a timely manner, my lady."

With that done, Bao and I retired to our bedchamber. He eyed me in a speculative manner. "I suppose we ought to sleep, huh? Big day tomorrow."

"No." I slid one hand around the back of his neck, tugging his head down for a kiss, feeling the familiar intimacy of our shared *diadh-anam* intertwining. "Unlike your Ch'in greatships, there will be precious little room for privacy aboard this one. *I* suppose we ought to thank Naamah for blessing our union, and celebrate it by offering up many hours of lovemaking as a prayer."

Bao smiled, wrapping his arms around my waist and pulling me against him. "Oh, good. I like your idea better."

Ah, gods! We'd come such a long way together; and we had such a long way yet to go. There was another ocean awaiting us, and beyond it, untold dangers. But for tonight, one night, it was enough to simply *be* together.

Piece by piece, we undressed each other, until there were no barriers left and we were naked before one another.

We kissed, long and luxuriantly.

We explored every part of each other as though it were new. I reveled in sheer sensation, in the rasping glide of Bao's palms over my skin, in the tug of his mouth on my nipples, his clever fingers teasing the cleft between my thighs, eliciting the moisture of desire. Kissing his throat, I inhaled the hot-forge scent of his skin. Working my way lower, I bit his nipples and smiled to see the ridged muscles of his belly contract beneath the caress of my trailing hair, his straining phallus bent upward like a bow.

I took him into my mouth and performed the *languisement* with all my hard-won skill, making him spend.

Pushing my thighs apart, Bao settled himself between them, gazing at me with half-lidded eyes, and returned the favor until I was breathless with pleasure.

Hard once more, he slid up my body and propped himself on his forearms, thrusting into me.

It was good; so good.

The bright lady smiled with brilliant approval.

There was a magic to lovemaking that never faded, an alchemy of the flesh that never failed to evoke wonder. We were two, and we were one. Joined by the spark of the Maghuin Dhonn Herself, an intimacy I'd never known with anyone else, nor ever would. Joined by flesh—

his flesh in me, hot and throbbing, mine encompassing his, wet and eager. Bao's hips rocked, and mine rose to meet them, enjoying the sensation of fullness advancing and retreating. Sweetly, tenderly, he kissed my lips, thrusting deep inside me all the while.

"Stone and sea!" I gasped, feeling the waves of climax burst within me, my inner walls squeezing his hard shaft.

Bao groaned, sinking hilt-deep inside me, a hot rush of seed spurting.

Afterward, we lay entwined together for a time, heading drowsily toward sleep. I rested my head on Bao's chest, listening to his strong, steady heartbeat while he toyed lazily with my hair.

"Moirin, when this is over, do you suppose we might start a family?" he asked. "Assuming we live through it, of course."

"You and your fat babies," I said sleepily.

"It's not a jest."

With an effort, I lifted my head. "I know."

"Well?" There was a rare vulnerability in his dark eyes. "I know that I am only a Ch'in peasant-boy, and I have done things in my life I'm not proud of. Do you think I would not make a suitable father?"

"Bao!" I sat upright, shocked. "No!"

"It's just—"

Whatever he meant to say, I silenced it with a kiss. "Having watched you with Desirée, and Ravindra before her, I think you will make a most excellent father." I gave the gold hoops in his ears a meaningful tug. "No matter what you've done. I've done foolish things, too. But you are my husband, and I love you, and if we live through this, yes, I will gladly light a candle to Eisheth and bear your fat babies." With one finger, I poked at his hard, flat abdomen. "Although I am still not convinced of their relative plumpness."

Bao's face relaxed into a smile. "You'll see. Round as dumplings."

With a sigh, I settled back against him. "Let us pray we have the chance."

He kissed my temple. "I do."

THIRTY-TWO

———— ✦ ————

At dawn on the morrow, we set sail for Terra Nova on the ship *Naamah's Dove*.

There was no ceremony, no great fanfare, all of that having taken place at the previous night's dinner, only a handful of folk saying one last farewell to loved ones. My father came to the wharf to see us off, looking out of place in his elegant priest's crimson robes, his oak-brown hair loose and shining on his shoulders.

"You have the letter for my mother?" I asked him.

He nodded. "I do. And I will deliver it in person, I promise."

For the first time, I saw that there were fine lines on his face, fanning from the corners of his green, green eyes.

It made my heart ache.

"Thank you," I whispered, embracing him. "Thank you for all the kindness you have given me."

My father held me. "How could I not?"

Aboard the ship, a sharp whistle sounded. Septimus Rousse leaned over the railing. "Lady Moirin!" he called in a good-natured tone. "Come aboard, won't you? We're losing daylight."

Reluctantly, I released my father.

He turned to Bao. "Keep her safe?"

Bao clasped one hand over his fist, bowing in the Ch'in manner. "It is my life's mission, Brother Phanuel."

And then there was nothing left to say, nothing left to do but board the ship. Another ship, another journey. We cast off from the wharf and began to make our way down the broad surface of the Aviline River. I stood in the stern and watched as the figure of my father dwindled to a crimson speck, and then vanished altogether as the white walls of the City of Elua fell away behind us.

"So we're off on another adventure," Bao said softly.

"Yes, and I expect it's going to be every bit as dreadful as I feared," Balthasar Shahrizai announced, joining us with Denis de Toluard in tow. "Have you seen the size of the cabins?" He shuddered. "Ghastly."

"At least you have a cabin, my lord!" one of the sailors called cheerfully to him. "If you want to see truly cramped quarters, come sling a hammock in the main berth!"

Balthasar gave the fellow a jaundiced look. "I think not."

Bao laughed and clapped him on the shoulder. "You'll get used to it."

He shuddered again. "Elua have mercy, I hope not! Months on end of living cheek by jowl with a motley group of increasingly malodorous, malnourished adventurers... no, no thank you."

"Are you going to carry on like this for the entire trip?" Denis de Toluard asked with asperity.

"I might," Balthasar admitted.

The other rolled his eyes. "You didn't *have* to come, you know. It would have been enough to back it."

"Actually, it wouldn't." Balthasar's gaze fell on me. "You may not think much of my sense of honor, Denis, but I couldn't have abided knowing a young woman's courage put mine to shame." He shrugged. "So here I am. Now, shouldn't we be singing sea shanties or throwing the old knucklebones or some such thing? Something nautical to while away the tedium?"

I laughed. "Give it a few hours, my lord. We've only just set sail."

He heaved a dramatic sigh. "It's going to be a very, *very* long journey, isn't it?"

For a surety, it was.

As the days passed, we settled into a routine. Bao and I shared a narrow berth in a small cabin off one of the two wardrooms, with the remaining five cabins occupied by Balthasar Shahrizai, Denis de Toluard, and three other ranking noblemen: a hot-tempered Azzallese baron's son named Alain Guillard; a steady L'Agnacite fellow named Brice de Bretel, younger brother of another baron; and the third son of a Namarrese comte, copper-haired Clemente DuBois, who had a tendency to make bad jokes whenever he was nervous.

Once we passed the harbor of Pellasus and left the relative placidity of the Aviline River for the open sea, that was quite often.

There were times when I could understand why sailors loved the sea, both for its endless beauty and the primordial challenge it offered; but I will own, they were few and far between. For better or worse, I was a creature of earth and trees and green growing things, and I didn't like being away from land. In my experience, sea voyages entailed long periods of tedium broken up by storm-tossed hours of terror.

Still, we endured.

As the only woman aboard the ship, not to mention a bear-witch of the Maghuin Dhonn whose vision had launched the expedition, I was an object of curiosity; but for the most part, both the crew and our force of fighting men were polite and respectful. Bit by bit, I came to know most of them by name.

On most evenings when the weather was good, Captain Rousse invited Bao and me, and usually Balthasar and Denis, to dine in his cabin, which was larger and more well appointed than our wardroom.

Septimus Rousse was a clever fellow beneath his bluff good cheer, and I soon came to value him. On our first evening together, he posed a blunt question to me.

"So tell me, Lady Moirin, what *did* your vision show you?" he inquired. "Do you know where to find his highness? What's befallen him?"

"I wish I did," I said with regret. "But no, I'm afraid not. All it told me is that Thierry's alive. That is the only thing of which I'm certain."

He sighed. "The gods are stingy with their directions, aren't they?"

I nodded. "That they are, my lord captain."

Septimus Rousse slapped a broad hand down on the table. If the table hadn't been bolted to the floor, it would have jumped; I know I did. "With your permission, I'd like to come with you, my lady."

I raised my brows. "On the search?"

"Aye, on the search!" He leaned forward. "Why not? I've got a good crew and an able first mate in Alaric Dumont, one of the best, a genuine descendant of Philippe Dumont. If anything were to happen to me, you'd be in good hands."

"Assuming whatever happened to you didn't happen to the rest of us," Balthasar Shahrizai observed.

"True enough." Captain Rousse grinned at him. "The jungles of Terra Nova! We could all die out there, couldn't we?"

"In ever so many ways," Balthasar agreed with a sidelong glance at Denis de Toluard. "Or so I'm given to understand."

Denis frowned. "Would you prefer I painted an unrealistic picture of the dangers we face?"

"His highness Prince Thierry was bound for a mighty river in search of this alleged empire, wasn't he?" Septimus Rousse asked shrewdly, ignoring their bickering. He reached around the table with one long arm, pouring each of us a measure of perry brandy from a decanter. "Tell me, what do the lot of you know about navigating rivers?"

Bao coughed. "Quite a bit, actually. There are mighty rivers in Ch'in." I kicked his shins beneath the table. "But doubtless not as much as you, lord captain," he offered.

"We would be grateful for your aid and expertise, my lord," I added. "If you are truly minded to accompany us, I accept the offer with gratitude."

Septimus Rousse hoisted his snifter of perry brandy, swirling and studying it before tossing it back in one gulp. "Done and done!" he proclaimed, slamming the empty snifter onto the table. "I'm coming with you."

I was glad.

Days wore onto weeks. We sailed and sailed, *Naamah's Dove* riding abreast the waves, bellying her way over the swelling crests, plunging into the troughs. Captain Rousse studied his charts, studied the night skies, consulted his sextant, plotting our course across the trackless ocean. His capable sailors went about their business, fearless and uncomplaining.

The rest of us simply did our best to stay out of their way and pass the time as best we might—reading or telling tales, playing at dice or card games, studying the Nahuatl tongue under Denis de Toulard's tutelage. It was every bit as tiresome and cramped as Balthasar had predicted, and with a limited supply of fresh water for bathing, we did indeed grow increasingly malodorous.

For me, there was also a certain loneliness at being the only woman in the expedition. Despite the fact that the men were polite and respectful, there was a rough-hewn sense of camaraderie among them that excluded me. Men have their own way of communicating, their own set of jests and boasts. When the seas were calm enough to permit it, they sparred with one another on the decks. Even when the seas were choppy, they scuffled and arm-wrestled and found ways of testing one another's strengths.

I didn't begrudge them, but it left me feeling isolated. It wasn't the first time I'd been the sole woman in the company of men, but never before had I been confined in close quarters with so many of them for such a long time.

When I dreamed of Jehanne some six weeks into our journey, it was a welcome relief.

Once again, I was back in the Palace, standing in the marble hallway before the door to my plant-laden bower.

This time, I smiled as I opened it.

"Hello, Moirin." Jehanne's blue-grey eyes sparkled at me. She was sitting curled on my bed clad in only a thin shift of white silk, her fair hair loose and shining over her shoulders. The wonderful fragrance of her perfume mingled with the green scent of sun-warmed plants. "Have you missed me?"

"Always." I closed the door behind me. "Have you a message for me, my lady? Have the gods deigned to grant you further knowledge?"

"Mayhap." Jehanne tilted her head. "Or mayhap it was your loneliness that drew me out of mine. Come and kiss me."

I obeyed gladly; glad, too, that in my dream, I was freshly scrubbed and clean, clad in clean attire.

"Again, please," Jehanne said; and there was a vast ache of loneliness in her voice, vast enough to put mine to shame. I climbed onto the bed beside her and slid my hands into the shimmering, silken curtain of her hair, pulling her against me and kissing her thoroughly and deeply. When at last I released her, she shuddered all over and sighed with profound gratitude. "Thank you."

I stroked her bare arm, marveling at how real it felt. "Is this about Thierry?"

"No." Her star-bright eyes were filled with candor and regret. "I wish it were."

I couldn't help sighing. "Why *are* the gods so stingy with their directions?"

She didn't answer right away, watching my fingertips trail over her fine, fine skin. "There is a balance that must be maintained, Moirin," she said at length. "Even gods dare not upset it with their interventions, lest all the worlds crumble. Did not the dragon tell you as much in Ch'in?"

I blinked. "You know about the dragon?"

Jehanne smiled with quiet sorrow. "I know many things, few of them useful. For instance, I know that Naamah has showered uncommon blessings on you, especially for one who had never pledged herself to her service. Would you not agree?"

"Aye, my lady," I said. "But—"

She laid a finger on my lips, silencing me. "You have served her in your own way, I know."

"You do?"

"Yes, Moirin." Jehanne glanced at me beneath her lashes. "I know about your Ch'in princess, and your broad-shouldered Vralian lad. I know about your wedding night. But I am here to tell you that the sacrifices Naamah asks of us may not always be so pleasant and easy. You have a hard choice coming."

"What is it?" I asked her.

She shook her head. "I am not allowed to say. Only to remind you that you have been blessed with uncommon grace."

"All right." I nodded. "Thank you. I will be mindful of it."

"Good." Looking relieved, Jehanne wound her arms around my neck. "Tell me you loved me best, Moirin," she murmured, kissing me. "At least among the women you've known. Lie if you must; I won't mind. I know I was not the most worthy among them."

"I loved you best," I said truthfully.

"Did you?"

I laughed. "Yes, Jehanne. Worthy or not, among the women I have known, I love you best."

She gave me a sparkling look. "I'm glad."

Ah, gods! It was true. I had come to cherish my friendship with my fiercely reserved Ch'in princess Snow Tiger, and I had delighted in her willingness to show her vulnerable side to me in asking for Naamah's blessing; and I would always be a little bit in love with my lovely Rani Amrita for her unfailing courage and the immense kindness she had shown me, not the least of which came about when I was tormented by Kamadeva's diamond, racked with desire beyond my control.

But neither of them was Jehanne, whom I had loved first and best.

In my dream, I demonstrated it at length.

I awoke to bells clanging, and shouting abovedeck.

THIRTY-THREE

Bao was already out of our narrow berth, reaching for his bamboo staff. I came out of sleep hard, still entangled in the remnants of my dream, imagining I could smell the lingering trace of Jehanne's perfume, feel the silken warmth of her arms wrapped around me.

"What is it?" I asked sleepily. A jolt of alarm raced through me, and I sat upright. "Ah, gods! Is it a fire?"

Bao shook his head. "I don't know."

Barefoot and sleep-disheveled, we raced topside, scrambling up the ladder, the other inhabitants of the wardroom hard on our heels.

On the main deck, we found a grim-faced Denis de Toluard with one of Rousse's sailors in his custody, others surrounding them. In the dim light of the safety lanterns hanging from the masts, I couldn't tell who Denis had in his grip.

"Denis?" I felt disoriented and bewildered. "What passes here?"

Captain Rousse pushed his way through the knot of sailors. "I'd like to know that myself!"

"Captain." Denis greeted him with a curt nod. "I couldn't sleep, so I came abovedeck for a bit of fresh air." He shook the fellow by the scruff of his neck. "I found this one slinking out of the chart-house."

"And this shoved under his shirt." Alaric Dumont, the first mate, showed the captain his thick logbook containing all his invaluable notes and charts. "Pried the lock on the case by the look of it."

"What?" Septimus Rousse sounded as bewildered as I felt. He peered at the fellow. "Edouard? What in the world were you doing?"

The sailor didn't answer. I recognized him now, a tall Eisandine fellow I knew only as a hard worker.

"Edouard!" The bewilderment in Captain Rousse's voice gave way to rising anger. He grabbed the front of the sailor's shirt in one fist. "Tell me! What in the seven hells were you doing with my logbook?"

"Nothing good," Bao muttered beside me.

The sailor kept his silence. With a roar of disgust, Rousse flung him to the deck, planting his feet and towering over him. *"Tell me!"*

Whatever he was about, this Edouard had courage. He kept his mouth stubbornly shut on his secret.

"All right, then." With an effort, Septimus Rousse took a step backward and collected himself. "Alaric, put him under guard." He glanced at the eastern horizon. "Come dawn, we'll see if a spot of keel-hauling will make him talk. Night shift, resume your posts." Turning to me, he bowed. "My apologies, my lady. I assure you, the matter will be dealt with."

The crowd gathered on the deck dispersed. Bao and I returned to our wardroom along with the others.

Now that the crisis had been contained, I was wide-awake, my nerves jangling. I daresay all of us were. We kindled a lantern and sat at the long table that bisected the room, discussing the matter.

"Why would anyone steal the captain's logbook?" Brice de Bretel mused. "Name of Elua! We'd be lost at sea without it!"

Balthasar studied his fingernails. "Precisely."

I swallowed hard. "You think he meant to sabotage the expedition?"

He shot me a look. "What else?"

"Rousse should have beaten a confession out of him!" Alain Guillard said in a fierce voice.

"Are you familiar with the practice of keelhauling?" Denis inquired. The other shook his head. "Believe me, the captain doesn't intend to go easy on him."

"What do you think, my lord Denis?" I asked him. "You're the one spotted the fellow. What was he planning to do with the logbook?"

"At best, hide it. At worst..." He shrugged. "Dispose of it."

"But that's madness!" Clemente DuBois' eyes were wide. He was alleged to be a skilled swordsman, but I wasn't overly impressed with his intellect. "Why would anyone do such a thing? It would doom us all!"

"Most likely," Bao said in a pragmatic tone. "I think that was the idea. For sure, it would doom the mission to failure."

Balthasar glanced up from his nails. "The more interesting question is, who put him up to it?"

There was silence in the wardroom. All of us, even slightly dim-witted Clemente DuBois, knew that the list of folk who stood to benefit from the failure of our expedition was a very, very short one.

"Would he?" I asked in wonder. "Would Duc Rogier do such a thing?"

Balthasar shrugged. "Unless the man's stark, raving mad, someone did. Someone provided a damn powerful incentive to get a man to risk throwing his own life away just to scuttle our mission."

"We need a confession from him," Denis said in a low voice. "We need to know if there are others, or if he was working alone. And whatever else happens, whether we succeed or fail, if we live to see Terre d'Ange again, our noble Regent can't be allowed to get away with this."

"It's not going to be easy," Bao commented. "Hard to get a man ready and willing to die to talk."

"He'll talk," Denis predicted. "Once he's had a taste of keelhauling, he'll talk. I saw it done to a sailor caught stealing rations on the first voyage." He shuddered. "He'll beg for a chance to talk."

In that, he was wrong.

Come dawn, I found out exactly what the process of keelhauling entailed. In theory, it was simple. A long rope was tied under the sailor Edouard's arms, and he was lowered overboard to be dragged alongside the ship. I thought the threat of drowning must be the worst of it, but it was only part. After weeks at sea, the sharp-edged barnacles that clustered on the ship's hull tore at the fellow's flesh.

Three times, Captain Rousse ordered Edouard lowered and dragged; and three times, he came up coughing and sputtering seawater and bleeding from increasingly numerous gashes, his clothing in tatters.

Each time, he refused to break his silence.

By the third time, Edouard was half-drowned, lying limp and listless on the deck, leaking fluids.

Septimus Rousse prodded him with a booted toe. "Would you rather the flogger?" he asked. "That's what's next for you, my lad."

I winced.

"My lord captain," Balthasar addressed him in a casual tone. "Forgive me for this breach of protocol, but I have a proposal." His dark blue eyes glinted, and I felt the uneasy stirring of his gift and a sharp taste like metal in my mouth. "As no doubt you know, members of House Shahrizai are well versed in . . . certain arts, which can be put to many uses. And it's been far, far too long since I had a chance to employ them." He bared his teeth in a smile. "Would you be willing to consider allowing *me* to question this man?"

On the deck, Edouard made a faint sound of protest.

The captain gave Balthasar a long, considering look. "You know, that's not the worst idea I've heard."

Balthasar's smile widened. "I'm glad you think so." He nodded at the prone sailor. "Have him cleaned up, put some dry clothes on him, and bring him to the wardroom. I don't want him dripping and bleeding all over the place. Yet."

Although I didn't want to undermine him in public, belowdeck I confronted Balthasar. "My lord, you're proposing to torture the fellow for your own pleasure! I cannot condone it."

"If it works, does it matter whether or not I take pleasure in it?" he inquired. "How is that worse than the punishment the captain's already meted out? Or the further punishment he had in store?"

"It's just…wrong!"

He sighed. "Moirin, listen. What I proposed and what I plan to do are not entirely the same thing. Tell me, have I earned a measure of trust from you?"

Reluctantly, I nodded.

"Then give it to me now." Balthasar's gaze was steady and grave. "I swear on my honor, I know what I'm doing."

Clemente DuBois essayed a feeble jest. "Couldn't you find something more convincing to swear on?"

Balthasar ignored him. "I would ask all of you to trust me," he said, glancing around the wardroom. "Watch, but don't intervene. And if I ask you to leave us alone, go immediately. Are we agreed?"

After a pause, everyone nodded.

"Good. Now someone go find out the fellow's surname for me."

In short order, one Edouard Durel was escorted to the wardroom with his hands tied behind his back. He was clad in dry clothing, and his wounds had been dusted with powdered alum to halt the bleeding. Although his expression was stoic, I could smell acrid fear-sweat on him.

I daresay Balthasar could, too. "Edouard Durel," he drawled in greeting, pointing at the long table with the tip of his belt knife. "Do have a seat, won't you?"

The fellow sat. The rest of us stood in the doorways of our cabins, watching while Balthasar paced around the table, toying idly with his knife. Light from the lantern glinted on its razor-sharp edges. The sailor tracked Balthasar's progress warily.

"Not a very pretty toy, is it?" Balthasar said apologetically, pausing to stroke the sailor's cheek with one keen edge. "Pity I didn't bring a set of flechettes, but I didn't think I'd have a chance to play." Leaning down, he whispered in the fellow's ear. "Thank you so very much for this opportunity. I've never inflicted pain on anyone against their will, but I must confess, I've always wondered what it would be like."

Cords in the man's neck tightened. "You commit heresy!"

"Do you think so?" Balthasar increased the pressure, opening a thin gash, which he then probed lovingly with the tip, working it beneath the skin. The sailor gritted his teeth. I caught my breath, and Bao squeezed my arm. "I don't see it that way at all. Mayhap you would be interested in hearing my perspective?"

The sailor didn't answer.

"You are a thief, Messire Durel." Balthasar prowled around the table and took a seat opposite the fellow. His eyes were unnaturally bright in the lamplight, pupils dilated with arousal. "That is not in question. And since your actions could quite possibly have doomed the lot of us to death by starvation or worse, one might consider you guilty of attempted murder. *I* do."

Edouard Durel looked away.

"Mighty Kushiel was in charge of administering punishment to the damned." There was a terrible tenderness in Balthasar's voice. "They say he loved his charges too well. You have condemned yourself to Kushiel's ungentle mercy, Messire Durel, and as a proud scion of Kushiel's line, it is my duty as well as my pleasure to administer it." He stroked the blade of his knife. "How well shall *I* come to love you, I wonder?"

"I didn't kill anyone!" Sweat beaded on the sailor's brow. "You can't punish me for something that never happened!"

Balthasar made a *tsk-tsk* sound. "Do you imagine Kushiel does not judge you for your intentions?" he asked, leaning across the table to tickle the fellow under his chin with the knife tip. "Hmm?"

Durel jerked his head backward. "*You* cannot prove it!"

"Ah, well, no. But I have the certitude of faith, and I am willing to risk my immortal soul for it." Balthasar prodded harder. "Tell me, did you intend to hide the logbook or toss it overboard?"

The sailor resumed his silence.

"No matter." Balthasar withdrew the knife and took a whetstone from his purse, running it over the blade's edge in a hypnotic rhythm, his overbright gaze fixed on Edouard's face. "More important, who are you protecting?"

Again, the fellow looked away, his jaw tight.

"Oh, I don't mean the Regent, or whoever put you up to this." Balthasar waved the knife in a careless gesture. "No, no. I'll come to that in time. Right now, I'm interested in getting to know *you*, Messire Durel." He leaned forward, propping his elbows on the table and resting his chin on his fists, still holding the knife and whetstone. "You attempted a heinous deed that might well have condemned you to a miserable death along with the rest of us. What stakes could possibly be high enough to prompt a man to do such a thing?"

Edouard Durel was sweating profusely now, sweat running in sheets down his face, mingling with the blood from the gash on his cheek. The wardroom stank of his fear, and I felt more than a little sick.

"Ah, now I begin to see! You got yourself in trouble, didn't you?" Balthasar asked softly. The sympathy in his tone sounded genuine, and for all I knew, it was. "Who was going to pay the price for it?"

"No one!" the sailor choked out.

"Aged parents, vulnerable in their twilight years?" Balthasar speculated. "A younger brother who fell in with a bad crowd? No?" He tapped the table with the hilt of his knife, thinking. "The wife and children?"

Durel flinched as though he'd been struck, tears filling his eyes and spilling down his cheeks. Kushiel's mercy, indeed. Somewhere, I thought I heard the sound of bronze wings clashing.

"Ah. And there we have it." Balthasar Shahrizai laid down the knife and whetstone, folding his hands atop the table. His handsome face was solemn and stern, and the air in the wardroom was thick with the barbed coils of his gift. "Edouard Durel, I speak for mighty Kushiel himself when I tell you that there is only one way to protect your loved ones from the consequences of your actions. Will you make your confession?"

It was not a pretty sight.

The sailor Edouard Durel broke into ragged, anguished sobs, his

broad shoulders heaving. Between sobs he stammered out a tale of
having fallen deep into debt after returning from the ill-fated voyage
to Terra Nova, drowning his sorrows and wagering at Bryony House.
He'd wagered and lost everything in his possession in a matter of days,
even down to the roof above his wife and six-year-old daughter's head.

And when it came to matters of finance, Bryony House was mer-
ciless.

At some point during the fellow's confession, Balthasar mimed for
Denis to cut his bonds and bring a bottle of brandy. He poured a gen-
erous glass, pushing it across the table. "Who approached you? Was it
Duc Rogier?"

Edouard Durel downed the brandy and shook his head. "His wife,
with that eldest son of theirs in tow." He shuddered. "Hateful lad."

I quite agreed.

Balthasar refilled the glass. "So she offered to make good on your
debt in exchange for your compliance?"

"Aye," he said wearily. "She promised they'd never want for aught
for the rest of their lives, that they'd live like peers of the realm so long
as I did what she asked and never, ever spoke a word of the matter."
He rubbed at his tears. "I thought... I thought there was a chance
we'd live through this. Captain Rousse is one of the most resourceful
sailors I've ever known. He might have found a way to plot a course
homeward."

"Gods, man!" Denis de Toluard interjected. "How could you possibly imagine you'd get away with it?"

The sailor looked at him with dull eyes. "I didn't. I reckoned I'd
be found out sooner or later. But as long as I kept my mouth shut, my
Adele and Mattie would be safe."

"And Prince Thierry and all his comrades doomed to whatever
fate befell them in Terra Nova!" Denis shouted.

Edouard Durel gave a broken laugh. "Do you really think you
stand a chance of finding them, my lord?" He gestured at me. "Just
because some half-breed bear-witch with a grudge claims to have had
a vision?"

"In fact, I do." Denis glanced at me. "I have more cause than most to put my faith in Moirin mac Fainche."

To that, the sailor made no reply.

"A few further questions, Messire Durel," Balthasar said. "Did you have an accomplice, or were you working alone?"

Durel shook his head. "If I'd had an accomplice, I'd have posted a lookout." He grimaced. "I wasn't expecting Lord de Toluard's midnight stroll."

"Did the Duchese de Barthelme approach anyone else with a similar offer?" Balthasar asked.

The sailor shrugged. "If she did, she didn't say anything to me about it." He picked up the refilled glass of brandy and downed it in a series of gulps, setting the empty glass on the table. "So far as I know, I'm the only traitor about the ship," he said in an unsteady tone. "That's what I am, isn't it?"

"I'm afraid so," Balthasar agreed. Reaching across the table, he put his hand over Edouard Durel's. "Don't worry about your wife and daughter. If we return safely, I'll make sure they'll pay no price for your sin, and be well cared for. And if we don't..." He smiled wryly. "Well, you've already seen to it that they'll be fine."

Fresh tears spilled from the fellow's eyes. "Thank you, my lord. I don't deserve your kindness!"

"No, you don't," Balthasar said judiciously. "But neither do they deserve to be punished for your folly."

Durel nodded. "What's to become of me?"

"That's the captain's business for now." Balthasar retrieved his whetstone from the table and stowed it. "Assuming we're all in agreement, I'd ask him to spare your life so that you might stand trial in Terre d'Ange and testify against the Regent's wife and her poisonous brat. I trust you're willing to do so?"

"Aye, my lord." Edouard Durel took a deep breath, his gaze on the knife still lying atop the table. "I was wrong to doubt you. I felt Kushiel's presence here. I am willing to accept whatever penance you give me."

"Ah." Balthasar plucked up his belt knife and sheathed it. "As it happens, I am more modest than I pretend. I will leave the matter of penance to the priests, and rest content with my role here."

With that, he sent Clemente to fetch the sailors to take Edouard Durel into custody once more.

When they had gone, Balthasar heaved a mighty sigh, running his hands over his face. "That," he remarked to no one in particular, "was challenging." He gave us all a surprisingly sweet smile. "Thank you for your trust."

"Don't thank me," Brice de Bretel said flatly. "I really thought you meant to skin the man alive."

Balthasar's smile tightened. "Nothing quite so crude, I hope."

I thought about the brightness of his eyes, the tenderness of his voice; and I thought that the sense of deadly desire it evoked was quite genuine. There was a part of Balthasar Shahrizai that would have relished giving in to his darkest urges and carrying out the punishment he threatened, and the most frightening part was that he would have done it out of a kind of love. "You wield a dangerous gift, my lord," I murmured.

He met my gaze. "Not lightly, Lady Moirin."

"No." I came forward to rest my hands on his shoulders, feeling the latent tension in them. Leaning down, I kissed his cheek. "It was well done. Thank you."

He nodded in acknowledgment.

Denis de Toluard shuddered. "Let's just hope there *aren't* any more. That was far too near a thing."

"Good thing you couldn't sleep, huh?" Bao observed.

"It is, isn't it?" A look of wonder touched Denis' face. "Ever since the King's death, I've had nightmares. I never thought I'd be glad of them."

"And I never thought I'd be so glad to have you on this expedition, my lord Denis," I said to him, inclining my head. "We all owe you a profound debt today. Were it not for your acuity, we'd be in dire straits, and Thierry's cause nigh hopeless."

"Hear, hear!" Balthasar hoisted the bottle of brandy and drank from it, wiping the bottle's mouth on his sleeve and passing it to Denis.

He drank, and passed it onward.

We all drank.

The ship sailed onward.

THIRTY-FOUR

W e were at sea for two more months.
It was an uneasy time, to say the least. Edouard Durel's attempt at sabotaging our mission had everyone on edge. Sailors and fighting men eyed one another uneasily, wondering if another traitor lurked in our ranks.

Captain Rousse called in every member of his crew for a private interrogation.

Balthasar Shahrizai spent countless hours in the crowded main berth, casually talking with and covertly eavesdropping on the force he'd assembled.

In the end, it seemed that no one else had been approached. Claudine de Barthelme had had a limited amount of time in which to operate in the City of Elua, in which to find and exploit vulnerable members of our expedition.

I dwelled on memories of her false smile, hating her. For my father's sake, I was glad it was her, and not Duc Rogier, behind the attempt.

I worried about Desirée.

New protocols were established to protect the captain's logbook. Edouard Durel was kept under restraint. Our ship, *Naamah's Dove*, rose and fell on the trackless grey ocean; bobbing like a cork in foul weather, riding out the crests and troughs of the storms that assailed us, sailing calmly over placid seas, her sheets filled with wind. Westward, ever westward.

When the cry of "Land ahead!" came from the lookout atop the central mast, I was profoundly grateful.

Everyone who could fit rushed abovedeck to catch our first glimpse of Terra Nova, at first little more than a green smudge on the horizon. Bit by bit, we drew nearer and the green smudge resolved itself into a vast, sprawling landscape dominated by a tall mountain in the distance, tall enough that the sun glinted on snow atop its peak. For the first time, I felt a sense of awe at venturing into a new land, a land that had remained undiscovered by the rest of the world for countless centuries. A plume of smoke trailed from the mountain's apex, white against the blue sky.

"The Nahuatl call it *Iztactepetl*," Denis de Toluard informed me.

"White Mountain?" I was pleased with myself for being able to translate the name; and pleased, too, at the omen, reminded of the dragon's beloved White Jade Mountain in faraway Ch'in.

Denis nodded. "Well done." He pointed at the smoke plume. "It's a volcano. The first of many things that can kill you in Terra Nova."

"Oh." Mayhap it wasn't such a happy omen after all.

Once we entered the wide harbor, I had to own I was a bit disappointed with my first look at the Nahuatl Empire. Thanks to Denis, I'd known that we would make landfall at the Aragonian port of Orgullo del Sol, but my head had been filled with the fanciful tales Cillian had told me years ago, when Terra Nova was first discovered. I'd had visions of marble temples rising from the jungle, folk going around adorned in shimmering feathers, gold and jade jewelry.

Instead, it was a rough and ready port still undergoing major phases of construction, and it was filled with Aragonians, none of whom were any too glad to see us. But while Captain Rousse was contending with the harbor-master, I saw my first Nahuatl folk as a number of men gathered to peer at the ship, looking expectant. They certainly weren't clad in feathers and jewels, but rather rough-spun garments, and they carried wooden frames on their backs, held in place with a braided thong around their foreheads.

"Porters," Denis said, following my gaze. "Members of the peasant class. The Aragonians hire them for menial work. Almost everything's carted on foot here. They've no pack-animals, and the Aragonians are careful not to trade in horse-flesh. It's one of the advantages they hold."

The lack of finery notwithstanding, I thought they were a good-looking folk with ruddy bronze skin, black hair and eyes, and strong, prominent features.

One of them caught my gaze and pointed, nudging the fellow next to him. All of them stared.

"I think they like you, Moirin," Bao remarked, leaning on his staff beside me.

"Name of Elua!" Denis drew a sharp breath. "I hadn't thought of *that*."

I was confused. "That the Nahuatl might like me?"

"No, Moirin." He shot me an impatient look. "They've never seen a European woman before."

"Not that our half-breed bear-witch exactly resembles the majority of them," Balthasar observed.

"But the Aragonians..." I gestured at the port city. "They've been here for years! Is there not a single woman among them?"

Denis shook his head. "Only men. If they want a woman, they'll take a native mistress. I keep trying to tell you, Terra Nova is dangerous. Too dangerous for women."

"You really don't know Moirin very well," Bao commented. "Did you know she can outshoot a Tatar?"

"I was lucky," I murmured.

Now the Aragonian harbor-master took notice of the staring Nahuatl porters and spotted me aboard the ship. He blinked and startled, and began questioning Septimus Rousse anew. Whatever the captain told him, it resulted in a deep, florid bow from the Aragonian official, and an invitation to disembark.

After months at sea, the solid quay felt unsteady beneath my feet. I did my best not to sway as the harbor-master proffered a second bow, his long mustaches tickling my hand as he took and kissed it.

"So lovely and so brave!" he said in heavily accented D'Angeline. "Doña Moirin, although I must advise against it, I admire your desire to discover the fate of your royal kinsman. Please, permit me to escort you and a few of your companions to the mayor's quarters. He would be furious if I allowed you to take coarse lodgings elsewhere."

I spared a glance at Septimus Rousse.

Our captain gave me a brusque nod. "Go, my lady. Don't worry, I'll see to what's needful here."

Along with Bao, Balthasar, Denis, a large cask of perry brandy for the mayor, and several Nahuatl porters carrying our personal baggage, I accompanied the harbor-master through the streets of Orgullo del Sol, drawing stares and startled looks along the way. I daresay no one had expected to see D'Angelines returning in the first place, and with my gender and Bao's distinctive Ch'in features, we made an unusual sight indeed.

The mayor's residence was one of the most ambitious buildings in the city, an elegant stone affair that stood in contrast to the wooden construction elsewhere. After a brief moment of shock and an exchange in Aragonian with the harbor-master, the steward hastened to fetch the mayor.

In short order, we were introduced to Porfirio Reyes, mayor of Orgullo del Sol. He was a short, thickset fellow with a bit of a paunch and drooping eyelids, but he had the same courtly manners as the harbor-master and a commendable ability to conceal surprise. Fortunately for me, he also spoke fluent D'Angeline with barely a trace of an accent.

"Such a sad tale, the loss of the young Dauphin!" He shook his head. "But it would be folly to compound the tragedy with your own needless death. Please, my lady, will you and your companions accept my hospitality, and allow me the chance to dissuade you from this madness?" He patted his substantial belly. "If nothing else, I assure you, you'll be well fed! After so long at sea, you must be yearning for fresh fare."

"And a bath," Balthasar murmured. "And the services of a laundress."

The mayor chuckled. "Ah, D'Angelines! Of course. I will gladly provide both, Lord Shahrizai."

I smiled at him. "It would be our pleasure."

Our baths were drawn by unsmiling Nahuatl women serving as maids, whom I tried without success to engage in conversation—whether due to my limited skills in the language, or their innate reticence, I couldn't say.

From what Denis de Toluard had told me, the Aragonians and the Nahuatl had an uneasy coexistence in Terra Nova. If the Aragonians could have seized the country outright, they would have done it, but the Nahuatl and their allies were too numerous. By the same token, the Aragonians' superior weapons, armor, and ability to fight on horseback made them hard to assail, and the Nahuatl tolerated their presence and engaged in ongoing trade because the Emperor hoped to acquire valuable steel and breeding stock.

Somehow, I doubted it was an arrangement that benefited the commonfolk of Terra Nova.

After bathing and changing into my least filthy gown, and entrusting the rest of my attire to the mayor's servants, I felt more myself.

Bao, himself cleaned and scrubbed, eyed me appreciatively. "A whole room to ourselves in the mayor's palace, huh? Not a tiny cabin in the wardroom where everyone knows everyone's business."

I kissed him. "Dinner first."

He grinned, wrapping his arms around my waist. "And later?"

"Later, we put our privacy to good use," I assured him.

The sun was setting over Orgullo del Sol when all of us joined Mayor Porfirio Reyes for dinner in a torch-lit courtyard patio. The air of Terra Nova was thick and moist, smelling of green, growing things.

Stoic Nahuatl servants brought course after course of food, including many unfamiliar fruits and vegetables, which were indeed a welcome sight, and flatbread made from a strange grain. The meal culminated in a delicious dish of fresh-caught fish simmered and slathered in a spicy red sauce comprised of yet another unfamiliar fruit, this one savory rather than sweet.

I reveled in its tang on my tongue. "What is this?"

"Do you like it?" Porfirio beamed. "The fish is called *huachinango*. It's quite good, I think. The sauce is made with a fruit the natives call *tomati*, and a blend of Aragonian spices." He took a judicious bite. "Yes, quite good. Unfortunately, we've not had much success in exporting *tomati* plants."

"Too delicate to survive the journey?" Balthasar inquired. "Or too difficult to cultivate?"

Bao gave me a speculative glance. "I bet Moirin could do it."

"Neither." The mayor dabbed his lips with a linen napkin. "Due to an unfortunate resemblance to the leaves of deadly nightshade, there's a persistent rumor that the fruits are poisonous."

Balthasar dropped his fork in alarm.

Porfirio Reyes laughed. "I assure you, it's utterly baseless. I've eaten my weight in *tomati* without a single ill effect."

I was hoping the mayor would serve *chocolatl* after the meal, remembering the exquisite taste of the frothy beverage, but instead he insisted on tapping the cask of perry brandy we'd brought him. He swirled the contents of his glass and inhaled deeply before allowing himself a sip.

"Delicious." Porfirio smacked his lips. "I can taste the sunlight on the pears as they ripen in the orchard." Setting down his glass, he regarded the four of us. Beneath his drooping lids, his eyes had a shrewd gleam. "Now, let us discuss this matter. First, I would like to know if your tale of romantic folly, this search for the lost Dauphin, is merely an excuse for a second attempt to undermine our trade with the Nahuatl."

"No, my lord," I said. "It's not."

"Although House Shahrizai does hope to recoup its investment," Balthasar said. "At least on this journey. But we plan no others."

The mayor's fingers drummed on the table. "You claim to be a seer, Lady Moirin?"

"Of a sort," I said honestly. "All I can tell you is that I'm very, very certain Prince Thierry is alive."

His expression softened. "It is highly unlikely, my lady."

"Nonetheless."

"You haven't the faintest ideas of the dangers you face." He waved one hand. "What little you've seen here is nothing compared to the jungle. Even the Nahuatl avoid it, and they're some of the most fearless folk I've ever met." He leaned forward. "Do you know what they seek to achieve as the measure of an ideal man? They have a saying for it. A stone face and a stone heart."

I shrugged helplessly. "My lord mayor, I know it's dangerous, but I *have* to go. Do you mean to prevent us?"

"I am considering it," Porfirio Reyes said frankly. "My conscience counsels against allowing a woman to undertake such a risk."

My *diadh-anam* flared in alarm. "Close your eyes."

He blinked at me. "I beg your pardon?"

"All of you, please," I added. "Or just glance away for a moment."

"I beg you grant the lady's request, my lord mayor." Denis de Toluard averted his gaze. "She means to summon her magic."

"Her what?"

"It will take only a few seconds, my lord," I said. "Please?"

The mayor shrugged his stocky shoulders and closed his eyes. "Never let it be said I refused a beautiful woman's earnest request."

As soon as the others followed suit, I breathed in deeply and summoned the twilight, blowing it around us. To be sure, it would have been more effective were the courtyard not already in dusk, but the twilight at once deepened and brightened everything, turning blue shadows to violet, making the torch-flames burn silvery-white.

When I bade him open his eyes, Porfirio gave me a startled look. "What trick is this?"

"Moirin's magic," Bao said with satisfaction.

One of the Nahuatl servants entered the courtyard, halted, and stared around in blank confusion, calling out a question to someone inside.

"What ails the woman?" Porfirio demanded. "We're right in front of her!"

"She can't see us," I said softly. "No one can until I release the twilight." As soon as the Nahuatl servant left, I let it go. The deep shadows lightened and the torches burned yellow and orange once more.

The mayor looked a trifle pale. "A sorceress, then?"

I shook my head. "'Tis a gift of the Maghuin Dhonn Herself to my mother's folk, and it is She Herself who laid this destiny on me—not for the first time. I have travelled the far reaches of the world before, my lord. I am not some pampered court noblewoman with a foolish romantic notion of heroism, and I beg you not to seek to protect me for my own good."

Porfirio Reyes swirled the brandy in his glass once more, and took another measured sip. "I see." He set down his glass. "All right, then. You'll need to travel to Tenochtitlan to obtain the Emperor's blessing on the venture."

"I know."

He rubbed his bearded chin. "Achcuatli's a clever fellow. He was under pressure from our side not to open serious trade with your Dauphin's party, but thanks to that physician's preventative treatment of the pox, he owed them a debt. He provided them with a map to the empire of Tawantinsuyo under the guise of a reward, but I'm not so sure it wasn't a convenient way of dodging the issue."

Balthasar raised his brows. "Is the empire real or not?"

"Oh, it's real," Porfirio said. "Or at least so I'm told. But if Achcuatli truly had your Dauphin's best interests at heart, he wouldn't have given them a map that sent them deep into the heart of the jungle."

"There's a better route?" Denis inquired.

The Aragonian mayor nodded. "Overland across the isthmus, and southward along the coast to the mountains."

"Doesn't matter," Bao said with his usual pragmatism. "We're not looking for the empire, we're looking for the missing prince. Which means we have to follow *his* route, not a better one."

Porfirio Reyes sighed. "Altogether too true."

"Into the jungle!" Balthasar hoisted his glass, contemplating its contents. "With its myriad dangers and flowers of surpassing beauty."

The bewildered Nahuatl servant who had found us missing returned to the courtyard and found us restored, all of us in our seats. Porfirio Reyes issued a series of commands, and she returned to refill our glasses with stoic efficiency.

"Whatever trade goods you've brought, you'd be well advised to use them in exchange for Emperor Achcuatli's aid," he told me. "I understand there are *pochteca* who have ventured into the green realms."

"*Pochteca*?" I asked.

"Merchants," Denis murmured. "Travelling merchants."

The mayor nodded again. "They guard their secrets fiercely, but Achcuatli has the authority to command them. Your chance of survival would be greatly enhanced by having a guide familiar with the territory."

Denis de Toluard flushed with anger. "All of this would have been most helpful to know before, my lord mayor. I may have been sicker than a dog, but I know there was no talk of better routes or knowledgeable guides; and in all the months that followed, Captain Ortiz y Ramos never breathed a word about either. If you ask me, that makes the lot of you complicit in Thierry's disappearance."

"May I remind you that you weren't welcome here?" Porfirio's tone hardened. "Aragonia has no desire to share trade relations with Terre d'Ange! Not only that, but when your physician shared his method of inoculation with the Emperor's *ticitls*, he took away one of our greatest weapons."

My stomach felt hollow. "You used the pox as a weapon? The killing pox?"

He gave me an apologetic look. "Not deliberately, of course. But it was cutting quite a swath through the Nahuatl population before the D'Angelines arrived. It seemed they had no natural resistance to it. In time, it would have reduced their numbers to a mere fraction, rendering the entire nation ripe for conquest."

Reminding myself that this fellow who had seemed so charming had the power to thwart our mission, I swallowed hard and said nothing.

"I know it seems ruthless, but believe me when I tell you that you'll find little to love in the Nahuatl," Porfirio said gently. "If you'd seen the steps of their temples running red with blood, you'd understand. They have no regard for human life, and they're capable of immense cruelty. They believe their god Tlaloc requires the sacrifice of young children to bring the rain, and they torment the little ones before death so that their tears dampen the earth; and that is but one of the gods they worship." He shook his head. "No, no. You'll find nothing to love about them. They're a barbaric folk, in some ways scarce better than animals."

Clearing his throat, Balthasar changed the subject. "If I may return to the matter at hand, we're most grateful for your counsel, my lord mayor. But if the Emperor did not see fit to appoint the Dauphin a guide, what makes you think he'll grant our request?"

The mayor laced his hands over his belly. "Because thanks to me, you know to ask for it. And you're not here to upset the balance of order, are you?"

"No," I murmured. "Only to attempt to find Prince Thierry and the others, I swear it."

"Listen, my lords, my lady." There was sympathy in Porfirio's drooping gaze. "I spoke truly when I said it was a sad tale. No one wanted your Dauphin and his men to meet a foul end. We hoped only that the rigors of the jungle would dissuade them, that they would accept defeat, turn back, and abandon the notion of encroaching on Aragonia's claim here. If I'd known what would happen, I would have turned him away here."

Bao stirred. "Why didn't you?"

He smiled wryly. "I didn't want to provoke a diplomatic incident; and quite frankly, our garrison here wasn't yet fully staffed. If the Dauphin had refused my order, I doubt I could have enforced it."

"Pity," Balthasar said. "It would have saved a lot of trouble."

"Indeed." Porfirio Reyes lifted his brandy glass and drank the last of its contents, then rose and patted his belly before giving us a sweeping bow. "And now I shall bid you good evening, my lady, my lords, and retire."

All of us took his cue. In the room Bao and I shared, both of us gazed at the wide-seeming bed with its comfortable pallet and clean linens.

"Do you…?" Bao asked uncertainly.

I shook my head. "I'm sorry. I've lost my appetite for lovemaking tonight."

"Oh, good," he said with relief, taking a seat on the bed and prying off his boots. "Never thought I'd say *that*."

I sat beside him. "It's a lot to stomach."

"It is." Bao put his arm around my shoulders and kissed my temple with uncommon tenderness. "Let's just get some sleep, huh? We've got a lot of work ahead of us."

It was sound advice, but sleep evaded me. Bao…Bao could sleep anywhere, no matter what the circumstances. I lay on the bed in the sheltering curve of his arm, trying to take comfort in his deep, even breathing, trying to dispel the images of bloodstained temples and crying children that haunted me.

A stone face and a stone heart.

You'll find little to love in the Nahuatl…

Mayhap it would prove true, but I'd found little to love in the Aragonians in Terra Nova thus far, too.

The killing pox…

I remembered summoning the fallen spirit Marbas with the Circle of Shalomon. While they had bartered in vain with a spirit who had appeared in the form of a lion, under no obligation to answer as a human, I had spoken to him in the twilight.

Among the many gifts Marbas could bestow was the cure for any disease. I had begged him to relent and give one to Raphael de Mereliot.

The lion's eyes had glowed. *It's not so simple*, he had told me. *To learn the charm to cure, you must learn the charm to cause. Leprosy, typhoid, pneumonia, plague…I can teach you to invoke and banish any one of these. Would you possess such knowledge? Would you put it into their hands?*

I had refused.

That, no one knew. I'd never told anyone. But after tonight's con-versation with Mayor Porfirio Reyes, I was convinced that that was one of the wiser decisions I'd made in my young life. Even without a fallen spirit's charm to invoke, the Aragonians would have gladly seen the vast majority of the population of the Nahuatl Empire wiped from the face of the earth by the killing pox.

And it was a piece of irony that even without Marbas' gift, Raphael de Mereliot had spared the Nahuatl from that fate.

A small part of me that had once loved Raphael was glad for his sake.

I hoped he was, too.

THIRTY-FIVE

———✦———

C ome morning, we broke our fast with the mayor of Orgullo del Sol, dining once more in the courtyard on fresh fruit, eggs topped with a spicy sauce, and more of the flatbread Porfirio Reyes told us was made from a grain called *maize*. It was the staple item of the Nahuatl diet.

As the mayor gave us further advice on our journey, my mind wandered.

I remembered dining on a dish of spice-laced eggs and flatbread made of lentils with the Rani Amrita and her son, Ravindra, in Bhaktipur, and I wished I were there instead of here. I wondered how tall solemn Ravindra had grown since Bao and I had left, and how the women and children we'd rescued from the Falconer's harem were faring.

I wondered if the vast change the Rani had implemented, banishing the practice of regarding no-caste people as *untouchable*, had begun to spread throughout Bhodistan or if it remained confined to Bhaktipur.

Thinking on the mayor's lack of compassion and gazing at his unlovely face, I thought I would give a great deal to see Amrita again, to hear her musical laugh as she teased me affectionately.

But Bhaktipur was far, far away. Our business was here in Terra Nova. With an effort, I made myself concentrate on Porfirio Reyes' advice. I might not like the fellow, but the truth was, he was being generous with us.

"...brought horses with you?" he was inquiring.

"Four pack-horses, all geldings," Balthasar replied. "Don't worry, we mean to respect the Aragonian ban on trading horse-flesh and steel weaponry."

"Good, good." Porfirio nodded in approval. "As long as you hew to the insistence that it's forbidden by your gods, Achcuatli shouldn't give you too much trouble. As much as he'd like to get his hands on them, he's a superstitious fellow, too. But if I may give you an additional piece of counsel, you'd be well advised to spare one of the horses that Lady Moirin might ride."

"Why?" I asked.

"In order to command respect," he said to me. "My lady, I've seen your magic, and I'm willing to believe you've a measure of experience in the world, but there's no telling what the Nahuatl will do when they get their first glimpse of a European woman. The more respect you can command, the better."

Balthasar raised his brows. "Do they practice heresy?" He clarified in the face of the mayor's incomprehension. "Do they force themselves on the unwilling?"

"Ah." Porfirio's expression cleared. "I'd forgotten that was the D'Angeline term. Given the opportunity, I don't doubt they would."

"Actually, it's not a common practice among the Nahuatl," Denis de Toluard murmured.

"It's not?" The mayor appeared surprised.

"I learned a few things about them during my time here," Denis said dryly. "I don't dispute their many cruelties, but that doesn't seem to be one of them."

"Even so, it's not a bad idea," Bao said.

"I don't want to ride while everyone else has to walk," I protested.

Bao gave me a look. "I made a promise to your father, Moirin—and you have a knack for finding trouble. If there is a chance the Nahuatl will be hopelessly inflamed by your green eyes and foreign beauty, and a chance that riding astride will help convince them that you are a great and powerful royal lady whose person must be respected, I will take it."

I shrugged. "All right, all right!"

Porfirio Reyes looked relieved. "A wise decision, my lady. I'll see that you're loaned a saddle."

Shortly after we'd concluded our breakfast, Captain Septimus Rousse came to report that all was in readiness for our journey. The sailors were lodged for the duration in an Aragonian inn, and Edouard Durel remained under guard. The ship was unloaded, trade goods distributed among our four pack-horses. He took the news that we were to lose one of them in stride.

"We'll hire a few of those porters," he said. "Our men are already burdened enough marching in armor."

"You might visit the slave market," Porfirio suggested. "In terms of cost, it's likely more effective to purchase several slaves and sell them when you reach Tenochtitlan." He caught my uneasy look. "I understand your discomfort, my lady, but it's the way things are done here. It's customary among the Nahuatl."

I shook my head. "The folk of the Maghuin Dhonn hold their freedom dear. I could not bear knowing I'd treated another human being as nothing more than chattel, no matter how briefly."

The mayor patted my hand. "Ah, I'd forgotten what the delicate sensibilities of real women were like! No doubt your captain can hire the services of a few free porters."

Porfirio Reyes insisted on accompanying us to the harbor where our party was assembled in preparation for departure. I had to own, they looked quite resplendent. House Shahrizai had seen to it that our fighting force was outfitted in a manner appropriate to the climate and the need for extended foot travel, and all forty of Balthasar's hand-picked men were clad in shirts of the finest chain-mail D'Angeline smiths could forge, over which they wore suede brigandines dyed Courcel blue and studded with rivets. Steel vambraces, greaves, and conical helmets that flared to protect their necks completed their ensemble, all polished to a high shine and glittering in the bright morning sun.

"This is going to be beastly hot," Balthasar predicted in a dire tone, donning his own helmet.

Bao eyed him. "Is it really necessary for the journey?"

Balthasar buckled his chin-strap. "If we want to command respect, unfortunately, yes."

Bao spun his staff with obnoxious good cheer, looking cool and comfortable in light attire. "Glad I fight better without it, then!"

"No need to gloat," Balthasar said sourly.

Septimus Rousse, the only other unarmored, bare-headed man in our party, oversaw the matter of unloading one pack-horse and procuring Nahuatl porters in short order, and the horse was saddled and bridled with the mayor's borrowed tack.

"Lady Moirin." Porfirio Reyes took my hand and bowed, kissing it. When he straightened, his heavy-lidded eyes were grave. "I would ask you one last time not to do this thing. I do not want your death on my conscience."

I felt guilty at having conceived a dislike for him, for he had shown us a good deal of courtesy and generosity. I did not think he was a bad fellow—just a man, with any man's faults and flaws. "I'm sorry, my lord mayor," I said gently. "But I must try. Please, be assured that this is on no one's conscience but mine. I am grateful for your assistance."

He released my hand. "Farewell."

There was a finality to the word. Like Duc Rogier de Barthelme, the mayor of Orgullo del Sol did not expect to see me alive again. To his credit, at least the latter did not welcome the prospect.

Still, I prayed I might prove them both wrong.

"Moirin?" Bao touched my shoulder. "Ready?" When I nodded, he cupped his hands to give me a boost into the saddle.

Unaccustomed to being ridden, the pack-horse sidled sideways and shook his head, ears flapping in protest at the change in routine. Leaving the reins slack, I touched its thoughts with mine, soothing it. "Be still, brave heart," I murmured in Alban, reverting to my mother-tongue for the sheer comfort of it. "I do not weigh nearly so much as the burden you were meant to carry, do I? And I am told we must command respect here, you and I." My mount planted his hooves and shivered; and then its head came up, ears pricked, and I stroked its withers. "Well done."

"I'd forgotten you talked to animals, Moirin," Balthasar remarked.

It evoked a long-ago memory of Jehanne, posing me a similar question in a sweet, poisonous voice, long before things had changed forever between us, long before Jehanne had become my unlikely rescuer, when she'd caught me whispering to the long-legged filly that had been Prince Thierry's gift to me. *Do bear-witches speak to animals?*

Ah, gods! Even the memories of her early unkindness hurt to remember.

"I do," I said in D'Angeline, echoing my long-ago reply. "It doesn't mean they speak back to me."

Balthasar Shahrizai, my unlikely ally, smiled at me. "Shall we go?"

I inclined my head to him. "By all means."

Thus began our journey to Tenochtitlan, the heart of the Nahuatl Empire.

For the first two days, we marched through tropical warmth, the men complaining and sweating through the padded gambesons they wore beneath their armor, the Nahuatl porters trudging uncomplaining in simple breech-clouts with packs on their backs and tump-lines bound around their foreheads; me feeling guilty at riding while others walked, feeling guilty at reveling in the palm trees that swayed above us, dreaming their hot, languid dreams. Whether or not Bao and Septimus Rousse felt guilty in their more comfortable attire, I could not say.

At last, the smoking White Mountain of Iztactepetl drew nearer, and we began to pass beneath its shadow, glancing apprehensively at the plume of smoke that trailed from its peak, hoping the volcano rested easy.

For now, it did.

On the third day, another footroad converged with ours, and we saw our first travelling Nahuatl merchant party.

Pochtecas.

The merchants were unassuming; later, I would learn that it was their way to appear modest and conceal their wealth. Indeed, whatever goods they carried would be hidden upon arrival in Tenochtitlan. There was a long line of porters—or more likely, slaves—carrying bundles in the same manner as ours.

But the warriors guarding the expedition—now, they were as resplendent in their own way as our company. They wore curious armor of quilted cotton that had been soaked in saltwater to stiffen it, and carried wooden shields on which devices had been worked with bright feathers. One of them was dressed head to toe in the skin of a spotted beast, and a great headdress of feathers towered above him.

I was so fascinated, I forgot to be frightened at first.

Balthasar held up one hand, and we all halted. The Nahuatl party halted too, conferring amongst themselves. Then the spotted warrior and the others strode forward, clearly intending to engage us in some way. At a glance, their numbers looked to be even with ours.

Now my heartbeat accelerated, and I silently cursed Porfirio Reyes for planting seeds of fear in me.

"They look like they're ready for a masquerade, don't they?" Clemente DuBois said nervously.

"Shut up, Clemente," Balthasar said in an absent tone. "All right, let's see what they want, shall we? Denis, you're our translator."

Surreptitiously, I strung my bow.

"No foolish ideas, Moirin," Bao warned me. "You're staying behind, and I'm staying right beside you."

"I'm just being prepared," I retorted.

The Nahuatl carried throwing spears and club-like weapons set all around the sides with rows of sharp obsidian blades. The good thing about the latter, Denis had told us, was that obsidian was brittle and shattered easily, especially against steel. The bad thing about the former was that the Nahuatl used handheld tools to hurl the spears with exceptional force, which Denis reckoned might be sufficient to pierce brigandine armor.

I made myself breathe through the Five Styles and remain calm.

The two parties met where the roads converged. Balthasar's men didn't draw steel, and the Nahuatl didn't raise their weapons. At one point, the spotted warrior glanced over at me. His expression was stoic, but there was a spark of curiosity in his eyes. He gestured with one arm, making an inquiry.

From atop my mount, I watched Denis reply. I did my best to keep my own face empty of expression.

After a brief exchange, the *pochtecas* and their porters advanced to join the warriors. Denis de Toluard beckoned to us. "Moirin!" he called. "They wish to meet you."

"Bad idea," Bao muttered.

I glanced down at him. "I'll never command respect if I show myself to be a coward at the outset."

He sighed. "You have a point."

I rode forward slowly, Bao walking beside me. Septimus Rousse stayed behind with our porters to keep a hand on the pack-horses' lines.

The Nahuatl eyed me with interest, but they made no move, threatening or otherwise. When I reached them, I drew rein. Bao moved a few feet away and held his staff in a deceptively casual defensive pose. My former pack-horse stood stock-still beneath me. I met the spotted warrior's gaze impassively.

"Lady Moirin, this is the Jaguar Knight Temilotzin." Beneath his steel helmet, rills of sweat streaked Denis de Toluard's face, but his voice was steady. "He is in command of this expedition."

I inclined my head a fraction. "*Niltze*, Temilotzin."

The spotted warrior gave me a fierce grin and touched his brow and his chest, speaking too rapidly for me to catch more than one word in three.

"Temilotzin says that it is clear the women of Terre d'Ange are braver than the women of Aragonia, who cower on the far shores of their ocean and dare not show their faces in the Nahuatl Empire," Denis translated for me. "He thanks you for allowing their party to precede us, since our progress is woefully slow. For our courtesy, he will put in a good word for us with the Emperor's chief advisor."

"*Tlazocamatli*, Temilotzin," I said politely. "Tell him I am honored by his gracious words, and I thank him for his kindness."

Denis obeyed.

The spotted warrior chuckled and repeated his gesture, touching his brow and chest, then turned to his party and issued a sharp order.

"Fall back to let them pass!" Balthasar called out.

All of us obeyed, clearing the junction. The *pochtecas'* party tramped past us at what was indeed a far more efficient pace than our own.

Once the last man had passed, Bao lowered his staff to rest the butt on the ground. "Guess they weren't hopelessly inflamed after all, huh?"

I gazed after their baggage-train as it began to dwindle in the distance. "So it seems."

"Be glad of it," Balthasar said wryly.

I laughed. "Believe me, I am."

THIRTY-SIX

All told, we were ten days on the road to Tenochtitlan.

We passed—or more accurately, were passed by—one more *pochteca* expedition on the course of the journey, an encounter even more uneventful than the first one, for which all of us were grateful.

Although the majority of our nights were spent making camp along the roadside, we found several inns catering to travelling merchants on the way, where we were treated with an odd dispassionate curiosity.

Our path ascended subtly into the mountains, tropical warmth giving way to cooler temperatures, palm trees giving way to conifers and oaks.

The men in armor began to breathe easier, and I felt relieved on their behalf.

On the tenth day, we reached our destination. From what Denis had told us, I knew that the city of Tenochtitlan was built on a lake in a vast valley surrounded by mountains, but even so, I wasn't prepared for the sight of it. We climbed atop the crest of the road and gazed down into the valley.

It was immense, and the city was well and truly built in the middle of the very lake. Ever the scholar, Denis explained how it had been done, expanding on one lone barren isle by creating artificial islands anchored in marshy ground that were built up and increased over many years, but I simply hadn't imagined it could be so vast.

"Elua have mercy!" Septimus Rousse breathed in awe. "It's nigh as grand as La Serenissima!" He gave a wry laugh. "I shouldn't have wasted all those months cooling my heels in Orgullo del Sol the last time."

"It's a considerable feat of engineering," Denis admitted. "Especially for a folk with no access to forged tools."

Here were the enormous temples I'd heard about so long ago, stepped pyramids rising high into the sky, dominating the city. The city itself was laid out in an orderly manner, looking as though a great deal of thought had gone into it. Reed canoes glided over the lake and through a system of canals, and three huge causeways stretched across the shining water from city to shore to provide access for foot traffic. Even as I watched, a movable bridge in the middle of a causeway was raised to allow a canoe to pass.

"Ingenious," Balthasar commented.

Denis nodded. "It is, rather. They raise the bridges at night to secure the city."

"Where is the Aragonian settlement?" I asked.

He pointed to a wooden fortress on the shores of the lake. "There."

It looked crude in comparison with the splendor of the city, but it was surrounded by high, sturdy walls.

"Well." Although I was infinitely more curious about the city, there was diplomacy to be considered. Before we sought an audience with the Emperor, the Aragonian commander must be assured that this wasn't a second attempt to encroach on their trade rights. "Let's go pay our respects, shall we?"

It took us the better part of three hours to descend into the valley, passing steppe after steppe carved into the sides of the mountain to provide arable fields spread thick with fertile muck dredged from the lake. Nahuatl men and women tending the fields gazed after us with that same odd mix of stoicism and curiosity.

At last, we reached the floor of the valley and made our way to the Aragonian settlement.

The tall oak gates were shut and bolted, but the guards on duty opened them with alacrity after peering through a peep-hole at us. As soon as they ushered our party through the gate and into the open square beyond it, one addressed Denis de Toluard in stern Aragonian, while another hurried away. The remaining dozen or so took up warning poses, hands on the hilts of their swords.

Denis argued in vain with the guard who'd spoken to him, both their voices rising. Not for the first time, I wished the gods had not seen fit to divide humanity with a thousand different tongues. I'd cudgeled my wits into mastering a number of languages, but Aragonian wasn't one of them.

As I waited for someone to tell me what transpired here, I noticed two things.

One was that the other Aragonian guards were staring at me with open lasciviousness. One of them caught my eye and made a deliberately lewd gesture, licking his lips, grabbing his crotch, and pumping his hips.

The other was that there was a palanquin adorned with gold sitting in the square, with a sturdy Nahuatl at each corner, along with a half dozen warriors with obsidian-studded clubs and another slender fellow in an elaborately embroidered mantle and a feather headdress standing beside it.

"What in the world passes here?" I asked no one in particular.

"I don't know," Bao said through gritted teeth, jerking his chin at the Aragonian guard who'd thrust his hips at me. "But I'm ten seconds from teaching that one a lesson."

I was on the verge of dismounting to seek out Septimus Rousse, whom I knew spoke fluent Aragonian, when the guard who'd left returned with another fellow, a handsome man with a pointed beard who I guessed to be Commander Diego Ortiz y Ramos.

He, too, began railing at Denis in a voluble tone, waving his arms in the air, all the while ignoring Denis' aggrieved replies. Balthasar attempted to inject himself into the conversation, and was roundly ignored by both of them.

I lost my temper, and loosed a shout at the top of my voice. *"Enough!"*

It rang loud enough that it startled them into silence.

I took a deep breath. "Thank you. Now, will someone please tell me what in the seven hells this is all about?"

The Aragonian commander spat on the ground. "Have you no shame?" he demanded in a thick accent. "And you!" He glared at Denis. "To use a woman thusly! I did not think even D'Angelines would fall so low!"

"Commander Ortiz y Ramos is under the mistaken impression that you're a gift for the Emperor, Moirin," Denis said wearily.

"What?" I stared at him in shock. "No!"

Diego Ortiz y Ramos pointed at the palanquin and the waiting Nahuatl. "Then why have they come to take you to him?"

"I don't know!" I said helplessly.

"Why don't we *ask* them?" Denis said in an acidic tone. "As I recall, your grasp of the Nahuatl tongue was uncertain, messire."

Once tempers had cooled, the matter was sorted out. It seemed our spotted warrior friend Temilotzin had indeed spoken favorably of our encounter to the Emperor's chief advisor, who in turn had reported it to Emperor Achcuatli himself. The tale of a D'Angeline noblewoman in Terra Nova had piqued the Emperor's curiosity. Without bothering to wait for a request, he'd sent Lord Cuixtli—that was the slender fellow waiting beside the palanquin, who explained the matter to Denis with an air of bored patience—to invite us to the palace for an audience.

"And the Emperor understands that I'm *not* a—a tribute-gift of some kind?" I was anxious to make that point perfectly clear.

Denis conferred with Lord Cuixtli. "Yes, of course," he reported. "That's why he sent the palanquin as a gesture of honor."

I sighed with relief, and offered a slight bow to the Nahuatl lord. "*Tlazocamatli*, Cuixtli."

He inclined his head in reply.

Grateful though I was, after ten days on the road, I'd vastly prefer to meet the Emperor after a bath and a good night's rest. Not trusting my tentative skills in the Nahuatl tongue, I asked Denis to ask Lord Cuixtli if it would give offense if I asked for a day's grace, adding assurances that I would hasten to accept the Emperor's generous offer if it would.

The Nahuatl lord considered the request, his face impassive, at length giving his reply.

"He says it would not give offense," Denis translated. He gave Diego Ortiz y Ramos an uneasy glance. "If anyone has given offense here today, it is the Aragonians. Lord Cuixtli will return tomorrow two hours after dawn to escort you and five men of your choosing to the palace."

I thanked him again, and he gave me a faint smile, flicking his fingers toward his brow and chest in a casual approximation of the salute the spotted warrior Temilotzin had offered me. At a gesture, the warriors fell in line and bearers picked up the empty palanquin and began trotting toward the gates after him.

"Well, then," Balthasar Shahrizai drawled. "Now that *that's* over, may I present Lady Moirin mac Fainche to you, Messire Ortiz y Ramos? As well as her *husband*, the esteemed Messire Bao?"

The Aragonian commander had the decency to look abashed. "Forgive me, Doña Moirin, Don Bao." He offered a courtly bow. "It was a misunderstanding. But may I ask *why* a D'Angeline noble-woman would choose to come to Terra Nova?"

"You may," I said. "If you're inclined to make amends with an offer of hospitality, I'd prefer to answer it over the course of a meal."

His chagrin deepened. "Yes, yes, of course! I will see that your men are lodged and fed, and you and your chosen companions must join me."

It was an awkward dinner. Although Diego Ortiz y Ramos did his best to make up for the misunderstanding with generous hospi-tality and courteous manners, the matter lay unspoken between us. He'd been quick to think the worst of me, quick to think the worst of Terre d'Ange—as though we would so profane Naamah's gifts in exchange for easy commerce. And, too, I could not forget that the commander had deliberately withheld advice that would have benefited Prince Thierry. While he was relieved to find that our intention was to trace the Dauphin's path rather than seek to establish trade with the Nahuatl Empire, it was clear he thought it madness.

Unlike Porfirio Reyes, he did not try to dissuade us.

I liked him less for it.

When the meal ended, it was a relief. I was grateful to retreat to a private chamber with Bao.

"Moirin." Bao whispered my name.

I buried my face against the firm curve of his throat. "Aye?"

"Nothing," he murmured against my hair. "Only that I love you." I felt his lips turn upward in a smile. "You cannot blame the man for thinking what he did."

"No?" I glanced up at him, uncertain.

Bao kissed me. "No. But only for all the best reasons."

"Tell me."

One by one, he did.

And in the end, it was a good night after all.

THIRTY-SEVEN

⟨ ✦ ⟩

Come morning, Lord Cuixtli returned.

I had to own, I felt a bit foolish climbing into the palanquin after all the formal introductions that had been omitted in yesterday's confusion had been made. I may have been descended from three royal lines, but at heart, I was still my mother's daughter, raised in a cave in the Alban wilderness.

But I'd learned the value of appearances in Terre d'Ange, and it was important to command respect here. So I took my seat beneath the ornate feathered canopy, and four strong Nahuatl bearers hoisted the palanquin onto their shoulders.

On Lord Cuixtli's command, we departed the Aragonian garrison and set out for the city of Tenochtitlan.

The great causeways connecting the city to the mainland were even more impressive than I'd reckoned, broad enough to allow five men to walk abreast in comfort, well nigh half a league in length. Here and there, the shallow lake was dotted with *chinampas*, artificial islands rooted to its marshy bottom, spread thick with rich soil and planted with crops. Whatever else was true, the Nahuatl were indeed an ingenious folk.

I wondered what the Emperor was like.

I wished I were more fluent in the Nahuatl tongue. Denis de Toluard had done his best to teach us aboard the ship during our long journey, but he was a natural-born scholar, a scion of Blessed Elua's most learned Companion Shemhazai, and he grew impatient when skills that came easily to him did not come easily to others. But in truth, I was allowing myself to rely too heavily on him here in Terra Nova. I resolved to make a greater effort, knowing I could do far better than I had thus far.

Still, I had chosen Denis to accompany me to the audience with Emperor Achcuatli, along with Bao and Balthasar and Septimus Rousse, rounding out my roster of five companions with Brice de Bretel, who had impressed me with his steadiness aboard the ship. Brice carried our tribute-gift for the Emperor, a large, very fine mirror set in a gilded frame studded with gems, wrapped in ornate brocade and gold braid.

I hoped it would find favor with him, and he would be willing to provide us with aid. One knowledgeable guide could mean the difference between success and failure, mayhap even life or death.

At last our company traversed the length of the great causeway and entered the city proper. We passed many low dwellings, as well as open squares where markets were held, throngs of folk buying and selling goods in a calm manner. Everything in Tenochtitlan seemed very clean and orderly.

It wasn't until we passed through a gate into the main central square where the great temples loomed that I began to feel uncomfortable.

The largest of the temples was truly immense, with twin staircases stretching up into the blue sky to reach a pair of shrines impossibly high above us. I glanced uneasily at it. All seemed quiet and there was no indication that the stairs had run red with blood anytime recently, but there was no mistaking its purpose. Tall racks of human skulls lined the base, hollow-eyed and grinning. There must have been tens of thousands of them altogether. Some were clearly ancient, long ago picked clean by scavenging birds and bleached by the elements.

Others still bore traces of weathered flesh and skin.

I swallowed hard, trying not to shudder.

Following my gaze, Lord Cuixtli spoke to Denis. I caught the gist of his words, which was that he understood the custom was distasteful to the strangers from beyond the sea, and no sacrifice was scheduled for today.

"When is the next?" I made my first attempt since Orgullo del Sol to hold an actual conversation in Nahuatl. "Soon?"

"Not soon, no." Lord Cuixtli shook his head. "Only during the high—" He used a word I didn't know. Seeing my lack of comprehension, he addressed Denis in a spate of rapid language. Denis nodded, listening with a mixture of repressed horror and a scholar's perennial fascination.

"It's as I told you before, Moirin," he said to me when the fellow had finished. "The Nahuatl have gone some way toward accepting Mithras Sol Invictus as a substitute for Tonatiuh, their sun god." He licked his lips as though they'd gone dry. "The Aragonians have imported sacrificial bulls for the sacred rites, and that appears to be…satisfactory. Lord Cuixtli himself is an initiate in the mysteries. But the Aragonians have no worthy substitute for the rain god or the war god, so as a precaution the Nahuatl continue to offer the appropriate sacrifices at the high festivals."

"I see." As I recalled from Porfirio Reyes' tale, the rain god was the one who required the tears of children. I pushed the thought away. It would do me no good to loathe the Nahuatl for their beliefs when we so urgently needed their goodwill.

The Emperor's palace was on the far side of the wall that bordered the ceremonial square. There, my bearers lowered the palanquin so that I might disembark and proceed on foot along with the others.

Although not so elaborate in construction as the Palace in the City of Elua, or the Celestial City in Shuntian, the palace was every bit as imposing in terms of scale. Inside, it reminded me more of the Celestial City in that there were a great many people going about their business with a sense of tremendous order and purpose.

The stone walls of the palace were thick, and I felt them pressing in on me, a sensation that had not troubled me for some time. My head felt thick, my skin felt hot, and there was an uneasy stirring in the pit of my belly.

"Are you all right, Moirin?" Bao murmured. "You look pale."

"Man-made stone." I made myself breathe the Breath of Wind's Sigh, inhaling deeply through my nose and drawing air into the space behind my eyes until my head began to clear. "I'll be fine."

Bao nodded, understanding.

After a brief wait, Lord Cuixtli ushered us into the throne room and the Nahuatl Emperor's presence.

Emperor Achcuatli was seated on a gilded throne inlaid with jade. He regarded us with an impassive mien, although it was to me that his gaze went first. He was a fellow of some thirty-odd years, with a warrior's bearing. His eyes were as black as obsidian and gave nothing away. There were round obsidian plugs in the lobes of his ears, and a plug of gold piercing the skin beneath his lower lip. He wore a feather headdress finer than any I'd seen, a mantle of feathers over his shoulders, and an embroidered cloth wrapped around his waist. His brown chest was bare, save for a collar of gold. On his feet, he wore sandals that laced to the knees, and the soles were made of solid gold.

My uneasy feeling returned.

All six of us bowed deeply to him. His sharp gaze passed over each of us, returning to me.

"So it is true," he said in Nahuatl, slowly and distinctly enough that I could understand him.

Unsure of the protocol, I inclined my head. The intensity of the Emperor's gaze made me raise it again.

His fingers drummed on the arms of the throne. "You seek your kinsman who came here before you?"

"Yes, my lord," I said, concentrating hard on every syllable. "We come to beg for help."

The Nahuatl Emperor made a sweeping gesture with one arm. "So beg."

Fearing my lack of eloquence might hurt our cause, I signaled Denis de Toluard with my eyes.

Clearing his throat, he stepped forward. "I do not know if his majesty remembers, but we have met. With your permission, I will speak for Lady Moirin."

In slow, careful Nahuatl, Denis outlined the reasons for our quest, describing it in glowing terms as a matter of honor. He exaggerated my status in Terre d'Ange, speaking passionately of the vision that had led me here and the hardship and sacrifice it entailed. He beckoned to Brice de Bretel, who approached the throne to offer our tribute-gift on bended knee, his head bowed.

One of the Emperor's attendants accepted it, untying the gold braids and unwrapping the thick brocade to reveal the mirror.

Achcuatli studied his reflection in it, tilting it back and forth. "Very fine. And?"

Denis described the goods we had brought to trade, especially the steel tools and implements, lingering over their superior efficacy. By the time he had finished, he was sweating. "All this, we are willing to trade for your aid, your majesty," he finished. "All we ask is that you assign a *pochteca* with knowledge of Tawantinsuyo to guide us in the search for our missing companions."

The Emperor was silent.

Pressure beat about my skull. I breathed the Breath of Wind's Sigh, but it didn't seem to help.

"This one is different." Achcuatli pointed at Bao. "Why?"

Bao smiled and narrowed his eyes.

"Ah..." Forgetting he wore a chain-mail shirt beneath his brigandine, Denis de Toluard wiped his brow with one forearm and winced. "Lady Moirin's husband is a prince from a faraway land, even farther than ours, across many seas. He gave up his throne for love of her, that he might accompany her on this quest."

"Is that even remotely true?" Balthasar whispered to me.

I hushed him.

The Nahuatl Emperor rose and descended from his throne. Attendants with handheld brooms bent low, hastening to brush the path before his gold-shod feet. They were forced to back out of the way when Achcuatli stopped before Bao and thrust his face close to Bao's, staring aggressively at him.

Bao planted the heel of his staff with a thump and stared back at the Emperor without blinking.

Someone chuckled.

Belatedly, I realized the Jaguar Knight Temilotzin was among the warriors attending Achcuatli.

The Emperor smiled, returning to his throne. Once again, he spoke deliberately enough for me to understand. "Before I consider this request, I must be assured your warriors have skill sufficient to protect any *pochteca* I might assign you." He made a careless gesture. "I know one who is curious. Temilotzin?"

The spotted warrior sprang into action, his obsidian-studded club raised high above his head.

"*Mine!*" Bao called out gleefully, already in motion, his staff a blur. No one contested him for it.

It was a short skirmish. It ended with the Jaguar Knight upended and sprawling on the floor of the throne-room, undone by unfamiliar tactics and weapons, the butt of Bao's steel-laced bamboo staff hovering over his vulnerable throat. Our D'Angelines looked startled and a bit sick at the suddenness of it all. I couldn't help but wonder if any of them could have dealt with the challenge as effectively, and if Temilotzin would have slain them if they hadn't. By the looks on their faces, they were wondering the same thing.

"Interesting," Achcuatli mused.

My skin prickled.

"Enough." With a flick of his fingers, the Nahuatl Emperor ordered Bao to disengage. Bao obeyed. Temilotzin climbed to his feet, massaging his throat. The Emperor regarded us. "Your company is worthy, but there is another matter to consider. *I* have been dishonored."

I shot Denis a bewildered look, and he gave his head a little shake, spreading his hands. "Forgive us, your majesty. Have we given offense?"

"You have not given it, but you have caused it." Achcuatli pointed at me. "The Aragonians thought this one was a gift for me."

"Yes, but it was a misunderstanding," Denis protested.

The Emperor's mouth hardened. "And did Lord Cuixtli misunderstand their shock and horror?"

Denis glanced at me.

I answered for myself, forcing myself to meet Achcuatli's black gaze. "No, my lord. He did not."

The Emperor nodded. "They take our women without a thought, and yet the thought of me taking one of theirs is—" He used a word I didn't know, but the meaning was clear. His fingers drummed. "I find that a grave offense."

My pulse hammered in the hollow of my throat. "I am not Aragonian," I said quietly.

"You are a stranger from across the sea." He kept his gaze fixed on me, hard and implacable. "I offer you the chance to make good on this offense." He held up one finger. "One day and one night. It is all I ask."

The uneasy feeling in my belly shifted, turning to the dove-winged flutter of Naamah's gift awakening. Belatedly, I remembered the warning Jehanne had brought me in a dream the night Edouard Durel had attempted to steal the logbook.

I am here to tell you that the sacrifices Naamah asks of us may not always be so pleasant and easy. You have a hard choice coming.

It seemed it was here.

THIRTY-EIGHT

On the heels of the Emperor's proclamation, the throne-room burst into a babble of D'Angeline voices raised in protest.

Only Bao and I were silent.

Ah, gods! For reasons I could not fathom, Naamah willed this. I felt it in every part of my being. She had showered her blessings on me even though I was not sworn to her service, allowing me to serve as a vessel of her grace when it pleased me, never asking for aught in return.

Until now.

I glanced at Bao. Whether he sensed Naamah's will through our shared *diadh-anam*, or he simply knew me well enough to read me, he returned my gaze with an expression as stoic as any Nahuatl warrior and said one word to me. "Bargain."

I raised one hand, and the D'Angelines fell silent. "You ask me to dishonor my husband, my lord." The Nahuatl words came more easily to me than before, as though Naamah's presence had graced my tongue—and mayhap it had.

Emperor Achcuatli permitted himself a small smile. "I offer an exchange. For one night, I will send my youngest wife to your husband." The various lords, warriors, and attendants in the throne-room murmured in surprise, and Achcuatli's smile took on a tinge of satisfaction. "That is more than enough honor for any man."

"Moirin, you don't need to do this," Balthasar murmured to me. "Thierry wouldn't want you to."

"He's right," Denis agreed.

I ignored them both. Naamah's gift was alive within me, coiling through my veins. The prickly heat I'd felt earlier had turned to glowing warmth. Achcuatli eyed me speculatively, his smile fading.

He felt it, too.

The Nahuatl Emperor had asked for me out of pride, not genuine desire, but he had invoked Naamah's presence nonetheless.

"I am a priest's daughter," I said softly. "I am the descendant of three royal houses. I have been a companion to queens and princesses. I am the Emperor of Ch'in's jade-eyed witch and swallower-of-memories, and the Rani of Bhaktipur's *dakini*. I have ridden in a dragon's claw, and I have seen the face of the Maghuin Dhonn Herself. If I agree to this, it is more than enough honor for any man."

Stone and sea! I wasn't sure where the words had come from; I wasn't even sure what language I'd spoken. And yet it seemed everyone in the room had understood them, at least their general meaning.

To be sure, Achcuatli had. Although his face remained expressionless, I could sense an answering heat rising in him.

"Agreed," he said, his voice taking on a slight edge of hoarseness.

The image of rows and rows of grinning skulls flashed before my eyes, threatening my composure. With an effort, I forced it away. "And if I do, will you grant our request and give us the aid we seek?"

The Emperor inclined his head. "In exchange for your tools of steel, I will supply your journey and order two *pochtecas* familiar with Tawantinsuyo to guide you." He glanced at the spotted warrior, who grinned. "As well as the services of Temilotzin here."

I took a deep breath. "Then we have a bargain, my lord."

Emperor Achcuatli smiled to himself and made a gesture of dismissal. "Go with Cuixtli. I will send for you."

As soon as we were escorted out of the Emperor's presence, the D'Angeline firestorm of protest reignited.

"It is contrary to Blessed Elua's precept!" Brice de Bretel fumed. "You should not have to do this thing because the damned *Aragonians* have given offense!"

"Not to mention the fact that the damned Aragonians will now think they were right about us all along," Balthasar said in a biting tone. "Don't mistake me, I'm a great advocate of Naamah's Service, but it's a sacred calling, and *never* meant to be coerced. And I speak as one who knows a great deal about coercion."

Once again, I ignored them.

Bao put his arms around me, blocking out the cacophony. "Are you all right?" he whispered in my ear.

"I think so." I laid one hand on his cheek. "Are you?"

He shrugged. "Ask me after I've had a look at the Emperor's youngest wife."

Despite everything, it made me laugh. "Bao!"

He gave me a wry smile. "I knew who and what you were when I wedded you, Moirin. And maybe I deserve this. Maybe it's fate's way of repaying me for running away from you for so long."

"Not to mention marrying your Tatar princess," I reminded him.

Bao kissed me. "That, too."

Lord Cuixtli cleared his throat with polite impatience.

Reluctantly, I left the safety of Bao's embrace. His arms fell to his sides, letting me go. Our bickering D'Angelines had fallen silent.

"I swear to you, I am not doing this because Emperor Achcuatli coerced me," I said to them. "I am doing it because Naamah wills it. I do not understand why, but the gods do not always make their reasons clear to us. So..."

I didn't know what else to say.

It was Septimus Rousse who responded first, addressing the void my faltering silence had left and laying his big hands on my shoulders. "No one doubts your word or questions your integrity, Lady Moirin," he said in a firm voice meant to warn the others as much as to assure me. "If you say it is Naamah's will, then it is so. *I* do not doubt you. It is well known in my family that the gods make unexpected choices, and use their chosen hard." Bending low, he kissed my cheek. "You have won a great boon for us today. May Blessed Elua keep and hold you."

My eyes stung. "Thank you, my lord captain."

One by one, the others followed suit.

And one by one, they departed for the Aragonian settlement, until only Bao and I were left with Lord Cuixtli.

He beckoned to us. "Follow me."

Apparently, the palace did not lack for guest-chambers. Lord Cuixtli led us to one and indicated that Bao was to consider it his own for the day.

"A servant will come soon," he said, speaking slowly for our benefit. "Ask for what you need. Come and go as you like. At sunset, the Emperor's youngest wife, Omixochitl, will be sent to you. Do you understand?"

Bao nodded. "Yes."

"Good."

By the time Lord Cuixtli escorted me to my own chamber, there were two Nahuatl women already present.

"They will serve you," Cuixtli said. "Ask for what you need. The Emperor will send for you when he is ready."

"I understand," I said. "Thank you."

Once Lord Cuixtli departed, there was an awkward silence as the two Nahuatl women and I eyed one another. Remembering the reticence of Porfirio Reyes' servants, I wondered if it was a part of the culture, if mayhap Nahuatl women were discouraged from conversing with foreigners, or even conversing at all.

But then the younger of the two broke the silence. "You come from across the sea?" she asked shyly.

I smiled at her. "Yes. Very far."

That was all it took. In short order, we were having a lively, albeit occasionally halting, conversation about what the land beyond the sea was like, about why I was here, and why no other women had ever made the journey. And while the women were not effusive, they were friendly and interested. I began to suspect the servants in Porfirio Reyes' house had cause for their reticence and cause to resent foreigners.

After a time, the elder of the two glanced out the window to ascertain the sun's position, and asked if I wished to partake of the *temazcalli*.

"House of heat?" I echoed the words slowly, not sure I'd understood.

She nodded. "For the rite of cleansing."

I knew the word for bath—all D'Angelines were quick to learn that one—and it was different. "I do not know this thing."

That made the younger one giggle. "Come, see!"

Curious, I consented.

The *temazcalli* was indeed a house of heat, or at least a heated room adjacent to an inner courtyard in the palace. It was a square chamber with a low ledge for sitting and a pit in the center of the room. My attendants assisted me in disrobing, and indicated that I should sit while they used water-soaked wooden tongs to place fire-heated stones from a kiln outside the room in the pit. Once that was done, water was ladled over the hot stones.

The stones hissed, clouds of steam arising. The Nahuatl women retreated, closing the door behind them.

I sat naked and cross-legged on the ledge, breathing slowly through the cycle of the Five Styles to allay any anxiety at being confined in a man-made place of stone, steam filling my lungs as I breathed in and out. A sheen of sweat broke out on my skin. All along my hairline, I began to sweat until it ran in rivulets down my temples. Droplets of sweat gathered in the hollow of my throat, trickled between my breasts.

Surprisingly, it felt good.

Cleansing.

After the purgative effects of the *temazcalli*, a cool bath felt wonderful. My attendants scrubbed me from head to toe with a soapy root that had a pleasant smell and produced a considerable lather.

You'll find little to love in the Nahuatl...

"Well, I have found one thing," I said aloud in D'Angeline to the absent Porfirio Reyes. "Mayhap that is why Naamah wills this."

"My lady?" one of my attendants inquired. "Is it well?"

I smiled at her. "It is well."

When we returned to the chamber allotted me, gifts from Emperor Achcuatli had arrived.

There was a sleeveless shirt and matching skirt of fine embroidered cloth, blue and yellow and green. There was a headdress of shimmering green feathers, bordered with embroidered bands of blue and gold. There was a mantle of multicolored, iridescent feathers that lay light as a whisper over my shoulders. And although they did not have soles of gold, there were sandals that laced to the knee.

But there was gold—armbands of solid gold, wrought with the faces of unfamiliar gods staring out at me.

Piece by piece, I donned everything.

Naamah, the bright lady, approved.

THIRTY-NINE

I did not expect kindness.

In that, I was mistaken. The Emperor Achcuatli gazed at me long and hard when I was escorted once more into his presence, and there was desire in his gaze, but there was also a gentleness he hadn't shown before. At length, he smiled. "It is pleasing to see you dressed in my gifts."

I bowed. "They are very beautiful, my lord."

He gestured to a chair across the table from him. "Come, sit. We will take *chocolatl*." At that, I must have brightened, for he laughed. "You know it?"

I sat opposite him. "Yes, my lord."

While attendants prepared the frothy concoction, sweetening, spicing, and whisking it, Achcuatli studied me. "You are not scared or—" The second word was unfamiliar. Naamah may have graced my tongue, but not my vocabulary—at least not in a permanent manner.

"No, my lord. I am not scared," I said. "I do not know the other word."

Achcuatli pressed a fist to his belly. "To feel sick inside at an unclean thing."

The image of the skulls flashed before my eyes again, and once again, I pushed it away. "There are things about the Nahuatl I find... hard to understand," I said slowly, choosing my words with care. "Desire is not one of them. It is a sacred thing to my father's people."

His obsidian eyes were intent. "Is that why it is so strong in me for you?"

Attendants set golden goblets of foamy *chocolatl* before us. I waited for the Emperor to drink before taking a sip, reveling in the wondrous mixture of bitterness and sweetness, the rich taste of it. "Yes."

"A sacred thing," he mused.

I took another sip. "I am a child of the goddess Naamah, to whom all desire is sacred."

Achcuatli's mouth twisted. "The men of Aragonia would have had us believe they were gods, too."

I shook my head. "I do not say that. Only that Naamah is—" I didn't know the word for ancestor. "My father's hundred-times-ago mother."

His face cleared. "I see. Yes, such things are known."

"Did you think it was true?" I asked. "About the Aragonians?"

"No." The Nahuatl Emperor was silent a moment. "I knew they were men. They fight and bleed and die like men. But I thought their gods had favored them, giving them knowledge to build great ships that cross the sea, giving them armor against which our *macahuitls* shattered and broke, and great beasts to master and ride. And so I let them stay. I was young, and knew no better."

It was on the tip of my tongue to ask why he did not send them away now, but not wanting to provoke a diplomatic incident, I did not voice it.

Achcuatli guessed anyway, giving me a shrewd look. "Now it is too late. There are too many to defeat with ease, and they have made bargains with other people, tribes we have conquered, who would be pleased to see this empire fall. Foolish people, who think the men of Aragonia would keep their bargains."

Once again, I held my tongue, grateful that I'd learned a measure of discretion.

And once again, he knew. "You do not wish to speak against them," he observed. "That may be wise. But I know what they wish. If they could defeat us and rule over this empire, they would." He shrugged. "I know what they say. They think their Nahautl servants are too stupid to learn their tongue, and we have let them think it. They speak freely before their servants. They think we are little better than animals."

"I do not think that," I said.

"No." Achcuatli considered me. "You are different. And yet Cuixtli tells me the sight of the *tzompantli* sickened you."

"Yes." I didn't need to know the word to guess it referred to the rack of skulls. And while I didn't want to give offense, I thought it best not to lie when doing Naamah's business. "It did."

The Emperor drained his goblet. "Come," he said. "I wish to show you something."

Obediently, I rose to accompany him. Attendants hastened to brush the ground before our path. Achcuatli dismissed them from the task with mild irritation. I noted that he'd exchanged his gold-soled sandals for more practical plain ones, and thought that the Nahuatl Emperor also knew a good deal about the value of appearances.

Followed by a discreet throng of attendants and guards, we exited the palace into an extensive pleasure garden, one so vast and ornate it made me catch my breath. There were oak trees, cypresses, and palms, and others I could not identify with thick barrels and wide, spreading leaves. There were countless flowers in a riot of color. All of them were healthy and vibrant, reaching exuberantly toward the sun. I breathed the Breath of Trees Growing, drinking in the green scent of the place.

Achcuatli led me toward a large structure. At a distance, I thought it a gazebo of sorts, but as we drew nearer, I saw that it was an aviary built of wood and wicker, filled with growing trees. There must have been a hundred birds inside it. I hadn't seen such brilliant plumage since leaving Bhodistan.

"See there?" He pointed to a bird with emerald-green feathers and a ruby breast. It perched on a branch, regarding us with big round eyes. Splendid green plumes as long as my forearm trailed from its tail. "That is the *quetzal*. It is a sacred bird."

I glanced at Achcuatli's headdress, recognizing the plumes, and lifted one hand involuntarily to touch the feathers on my own.

"Yes," he said as though in answer to an unasked question. "It is an honor to wear them."

"You are kind."

Achcuatli touched my cheek, a feather-light touch. Even so, I felt a spark of desire leap between us. It was the first time he had touched me. "I would have the world know that the Nahuatl know how to honor a woman."

"I will tell them," I said.

His black eyes glinted. "Good."

When he withdrew his hand, I felt a pang of loss; and at the same time, a pang of guilt, thinking of Bao. But Naamah's gift enfolded me, assuring me that I was doing her will. I put my guilt aside. Later, there would be time to confront it.

As if the aviary wasn't impressive enough, there was a bestiary, too. Upon visiting it, Achcuatli stood for a long time before a cage that contained a pair of immense spotted cats that paced back and forth, lashing their tails. Now I knew where Temilotzin's hides came from. Brushing their thoughts, I felt a mixture of boredom and frustration.

"Some days I feel like them," Achcuatli said at length. "Trapped in a cage I did not make."

"So free them," I murmured.

He shook his head. "It would be a terrible omen."

I wondered at the Emperor speaking so freely to me; but then, betimes it was easier to confide in a stranger. And I was a foreigner. I would not think less of him for revealing he did not possess a stone face and a stone heart. Indeed, quite the opposite.

We left the bestiary to stroll the garden. As odd as the situation was, I couldn't help but take pleasure in the lush greenery. Achcuatli paused before a bed of vivid dahlias, stroking their intricate petals with one finger.

"Greet the sky and live, blossom!" he said unexpectedly. "Yet even as the wind stirs your petals, flowers fall. My flowers are eternal, my songs live forever. I lift them in offering; I, a singer. I cast them to the wind, I spill them. The flowers become gold, they come to dwell inside the palace of eternity."

Something in the words caught at my heart. "Is that a poem?"

"Yes. It is part of a famous poem." He met my gaze. "It is in honor of life and death. Your people honor life, but they do not honor death." He broke the stem of a purple dahlia, lifting the blossom. "To me, the skulls in the *tzompantli* are no different from this flower, and are as beautiful in their own way."

I took a long, slow breath. "I am trying to understand, my lord. But the flower does not feel pain. The flower does not bleed."

Achcuatli nodded gravely. "And that is why the flower's death is not enough to feed the gods. Blood is needed."

I looked away. "What if you're wrong?"

He touched my hair. "Who are you to teach the Nahuatl about their own gods?" For a mercy, he sounded more amused than offended.

"A child of my mother's people," I said in a low tone. "Who lost a great gift because we did not understand the will of our god. One who has seen for herself that men try to shape the gods' will to serve them." I thought about Raphael de Mereliot. "One who did the same when she was young."

Achcuatli chuckled. "You are still young."

Without looking at him, I laid a finger on the tightly furled bud of an unopened dahlia blossom. Summoning the merest hint of the twilight, I exhaled softly and coaxed it to grow. It opened obligingly, its myriad petals unspiraling to reveal a crimson blossom with a yellow center.

Beside me, the Nahuatl Emperor drew a sharp breath.

I glanced up at him.

His eyes were narrowed. "What *are* you?"

"Myself," I said simply.

Beneath the thin veneer of stoicism, warring emotions crossed his mien. Without warning, he seized my face in his hands and kissed me hard, his tongue thrusting past my lips, the gold plug in his chin digging into mine. Just as quickly, he released me and took a step backward.

"I must think." Achcuatli beckoned to the entourage trailing us. "My servants will return you to your chamber. I may send for you tonight, or I may not."

I inclined my head, knowing he would.

FORTY

The summons came an hour after sunset.

Once again, my two attendants helped me dress in Nahuatl finery. I was escorted with ceremony through the halls of the palace to the Emperor's bedchamber.

I could sense Bao's *diadh-anam* not far away. I could not help but think that within these same walls, Bao was consorting with Achcuatli's youngest wife; and I could not help feeling a pang of jealousy. I set it aside along with my guilt, to be dealt with later.

The Emperor's bedchamber was aglow with lamplight, hung about with intricate feather tapestries. His gaze was avid, but his expression was set and hard. "I do not know if this is wise."

I shifted my hands into a soothing *mudra*. "Nor do I."

The admission eased him. "No?"

I shook my head. "No, my lord. Only that Naamah wills it."

"Are you sure?" There was a note of wry humor in his tone. "You said you have mistaken the will of the gods before."

I smiled. "Not this time."

He extended one hand. "Come, then."

"I must pray to Naamah first, and ask her blessing." I'd brought an unlit taper in a silver candle-holder from my chamber. Now I kindled it at a lamp, setting the holder on an elaborately painted chest. While Achcuatli watched curiously, I knelt and gazed at the flickering flame, praying silently

"Do you do this every time?" he asked.

"No." I concentrated on opening my heart to Naamah that she might speak through me if that was her will. I thought about what Porfirio Reyes had said, and what I'd learned to love about the Nahuatl in this brief time. Achcuatli had shown me kindness and generosity. He had spoken openly and honestly to me. And although I could not help but recoil from the thought of the skulls lining the racks of the *tzompantli*, I'd caught a glimpse of it through his eyes, and I understood that we saw very different things.

I saw the horror of thousands upon thousands of needless deaths. The Nahauatl Emperor saw a sea of flowers, their hearts' blood shed to nourish the gods so that the sun might rise and the rains might fall.

And since the Aragonians had come, he was walking a narrow and difficult path, trying in his own way to be a good shepherd to his people.

I breathed slowly and deeply, my hands resting on my knees palm upward, feeling Achcuatli's gaze on me.

When the words came to me, they seemed to come from a distant point beyond the candle-flame, a place of tremendous brightness. "Blood is not the only sacrifice," I heard myself say. "And heaven is not the only reward. The roots of the tree of Aztlan have been well watered. Let its branches spread far and wide, and its seeds fall on fertile ground."

Naamah's grace settled over the chamber, as delicate and ephemeral as the feather cloak Achcuatli had given me.

I glanced at him to see his obsidian eyes were bright with unshed tears. "Do you know the meaning of those words?" he asked me.

"No, my lord," I said softly. "Do you?"

He nodded. "I believe I do."

Rising to my feet, I went to him. I laid one hand on his bare chest, feeling his heart beat beneath my palm. He put his arms around me, Naamah's blessing doubly enfolding me. I felt his warm breath stir my hair.

It had been a long time since I'd been with someone who was scarce more than a stranger to me. I had to own, there was a certain fearful thrill at the newness and difference of it, and in giving myself over wholly to Naamah's will.

Despite his abrupt kiss in the garden, Achcuatli was gentle. He undressed me with reverence, untying the feather cloak, setting aside the feather headdress with the long emerald *quetzal* plumes that were his gifts. He removed my clothing and left me adorned in golden armbands, gazing at me with heavy-lidded eyes.

"You are very beautiful," he said at length.

I kissed him, learning how to angle my head to avoid the golden chin-plug. "Thank you."

In turn, I undressed him. His skin shone coppery in the lamplight. In the course of undressing him, I performed many of the kisses and caresses and love-bites that were part of Naamah's arts, raising his desire to a feverish pitch. After I knelt to unlace his sandals, I wrapped my long hair around his erect phallus with a deft twist of my head, drawing back to pull away in a long, silken glide.

At that, Achcuatli groaned and pulled me to my feet, his fingers digging hard into my shoulders. "Enough!" he said in a hoarse voice.

The bed was soft, a pallet filled with feathers. I sank into it under the weight of Achcuatli's body on mine. With Naamah's gift beating in my veins, I spread my thighs to welcome him.

Slowly and steadily, Achcuatli thrust himself into me. The absence of a shared *diadh-anam* brought home the strangeness of it all. His strong-featured, unfamiliar face hovered over mine, his gaze hard and intense as he moved in and out of me. I wanted to close my eyes, but some prompting of Naamah's told me not to.

Blood is not the only sacrifice.

I offered up my own pleasure as a sacrifice, my own deep wellspring of desire. I felt the fluttering of Naamah's doves in my belly, the deeper waves of climax fluttering lower. I watched Achcuatli's face break into a fierce grin of pride as my hips rose to meet his, my back arching, nails scoring his back.

And I understood that there was a deeper wound beneath the slight that the Aragonians' disgust and dismay had provoked, that it was symbolic of the profoundly injured pride of the entire Nahuatl folk, regarded as little better than animals by these strangers from across the sea who would gladly have razed Tenochtitlan to the ground if they could.

Naamah's blessing was not enough to heal the wound, but it could spread balm over it, that healing might begin.

With a low groan, Achcuatli buried himself deep inside me and spent.

Afterward, he lay quiet and thoughtful, idly stroking my skin, gazing at the ceiling with open eyes.

"What did it mean to you?" I asked at last, unable to resist my curiosity. "The words I spoke?"

He glanced at me. "It is a thing my advisors and I have discussed. I told you that the Aragonians made alliances with tribes who resent our rule." I nodded. "We have discussed making our own peace with enemy tribes, and bringing them more fully into the fold of our empire."

"Instead of making war on them to gain captives to sacrifice?" I asked.

"Yes." Achcuatli studied me. "No one put those words in your mouth?"

"No one but Naamah, I swear."

"Why would a foreign goddess speak to me through a stranger when our own gods are silent?" He shook his head in frustration. "I do not understand."

Rolling onto my side, I propped my head on one arm. "Years ago, I had a teacher who taught me that all ways lead to the Way," I said slowly, thinking. "That there is a great truth behind all the truths of the world, and the faces of the gods are masks that may be changed at will. Mayhap Naamah is not so foreign as you think."

The Nahuatl Emperor traced the curve of my waist with one finger, then settled his hand on my hip. "We worship a goddess of desire, too. Xochiquetzal's festival is celebrated with flowers and masks."

My skin prickled. "Truly?"

He nodded. "It is said she appears as a young and beautiful woman, followed everywhere by birds and butterflies." He smiled a little. "I would not be surprised to find birds and butterflies following you."

I smiled, too. "I am mortal, I promise."

"I will think on what you have said to me," he said. "I will take counsel with my priests and advisors. The world has changed since I was a boy. Perhaps the will of the gods has changed with it."

I kissed his shoulder. "Thank you, my lord. I am glad."

Achcuatli's grip on my hip tightened, and there was heat rising in his gaze. "But for now, the night is not over."

It was a long night.

In the morning, I was tired and sated, filled with a complex mixture of emotions, pride and guilt warring in me. I was glad to have served Naamah's will, glad that mayhap it would help steer the Nahuatl a measure farther away from their harsh practices, leading them to question the gods' will and altering the tenuous balance of power in Terra Nova for the better. Naamah's blessing was a pebble tossed into a lake the depths of which I could not fathom. All I could do was hope that the ripples would carry onward.

But I felt guilty, too.

To his credit, Achcuatli continued to be gentle with me. We broke our fast in the bedchamber, where servants brought *chocolatl* and an array of fresh fruits.

"I wish you would not go on this quest," the Emperor said softly. "It is very, very dangerous."

"I know."

He shook his head. "You think you do, but you do not. Very few *pochtecas* have undertaken it in my lifetime, and most have not returned. It was not easy to find guides."

I sipped my frothy *chocolatl*. "You sent Thierry into danger on purpose, didn't you?"

He was silent a moment. "I thought he would turn back, and the problem he posed would go away."

"He didn't."

Achcuatli searched my face. "You know it is likely he is dead? That they are all dead?"

I nodded. "It is likely, yes. But they are not."

He sighed. "You are very stubborn."

With an unexpected pang, I thought of my mother. "Aye, I am."

The Emperor picked at the fruit on his plate. "I will keep my promise. I will give you the aid of my *pochtecas*, and anything else I may. All will be arranged within a day. While you are here, you are under my protection. But once you leave, I do not expect to see you alive again, Moirin."

I hoisted my goblet to him. "Believe me, my lord, you are but the latest in a long list of men who feel the same way. I will do my best to prove you wrong."

His obsidian eyes glinted. "I hope you do." Achcuatli paused, his expression turning grave. "There is another warning I would give you. Last night, you said to me that blood is not the only sacrifice, and I took heed of the words your goddess sent you. Perhaps it is true, that the roots of the tree of Aztlan are soaked, and the gods are sated for now. Do not forget, that does not mean it holds true elsewhere in the land."

"I will not," I promised.

The Nahuatl Emperor inclined his head in approval. "Sometimes when the gods thirst, blood *is* the only sacrifice."

FORTY-ONE

In the courtyard outside the palace, Bao and I were reunited.

My *diadh-anam* rose and danced within me at the sight of him, at his wry, regretful smile.

All the guilt I had repressed crashed down upon me. It didn't help to have Lord Cuixtli and the Nahuatl porters and warriors standing by, my palanquin loaded with the Emperor's gifts.

But it was Bao.

My Bao.

I hugged him, burying my face against his throat and breathing in the scent of his skin. "Are you well?"

"Well enough." He slid a hand beneath my hair, cupping the back of my head. "And you?"

I nodded, blinking against the sting of tears. "How was the Emperor's youngest wife?"

"Young," Bao said in a laconic voice. "Young and terrified. No one consulted her or asked for her permission in this bargain, and the Emperor's senior wives had filled her head with terrible tales of the strangers across the sea and their depravities. For all I know, half of them were true." He shrugged. "I didn't lay a hand on her, Moirin."

I was glad.

And I felt guilty for it.

Bao looked sideways at me. "And how was the Emperor?"

I glanced at the palanquin, noting that several bags of the *cacao* beans that served as currency in the Nahuatl Empire had been added to it. "Generous."

"So he ought to be." Bao pressed a kiss against my hair, silently absolving me. "Shall we return to our companions?"

I nodded. "Yes, please."

Once again, I travelled across Tenochtitlan in a palanquin. This time, it was different. There was a quiet respect in the Nahuatl gazes that followed our progress; and whether it was due to the honor Achcuatli had accorded me, or the salve my actions had spread on their pride, I could not say.

In the ceremonial square, I asked Lord Cuixtli to halt before the great temple dedicated to the rain god Tlaloc and Huitzilopochtli, the god of war. My bearers lowered the palanquin, and I disembarked. Beneath the bright blue sky, I gazed upward at the towering twin staircases, faint traces of blood rusty in the creases where the stones were joined.

I stared at the hollow-eyed skulls in the *tzompantli*, trying to envision a sea of cut flowers. The skulls stared back at me, jaws parted in mockery, teeth bared in an eternal cheerful grin.

I touched one, feeling the smooth, sun-warmed bone beneath my fingers. "Greet the sky and live, blossom."

"Moirin?" Bao gave me an inquiring look.

I shook my head. "I am trying to understand, that's all."

He frowned at the *tzompantli*. "Why? I do not think the Nahautl would celebrate death so if they had endured it."

I touched his cheek, feeling warm, living skin. All too well, I remembered Bao's death and rebirth. "The Emperor said somewhat to me before I left that made me think. And I believe we may have need of understanding before this is done, my magpie."

"A vision?" he asked.

I shook my head. "Only a feeling."

Bao sighed, rolling his shoulders. "Moirin, I will be glad when this is done, and we can get down to the business of making fat babies."

I smiled. "So will I."

Our journey across the long causeway to the Aragonian fortress on the distant shore was an uneventful one; but on the far side of the lake, the reception we found among the Aragonians was markedly unpleasant.

It was a dreadful scene.

"Whore!" Diego Ortiz y Ramos spat the word at me as soon as I stepped from the palanquin. The guards had spotted our approach from the watch-towers and the commander was awaiting us in the square, his cheeks flushed and hectic with color, the point of his neatly trimmed beard quivering with indignation. "You lied!"

I felt an answering flush of anger rise. "No, my lord," I said in a precise tone. "I did *not* lie. If you and your men had not offended the Emperor, I would not have been driven to make the bargain I did."

"Do you expect me to believe that?" He pointed a finger at me. "Half-breed or no, you D'Angelines are all alike with your filthy morals, your filthy gods, and your filthy ways! You came here with every intention of using sex—"

Without warning, Bao swung his staff, connecting hard with the Aragonian commander's steel helmet. There was a dull ringing clang, as though he'd struck a defective bell. The fellow gaped at him in disbelief, wobbling on his feet. Knowing Bao, I guessed he'd used exactly the amount of force he intended to rattle the man without knocking him down.

It happened so fast, the Aragonian guards stood staring for several seconds before drawing steel. Lord Cuixtli gave a sharp command, and the Nahuatl warriors took offensive stances and raised their studded clubs. There were only six of them, but they represented an entire empire.

Balthasar Shahrizai arrived at a run, followed by most of our company. Sizing up the situation at a glance, he ordered them to stand down.

Bao ignored them all. "Apologize," he said in a flat tone.

The commander looked blankly at him, one hand on his helmet as though he wasn't sure what had struck him. "Are you mad? I'd be within my rights to put you in chains for assaulting a commanding—"

"You will apologize to my wife, or I will beat you very badly," Bao said with unnerving calmness. When the commander dropped his hand and made a move toward his sword-hilt, Bao feinted a jab at his face.

Diego Ortiz y Ramos flinched, but held his ground. "I will not!" He glanced at Balthasar with indignation. "You are a sensible man, Lord Shahrizai. Our countries are allies. Do you want to provoke a diplomatic incident here?"

"Oh, mayhap," Balthasar said in his languid drawl. "Mayhap I'll send a few of my men here back to Terre d'Ange to report that the Aragonian commander withheld information that might have saved the Dauphin's life. Do you reckon that will sit well with your patrons in Aragonia?"

Diego blanched. "You would not send away your only ship!"

"Why not?" Balthasar shrugged. "The consensus seems to be that none of us are coming back from Tawantinsuyo alive."

The commander turned to me, his face still livid. "This is absurd. Doña Moirin, call off your husband."

"No," I said thoughtfully. "I don't think so."

"I have just spent an entire night trying to convince a very frightened young woman that I did not intend to harm her, while my wife paid for the offense you and your men gave the Emperor." Bao whipped his staff upright, planting it with a thud. "If you do not wish to apologize, so be it. Draw your sword, and we will fight like men."

The Aragonian commander hesitated. Lord Cuixtli and the Nahuatl watched the proceedings with interest.

Balthasar contemplated his fingernails, picking idly at a flaw. "If I were you, Commander, I would swallow my pride and apologize. Messire Bao has the reach of you with his pole, and he's *very* skilled at wielding it." He nodded toward the Nahuatl. "Also, it would be wise not to offend them a second time."

The fellow's struggle was reflected on his face. At length, he forced himself to say the words in a wooden tone. "Forgive me, Doña Moirin. I apologize."

"And I accept." I paused. "Denis?"

Denis de Toluard came forward. "My lady?"

"Will you translate something into Aragonian for me?" I asked him. "I would have the commander and all his men hear it."

"Of course."

I thought about what I wanted to say. "Although I did not choose this bargain, I do not regret it. Emperor Achcuatli showed me kindness and respect. He treated me with honor, and I am grateful for it."

Denis translated my words. Diego Ortiz y Ramos and his men heard them with sullen disapproval, but I saw Lord Cuixtli's lips curve in a faint smile, and I knew my message had found its intended audience.

"We will not presume on your hospitality much longer, my lord," I added to the commander. "I am sorry for having unwittingly provoked unpleasantness here." Beckoning to Denis, I pointed at one of the bags of *cacao* beans in the palanquin. "Please accept this as a token of my apology, and in compensation for lodging and feeding our company."

It embarrassed the fellow. "No, no!" He waved a hand in dismissal, his Aragonian sense of chivalry belatedly asserting itself. "You have accepted *my* apology, and that is payment enough."

I smiled sweetly at him. I did not want any debt between us. "Oh, but I insist."

Without waiting for a word from me, Denis tossed the sack at the nearest guard, who caught it out of reflex.

"And now I would like to retire for a few hours," I announced. Turning to Lord Cuixtli, I inclined my head to him. "Please thank the Emperor again for his generosity," I said in Nahuatl.

Lord Cuixtli touched his chest and brow in a gesture of respect far less casual than his salute at our first encounter. "I will tell him."

Once we had returned to our shared chamber, Bao was restless and moody, pacing the small space, moving in and out of the sunlight that slanted through the crude window and spinning his bamboo staff in his hands. I sat quiet and still on the coarse reed-stuffed pallet atop the wooden bed-frame, watching him pace through light and shadow, not wishing to disturb him.

"I was not angry until that idiot opened his foul mouth," he said abruptly. "Then..." He shrugged. "I was."

"I'm sorry," I murmured.

"It's not your fault." Bao sighed. "I meant what I said, Moirin. I knew who and what you were when I wed you."

"That doesn't make it any easier," I said.

"No." He twirled his staff in an intricate pattern. "It doesn't. And fellows like that Aragonian make it harder. I shouldn't have hit him, should I?"

"I think you needed to." I smiled. "For my part, I found it quite satisfying."

That earned a reluctant answering smile from Bao. "Did you see the look on his face?"

I nodded. "He was gaping like a fish on dry land."

Laying down his staff, Bao sat beside me and took one of my hands in his, lacing our fingers together. "I am not angry at you, Moirin. I swear it."

"I know."

"I have been thinking of what you said to Desirée at her father's funeral," he said. "That it was all right to be angry at the gods sometimes. You told her that the gods understand sorrow—and anger, too."

"She asked why they send so much of it," I said, remembering. "And you told her it was to make us stronger. That it was hard, but it was the only way."

"Yes." Bao took a deep breath, exhaling slowly. "It helps to remember why we are doing this."

"For Desirée?"

He squeezed my hand. "Yes. For her, I can be strong."

"Strong like a dragon?" I asked, echoing the young princess' words.

Bao smiled. "Exactly."

FORTY-TWO

A day later, all was in readiness.

The steel tools we had brought had been delivered to the Emperor's palace, keeping back only the hatchets and adzes that Septimus Rousse gauged we might need to create vessels to navigate the jungle rivers.

For that alone, I was grateful that he had chosen to accompany us. Even Bao, my resourceful magpie, admitted such a need would not have occurred to him.

Emperor Achcuatli assigned two *pochtecas* to guide us into the verdant wilderness of Tawantinsuyo.

It was strange to see him once more after the lone day and night we had shared. Truly, we were intimate strangers. His obsidian gaze lingered on me with a certain tenderness as he made the introductions. I could not but help remember his weight upon me as I sank into the feather pallet, the feeling of him inside me.

I pushed those memories away.

Bao maintained an expressionless face.

The *pochtecas* were an uncle and nephew. Neither were young; indeed, the elder of the two, Eyahue, was a wiry old fellow with skin tanned like leather by time and sun, his black hair gone to grey, his mouth sunken around missing teeth. At least he looked to be in reasonably good spirits regarding the journey. His nephew, Pochotl, was a sturdy fellow in his late forties, and he looked none too happy to obey the Emperor's order.

Rounding out our company was the spotted warrior Temilotzin, and he looked downright cheerful at the prospect. I had the impression Achcuatli had assigned him the duty simply because Temilotzin had taken a liking to us.

Standing atop a gilded dais in the great temple square of Tenochtitlan, the Nahuatl Emperor bade us a ceremonial farewell, publicly announcing that we were under his protection as far as the empire extended. He invoked the blessing of the gods on our journey, adding that offerings of flowers and honey would be given to Xochiquetzal, goddess of desire, in my name—every day until our return, or a year had passed.

I found myself unexpectedly touched by the gesture. The Nahuatl folk seemed to approve.

Bao raised his brows at me, but he kept his silence.

And then it was done, and there was nothing left but to bow deeply to Achcuatli, offer thanks for his generosity, and take our leave.

I cannot imagine what an odd sight our caravan made as we departed the city of Tenochtitlan and crossed the broad southern causeway for what might well be the last time. Forty D'Angeline warriors, sunlight bouncing off their steel helmets, bright reflections wavering in the placid water of the lake along which they marched. Our two *pochtecas*, one wizened, one sullen. Temilotzin in his jaguar hides and a wooden helmet with a feathered crest, a club in one hand, spear in the other, his wicker shield slung over his shoulder. Bareheaded Septimus Rousse, his coppery red hair a blaze beneath the blue sky. Bao with his staff lashed across his back, resembling no one else in our company. Three laden pack-horses, and me riding astride the fourth.

Nahuatl fishermen in reed boats and farmers on the artificial islands watched us go. It felt as though we were marching into history, never to be seen again. The Aragonians would tell the tale of the D'Angeline expedition that had tried to whore its way into the Emperor's graces with disdain.

Mayhap the Nahuatl would tell the tale as a tragic romance, the doomed expedition led by a woman from across the sea, who left behind the Emperor to lay flowers on Xochiquetzal's altar in vain.

And back in Terre d'Ange, my name would become a hallmark for folly, the half-breed bear-witch whose pride and arrogance compounded the realm's grief.

I prayed to Blessed Elua and his Companions, and to the Maghuin Dhonn Herself, that it would not be so.

The first weeks of our journey were easy enough as such things go. We were within the confines of the Nahuatl Empire. Achcuatli had sent out runners carrying word that we were under his protection, and no one troubled us. While one could not exactly say Balthasar and his recruits were inured to the hardship of marching beneath the hot sun in chain-mail and brigandines, they bore it more easily. As soon as we were out of sight of Tenochtitlan, I'd dismounted and taken to walking like the others, reckoning sharing the hardship was the least I could do. I'd done my part to command respect, and my mount was better used carrying supplies and trade goods, which we redistributed accordingly.

Every few days, we came across inns catering to the large parties of *pochtecas*, where we were able to refresh ourselves with baths and skillfully cooked meals. Septimus Rousse, who had served as a galley-cook as a lad, had taken on himself the duty of overseeing the preparation of meals in the field, but many of the ingredients in the stores we'd bartered for were unfamiliar to him. His overgenerous use of dried chiles to flavor the *maize* porridge he made had my eyes watering more than once.

As an added benefit, we were able to inquire if anyone remembered a party of fair-skinned strangers from across the sea passing through over a year ago. More often than not, we were able to confirm that we were still on the trail of Prince Thierry's expedition, something that heartened all of us and made the following day's journey easier to bear.

And at the first inn we visited, I introduced Bao to the pleasure of the *temazcalli*, the Nahuatl steam-bath.

It had the purgative effect I'd hoped for. Although I knew Bao had spoken truly when he said he was not angry at me, I knew he was angry nonetheless, and matters had been uneasy between us since he'd struck Diego Ortiz y Ramos.

There in the *temazcalli*, the tension melted away. We sat cross-legged and side by side on the stone ledge, wreathed in steam, breathing it deep into our lungs, sweat streaming down our naked bodies.

When Bao glanced sidelong at me through the steam, there was a familiar gleam in his eyes. "You look...slippery."

I eyed him, noting his phallus was hard and erect, curving toward the shining trail of sweat trickling down his flat, lean-muscled belly. "You look...interested."

"Did you do this with *him*?" he asked. "In the steam-bath?"

I shook my head. "No."

Bao smiled, unfolding his legs. "Good."

And it was good; slippery and awkward and good. The hard stone of the ledge dug into my knees as I straddled him, my hair falling from its lover's-haste knot in damp tendrils that clung to my cheeks. Bao braced me as we kissed, his hands firm on my hips, our tongues dueling. Skin slid against sweat-slick skin as I reached down and fitted his phallus to me, sinking onto him, leaning against him to press my breasts against the hard plane of his chest, clinging to his shoulders, rising and falling to impale myself on him amidst the clouds of steam.

Whether or not our Nahuatl innkeepers knew and were scandalized, I never knew. If they were, they did not say.

Afterward, things were easier between us. An unspoken accord had been reached, and I felt lighter in my heart for it.

As our unlikely caravan journeyed farther and farther southward, all of us came to know one another better.

Eyahue, our senior *pochteca*, was unexpectedly garrulous for a Nahuatl, telling long, rambling tales of heroic trade expeditions he'd undertaken during his younger days. Due to his missing teeth, his diction was imperfect and I often had a difficult time understanding him, but the Jaguar Knight Temilotzin found his tales worthy of thigh-slapping hilarity, roaring with laughter. Bit by bit, I came to gather that Eyahue had ventured into the river-laced jungles of Tawantinsuyo in pursuit of various herbs that could be obtained nowhere else, the specific details of which the old fellow was cagey about revealing.

"All you need to find is your missing prince, right?" he said to me, sucking meditatively at his remaining teeth. "You did not come for herbs, so it does not matter, eh?"

His nephew was another matter. Unlike his uncle, Pochotl maintained the traditional stone face and a stone heart.

My initial impression was correct. While the stolid, middle-aged Pochotl had accompanied his uncle on previous journeys, he had no desire to undertake another. He had made his fortune, and he resented the Emperor's order for disturbing his comfortable life.

I could not blame him for it.

But I could not like him, either.

In addition to proving surprisingly talkative, Eyahue had a prodigious libido for a man of his years. He reminded me of the old Tatar guide who'd led me across the desert and had been so taken with Master Lo's Camaeline snowdrop tonic, except Eyahue had no need of aphrodisiacs. At nearly every inn or village we visited along the way, the old fellow managed to find a woman willing to accommodate him. Although the goddess Xochiquetzal did not have an equivalent of Naamah's sacred service, it seemed a casual form of prostitution was not unknown among the Nahuatl.

"I'll tell you, he's an inspiration," Balthasar observed, watching Eyahue steer a broad-hipped woman back to his chamber, one hand firmly planted on her buttocks. "I don't know where the old codger finds the energy."

"He's not marching in sodding *armor*, for one thing." Brice de Bretel rubbed the back of his neck. "I'm beginning to wish someone would damn well attack us just to justify slogging along in it."

Denis shook his head at him. "Don't wish for trouble. Once we're past the boundaries of the Nahuatl Empire, we're likely to find enough of it."

It was a prospect I regarded with equal parts dread and eagerness. Terra Nova was vast, vaster than I'd reckoned. We trudged through mountain passes and descended into fertile valleys, pausing to let the pack-horses graze whenever we were able, a necessity that further delayed our progress.

We followed long, winding rivers, where I had some success shooting waterfowl for the pot. For reasons I didn't entirely fathom, Temilotzin found my skill with a bow well nigh as hilarious as Eyahue's tales and took to calling me his little warrior.

On and on we travelled.

A part of me wondered if mayhap the Dauphin had simply misgauged the distances involved and his party was somewhere ahead of us, marching across the endless landscape, an ever-receding target.

Balthasar and Denis, who knew Thierry de la Courcel better than I, assured me it was not so. The prince had given his word that he would return in a year's time. He would have turned back rather than break his oath.

At two months into our journey, we entered the farthest reaches of the Nahuatl Empire. The folk there were not native Nahuatl speakers. According to Eyahue, they had been conquered by Achcuatli's father, and chafed under the rule of the Nahuatl. They regarded us with curiosity and suspicion, but they were willing to trade to replenish our dwindling stores, and fortunately, Eyahue and Pochotl spoke their tongue.

In the market-place of the first such city, it struck me that if our stores were running low, Thierry's must have been, too. Travellers' inns were becoming fewer and farther between, and it had been well over a week since we'd had confirmation.

As Temilotzin cheerfully observed, there was no way of knowing if the Dauphin's party had succeeded in reaching Tawantinsuyo; and we had entered territory that was potentially hostile.

So I dispatched Eyahue and Pochotl to comb the market-place in search of any merchant or farmer who remembered the strangers from across the sea trading for food goods. For a mercy, they returned with an affirmative answer.

Our journey continued.

At every settlement, we repeated the same process, the *pochtecas* questioning the local folk.

I could not help but think of the tale of the D'Angeline Prince Imriel de la Courcel, who had tracked my ancestor Berlik all the way to the Vralian wilderness using a similar method, seeking to avenge the death of his wife and unborn child.

It was a piece of irony that it now fell to me to follow in the footsteps of Prince Imriel's descendant on the opposite side of the world, venturing deeper into the increasingly torrid southern heat, even as he had followed Berlik into the frigid, snowy wild.

When I mentioned it to Bao during the course of a day's journey, he shrugged. "It seems to me the gods often laugh at our expense." He wiped one tattooed forearm across his brow, dashing away beads of sweat. "Do not torture me with talk of snow, Moirin."

"I don't mean to." I paused. "Do you think the gods are mocking us?"

Bao heard the uncertainty in my voice and responded to it. "No," he said in a firm tone, giving me his full attention. "No, I do not. Forgive me, I did but speak in jest. Moirin, I believe the gods have their own way of restoring balance in the world—or at least that the world ever seeks to return to balance, even as water seeks to return to its source."

"All ways lead to the Way," I murmured.

He nodded. "So Master Lo Feng always said, and he was the wisest man I have ever known."

I sighed. "I wish he were here."

Bao smiled wryly. "So do I. But if he were—" He touched his chest, where the spark of our shared *diadh-anam* flickered. "I would not be."

"Master Lo made his choice," I said.

"Yes." His fingers brushed my cheek, lingering. "And I am at peace with it."

I smiled back at him. "I'm glad."

Temilotzin poked me from behind with the point of his spear. "Keep walking, little warrior!" he said in a jovial manner. "We have a long way to go yet."

"How far?" I asked him.

He laughed. "Far."

FORTY-THREE

S everal days later, we passed at last beyond the ultimate boundaries of the Nahuatl Empire.

In faraway Ch'in, the border between the Celestial Empire and the Tatar territories beyond it had been marked by an immense wall. Here in Terra Nova, there was no such thing, only a careless remark by Eyahue that we had come to the end.

"Are the folk beyond hostile?" I asked him.

He shrugged. "The Cloud People? They may be, or they may not. It depends on their mood. But I have traded with them before."

I learned that the Cloud People called themselves thusly because they built their settlements atop high mountains. Once again, I dispatched our *pochtecas* to query the inhabitants, this time giving them some small trinkets to trade for information, hoping it would generate goodwill among the Cloud People. On Temilotzin's advice, we made camp on the plains below the mountain, reckoning that if the Cloud People did prove hostile, there was no point in exposing our entire party to danger.

When Eyahue and Pochotl did not return by the day's end, I wasn't overly worried. It was a long journey on foot to the mountaintop settlement and back, and the *pochtecas* knew what they were doing. But as the second day wore onward, I began to fret.

"I'm sure they will be fine, Moirin," Bao said to me. "Anyway, we could all use a day's respite."

So we spent the day tending to necessary chores, bathing in the brisk river that spilled down from the mountains to meander across the plain, washing clothing and spreading it to dry, mending torn fabric and broken straps, tending to our stalwart pack-horses. The D'Angelines were grateful for the chance to shed their armor for a day, many going bare-chested beneath the bright sun, and consequently paying a price as their fair skin reddened. But even sunburn wasn't enough to cloud their high spirits at a day of rest, and I smiled to see them acting like boys at play in the river, dunking and splashing one another.

Still, by late afternoon, I found myself wondering what in the world we would do if our *pochtecas* didn't return. Now that we'd left the Nahuatl Empire, we were more reliant on them than ever.

If they had been taken prisoner or enslaved, Bao and I could enter the city cloaked in the twilight and search for them, but it would not be an easy task without having the faintest idea where they might be held.

I was mulling over the possibilities when Bao nudged me and pointed across the plain. Two familiar figures were approaching in the late amber light. When they drew near enough for me to see that Eyahue wore a gap-toothed smile, I sighed with relief and allowed myself to relax.

"You found word of them?" I asked.

The older *pochteca* clapped his nephew on the shoulder. "Pochotl did. Took a lot of asking. Your prince and his men passed the city by, but Pochotl finally found someone who saw the white-faced strangers on the road."

"Thank you," I said to the younger trader. "I am grateful."

Pochotl went so far as to offer me a brief, unsmiling nod of acknowledgment.

Since it was too late to break camp, we resolved to pass another night on the plain. The men drew straws for sentry duty, the losers grumbling. Early on, some had questioned the necessity of posting sentries, but Temilotzin and Bao had been equally insistent. Now that we'd passed beyond the boundaries of Emperor Achcuatli's protection, no one questioned the practice.

I retired to the small tent I shared with Bao, a concession to modesty that Balthasar Shahrizai had surprisingly insisted on. The others rolled themselves in cloaks or mantles and slept beneath the stars.

Worn out by a day of worrying, I fell asleep quickly and slept without dreams.

I awoke to the sound of someone hissing my name, and the knowledge that someone else was in our tent.

For a moment, I was disoriented, imagining myself once more in a tent high in the thin air of the Abode of the Gods, with Manil Datar bent on committing heresy on me. But Bao came out of sleep moving quick as a snake, rolling over and whipping his staff in the direction of the intruder.

The shadowy figure pulled back. "Hold, for Elua's sake, hold! It's me, Denis!"

"Denis?" I sat upright, rubbing my eyes. "What is it?"

From what I could make out of his expression, it was grim. "It's happened again. Someone's betrayed us."

"What?" My thoughts were fuzzy. "How?"

Denis' voice trembled a bit. "I just found Clemente DuBois with his throat slit. He was on sentry duty."

"What?" I was fully awake now. "Why would anyone—?"

"Only one reason to kill a sentry." Bao scrambled out of the tent, pushing past Denis, staff in hand. "We're about to be attacked. Moirin, call your twilight and stay safely out of the way. Denis, get armed, now!"

Denis gulped and nodded.

Without waiting to see if I obeyed him, Bao raced to the center of our campsite, where the banked coals of our campfire glowed faintly beneath the silvery light of the full moon high overhead. He began banging furiously with his staff on the large iron pot resting on the ashes, sounding a clanging alarm. "Ambush!" he shouted at the top of his lungs. "Get up, get armed! Now, now, now!"

Not far away on the plain, howls of anger rose in reply.

Ah, gods! All that armor—the chain-mail shirts, the brigandines, helmets, vambraces, and greaves—that our men had labored under for so long had been removed for the night. Mayhap half of our sleeping fighters responded with alacrity, reaching to don whatever was closest at hand.

The other half blinked in stupefaction. Ignoring Bao's order, I grabbed the nearest D'Angeline and shook him. Spotting links of chain-mail glinting in the moonlight, I hauled his armored jerkin free and threw it in his lap. "Get up, get armed, *now*!"

Moving sluggishly, he struggled into it.

Bao spotted me. "Moirin, *call your twilight*!"

"I'm doing more good this way!" I retorted, shoving a helmet on the fellow's head.

Seeing what I was about, Septimus Rousse began to emulate me. Between the two of us, we managed to get a dozen or so of our men upright and partially armed. Those who were more alert worked at lightning speed to pull brigandines over their chain-mail and buckle valuable greaves and vambraces in place.

Temilotzin, effortlessly prepared and ready, leaned carelessly on his throwing spear and peered across the moonlit plain. "Here they come," he remarked. In one smooth move, he fitted the butt of his spear into the throwing-tool and hurled it into the night.

There was a lone choked cry, followed by a fresh chorus of angry howls and the sound of feet pounding.

With a fierce grin, Temilotzin hefted his studded club. "And here they are!"

With that, the night erupted in chaos as our attackers fell upon us. I dashed into the tent to retrieve my bow and quiver, then retreated some distance from the fray, trying to identify a suitable target.

It was impossible. It was all hand-to-hand fighting, the combatants too closely engaged to risk a shot. It appeared our attackers outnumbered us, but not by a great many. Bao was a dervish in the thick of battle, his bamboo staff moving too quickly to track. Temilotzin was singing a war-song, his obsidian-studded club rising and falling, his sandaled feet stomping out a rhythm known only to him. Here and there, D'Angelines I couldn't identify were acquitting themselves with skill.

But some had fallen, easily recognized by their fair skin in the moonlight. I felt sick at heart.

"Moirin!" Septimus Rousse appeared beside me, pointing across the plain. Beyond the outskirts of the battle, a pair of dark figures were racing for our picket-line. "They're after the horses!"

"Ah, no!" Giving the battlefield a wide berth, I ran to intercept them, my heart beating in my throat. I loosed my first arrow at a dead run, and it went wide. Skidding to a halt, I nocked another. The nearest fellow was trying to grab a frightened pack-horse's halter and had his back to me.

Swallowing hard, I loosed my bow and shot him from behind. He toppled forward and lay still. The pack-horse squealed and tossed its head, tugging at the picket-rope.

The second fellow blinked in consternation, then came at me with a roar, raising a stone-headed war-club high overhead.

Reaching into my quiver, I nocked another arrow and shot him, too.

With a look of profound surprise, he sat down hard, glanced once at his chest, then slumped sideways.

Septimus caught up with me, breathing hard. "Nice work, my lady."

"My thanks, lord captain." All along the picket-line, horses whickered and stamped in protest. I caught sight of a third figure, stooped and lurking beyond the horses' shifting bodies. Nocking and drawing another arrow, I moved around the end of the line to get a clean shot at him.

The figure straightened, an obsidian dagger in one hand.

I stared at Pochotl. *"You?"*

He permitted himself a tight grimace and said nothing.

"Lazy, greedy, stupid, good for nothing sister-son!" Eyahue emerged from the moonlit darkness, ranting with fury. Gnarled hands extended, he flung himself on his nephew, clamping his fingers around Pochotl's throat and attempting to throttle him. "You did this, didn't you? No-good, cowardly, idiot excuse for a *pochteca*! You disgrace us!"

With an effort, Septimus Rousse pried Eyahue loose and subdued him in a firm grip. Rivulets of tears ran down the old fellow's creased cheeks, but his expression had turned to one of traditional Nahuatl stoicism, cold and hard.

"You disgrace us," he repeated with dignity.

"You are a fool, old man," Pochotl muttered. "Shall we both suffer for the Emperor's whims?"

I moved between them, keeping an arrow trained on the traitor.

Behind us, the sounds of battle were beginning to fade. A cry in an unknown tongue was raised and repeated.

"The Cloud People are retreating," Eyahue said in a flat tone. "Tonight, we are victorious."

I wondered at what price.

FORTY-FOUR

Six dead, several others wounded.

That was the price of our victory.

Sensing through the bond of our shared *diadh-anam* that I was alive and well, Bao turned toward tending the wounded. As a result, the spotted warrior Temilotzin was the first to seek me out and discover the prisoner I guarded.

"What passes here, little warrior?" he asked in an ominous tone rendered all the more ominous by the fact that he was splashed with blood from head to foot. "What has this one done?"

I gestured with the point of my arrow. "Betrayed us."

With a guttural roar, Temilotzin hoisted his obsidian-studded club. "Then he will die!"

"No, please!" Lowering my bow, I caught at his arm. It felt like tugging on an oak log. "We need to question him."

Reluctantly, Temilotzin relented. The expression on his blood-spattered face was implacable in the moonlight. If I'd had any doubt that a stone face and a stone heart lay beneath his easygoing manner, it vanished then and there. He jerked his chin at Eyahue. "And him? Did he betray us, too?"

"Never!" the old man said with fierce indignation.

"I believe he speaks the truth," I said. "But we need to know more. Can you guard them without killing anyone?"

He grunted. "I will try."

Accompanied by Septimus Rousse, I went to help take stock of the situation. Brice de Bretel and another level-headed L'Agnacite fellow named Jean Grenville were working to stoke the campfire and give us more light by which to assess the damage to the wounded. Balthasar Shahrizai, who looked pale but otherwise unharmed, was directing other uninjured men to set up sentry posts farther afield where their night vision wouldn't be compromised by the blazing fire.

It didn't surprise me that Balthasar had maintained the presence of mind to fully arm himself. For all his insouciance, there was steel in him.

Aside from poor Clemente DuBois, the dead were those who *hadn't* kept their wits, and whom Septimus and I hadn't been able to aid in time. All five had plunged into battle bare-headed or with unbuckled helmets that had come loose in the fray. The war-clubs of the Cloud People may have been crude weapons, but they were capable of wielding them with deadly force on unprotected flesh.

Bao, kneeling beside a groaning warrior with a broken arm, glanced up at our arrival. "Moirin. You didn't listen to me, did you?"

It occurred to me that if Bao wasn't so skilled at keeping his opponents out of reach, it could well be him lying among the dead with a crushed skull. "No, I did not." I pointed toward the picket-line. "Which is the reason we still have pack-horses, and Temilotzin is standing guard over the traitor Pochotl. Now, tell me what to do."

"Pochotl, eh?" He sounded tired.

I nodded. "He's safe enough for now. Tell me how I can help."

"And me," Septimus added.

Bao gathered himself. "I need the sharpest blade you can find. We're going to have to cut off his brigandine. And branches, as straight as you can find. I'll need to splint his arm once I get it set."

"I'll help." Denis de Toluard limped into the circle of firelight, nursing a bruised thigh. "I understand a bit, at least in theory. Raphael used to discuss his practice with me."

"Good," Bao said with curt approval.

The aftermath of battle is a terrible thing. In some ways, this was not the worst I had known. The scale of devastation wrought on human flesh by the weapons of the Divine Thunder in Ch'in was almost more than the mind could encompass.

But this time, *I* was responsible.

And we were deep in hostile, unfamiliar territory. Our victory was tenuous at best, and the road ahead of us long and hard. The dead would be buried far from home. There was no respite for the wounded, no safe haven where they could heal.

I found the sharpest knife in the camp—one of Balthasar Shahrizai's well-honed daggers. I held Arnaud Latrelle's good hand and hummed one of Sister Gemma's healing Eisandine tunes to the best of my ability while Bao sawed relentlessly at the suede arm of his brigandine with Balthasar's dagger.

He was a young one, Arnaud Latrelle, younger than me. "Guess I should have taken the time to put on chain-mail?" he gasped.

I stroked his sweat-damp brow. "Next time, aye, that would be a good idea."

He choked back a scream of pain when Bao and Denis maneuvered the broken bones of his forearm into place, lashing them firm with strips of torn cloth and straight pine-branches Septimus Rousse had procured from a nearby copse.

There were others.

I checked the dilated pupils of two men struck hard on the steel helm by the war-clubs of the Cloud People, soothing them while they retched and vomited.

I comforted another with a broken clavicle, who bit his lip and writhed with agony as Bao eased his chain-mail shirt over his head, Denis holding his legs to keep him as still as possible while Bao wrapped him in makeshift bandages to stabilize the break.

All in all, it was a long night.

Dawn broke over the plain, finding us all weary and exhausted. Brice and some of the others had shifted the corpses of the slain Cloud People warriors some distance from the camp. Our own dead had been arranged in a somber row.

"Should we . . . ?" Balthasar gestured uncertainly at them.

"Bury them?" Bao gave a tired nod. "We can't leave them for scavengers."

"What of their weapons and armor?" Balthasar looked ill. "No one wants them to fall into enemy hands, but we can't afford the extra weight."

"No." Bao pressed the heels of his hands against his closed eyes. "And if we bury them in armor . . ." He dropped his hands and glanced across the empty plain toward the Cloud People settlement atop the mountain. It looked quiet and peaceful from a distance, but appearances were deceiving.

"They very well might dig them up," Balthasar finished the thought for him.

"Take the armor downstream and throw it in the river," I suggested. "It's deep and fast enough in places that they'd be hard-pressed to retrieve it if they even thought to look there."

Bao gave me a grateful look. "And the water will rust them in time. Well thought, Moirin."

Accordingly, Balthasar recruited one team to set about the grim business of stripping the dead of whatever armor they'd managed to don in their haste and gathering those pieces they hadn't, and another team to begin hacking a common grave out of the soil, using the hand-axes and adzes we'd brought for the purpose of building vessels.

While they worked, Bao and I went to question Pochotl. We borrowed Denis and Balthasar—the former because I wanted someone else skilled in the Nahuatl tongue to hear what was said, and the latter for his keen interrogation skills.

As it transpired, Pochotl was more than willing to talk. After months of sullen reticence, he was downright forthcoming. When I asked him why he'd done it, he stared at me as though I'd gone mad.

"To make an end to this!" He waved one hand, indicating the campsite. "I do not fear to risk my life for *my* people, but why should I do so for *yours*?"

"Because the Emperor ordered it," Temilotzin growled. "Do you think he would thank you for giving steel weapons and horses to our enemy?"

Pochotl shrugged. "It is only one small city. None of the Cloud People know how to use these weapons. They do not even have *maca-huitls*. We could have come back with an army and defeated them, taken their weapons and horses. The men of Aragonia are too far away to stop us. The Emperor could not be angry at us, because *we* did not harm the foreigners under his protection."

Temilotzin scratched his chin, dislodging flakes of dried blood. "That's a pretty good plan."

I scowled at him.

The Jaguar Knight grinned at me. "Peace, my little warrior. I did not say I agreed with it." He thumped the spotted hide over his chest, loosing a further dusting of dried blood. "I keep my word. Shall I kill him now?"

"Yes!" Eyahue said in a fierce voice.

"No!" I said in alarm. "No, we need to know for sure if he acted alone, or if Eyahue knew." I glanced apologetically at the old man, who shrugged, taking no offense. "We need to know if the Cloud People are gathering for another attack, and if we'll find them enemies from now onward."

"Oh, those are good questions." Temilotzin turned to Pochotl with a cheerful smile. "Answer them, or before I kill you, I will peel the skin from your flesh and dance before you wearing it like a priest of Xipe Totec."

"Xipe Totec?" I asked.

"You don't want to know," Denis murmured.

Balthasar, doing his best to follow the conversation, shuddered. Even Bao looked a bit nonplussed.

For a mercy, Pochotl continued to answer freely. No, Eyahue had known nothing of his plan, which he'd conjured on the spot once they'd parted ways in the city. The Cloud People were of two minds whether or not to trust him, and decided to send a small raiding party of fifty or sixty warriors to see if it was indeed possible to kill us all in our sleep.

"Not you, Uncle," he added. "I made them promise to spare us."

Eyahue glared at him. "Idiot sister-son! You trusted them to keep their word?"

Temilotzin rubbed his chin again. "That is a flaw in your plan."

"They had no reason not to!" Pochotl defended himself. He gestured at the campsite. "In their eyes, I would have given them a great gift!"

"No," Eyahue said as slowly as though he were speaking to a dim-witted child. "In their eyes, you would have proved yourself an oath-breaker unworthy of trust. It is likely they would have killed us rather than take any chances. *That* is why a *pochteca's* word of honor is so important. Trade is built on trust. I am sorry you never understood this." He glanced at me. "The Cloud People attacked us. They will not hold us to blame for their defeat, and I do not believe they will try again." He nodded at Temilotzin. "You may kill him now."

Obligingly, the spotted warrior raised his club.

"Wait!" I pleaded once more. Temilotzin sighed and lowered his club. I turned to Pochotl. "You said you found someone among the Cloud People who had seen Prince Thierry's party on the road. Was that true?"

Pochotl gave me a flat stare. "No," he said. "I lied."

"*Now* may I kill him?" Temilotzin asked in a tone of long-suffering patience.

I thought of Edouard Durel held under guard in Orgullo del Sol. He had betrayed us as surely as Pochotl had, but gods willing, he would be returned to Terre d'Ange to bear witness against Claudine de Barthelme and her son. He would be tried fairly in a court of law, and mayhap even granted some form of clemency for cooperating.

Executing a man in cold blood was not a deed that sat well with me.

But Pochotl *had* betrayed us; and if his plan had succeeded, there was no chance we would have survived. The Cloud People would have crept into our camp and bludgeoned us to death in our sleep. Pochotl had slit poor Clemente DuBois' throat with his own hand, and five other men were dead because of his treachery. He had disobeyed the Nahautl Emperor's direct order.

By the implacable looks on Eyahue and Temilotzin's faces, I could see that there was no sparing him.

"Yes," I said to the latter. "You may."

The Jaguar Knight hoisted his obsidian-studded club. "You may wish to stand back," he warned us. "This will be messy."

The rest of us retreated a few paces.

Pochotl stood unmoving, his expression stoic. Temilotzin swung his *macahuitl* club in one hard, level blow at the fellow's neck. The edges of the obsidian flakes lining his club may have been brittle, but they were razor-sharp. His strike sheared Pochotl's head clean away from his body. The head bounced and rolled on the plain, while blood jetted in a crimson geyser from the stump of his neck. The headless body remained upright for the space of a few heartbeats before crumpling to the ground.

Denis de Toluard turned away and vomited.

I would have liked to do the same, but I fought against the surge of nausea, swallowing bile and struggling to keep my face expressionless. Temilotzin gave me an approving look, then clapped Denis on the shoulder. "Your stomach will grow stronger in time," he assured him, then stooped to pick up Pochotl's head by its long black hair. "Do you want him buried with the others, old man?" he asked Eyahue.

The old *pochteca* regarded his nephew's disembodied head with disgust. "No," he said. "Leave him to the scavengers."

We did.

FORTY-FIVE

In the wake of our first battle, once the worst of the aftermath had been dealt with, I found I had a rebellion on my hands.

Alain Guillard, the hotheaded Azzallese baron's son who had bunked in one of the wardroom's cabins aboard *Naamah's Dove* with us, was arguing that we should turn back; and he'd convinced at least three others.

"This was madness from the beginning!" he railed. "What in Elua's name were we thinking, any of us?"

"*I* was thinking I abandoned some of my dearest friends and the Dauphin of Terre d'Ange to their fate!" Denis de Toluard retorted with unexpected force. "And that I'd been given a chance to redeem myself!"

"That's your burden, Denis," Alain said in a remorseless tone. "*I* didn't."

"Be glad I carry it!" Denis shouted at him. "It gives me nightmares until I can't sleep at night!" He jerked his chin at the waiting common grave dug into the earth and the line of D'Angeline dead nearby, stripped of their armor. "If it didn't, we'd all be like them!"

"And so we all will sooner or later!" Alain shouted back at him. He gestured savagely in my direction. "She doesn't know where she's going, Denis! None of us do!" With an effort, he wrestled himself under control. "We've been on the road for months, and we're not even in sight of these fabled jungles. Now we're supposed to rely on people like to slaughter us in our sleep to assure us we're on the right track?" He shook his head. "We're only days away from the borders of the Nahuatl Empire. If we turn back now, we stand a chance of surviving this."

His allies murmured in agreement, and others looked uncertain.

"Don't let him get the upper hand, my lady," Septimus Rousse murmured in my ear. "If you do, he'll never relinquish it."

Bao nodded. "He's right, Moirin."

I took a deep breath. "My lord Guillard speaks the truth! I *don't* know where we're bound. The task is harder, and the journey longer, than I knew."

"That is not what I had in mind," Bao muttered.

I ignored him. "But I *do* know that Thierry de la Courcel lives, and I know it is my oath-sworn duty to attempt to rescue him." The spark of my *diadh-anam* blazed steadily in my breast, lending me strength. I pointed at Alain Guillard. "You volunteered for this, my lord. All of you did. You begged for the chance to accompany us. Will you turn back now, just because it is *hard*?"

A few men chuckled.

Alain glared at me. "Do you think it is easy for one of Azza's scions to admit he made a mistake?"

"No," I said softly. "I don't." I glanced at the D'Angeline dead lined up beside the open grave, at Clemente DuBois, his slit throat gaping, his empty blue eyes gazing at the sky. He would never make another nervous jest.

Stooping beside his body, I closed his eyelids gently.

I straightened. "If anyone wishes to turn back, now is the time," I announced. "My lord Guillard is right. In a few days' march, you may return to the protection of Emperor Achcuatli's realm." I glanced at Arnaud Latrelle with his arm in a splint, and Gregoire d'Arnes, the fellow with the broken clavicle. To be sure, there was no point in their continuing onward. "You can escort the injured to safety. You can carry word to the crew of *Naamah's Dove* in Orgullo del Sol that the journey to Tawantinsuyo is harder and longer than we knew, and order them to wait for us. I will not compel anyone to accompany this expedition. But *I* mean to press onward. I mean to find Prince Thierry, and restore him to the throne of Terre d'Ange as the rightful heir to his father's realm."

At that, there were cheers, and a few murmurs of dissent.

I ignored the latter. "Who is with me?"

As it transpired, quite a few—but not all. We lost Alain Guillard and two out of his three allies. The third, a fair-haired young man named Mathieu de Montague, changed his mind.

"Will you trust me to address them, my lady?" Balthasar asked me discreetly.

I nodded. "Of course."

"D'Angelines!" Balthasar got their attention in a ringing tone. "All of you who are hale and unharmed, think well before you make your final choice here." He locked gazes with Alain Guillard, contempt creeping into his voice. "Will Azza's famous pride allow *you* to sleep at night knowing yourself a coward and a quitter, Alain?"

The fellow reddened, but did not reply.

Balthasar turned to Mathieu de Montague. "And you, Messire de Montague! Do you imagine you can have another change of heart at the next skirmish?" He shook his head. "Don't. Lady Moirin is overly generous. She is in command of this expedition, but I am in command of *you*." He glanced around at all the men. "I will not attempt to gainsay her generous offer, but I will say this. It will not be repeated. Make your choices here and now. From this day forward, anyone who argues for turning back will be considered guilty of fomenting mutiny!" His voice hardened. "Is that clear?"

There were nods all around.

"See, Moirin?" Bao said to me. "*That's* what they needed to hear."

"I suspect they needed to hear both things," Septimus Rousse said diplomatically. "Commanding men unwilling to serve is a dangerous business." He nodded toward the picket-line. "That is a lesson we may take from Pochotl's betrayal."

And a bitter lesson it was, too,

Once the matter of rebellion was settled, we buried our dead. Each of the slain men was wrapped in a cloak and lowered into the grave as gently as possible.

I'd witnessed battles and tended to the dead before. In Kurugiri, Bao and I had been the only ones willing to handle the corpse of Jagrati the Spider Queen, winding her into a shroud to lend a measure of dignity to her death. But I'd never been responsible for the actual burial of the dead.

There was a terrible finality to it. Once the last body had been lowered into the grave, we stood about uncertainly. I did not know the protocol for such matters, but I suspected I knew who did.

"My lord captain," I addressed Septimus Rousse. "Would you be willing to offer an invocation?"

He inclined his head to me. "Of course." He knelt to gather a handful of loose soil, then rose and stretched out his closed fist, holding it over the grave. "Today we bid farewell to six dear companions," Septimus said in a firm, steady voice. "They perished in pursuit of a noble cause. May they pass through the bright gate into the Terre d'Ange-that-lies-beyond, and may Blessed Elua and his Companions receive them gladly." Opening his hand, he let the soil trickle into the grave. "Blessed Elua hold and keep you." He nodded at Balthasar. "Will you commence the speaking of their names, my lord?"

Balthasar stepped forward to gather a fistful of soil. "Clemente DuBois," he murmured. "You were the most annoying companion with whom I've ever shared a living space. Now I will miss your dreadful jests."

There was a brief, shocked silence; and then men laughed and groaned in rueful acknowledgment. With a quiet smile, Balthasar sprinkled dirt on the grave.

Another fellow came forward. "Richard de Laroche," he said in a ragged tone. "You were a good man and a good friend to me. I promise not to tell your mother that you died because you couldn't manage to buckle your helmet properly."

One by one, others came forward.

All the dead were named, all were acknowledged with a last tribute and a fond jest. When it was done, the mounds of dirt painstakingly hewed from the plain were shoveled by hand into the grave and tamped into place.

And then there was nothing left to do but carry onward. Men with damaged gear sorted through the armor and weapons of the slain, replacing pieces as needed. Septimus Rousse outfitted himself with a full set of gear. Bao declined an opportunity to do the same.

"You might at least consider a helmet," I said to him.

He shrugged. "It does not suit the style of a stick-fighter. The weight would unbalance me. Besides, I have a very hard head, Moirin."

I eyed him. "The gods know that's true."

In accordance with our plan, all the unclaimed armor and weapons were loaded onto a pair of pack-horses and carried half a league downstream to be dumped into the deepest part of the river. Temilotzin and Eyahue regarded this development with obvious regret, but neither of them spoke against it.

Despite Balthasar Shahrizai's speech, there had been no shifting in the lines of rebellion that had been drawn. Alain Guillard and his two allies remained firm in their resolve to turn back. Our injured fighters raised no protest. Although they were not happy about the prospect, they recognized their limitations. And having relocated his courage, Mathieu de Montague remained desperately adamant that he would not lose it a second time.

I could not help but pity the lad, who was another of the youngest members of our party.

"There's no shame in it," I said gently to him. "A warrior's path is not for everyone."

Young Mathieu flushed, the blood creeping in a crimson tide beneath his alabaster skin. "Do you think me unworthy, my lady?"

"No!"

"Moirin, don't coddle him," Balthasar said in passing, slapping the lad on the back. "You'll do, won't you?"

"I will!" the lad said fiercely,

"That's the spirit," Balthasar noted with approval. "Remember, if *I* can do this, anyone can."

Keeping a sharp eye on the distant mountain-top settlement of the Cloud People, our fighting men at last allowed themselves to wash the dried gore of battle and the dirt of its aftermath from their skin in the river.

I consulted with the knowledgeable Septimus Rousse and the *pochteca* Eyahue regarding what we could spare from our goods to aid those turning back toward the Nahuatl Empire in their journey.

Some hours past noon, we parted ways. It might have been wiser to wait, but no one wanted to linger on the plain beneath the shadow of the Cloud People's mountain where their dead awaited retrieval.

I'd allotted one pack-horse, a sack of ground *maize* and a quarter-full sack of *cacao* beans to our rebels, reckoning it generous.

"You needn't do this, my lady," Alain Guillard said in a stony voice, not meeting my gaze. "We'll find a way to manage."

"I am not doing it for you," I said calmly, nodding toward the injured men. "I am doing it for *them*."

He said nothing.

And so we parted, trudging across the plain in opposite directions.

Terra Nova stretched endlessly before us.

FORTY-SIX

For many days afterward, our company was on edge, nerves raw and frayed. We took it as a matter of faith that we remained on the trail of Prince Thierry's expedition. We posted shifts of multiple sentries at night and avoided settlements of the Cloud People whenever possible.

But it seemed Eyahue was right. There were no further attacks. And bit by bit, we began to relax. Grumbling over the rigors of the journey, which had abated in the wake of the battle and subsequent rebellion, resumed. It seemed to be of a harmless nature, and I was content to let the men complain.

We'd been so long on the road, I almost didn't believe Eyahue when he announced we had reached the isthmus that connected the northern land-mass of Terra Nova to its southern counterpart. But several days onward, our trail ascended into a forested mountain range, following along the shoulder of a long, winding spine that snaked southward.

And when we scaled the first peak, we caught a glimpse of the sea—not the sea we had crossed on our journey to Terra Nova, which lay to the east of us, but a vast, uncharted sea to the west.

All of us stared at it in awe.

"Name of Elua!" Balthasar murmured. "What do you suppose lies on the other side of it?"

"We can't confirm it without navigating it," Septimus Rousse said. "But if the theories are correct, I'd say Messire Bao's homeland."

Pointing to the highest peak some leagues ahead of us, Eyahue informed us that if we were to climb to the very top, we would see both the eastern and western seas from its heights.

Septimus' eyes gleamed. "I'd like to see that! Is there perchance a river that connects the two?"

Eyahue shook his head when the question was translated for him. "No. Many rivers, yes, but not one such as that."

"A pity," Septimus said with disappointment. "One could sail all the way around the world if there were."

Denis de Toluard unbuckled his helmet and removed it to ruffle his sweat-damp hair. "Waterways can be built," he said thoughtfully. "Look at what the Nahuatl accomplished with canals in Tenochtitlan, or the Caerdicci in La Serenissima. If the isthmus is as narrow as Eyahue says, it might be possible to devise one using existing rivers."

The two men exchanged a glance.

"It would be a mighty endeavor," Septimus mused.

"Aye, and it's an endeavor for another day," I said firmly. "If we live through this, you can plan it."

It was a lush land, and a sparsely inhabited one. There were no great settlements, only small villages along the way whose denizens appeared peaceable and regarded us with wonder and curiosity.

Eyahue assured us with disdain that they were beneath a *pochteca's* notice and had nothing worth trading for save food goods. They spoke myriad dialects, of which he spoke but a smattering. Whenever he was able to question villagers regarding a party of white-faced strangers passing through before us, he received blank looks and head-shakes in reply.

"Do not worry." Eyahue patted my hand after the third such failed attempt. "It is likely that they took a different route thinking it would be easier to travel through the lowlands. They were wrong. That is why you are lucky to have me."

I prayed he was right.

There was abundant animal life in the unpopulated areas between villages, and thanks to the absence of human predators, they were quite fearless. On several occasions, I was able to procure deer with very little effort, although I could not help but feel a pang of guilt shooting creatures that stared at me with the same mild wonder as the villagers. Temilotzin, who had equal success with his throwing spear, laughed at my discomfort.

At length, our path descended from the shoulder of the mountain range into the dense lowland jungles.

"The worst is ahead of us," Eyahue announced. He pointed south. "This jungle is not so bad. But in two, three days, we will reach the swamp. That will be bad."

It was.

I didn't mind the jungle. It was hot and dense, and I felt awful for the men laboring in their armor, but it was beautiful, too. We travelled along narrow footpaths through the thick greenery. Here, we began to see the flowers of surpassing beauty that Denis had mentioned so long ago—an incredible array of orchids that sprouted from the trunks of living trees or rose defiantly from the decay of fallen trunks, ladders of delicate blossoms nodding on long, slender stems, impossibly lovely.

Iridescent emerald hummingbirds darted here and there amidst the blossoms, their wings a buzzing blur. Monkeys chattered at us from the trees, and birds with dazzling plumage took flight with raucous cries.

"It reminds me of Bhaktipur," Bao said to me.

I smiled wistfully. "It does, doesn't it?"

But all too soon, as Eyahue had predicted, the jungle turned to swamp. Firm trails turned into a quagmire, with as much as half a foot of standing water underfoot. Everything smelled of vegetal rot. The thick muck sucked at our feet, making every plodding step an effort. I did not know who fared worse, the men in armor struggling to make progress, or our poor pack-horses, who sank knee- and hock-deep in the mire at times, plunging free with difficulty.

I did my best to encourage the former and soothe the latter, but stone and sea! It was hard going.

"How far, Eyahue?" I gasped on the first day

The old *pochteca* grunted. "Tomorrow or the next day. You are lucky to have me," he added again. "I know the best paths."

I daresay it was true.

Thanks to Eyahue's guidance, we were able to make camp the first night in the swamp on land that, while not precisely dry, was merely muddy. After gnawing on stale flatbread, men rolled themselves into their cloaks and dropped into an exhausted sleep. While well watered, our pack-horses went hungry for the night.

The second day was worse; and the second night worst of all. There was no solid land, dry or muddy, to be found. We slogged through the swamp until the light failed us, and dozed as best we could, soaked and miserable, wedging ourselves in the crooks of the hardy trees that sank their roots deep into the mire.

On the third day, we won clear of the swamp. Bit by bit, the ground grew more solid, the trees sparser, until a vast savannah of grasslands stretched before us.

Balthasar Shahrizai whooped in approval, flinging his arms into the air. "Blessed Elua be praised!"

"We've not reached Tawantinsuyo yet," Eyahue said in a testy manner. "There's a long way to go."

"But you said that was the worst of it?" I asked him.

He pursed his wrinkled lips. "The worst until we reach the river passage."

Although there were hours of light left, everyone was exhausted and the horses were famished. We unloaded them and turned them loose to graze, then set about building a roaring bonfire despite the heat, propping our sodden clothing on stakes to dry, the men tending to their gear. Septimus Rousse made a hearty porridge of sweet potatoes and *maize* from our stores, and all of us felt better for having a warm meal in our bellies.

"It really does feel like a whole new world," Denis said in a contemplative tone, gazing across the sea of waving grass. "And to imagine that for thousands of years, no one knew it was here."

"Except for the millions of people who lived here," Bao pointed out.

Denis waved a dismissive hand. "Oh, you know what I mean! I've never been to Ch'in, but I knew it was there, as surely as you knew Terre d'Ange existed before you set foot on it."

Bao stifled a yawn. "I never thought about it. I would not have left Ch'in were it not for Master Lo." He gave me a tired smile. "And I would not have left it a second time were it not for Moirin."

"Denis, why did Thierry want to come here so badly?" I asked him. "I know he did, but I never fully understood why."

"Glory," Balthasar murmured when Denis did not reply right away. "Adventure. All his life, Thierry felt overshadowed by the deeds of his ancestors in the past, and stifled by the tragedies that befell House Courcel in his father's lifetime. He wanted to live life to its utmost, to walk the knife's edge between terror and exhilaration. He wanted to pit himself against the greatest challenge he could imagine. In our lifetime, that's the exploration of Terra Nova."

There was a little silence.

"What the Circle of Shalomon attempted didn't help," Denis said quietly. "Seeking to explore a different kind of uncharted territory. It further convinced Thierry that Terre d'Ange needed to find a way to seek greatness." His mouth twisted. "One that didn't involve loosing a fallen spirit on the world."

To that, I had no reply.

"You didn't help, either, Moirin," Denis added. "I'm not saying it was your fault." He shook his head. "It wasn't. But when you sailed off on that enormous Ch'in ship in pursuit of some arcane destiny, it fanned the flame within him."

I felt guilty. "I didn't *want* to go."

Bao stirred. "Hey!"

"I'm glad I did," I said to him. "But I didn't want to. I didn't choose my everlasting destiny!"

"Thierry did," Balthasar said. "Or at least he tried to. And he would have chosen it with or without you idiots attempting to summon demons, or Moirin's date with a mysterious destiny."

"Why didn't you accompany the Dauphin, my lord Shahrizai?"

Mathieu de Montague asked with curiosity. "It seems you knew him so very well."

Balthasar smiled wryly. "Cowardice."

Bao scoffed.

"I don't think anyone's going to believe that excuse anymore, my lord Balthasar," I observed.

He shrugged. "All right. Mayhap I'm not a coward, but I like my comfort and luxury. I don't mind a stiff challenge so long as at the end of the day, there's a hot bath and silken sheets, and some pretty lad or lass begging for sweet discipline. Thierry knew that about me. He never expected me to go."

"Do you suppose he ever imagined you'd come after him?" Mathieu asked.

Balthasar laughed with genuine amusement. "No." He ran one hand over his sweat-streaked, grimy face, flicking his fingers with disgust. "No, I think Thierry de la Courcel will be surprised as hell to see me when we find him."

"If we find him," someone on the far side of the fire muttered.

"*When* we find him," Balthasar corrected him. He glanced at me. "He's still alive, right?"

I stared into the dusk falling over the savannah, the trackless sea of grass rippling in the evening breeze. I wished we'd had a confirmed sighting to assure us we were on the right path; and I wished that Jehanne had returned to my dreams to tell me once more that her step-son lived, or give me any kind of guidance.

Bao nudged me. "Right, Moirin?"

"Absolutely," I said. "Without a doubt."

FORTY-SEVEN

We marched across the savannah.

Our gratitude at having reached dry land with ample grazing soon gave way to frustration at the lack of drinking water. Eyahue had cautioned us to conserve our stores, but he hadn't fully reckoned on the needs of our pack-horses, being unaccustomed to taking them into consideration.

At every stream and drinking hole, we drank our fill and refilled our waterskins, doling out the contents parsimoniously to men and horses alike on the long stretches in between. Onward we marched beneath a broiling sun, throats parched and dry. Eyahue taught us the trick of holding pebbles in our mouths to generate saliva.

"Keep going, keep going! You'll have plenty of water on the river." The old *pochteca* chortled. "More than you ever wanted!"

On the tenth day, one of our pack-horses foundered. We had done our best to tend to the horses, but this one had developed an infection in the frog of its hoof on the left foreleg after slogging through the swamp, and it had only worsened over the course of the journey. When it began to limp too badly to keep pace with our caravan, we made the decision to put it down.

The Jaguar Knight Temilotzin did the deed, cutting the big vein that pulsed alongside the pack-horse's neck with a keen-edged obsidian dagger. The horse sank to its knees and toppled slowly onto its side, its eyes rolling in what looked like relief, bleeding profusely into the grass. Its sides rose and fell several times, and then went still.

We butchered it and ate the meat. We redistributed its load among the men and continued onward. And we still had no confirmation that the Dauphin's party had passed this way.

"What if they misread the map?" I asked Eyahue. "What if they missed the river?"

He shook his head. "Doesn't matter if they read the map wrong. Sooner or later, they will meet the river."

And sooner or later, we did, too.

Even as the swamp had given way to savannah, the savannah gave way to the jungle once more.

There were signs of cultivation on the outskirts of the jungle. It was Brice de Bretel who let go a startled cry, pointing. "Look!"

At a glance, it seemed an unremarkable sight. One of the local inhabitants was tilling a field, walking behind the patiently plodding horse that drew his rough-hewn plow, the fellow's strong hands gripping the handles as the two-pronged wooden plow dug furrows in the earth. I had to look twice before it struck me.

His *horse*.

There were no horses native to Terra Nova, and the Aragonians hadn't explored this far. There was only one explanation for it: Thierry's party had been here before us.

"Do you suppose we've found them?" someone asked nervously. "Or... what became of them?"

I asked Eyahue what he thought.

"No," he said dismissively. "I know these people. I speak their tongue. They are peaceful farmers and fishers." He pointed toward the jungle. "The river is only an hour's walk away. It is likely that your prince traded horses for canoes."

Temilotzin scowled. "So your people will give horses to peasants, but not to the Emperor?"

"I doubt they had a choice," I said. "Nor will we. It's barter or turn them loose. But they're geldings, not breeding stock."

That mollified the spotted warrior. The fellow with the plow had caught sight of us, and he and a handful of others working the field were staring. Eyahue went to speak with them, then beckoned us over, grinning from ear to ear.

"Yes, your white-faced strangers were here," he informed us. "Tipalo says many months ago. They traded two horses for help building canoes. One of the horses died. He would like more."

At last, I let myself feel relief. "Does he have any idea what happened to them?"

"No," Eyahue said. "They paddled down the river and never came back. That is all he knows."

"It's more than we knew yesterday," Bao said pragmatically. "We know they reached the river, and we're still on their trail."

Whether it was due to innate hospitality or eagerness at the prospect of gaining two more horses, the folk of Tipalo's village gave us a generous welcome. The village was located some distance into the jungle, before it began to thicken to the point of impassability, near a river that Eyahue said was a tributary of the big river.

It was a rustic place with a circle of wooden huts sporting roofs of thatched palms built on hard-packed earth, but the folk seemed relaxed and agreeable. Dozens of near-naked children regarded our sweltering men in their steel armor warily, but they swarmed Temilotzin, giggling and scattering when he roared and waved his arms and stamped his feet in mock-threat. Remembering the casual ease with which our Jaguar Knight had beheaded Pochotl, I could not help but marvel at the contrast and think that human beings were complex and contradictory creatures.

"Aside from the insects, this isn't as bad as I imagined," Balthasar remarked, swatting at a swarm of mosquitoes.

"No," Denis said. "But I daresay there's worse to come."

"I'm sure there is, my doom-saying friend," Balthasar said mildly. "So let me enjoy myself while I can, won't you?"

Over the course of our journey, Eyahue had endeavored to teach us a bit of Quechua, the native tongue of the folk of Tawantinsuyo.

I'd hoped that when it came time to barter, I'd be able to understand a bit, but we had not yet reached the boundaries of the empire, and these folk spoke a dialect of their own.

So it fell to our crafty old *pochteca* to barter for us; and in all fairness to him, it appeared he struck a decent bargain.

"Tomorrow, we will go to the big river," Eyahue announced. "Tipalo and the others will help us fell *marupa* trees and build canoes." He cast a critical eye over our company. "At least nine will be needed. It is a great many trees. For this and additional supplies, we will give them your horses. If we survive and return to reclaim these horses..." He shrugged. "Well, then we will strike a new bargain."

"Do you not expect to survive this journey?" I asked him.

Eyahue sucked his remaining teeth in a meditative fashion, rocking back on his heels and reaching out to sling one wiry arm around the waist of a giggling village woman who may or may not have been part of the bargain he'd struck on our behalf. "I have survived it before," he admitted. "Many times. But I am old now."

"Not *that* old," Balthasar observed.

"Old enough." He squeezed the woman's buttocks, eliciting further laughter. "But young enough, too!"

On the following day, we hiked deeper into the jungle and got our first look at the big river. At a glance, it didn't look as intimidating as I'd feared. It was a wide swath of slow-moving milky-green water that led deeper and deeper into the depths of the jungle. But Eyahue had proved himself right time and time again, and when he assured us that the placid river would develop deadly rapids in the leagues ahead of us, I did not doubt him.

The *marupa* trees grew tremendously tall, with very straight trunks ideally suited for making long dugout canoes. The villagers indicated two that would be acceptable and set out scouring for others while our party began the task of felling and hollowing the first two trees, sharpening hatchets and adzes dulled in the digging of a mass grave after the attack of the Cloud People.

Even with so many willing hands and the aid of the villagers, it was a considerable job, and we were at it for days. The men worked in shifts, taking turns with our limited number of tools.

My offers to help were rebuffed, so I spent the time in the village getting to know its inhabitants as best I could without a shared tongue, relying on the knack of nonverbal communication I'd developed during the long winter I'd spent among the Tatars.

The women were hard at work knotting sturdy hammocks out of sisal fiber, part of the supplies for which Eyahue had bartered. They showed me how to tie the intricate knots, although I could not match the swift dexterity of their practiced fingers. They also showed me how to weave palm fronds into mats. They used the mats for seating, but the women indicated to me with gestures that they could also provide shelter from rainfall.

Between the outskirts of the savannah and the inner verges of the jungle, the villagers grew a fair number of crops. There was no *maize* here, but there were many of the other fruits and vegetables I'd come to know since we'd landed on Terra Nova: nourishing sweet potatoes, rich, silken-fleshed avocados, tart fruits that resembled overgrown pinecones topped with a tufted shock of leaves, papayas like melons that grew on trees.

Using nets and basket traps, they caught a variety of fish: big whiskered bottom-dwellers, long eel-like fish, fierce little fish with deceptively sharp teeth. I learned quickly to be wary of the latter.

All in all, it was a rather idyllic existence; but Eyahue warned us time and time again not to be deceived.

There would be no crops in the jungle save those stores we brought with us. What could be cultivated within its depths was guarded by wary, hostile natives who did not welcome intruders. There were fish and game, but hunting was notoriously difficult in the dense undergrowth, and even fishing was likely to prove an exhausting endeavor after a hard day's travel.

And so I paid attention to the village children. When they weren't engaged in play, they spent much of their days gathering less orthodox fare to augment the village's diet. They taught me how to chisel open rotting palm logs using a sharp-edged rock to get at the thick, wriggling grubs inside, which they plucked out and wrapped in palm leaves to cook.

Balthasar Shahrizai stared at me in outright horror when I sampled one. "Elua have mercy! That may be the most disgusting thing I've ever seen."

The flesh was chewy, but the taste was palatable. "If it's a matter of survival, you'll eat them too, my lord," I said to him.

He shuddered. "I'm not sure I wouldn't rather die."

Bao reached over and popped one in his mouth, chewing with relish. "Not so bad," he pronounced.

The children also caught lizards and frogs when they could, showing me which were good to eat. When I spotted a brilliant blue fellow with black speckles clinging to the bark of a tree with his webbed feet, I indicated it inquiringly. They batted my hand away with alarm, shaking their heads vehemently.

One of the older boys pointed into the depths of the jungle, then smeared his palms over his cheeks in a gesture I didn't fully understand, although its meaning seemed clear to the others. He acted out a stealthy pantomime of hunting and stalking, raising a clenched fist to his lips and blowing sharply through it in the direction of one of his mates, who clutched at his throat and toppled over in mock rigor.

I got the message.

Later, Eyahue confirmed it. "Oh, yes. Anything brightly colored is like to be poisonous. Snakes, frogs, lizards." He shrugged. "Here's a simple rule. If it's pretty to the eye, don't touch it, lady."

"The hostiles hunt with poison?" I asked him.

He nodded. "Blowpipes and arrows. But don't worry." The old *pochteca* patted my arm in a fatherly gesture. "They are very skillful in the ways of the jungle. If they decide to kill you, you'll never even see it coming."

This was not exactly comforting.

FORTY-EIGHT

———✦———

Several days after our arrival in Tipalo's village, we took our leave of it.

We had nine dugout canoes built of *marupa* wood; light and brittle, excavated and hewn to sophisticated sleekness with a combination of native expertise and Septimus Rousse's knowledgeable counsel, each vessel capable of sitting up to four men.

We left behind two pack-horses, but we had replenished food stores, as much as we could carry stuffed in satchels lashed to a cross-bar in the center of each canoe. We had a woven sisal hammock for each man among us, and an assortment of nets and fish-traps.

I prayed it would be enough.

Everyone with any kind of skill with a paddle had been assigned a vessel. The rest had been decided by lot. Wary of being dragged down and drowned by the weight of their armor, most of the men had elected to pile it in the bottoms of the canoes, wearing only their helmets with the chin-straps unbuckled.

One by one, our canoes were launched.

Standing along the banks of the big river, the villagers waved farewell to us, calling out encouragement.

Eyahue's canoe went first, with Captain Rousse following close behind him. Bao and I were in the third vessel, Temilotzin in the fourth. After that, it was catch as catch can.

On the morning of the first day, it began to rain, fat drops dimpling the milky-green surface of the river. We paddled through the rain. An hour or so after it had begun, the skies cleared and the sun returned.

Come noon, the sun stood high overhead, beating down on us like a hammer. The jungle steamed like a *temazcalli*, the air thick and hard to breathe. Everyone sweated profusely, and clouds of mosquitoes and gnats enveloped us.

"Gods!" Balthasar, seated behind me, leaned over and spat into the river. "Seems I'll be eating my share of insects after all."

I was hot, itchy, and miserable, my arms aching with the unfamiliar strain of paddling, but I did my best to bear it without a complaint. Eyahue reckoned we had three weeks on the river before we reached the city of Vilcabamba, the easternmost stronghold of the empire of Tawantinsuyo. With the worst yet to come, there was no point in complaining at the outset of this leg of the journey.

With an hour's daylight left, Eyahue spotted a stretch of rocky shoreline large enough to beach all nine canoes and ordered us to make camp. It felt as though we'd travelled a great distance into the jungle. Tipalo's village might have been only a day's journey behind us, but it lay upriver and would not be so easily regained. Assuming we survived, our plan was to return via a land passage. According to Eyahue, there was another river farther south that flowed from west to east through the jungle, an even greater river with hundreds of tributaries, but not even he had traversed it.

In the absence of other human inhabitants, or at least none we could see, the jungle seemed denser and more wild. To me, it felt like one great living creature, the trees and plants growing so thick and close-packed that I couldn't pick out individual senses among them— just one enormous green being with its own heartbeat pulsing, inhaling and exhaling in long, slow breaths.

Despite my fatigue and aching muscles, I found it exhilarating.

The rest of our company did not.

Almost to a man, they found the jungle ominous and frightening. Only Eyahue seemed inured to it, selecting the best place to sling his hammock and nap while the rest of us endeavored to make camp and prepare a meal.

With thirty-odd folk in our company, it was necessary to spread out and venture some distance into the jungle to find sufficient sites for our hammocks. A full half the men elected to forgo them, clearing spaces on the rocky shore and wrapping themselves in cloaks.

I had to own, when night fell, even I was uneasy. Beneath the canopy of the jungle, the darkness was absolute. Creatures that slept during the day came alive under the cover of darkness, and the night was filled with sounds—small sounds like the incessant whine of insects, and other, more menacing sounds.

Thanks to my sojourn in the palace gardens in Tenochtitlan, I recognized the deep, coughing roar of a jaguar.

"Moirin?" Bao whispered from his nearby hammock.

"Aye?"

"It's going to be all right," he said with an assurance I knew he didn't feel. "We're going to be fine."

Grateful for the lie, I returned it. "I know."

In the morning, those who had chosen to sleep on the ground regretted their decision, waking to find themselves stiff and bruised from sleeping on the stony shore, and bitten by an array of insects that hadn't troubled those of us in hammocks. Denis de Toulard in particular scratched himself furiously, his nose twitching all the while.

"Gods, man!" Balthasar, who had slept in a hammock and looked reasonably well rested, eyed him. "What ails you? Have you got the palsy?"

"Ants," Denis said briefly. "They're everywhere."

I winced, having forgotten. The fallen spirit Caim with his owl's eyes and a bird's nest in his antlers had taught the language of ants to all the members of the Circle of Shalomon save me—and it had proved nothing but a plague and a nuisance to them. It was the reason Lianne Tremaine, the former King's Poet, lived in a tower chamber at Eglantine House. Given the terrain through which we'd already passed, the fact that Denis hadn't evinced his discomfort until now was a testament to his will.

"Stone and sea! I'm so sorry, my lord," I said to him with genuine remorse. "This must be the worst place in the world for you."

Denis gave me a wry glance. "It's no more than I deserve, Moirin. Raphael must have suffered the same." He shrugged. "Mayhap it's the gods' way of allowing us to atone for our sins."

Balthasar examined his fingernails. "As a scion of mighty Kushiel, I assure you, he does not use *ants* as an instrument of atonement."

I ignored him, approaching Denis and laying one hand on his cheek. "My lord, you have atoned and more," I said softly. "You have saved us twice over—once aboard the ship, and secondly when the Cloud People attacked us. Were it not for your warning, they would have slaughtered us in our sleep. I daresay the gods have forgiven you."

His eyes brightened with emotion. "You truly think so?"

I nodded. "I do."

Denis let out his breath and rubbed his twitching nose. "Let's go find Thierry and the others," he said with renewed resolve.

Once again, we launched our canoes, carrying them over the rocks, mindful of the brittle wood.

The first few days on the big river were days of sameness. The river unfurled before us like a broad, milky-green ribbon, leading us ever deeper and deeper into the depths of the jungle. We rode atop its breast in our canoes, paddling, ever paddling. Our arms and shoulders grew stronger, muscles toughening as we journeyed.

It rained almost every day, but not for long. We grew accustomed to ignoring the rain, bailing out our vessels as necessary, trusting that the rain would end. Sooner or later, the sun came out and steamed us dry. By day we paddled; by night, we made camp along the banks of the river, eating fruits and roasted sweet potatoes and sleeping in hammocks strung between trees, all of us doing our best not to heed the sounds of the jungle at night. Bit by bit, we began to relax a little.

That was a mistake.

I was fishing when we took the first casualty of our river journey. Calling on the skills of my youth, I'd gone a few dozen yards downstream with Bao, summoning the twilight once we were out of sight. Lying on my belly on a rocky promontory, I coaxed the bottom-dwelling whiskered fish into my hands, grabbing them and tossing them to Bao, who stuffed them deftly into a reed creel.

While immersed in the business of procuring food, we heard cries from the campsite behind us.

Bao and I exchanged a glance. "We'd better go," he said.

I nodded, releasing the twilight. "Don't forget the fish."

When we reached the campsite, we found one of our men on the ground, his chest heaving as he struggled futilely for air—Eric Morand, a mercenary from Camlach province.

My own throat tightened. "What happened?"

"Went gathering firewood and got bitten by a snake." Eyahue nodded at Temilotzin, who held up a headless, writhing length of crimson-banded serpent, his broad face dispassionate. "I told you, if it's pretty to the eye, don't touch it."

I stared in horror at Eric Morand, who stared back at me with wide, stricken eyes. "Can't we do something? Anything?"

Eyahue shook his head. "Nothing but give him the mercy blow," he said gently. "Do you want it?"

Kneeling beside the Camaeline mercenary, I asked him if he wanted the mercy blow. "Can you blink?" I asked, tears streaming down my face. "If you can, blink once for yes."

His eyes closed once, and opened.

I beckoned to Temilotzin, who stooped beside me. He placed one hand on Eric Morand's brow with unexpected tenderness. With the other, he placed the tip of his obsidian dagger over his heart, driving it home with one efficient thrust.

Eric Morand went still forever.

A stark mood settled over the camp that evening. It was impossible to dig a grave in the dense, root-packed floor of the jungle, so we built a cairn instead, gathering stones and heaping them over our fallen comrade's body. Once again, Septimus Rousse gave the invocation. This time, there were no fond jests.

No one had much of an appetite for the fish I'd caught, but we roasted them and ate them anyway, doling out a few bites for every-one, aware that we couldn't afford to waste food. The cairn loomed in the gathering darkness, a harsh reminder of the day's tragedy.

When we launched our canoes the next morning, I felt as though Eric Morand's stricken gaze followed us from beneath the cairn, watching as we journeyed farther down the river, abandoning him.

And when the rain began to fall, it almost seemed appropriate—at least at first. But instead of tapering off by mid-day as it had in the past, it only rained harder and harder. The placid river began to swell, the current increasing until we were no longer paddling to propel our vessels, but merely to control them. The rain fell in sheets, blinding us and throwing a thick veil over the world.

Through the downpour, I could dimly make out Eyahue's canoe ahead of ours veering sharply to the left. In the prow, Bao loosed a shout of alarm at the sight of a nearly submerged boulder.

"Left! Left, as hard as you can!" he yelled.

Paddling madly, we managed to pass it, calling out warnings to the vessels behind us. Ahead of us, Eyahue pointed frantically toward the shore. It took all our strength to paddle hard enough to cut across the current.

Alas, not everyone behind us was as fortunate.

I was helping drag our canoe ashore when the cries went up on the river. Shielding my eyes against the rain with one hand, I saw that one of the vessels had struck the boulder and overturned. Free of its burden, the canoe shot away downriver, carried by the swift current, leaving four men struggling against it.

Others were trying to help, but it was impossible to fight the current long enough to drag them into the canoes. Two of the men began swimming hard toward the shore, making slow headway. One was clinging to the boulder, and I could no longer see the fourth.

Bao plunged into the river without hesitation, wading armpit-deep into the water and shouting encouragement to the swimmers. How he kept his footing in the current, I couldn't imagine. All I knew was that it terrified me.

"Your husband is a madman," Balthasar muttered before going after him, picking his way with obvious difficulty.

Together, they managed to help the exhausted swimmers to shore, and I do not think those men would have made it to safety without them.

"Who's left out there?" Balthasar gasped.

The L'Agnacite Jean Grenville coughed and retched and spat out river water. "De Montague's on the rock," he said hoarsely. "Didn't see what happened to Longchamps."

One by one, the remaining canoes reached the shore. The downpour continued unabated. In the middle of the rising river, Mathieu de Montague wrapped his arms around a boulder that would soon be wholly submerged.

"Can we reach him on foot?" Bao asked Jean Grenville.

He shook his head. "Too deep."

Balthasar pushed the sodden hair from his eyes. "Can he swim? If he can't, in another ten minutes, he'll be swept away."

Jean gave a weary nod. "A little, I think. Just not well."

"We'll get as close as we can," Bao said decisively. "Link arms, make a chain. It's our only chance."

I watched with my heart in my throat as ten of our strongest men put Bao's plan into action, clasping each other's wrists and plunging into the raging water in a long chain, a bit downriver of where Mathieu clung to his increasingly tenuous perch, straining to keep his head above water.

Our redoubtable Jaguar Knight Temilotzin anchored the chain, his feet planted firmly on the shore.

Of course, Bao led it.

Once again, he waded up to his armpits in the fierce current. Balthasar maintained a hard grip on Bao's left wrist, his other hand clasped around Brice de Bretel's wrist. Bao reached out his right hand in Mathieu de Montague's direction.

Between the hissing rain and the torrent of the river, I couldn't hear what Bao shouted to the lad, but Mathieu shook his head in terrified refusal. The rain fell harder and the river rose further

Bao shouted at him again.

Whatever he'd shouted, it didn't matter. A fresh surge of water dislodged Mathieu from his rock. Paddling dog-wise, his neck craned at an awkward angle, he made his way toward Bao's extended right hand.

Ah, gods!

It was close, so close. Peering through the rain, I saw Mathieu sputter and put out his hand with only a few feet between them. Bao lunged for him and came up short, his empty fingers grasping at air. The entire chain of men lurched forward, staggering in the current, every last one of them in danger of losing their footing and being swept away.

On the shore, Temilotzin grunted and heaved backward, stabilizing the chain.

Bao made one last desperate lunge in vain, his effort curtailed by Balthasar Shahrizai's death-grip on his wrist.

In the space of a single heartbeat, the moment passed and the opportunity vanished. The ferocious current carried Mathieu de Montague downriver past Bao's reach, his open mouth gaping in dismay.

The river swallowed him, and he was gone.

Depressed and defeated, our men retreated, helping one another straggle ashore, dropping with exhaustion once they reached it.

The green walls of the jungle rose around us in mockery.

And the rain kept falling.

FORTY-NINE

It rained for three days.

Our campsite was a sodden, miserable place plagued by guilt. For a surety, there was plenty of it to go around. We had lost two men in the accident—Mathieu de Montague, whose fate everyone had seen, and a fellow named Uriel Longchamps, who had sunk and vanished without a trace after the canoe had overturned. Although we'd searched along the bank of the river until nightfall, there was no sign of either of them.

"It is my fault," Eyahue said in a morose tone. "I knew the river was too high. I should have called for a landing sooner."

Bao studied his hands. "I was *so close*! I should have had him."

"Mathieu de Montague wanted to turn back," I murmured. "He was afraid. And we talked him out of it."

"*I* did," Balthasar corrected me. "I shamed him. I should have let him go."

"You should have let me go after him in the river," Bao accused him.

"I should have done no such thing, messire!" Balthasar retorted. "Are you strong enough to swim for two in that current?" He shook his head. "None of us are. You would either have been carried away with him or forced to let him go. I'll not apologize for sparing you that choice."

While we grieved and bickered, the rain continued to fall. Our food stores were dwindling at an alarming rate, fruit rotting in the incessant damp, and a portion of our supplies lost in the canoe that had been swept away. With current running as high and fast as it was, fishing proved a futile endeavor.

Gear rusted, soaked clothing began tearing at the seams. Insects plagued us day and night. Their bites itched and festered. Minor injuries, cuts and scrapes and blisters, grew dangerously infected. My own palms were badly blistered from all the paddling, great water-logged blisters that showed no sign of healing. At times I could have wept for the sheer physical misery of it all.

But I reminded myself that we were all lucky to be alive to endure it, and distracted myself by weaving mat after mat of palm fronds, teaching some of the men to do the same. With his Siovalese affinity for engineering, Denis de Toluard directed others in building a rough shelter on the verge of the jungle where at least we could huddle beneath the scant protection our mats afforded.

And on the second day, Eyahue vanished into the jungle for several hours, borrowing a sword to hack his way through. He returned with a satchel full of leaves that released a crisp, astringent odor when bruised, ordering us to grind them to a paste to smear on any open wounds.

It stung like fury, but it seemed to help. By the next day, my blisters were no longer seeping.

"Is that one of your secret herbs?" I asked Eyahue.

He nodded reluctantly. "The *ticitls* pay a great deal for this medicine."

I smiled wearily at him. "Thank you for sharing it with us."

After three straight days of rain, waking to clear skies seemed like a gift of the gods. The rain had stopped in the small hours of the night, and already the river was visibly lower, no longer a raging torrent.

Everything sparkled in the light of dawn, rain-washed and glistening, drops still sliding from the leaves. It was like being in a vast green temple, and for the first time in days, my sense of wonder at the enormity of the jungle returned.

For a mercy, it was an uneventful day on the river. Although we'd lost one canoe, sadly, due to the casualties we'd sustained, there were enough seats to go around in the remaining eight. We searched in vain for the bodies of our lost men as we paddled, regretfully concluding by the day's end that there was no chance of retrieving them.

At Septimus Rousse's suggestion, we built a small cairn in their honor, and he once again gave the invocation.

Our journey continued.

Some days after our loss, we had our first encounter with hostile natives—or at least a near-miss of an encounter. We were some hours into the day's travel when I heard a series of sharp buzzing sounds. Glancing around to see what new swarm of insects had come to torment us, I realized belatedly that the sound I'd heard was arrows in flight.

There was no telling where they'd come from. On either shore, the jungle looked as impenetrable as ever. Even as I searched, a second flight was launched. There was a metallic ping and a startled cry behind us as an arrow struck someone's helmet.

In the lead canoe, Eyahue was shouting. "Get low! Get low and paddle hard!"

My pulse hammering, I hunched as low as I could, paddling awkwardly. The dugout canoe afforded little in the way of protection. For once, I envied the men their heavy steel helmets.

A third volley hissed above us, and then there was silence. Still, we paddled in a crouch until Eyahue announced it was safe to sit upright.

Shouting up and down the river and taking stock of the situation, we determined with relief that our company had sustained no casualties in the attack. It was a Namarrese fellow named Marcel d'Aubrey who had taken a strike to the helmet, and although he was shaken, he was unharmed.

Once we had ascertained that there were no injuries, I asked Bao to bring us alongside Eyahue's canoe.

"You said if the hostiles decided to kill us, we'd never see it coming," I reminded the old *pochteca*. "So what passes here?"

"That?" He rested his paddle across his knobby knees and scoffed. "Oh, that was just a warning. They were just telling us to keep moving."

"If Messire d'Aubrey hadn't been wearing a helmet, they would have killed him," I observed.

Eyahue sucked his teeth. "True," he admitted. "I imagine they were curious about those shiny head-pieces." He shrugged. "Now they know."

It was an effective reminder of the myriad dangers the jungle held, but in the days that followed, it grew obvious that hostile natives were the least of our concerns.

First and foremost was the shortage of food. Already, we were eating but two meals a day while expending considerable energy. The last of our fruit was long gone, and if our stores were to last until we reached Vilcabamba, we were down to half a roasted sweet potato a day for every person in our company.

It wasn't enough.

Our bellies complained, and our strength waned, leaving us weak and listless. Our efforts to fish with nets and traps yielded meager results. I had better luck fishing with my familiar childhood methods, calling the twilight and coaxing fish into my bare hands; but where a catch of four or five good-sized fish would have provided a veritable feast for my mother and me, it didn't go far among thirty-some starving men.

Eyahue found my success suspicious. "How do you and your husband catch more fish than anyone?" he asked. "Why do you always go away alone to do it instead of sharing your secret?"

"It's a gift from my mother's people," I told him. After the way the Emperor had reacted to the small gift of magic I had displayed in his gardens, I was wary of the *pochteca's* response if I told him the whole truth. "It cannot be taught, and the fish will not come if there are others present."

Gods knew, that was true enough, and it seemed to mollify Eyahue.

It was a good thing I'd paid attention to the children in Tipalo's village, for it wasn't long before we were relying on their lessons. Several of our men became quite expert grub-hunters, and we discovered that they were slightly more palatable when skewered and roasted. True to his word, Balthasar held out and refused such fare. I wished he wouldn't, for he was developing a feverish look I didn't like. More than once, I'd caught him shivering in the heat and trying to hide it.

"Bao's right," Denis said to him, chewing a mouthful of grub-worm with fierce determination. "It's not so bad."

"Not so good, either," someone muttered.

Although we scoured the outskirts of the jungle and plundered the river for edible game as best we could, it still wasn't enough. There were just too many of us.

The day we spotted a herd of *capybaras* wallowing and grazing along the edge of the big river, I thought mayhap our luck had changed. They were odd-looking beasts; extraordinarily oversized rodents with coarse coats, squealing and grunting and nudging one another as they swam and rooted among the weeds.

"Bao!" I whispered, setting down my paddle. I scrabbled for my bow and nocked an arrow. "Bring us close!"

He nodded, paddling.

We drifted sideways alongside the herd. They ignored us. Rising carefully to one knee in the narrow vessel, I picked my target and took aim at a big, fat, well-fed fellow. I thought to myself that he would make a meal for all of us, and if I were quick, I might even be able to kill two of them.

Before I had a chance to loose my arrow, the water erupted. To call the creature that emerged a snake didn't begin to do it justice. It *was* a snake, but it was far, far bigger than any snake I'd ever seen in my life, as long as two of our canoes placed end to end, a thick, sinuous, shining length of mottled yellow and black.

I let out a scream.

Everything seemed to happen at once. The snake lunged at the fat *capybara* I'd chosen as my prey, sinking its teeth into it and twining around it. In a trice, it had the creature wrapped within its coils.

The canoe rocked violently to one side as all of us recoiled in shock, then pitched hard to the other as everyone overcompensated in an effort to stabilize it. If I'd been seated, I daresay it wouldn't have mattered, but I was kneeling and unbalanced, and the momentum flung me overboard.

I hit the water. It was churning with the force of the snake's attack, the flight of the other *capybaras*, the splash of my impact. Underwater, the snake's yellow and black coils rotated before my open eyes through the rising sediment, impossibly thick.

Flailing backward, I got my head above water and found myself face-to-face with the serpent, its dull eyes regarding me impassively above the jaws locked onto its prey. Having a good rapport with animals, I'd never been one to harbor an unreasonable fear of them, but the suddenness of the snake's attack and the incomprehensible enormity of it, coupled with my very, very vulnerable position, struck terror into my heart.

In the canoe, everyone was shouting. I felt hands grasp beneath my arms as Bao and Balthasar hauled me forcibly into the canoe.

"Go!" Bao shouted to Brice de Bretel in the stern. "Go, go, go!"

Paddling frantically, Brice managed to propel us some yards away, the canoe rocking dangerously as the others scrambled to regain their positions. I sat on the floor of the dugout, gasping and shuddering, my bow still gripped in one hand.

Behind us, the snake unhinged its jaw to an unholy degree as it commenced the process of swallowing its prey whole.

That night at camp, the giant snake was the topic of much discussion. Temilotzin was disgruntled. "You should have killed it once it began to feed," he said to me, making a chopping gesture with one hand. "Cut off its head. That is when they are the least dangerous."

"I'm sorry," I said humbly. "We didn't know."

Temilotzin pointed at the three men who shared his canoe. "After we passed you, I tried to make them turn back so I could do it myself. But they pretended not to understand." He jerked his chin in disdain. "They were scared."

"We all were," Bao murmured.

Eyahue assured us that the giant snakes very rarely attacked humans. "Unless you're stupid enough to fall right on top of it," he added, laughing at his own jest. "Lucky for you he already had his prey! Too bad, though." His expression turned rueful as he rubbed his sunken belly. "We could have been eating meat."

"I'm sorry," I repeated.

"How did you not see somewhat so big?" Denis asked me.

"I don't know," I admitted. "If I caught a glimpse of it, I must have thought it was a log. I was concentrating on the *capybara*."

"None of us saw it," Bao agreed. "It wasn't Moirin's fault." He stroked my hair. "Please do not frighten me so again."

"Believe me, I'll try not to." I sighed, rotating a skewer of sizzling grubs over the campfire. "Gods bedamned snake! I had a clean shot, too." I glanced over at Balthasar, who was unwontedly quiet, his arms wrapped around his knees, trying to suppress a shiver in the warm evening air. "Will you not try them, my lord?" I entreated him, holding out the skewer. "Just once?"

He shook his head. "I'm not that hungry."

"How can you not be?" one of the men grumbled on the far side of our campfire. "Name of Elua! Send them my way, won't you?"

"You're not well," I said softly, ignoring the complaint. "You need to eat and keep your strength up."

Balthasar lifted his head and glared at me. Famine had whittled away at his beautiful features until his cheekbones stood out like blades, his dark blue eyes set in sunken hollows above them. "Leave be, won't you? I'm fine, Moirin!"

He wasn't.

And that was the second worst of our problems.

FIFTY

<hr/>

It wasn't just Balthasar Shahrizai. Over the course of days, seven other men began showing signs of fever, alternating between shivering despite the day's heat, and sweating even more profusely than the rest of us. I was sorry to see that Jean Grenville, one of our steady L'Agnacites and best foragers, was among them; but Balthasar was the worst of the lot by far, his condition deteriorating at an alarming rate.

Ah, gods! Truth be told, all of them worried me, more than I cared to let on. Every night, I prayed.

We reached stretches of perilous rapids that took all our hard-won skill to navigate, twisting and plunging through narrow passages between rocks. Whenever possible, we disembarked and transported the canoes and their goods manually along the shore, which was infinitely more exhausting, but far less dangerous.

All of us were weaker than we had been for lack of food, but the sick men labored harder at both chores. When we made camp at night, they lacked the strength to do aught but sweat and shiver.

I was afraid for them, and afraid for the rest of us, too. If the disease passed to our entire company, we wouldn't be able to continue. We would simply starve to death here in the jungle.

"It is not that kind of sickness," Eyahue told me. "It does not pass from one person to another." He blew out his breath. "Bad spirits in the air cause it."

"Is there anything we can do?" I asked him.

He nodded. "Smoke will help drive them away. Put green wood on the fire."

Whether or not it helped, I could not say. No one else took ill, but those who were already sick continued to worsen.

When we found a campsite not far from a slow-moving segment of river where the whiskery fish were particularly abundant, I called for a day's rest. While others foraged for frogs and grubs and the sick men rested, Bao and I spent the entire day downriver cloaked in the twilight, catching fish.

By the day's end, we had over two dozen. We wrapped them in leaves and steamed them over the fire, everyone cramming the slightly gamey flesh into their mouths with their fingers. I made sure all of the sick men had an entire fish to themselves, hovering over Balthasar to be certain he ate every last bite while he scowled at me, squinting against the green-wood smoke of our campfire.

I hoped it would help.

It didn't.

Come daybreak, the sick men were no better, and Balthasar's condition had worsened markedly. He was shaking so hard he could barely sit upright, and in the clear light of dawn, I was shocked to see that the whites of his eyes had turned a vivid hue of yellow, eerily bright in contrast to his dark blue irises. Until that moment, I'd doubted Eyahue's talk of bad spirits, but now I wondered.

The old *pochteca* called me aside. "Your friend is going to die before we reach Vilcabamba," he said bluntly. "Maybe others, too. Today's journey will be very hard. They are too sick. It would be better to leave them now."

My heart ached. "Is there nothing else we can do? No way to save them?"

He hesitated.

"Eyahue!" I grabbed his scrawny shoulders and shook him. "If you know something you're not telling me, I swear by stone and sea and all that they encompass, I will kill you myself!"

"All right!" He fended me off. "Yes, maybe. Maybe! But it is dangerous." He pointed downriver. "First, we must pass through a gorge with fast rapids. There is no place to carry the canoes and your sick men will be no help. But if we make it through, there is a tree that grows in the heights whose bark is poisonous to the bad spirits."

"It will cure them?" I asked, hoping against hope.

Eyahue scowled at me. "*If* I can find it, and *if* I do not get killed trying. Where it grows, there are hostiles for sure, the last of the wild forest tribes before we reach Vilcabamba."

"We have to try," I said. "Please?"

He sighed. "If we survive the rapids, I will try."

I kissed his wizened cheek. "Thank you, Eyahue."

I explained the situation to the others. No one wanted to leave ailing men behind, although Balthasar protested the decision.

"As one of the sponsors of this expedition, I must advise against this as a bad investment," he said in a wry tone that did nothing to belie his underlying seriousness. He regarded us with those uncanny yellow-and-blue eyes and tried unsuccessfully to fight off a violent bout of shivering, his teeth chattering. "I'll only be a burden to you." He clenched his jaw to silence them, gritting out his words. "Leave me. I'm not jesting. This is a bad idea. Save the others who aren't as far gone." He coughed. "If you want to give me a fitting tribute, gather a few flowers of surpassing beauty to strew over my impending corpse before you go, won't you?"

Bao poked him with the butt-end of his staff. "No. Don't be stupid. Now get up and get in the canoe."

Balthasar smiled bitterly, holding out one trembling hand. "What if I can't?"

"I'll carry you," Bao retorted. "Shall I?"

It was a test of wills, and I daresay it may have been the first Balthasar Shahrizai lost in his lifetime. Beneath Bao's unrelenting stare, he heaved himself upright with a considerable effort, wavering on his feet. Bao handed him his bamboo staff and Balthasar leaned on it, breathing hard, his breath rasping in his lungs, his free hand on Bao's shoulder to steady himself. "You're a stubborn one, aren't you?"

"He is," I agreed.

Bao looked sidelong at me, a world of fond intimacy in a single glance. "No more than you, Moirin."

For what felt like the hundredth time, we launched our canoes. At Septimus Rousse's sensible suggestion, we had redistributed our company so that every canoe held but one of the fever-stricken men, seated in the third slot.

In the first hour of our journey, we paddled along the serene face of the river. It rained for a time, and then the skies cleared once more. And then the river began to quicken. The banks rose and narrowed, the current picking up pace. Protruding boulders began to place obstacles in our path, water breaking around them in telling patterns.

At first, I tried to pay attention to the entire company, but once we entered the rapids, it was impossible. Stony walls rose around us, the river hurtling us onward beneath their shadow. In the prow, Bao called out orders.

"Left!" he called, digging his paddle in at a sharp angle. "Now right, right, hard right!"

The river rose and fell, crashed and thundered.

Everywhere, spray spurted, stinging my face.

I narrowed my eyes and kept paddling. Behind me, Balthasar huddled and shivered. In the stern, Brice planted his paddle as ordered, grunting with the effort of trying to keep us in a clear channel through the raging waters.

In the prow, Bao had risen to his knees, paddling fiercely on either side of the canoe, maneuvering us around boulders. Master Lo's magpie had always claimed he could do whatever was needful. As ever, he was as good as his word. Our canoe shot through the rapids like a cork.

We emerged into a scene of tranquil beauty. Beneath towering cliff walls covered with emerald moss, the river widened once more, turning placid despite the influx of a slender waterfall that spilled over the crags, sparkling in the sunlight. Ahead of us, Eyahue's canoe was making landfall on the rocks at the base of the cliff.

Instead of following him, Bao turned us sideways to the rapids behind us, idling on the water and watching to make sure the other six vessels made it safely through the dangerous passage.

The first four made it through without incident, canoes bucking and plunging like wild horses, shooting through the final gap into the calm bay.

The fifth was not so lucky.

The fellow in the prow, an Eisandine fighter named Gaston Courtois, misjudged the angle of his approach. There was a sharp, splintering crack as the canoe struck the rocks on the starboard side. The force of its momentum carried it into the calm waters, where it drifted slowly into two pieces, the entire hull split in half. Dazed men clung to the pieces of their broken vessel while four sets of armor sank slowly to the floor of the river.

And behind them, the sixth canoe was making its inexorable way through the rapids, unable to slow its progress.

"Get out of the way!" Bao cupped his hands around his mouth and shouted. *"Get out of the way!"*

Gaston Courtois and the fellow behind him heard Bao and kicked frantically, propelling their half of the broken vessel clear of the gap.

The other half floundered, one man barely able to cling to the splintered wood, the other helping him keep his head above water, neither able to get out of the path of the oncoming final vessel.

"It's Jean," Brice said in anguish. "He's too weak!"

Bao stood with care, our narrow canoe rocking as he balanced on the balls of his feet. "Hold steady," he cautioned us before diving into the water, setting the canoe to rocking further.

Once again, it was a near thing. But this time, luck and the gods favored us.

Swimming strongly, Bao reached the shattered half of the canoe. Swearing and cajoling, one arm draped over the splintered *marupa* wood, his legs kicking, he did his best to drag it out of the collision path as the last vessel shot through the gap, daylight showing between its hull and the water.

And for a mercy, the very capable Septimus Rousse was at the helm in the prow of that vessel, anchoring our lineup along the course of the river with his expertise.

"Starboard!" he roared, digging in with his paddle and suiting actions to words. *"Starboard!"*

There was no collision.

Exhausted and weary, we dragged ourselves to shore one way or another. Most of us paddled our canoes.

Some swam.

Some drifted, clinging to spars. In time, all of us fetched up along the shore. The sick men were as sick as ever or worse. Jean Grenville shivered incessantly after his dunking, muttering incoherent apologies.

Balthasar regarded me with his uncanny yellow-and-blue eyes. "You should have left me. Now that we're down another canoe, you have no choice."

I shook my head. "No."

"There aren't enough to carry all of us, Moirin."

I gazed up at the moss-covered cliffs. "We'll deal with that problem later. We're not done here, my lord."

FIFTY-ONE

They're up there?" I asked Eyahue. "The trees with the bark we need?"

The old *pochteca* grunted in assent. "Maybe. But like I said, there are hostiles, too. I make no promises."

A sense of calm settled over me. "I'm going with you."

He shook his head. "No point. You'll only give them another target."

"I can conceal us," I said to him. "You wanted to know how I'm able to catch more fish than anyone else? They can't see me. That's the gift of my mother's folk. We're able to conceal ourselves."

Eyahue eyed me uncertainly. "Are you mad?"

"No." I led him some distance away until no one was watching, and bade him close his eyes. When he reluctantly obeyed, I summoned the twilight and wrapped it around us both. "Open your eyes."

He let out a sharp cry at finding the vivid green daylit jungle turned dim and silvery in the twilight. "What is this? Can you turn day into night?"

"No, no." I considered my words. "Our elders say it is a way of taking half a step into the spirit world, where eyes in the mortal world cannot see us. We are a peaceful folk. This is a gift our goddess gave us to protect us from our enemies."

Ignoring me for the moment, Eyahue returned to our landing site. He planted himself in front of Temilotzin, waving his arms at the spotted warrior. "Hey! Hey!"

"He cannot hear you," I said. "Not unless you *will* him to hear you."

Eyahue leaned forward. "Hey!" he shouted. Temilotzin startled, his eyes stretching wide as he glanced from side to side in confusion. Eyahue chuckled. "That's a pretty good trick." His amusement faded, giving way to stony regard. "Why didn't you use it the night Pochotl betrayed us?"

"It is a small gift," I said. "I cannot conceal an entire army, and I cannot use it when there are already eyes upon me." I pointed at the cliffs. "But I can conceal us from the hostiles for a time."

Eyahue sucked his teeth. "Did the Emperor know about this?"

"He knew I possessed a gift, yes." Having told a half-truth, I gambled with a whole one. "But I thought it might make you afraid if you knew."

It stung his Nahuatl pride. "Of you?" he scoffed. "I've survived a thousand and one dangers. Why would I fear a girl with a gift for hiding in the shadows?"

"Then you'll let me come with you?" I asked.

He nodded. "I will."

With relief, I let the twilight fade, causing Temilotzin to jump nearly out of his skin. Chuckling once more, Eyahue patted the Jaguar Knight's arm. "There's something I need to tell you about your little warrior," he said to him.

Although the shore wasn't suitable for making camp, there was a good-sized cave halfway up the cliff, accessible by a steep path among the moss-covered rocks. When we reached it, there were signs it had been used before, markings etched onto the walls of the cave and ashes from an old campfire. It made the presence of unseen hostiles all the more palpable.

Still, it was shelter and a level space on which to make camp, and we had little choice but to avail ourselves of it. With some difficulty, we managed to get everyone into the cave, the hale helping the ailing make the ascent.

"I know what you're about, Moirin," Bao said to me as we half carried, half dragged Balthasar into the cave. "You don't imagine I'm letting you go alone into the jungle with that old man, do you?"

I smiled tiredly at him over the top of Balthasar's sagging head. "Not for a minute."

He eased Balthasar to the cavern floor. "Good."

"I wish to Blessed buggering Elua that both of you would listen to reason." Slumping against the cave wall, Balthasar closed his eerie eyes, his breath rattling in and out of his lungs. "Stop wasting time. I'm dying." He shivered, wrapping his arms around his knees. "Don't pretend I'm not. This jungle is killing me. The bad spirits have won. They know I don't belong here. They're burning me up from the inside out. Do you really think there's some magic *tree bark* out there that will cure this?"

"Actually, I do." Bao hunkered on his heels before him. "Balthasar, listen to me."

The blue-and-yellow eyes cracked open.

"It's not bad spirits," Bao said firmly. "It's a disease that insects carry. We've known about it in Ch'in for four thousand years. My mentor Master Lo would have prescribed *qing hao* to cure you. It would have worked, too. I've seen it before."

Balthasar tilted his head back, regarding him under his eyelids. "You didn't see fit to mention this earlier?"

Bao shrugged. "That herb does not grow here. Until today, I did not know there was another medicine that might prove effective." Reaching out, he took one of Balthasar's limp hands in his own. "Try not to die until we find it, huh?"

Balthasar's laugh turned quickly to a rasping cough. Closing his eyes once more, he rested his chin on his knees. "I'll try."

Once our company was situated, we set out for the top of the cliff, following a narrow, winding path that forced us to climb with hands and feet, nails digging into the moss-slick rocks, the river dwindling beneath us as we ascended into the jungle heights. Our wiry *pochteca* Eyahue led the way, with Bao and me close behind him. Brice and a handful of others followed us in order to forage for firewood.

Behind us, we left Septimus Rousse in charge of the expedition, with Temilotzin to provide whatever guidance he might should we fail to return.

Atop the cliff, we parted ways.

Brice de Bretel inclined his head to me. "Good luck, my lady. I will pray for your success."

I nodded. "Thank you."

Eyahue beckoned, pointing to a faint path. "This way."

As soon as we were out of sight of the others, I called the twilight. Safe in its embrace, we followed thin trails forged by hostile inhabitants, many of them doubling back on themselves in an inexplicable fashion. The soft dusk of the twilight made everything dim, frustrating Eyahue.

"I cannot *see*!" he complained. "I cannot tell one tree from another!"

"Hush." Bao pointed. "Moirin?"

A small flock of ground-fowl rooted in the undergrowth before us. My heart quickened. Unslinging my bow from my shoulder, I nocked an arrow and took aim. I got two shots off before the flock scattered, taking down two plump birds.

Eyahue smacked his lips. "At least it wasn't a wasted trip! But if you want me to find you a *cinchona* tree, you're going to have to let your magic go."

Bao and I exchanged a glance. "It's your decision," he said.

I swallowed. "If I concentrate on paying attention every moment, I ought to be able to tell if someone's coming."

"Do it." Bao glanced at the silvery disk of the sun overhead. "If we don't find one within two hours, we'll turn back."

Apprehensively, I released the twilight. The world returned in a hot, humid rush of greenery, the sun blazing once more. Bao retrieved the ground-fowl I'd shot, which proved to be a rufous brown with striped tails in the daylight.

We set out once more, Eyahue poking at trees and muttering to himself. I paid him scant heed. I breathed the Breath of Earth's Pulse to ground myself and the Breath of Trees Growing, extending my senses into the depths of the jungle.

At home in the Alban wilderness of my childhood, I could have done this handily, especially if I'd had the luxury of staying very still in one place. But the need to keep moving made it more difficult, and the jungle was so profoundly dense and alive, it confounded my senses.

The sun crept across the sky. Even with the faint trails, it was hard going. Foliage caught at us, roots tripped us up. Sweat trickled between my shoulder blades, and gnats sought to crawl into my eyes. From moment to moment, my concentration wavered. I sent a wordless prayer to the Maghuin Dhonn Herself to lend me strength, and to Eisheth, the D'Angeline goddess of healing, to aid us in our quest.

On the edge of a small clearing, Eyahue scratched at a tree trunk with his obsidian dagger, peeling away a strip of bark and sniffing it. Bao busied himself with plucking one of the ground-fowl, glancing periodically at the sun with a worried look. I took the moment's respite to close my eyes and concentrate harder, casting out the net of my senses once more.

The thoughts of humans are as different from those of animals as animals from plants—keener, flowing inward and outward at the same time.

I sensed them now; men, several of them, considerably closer than I would have guessed, moving in our direction and spreading out to encircle us.

My skin prickled, and I opened my eyes. "Eyahue, there are men coming. Is that the tree?"

He glanced at me. "Eh? No, no." He tossed the strip of bark away. "Sorry, lady. Better call your magic."

Although I felt sick at heart at the prospect of failure, it was a relief to return to the dim, sheltering arms of the twilight, the green world fading once more; and all the more so when five figures emerged from the jungle surrounding the tiny clearing, moving with such stealth that not a single sound betrayed their passage.

They wore little in the way of clothing, only crude belts around their waists, woven headbands laced with palm fronds, and decorative shards of bone piercing the septums of their noses. Two carried bows and three carried blowpipes, all of them poised to take aim. Their faces, which oddly appeared to be a different hue than their bodies, reflected their confusion at finding their quarry vanished. They lowered their weapons and began calling to one another, arguing in a bewildered manner.

"Shall we slip past them?" Bao murmured.

A thought struck me. "Eyahue, they're speaking Quechua, aren't they? Would they know where to find the trees we need?"

"Them?" He jerked his chin at the hunters. "Of course."

"Are you *sure* they're hostile?" I asked. "Have you never traded with them?"

The old *pochteca* scratched his chin. "I haven't, but I've heard tell they've been known to trade with the civilized Quechua in Vilcabamba from time to time." His eyes took on a cunning gleam. "If you've a mind to take a risk, I've an idea." He nodded at the ground-fowl Bao carried. "What happens if he puts them down? Can the jungle folk see them?"

"Aye," I said uncertainly.

"And they can hear me if I will it?" Eyahue asked. I nodded. He chortled, rubbing his palms together. "Let's offer them a trade."

On Eyahue's orders, Bao set down the two plump birds I'd slain and backed away from them.

The hunters pointed and shouted at their sudden appearance.

Taking a deep breath, Eyahue addressed them in as sonorous tones as he could manage in his reedy voice. I caught enough words I recognized to ascertain that he was offering the birds in trade for guidance to the nearest *cinchona* tree.

The hunters looked around frantically, here and there and everywhere, raising and lowering their weapons in their confusion.

Eyahue laughed so hard I thought he might wet himself, doubling over and slapping his scrawny thighs. "They think we are spirits! You should have more fun with this gift!" he said to me

I scowled at him. "Tell them we offer friendship in exchange for their aid."

He looked dubious. "Friendship?"

I thought about all the unlikely friends I'd made over the course of my life's journey, following my everlasting destiny; friends who had humbled me with their kindness. I thought about how I'd feared and avoided the Tatars due to their fearsome reputation, only to find generosity and hospitality among Batu's tribe on the Tatar steppe when I couldn't have survived without it. I nodded. "Tell them."

Reluctantly, he did.

The jungle folk conferred amongst themselves. One strode forward, addressing the empty air in a firm tone.

"They want to see us," Eyahue informed me. "They will not agree unless we show ourselves."

I took a deep breath. "Then we will do so. Ask them to lay down their weapons as a gesture of trust."

It was a tense moment. At last, the five men stooped and set down their weapons, glancing around uncertainly. I lowered my own bow to the ground. Bao unslung his staff, leaning unobtrusively on it.

I let the twilight go.

All of us stared at one another. The hunters' appearance in the daylight was startling, their faces painted bright red. I remembered the boy in Tipalo's village smearing his cheeks as he mimed a hunter with a blowpipe. The gesture was more ominous in retrospect; and yet there was fear in the hunters' eyes, more than I thought our emergence from the twilight warranted.

Their leader addressed us.

"He wants to know if we are spirits from the black river," Eyahue said in a puzzled tone.

"What does that mean?" I asked him.

The old man shrugged. "No idea."

"Tell him no," I said. "Tell him we are harmless, and we seek their help because our magic is weak here."

"I'm not telling him that!" Eyahue gave me a withering look. "You don't know the first thing about bartering, do you?"

"Moirin knows a great deal about befriending people," Bao said quietly. "I suggest you do it."

Grumbling, the *pochteca* acceded.

The hunters relaxed visibly. Moving slowly, I extended my hands palms upward, then placed them together in the soothing *mudra* of reassurance that the Rani Amrita had taught me so long ago. *"Sulpayki,"* I said carefully, bowing toward them. "Thank you."

Unexpectedly, the leader grinned, his teeth white against his crimson-painted face. He mimicked my gesture and replied in a rapid spate of Quechua, while one of the others picked up the ground-fowl and examined them with approval.

I glanced at Eyahue, who was looking thunderstruck. "He says they are honored by our visit," he said. "They saw our boats and our sick men and wondered if they should kill us before we joined the black river and grew stronger. But now that they know we are good spirits bringing gifts, they will help us." He nodded at the leader. "His name is Paullu. He says we should bring our people to his village, where they already have *cinchona* bark. The shaman there will heal them."

I bowed a second time. *"Sulpayki,* Paullu."

The naked hunter with the crimson face-paint returned my salute with dignity. *"Imamanta,"* he replied.

You're welcome.

FIFTY-TWO

⟡

itter!" Balthasar said in protest, making a face as he drank a
concoction of dried, powdered *cinchona* bark. "Ah, gods! It's so
bitter."

I folded my arms. "Just drink it."

Wincing, he did.

It had not been an easy task to escort eight feverish men up the
steepest part of the cliffs and trek for an hour through the jungle to
Paullu's village, but we had done it. Putting our trust in the hospitality
of our new friends, we'd left behind the last of our food stores with the
majority of our crew. Under Septimus Rousse's direction, they were
searching for a *marupa* tree to replace our lost canoe. In exchange for
the generosity of Paullu's villagers, we brought an array of glass and
crystal beads and a couple of hand mirrors that delighted them to
no end.

I found myself liking them.

Like the Maghuin Dhonn, they lived close to nature; and yet in
some ways, they were more sophisticated than my mother's solitary,
reclusive folk. The village was a surprisingly elaborate configuration
of thatch-roofed wooden buildings, often linked by bridges and walk-
ways. They fished and hunted and foraged, but they grew crops in the
jungle highlands, too.

Bao, who knew a great deal more about it than I did, praised their
shaman's knowledge of herb-lore.

"Look, Moirin." He plucked a leaf from a shrub the shaman Atoc had shown him, rubbing it on his forearm and releasing a sharp, not displeasing, odor. "It helps keep the mosquitoes at bay."

"I wonder how Eyahue missed that one in all his travels," I said ruefully. "Mayhap it amused the local folk to see him suffer. Would that we'd known of it sooner."

Bao shrugged. "Better now than never."

Mindful of my role as a good spirit bearing gifts, not to mention the additional burden our numbers placed on their stores, I made it a point to contribute every day with a gift of fish or game. Thanks to the narrow hunting trails that laced the usually impenetrable jungle, I was able to procure several more of the tasty ground-fowl over the course of our stay.

Bitterness notwithstanding, the *cinchona* bark proved an effective cure. Within three days in the village, all the afflicted men's fevers broke. There was no more incessant shivering, and the whites of Balthasar's eyes began to clear, their uncanny yellow hue fading.

And for another mercy, we were able to determine that an earlier company of white-faced strangers had passed this way. It seemed they were reckoned bad spirits from the black river, something that remained a mystery. Despite having referenced it upon our initial meeting, Paullu was reluctant to discuss the black river.

"It is bad," he said stubbornly. "Bad luck!" He shook his head vigorously. "You are good spirits, but you are no match for it. No one is. I should never have spoken of it. You should not go there. No one should go there anymore."

"Where?" I asked, pointing downriver. "Vilcabamba?"

Paullu flinched. "Yes."

"Why?"

He would not say. No one would. Only that it was a very bad thing, and to speak of it was to risk summoning it.

"It must have been a flood," Eyahue determined. "Farther into Tawantinsuyo, in the highlands, the rivers that flow down from the mountains sometimes run black with silt." He nodded at the narrow river that ran past the village, making its way to the big river. "I bet it flooded the day your prince passed through and turned black, maybe swept away a few people." He chuckled. "You know how superstitious these jungle folk can be."

I eyed him, thinking of the racks of skulls in the *tzompantli*. "I don't see any signs of a major flood here."

He shrugged. "It was a long time ago. The jungle grows back fast."

Whatever the truth, we got no more out of Paullu and the villagers. The mystery of the black river remained unsolved.

By the end of the third day, it was obvious that Balthasar and Jean and the others would be well enough to travel. Septimus Rousse reported that the replacement canoe was ready to launch. Since the beads had proved so popular among the villagers, Eyahue managed to barter several more strands for a renewed supply of sweet potatoes.

"We must have a feast before you go," Paullu announced. "You are good spirits, but you are weak. You will help our women prepare *masato* to give you strength."

I smiled at him. "You are kind."

Eyahue translated my words, and Paullu's face took on a serious expression. Reaching for my hand, he pressed it between his callused palms. "You do not know what you face. I tell you once more, you should not go to Vilcabamba."

My *diadh-anam* flared in protest. "I have to," I said simply.

Atoc, the village shaman, spoke. He was a cryptic fellow of indeterminate years, his dark eyes old and wise in his unlined face.

"He says you speak the truth," Eyahue reported in a somber tone. "And he will ask the spirits of the forest to bless you."

"*Sulpayki*, Atoc," I murmured, thanking him.

The shaman bent his head toward me. "*Imamanta.*"

"*Masato* will give you strength," Paullu repeated. "We will have a great feast in your honor."

I wondered what *masato* was and soon found out, somewhat to my dismay. It was a fermented beverage made by boiling and mashing manioc root, which was then chewed and spat into a large wooden tub, repeating the process over and over; a village endeavor undertaken collectively by all the women, one in which I was expected to participate.

Balthasar was horrified. "I think I'd rather eat grubs."

I had to own, the first warm, grainy mouthful made my stomach churn, but the village women were laughing and jesting, enjoying the communal nature of the process. Paullu's wife, Sarpay, pointed at Balthasar and made a suggestion that had all of them giggling.

"She says that since you are as pretty as a girl, you should help prepare the *masato*," Eyahue informed Balthasar.

The latter fixed the old man with a death glare, which only made the women laugh harder.

Water was poured over the macerated manioc, and the resulting liquid was left in the hot sun to ferment for long hours. Paullu and his men returned from hunting with great fanfare, having trapped and slaughtered a wild pig. This was butchered with care, wrapped in leaves and set to cook in a firepit. By the end of the day, the scent of roasting pork made my mouth water.

Before the feast commenced, the shaman Atoc summoned Eyahue, Bao, and me, the three good spirits, for a ceremonial blessing. First he brushed us all over with a whisk of palm fronds, calling on the spirits of the forest to protect us. Then, crouching over a bowl, he ignited a mixture of herbs. Drawing up the smoke through a hollow reed, he blew it into our faces while the villagers watched.

"That is strong magic," Paullu said in approval, fingering the strand of pale pink beads of rose quartz he now wore around his neck. "It will not keep you safe, but it will help."

Bowls of *masato* were filled from the tub and given to everyone. The milky beverage was largely tasteless, but the fermentation made it slightly fizzy, and after the second bowl, I could feel its effects. Despite his grumbling, I was pleased to see that Balthasar's sense of propriety overrode his reservations. With only the slightest grimace, he drained the bowl that Paullu's wife, Sarpay, offered to him

"If I didn't know how it was made, it wouldn't be that bad," he admitted, wiping his mouth. He smiled at our hostess. "*Sulpayki*, Sarpay."

With a delighted smile, she trotted off to refill his bowl.

Children shouted and clapped as the roasted pig was exhumed from the firepit, the rich, fatty aroma filling the air. We ate with our fingers, reveling in the abundance. Not even Balthasar could find fault with the pork.

Afterward, there was more *masato*, while the men danced with handheld drums, spinning in circles. And mayhap it was the effects of the manioc beer, but I found myself thinking that there was something poignant about the symbolism of the process by which it was made. As I knew all too well, thanks to the instruction of the Patriarch of Riva, in the Yeshuite faith, the sacrifice of the One God's son is celebrated by partaking in the Eucharist, the bread and wine symbolizing the body and blood of Yeshua ben Yosef. This was a more literal affair, celebrating the hard-won bounty of the jungle and the deep reserve of strength found in the bonds of a tightly knit community.

When I tried to articulate the thought to Bao, he laughed at me. "I think you're a bit drunk, Moirin." He leaned close, whispering in my ear. "Don't drink too much *masato*. I have a surprise for later."

"Oh?" I raised my brows, but before Bao could give any further hints, Paullu came to pull him into the men's dance, handing him a drum.

While the rays of the setting sun gilded the lush jungle around us, Bao spun in dizzying circles, bare-chested among the naked hunters, beating out a complex rhythm on the drum he held. I could not help but remember the performance he had arranged with the acrobats of Eglantine House in honor of the Montrèvan oath-swearing ceremony. It seemed so long ago and far away, it might have taken place in a different lifetime.

I thought of Desirée with a pang, and prayed that she was well. And then I pushed the thought aside with regret, for there was nothing I could do about it.

Bao spun, drumming.

The women clapped in approval, calling out jests and teasing their own men for failing to keep up with him.

"Friendship, eh?" Eyahue mused beside me.

I smiled. "Aye."

At last the dusk began to deepen. The nocturnal creatures of the jungle began to emerge. Bats flitted in the high treetops, and ghostly moths with wing spans the size of a grown man's two hands haunted the branches. One by one, the village folk began to drift away, carrying sleepy, satiated children to their dwellings.

Bao fetched up before me, the drum wedged under his arm, sweat glistening on his brown skin. "Paullu and Sarpay have agreed to lend us the privacy of their home for the night," he announced. "That's my surprise. Do you like it?"

I stood and kissed him, tasting salt. "Very much."

His dark eyes gleamed. "Good."

FIFTY-THREE

It had been a long, long time since Bao and I had been alone together. With the walls of a dwelling sheltering us from the sounds of the benighted jungle and the gazes of our companions, we made love into the small hours of the night; sharing our bodies, sharing our breath, sharing our entwined *diadh-anams* until neither of us was sure where one began and the other ended.

That, too, was a kind of communion.

In the morning, both of us were heavy-eyed for lack of sleep. The others regarded us with good-natured amusement, but no one begrudged us a night of pleasure, although Balthasar had a few choice words of warning for us.

"Don't let it make you careless," he said. "I didn't survive an infestation of bad spirits to capsize and drown on that damn river."

Bao yawned. "It won't. And I told you, it wasn't bad spirits."

"It might as well have been." Balthasar hefted a satchel of powdered *cinchona* bark that Atoc had given us. According to the shaman, if our recovering men didn't continue drinking the brew, the fever would return. "Gods know, this stuff's vile enough to keep a host of bad things at bay."

Paullu and a handful of villagers accompanied us on our return journey to the big river, where the rest of our company hailed our arrival with obvious relief. We redistributed our renewed stores, and in short order, were ready to depart once more.

"*Sulpayki*, Paullu." I offered him a final bow in parting. Once again, he returned it with dignity. "Thank you for all your kindness."

He nodded, but made no reply.

One by one, we launched our canoes while Paullu and his hunters climbed the emerald cliff alongside the sparkling waterfall. Before we resumed our journey downriver, I turned back to see the villagers arrayed in a line atop the cliff, their crimson-painted faces vivid in the morning light.

"Does anyone else have the impression they think we're headed to our deaths?" Balthasar inquired wryly.

In the prow of our canoe, Bao began paddling purposefully. "Who along the way hasn't thought the same?" he retorted. "And yet we're still here."

"Not all of us," I murmured.

"No." Bao gave me a somber glance over his shoulder, reminded of our losses. "Not all of us."

By Eyahue's estimate, we were still a week's travel away from Vilcabamba. The days of sameness resumed. We paddled through rain showers until the sun reemerged to steam us dry. When the river was wide and placid, we bent our backs to the labor, paddling hard, our palms toughened and our muscles long accustomed to the effort. Where it ran swift, we forged paths through rapids, all of us grown to be expert navigators.

In the evenings, we made landfall along the rocky shores, slinging our hammocks along the verges of the jungle.

We fished and foraged, augmenting our stores of sweet potatoes that ever dwindled too quickly.

I didn't bother keeping count of the days. I'd long ago lost track of the length of our journey. And despite Balthasar's and Denis' assurances to the contrary, I privately thought that Thierry de la Courcel must have done the same.

It was the sameness.

The sameness was mesmerizing; the endless river, the endless green of the jungle. The incessant heat, the constant clouds of mosquitoes and gnats. The gnawing sense of hunger that never quite went away as there was never quite enough to eat. The myriad deadly dangers to be avoided. The ever-present sound of rushing water; whispering at times, roaring at others. It lulled one's mind into a strange state of wary torpor, where one's only thoughts were of survival and the never-ending journey.

And yet all journeys end.

"Tomorrow, I think," Eyahue announced unexpectedly one evening, using a stick to poke at a sweet potato roasting in the ashes, rolling it within reach. "Tomorrow, we will come to Vilcabamba."

I lifted my head to stare at him. "You're sure?"

He grabbed the potato and dropped it with alacrity, sucking his burned fingers. "Sure, no. But I think so."

The rumor spread through our camp, raising hope and dispelling the torpor that all of us felt.

"What is it like there?" someone asked. I translated the question for Eyahue.

"Very fine." The old *pochteca* cackled and exposed his gums and remaining teeth in a broad grin. "Oh, yes! Very fine indeed."

Eyahue spun a tale of a great city of stone rising from the jungle, accessed by hanging bridges built over vast chasms in the earth. It was the easternmost stronghold of the empire of Tawantinsuyo, a name that in itself referred to the four disparate quarters of the empire of the Quechua folk. They possessed gold in abundance, he told us, for it was sacred to the sun god Inti they worshipped. The Emperor of Tawantinsuyo made his permanent residence in another city far away in the mountains, but Vilcabamba, where his sacred plant was cultivated, was one of his seasonal refuges.

"That's what you came to trade for, isn't it?" I asked him. "This sacred plant?"

He put a finger over his lips and winked at me. "Shh! Only Quechua royalty are permitted to use it."

The spotted warrior Temilotzin chuckled.

The following day, we set out on the river in higher spirits than usual, hoping that there actually was an end in sight to the journey.

It was in the late morning when I noticed a phenomenon along the southern bank of the river, a trickle of darkness moving toward us, oddly shiny in the sunlight. It wasn't until our paths converged that I was able to make out what it was.

Ants.

Tens of thousands of them, pouring in a stream over the rocky shore, black bodies glistening.

I had to own, it made my skin crawl.

We pulled alongside Eyahue's canoe to ask him about it.

"Nasty buggers," the old *pochteca* confirmed. "They hunt as an army. We'll want to stay out of their way."

"How dangerous are they?" I asked.

Eyahue sucked his teeth. "Their bite stings like fire. I've never known them to take down prey as big as a man ... but I wouldn't like to be lying injured in their path, either." He looked askance at the teeming shore, his expression apprehensive. "Can't say I've ever seen quite so many in one place before."

As our canoes glided past the stream of ants, the head of the column roiled in confusion, doubling back on itself and reversing direction, following our course. Here and there, I could make out individual insects, antennae twitching as they appeared to regard our progress with their faceted eyes.

And there were more coming, thin trickles emerging from the depths of the jungle to broaden the stream.

"Poor Denis," Bao murmured, paddling steadily. "This must be driving him mad."

"Bao?" My voice shook a little. I pointed to the shore. "Would you call that a black river?"

He shot me a grim look over his shoulder. "Not yet. But I might if it continues to grow."

"Drop back," I said to him. "I want to know what Denis thinks."

We back-paddled on the placid surface of the river, drifting on the milky-green waters, letting the canoe in which Denis de Toluard rode catch up to us.

In the stern of his canoe, Denis was restless and uneasy, his nose twitching, his paddle idle in his hands. "Go," he said unasked when they drew alongside us. "Go, go, go! That is what they say. Go and see, call the others. Call them all from the depths of the jungle, every last colony." He rubbed violently at his nose with one knuckled fist. "Not *see*, no. They cannot *see* as we understand it. But they can scent us, and they do."

On the shore, the stream grew still for a moment. Antennae perked and twitched, echoing Denis' movements.

"Can you tell if they mean us harm?" I asked quietly.

His haunted gaze met mine. "I don't think so. They feel like... sentries?" He nodded to himself. "Sentries, yes."

We continued onward and the army of sentries streamed alongside us, growing ever larger. The ants foraged as they went, taking down beetles and lizards in their path, stripping them in seconds. They poured over rocks, divided around boulders, the moving mass of them looking for all the world like a black river.

A sick sense of apprehension settled in the pit of my stomach. Not even Eyahue's victorious shout as he pointed to terraced fields arising in the heights beyond a vast bend in the river could alleviate it.

But then the stream of ants altered their course, turning away from the river to plunge back into the jungle, heading overland toward the distant terraces. I wasn't entirely reassured, but my sense of dread lessened.

A little later, we came around the bend and got our first sight of Vilcabamba.

Eyahue hadn't lied.

The Quechua city was perched in the highlands, spilling down the western slope of a mountain into the valleys below. It was protected by deep chasms spanned by hanging bridges. Buildings in the valleys were built of wood and thatch, but in the heights, there were palaces wrought of carved and painted stone. Streams trickled down to join the big river, churning the waters ahead of us.

All of us drifted and stared, unable to believe our eyes, unable to believe that we had reached the outermost stronghold of Tawan-tinsuyo.

Belatedly, I realized that we were approaching a long quay with a handful of canoes docked there. On a ridge above it stood a double line of Quechua warriors clad in quilted cotton armor. They carried wooden shields, spears or stone-headed war-clubs, and their faces were impassive.

Eyahue called out to them, telling them that we were traders in search of a party of white-faced strangers. One of the Quechua warriors pointed at the quay without replying, indicating permission to tie up.

"Should we arm ourselves?" Balthasar murmured.

Seeing the splendid city, I was acutely aware of our unimposing appearance. We were sweaty and hungry and grimy, hardly in any condition to impress anyone. At least the armor would help. "I think we'd better."

So we docked at the quay, unloading those trade goods we had left in store. The men donned their armor—or at least those who had not lost it to the river, for we were a few sets short by now. Of that which remained, much of it was rusted, the leather straps half-rotted by the jungle's damp heat. The shining company that had set out from Orgullo del Sol was considerably diminished. Still, it was something.

The Quechua watched without comment. Bao nudged me, pointing with his chin. Following his gaze, I saw that there were more black ants swarming atop the ridge above us, winding in streams around the warriors' sandaled feet. The Quechua ignored them utterly.

The sick feeling returned.

I glanced at Denis, who shook his head. He looked as ill as I felt. "I don't know, Moirin. They want...I don't know." He rubbed helplessly at his twitching nose. "Whatever it is, it's unnatural."

Eyahue repeated our inquiry regarding the white-faced strangers, addressing the Quechua in a cajoling tone. This time, the lead warrior inclined his head and replied. "He says we are expected," Eyahue reported, sounding puzzled. "And they will escort us into the presence of Lord Pachacuti."

"What about Prince Thierry and his men?" I asked.

The old *pochteca* shook his head. "He said nothing of them."

The Quechua leader beckoned, then turned and began to climb a series of steps carved into the side of the mountain, his men falling in behind him. On the ridge, pools of ants awaited us.

Bao and I exchanged a glance. "I go first," he said firmly, unslinging his staff. "No arguments."

Swallowing hard, I nodded. "None here."

Following the Quechua, we climbed the steps to the ridge, where the pool of ants parted for us, transforming itself into a divided stream. As we climbed the next set of stairs, ascending into the heights, twin rivulets of ants poured alongside us, following our progress. Although their presence unsettled me, I did my best to ignore them.

"Do you know this Lord Pachacuti?" I asked Eyahue.

"No." He shrugged. "He's new since last I was here. Some ambitious son of the Emperor, I reckon."

"Why's that?" I asked.

Eyahue grunted. "The name means 'Earth-Shaker.' It was the name the first Emperor of Tawantinsuyo took for himself; the *Sapa Inca*, they call him." He eyed the stream of ants with distaste. "The Quechua believe one worthy of the name comes every so often to reorder the world."

"Oh."

We reached the first hanging bridge. It swayed underfoot, jostled by the tread of the Quechua who preceded us. I reached out with both hands to steady myself on the thick cables woven of sisal, and flinched. They were crawling with ants.

Bao turned back. "Steady, Moirin," he said in a calm voice. "You can do this. We've endured worse."

I smiled gratefully at him. "We have, haven't we?"

Fighting to maintain my balance, I averted my gaze from the green chasm yawning beneath us and kept it fixed on Bao's back, comforted by his sure-footed tread. We crossed the bridge and continued. Upward and upward we climbed, passing terraces cut into the face of the mountain. Farmers labored beneath the hot sun, unperturbed by the sight of armored men and our entourage of ants.

At last we reached the palace, passing through tall wooden doors emblazoned with gold disks depicting the Quechua sun god.

Far from being deterred, the ants streamed through the doors alongside us. With the sounds of the jungle hushed by thick stone walls, I could *hear* them, a faint rustling sound that set my skin to crawling anew. No one we passed seemed to find it the least bit unusual, which unnerved me all the more.

Our reticent escorts led us to a vast hall where dozens of young women danced attendance on the figure seated on a throne before an elaborate wall hanging wrought of feathers, a figure clad in a robe of fine-combed red wool, a great collar of gold, and a flared gold head-dress.

"Lord Pachacuti," the lead guard announced. All of them knelt, touching their brows to the floor.

The ants flowed forward, clicking and rasping, forming a teeming black pool around the base of the throne. The maidservants moved out of their way with the grace of long practice. The man on the throne smiled, reaching into a basket and tossing a handful of leaves to the swarming mass of ants.

I caught my breath, my *diadh-anam* flaring.

From his throne, Raphael de Mereliot turned his smile on me; and it was a terrible smile, cold and hard and cruel. "Well met, Moirin," he said. "I've been waiting for you."

FIFTY-FOUR

There was a shocked silence in the throne room.

It was Denis de Toluard who broke it with a short, wondering laugh. "Raphael!" He unbuckled his helmet, running a hand through his damp hair. "Blessed Elua bugger me, I'm glad to see you!"

"Denis." Raphael's hard smile softened into ruefulness. "Would that I could say the same, old friend."

"What do you mean?" Denis blinked at him, then glanced around. "Where's his highness? Where are the others?"

"Safe." Raphael rose from his throne. Despite his foreign attire, he looked the same as I remembered him, with his tawny gold hair, grey eyes, and D'Angeline beauty; and yet he looked utterly different, too. He approached Denis with one hand extended. "I'm so very, very sorry about this, but I simply can't take the chance."

Denis clasped his hand in bewilderment, raising the other to rub his nose. "What do you mean?" he asked again.

Raphael's free hand shot up, steel flashing as he planted a dagger under Denis' chin and shoved it home with one ruthless thrust.

I let out an involuntary cry.

"I'm so sorry," Raphael repeated, catching Denis as he sagged and wrenching his dagger free, lowering him to the floor. "Truly."

The black river of ants flowed forward, chitinous mandibles clicking.

Raphael de Mereliot glanced over his shoulder. "No," he said to them. "He was my friend."

The tide subsided.

For a long, stunned moment, no one moved; and then Bao sprang into action with a hoarse shout, his staff whipping through the air.

Before it could make contact the tide of ants surged once more, pouring over Bao, crawling up his legs with impossible speed, enveloping him like a living carpet despite his frantic efforts to brush them off, all thoughts of attack abandoned.

"I suggest you hold still," Raphael said in a mild tone. "They'll eat you alive if I order it, starting with your eyes." He peered at Bao. "Master Lo Feng's surly lad, is it? Where's your master?"

Bao glared at him through a mask of writhing ants and gritted his teeth. "Dead."

"I'm sorry to hear it." Raphael's regret sounded unnervingly genuine. "He was a wise man, and I always admired him." He plucked Bao's bamboo staff from his hand. "So this one serves you now?" he asked me. "Is that how it is?"

"No," I whispered, shaking with terror. "He's my husband. Please, Raphael, call them off him, won't you?"

He laughed. "Your *husband*?"

I nodded.

"How low you've fallen, Moirin," Raphael remarked. "Naïve as you always were, I suppose I shouldn't be surprised. But it's a long way from sharing the bed of Jehanne de la Courcel, Queen's Companion." He met my gaze, sparks flickering in his implacable storm-grey eyes. "You know I blame you for her death?"

"Aye," I murmured. "So do I."

Bao closed his eyes, ants crawling over his eyelids.

Balthasar Shahrizai cleared his throat. He was pale and trembling, but his voice was steady. "My lord de Mereliot?" he inquired. "Or should I address you as Lord Pachacuti? Which do you prefer?"

Raphael shrugged. "Either will suffice." He eyed Balthasar. "I'm surprised to find *you* here, Shahrizai."

"No more than I." Swallowing with a visible effort, Balthasar glanced uneasily at the black, seething statue that was Bao. "My lord de Mereliot, if you mean to kill him, I beg you, at least do it cleanly."

"Oh, I don't think killing him will be necessary." Raphael smiled at me. "I suspect he'll be quite useful to me in keeping Moirin in line—and vice versa. But he needed to be taught a lesson. Have you learned it?" he asked Bao.

"Yes," Bao whispered.

"Very well." Raphael waved one hand and the black tide of ants receded. I was weak-kneed with relief as Bao's figure reemerged unharmed, his face rigid with anger and horror.

"Elua have mercy, man!" Septimus Rousse's voice cracked. "Why in the name of all that's sacred are you doing this?"

"I said I was sorry about Denis," Raphael said irritably. "Gods! I didn't *want* to kill him. He was my friend! I just couldn't take the chance. Moirin knows why. Don't you, Moirin?"

"Caim's gift," I said faintly. "The language of ants."

Raphael nodded in approval. "Exactly so. Mind you, I'm not sure if Denis *could* have learned to control them," he said thoughtfully. "It is no easy thing to learn to coax one's glands to produce the proper scents. I did, but I'm...special."

I stared at his beautiful face, at the sparks flickering in his eyes like the tail end of a lightning strike barely glimpsed, and I remembered the spirit Focalor, the Grand Duke of the Fallen, with his incandescent eyes breathing Claire Fourcay's life-force into me, attempting to pour his own essence into Raphael de Mereliot. "He's still inside you, isn't he?" I asked. "Focalor?"

"A mere pinch." Raphael demonstrated with thumb and forefinger. "But it's growing stronger. Like all numinous beings, it thrives on worship." He glanced at the ants and the Quechua with equal affection. "And with your aid, Moirin, I believe I'll be able to summon the rest of him on my own terms this time."

"No." I shook my head. "I won't do it."

Raphael lifted one finger. The river of ants poured over Bao's feet, climbing to his knees. "You may wish to rethink that position."

"Don't," Bao said through gritted teeth. "Gods! Forget about me! Someone just kill him!"

"Oh, I don't advise any of you try." Raphael circled his finger and the black river divided into multiple streams, ants flowing across the floor, scaling new targets, crawling over clothing and under armor. Someone choked back a sob.

"Stop!" I cried. "Raphael, please!"

He looked mildly at me. "Then you agree to aid me?"

"This isn't you," I said to him in despair. "Name of Elua! Raphael, no matter what's passed between us, you're a healer! *That's* who you are, what you are!"

"No." Tucking Bao's staff under his arm, Raphael regarded his hands. "That's what I was. The gods gave me a gift, and saw fit to mock me with it." When he looked back at me, his expression was bleak. "They took my parents when I was a boy, and too weak to save myself. They gave me a taste of power with you, and took it away." He raised his voice. "They took Jehanne from me, Moirin! She died hemorrhaging before my eyes, bleeding out her life to give birth to another man's child, and there was nothing I could do to stop it, nothing I could do to save her, because *you weren't there*!"

"I know!" I shouted at him, helpless tears in my eyes. "Do you think that knowledge is not a dagger in my heart?"

"Moirin," Bao murmured, glancing at the ants covering his lower legs. "I do not think you should antagonize him."

"Even that was not enough!" Raphael shook his head, his face grim. "They took my sister Eleanore from me, mocking me with a disease I could not cure. Do you know that great feat of healing I've accomplished on my own?" He pointed at Eyahue and Temilotzin, both of whom had been motionless and dumbstruck since we entered the throne room. "I taught a nation of bloodthirsty savages to inoculate themselves against the killing pox so that they might go on worshipping death and sacrificing innocent victims." His face twisted. "What a piece of irony is that?"

"We can't know the will of the gods," I said softly. "What you did was a wondrous thing. Mayhap it will alter the course of history for the better."

"I am past caring what the gods will." Raphael's voice was hard, hard as stone. "I will do what *I* will. Now, Moirin." He gestured, and the tide of ants crawled higher. Behind me, someone was weeping in fear. "Will you aid me?"

"Aye," I said in defeat. "I will."

"Swear it," Raphael said. "Swear it on the sacred oath of your people."

I licked my dry lips. "I swear by stone and sea and sky, and all that they encompass, that I will aid you. I swear it by the sacred troth that binds me to my *diadh-anam*. Now call them off!"

To a chorus of relieved sighs, he did. "Don't imagine I have any illusions about your loyalty, Moirin," he warned me. "I know you'll try to find a way to wriggle out of keeping your oath just like you did before."

I was silent.

Raphael paced the room, returning to his throne. The black river flowed alongside him. He sat, Bao's staff over his knees, contemplating us. "So long as you behave, I've no cause to harm the rest of you unless Moirin gives me one," he said. "You'll be put to labor in the fields with the others." Dipping into the basket beside him, he scattered another handful of leaves onto the seething floor, smiling indulgently. "It's hard to keep these little darlings fed. Bear in mind that they do prefer flesh, they're everywhere, and they're *always* watching." He laughed. "Well, not exactly watching, of course. They don't see as we do."

It was so near an echo of the words Denis had spoken only that very morning, it struck me like a fist to the gut.

"If you attempt to escape, they will know," Raphael continued heedlessly. "If you think to attack me . . ." He shrugged, stroking Bao's bamboo staff. "Well, I think you have seen what will ensue. Is that understood?"

Everyone nodded.

"Good," he said briskly. "Now strip off all armor and weapons. I daresay my Quechua warriors will find them useful when we overthrow the *Sapa Inca*."

I startled. "*What*?"

"Oh, yes." Raphael smiled at me. "There are sacred places on this earth, Moirin, sanctified by centuries of worship. In Tawantinsuyo, it is the Temple of the Ancestors in the city of Qusqu. That is where I must be coronated. We have a great deal to discuss, you and I. But for now it can wait." He pointed with Bao's staff. "Arms and armor! Strip! Moirin, I'll have your bow as well."

One by one, the men complied; and so did I, surrendering my yew-wood bow with a pang of regret.

For a moment, I thought Temilotzin would resist. The Jaguar Knight glowered, clutching his obsidian-studded club. Streams of ants skirled and chittered around his sandaled feet.

"Don't," I pleaded with him in Nahuatl. "Please, don't!" I glanced at Denis de Toluard's lifeless body, my heart aching. "I'm not sure I could bear it. Wait, and let me try to find a way out of this."

With a growl, Temilotzin hurled his club to the floor, shards of obsidian shattering on the stone. "I do not like this prince of yours, my little warrior," he said in disdain. "Better we had never found him!"

"I agree," Eyahue muttered.

Overwhelmed by the shock of the encounter, I was ashamed to realize I'd altogether forgotten the purpose of our journey.

Now I remembered.

"He's *not* our prince," I said firmly. "Raphael? My lord de Mereliot?"

Idling on the throne, being attended by his ants and handmaidens, he lifted his head. "Hmm?"

"You told Denis that Thierry and the others were safe," I said. "Was that true?"

"Of course it's true!" Looking offended, Raphael waved one hand. "They're laboring in the fields just like these men will. And *they* will confirm the folly of attempting to escape," he added. "One tried. He died screaming."

I closed my eyes briefly, fighting a wave of nausea. "But the Dauphin and the others are well?"

Raphael shrugged. "All that made it safely to Vilcabamba. We lost a few along the way." He fixed me with a hard stare. "Do you suppose I'd murder them all outright? What do you take me for, a monster?"

I gazed back at the man I'd once thought I'd loved, the man I'd believed my destiny—the man whose bed I'd been so eager to share, the man with the golden healer's touch, the man I'd let charm me into folly and self-sacrifice, the man who had saved my father's life.

The man who had just stabbed one of his best friends in the throat, the madman who held us all captive and hostage with his terrible army.

If he was a monster, he was a monster *I* had helped to create. My *diadh-anam* had spoken truly all those years ago, but I hadn't understood it. Whether he was mad or no, Raphael was right about one thing. The gifts of the gods were often double-edged. My destiny was indeed entwined with his, but what I hadn't known was that I'd forged every link of the chains that bound us myself.

"Well?" Raphael raised his brows. "Answer the question, Moirin. Do you take me for a monster?"

"Aye," I said. "I do.

Trailing his fingers in the black river of ants, Raphael just laughed.

FIFTY-FIVE

I was a prisoner without a cell.

Raphael had no need to confine me. The threat hanging over the heads of Bao and all our company was enough to compel my obedience. Once the men had been escorted away by the Quechua warriors and a column of ants, presumably to labor in the fields or to whatever lodgings they were allotted, Raphael proved surprisingly magnanimous.

He gave me a suite of rooms that opened onto a small, sunlit courtyard filled with fruit trees and a bathing fountain in a stone channel that poured down the terraced mountainside. In other circumstances, it would have been charming...were it not for the presence of the ants.

I eyed the black stream exploring the courtyard. "Surely they're not...staying?"

"Just one small colony," Raphael assured me. "Don't worry, I've assigned one of my handmaidens to look after you and care for them."

I shuddered.

He sent for the handmaiden, a pretty young Quechua woman named Cusi, who seemed awestruck at being in his presence. Raphael stroked her hair absentmindedly. "Cusi here was raised to be a Maiden of the Sun," he remarked. "To serve royalty, or even at a time of great need, to serve as a holy sacrifice."

"I thought you disdained such practices," I murmured.

Raphael frowned at me. "As the Nahuatl practice it, yes, of course. It is barbaric and...wasteful. But sometimes blood is necessary, Moirin. Sometimes blood is the only sacrifice that will suffice."

I remembered the Nahuatl Emperor saying much the same words to me, and kept my mouth shut on the thought. It seemed a bad omen.

"But that time is not yet upon us, is it?" Raphael smiled at the handmaiden. "I chose her especially for you, Moirin. She's a pretty girl, isn't she?" His voice took on a taunting edge. "Make her your own little royal companion, if you wish. I've ordered her to please you in any way you might desire. Customs being what they are, I'm not sure she understood what I meant, but..." He shrugged. "You will find the Quechua wholly unsophisticated, but not unteachable."

A surge of bile rose in my throat, and I fought to swallow it. "You're very generous, my lord."

"I need you," Raphael said simply. "And I need you healthy and hale, Moirin. We have a great undertaking before us."

I rubbed my face with both hands. "How did you know I would come?"

"I dreamed it," he said. "Over and over. I dreamed of you, and blood, and a doorway filled with darkness."

"Did you dream of Jehanne?" I could not help asking.

His face hardened. "No," he said in a curt tone. "Do not speak her name to me, Moirin. I cannot bear the sound of it on your lips, and it will be better for all of us if I do not despise you more than I already do."

Silently, I nodded my understanding.

Raphael patted my shoulder. "Good. There is just one more small thing. Sooner or later, it will occur to you that if you're willing to bloody your hands, you might simply summon your twilight and dispatch me at your leisure." He smiled. "Know that if any harm befalls me, my Quechua warriors have orders to put every D'Angeline in Tawantinsuyo to death, so I suggest you pray for my health and well-being. Do you understand?" I nodded again. "Very well. The day grows late. You should bathe and eat and rest. You've had a long, hard journey, and another awaits you. We'll speak further in the days to come."

With that, he left me.

True to his word, a colony of ants remained. When Raphael had gone, taking the bulk of his insectile entourage with him, they swarmed up a sisal rope hanging from the ceiling of my bedchamber, climbing over one another in layers until they formed a large, glistening black ball that regarded me with a thousand faceted eyes.

I sank onto the feather-stuffed pallet atop my bed, buried my face in my hands, and wept.

The distraught handmaiden Cusi knelt beside me and sought to offer comfort, her hands fluttering impotently over my hair and skin, a stream of soothing Quechua words I barely understood pouring from her lips.

With an effort, I wrestled myself under control, catching her fluttering hands in mine and stilling them. "*Sulpayki*, Cusi," I said to her. "Thank you. I'm sorry, I don't mean to trouble you. *Pampachayuway*. I am sorry."

She gave me a timid look beneath long lashes. "*Mana?*"

"No," I agreed. "No trouble."

Freeing her hands from mine, Cusi laid one soft, warm palm against my cheek. "I speak little D'Angeline," she said slowly, her eyes gazing intently into mine. "You eat and sleep. Lord Pachacuti said to. He is a god, yes?"

I did not answer.

Her dark eyes widened. "*Arí*? Yes?"

I shook my head. "No."

Clearly disturbed by my heresy, Cusi sucked in a long, deep breath, glancing around the bedchamber. "Eat," she said firmly, reverting to Quechua and miming actions to suit her words. "Drink. Sleep. Grow strong."

Too weary to argue, I obeyed. With the sun fading in the west, I bathed in the man-made waterfall, then donned clean attire and ate the food that Cusi brought: roasted fowl, *maize* flatbread, and an array of fresh fruits. My body accepted the gift of food with gratitude, and despite the menacing presence of the writhing ball of ants hanging in my bedchamber, I succumbed to exhaustion and slept.

Slept—and dreamed.

This time, I caught the heady fragrance of Jehanne's perfume before I saw her; and this time, the dream did not take place in the enchanted bower she'd had made for me, but in another room I'd once known well: Raphael de Mereliot's bedchamber. Glancing around, I found Jehanne standing on the balcony, gazing out at the garden.

Jehanne turned around, and there were tears streaking her exquisite face. "I wanted to remember him the way he was."

"You didn't know?" I asked softly.

She shook her head. "Not until now."

I joined her on the balcony. With a soft sigh, Jehanne rested her head on my shoulder. I put my arms around her, holding her close, breathing in her scent. For a long moment, neither of us spoke.

"I just didn't expect it to be so awful," Jehanne said at length.

"Nor did I," I murmured.

She turned in my arms, searching my face with her starry gaze. "What will you do?"

"I wish I knew," I admitted. "Break my oath if I must. Do you have no counsel for me, my lady? You said I would have need of you before the end."

Jehanne frowned in thought. "The end isn't upon us yet. But I do think Raphael made one mistake. He shouldn't have given you the girl."

"I don't *want* the girl," I said. "And I suspect she's meant to keep watch over me and report to him."

"Yes, of course," Jehanne agreed. "But you've a way with women that Raphael underestimates." She laughed at my expression. "I don't mean for you to seduce the poor child, Moirin!" She kissed my lips, tender and lingering. "Win her trust. It's what you do best."

"Aye?"

She nodded. "You won mine, and that was no easy feat. In many ways, it is very much a man's world. Too many women regard one another as competitors, and too many men regard women as nothing more than useful tools."

My skin prickled. "The fallen spirit Focalor called me as much," I said. "He said I was nothing more than a useful tool for other hands to wield."

Jehanne's face was enigmatic. "I know."

Letting go of Jehanne, I paced the narrow balcony, thinking aloud. "Raphael spoke of blood sacrifice. He was talking about these women, the Maidens of the Sun. They're the key, aren't they? Somehow, I need to turn them against him. Is that what you're telling me?"

Jehanne was silent.

"Have you said as much as the gods allow?" I asked ruefully.

"Not entirely." She gave me a deep look. "I may say that I do not blame you for my death, my beautiful girl, and nor should you. Both of us know that a far greater fate hung in the balance. And I will tell you not to hold yourself wholly to blame for what Raphael became. I knew there was tremendous passion and ambition in him. It is a part of what drew me to him; but I was selfish, too. I fed his hunger without ever truly slaking it."

"You loved well and truly, my lady," I said. "It is all Blessed Elua asks of us."

She gave a graceful shrug. "And yet if I had given Raphael de Mereliot the whole of my heart, he might have been content."

"Or not," I said.

"Or not," Jehanne agreed. "If I had given my husband, Daniel, the whole of my heart, he might not have succumbed to despair. Such things are never given us to know." She smiled at me with profound and abiding affection tempered by a hard-won understanding I could not yet fathom. "And mayhap the gods in their infinite wisdom are right, for I would not like to regret the piece of my heart I gave to you, Moirin."

I smiled back at her. "Nor would I." Placing my palms together, I bowed to her in the Bhodistani manner. "Thank you. You have given me hope."

Jehanne de la Courcel cupped my face and planted a kiss on my brow. "Hold fast to it," she whispered. "For my daughter's sake—for all our sakes."

I awoke with a start.

Sunlight filled the bedchamber. A few yards away, the bulging knot of ants clinging to the sisal rope regarded me with their multi-faceted eyes. Ignoring them, I dragged myself upright.

Cusi pattered into the room from the adjoining antechamber. "Sleep good?" she asked in hopeful D'Angeline. "More food?"

Yawning, I rubbed my eyes. "*Arí,*" I said. "Yes, please. *Sulpayki,* thank you." Reaching out, I caught her hand and squeezed it in thanks. "You speak Lord Pachacuti's tongue very well. Did he teach it to you himself?"

Cusi smiled with modest pride, all dimples. "No. Lord Pachacuti teach to Ocllo. She is old and wise. She teach to me."

"I see." I contemplated the girl, wondering how I was to win her trust and turn her against a man she reckoned a god. In truth, I could not blame her. The Aragonians had tried and failed to convince the Nahuatl that they were gods; but the Aragonians had not been attended by a mile-long entourage of ants that did their bidding. There were no hints of lightning flickering in Diego Ortiz y Ramos' eyes as there were in Raphael's.

Truly, Lord Pachacuti the Earth-Shaker had overturned the order of the world.

Well and so. My own small gifts might be no match for Raphael's ants; but they were mine by right of birth. At least I could show my handmaid that Lord Pachacuti was not the only one with the ability to reorder the world. It would not win her trust, but it might suggest to her that my words were worth heeding.

Rising from my bed, I made my way into the courtyard. Cusi trailed uncertainly behind me, the ball of ants unknotting themselves to trickle after us.

I breathed the Breath of Trees Growing, taking in the vast energy of the jungle surrounding us, and chose a small tree. It bore a fruit that was unfamiliar to me, small green fruits that were hard and unripe.

Laying one hand on its slender trunk, I felt its lively thoughts. My *diadh-anam* burned brightly within me. Beneath Cusi's watchful gaze, I summoned a hint of the twilight and exhaled softly over the branches, pushing.

The unripe fruits swelled and grew, green skin taking on a crimson blush. I plucked one and split the tough skin with my thumbnail, prying it in half. The flesh inside was pink and smelled sweet. Stooping, I laid the fruit in the ants' path. They swarmed over it, devouring it in seconds.

Cusi stared, her mouth agape.

I plucked another ripe fruit from the tree and handed it to her. She took it without thinking, her eyes wide and wondering.

"What are you?" she asked.

"Not a god," I said. "And neither is Lord Pachacuti."

FIFTY-SIX

After my display in the courtyard, Cusi was more reserved. I chose not to push the matter further for the time being. Gods knew, I'd learned during my time in Vralia that sowing doubt in the faithful was a delicate business.

And even then, I'd failed with Aleksei. He'd come to it in his own time, but if it hadn't been for his mother, Valentina, it wouldn't have been soon enough to save me. I would have been stoned to death on the Patriarch's orders.

Were it not for Jehanne's visit, the thought would have disheartened me; but when I thought further on it, I realized Jehanne was right. It was Valentina who had been the key all along, not Aleksei.

I prayed I could find the key that would unlock the trust of the Quechua women, and learn how it might aid us all.

But before I did aught else, I needed to assure myself that what Raphael had said was true. I could sense through Bao's *diadh-anam* that he was unharmed, but I needed to know the others were safe, and that Thierry de la Courcel was alive and well.

When I announced my intention to Cusi, she gave a resigned shrug. "Lord Pachacuti say you ask this."

"Did he forbid it?" I asked.

She shook her head. "No."

I considered this as we descended several terraces and made our way around to the far side of the mountain, accompanied by a rivulet of ants. When I had been with Raphael in the City of Elua, he'd strung me along with expert finesse; playing on my belief in our shared destiny, playing on my infatuation with him, playing on my sense of guilt. He'd alternated between doling out affection and recrimination, keeping me compliant and desperately eager to please him for far too long.

In some ways, this was not so different.

Raphael de Mereliot *needed* me. And once again, he needed to keep me compliant. If he executed his threat, he ran the risk of pushing me to the point where I had nothing left to lose.

I supposed he could begin killing men horribly one by one, keeping in reserve those whose deaths would cause me the most agony. But the fact that he hadn't yet done so, assuming he was telling the truth, suggested to me that mayhap there was a shred of decency left in him, and that he was more comfortable relying on familiar patterns, doling out rewards along with punishment, dangling the hope of survival, and mayhap freedom, before me.

At least the knowledge gave me a small measure of leverage; and I daresay I knew Raphael better than he knew me. I'd grown far from the love-struck backwoods maiden he had manipulated so easily.

Although it was also true that the Raphael I'd known had been sane.

For a mercy, it seemed he *had* told the truth. Cusi led me to a terraced field where dozens of men were bent over with digging-sticks, planting potatoes under the hot sun. When I caught sight of the familiar copper-red brightness of Septimus Rousse's hair, I laughed aloud with relief.

Across the field, heads rose.

"Moirin!" Bao raced toward me, vaulting rows. I flung my arms around his neck, burying my face against his sweat-slick skin. He wrapped his arms around my waist and held me hard. "You're all right?" he asked in a fierce voice. "He didn't harm you?"

"Fine," I murmured. "He won't. He needs me."

Reluctantly, Bao released me. "There's someone here I think you will very much want to see."

For the space of a few heartbeats, I didn't recognize the gaunt, work-hardened, sun-browned man approaching me—and then I did.

"Thierry," I whispered.

The Dauphin of Terre d'Ange tried to summon a smile, but his dark blue eyes were red-rimmed with grief. "Moirin mac Fainche of the Maghuin Dhonn. You shouldn't have undertaken this journey. Neither of us should."

"Oh, gods!" I covered my mouth with both hands, realizing that he would only just have heard the news from home. Tears stung my own eyes. "Oh, Thierry! I'm so sorry about your father!"

"Thank you." Thierry embraced me, kissing me on both cheeks. "I'm sorry to have led you here."

One by one, others came to join us. It pained me to see the faint glimmer of hope in their eyes at the sight of my freedom.

"Any chance of talking sense into the Mad Lord de Mereliot?" Balthasar inquired. He looked around at the stream of ants that ringed the field, my own entourage having merged with their sentries. "I'm really not fond of insects."

I glanced at Cusi, who appeared to be straining her ears and concentrating hard. "Not yet, no."

Balthasar followed my gaze. "Ah."

"She spies for that idiot Lord Lion Mane?" Bao asked me in the Shuntian scholar's tongue.

I nodded. "Oh, yes. She believes he is a god."

Bao's jaw hardened. "Figures."

Gazing at Prince Thierry, a thought struck me. "Your highness, Raphael de Mereliot knows no more than you did of the tragic events that have passed in Terre d'Ange. If he has any lingering care for Jehanne's daughter, it may be that they will move him. I do not think I can sway him from his course here, but mayhap I can persuade him to free you to return to Terre d'Ange."

Thierry gave a hollow laugh. "Do you think I'd stand a chance of reaching it? I barely survived this journey."

I beckoned to Eyahue. "Would you guide him?"

The wiry old *pochteca* dug in his ear with one finger. "Eh?"

"Would you be willing to guide the prince back to Tenochtitlan if it could be arranged?" I asked patiently. "You and Temilotzin?"

"Oh, aye!" Eyahue brightened. "Anything to get out of here!"

"My ship *Naamah's Dove* waits in Orgullo del Sol to carry you home, highness," Septimus Rousse added. "Commanded by my able second, Alaric Dumont. It would be an honor to provide that service."

"I would not save myself at the expense of the rest of you," Thierry murmured. "Do not shame me."

"You wouldn't be saving yourself," I said to him. "And there is no shame in attempting this. You would be saving your young sister, Desirée, whom I have sworn an oath to protect, and the rule of law in Terre d'Ange, which has currently been usurped by the Duc de Barthelme. Is that not worth doing?"

After a moment, Thierry de la Courcel nodded, his sun-browned face leaner and older than I remembered it, faint lines etched in the corners of his eyes. "In my father's memory, yes."

"I will try," I promised him.

"What happens if you fail?" Balthasar asked me.

I shrugged. "We try somewhat else."

My handmaid, Cusi, was quiet most of the way back to the palace, her features screwed up in thought. "I think there are many things I do not understand," she said slowly. "Many things."

"Ask, then," I said. "I will tell you whatever you want to know."

She gave me a startled look. *"Arí?"*

"Arí, yes," I agreed.

Cusi frowned. "No. I think I am not wise to know what question to ask or what answer to believe."

Despite everything, I laughed aloud. "If you know that much, you're already wise beyond your years."

It won a shy smile from her, the first since I'd quickened the fruit tree. "Yes?"

"Yes." I laid one hand on her arm. "I will make you a promise, Cusi.

No matter what you ask, I will answer it truthfully. I know you may not believe me, but I promise it nonetheless. I will not lie to you."

She was silent a moment. "I will think."

I nodded. "For as long as you like. I will answer whenever you are ready."

Upon returning to the palace, I sent her to request an audience with Lord Pachacuti. It seemed to shock her a bit that I would dare to presume such a thing, and all the more so that he granted it.

Raphael heard me out in the throne room, his face expressionless as he dipped into his basket, feeding leaves to his crawling horde. From time to time, he popped a leaf into his own mouth, chewing it leisurely. For some reason, that unnerved me as much as anything else.

I opened with humility, hoping it might soften him. "Thank you for permitting me to visit Prince Thierry today, my lord. Forgive me; I apologize for having doubted you."

Raphael snorted. "False humility doesn't become you, Moirin. What do you want?"

So much for that gambit. "A boon," I said. "You never asked what brought me to Terra Nova. May I tell you?"

He cocked his head, considering the request, then spat out a wad of chewed leaves into the waiting hand of one of his maidens. "All right."

I spun out the tale of Denis de Toluard's return with the news of Thierry's disappearance that had led King Daniel to take his own life, the rise of Duc Rogier de Barthelme to the regency, and his swift move to declare Desirée's betrothal to his loathsome son.

Not wanting to give him further leverage over me, I did not tell him I was Desirée's oath-sworn protector. But I told him of my vision that Thierry was alive, taking care not to mention that it was Jehanne who appeared in my dreams, and of Edouard Durel's attempt to sabotage our mission at the Duchese de Barthelme's behest.

It disturbed him. Raphael rose to pace the floor as he listened, streams of ants skittering out of his path. "You're right," he said when

I'd finished. "This is unacceptable. But don't worry, I'll deal with it when I return to Terre d'Ange."

I blinked. "My lord?"

Raphael laughed. "You didn't think I intended to remain in Terra Nova, did you?" He gestured carelessly. "Among these savages?"

One of the purported savages' eyelids flickered briefly, and several others stiffened.

"I thought you had adopted them as your people." I hoped Raphael would further refute my claim, but he caught himself.

"Yes, of course." He bestowed a charming smile on his hand-maids, who relaxed. "But I am D'Angeline, after all. Once I have been acknowledged the *Sapa Inca*, I will appoint a regent of my own and return home. The matter has already been decided. The Quechua in Vilcabamba understand this."

Clearing my throat, I sought to steer the conversation back on course. "That is some time away, my lord. There is a swifter resolution to the troubles at home at hand. Were you to free Prince Thierry and a few guards, the *pochteca* Eyahue will guide them back to the Nahuatl Empire, where a ship awaits."

Raphael raised his brows. "I see no urgency to the matter, Moirin. Betrothal or no, a royal wedding would be many years in the offing."

I shook my head. "The damage would be done long before that day." My palms were sweating, and I wiped them unobtrusively on my gown. "She's her mother's daughter, Raphael," I said softly. "High-spirited and willful, a handful even as a child. But she *is* a child, and spirits can be broken. Desirée's will be. I've seen it."

His storm-grey eyes seemed to darken, sparks flashing in their depths. "I asked you not to speak of Jehanne!"

"You asked me not to speak her name," I said. "And I am speaking of her daughter."

"*Daniel's* daughter," he retorted.

I held his gaze with an effort. "Daniel de la Courcel could barely bring himself to look at the child, so much the image of her mother is she. He took his life and left her an orphan, with no one in Terre d'Ange capable of protecting her interests. I tried and failed. Thierry is her brother, and the rightful heir to the throne. I am begging you to let him go. It will change none of your plans here."

"The image of her mother, eh?" Raphael mused.

I nodded.

He returned to his seat on the throne, lost in thought for a long moment. When his gaze returned from the distance, it was keen and clear. "Mayhap that was what was destined all along. I do not intend to return to Terre d'Ange as a mere lord, Moirin—nor a mere mortal. I intend to return as the God-King of Terre d'Ange and Terra Nova alike." He smiled at me. "And based on what you tell me here today, I do believe I intend to take Desirée de la Courcel as my bride."

I stared at him in horror. "You can't be serious!"

"Oh, but I am." Raphael drummed his fingers on the armrests of his throne. "Once the summoning of Focalor is complete, I will have all his gifts. The wind will blow at my command, the lightning strike, the seas rise and fall. I shall be as powerful as the legendary Master of the Straits, and far, far more ruthless."

"But Jehanne's *daughter*," I protested. "Surely—"

"I told you not to speak her name!" he shouted at me. The restless river of ants stirred, and the Quechua handmaids grew still.

"It is no way to honor her memory," I whispered. "You loved her, my lord! I know you did."

His face had turned stony. "And how did she repay that love? With too little, always too little."

I said nothing.

"It will be different with her daughter," Raphael said. "As you say, she is a child yet, and malleable." He nodded to himself. "Yes, this is what destiny held in store for me. I will not break her spirit, no. But I will mold it to suit my own." Dipping into his basket, he tossed a handful of leaves to the ants and shoved a few more into his own mouth, chewing. "Thank you, Moirin," he said to me. "This has been very helpful. You may go now."

Sick at heart, I went.

FIFTY-SEVEN

N o?" Thierry asked the following day, reading my expression.
I shook my head. "No. I'm sorry, your highness. I tried. I
fear I only made matters worse."

A sigh of regret rippled through the remnants of our company.
Cusi, who had not yet availed herself of my offer to answer her questions, glanced from face to face, her gaze intent. She was not the most
subtle of spies.

I'd feared Thierry might succumb to despair after having his
hopes raised and dashed, but instead it seemed to instill a new resolve
in him. "This uncanny gift of Raphael's and the undertaking he has
planned," he said. "It all goes back to the Circle of Shalomon, doesn't
it?" I nodded. "Explain it to me." He glanced at Cusi. "To the extent
that you deem prudent."

I shrugged. "I promised not to lie to her. Let her hear the truth
and make of it what she will."

I described the summoning of spirits; of Caim and the gift of the
language of ants he had bestowed on the Circle; of Focalor, and how
the fallen spirit had nearly taken possession of Raphael. How a piece
of his essence endured, fed by the worship of the Quechua people, and
how Raphael believed that with my aid he could summon and control
the spirit in its entirety once he was coronated as the *Sapa Inca* and
worshipped by the whole empire.

"Can he do it?" Thierry asked me steadily.

"I don't know," I admitted. "I wish I did, but I don't. If Raphael believes it, it's certainly possible." Sorrow brushed me. "I would that Denis de Toluard were alive. He would have known better than I."

"At least he redeemed himself twice over on the journey," Balthasar murmured. "It meant a great deal to him."

Wiping my eyes, I nodded.

"This oath you swore," Thierry mused. "It's of grave import to your people, is it not? And there are dire consequences for breaking it?"

"Aye." My *diadh-anam* flared painfully within me. Swallowing, I glanced at Bao. "More dire than ever, I fear. I would lose the spark of the Maghuin Dhonn Herself and be cast out of Her presence forever. And Bao…" I couldn't say the words.

"I'm not afraid to die, Moirin." Bao smiled wryly at me. "After all, I've done it before."

Cusi let out a stifled shriek, then clapped a hand over her mouth, her eyes wide and fearful above it.

Thierry gave Bao a puzzled look. "Whatever do you mean?"

"That's right, you haven't heard the myriad tales surrounding our Messire Bao, your highness," Balthasar remarked. "Among other things, he died in faraway Ch'in and was restored to life by Moirin's magic."

"You can bring men back from the dead?" Thierry stared at me.

"No," I said. "Not exactly. It was our mentor, Master Lo. He gave his life to restore Bao's; but it required half my *diadh-anam*, too. It's what binds us together."

"*Dispinsayuway*," Cusi whispered unexpectedly, tugging at my sleeve. Her brown skin looked ashen. "Excuse, please! I go now." She gestured in the direction of the palace. "You can find?"

"Yes, of course," I said to her.

She gave me a bobbing salute. "Later I come, yes?"

"Yes, fine. Are you well?" I asked. "Sick?"

"No, no." Cusi shook her head. "Later!" With that, she took off at a run across the terraced field, clutching her skirts and raising them above her ankles. My attendant ants roiled briefly in confusion before rejoining the stream of field sentries.

Balthasar gave a humorless chuckle. "Scared of ghosts, do you reckon?"

"I'm not sure," I said slowly. "My lady Jehanne came to me in a dream last night. If I understood her aright, gaining the trust of the Quechua women is somehow the key to thwarting Raphael."

"You're good at that," Bao commented.

"Aye." I gazed after the receding figure. "But she's not opened to me, and I've only been making a muddle of things." I sighed. "My oath . . . Bao, I fear I'm forsworn no matter what I do."

He frowned. "What do you mean?"

My lips had gone dry again, and I licked them in vain. "Raphael . . . he's conceived this notion of returning to Terre d'Ange and wedding Desirée himself. A younger version of Jehanne he can mold to his liking."

Thierry swore violently.

"I'm sorry, your highness!" My eyes burned. "I'd no idea he'd imagine such a thing! And I'm Desirée's oath-sworn protector. If I fail to aid Raphael, I break my oath to him. If I *do* aid him, I break my oath to her." I tried to laugh, but it came out as a sob. "I'm sorry. It doesn't change anything, not really. When the moment comes, I have to break my oath to Raphael, I know I do. And once it's done, my magic will die with my *diadh-anam*. That door will be closed forever. And . . . and Bao . . ." I wiped my eyes. "Ah, gods! You died a hero. I hope the Maiden of Gentle Aspect will still be waiting for you in the afterlife to spare you judgment of the Yama Kings."

Bao grabbed my shoulders and gave me a little shake. "Moirin, it would solve nothing. Your prince would still be trapped with the Mad Ant-Lord of Tawantinsuyo, and Desirée would still be betrothed to that loathsome little wretch. Calm down. Be patient. There has to be another way."

It did calm me. "Do you have any ideas?"

"Listen to the White Queen," he said. "Raphael's still mortal, isn't he?" He shrugged. "Maybe it's as simple as convincing one of the women to poison his dinner or stab him in his sleep, huh?"

"I have to say, I like the way your mind works," Balthasar said to Bao.

I took a deep breath. "I would that it were that simple. I'd call the twilight and kill him myself if it were. But Raphael's made it clear that if any harm befalls him, we'll all be put to death." My voice hardened. "Still, you're right. There must be a way. The gods would not have sent us here if there were not. Whatever it is, I will find it."

Bao grinned, his dark eyes gleaming. "Good girl."

Accompanied by my escort of ants, I made the long trek around the mountain and over the terraces.

I felt guilty at having given in to fear and weakness. The miserable failure of my attempt to appeal to Raphael's better nature, which had had the exact opposite effect I'd hoped, had shaken me more than I reckoned, making me unsure of myself. But the memory of Bao's fierce grin bolstered me. If my stubborn peasant-boy was nowhere ready to surrender, neither was I.

In the palace, I found my quarters empty. The ants swarmed up the sisal rope, forming their writhing ball.

"It's not your fault," I said to them. "You didn't choose this either, did you? I do not blame you."

The outermost layer clicked their mandibles at me. With reluctance, I touched their thoughts.

They were hungry.

Cusi was supposed to attend to their needs, but she was nowhere in sight. I ventured into the courtyard garden, the ants swarming back down the rope to follow me. One by one, I gathered all the fruits from the tree I'd quickened, splitting them open and laying them on the ground.

The grateful ants poured over them, devouring the sweet pink pulp from the inside out. I spotted their queen among them, several times larger than her subjects.

It occurred to me that if I could touch their thoughts, mayhap I could influence them, too. I could do it with larger, more sentient animals. For the better part of an hour, I tried to no avail. Their hive mind was too alien, responding only to their own language of scent. I wondered how Raphael had learned to manipulate his own.

I wondered, too, what would happen if I killed the queen of this colony—if it would render them rudderless, or if Raphael somehow functioned as the queen of queens in the ant world.

Although I was tempted to try the experiment, in the end, I stayed my hand; partly from the knowledge that there must be hundreds of colonies functioning under Raphael's command with queens to spare, and partly out of fear that this one might turn on me if I did. The thought of being swarmed by thousands of bereaved drones made my skin crawl.

At least I felt as though my wits were working once more, which made the situation seem a little less hopeless.

To wash away the illusory sensation of ants crawling over me, not to mention the day's sweat, I bathed in the artificial waterfall. After scrubbing myself thoroughly with a soapy root, I closed my eyes and let the water pour over me, willing it to further clear my thoughts.

When I opened my eyes, through the streams of water cascading over me, I saw two figures standing in the courtyard.

Stifling my surprise, I stepped naked from the waterfall. One of the figures was Cusi, biting her lower lip and eyeing me uncertainly. The other was an older woman with iron-grey streaking her black hair. She had intelligent, watchful eyes and a bearing that indicated she was someone of status.

Ignoring my nakedness, I shifted my hands into a *mudra* of respect and inclined my dripping head to her. "*Rimaykullaykil*, my lady."

The old woman pursed her mouth and looked me up and down, her face impassive. Murmuring apologies in two tongues, Cusi darted forward with a clean garment of fine-combed wool dyed a bright saffron hue, helping me to don it.

"This is Ocllo," she said to me, indicating the other woman. "She is old and wise. Not like me."

I smiled at Ocllo. "Well met, my lady."

She folded her arms over her chest, glowering, and declined to return my smile. "Cusi say you make the *guayabo* tree's fruit to ripen." She pointed at the tree with its branches barren of aught but dark green leaves. "But I do not see it."

I pointed to the stream of ants circling the courtyard. "I fed it to them."

Ocllo's nostrils flared. "True?"

"True," I said.

"Do it again," Ocllo demanded. "Do it for me!"

I shook my head. "That tree is tired. I forced it past its season. It is too soon. Choose another."

Stalking the courtyard, the old woman examined various trees and shrubs, settling on a tough, woody vine that stretched between two trees, narrow leaves and tight-knit buds dotting its length. "This one."

I summoned the twilight.

I touched the vine and breathed on it.

One by one, the furled buds opened and blossomed, pink and crimson petals spreading to greet the sunlight.

"Well!" Ocllo studied the vine, poking and prodding, nodding to herself. "Well, well, well! It seems Cusi speaks true."

"Yes," I agreed. "Why are you here, my lady? Have you questions for me? I promise, I will answer them honestly."

Ocllo fixed me with a gimlet gaze. "What do you know of the Temple of the Ancestors?"

It was not a question I had expected, and I blinked at it. "I know it is where Lord Pachacuti intends to be coronated."

"Nothing more?" she pressed me.

"Do you ask about the spirit he intends to summon there?" I glanced at Cusi. "I know you were listening; there's no point in pretending otherwise."

"I will ask about the spirit later," Ocllo said impatiently. "Now I ask about the Temple of the Ancestors. What do you know of it?"

I spread my hands. "I know it is located in the city of Qusqu, nothing more."

The old woman leaned forward, her face inches from mine as she searched my gaze. "Who betrayed the secret of the ancestors to you? Is it the old Nahuatl trader? I know that one from years before. Always trying to seduce the Maidens of the Sun. If anyone finds it, it is him, even though it is forbidden."

"I've no idea what you're talking about!" I said in frustration. "I'm sorry, my lady! I cannot tell you what I do not know."

The women withdrew a few paces and conferred in rapid Quechua in low voices. After a moment, they returned.

"There is one among your men who is not like the others." Ocllo pulled at the corners of her eyes, then mimed Bao's gold hoop earrings and the zig-zag tattoos on his forearms. "The one you say to Lord Pachacuti is your husband."

"Aye, his name is Bao," I said. "He is from Ch'in, from a country far away, farther than Terre d'Ange."

Her dark eyes were intent. "Cusi says that one says he have died before."

I was silent a moment, remembering the Patriarch of Riva. He'd reckoned the claim a sin, and forced me to recant it. I knew very little of Quechua faith and I feared to give offense. But I had promised to speak the truth; and anyway, Cusi had already heard the claim. "Yes," I said at length. "It's true."

"He went to the land of death?" Ocllo asked. "All the way? And came back?" She pointed at the flowering vine. "You brought him back like so?"

"Not alone," I said. "There was another man, a man who loved Bao like a son. He gave his life for him."

Ocllo inhaled sharply. "I see."

"May I ask what all this is about, my lady?" I inquired politely. "I'm sorry, I don't understand at all."

"No." She shook her head. "It is too soon. Later, maybe. I do not know." She made a magnanimous gesture. "You may ask something else."

I thought. "Does Lord Pachacuti know the secret of the ancestors?"

The old woman's shrewd eyes glinted. "If he is a god, yes."

I held her gaze. "And if he is not?"

"Then we will see." Ocllo glanced at the sun. "Now I must go and you to make ready. Lord Pachacuti wishes to dine with you."

More confused than ever, I watched her go.

FIFTY-EIGHT

One thing was certain, Lord Pachacuti lived very well in Vilca-bamba. The wealth of the Quechua had not been exaggerated. The meal was a veritable feast, all of it served on plates of solid gold.

It felt strange to sit across the table from Raphael as I had so many times in his townhouse in the City of Elua; only this time, we were enemies in a foreign land, served by Quechua maidens with down-cast eyes, a seething ball of ants hanging near our table. From time to time, one would scuttle down the rope and across the table, and Raphael would dip into his basket and place a leaf before it as though rewarding a favored pet.

"Do they all obey you?" I asked him. "Or is it just the queens who take their orders from you?"

"Plotting, Moirin?" Raphael smiled sidelong at me, stroking the thorax of his latest visitor with one fingertip.

"Curious," I said. "And I must confess, I cannot imagine how you learned to do it."

"That is because you lack Caim's gift, as well as a physician's inti-mate knowledge of the body's humors." A dreamy expression crossed his face. "I spent many hours in the jungle learning to discipline mine and assert my dominance. Many, many hours." His face clearing, he fed the ant a leaf. "Allow me to spare you the effort. All of them answer to me. You'll get nowhere by attempting to kill my queens."

"My thanks," I said. "It's generous of you to acknowledge it."

Raphael shrugged. "I'm fond of them and I'd prefer you didn't attempt to stomp them to death for no good cause."

I glanced around the room. All of the maidens, including Cusi, avoided my gaze. "Why did you ask me here tonight?"

"Would you believe I'm lonely?" he asked wryly.

I considered him. "Aye, I would."

He looked away. "What I mean to do is a glorious undertaking, Moirin. It will remake the world itself. I'd ask you to attempt to understand it."

"Explain it to me," I said.

Raphael shook his head. "We'll speak more of it later. Tell me more of this curiosity of yours. I'm interested in knowing how you think to wriggle out of your oath. What else are you *curious* about?"

I pointed at the basket of leaves. "Those."

"Ah." His brows rose. "The sacred herb of emperors." He pushed the basket across the table toward me. "Try it."

I hesitated.

"It's not poison, Moirin." Raphael plucked out a few leaves, shoving them into his mouth and chewing them into a wad he tucked into his cheek. "Just try it."

I did.

The leaves had an astringent taste and spread a tingling numbness over my lips and tongue, trickling down my throat. But as I chewed them, I began to feel more optimistic, energized, and clear-headed than I had for many days. Another time, it might have been pleasant. Under the circumstances, it was a bit unnerving. I didn't dare allow myself to trust the sensation.

Discreetly, I tried to spit out the wad of chewed leaves; but Cusi's small, brown hand intercepted it.

"*Sulpayki*," I murmured to her, feeling terribly self-conscious. "Thank you." She gave me the tiniest of nods.

"She pleases you?" Raphael inquired.

"For a spy, yes," I said.

He laughed. "What else are you curious about?"

I smoothed my gown with my hands. "Where does the wool come from? I did not think there were sheep in Terra Nova."

"What a remarkably banal question," Raphael observed. "I must say, I'm disappointed."

I shrugged. "You asked."

"The Quechua in the highlands of Tawantinsuyo raise animals they shear for wool," he said. "Even finer than sheep's wool. What else?"

I met his eyes. "Why the Temple of the Ancestors?"

"Ah, much better! Perhaps now we shall engage in a discussion worth having." Raphael waved one hand. "Leave us!" he ordered. "I will call for you once more when I am ready."

The handmaids withdrew.

"The Quechua are not a wholly barbaric folk, Moirin." Raphael leaned back in his chair, warming to his topic. "They have a very fine system of service and labor that ensures everyone contributes fairly, and a means to distribute food goods so that no one in the empire of Tawantinsuyo ever need starve. Nor are they the only folk to honor their ancestors; to be sure, many others do. But they *are* a simple and literal-minded people. They preserve the bodies of their royal dead and venerate them."

"Oh?" I asked.

Raphael shuddered. "It's true. They worship the rotting corpses of every man to have held the title of *Sapa Inca*, reckoning each and every one of them to be descended from their sun god. Their bodies are housed with honor in the Temple of the Ancestors. On special occasions, the Quechua bring them out and make offerings to them." His eyes took on a hectic sheen, sparks dancing in their depths. "When that worship is transferred to me, everything will change. *I* will show them a god incarnate."

I was silent.

"I will free them from the shackles of superstition, Moirin." His voice took on an impatient tone. "I will bring civilization, *true* civilization, to Terra Nova. Do you know how the Nahuatl write? They draw pictures! Do you know how the Quechua keep accounts? They tie knots in string! When I am God-King of the world, I will teach them knowledge! How can you argue against this?"

I chose not to answer. "How do you plan to summon Focalor without the Circle of Shalomon?" I asked instead.

He tapped his chest. "There is a part of his essence inside me. It will call to him. All I need is for you to open the door."

"Focalor nearly consumed you whole last time, Raphael," I said softly. "What makes you think this time will be different?"

His eyes flashed. "I've had years of learning to contain him! And it is *me* the Quechua worship, not the fallen spirit. It feeds me and gives me greater power." He laughed. "I know you are trying to tell them I'm not a god. It doesn't matter. Nothing you say matters." He gestured at the ants. "They can see that I have a great gift worthy of worship; and afterward, I will be a living god."

"If you are wrong, you unleash great devastation on the world," I murmured. "I saw storm-tossed waves and a thousand sinking ships in Focalor's eyes."

"I'm not wrong!" Raphael shouted. "Gods! Why must you always argue against my destiny, Moirin?" With an effort, he calmed himself. "Did you see the temples of human sacrifice in Tenochtitlan? The tens of thousands of human skulls?"

"Aye," I said. "But—"

"But nothing!" Lightning flickered in his eyes. "Once Focalor's power is mine, I can put a stop to it with a word. After I am made the *Sapa Inca*, I can lay claim to the Nahuatl Empire, too. I will not even need an army. I can threaten to sink the entire city beneath the lake; or withhold the rains until they starve."

"The Master of the Straits never used his power thusly," I noted.

Raphael sighed. "Yes, and think how much good he might have done had he dared. How is it that you will not see this, Moirin?" He made his voice gentle. "I will make the world a better place."

I gazed across the table at him and saw a vision of the future unfurling between us. I saw the great temples and palaces of Terra Nova fallen into ruin, neglected and abandoned, some reclaimed by the jungle, others razed to the ground. I saw the hollow-eyed skulls of the *tzompantli* crushed to splinters by booted feet. I saw complex hanks of knotted thread and scrolls of pictographic writing consumed by flames. I saw a sea of copper-brown faces set in expressions of stoic despair.

I saw Desirée seated on a throne beside Raphael, blank-faced as a doll.

"No," I whispered. "It does not work that way, my lord. Ah, gods! Raphael, I fear that if you seek to order the world to your liking, you will set in motion forces you do not understand. You cannot know the consequences."

His face went stony. "And you do?"

"I *see* them," I said helplessly.

In an abrupt motion, Raphael pushed his chair back from the table. The ants stirred attentively, hurrying down the rope. "Do you think I do not know the history of your folk?" he asked. "The Maghuin Dhonn failed to use the gift of sight wisely, and your bear-goddess herself took it from you long ago, Moirin. Didn't she?"

"Aye, but—"

He loomed over me. "You claim to see. Have you ever glimpsed a vision of the future that proved true?"

I hadn't.

I hadn't, because every dire vision I'd been afforded, I'd found a way to avert. But I could not say so to Raphael, and so I held my tongue.

"I didn't think so," he said with satisfaction. Picking up a small earthenware bell, he rang it, summoning his handmaidens, my inept young spy Cusi among them. "Take your mistress back to her quarters, little one," he ordered her. "I've no further taste for her company tonight."

Eyes downcast, Cusi bobbed in her approximation of a curtsy. "Yes, Lord Pachacuti."

A stream of ants followed us back to my quarters. Elua help me, I was beginning to take their presence for granted.

My thoughts chased one another in a futile endeavor, like a dog seeking to catch its own tail. Somewhat that Raphael had said tonight teased at my thoughts, but I could not catch it, only circle around it. Remembering Master Lo's teaching, I did my best to let go, breathing the Five Styles, willing my mind to be still and letting one thought give rise to another.

Beside me, Cusi shivered despite the warmth of the evening.

It came to me that I was paying attention to the wrong things.

I watched her bustle around my quarters when we reached them, kindling a lamp filled with oil that burned with a pleasant, nutty smell, turning down the blanket that covered the feather pallet on my bed. "Cusi? Why are you frightened?"

She shot me an unreadable look. "*Pampachayuway.* I am sorry, very sorry! I was not having such fear before."

"Why now?" I asked. "Do I frighten you?"

Cusi shook her head vigorously. "Not you, no. Not you, lady."

"Lord Pachacuti?" I guessed.

Her slender shoulders rose and fell. "Always, a little. But it is not that. I cannot say. It is not for me to say. I am not wise enough." She cast a yearning look at my feather pallet. "Lord Pachacuti say maybe you want me to sleep beside you some night, yes?"

Ah, gods!

Whatever Raphael had said to her, for a mercy, she hadn't understood it. There was naught but a scared child's innocence in the question, enough so that it made my heart ache for the girl. She was so very, very young. Maybe fifteen, no older than sixteen. Too young for whatever was being asked of her.

"Would it make you less afraid?" I asked gently.

Cusi nodded wordlessly.

I sat on the feather pallet and patted it. "Come."

The simple comfort of human contact is a thing that transcends all boundaries. Beneath the woven blanket, Cusi burrowed against me, hiding her face against my shoulder. I put one arm around her and breathed the Breath of Ocean's Rolling Waves, slow and deep, until I felt her own breath deepen into sleep and her body slacken.

I lay awake.

"What is the secret of the ancestors?" I asked the darkness. "What does it have to do with Bao? And why is Cusi afraid when she was not before?"

In her sleep, Cusi whimpered.

I stroked her hair. "Hush," I whispered. "Hush, and sleep."

She did.

In time, I did, too.

FIFTY-NINE

I awoke to an empty bed.

I found Cusi in the courtyard, tending to the ants. She had a pair
of good-sized lizards in a basket. While I watched, she slit each one's
belly with a little bronze knife, carefully laying their still-twitching
bodies amidst the swarming ants. Within a matter of seconds, both
lizards were stripped to the bone.

Cusi gave me an apologetic look. "It is not nice to see. I try to do
while you sleep."

"It's all right," I assured her. "Lord Pachacuti told me that they
prefer flesh."

"Yes." She closed the empty basket. "It make them strong."

In the daylight, she no longer looked so frightened, but there were
dark circles below her eyes, and it seemed to me that a shadow hung
over her. I tapped my lips with one finger, considering her.

"Why do you look at me so?" Cusi asked.

"I am wishing you would tell me what frightens you," I said.

She looked away. "I cannot."

"Ever?"

Her haunted gaze came back to me. "It is not for me to say."

"Forgive me," I said to her. "I will stop asking. After I break my
fast, I would like to visit my men again. Will you come or would you
rather not?"

"I will come." She gave me another apologetic look. "You know I listen for Lord Pachacuti?"

"I know," I said. "You are in his service. I understand this, Cusi. You are only doing as he asks." I smiled wryly. "And Lord Pachacuti tells me nothing I say matters. I think it pleases him to watch me scuttle around like one of his ants."

She shook her head. "That is not true."

"I have known him for many years," I said. "Even before he was given a gift by the bad spirits. There is a streak of cruelty in him."

"Not that," Cusi said. "The other thing."

With that, her face took on a shuttered look, and I did not press her. If I understood aright, she was denying that nothing I said mattered. All the more reason to choose my words with care.

Upon reaching the field where our captive men labored, I received a piece of unwelcome news.

"Your Nahuatl have deserted us," Thierry informed me grimly. "They've entered Raphael's service."

"*Both* of them?" It didn't surprise me that Eyahue would do such a thing; the old *pochteca* was nothing if not an opportunist. It was a part of what had brought him such success as a trader. But Temilotzin's desertion stung. I'd thought our Jaguar Knight would prove more loyal.

"I'm afraid so, my lady," Balthasar confirmed. He pointed toward a row of distant huts. "Along with that damned *cinchona* bark, we had a few sacks of trade goods, beads and mirrors, that de Mereliot didn't bother to confiscate. That old rascal purloined everything but the bark. I daresay he means to use them for bribes."

"Aye, and trade them for the sacred herb of emperors if he can," I muttered. "But why Temilotzin?"

Bao dusted dirt from his hands. "He said such work was beneath a warrior's honor, Moirin. That if there is fighting to do, that is where he belongs." He shook his head. "I'm sorry, I know you harbored a fondness for him. And I do believe he waited to see if Raphael would honor your request to allow his highness to leave. If he had, he would have accompanied your prince. But in truth, Temilotzin has no cause to care who wins the battle for Tawantinsuyo."

I thought of my vision. "Temilotzin is mistaken," I said. "If Raphael succeeds, he means to overthrow the Nahuatl Empire, too."

I thought the revelation might draw some reaction from Cusi, but she was staring at Bao with morbid fascination, like a dove transfixed by a serpent. Her little bronze knife was clutched in trembling hands.

Bao eyed her in turn. "Moirin, why does your spy look at me as though I mean to eat her?" he asked in the Shuntian scholar's tongue.

"I've no idea," I replied in the same.

"It doesn't appear you're winning her trust," he observed. "Should I disarm her? I don't like the way she's clinging to that knife."

"Not unless necessary." I shook my head. "And it's not that she distrusts me. I don't think that's entirely true. There's somewhat I don't understand at work here. Give me time."

"I don't know how much you have." Bao kept a watchful eye on the girl. "According to Eyahue, there's talk that the army will march soon."

My stomach sank. "I need to speak to Temilotzin. I need to tell him he's making a mistake."

Bao nodded. "Good luck."

Once again, Cusi and I made the trek across the terraced fields back toward the palace, a stream of happy, well-fed ants chittering alongside us. Cusi's brows were knit in thought, a narrow furrow etched between them. Trusting my instincts, I kept silent and waited for her to speak as we trudged beneath the hot sun.

At length, she did.

"The tongue you speak with *him*," she asked in a tentative tone. "Is it the tongue of the dead?"

"No," I said. "It is a tongue from the land of his birth. Do you think Bao is a ghost, Cusi?"

"I do not know this word."

"Not alive?" I hazarded. "Living dead?"

She shook her head. "He died and lives. It is not the same."

I nodded at the bronze knife she yet held. "You do not need to fear him. Bao does not mean to harm you."

Cusi gave me a stricken look. "I know."

Stone and sea! I could no more make sense of what was going through the child's mind than I could fly. And so I gave up trying for the time being, and concentrated on ascertaining Temilotzin's whereabouts. I was not worried about Eyahue—like as not the wily old fellow could look out for his own interests—but Temilotzin was a formidable warrior, and I could not bear to see him work toward the downfall of his own nation.

It was a blessing that Raphael feared me so little that I was given free access wherever I sought to go. Asking around with Cusi's aid, I found Temilotzin overseeing men training in a vast courtyard.

In a day's time, our Jaguar Knight had risen high in Lord Pachacuti's estimation. If nothing else, Raphael recognized skill and sought to put it to good use. Temilotzin had traded his spotted hides and his shattered *macahuitl* club for steel armor and a sharp sword, drilling almost thirty similarly outfitted Quechua in their usage. Clearly, he'd learned from watching our D'Angeline fighters along the way.

He scowled at the sight of me, gesturing to the Quechua to stand down.

"Temilotzin—" I began.

"Listen well, my little warrior!" he shouted at me. "None of these men understand a word of Nahuatl! Does your maid?"

I glanced at Cusi. "No, I don't think so."

"Good!" Temilotzin planted his fists on his hips, glowering at me. "You will pretend we quarrel! Eyahue and I have told Lord Pachacuti that Emperor Achcuatli forced us to serve you against our will. That is the truth you will tell if asked!"

I folded my arms and glared back at him. "I understand!"

His mouth twitched in a near-smile, quickly recapturing its hard scowl. "You needed someone on the inside. Lord Pachacuti would never have trusted the others. Tell me how we may help."

I made my voice low and bitter. "I need to know the secret of the ancestors. And if there is aught else you deem worthy, I would know it."

Temilotzin laughed contemptuously. "I will ask, little warrior! Whatever I learn, the old man will find a way to get word to you." He made a dismissive gesture. "Now go."

I spat at his feet.

His mouth twitched again. "Do not make me laugh, little warrior!" the Jaguar Knight roared. "Go!"

Turning on my heel, I went, Cusi trailing behind me.

For two days, I heard nothing further from Temilotzin, no word from Eyahue. The old woman Ocllo paid me no further visits, and Cusi seemed to withdraw further into herself, quiet and introspective. She appeared grateful for my company, grateful to dispel a measure of her fear and loneliness by sharing my bed at night, but whatever secret she was guarding, she kept it stubbornly to herself.

I saw very little of Raphael, who had immersed himself in planning for the conquest, consulting with strategists. The palace bustled with activity, and laborers in the fields worked overtime to harvest the crops that would be needed to supply this undertaking, a task rendered all the more difficult by the massive army of ants that would accompany it.

Condemned to helplessness, the men of Terre d'Ange were restless and angry. Our arrival had sparked something deep within Thierry de la Courcel, and I feared that he meant to attempt some sort of rebellion. Not even the news of Temilotzin and Eyahue's deception placated him.

"Tell him to be patient!" I pleaded with Bao in the scholar's tongue. "Even if it weren't for those gods-bedamned ants, there are too few of you, and too many Quechua loyal to Raphael!"

"I know." He sighed. "And they've the armor and weapons we carried with such effort only to deliver them into Raphael's hands, while we've nothing but digging-sticks. Believe me, I know. But it's frustrating, Moirin."

"I know." I touched his cheek. "Just keep him from trying anything foolish. If there's a time for desperate heroics, it's not yet on us."

Bao nodded. "Be glad that Balthasar came with us, and Captain Septimus, too. They're good at talking sense into the prince."

The following day, Eyahue paid me a visit in my quarters. I was so glad to see the old *pochteca*, I could have kissed him. Only uncertainty over how he wanted to play the encounter restrained me.

For Cusi's benefit, Eyahue hemmed and hawed, avoiding my eyes and acting abashed. "I come to apologize, lady," he said in careful Quechua. "And to explain. It was Temilotzin's idea to serve Lord Pachacuti. He is a warrior. It is his right."

"You are no warrior, old man," I retorted.

"Yes, I am old! Too old to work in the fields!" Eyahue said in a querulous tone, holding up one skinny arm. "Look at me!"

I jerked my chin at the fine wool of his tunic. "You steal from us. Now you wear good clothes. Did you trade stolen things for them?"

"Let me explain, lady," he wheedled. "I will explain in Nahuatl. Easier for you to understand, yes?"

Once again, I folded my arms sternly. "Go ahead."

Taking a deep breath, Eyahue shuffled his feet. "The Jaguar Knight says that you'll get nowhere trying to turn this tide," he said, rapid and cajoling. "The Quechua men are eager for this battle, eager to use their new weapons in the service of the mad Ant-Lord. Prince Manco believes that one will appoint him Regent."

"Who's Prince Manco?" I asked.

Cusi glanced over with a flicker of interest.

Eyahue coughed into his fist. "Sorry, didn't mean to use names. You're a clever lass; tell the maid some lie if she asks. He's the fellow your Ant-Lord deposed here. Stepped down willingly to serve the mad god, looks to be appointed to rule in his stead. He's the fifth son of the Emperor, and reckons this is his best chance at getting near the throne. One way or another, this battle is coming."

I raised my brows. "And the secret of the ancestors?"

Eyahue held out his hands palm upward and gave a helpless shrug,

"No man knows, only that it is rumored to exist. It is a secret the Maidens of the Sun keep, and not even *I* could pry it loose." His voice took on a hint of genuine indignation, one hand forming a fist to thump his sunken chest. "And you know how skilled I am in the ways of women!"

Gazing at the wiry old fellow, I bit the inside of my cheek in an effort to stifle a laugh. "Aye, I do."

He drew himself up with dignity. "Do you mock me?"

"No." I shook my head. "No, my lord Eyahue. It is clear to me that your goddess Xochiquetzal has blessed you, and you take joy in it. I laugh because it is true, and because it is better to laugh than weep."

He bared his mostly toothless gums in a rueful smile. "True words, lady."

I sighed. "I do not know what to do, Eyahue."

"And I do not know what to tell you." He patted my arm. "Do not lose heart, child. You have come too far to fail. Surely the gods are not done with you yet." He shifted back to speaking Quechua, wheedling once more. "So, lady? Do I have your forgiveness?"

"Aye," I said. "You do. Now go."

Bowing, he went.

"He is no good, that one!" Cusi said fiercely after Eyahue had departed. "He asks too many questions, questions he should not know to ask! You should not forgive him, lady. He is a danger to you."

I had the sense of a chasm looming between us.

I had promised Cusi I would not lie to her, but I had. I had deceived her twice over, first with Temilotzin, now with Eyahue. More than once, I had plotted to her face, dissembling and relying on tongues she did not speak.

And yet she sought to protect me.

A promise was not the same thing as a binding oath. But it should be. There should be no difference between the two.

None.

My *diadh-anam* flared in agreement. In memory, I saw the look of profound acceptance and approval in the eyes of the Maghuin Dhonn

Herself. It was time to cast caution to the winds and leap into the chasm.

"Eyahue does but seek to aid me," I said simply. "Temilotzin, too. All else is pretense."

Cusi drew a sharp breath, studying my face. "Truly?"

I nodded. "Truly. And now you hold their fate in your hands, Cusi. Lord Pachacuti will not harm me if you tell him. He needs me. But he will punish Eyahue and Temilotzin, mayhap put them to death. The choice is yours."

Her expression turned to one of dismay. "I do not want it! It is too big for one such as me."

"I know," I murmured. "The gods use their chosen hard, Cusi, and it seems yours have chosen you for this burden. Whatever secret it is you keep, whatever the secret of the ancestors may be, you've guarded it well. You keep telling me it is not for you to say, that you are not old and wise enough. Are you sure that your gods have not decreed otherwise?"

She looked away, her chin trembling. "I am afraid."

"I know," I repeated. "Nonetheless, you must choose."

SIXTY

I slept, and dreamed of falling. Downward and downward, as though I'd leapt into an immense chasm, until at last I struck bottom and woke with a violent jerk, unsure if I was awake or dreaming, alive or dead.

There was a hand clamped over my mouth.

For a moment, I was confused, once again imagining myself in a tent in the Abode of the Gods with Manil Datar assaulting me; but there was no knife at my throat, no scent of his cloying perfume. I squinted in the faint moonlight filtering into my bedchamber and made out the face of the old woman Ocllo above me.

"Be still!" she hissed.

I nodded my understanding. Ocllo withdrew her hand and straightened. I sat upright to see the shadowy figures of several other women in my chamber, Cusi among them, her pretty face somber. Ocllo beckoned imperiously to her.

"*Pampachayuway*, lady," Cusi whispered to me, taking a seat beside me. "I do not wish to pain you, but I must do this thing. Give me your hand."

I hesitated.

Her dark eyes were grave, and older than her years. "You put the lives of your Nahuatl men in my hands. Will you not put your own?"

Slowly, I extended my right hand. Wrapping her fingers around my wrist, Cusi pressed the tip of her little bronze knife against the heel of my palm. With one surprisingly powerful thrust, she sliced open my palm.

Bronze does not take a point or hold an edge like steel, and it hurt a great deal more than I would have reckoned. I bit back a cry and breathed the Breath of Wind's Sigh, willing my mind to distance itself from the pain while my cupped palm filled slowly with blood, dark and shiny in the faint light. Releasing my wrist, Cusi administered the same treatment to her own right hand, opening a gash without flinching.

"Now." She held out her hand to me, blood dripping from it. On their sisal rope, the ball of ants stirred with interest. The other women in the chamber watched with silent concentration.

I clasped Cusi's wounded hand with my own. It was slippery with warm blood. She returned my grip firmly. I could feel my pulse beating in my palm, and imagined I could feel hers, too, every beat a throb of dull agony.

It went on for a long time, until at last Ocllo nodded in approval and beckoned to two more women. Cusi relinquished her grip. One of the women came forward with a golden bowl full of water, kneeling and gently bathing Cusi's and my injured hands, after which the other woman bandaged them gently.

"Now you are of one blood," Ocllo murmured. "Now you are as sisters. Now you may enter the Temple of the Maidens of the Sun, lady." She beckoned to me. "Come."

After exchanging my thin sleeping-shift for a gown, I exited the palace and followed the Maidens of the Sun through the streets of Vilcabamba, accompanied by the ever-present stream of ants.

The city was quiet and sleeping, for Lord Pachacuti had no need to post sentries. His ants would respond to any intruder, or anyone seeking to flee. We were neither, and there was no one to take notice of us. We passed through the city like silent ghosts. My hand continued to throb, slow blood seeping through the bandages.

I daresay the Temple of the Maidens of the Sun was a glorious place in daylight, when the sun was meant to be worshipped. By night, it was a vast, eerie space. Low flames flickered in a firepit in the center of the main temple chamber, shedding enough light to illuminate a massive golden disk depicting the Quechua sun god Inti on the far wall, not enough to chase the shadows from the corners or the high ceilings.

More silent women awaited us, many of them young and pretty.

After the black stream of ants had finished pouring over the threshold, the doors to the temple were closed.

"So!" Ocllo's voice echoed in the vast chamber. "You say Lord Pachacuti is not a god!"

There was a soft, murmuring echo as someone translated her words from D'Angeline into Quechua.

"I do," I said.

She gestured at the thousands upon thousands of ants. "Yet he has great power. What other man can do such a thing?"

"None here," I said. "Lord Pachacuti killed the only man in our company to possess the ability to understand them."

Ocllo frowned. "You say his gift comes from bad spirits, yet you have a gift, too. I have seen it."

I nodded. "It is a gift from my gods."

Her shrewd eyes narrowed. "How is that different?"

"I did not ask for it, my lady," I said honestly. "I was born with it. Lord Pachacuti *asked* for his gift."

"And the gods gave it to him," Ocllo observed.

"A fallen spirit who was once a god's servant, yes. With my aid— aid I gave him because I was young and foolish and knew no better. And the gift that was given him, the gift of the language of ants, was not even the gift he sought. It was given him as a *jest*, one he has turned to dire ends I daresay not even the spirits themselves could have foreseen." I opened my arms. My wounded right hand throbbed, wrapped in blood-stained bandages. "My lady, I do not lie. If Lord Pachacuti succeeds in this conquest, he will become more powerful than ever. He will become a god in truth." I shook my head. "But if you think he cares for the people of Tawantinsuyo, you are wrong. In the end, only bad will come of it."

Ocllo pursed her lips. "So you say."

I raised my voice in frustration, unwanted tears stinging my eyes. "I've *seen* it! How can I make you understand?"

"Hush." Ocllo's voice deepened, unexpectedly soothing. The corners of her eyes crinkled. "There is one way, child. But I fear it cannot come from you."

"The ancestors?" I asked.

Cusi's bandaged hand found mine and squeezed it. Despite the pang of pain, I welcomed her grip.

Finding herself with a captive audience, Ocllo paced the floor of the temple in a leisurely manner, treading with care and drawing her skirts to avoid the ants. "It begins many, many years ago with the first Earth-Shaker," she said conversationally. "The first Lord Pachacuti, the first *Sapa Inca*. He told the secret to his Queen, his Queen of Queens, his first wife, the great Mamacoya, and swore that she and her descendants must keep it always." She nodded to herself. "So we have, every one of us. Have we not?"

Voices murmured in agreement.

My skin prickled. "Will you speak of it now?"

She fixed me with her gimlet gaze. "You say to me that the man who is your husband died, and lives. I ask again, is it true?"

"Aye, it is."

Ocllo snorted. "I do not mean that he was struck on the head and slept for a time."

"Bao *died*," I said simply. "Everything I told you is true. He was killed by a poisoned dart. He drew no breath, no blood beat in his veins. I felt his body myself, felt it grow cold and stiff. For a long time, not a short time. He journeyed to the Ch'in underworld, and remembers it. And I do not know why this matters to you, but it is true."

"Because the first *Sapa Inca* said that one who had returned from death would wield the key to call on the ancestors in our hour of need," she said. "Call them out of death into life to save their people."

I stared at her, open-mouthed. "You think Bao can do this? But... but they're not *his* ancestors!"

"No." Ocllo frowned. "That is why we are uncertain. But the prophecy does not say the twice-born would be the one to call them, only that he would wield the key." She held up a bronze knife like Cusi's. "This."

"I don't understand," I whispered.

Cusi's hand tightened on mine. "He would be the one to offer the sacrifice," she murmured. "It is the sacrifice that calls the ancestors."

And then I did understand, and I wished that I didn't.

"You," I said, my throat tight. "You're the sacrifice. That's why you're afraid, isn't it?"

Her chin lifted. "I was not afraid when Lord Pachacuti chose me," she said with dignity. "It was an honor. But I am afraid now..." Her voice broke. "Afraid to be wrong and anger the gods. If I am wrong, they will cast me aside."

I gazed at her in horror, then glanced at Ocllo, at the other women in the temple. "Is there no other way? Surely there must be!"

One by one, they shook their heads. "You claim Lord Pachacuti is not a god, but you cannot prove it," Ocllo said, not without sympathy. She gestured at the ants again. "And he holds the power of death in his hands. If the hour of our need is here, the ancestors will answer. It is the only way to be sure. But it must be a true sacrifice, a willing sacrifice, of one of their own."

"*Why?*" I could hear a child's resentment at the unfairness of the world in my voice.

"It is necessary," the old woman said soberly. "You know this in your heart, lady. You told me that the man who loved your husband like a son gave his own life for him. To call the ancestors out of death, a life must be given." She laid a hand on Cusi's shoulder. "And Cusi has already been chosen. I think maybe it is no accident that she is the one to find the twice-born who wields the key."

There were solemn nods all around.

"No, of course it's not!" I said helplessly. "Because gods-bedamned Raphael de Mereliot, Lord Pachacuti, *gave* her to me knowing he'd already chosen her as the sacrifice, knowing it would cause me pain! That's the only reason Cusi met Bao, and learned what she did!"

"Did Lord Pachacuti know your husband was twice-born?" Ocllo asked me.

It brought me up short. "No. No, I don't think so."

"So mayhap it was the will of the gods after all, and Lord Pachacuti erred because he does not know the secret of the ancestors," she said softly. "Or maybe you are wrong, and he is only testing our loyalty. Either way, it is not for you to decide the fate of the Quechua. It is for us." Her gaze settled on Cusi. "And in the end, the choice falls to the chosen one. No one else can make it."

A faint sigh echoed throughout the temple.

Cusi glanced at me, tears glimmering in her dark eyes. "It is as you told me, is it not, lady? I must choose."

"I did not know the stakes," I murmured.

"I did." Releasing my hand, Cusi clasped hers together before her. "I have chosen," she announced in an unexpectedly firm voice. "I choose the path of the ancestors."

SIXTY-ONE

⬥

Our midnight gathering concluded, the Maidens of the Sun dispersed to their quarters in the temple. Cusi and I made our way back to my quarters in the palace, the ants streaming alongside us, chittering softly and clicking their ever-hungry mandibles in the moonlight.

She was calm, a mantle of grace and acceptance settled over her small figure.

I was not.

My mind reeled from revelation to revelation. Ah, gods! It seemed cruel, too cruel. I wanted to doubt it, and yet, in my heart of hearts, I could not. From the far side of death, Jehanne had told me the women held the key to thwarting Raphael; had told me Raphael had made a mistake in giving me the girl. And before I'd even embarked on this quest, the Nahuatl Emperor Achcuatli had warned me that I did not understand the ways of Terra Nova. Mayhap Naamah had meant for him to hear the words of her blessing—but she had meant for me to hear his words, too.

Sometimes when the gods thirst, blood is *the only sacrifice.*

Now I believed. But stone and sea, it hurt.

The ants swarmed up their sisal rope, clambering into a ball. Moving quietly about the bedchamber, Cusi kindled a lamp and turned down the blanket, then turned to leave.

"Will you not stay?" I asked her.

Pausing, she shook her head. "No." Her voice was soft with regret. "I think it is time for me to be alone and pray, lady. I will pass the night in the far chamber, and in the morning, I will ask Lord Pachacuti to send another handmaid to you. I will tell him it is a sacred matter, for it is true."

It was on the tip of my tongue to say that I did not want another handmaid, that in a very short time I had grown fond of Cusi—of her dimpled smile, her youthful innocence, and her woefully obvious spying.

But that was the girl I'd known yesterday—or the girl I'd thought I had known. All along, she'd known herself to be a chosen sacrifice. And all along, I had been ignorant of the stakes.

Now the choice was truly hers. It had not been mine to make, and it was not mine to belittle or diminish. Only to understand as best I could.

I inclined my head to her. "*Sulpayki*, Cusi. I will miss you."

She smiled a little, one cheek dimpling. "You will see me again, lady. It is only that I cannot be a part of..." She gestured vaguely. "This. I cannot be pulled in two ways any longer."

I understood.

There was a long road yet to travel between the jungle city of Vilcabamba and the Temple of the Ancestors in the distant capital of Qusqu, a road filled with planning and plotting, warfare and strategy, logistics and subterfuge. I'd no idea how we would make it all work; and there was still the matter of my conflicting oaths to be resolved. There were a thousand details to be considered.

But Cusi was right, that should not concern her now.

Only her choice mattered.

"I pray your gods and ancestors bless you," I said to her. A rueful smile tugged at my lips. "And I pray I can explain this to Bao. He will not like it. Not at all. I cannot promise that he will agree to it."

"He has to," Cusi said simply.

"One does not tell Bao what he *has* to do," I murmured. "But I will try."

She paused. "Can you tell me one thing, lady? Why does Lord Pachacuti seek such power if it is wrong?"

"There is a hunger in him," I said. "Nothing has ever been enough to fill it."

"Like the ants," she said.

"Very like the ants," I said. "But Raphael is a human being. He has been hurt badly by many losses. It has twisted his hunger into something unnatural, just as he has turned the ants' hunger to unnatural ends."

She cocked her head. "But it is not why you came, is it? You say to him that you came because of a child, a little girl."

"Aye." I nodded. "Far, far away, she is in danger. I came because I swore an oath to protect her, and the only one who can do this is her brother, Prince Thierry. I came to bring him home. But it is complicated, Cusi. I am responsible for Lord Pachacuti's gift, too. I believe the gods meant for me to attempt to stop him." My throat tightened. "But I never knew it could come at such a cost."

Cusi patted my uninjured hand gently. "Do not cry for me, lady. We are also to blame. We took him to be a god." A frown creased her brow. "Or do you think I am not worthy of paying the price?"

"Not worthy!" I laughed through the tears that stung my eyes. "Oh, Cusi, no! I think you are more than worthy. It just seems cruel that the gods, or the ancestors, require the fairest and brightest of blossoms, one only just beginning to bloom."

Blushing a little, she ducked her head. "Should we offer them anything less?" she asked in a low tone.

"No," I said after a long moment. "No, I suppose not. But I cannot help being sad, and you will have to forgive me for it. I do not mean to dishonor your courage."

"You have a kind heart." Cusi glanced shyly up at me. "Lord Pachacuti knows this, too. Now that I know you, I see the ways he tries to hurt you. Tomorrow you must tell Lord Pachacuti you are angry at him for choosing me to serve you. He will expect you to be angry and shout."

I wiped my eyes. "He will, won't he?"

"Yes." She took my bandaged hand. "I think the bleeding has stopped. Do not let him see this, or he may wonder. I will be careful, too."

I wanted to answer, but no words came.

Letting go my hand, Cusi gave me an impulsive hug, pressing her soft cheek against mine. "I am glad I have chosen," she whispered. "And I am glad we share blood, and you are a sister to me now."

I returned her embrace, kissing her cheek. "You honor me."

With that, Cusi took her leave, retreating to her cot in the outer chamber. I lay awake while the lamp burned low and guttered, leaving me in darkness. At last I fell into a fitful sleep.

I dreamed of blood trickling over stone, rivulets swelling to streams. I dreamed of a vast doorway filled with darkness; and beyond it, a living storm, a churning maelstrom of wings and thunder and lightning.

I dreamed of flowers; of a field of marigolds bursting into blossom, of dahlias quickening beneath my touch, liana blossoming on the vine, thousands upon thousands of blossoms raising a humble, fragile bulwark against the coming darkness and the gathering storm.

I dreamed of bones, ancient bones, beginning to stir.

And I awoke to sunlight, and emptiness.

Cusi was gone.

SIXTY-TWO

Does your cruelty know no bounds, my lord?" I shouted at Raphael. "Gods bedamned, Raphael! You *knew*! You sent poor Cusi to attend me, knowing you meant to sacrifice her all along!"

Lounging on his throne, Raphael de Mereliot shrugged and stuffed a few leaves into his mouth. "Forgive me, Moirin. It amused me."

I clenched my wounded hand into a fist, the pain anchoring me. "I do *not* forgive you."

"You don't have a great deal of choice, do you?" Raphael's gaze hardened. "Anyway, I do but honor the lass by bestowing the gift of sacrifice upon her. She volunteered for it." He gestured carelessly around the throne room at his handmaidens. "They all volunteered, Moirin. Each and every last one of them."

I glowered at him, not needing to feign bitterness.

He laughed. "Such a look!" Swinging himself upright, Raphael rose and paced across the floor, accompanied by a skittering stream of ants. "Ah, Moirin." His fingers trailed across my cheek, down my throat. Once upon a time, I would have ached to have him touch me thusly. Now it made my stomach roil. "My hot-tempered little bear-witch, my useful tool. Tell me, who would you choose to take Cusi's place?"

"No one," I murmured.

"Oh, but you must if you wish to spare the lass." He pointed at a pretty Quechua maid, and then another. The young women blanched, trembling, and trying not to show it. After last night's revelation in the temple, none of them were so eager to sacrifice themselves for Lord Pachacuti's sake. "Her? Or mayhap her?"

I shook my head. "I will not play this game with you, Raphael."

His fingers tightened like pincers on my throat, digging in hard enough to bruise. "Then do not complain to me, Moirin mac Fainche of the Maghuin Dhonn!" With an abrupt gesture, he thrust me away. "I find it tiresome."

I staggered and caught myself, massaging my bruised throat. "No more than I, I assure you."

Returning to his throne, Raphael waved one languid hand. "Go, then."

I turned to obey.

"Wait."

I halted.

"Why did you wed him?" There was a genuine note of curiosity in Raphael's voice. "Master Lo's surly lad?"

"Why do you care?" I turned back, unnerved by his mercurial mood shift.

He shrugged. "I'm curious. Indulge me, won't you? Otherwise, I might have to, oh, forbid you to see him. I haven't done that yet, have I? All in all, I think I've been quite generous with you."

"All right." I took a deep breath. "First of all, he's a man, not a lad. And he's not surly. If he seemed so in Terre d'Ange, it was only because D'Angelines had given him little cause to love them." I gave him a tight smile. "You, in particular."

"I never said a word to the lad!" Raphael retorted in an offended tone.

I raised my brows. "Aye, and I suspect that may have had somewhat to do with it, my lord. Bao is stubborn and proud. You treated him as less than a man. You're doing it still. Do you blame him for resenting it?"

Raphael blinked. "I treated him as I would treat any servant."

"No." I shook my head. "I lived in your household, Raphael. You treated your servants with a courtesy you never afforded Bao, with a courtesy you do not afford your Quechua handmaids."

He lowered his voice. "They are a simple folk, Moirin! They worship their rulers. If I treated them otherwise, they would not respect me."

"Mayhap," I said. "Or mayhap it is that like many D'Angelines, you think so very highly of yourself, you have a hard time reckoning others your equals."

Raphael scowled at me. "Mayhap it is your own bitterness that speaks!"

"Mayhap it is," I admitted. "How many times did you see fit to remind me that I was naïve and unsophisticated? I grant you, it was true, but it did not make me *less* than you. Different, but not less. You never saw me as aught but a useful tool for your hands to wield, the very thing you called me today."

"And so you are." Leaning his head against the back of his throne, Raphael closed his eyes. "One that grows tiresome once more. Never mind. Go away, Moirin."

"No." I stood my ground. "Since you asked, I will answer your question. I wed Bao because I love him. I love his pride and stubbornness, even when it exasperates me. I love his refusal to succumb to despair. He makes me laugh. And he makes me feel . . . safe."

Raphael's eyes cracked open. "That sounds dull."

"It's not," I said.

"*I* think you harbor a deep-seated resentment against full-blooded D'Angelines," he said.

I laughed out loud. "If I did, would I have travelled to the far side of the world to rescue one of them? No." I shook my head again. "I have found much to love in Terre d'Ange. I find the worship of Blessed Elua and his Companions, the celebration of love and desire, to be beautiful and unique among realms. I found my father, and my lady Je—" I stopped myself before I said Jehanne's name. "I have found myself guilty of misjudgment," I said instead, "and discovered that a beautiful face and a facile wit can conceal great strength of character."

He stirred. "Do not speak of her!"

"I wasn't," I said. "If anyone misjudged her, it was she herself. I was speaking of Balthasar Shahrizai."

"Oh." Unexpectedly, Raphael's mouth quirked. "I imagine he's despising every minute of this, isn't he?"

"Indeed," I agreed.

The thought seemed to cheer him. "All right, you've had your say. Now be gone with you. I mean it this time, Moirin."

I took my leave with alacrity, glad to be out of his presence. Raphael had always been tempestuous, but he had never been violent. The bruises on my throat were a reminder that everything was different now. Cusi was right, I had to do what he expected to avoid arousing suspicion, but I needed to be careful about provoking him. It was a piece of luck that my reference to Balthasar had amused him, pandering unwittingly to the streak of cruelty within him.

Upon returning to my quarters, I found that Cusi's replacement had already been assigned to me, a serious-looking young woman named Machasu, a few years older than Cusi. She pointed gravely at my injured hand. "Sister of one, sister of all," she said in softly accented D'Angeline.

It was a relief to hear. "*Sulpayki*, thank you. Yes."

Machasu nodded. "Eat now, lady?"

I shook my head. "I must speak with my men. Lord Pachacuti hasn't forbidden it, has he?"

"No." She fixed me with an intent gaze. "But I have to tell him what you do and say. Ocllo says, say what you tell me. This, I will do."

"I am grateful." I hesitated. "Machasu, is it just the Maidens of the Sun who are willing to help, or are there others?"

"No others yet, but some women may help if Ocllo asks." Her grave look deepened. "But she must be very, very careful."

"I understand," I said. "What about the men?"

"No." Her tone was flat.

"I would like to speak to your Prince Manco nonetheless. Not about this," I hastened to add, raising my wounded hand as Machasu's expression turned to one of alarm. "Not about the secret of the ancestors. But about Lord Pachacuti."

"Prince Manco will not listen to you," she said with distaste. "He thinks he is a great warrior chosen by the gods. You cannot trust him. Anything you say, he will say to Lord Pachacuti."

"I know," I said. "But it only amuses Lord Pachacuti to see me try and fail. And it may be that seeds of doubt planted now will blossom later."

Machasu looked dubious. "I will ask."

Another thought struck me. "Machasu, I may have to reveal the secret of the ancestors to all my men, not just Bao. If I ask them to trust blindly, knowing nothing, I fear they will rebel. But I do not want to betray the trust of the Maidens of the Sun, either."

She was silent a moment. "You are our sister," she said at length. "Ocllo trusts you. Do as you must."

With that, we set out to trek across the terraced fields.

My heart ached at the sight of Bao's indomitable grin as he caught sight of me. Everything I had told Raphael was true, but it didn't begin to encompass the bond between us. There was the way my *diadh-anam* quickened with joy at being reunited with his, a sensation I couldn't even begin to describe. There was an unshakeable solidarity born of having survived so many trials and hardships together—aye, and wonders, too.

There was love, always love.

I did not relish the task of telling him what I had to tell him today. In the benighted Temple of the Sun, it had seemed at once a noble sacrifice and a necessary horror. In the bright light of ordinary day, sweat trickling beneath my gown, it merely seemed a horror, an unthinkable horror.

But it *wasn't* an ordinary day. No day under Lord Pachacuti's rule was ordinary. A living, seething moat of ants ringed the field, an ever-present reminder of the unnatural straits in which we found ourselves.

Bao read my expression, his grin faltering. "What is it, Moirin? More trouble?"

"No." My eyes stung. "Worse. Hope, but it is a grim one."

His sharp gaze skated over Machasu. "That is a different maid," he said in the scholar's tongue. "Is she also a spy?"

"No," I said. "An ally."

The others began to gather, eager for news. There was not a man among them one would have taken at a glance for the pampered, gossip-loving scions of D'Angeline nobility many of them had been, quick to revel in luxury and indulgence. They were lean and work-hardened, hands callused by paddles and digging-sticks, fair skin burnt brown by the sun. But there was a fierce light in their eyes. Whatever fight there was to be fought, they were ready for it.

"Lady Moirin." Prince Thierry de la Courcel, naked above the waist, greeted me with a courtly bow that did not disguise the hunger in his expression. "Tell us, what passes?"

I swallowed. "I would speak to Bao alone."

A muscle in Thierry's jaw twitched. "Why?"

Balthasar Shahrizai laid a grimy hand on Thierry's shoulder. "They're husband and wife, man," he said in a deceptively easy tone. "Give them a moment, won't you?"

Prince Thierry kept his gaze hard on mine. "Whatever news you have to deliver, it concerns all of us, does it not?"

"Aye," I said. "But none more than Bao."

The rightful heir to the throne of Terre d'Ange hesitated, then nodded, taking a step backward. "Of course. As you will, my lady."

A stream of ants detached from the river to follow Bao and me into the field as we went some distance from the others. The sun-warmed earth between the rows of growing potatoes was soft and crumbling beneath my sandal-shod feet. Once we were out of earshot, Bao took my arm in a firm grip.

"Tell me," he said.

I did.

I told him the whole of what I had learned from Ocllo and Cusi and the Maidens of the Sun. I told him the secret of the ancestors, and their belief that one who was twice-born would wield the key—would wield the *knife*—to offer the blood sacrifice that would call forth the ancestors out of death into life.

When I had finished, Bao walked away.

He did not go far, only a few paces. But he stood with his back to me, his head bowed, hands clasping his elbows. I gazed at him, seeing the bright shadow that had hung over him since his death gather and darken.

"Bao..." I whispered.

"Do you think it will work?" he asked without turning around. "This business of sacrifice?"

I went to him then, wrapping my arms around his waist, pressing my face against the back of his neck and inhaling the scent of his skin. "I think it is our only hope."

Bao took a deep breath, his ribcage rising and falling beneath my arms. "I should have known there would be a further price to pay," he said. "There is always another price. I do not wish to do this thing, Moirin."

"I know," I said.

"She's scarce more than a child!"

I leaned my brow against his taut shoulder blades. "I know. Ah, gods, Bao! I know. But it is her choice, and she has chosen."

"I want to speak with her," Bao said abruptly.

"Cusi?"

He turned in my arms. "Yes. I do not doubt you, Moirin. I don't. But for my own sake, I must hear it from her lips."

I nodded. "Then I will make it happen. What will you tell the others?"

Bao shrugged. "Whatever is needful."

SIXTY-THREE

Time was running short. Upon returning to my quarters, I was visited by Eyahue, who brought the latest details of the conflict to come.

"Lord Pachacuti has sent *chasquis* to Qusqu to demand the *Sapa Inca* Yupanqui's surrender," he announced to me in Nahuatl. "Swift runners stationed throughout Tawantinsuyo to relay messages. Once he receives a reply, he will move."

"How long?" I asked.

"Soon," Eyahue said. "Days. The *chasqui* system is very efficient."

"What do you think the *Sapa Inca* will do?"

He sucked his teeth. "I think he will refuse. I do not think Yupanqui will believe Lord Pachacuti's threat. It is as I said before, lady. Neither Temilotzin nor I think you can stop this from happening."

"Nor do I," I said. "Not here, anyway. My thanks, Eyahue."

"Is there aught else I can do?" he asked.

I shook my head. "For now, no. I'll send word if there is. This is Machasu," I added, indicating my new handmaid. "You may trust her."

"Oh, aye?" Eyahue eyed her with shrewd interest. "Got rid of the other one, did you?"

"It seems she had other duties." I trusted the old *pochteca* to a degree, but not enough to give him leverage over us. He was too garrulous and too much the opportunist. When the time came, I would tell him.

After Eyahue's departure, I dispatched Machasu on a pair of errands; the first to seek an audience on my behalf with Prince Manco, and the second to carry word to Ocllo that I needed to arrange a meeting between Cusi and Bao.

While she was gone, I sat cross-legged in the courtyard and breathed the Five Styles, trying to clear my mind and focus my thoughts.

I wondered what Bao was telling the others. I did not think they would be pleased to receive the news that the entirety of my plan was to stake everything on a long-kept Quechua secret and one young woman's sacrifice. And yet it seemed to me that all the signs indicated it was our only hope.

But the gods knew, I'd been wrong before. If I hadn't misread my destiny in the first place, we wouldn't be in this dilemma.

I prayed that Cusi, who was even younger than I had been, had not mistaken her own destiny; and then I felt horrible for it, and wished again that there was another way.

If there was, I could not see it.

And so I turned my thoughts to the matter of my conflicting oaths. I couldn't see a way out of this bind, either. So long as Raphael was hell-bent on taking Desirée as his bride, I could not keep my oath to one without breaking my oath to the other.

It seemed likely to me that the sacrifice would be the last ritual before Raphael called on me to open a gateway between the worlds so that he might attempt to summon Focalor. Mayhap the Quechua ancestors would intervene before that final step. I could not imagine how such a thing might come to pass. But Raphael had mocked the Quechua for worshipping their dead—and yet he himself had claimed that worship fed power.

I made a note in my thoughts to ask Ocllo if she knew exactly *how* the ancestors would be called out of death into life to save their descendants.

Or mayhap, I thought reluctantly, it was simply what was destined, the further price that Bao had spoken of.

Once my *diadh-anam* was extinguished, the door would be closed forever. I would be powerless and estranged forever from the Maghuin Dhonn Herself, and Bao . . . my twice-born magpie would die a second death, returning to the Ch'in afterworld of Fengdu, where I prayed the Maiden of Gentle Aspect awaited him.

Raphael would still have his army of ants, but if the desiccated bodies of the ancestors rose to denounce him, the Quechua would turn against him. Raphael ruled in Vilcabamba with their consent, as he planned to rule in all of Tawantinsuyo, worshipped as a God-King. As terrible as the ants were, they wouldn't suffice to keep an entire hostile empire at bay.

There might be a few casualties, awful, unthinkable casualties, but all it would take was one well-thrown spear to kill Raphael. If I could get my hands on my bow, I'd gladly kill him myself.

And then it would be over.

Ah, gods! With the revelation of Cusi's intended sacrifice so fresh in my mind, it seemed terribly selfish to pray that matters would not come to pass thusly, but I couldn't help it.

If she was right, at least she had the solace of eternity.

I wouldn't.

So I prayed wordlessly to the Maghuin Dhonn Herself to guide me; and I prayed to Blessed Elua and his Companions, most especially to my patron gods Naamah and Anael, over and over.

"Did I not say you would have need of me before the end?" a light, familiar voice inquired. "Do not fret so, Moirin. I will be there."

I startled awake, realizing belatedly that I'd fallen into a doze in the hot courtyard, worn out by lack of sleep and worry.

"Jehanne?" I said aloud.

"Lady?" Machasu gave me an odd look. "I am sorry. Do you wish to be alone? I will go."

"No." I rubbed my eyes. "Did you say something just now?"

"No," she said. "I came to tell you that Prince Manco will see you in a short time. But Ocllo says it is not safe for Cusi to leave the temple now. It will only make for dangerous questions."

I took a deep breath. "Well, then, I will have to bring Bao to the temple."

Machasu's eyes widened. "That is worse! He cannot leave the fields! One tried, once." She pointed to the ants. "They ate him. Alive."

"I know." My stomach churned. "But the ants will not see him. No one will see him." I held up my injured hand. "Do you trust me? Does Ocllo trust me?"

Slowly, Machasu nodded.

"Then tell her I will bring the twice-born to the Temple of the Sun when the moon is high tonight to meet with Cusi." I fought a yawn. "Tell her I swear no one will know. It is a secret I have not told her yet, a gift I have not shown."

"I will tell her." She gave me a stern look. "And I will bring food. You must eat, lady. You must stay strong."

"You are right," I said. "Thank you."

After I had bathed and eaten, I paid a visit to Prince Manco. As Machasu had predicted, it was a useless endeavor.

The deposed Quechua prince received me in his own garden courtyard where he was engaged in practicing his fighting skills, clad in a full set of D'Angeline armor. I was forced to wait and observe his dubious prowess as he stomped and clattered and slashed his way across the garden. At length he paused and beckoned for an attendant to hold up one of the small hand-mirrors that Eyahue had stolen to trade.

When at last he was done admiring himself, Prince Manco turned to me, unbuckling and removing his helmet. Without it, he was revealed to be a weak-chinned young fellow with close-set eyes.

"What is it you want?" he demanded of me.

Placing my hands together, I bowed to him. "I come to warn you, highness. Lord Pachacuti is not the god you take him to be."

He scowled at me and thumped a gauntleted fist on his breastplate. "Oh? What gifts do you bring, woman? Armor that shines like silver, yet is as hard as stone?" He gestured at my insectile entourage. "Can you command the black river?"

"No," I murmured. "But actually, the armor—"

"I do not care!" Prince Manco's nostrils flared. "I will not listen to your lies! Lord Pachacuti told me not to! You think you are clever, yes, but I agreed to this only so I might tell him what you say!"

I sighed. "Lord Pachacuti will use you and discard you, along with all of the Quechua folk."

He glared at me. "Lord Pachacuti will give me Tawantinsuyo to rule once he returns to his homeland!" His sword cut the air. "Everyone will fear me. My father's head will roll! My brothers will kneel and beg for their lives!"

Ignoring him, I turned to his attendants. "Remember that I brought this warning," I said to them. "Tell others."

"You do not speak to them!" Prince Manco shouted at me. "Go away!" He hefted his blade, menacing me awkwardly. "I do not know why Lord Pachacuti lets you live. I should kill you for him!"

I stared at him. "Lord Pachacuti *needs* me. Do it, and you will answer to him." I nodded at the ants. "Or them."

Manco lowered his blade. "Go away," he repeated. "I do not want you here."

I went.

"I am sorry," Machasu said to me. "It is as I told you."

"It is," I agreed. "Still, I had to try."

In my quarters, I lay down on my bed for a few hours of much-needed sleep, instructing Machasu to wake me when the moon began its ascent into the night sky. It seemed only minutes had passed before she shook me gently awake.

"So soon?" I mumbled.

"Yes, lady," she said apologetically. "The moon begins its climb."

I ran my hands over my face. "Look away a moment, will you please?" The glistening black ball of ants on their sisal rope caught my eye. "And stand between me and them," I instructed her. Mayhap the ants could not see in truth, but their faceted eyes disconcerted me, and I did not want their blind gaze upon me.

Machasu obeyed.

I summoned the twilight. It came with a gentle rush, embracing and easeful, softening the world into muted hues.

"Lady?" Machasu glanced around with sudden alarm, finding me vanished.

"I am here," I said, willing her to hear me. "All is well. Rest, and be calm. When you awake, I will have returned."

She drew a shuddering breath. "What magic is this?"

"Mine," I said. "And it will not harm you."

The trek across the terraces to the far side of the mountain took the better part of an hour, but it was the first time I'd made it *alone*, free from the ever-present stream of ants. I sensed Bao's wakeful presence in the distance, his *diadh-anam* quickening as mine drew nigh. There were a handful of thatched huts at the foot of the field.

When I entered the one that contained Bao, he sat upright, wedged on the floor between a pair of slumbering D'Angelines.

A sisal rope like the one in my bedchamber hung from the rafters of the hut, and its ball of nesting ants began to stir.

"Be still," I whispered to Bao.

He nodded.

I breathed the twilight over him, encompassing him. The ants settled. I held out my hand to Bao, beckoning.

He threaded his way deftly through sleeping figures in the hut. "Moirin," he breathed, wrapping his arms around me.

Safe.

Raphael was wrong, so wrong! There was nothing dull about the feeling, nothing at all. I buried my face against Bao's throat, reveling in the comfort of his presence. Although I wanted it to last forever, I knew it could not. "Come with me, will you?" I made myself say. "Cusi is waiting."

Reluctantly, Bao released me. "Lead on."

By the time we made our way back to the city, the moon was standing high overhead, silvery-dim in the twilight. The door to the Temple of the Sun was unlocked, opening to our touch.

Inside, there was a faint gasp as the door opened onto apparent nothingness. Ocllo and Cusi and several of the other Maidens of the Sun awaited us around the sacred fire, its flames burning silver-white. Their gazes darted all around the temple as I closed the great door softly behind us.

All save Cusi's. She was gazing directly at Bao as though she could see him despite the twilight, and I wondered if it were true, if by dint of her choice, she already had one foot in the spirit world. Her lips parted as I released the twilight, but unlike the others, Cusi did not jump and startle, and her gaze remained fixed on Bao.

"You wish to speak to me?" she asked softly.

He inclined his head, his gold ear-hoops glinting in the shadowy light. "I do."

Cusi beckoned to him. "Come."

Out of respect, the rest of us withdrew out of earshot as they went to stand beneath the immense golden disk of the sun god, where it appeared Bao questioned Cusi, who in turn spoke earnestly at length to him. Although I wondered what passed between them, I sensed it was a sacred and private matter.

"So it is true," Ocllo murmured to me. "You were able to approach the temple and enter it unseen. Is this also a gift of your gods?"

"Aye," I said. "A small gift for a dwindling folk, that we may conceal ourselves from hostile eyes."

"Why do you not simply escape?" she asked.

I smiled ruefully. "If I could, I would, my lady. But I came to rescue our prince and his men, and I am not strong enough to hold the magic for so many or so long. And I do not think it is what was meant to be, nor what our gods and your ancestors intended."

Ocllo nodded toward the golden disk. "This, then?"

"I fear so."

She touched my arm. "If it is meant to be, you should not fear it, little sister."

I glanced at her. "My lady, does the legend say exactly what will come to pass when the ancestors are called out of death into life? How they will save their folk?"

"No," Ocllo said with regret. "Only that they *will* come in our hour of need, in answer to a willing sacrifice offered by one who has walked in the land of death and returned." She paused. "Do you doubt?"

At the far end of the temple, Bao sank to one knee, his head lowered. Cusi placed both hands on his bowed head, her lips moving in a prayer of benediction, his bright shadow enveloping them both. My skin prickled at the sight, and a soft sigh echoed throughout the temple.

"No," I whispered. "I do not doubt."

Taking a step backward, Cusi held out her little bronze knife with both hands, offering it to Bao.

He remained still.

Her lips moved again, repeating the offer, a small furrow forming between her brows. Reluctantly, Bao's head lifted. She held out the knife to him a second time; and this time, Bao accepted it.

Cusi smiled, dimpling.

My heart ached.

Rising to his feet, Bao tucked the knife into the waistband of his breeches and bowed deeply to the young maid. She stayed where she was, her hands clasped before her, while he crossed the floor of the temple toward us.

"Is it enough?" Ocllo asked him simply.

Bao nodded. "It is enough."

SIXTY-FOUR

On our trek back to the potato field and the thatched huts, wrapped in the twilight, Bao was quiet. I kept my own silence for a time, not wanting to disturb him, but there were too many questions to let the opportunity pass.

"How did Thierry and the others take the news?" I asked.

He glanced sidelong at me. "I have not told them yet. I needed to speak to the girl first."

"And now?"

Bao took a deep breath, exhaled hard. "I hate this so very much, Moirin. But having spoken to Cusi, I believe. I will tell them so." His mouth twisted. "They will not like it. I do not know if I can make them understand."

"I am not sure I understand it myself," I murmured.

"You do," Bao said. "We both do. But it is not a thing one can put into words, is it?"

"No," I agreed.

"Have you any idea how we will accomplish it?" he asked. "I do not imagine it will be easy."

I shook my head. "Not yet."

Bao searched my face. "And the conflicting oaths you have sworn?"

I sighed. "I don't know. I think...I dreamed today, briefly. At least I think I did. And I heard Jehanne's voice telling me not to fret, telling me she would be there at the end." I shrugged helplessly. "It's somewhat to do with her."

Outside the thatched hut where he lodged, Bao wrapped me in his arms, and I clung to him. "We could flee this place, couldn't we, Moirin?" he whispered against my hair. "You and me, alone, tonight."

"Aye," I whispered back. "But that would mean breaking my oath to Raphael, and the loss of my *diadh-anam*. It would resolve nothing."

"I know." His arms loosened, one hand dropping to touch the hilt of the bronze knife shoved into his waistband, a reminder of what was to come. "So we will do what we must instead, huh?"

I nodded.

Bao kissed my lips. "Later?"

"Later," I agreed. "We will speak further as matters develop. Come Qusqu, we will make a plan."

Once again, I made the long journey back to the palace, where I found Machasu half dozing in our quarters. She roused and blinked sleepily as I released the twilight, shuddering a little at my sudden reappearance.

"Is all well, lady?" she asked.

"Aye." I yawned, a profound wave of exhaustion overcoming me. My legs felt leaden and my eyes were raw for lack of sleep. "As well as it can be. Do me a kindness, and let me sleep until noon."

"Yes, lady."

The deep abyss of sleep claimed me almost the instant I laid my head down, and I slept without dreaming. All too soon, I awoke to sunlight and commotion, the sound of Machasu's voice pleading in Quechua, and men's deeper voices answering her in the negative. I shook myself awake, rubbing my hands over my face.

"What is it?" I called.

Machasu entered the bedchamber, bobbing an apology. "Lord Pachacuti has sent for you. His guards are waiting."

"All right." I dressed wearily and found Temilotzin and two other guards awaiting me in the antechamber.

Temilotzin scowled at me. "Why so tired, little warrior?" he asked in Nahuatl. "Are you ill?"

"No. What passes?"

His scowl deepened. "Your men were fighting in the fields this morning. Lord Pachacuti is displeased."

"What does that have to do with me?" I asked tiredly.

"I suspect Lord Pachacuti wishes to ask you that very thing," Temilotzin replied.

In the throne-room, the disgruntled Lord Pachacuti had summoned six of our men: Bao, Balthasar and Septimus, Prince Thierry and two of his companions I didn't know by name. All save Bao were scraped and bruised, and Thierry sported a swollen knot on one cheek. It was obvious that they had been fighting, and obvious that their camp had divided into two factions since yesterday.

I suspected they hadn't taken Bao's news well. Catching my eye, he gave me a somber nod.

"Moirin!" Raphael greeted me, a hectic gleam in his eyes. "I'm so pleased you could bestir yourself to join us." He gestured at the six men. "Would you care to tell me what this is all about? *They* don't seem inclined to."

"I haven't the faintest idea, my lord," I said.

He drummed his fingers on the arms of his throne. "Are you sure?" Reaching into his ever-present basket, he tossed a few leaves to the skirling eddy of ants at his feet. "I can resort to more...persuasive... methods."

"Do it, then, Raphael!" Thierry shouted unexpectedly, his fists clenching at his sides. "Gods! You keep us alive only to torment us!"

"Is that what you think?" Raphael shook his head slowly from side to side. "You wound me, Thierry. I saved your life in the jungle, didn't I? Were it not for the guidance and aid of my little friends, our company surely would have perished before we reached Vilcabamba."

"Mayhap it would have been better if we had," one of the others muttered.

Raphael gestured carelessly, and one of the Quechua guards

promptly drew his sword and laid its edge against the man's throat. "Is that your wish, Michel?" Raphael inquired. "I'm willing to grant you a clean death if it is. After all, I am not without mercy."

The fellow's throat worked. "No."

Another gesture, and the blade was lowered. "Let's try this again," Raphael said in a conversational tone, circling one finger. Ants poured across the floor, scaling Bao's legs, turning the lower half of his body into a writhing mass of blackness. A few essayed higher, crawling over his face. "Messire…Bao, is it? Moirin tells me I do not accord you your due, but see what respect I have for your courage. Few men could abide such a torment once, let alone twice. Will you not tell me why you and Thierry fought?"

Bao stood very still, his face unnaturally calm. "No."

"I wonder that you can abide the sight, Moirin," Raphael remarked to me. "Claiming to love him as you do." He flicked his fingers, and the tide of ants climbed higher. "Shall I bid them to bite?"

A faint sound of protest escaped me.

"For the love of Elua, enough!" Balthasar Shahrizai took a deep, shaking breath. "We quarreled over a plot to escape, Raphael."

Sparks flickered in his eyes. "And how in the world did you think to accomplish such a thing, my lord Shahrizai?"

Balthasar was silent.

"Ah." Understanding dawning in Raphael's expression. "You sought to find a way to kill me, didn't you?"

"Do you blame us?" Balthasar asked. "My lord de Mereliot, we are desperate. And yet I know you do not keep us alive to torment us."

"Oh?"

"No." Balthasar shook his head, his face pale beneath the sun's tan. "You're sick, Raphael. Sick with madness. And the healer within you knows it. It's what stays your hand, and keeps you from slaying your countrymen." His voice was filled with terrible compassion. "Raphael, I beg you, listen to me. It's not too late to turn away from this path. Pray to Blessed Elua for forgiveness, to Kushiel for mercy, and to Eisheth for healing."

"Gods bedamned! Do you not understand that the gods *failed* me!" Raphael shouted at him. "Over and over!"

"Did they?" Balthasar asked steadily. "Or did you fail *them*?"

Raphael gritted his teeth. "Kill him," he said to his guards. "You heard him, he has confessed to an attempt on my life."

"No!"

The outcry arose from multiple throats, mine included. But it was Thierry de la Courcel's that rang the loudest. "Neither Balthasar nor Bao nor Captain Rousse argued for attempting to kill you, Raphael," he said. "*I* did."

Raphael's fingers drummed restlessly. "Did Moirin not warn you that should anything happen to me, all your lives are forfeit?"

Thierry met his gaze. "She did. I thought it a risk worth taking. I thought the Quechua might have more respect than you reckon for a man able to kill a god, and acknowledge me their new leader."

"You know, that's not badly reasoned," Raphael commented. "You're wrong, of course, but it wasn't a bad notion." He leaned forward, propping his chin on one fist. "Tell me, how did you plan to do it? You're hardly in a position to plot an assassination."

"Does it matter?" Thierry asked.

Raphael shrugged. "Indulge me for Messire Bao's sake, won't you?"

Thierry glanced at Bao. "You'll call off your ants if I do?"

"I will."

"Very well." He looked back at Raphael. "I meant to seek an audience with you under the pretense of offering to fight in the coming battle in exchange for our freedom. I don't expect you would have trusted me enough to accept the offer, but you would have granted the audience for the pleasure of rejecting it to my face. You would have let me get close to you."

Raphael raised his brows. "Did you then intend to kill me with your bare hands?"

"No." Thierry hesitated only slightly. "A digging-stick hardened in the fire and sharpened to a point."

Or a bronze dagger, I thought, suspecting it might have been what gave him the idea.

"Ingenious." Raphael leaned back in his throne. "You've fire in you after all, Thierry de la Courcel. I thought whatever spark of lingering greatness your House once possessed was extinguished when this adventure went so very awry, but it seems I was mistaken. What fanned its flames? The arrival of Moirin and her lot?" He laughed. "It's ironic that they should raise your hopes, then dash them."

Thierry was silent.

"Why *did* you oppose his plan?" Raphael asked Bao. "Oh, right, forgive me." He gestured, and the ants retreated. Bao eased marginally, his dark eyes watchful. "Well? Did you lack the nerve? It doesn't seem so." He laughed again. "Did you lack faith in Thierry and his digging-stick?"

"I believe your threat is a valid one," Bao said in a low voice. "I do not fear risking my life. But I was not willing to risk Moirin's."

"How touching."

Bao shrugged. "You asked."

"Shall I show you why Master Lo Feng's esteemed apprentice is correct?" Raphael asked Thierry. Without bothering to wait for a reply, he gestured to his handmaids, who pulled back the feather tapestry behind the throne to reveal an alcove in which the odious Prince Manco had concealed himself. He strode forth with a satisfied grin, armor rattling, and bowed to Raphael.

Our men looked bewildered.

"Oh, of course!" Raphael said in mock sympathy. "You've no idea who this is. But Moirin does, don't you? This is Prince Manco, who will rule in my stead one day. She tried in vain to suborn his loyalty." He turned to the Quechua prince. "You're looking very fierce in your armor, highness! Tell me, would you pledge your loyalty to a man unwilling to use such fine weapons to conquer Tawantinsuyo?"

The prince glared. "Never!"

"In the unlikely event that their plot had succeeded, what *would* you have done?" Raphael asked him.

Manco laid one hand on the hilt of his sword, and the other guards followed suit. "Put them to death," he said promptly. "All of them."

Raphael smiled. "There you have it," he said to Thierry. "My threat is indeed a valid one. You have nothing to offer the Quechua. I do. If you think to act against me in any way, they will retaliate. Is that understood?"

Thierry's eyes blazed with fury, but he restrained himself. "It is."

"Excellent." Raphael dipped into his basket, shoved a few leaves into his mouth, and chewed in a meditative fashion. "I'll have need of all hands to transport goods on the journey to Qusqu. I need to know you'll remain compliant. Will you?"

A muscle in his jaw twitched. "For the sake of my people, yes."

"Kneel and swear it," Raphael ordered him. "Swear on the honor of House Courcel that you will not raise a hand against me."

Thierry hesitated.

"Do it or I put them *all* to death, guilty or no!" Raphael shouted. "Every last man of you!"

Dropping to one knee, Thierry bowed his head. "On the honor of House Courcel, I do so swear."

"Good." Relaxing, Raphael rose from his throne and placed an approving hand on Thierry's bowed head in an eerie echo of the blessing that Cusi had bestowed on Bao in the Temple of the Sun...last night? Gods, it was only last night. "That wasn't so hard, was it? I fear it's the next part that will be."

Thierry glanced up at him.

"You didn't imagine this attempt could go unpunished, did you?" Raphael inquired. "You, my friend, I will spare, because... well, technically, you're the rightful King of Terre d'Ange until that title is accorded to me, and I'd rather not commit regicide unless it's absolutely necessary. But I fear you must be taught a lesson on the repercussions of ruling unwisely. So..." He nodded to Prince Manco. "You, I think, have earned the opportunity to see how sharply your sword cuts."

"Raphael..." I murmured helplessly.

"Be quiet, Moirin!" Lightning flashed in his eyes. "Be glad I have need of you, else I'd have *you* slain for meddling! My tolerance has its limits."

I fell silent.

"This one is yours," Raphael said to Prince Manco, indicating the fellow he'd addressed as Michel. "And for the other..." He tapped his lips, beckoning to Temilotzin. "I do believe I'd like to use this opportunity to garner proof of your loyalty, Nahuatl." He indicated the second of Thierry's companions. "This one, you will kill for me. Do you understand?" At Temilotzin's blank gaze, he repeated the words slowly in Quechua, slicing his hand across his throat and pointing to the fellow. "Do you understand?"

Temilotzin nodded impassively.

Raphael returned to his throne, raising one careless hand. "Do it."

The Jaguar Knight struck without hesitation, his sword rasping clear of its scabbard. Pivoting on one foot, he leveled his blade in a hard, flat swing, beheading Thierry's comrade with the same remorseless efficiency with which he had dispatched the traitor Pochotl, gouts of blood spraying everywhere, the poor fellow's head rolling as his body slumped.

As horrible as it was, Prince Manco's inept effort was worse.

He wielded his sword like a club, hacking frantically at his victim, who fell to his knees, keening, raising his hands in a futile effort to defend himself, his palms and forearms slashed and bleeding.

I clenched my own wounded hand into a fist. "Temilotzin, please!" I begged in Nahuatl. "Make an end to it, won't you?"

Without acknowledging me, the Nahuatl warrior strode forward and shouldered Manco out of the way, thrusting the point of his blade into the fellow's chest and shoving it home.

Sighing, he died.

The coppery-sweet scent of blood hung in the air, thick and cloying. The black tide of ants advanced and retreated, mandibles clicking.

"Yes," Raphael mused aloud. "I think you've earned the right, my

little darlings, and these men have forfeited theirs. Go ahead." In a
trice, the tide surged forward and poured over the fallen bodies of the
slain, covering them in a living carpet as the ants began to feast.

Still on one knee, Prince Thierry retched.

"I *am* sorry that this was necessary," Raphael said apologetically.
"But I fear it was. You understand, don't you?"

No one answered him.

I made myself meet his gaze. "Aye, my lord. Your point is clear."

Raphael smiled at me. "I am glad."

SIXTY-FIVE

hree days later, word came.

The *Sapa Inca* discredited the tales the runners had carried of a living god in Vilcabamba with the power to command a black river of death. He had no intention of entertaining the notion of surrender.

We were going to war.

The fields were plundered in preparation, every ripe tuber, vegetable, or fruit harvested. The trees in the sacred orchard were stripped bare. Flocks of fowl were slaughtered, their meat dried and smoked. Thousands of baskets were woven for the transporting of goods.

The Maidens of the Sun took part in the latter task, and I did my best to assist them, since it afforded a chance to further our plans.

Ocllo shared her knowledge of the Temple of the Ancestors with me, having visited it many times as a young woman in Qusqu before she was sent to Vilcabamba to teach the maidens there.

"Here is where the ancestors sit," she said, sketching on the floor of the Temple of the Sun with a charred stick. "They face the altar before which Lord Pachacuti will be declared the *Sapa Inca*."

I glanced at Cusi, her deft hands weaving palm fronds, her face tranquil. "The altar where...?"

Ocllo shook her head. "The prophecy says it is to be done in a high place in the temple." She drew a jagged stairway between the seated figures of the ancestors. "Here is where the high priest would enter with the sacrifice from a hidden chamber." She tapped the top of the stairway. "So I think it is here. It is the highest place."

"A high place, yes," Cusi agreed calmly.

I studied the drawing. "How do we get Bao into the hidden chamber? And what is to keep Lord Pachacuti from ordering him killed the minute he shows his face?"

"The first thing, I do not know," Ocllo admitted. "It will not be easy. But the twice-born does not need to show his face." She pointed at the sun disk on the far wall of the temple. "The high priest wears a golden mask with the image of Inti."

I sighed. "So we'll need that, too."

"Yes." Ocllo looked troubled. "But you must not harm the high priest, or any of the priests."

"Can you persuade them to aid us?" I asked.

"I do not think so," she said reluctantly. "The Maidens of the Sun have kept Mamacoya's secret too well, for too long. I do not think the priests will believe us now. They are jealous of their power. And I am afraid if I ask, they will betray us."

"Well." I studied the drawing some more, my mind working futilely. "We'll just have to think of something."

On the heels of Thierry's failed plot and my own useless attempt to convince Prince Manco of his folly, Raphael had at last abandoned his policy of lenience toward me, and forbidden me further contact with anyone but the Maidens of the Sun.

"Your crude machinations no longer amuse me, Moirin," he informed me. "I have too many other concerns. You'll see your husband and your companions on the road with the other porters. For now, you'll stay where my handmaids can keep an eye on you."

Since there was no point in antagonizing him, I merely inclined my head in acknowledgment, taking what comfort I could in the knowledge that Raphael's faith in the loyalty of his handmaids was misplaced.

And Raphael could order me all he liked, but at least in this, he could not compel me. During the small hours of the night, I simply summoned the twilight and slipped out across the fields once more.

Sensing my approach, Bao was waiting for me, and Prince Thierry with him. I drew them into the twilight, and we took counsel in the field.

"Moirin." Thierry's face looked haunted. "I can but beg your forgiveness. I cost Michel and Jean-Robert their lives, and nearly cost the rest of us ours as well."

"You took a bold risk, your highness," I said softly. "Had it paid off, I would have been begging *your* forgiveness."

"It's just..." He passed his hands blindly over his face. "This scheme, this business of blood sacrifice and an ancient wives' tale..." His voice broke. "How can you ask us to trust to such madness?"

I took a deep breath. "I've no good answer for you, my lord. Nothing is sure. I have made mistakes before. But I set out across the sea to find you because Jehanne came to me in a dream to tell me that you were alive and I needed to fetch you back—and it was true. And it was Jehanne who told me that winning the trust of the Quechua women was the key to defeating Raphael."

"You put a great deal of trust in dreams," he murmured.

"These dreams, aye," I said. "And if the dead may guide me, how can I not believe the Quechuas' ancestors may aid their own folk?"

Thierry looked away. "It is a great deal to ask."

Bao laid a hand on his shoulder. "I find purpose in it, your highness," he said. "It gives meaning to my own death."

Thierry gave him a stricken look, eyes glimmering in the twilight. "How can you think our salvation lies in killing an innocent girl in cold blood? It's monstrous!"

"I do not think it is *our* salvation," Bao said somberly. "I believe it is *theirs*. There are two tales being played out here, your highness, two destinies converging—the destiny of Terre d'Ange and the destiny of Terra Nova. The Quechua have a right to choose their own, and the maid Cusi has chosen hers."

"You believe this?"

Bao nodded. "I do."

The prince was quiet for a long moment. "Raphael spoke truly the other day," he said at length. "Mad though he may be, he was right. I yearned to restore House Courcel to greatness with this adventure, and I nearly succumbed to despair knowing I had failed so horribly. But glory is not always found where it is sought. Raphael taught me a bitter, bitter lesson. My father is dead, and the throne of Terre d'Ange is occupied by a usurping regent. I need to begin thinking like a King, not a would-be adventurer and hero." His gaze rested on me. "When a bedraggled courtesan and a renegade Cassiline Brother stumbled out of the Skaldic wilderness with a wild tale of intrigue, betrayal, and mystic portents on their lips, the great Ysandre de la Courcel did not discount them," he said slowly. "She heeded their warning, and gave them whatever aid she could to accomplish an impossible task."

I held my breath, watching Thierry come to a decision.

"So be it," he said in a firm voice. "I will do no less. Moirin, your visions have guided you truly thus far. I will trust that the gods have sent you, and put my faith in them. Whatever I may do to aid you, I will do."

My eyes stung. "Thank you, my lord. I will try to be worthy of it."

Thierry smiled wryly, turning his empty hands palm upward. "I fear it is a hollow gesture. I have little aid to give."

"You've your wits," I said. "I've need of good counsel. In Qusqu, we must find a way for Bao to take the place of the high priest in the Temple of the Ancestors. And we must do so without harming any of the priesthood."

"Is there aught with which you might drug them?" Thierry suggested promptly. "In the tales of yore, Phèdre nó Delaunay used a tincture of opium to drug the men of Daršanga."

I blinked at his swift reply. "No, not that I know of... but if such a thing exists here, I know who *would* know it."

"Eyahue," Bao said.

I nodded. "Exactly."

Thierry frowned. "Are you sure you can trust those Nahuatl? The big warrior obeyed Raphael without a moment's hesitation."

"It is their way," I said. "Temilotzin knew your men were doomed, your highness. He granted a swift death to one, and the mercy blow to the other when I begged him."

"Through great hardship, Eyahue and Temilotzin have shown great loyalty," Bao added. "I trust them as much as any man in our company."

After a pause, Thierry nodded. "I take you at your word. What, then, of the coming war? Is there no way to avert it?"

"I fear not," I said soberly. "It is not only Raphael who hungers for it. You saw Prince Manco in the throne-hall. He is a bloodthirsty idiot eager to see his own father overthrown. The men of Vilcabamba are eager for this war."

"Yearning for greatness," Thierry murmured. "Even as my own yearning set this tragedy in motion."

I took his hands in mine. "It is not a tragedy yet, my lord. Let us pray that we may yet avert the worst."

He squeezed my hands in reply. "I do."

SIXTY-SIX

Since I was forbidden contact with anyone save the Maidens of the Sun, the following day, I sent Machasu to arrange for a clandestine meeting with Eyahue in the living quarters adjacent to the temple.

"Why do you want such a thing?" the old *pochteca* asked upon hearing my inquiry. "Do you think you can drug Lord Pachacuti and escape?" He waved one hand at my entourage of ants. "You cannot drug *them*."

"I know," I said. "Eyahue, at this point, the less you know, the safer you are. Only tell me, do you know of such an herb? Could you obtain it?"

He pursed his wrinkled lips. "There is one, but it is dangerous. Very dangerous. *Wurari*. It is the poison the blow-dart hunters use."

"I don't want to kill anyone!" I said in alarm.

"In very small amounts, it does not kill," Eyahue said. "It only makes the victim unable to move for a time." He shrugged. "But too much, and they cannot breathe—and I do not know the amounts."

"You could try it on me, lady," Machasu offered, her voice trembling a little. "I do not mind."

I winced. "No. It's too dangerous."

"Or you could try it on small animals first," Eyahue suggested pragmatically. "That is what the hunters do to be sure they have a killing dose."

"A much better idea," I said in relief. "Can you obtain it?"

He gave me a long, unreadable look. "Aye, I can. And I will do so now with no questions asked. But before you put it to its final use, I want to know what your purpose is. Do you swear to tell me?"

"I do." I hugged him. "Thank you, Eyahue!"

He scowled at me. "Thank the Emperor Achcuatli for giving you such a wise guide!" His scowl turned into a leer. "You must have given him quite a night's pleasure to inspire such generosity."

Despite everything, I laughed. "You may be sure of it, old man."

Eyahue was as good as his word. In a day's time, a small earthenware jar sealed with wax and a wooden stopper was sent to me in care of the Maidens of the Sun. Machasu delivered it to my quarters, along with a brimming bowl of liquid made from fermented *maize*.

"*Chicha*," she said in explanation. "The Maidens of the Sun brew it. It is drunk at all great celebrations."

"So we are to mix the poison in it?" I sniffed at the bowl, then glanced at the half-dozen caged lizards that were to be the subject of our first experiments. "I am not sure they will drink it."

Machasu shook her head. "It is not for drinking. The poison cannot be taken by mouth. It must go into the blood, as with a dart. Your guide said it would be better to weaken it with *chicha* than water." She hesitated. "I fear you have only a day to try this, lady. Lord Pachacuti has given the order. Tomorrow we go."

I pried at the wax sealing the stopper. "Then we'd best begin."

It was a grim series of experiments we conducted in the courtyard under the interested gaze of my attendant ants. At my request, Machasu procured another bowl and a hollow reed while I gathered a handful of long, spiny thorns from one of the flowering plants.

First, I tested the *wurari* on one of the lizards. In its undiluted state, the poison was thick and syrupy. Dipping a thorn into the liquid, I pricked the lizard. Within a minute, the poor creature was dead, and I gave it to the ants.

After that, I used the hollow reed to measure out ten drops of poison into the mixing bowl. Drop by drop, I began adding *chicha* beer to dilute it, testing at every stage and scratching notations onto a flagstone with a sharp rock.

Silently, I blessed Master Lo for his attempts to teach me the rudiments of medicine. Although I'd not had an affinity for it, at least I understood the elemental techniques of mixing potions.

It took every last lizard we had, but after being pricked by a mixture of one measure poison to three measures of *chicha*, the final subject did not die. It crouched motionless on the flagstones, its scaled sides rising and falling almost imperceptibly while the restless ants circled in a stream, and Machasu and I watched intently, glancing at the sun to gauge the time. I reckoned an hour's time had passed when the lizard began to stir once more, seemingly unharmed. I returned him to his cage, granting him a temporary reprieve.

Machasu let out her breath. "That was very clever, lady."

I frowned. "A man is much bigger than a lizard. I cannot be sure it will work at the same proportions."

She was silent a moment. "Then you must try it on me after all."

"No."

"Lady, the lives of my people are at stake." Machasu did her best to make her voice firm this time. "I am no more afraid than Cusi to do my duty."

"No," I said again. "I do not dishonor your courage, Machasu. But we are a long way from Qusqu yet, and many things are uncertain. If it is necessary when the time comes, I will accept your offer."

"It is true that many things are uncertain, lady. Because of that, you may not be able to choose the time." Before I had any inkling of her intentions, Machasu picked up a thorn and dipped it into the mixture, jabbing the soft flesh of her inner elbow. A pin-prick of blood blossomed. "Better to know now."

"Machasu, no!" I cried, too late.

She essayed a faint smile. "It is done."

Time seemed to slow to a crawl as we waited together. The sun moved sluggishly above the courtyard. Beneath my gown, sweat trick-led down my back. The lizard in his cage blinked and dozed. The ants foraged idly, eating leaves that had fallen.

I was on the verge of concluding that the proportion was ineffec-tive on a human when Machasu began to shiver.

"Machasu?" I said urgently. "What passes?"

"I do not know," she whispered. "I feel . . . weak. It is hard to move my arms. My legs, too."

"Can you breathe?" I asked.

She nodded.

"Good, very good. Keep breathing, low and steady, and all will be well." Praying it was true, I felt at the pulses in her wrist as Master Lo had taught me. For a short time, they raced and her skin was hot to the touch; and then her pulses dropped, and her skin grew cold beneath my fingertips.

Machasu's eyes rolled back in her head, showing only the whites.

"Stupid girl!" I muttered, dashing away tears. "You did not need to take such a risk. Not here, not now."

Limp, she made no response.

Her pulse continued to beat at an alarmingly slow rate. Laying a leaf atop her slack lips, I saw that it fluttered faintly. I cradled Machasu's head in my lap and glared at the skittering ants in the courtyard. "Stay away!" I warned them fiercely. "Lest I stomp your queen to death!"

Although it seemed an eternity, it was no more than an hour before Machasu stirred, her eyes returning to their proper orbit. Her skin warmed, her pulse quickening and her breath deepening.

"Can you hear me?" I asked.

She blinked.

I whispered a prayer of thanks to Eisheth, the D'Angeline god-dess of healing. "I am very, very glad. You should not have done that, Machasu."

Her breast heaved in a shallow cough. "But now you know, lady. It works. One part to three, aye?" One feeble hand rose, feeling at her throat. "It is only that it takes longer to work on humans."

"Aye," I murmured. "So it does."

It took the better part of another hour before Machasu was strong enough to walk with my aid into our quarters. Slipping her arm from my shoulders, I lowered her to rest on her pallet in the antechamber, where she slept long and hard.

In the courtyard, I tidied away the evidence.

The white-boned carcasses of the lizards did not concern me. They were the ants' rightful prey, and no one would question their deaths. But I was careful to measure out the amount of *wurari* poison in the stoppered jar, pouring it into the mixing bowl, which I had cleaned. I added three drops of *chicha* for every drop of poison. When it was done, I tipped it back into the earthenware jar, and shook it, shoving the wooden stopper in place, making it ready.

Lighting a taper, I sealed it with wax. I gathered several dozen more spiny thorns, wrapping them in a length of cloth. I stowed away both the jar of poison and my roll of thorns in the bottom of a satchel, and washed the mixing bowl one last time.

By the time I had finished, the sun was beginning to set. I checked on Machasu, and found her sleeping soundly. Her skin was damp and overly warm, but her breathing was reassuringly steady. I sat beside her for a time, breathing the Breath of Ocean's Rolling Waves, stroking the hair back from her brow, thinking on how the courage of these Quechua women humbled me.

When the shadows began to gather in the corner of the chamber, I retreated to my own room. The ants made their nightly foray up the sisal rope, clustering in their customary ball.

Tomorrow, we marched to war.

All I could do was pray that it ended swiftly.

SIXTY-SEVEN

✦

If I had thought our caravan that departed from Tenochtitlan all those months ago was an unlikely one, it was nothing to the procession that set forth from Vilcabamba.

It took hours simply to exit from the jungle fasthold, our company winding down the terraced steps and crossing the narrow, swaying bridges, forced to walk no more than two abreast, the hand-ropes on either side blackened by a stream of ants. The armored warriors under the ostensible command of Prince Manco led the way, steel glinting green in the sunlight that filtered through the canopy. Behind them marched a thousand more warriors in traditional Quechua gear, quilted cotton armor and wooden shields, wooden clubs with stone or bronze heads.

Raphael de Mereliot, Lord Pachacuti, was carried behind the army on a splendid litter. Mayhap in other circumstances he would be reviled for taking a position of safety, but Lord Pachacuti was a special case. He commanded the black river itself, an army more terrifying than any human one.

A dozen of Raphael's favorite handmaids from the Temple of the Sun marched behind him with Cusi among them, along with Ocllo to supervise them and a bevy of servants to help them attend to his every need.

On Raphael's order, I marched alongside them. Behind us was an endless line of porters and servants carrying supplies in woven baskets lashed to their backs, our D'Angeline company somewhere among them, lost in the throng. I would have worried, but I could sense Bao's *diadh-anam*.

Once we cleared the gorges surrounding Vilcabamba, the road widened and our pace quickened. The ants spread out through the adjacent foliage in a carpet of living blackness, scavenging as they went, seemingly tireless.

I could not help but wonder at the cost to the environs. Raphael was using the ants to unnatural ends. The highlands that lay many leagues before us were not their natural habitat, and I feared they might lay waste to it. And what of the jungle that we would leave behind us? The ants played a vital role in maintaining the balance of nature. Whatever damage their enslavement had already done would be magnified ten-fold in their utter absence as their natural prey was left to multiply unchecked.

But I supposed such concerns were beneath Lord Pachacuti on his quest for godhood.

Our first days during the long march to Qusqu were uneventful, unless one considered the logistics of managing such an undertaking to be of interest. The road followed a river that ran eastward from the highlands. We camped in a long train, foot-weary servants shuttling back and forth to tend to the needs of men and ants alike. There were tents for Prince Manco and Lord Pachacuti, and one for the Maidens of the Sun. I was glad of the latter for I worried about Machasu, who had a lingering fever from the effects of the *wurari*, but after three days, it passed.

Everyone else slept in the open, taking their chances with the elements.

On the first night, I ventured to visit Raphael's tent and upon being granted admittance, I asked his permission to seek out Bao, reminding him that he had told me I might see them on the road.

"I did, didn't I?" Raphael was in good spirits and well rested, being the only one among us who had not walked for leagues. He had Cusi in attendance on him, and Bao's bamboo staff in his hand, twirling it inexpertly.

I eyed him. "Did you bring that just to torment me?"

He laughed, nodding toward a corner of the tent where my yew-wood bow and quiver were propped. "No. I brought *those* to torment you." He tucked Bao's staff under his arm. "This I brought in case I need to remind your Ch'in husband that he is powerless here. I find his stubborn refusal to show a proper degree of fear quite vexing."

"You would not be the first to find Bao vexing," I said. "May I see him?"

Raphael shrugged. "I suppose so. You haven't forgotten your oath to me, have you, Moirin?"

I wished I could, for that bedamned oath preyed on my mind. "No, my lord. Believe me, I have not forgotten. You know full well that the Maghuin Dhonn cannot afford to take such things lightly."

"Good." He waved me away. "Go."

I inclined my head. Cusi caught my eye as I straightened, giving me the hint of a sweet, trusting smile that made my heart ache for her all over again. Ah, gods! She was young, so young.

Following the urging of my *diadh-anam*, I located Bao and the others half a league down the road. He rose to embrace me, his cheek pressed against my hair. "Was Eyahue able to aid you?" he whispered into my ear.

"Aye," I murmured in reply. "He was. It seems we have the means to incapacitate the priests for an hour's time without harming them. But I fear it will not be an easy feat to accomplish."

Loosening his arms, Bao kissed me. "In our lives, what is?"

I smiled ruefully. "Precious little. Is all well with you?"

Bao nodded. "I do believe your missing prince has come into his own, Moirin. If we survive this, he'll make a fine ruler."

For a mercy, it appeared to be true. The mood in the D'Angeline contingent was calm and resolved. There were no more factions between them. Since his decision, Prince Thierry seemed to have matured into his role as a King in exile, taking on a mantle of authority that he had not possessed before.

It heartened me to see it.

I prayed it was not too late.

On the fourth day of our march, we passed our first settlement, a small fishing village along the banks of the river.

The villagers stared, for which I could not blame them. They stared at the vanguard of men marching in bright, shining armor; they stared at the Quechua in traditional gear who followed. They stared at Raphael in his feather-canopied litter, and the stoic bearers who carried it. Most of all, they stared fearfully at the black tide of ants that accompanied us.

So it went.

Jungle gave way to lowland plains. The ants scoured the earth, augmenting their diet with aught they could devour. Despite the vast supplies our porters carried, it was not enough, never enough. Store-houses along the way, meant to protect the folk of Tawantinsuyo from starvation, were raided and emptied.

Days passed; and then weeks. The swift *chasquis* running relays might be able to make the journey in mere days, but our plodding caravan could not.

Rumor ran ahead of us, carrying the bitter truth. The *chasquis* sent forth from Vilcabamba had spoken truly.

Lord Pachacuti the Earth-Shaker and his black river of death were a reality.

Our first pitched battle came in the foothills of the mountain range in which the capital of Qusqu was located. Determined to test his opponent, the *Sapa Inca* Yupanqui had sent several thousand of his best warriors to make a stand in a low, flat valley. They outnumbered us three-fold or better.

It was no contest.

I saw it from a distance, on the slope of the hill that led into the valley. The *Sapa Inca's* men were arrayed in a line across the far end of the valley. Raphael called for a halt. Keeping the ants in reserve, he sent forth a herald, a barrel-chested fellow with a deep, booming voice. The herald strode down the hill and within earshot of our opponents.

"The Divine Lord Pachacuti offers you mercy!" he cried. "All who wish to join him are welcome! Lay down your weapons, and they will be returned to you in exchange for your loyalty!"

The *Sapa Inca's* men roared in refusal, beating their wooden shields with the butt-ends of their clubs.

The herald repeated the offer once more, and once more, it was refused. He returned to our company, and our warriors parted ranks so that Raphael's litter might be brought to the forefront of their lines.

The litter was lowered, and Raphael stepped forth from it. He wore a long red tunic of fine wool, a great collar of gold, and a flared golden headdress atop his tawny mane. As much as I had come to loathe him, I had to own that he cut a stunning figure. Standing atop the hillside, he raised one hand, then lowered it in an abrupt gesture.

From behind our lines, the black river moved forward, trickling between men and gathering to form a vast tide that poured down the hillside, blanketing the valley.

It was a sight to make anyone's skin crawl. I daresay the *Sapa Inca's* men were brave enough, for they held their line until the black river was almost upon them, but the ants in mass were too uncanny, too terrifying. The men broke ranks and began to flee, stumbling over one another in the chaos.

Those who fell were instantly engulfed, writhing and screaming; and at that, I had to look away.

With a slight smile of satisfaction, Raphael issued a silent command for the ants to withdraw and divide. The black river parted in obedience, forming a wide swath and going still. Now our human army marched down the hillside into the swath, the herald shouting out his offer for a third time.

A few of the *Sapa Inca's* men fought nonetheless, war-clubs clanging futilely on the steel armor of the warriors in our vanguard; and mayhap a third of their number staged a successful retreat into the foothills, having outrun the fearsome tide.

But the majority heeded the herald's offer, flinging down their weapons and raising their hands in an age-old gesture of surrender.

We made camp in the valley. The surrendered weapons were gathered and stacked in a pile, returned one by one as each of their owners came forward to swear loyalty to Raphael de Mereliot, Lord Pachacuti.

There was awe in their faces, and I could not fault them for it. They had never seen anyone like Raphael. With his fair skin, his gilded-bronze hair, and sparks of lightning flashing in his storm-grey eyes, he well nigh appeared to be the offspring of some elemental gods; and there were the ants, ominous proof of his unnatural power. Lest anyone doubt it, a dozen skeletons littered the battlefield, bones picked clean.

"Lord Pachacuti is pleased," the herald announced after the last of the *Sapa Inca's* men had pledged loyalty.

Raphael inclined his head in acknowledgment.

"Lest any man among you have sworn falsely," the herald continued, "know that the black river is ever watching." He indicated the vast mass of ants with a sweeping gesture. "To raise a hand against Lord Pachacuti is to be devoured by it."

They believed.

Since it was true, I could not fault them for that, either.

SIXTY-EIGHT

———✦———

Three days later, we reached the city of Qusqu.

There were no further battles along the way. The *Sapa Inca's* men honored their oaths and proved loyal to Raphael—or at least too fearful of the black river to resist him. We marched over wrinkled green terrain, ascending ever higher into the mountains, the climate growing colder and the air turning thinner.

Qusqu was a jewel of a city, set amidst the arid heights. Like the Nahuatl, the Quechua were skilled engineers, quarrying stone without the aid of steel implements, building terraces planted with an array of hardy crops, harnessing the power of the river that plummeted from the peak of the mountain, taming it into canals that interlaced the city, providing fresh drinking and bathing water for all before spilling into the rich valleys below.

We found the city partially abandoned and ripe for occupation. Laborers and merchants remained, but the *Sapa Inca* Yupanqui and his army had withdrawn.

"My first conquest." Seated in his litter, Raphael drew a deep breath as we entered the city walls, as though to take possession of the air itself. "But where is the *Sapa Inca*?" He frowned. "He must surrender to me."

One of the Quechua pointed. "There."

There was a fortress that loomed above the city, perched atop it like a falcon hunched over its prey, defended by high walls. A hastily dug moat surrounded it, filled with churning water diverted from the river and channeled back into the canals.

Prince Manco scowled. "My father thinks to make a stand."

Raphael smiled. "Oh, he does, does he? Well, let him. We'll take the fortress at our leisure."

Standing close enough to hear the exchange, I eyed the myriad streams of ants scuttling along the streets of Qusqu. "Do not delay overlong, my lord," I said quietly. "The mountains do not possess the abundance of the jungle. Your black river may starve us all in this place."

Raphael narrowed his eyes at me. "Do not presume to tell me my business, Moirin. I have no more patience for your insubordination."

I held my tongue.

Beneath the shadow of the fortress, we settled into the city. Raphael took possession of the palace, lodging his men in its myriad rooms. He sent forth criers to announce that Qusqu was under the rule of the Divine Lord Pachacuti, and that the surrender of the *Sapa Inca* was imminent. The inhabitants left behind acknowledged his sovereignty with alacrity, terrified by the roving streams of ants. Even my own attendant entourage had been absorbed into the rivers that roamed the streets.

On Raphael's orders, I lodged with the Maidens of the Sun, which suited my purposes better than he could have known. On that first night, Ocllo secluded herself with the high priestess for many long hours. I slept fitfully, fearing that she did not tip our hand unwisely, praying that the religious women of Qusqu would aid us. I wished I could confer with Bao and the others, but it could wait until I knew more.

In the morning, Machasu brought word that the high priestess had sent for me.

The high priestess Iniquill received me with Ocllo in attendance. She was an elderly woman with hair turned pure silver and sharp eyes beneath wrinkled lids, and one could see from her strong bones that she had been beautiful in her youth. She beckoned me close, studying me for long minutes.

"Lord Pachacuti commands an army of death and hunger with his magic," she announced in Quechua. "This I have seen. My sister-maiden Ocllo tells me you command the gift of life with yours. This I would see." She pointed at a wilting shrub in an earthenware pot. "If you can bring forth blossoms, I will believe."

I bowed to her. "As you will, my lady." Kneeling, I thought of my dream of a bulwark of flowers raised against the darkness. I brushed the plant's broad, hairy leaves with my fingertips. "It wants water."

"Anyone can water a plant," Iniquill said dismissively.

"Aye, my lady," I said. "But it can draw no more moisture from the soil than what is in the pot. If I coax it to bloom, it will die soon after, and it is a gift of life you asked to see."

The high priestess relented grudgingly and there was a brief delay as one of the maidens was summoned to fetch a jar and water the plant until the soil was sodden, doing her best to hide her curiosity.

When she had been sent away, I knelt once more. I breathed the Breath of Trees Growing and summoned a flicker of the twilight, exhaling softly over the shrub's wilted leaves.

The leaves stiffened and brightened, dark green lightening to a more vivid hue. The muddy soil dried visibly as the shrub brought forth dangling buds that elongated before our eyes, peach-colored petals furling back to reveal trumpet-shaped blossoms.

I glanced up at the high priestess Iniquill.

She turned her keen gaze toward Ocllo. "And you vouch for the one who is twice-born?"

"I do," Ocllo said calmly. "The holy sacrifice Cusi has spoken with him. The gods have granted her true sight, and she saw the shadow of death upon him. He has knelt for her blessing and received the blade from her own hands."

"Then it seems I must believe." The elderly priestess' wrinkled eyelids flickered. "But this strange and terrible Lord Pachacuti has not yet won the throne of Tawantinsuyo. It may yet be that the *Sapa Inca* Yupanqui will defeat him."

"My lady, I would not be sorry to hear it," I said honestly. "But I fear it is only a matter of time."

In that, I was right.

Despite his irritation at my warning, within a day's time Raphael was already at work solving the dilemma that the moated fortress presented. He ordered laborers onto the slope of the mountains where a sparse forest of evergreens grew. Trees were cut, their trunks shorn of branches and dragged through the city to the base of the fortress.

The *Sapa Inca* did not accept the inevitability of defeat. His warriors clustered on the high walls of the fortress, hurling spears and rocks down on the men who sought to wrestle the trunks in place across the moat, forming crude bridges.

If they had been men in ordinary Quechua gear of padded cotton and wooden shields, it might have proved an effective tactic. But Raphael set his trusted vanguard to accomplish the task—Prince Manco, Temilotzin, and the others clad in steel D'Angeline armor, the armor my own company had labored so hard to bring to Tawantinsuyo, never reckoning it would be seized by their own countryman and put to such a purpose. While I daresay Raphael's men sustained many an unpleasant bruise, none took a serious wound.

Once it was done, the bridges were in place.

I saw the final battle because Raphael de Mereliot wished it so, summoning me to his side.

"All genius craves a witness, Moirin," he said to me in a companionable manner, slinging a careless arm over my shoulders. "In that if nothing else, I am no exception—and you are *my* witness." He squeezed me. "Does that please you?"

I shuddered beneath his touch. "No."

"Pity," he said absently, loosing me to raise one arm. All along the banks of the churning moat, hungry ants gathered. And they *were* hungry. I could sense it in their inchoate thoughts, hear it in the clicking of their mandibles. Their antennae twitched, waiting for orders, waiting for a promised feast.

With a smile, Raphael lowered his arm. "Go!"

The crude bridges would not have sustained a human army—but they did not have to. The black river of ants divided into a dozen streams, swarming the fallen trunks laid across the moats.

Even then, the *Sapa Inca's* men fought. From atop the ramparts of the fortress, they emptied vessels of oil into the moat. They threw down flaming brands, and the surface of the water caught fire.

"Oh, clever!" Raphael said in admiration, gripping my arm. "Very clever!"

I pulled away from him.

He glanced at me. "You yearned for my touch once, Moirin."

I wrapped my arms around myself. "That was a long, long time ago."

Through the flames, the ants persevered. There were just too gods-bedamned *many* of them. Thousands after thousands, they clambered across logs crumbling into glowing embers, they forged living, writh-ing bridges across the moat.

Some died, sizzling. Some were swept away in the torrent and car-ried into the canal system.

Still, they kept coming and coming until the moat was black with their bodies. Ant crawled over ant, obedient to Raphael's orders. They scaled the walls of the fortress in a relentless rising tide. The fortress could have held out against a human onslaught for as long as its stores lasted. It was not built to withstand this.

Soon there were screams.

I felt sick. Raphael stood beside me, his eyes wide and unseeing, his nostrils twitching as he received messages borne on the air by his unnatural insect army. "They are beginning to flee," he informed his herald. "Tell the men to make ready."

The herald called out the order and the men spread out around the moat, weapons at the ready.

It was only a matter of minutes before the doors to the fortress were unbarred from within. Quechua warriors in padded armor staggered out, brushing frantically at themselves, plunging heedlessly into the waters of the moat.

The first wave of the *Sapa Inca's* men to struggle ashore through the waist-deep water were cut down ruthlessly, hacked by swords and bludgeoned by clubs. It was not until those behind them began to cry out in supplication that Raphael ordered his men to stay their hands.

"You did not need to kill them!" I whispered in horror. "They're fleeing!"

"They opposed me," he replied in a pitiless tone. "Bloodshed is the only language men such as these understand."

Ants streamed out of the fortress, regrouping in twin columns on the far side of the moat, apparently held in abeyance once more by Raphael's order. Between the columns of ants, grown men shivered and wept, jostling one another as they cast terrified glances at the waiting ants.

One who was not weeping pushed his way through the throng, his face impassive. Plates of gold were sewn into his armor, immense gold plugs stretched his earlobes, and he wore an elaborate gold headdress adorned with feathers and red woolen fringe. A pair of younger warriors flanked him.

Raphael smiled. "At last."

The *Sapa Inca* Yupanqui approached the edge of the moat and halted, his gaze seeking Raphael's. "You are the one who calls himself Lord Pachacuti." He cast a raking glance over the steel-clad warriors. "I see you have my most useless son with you."

"May I kill him myself, Lord Pachacuti?" Prince Manco called in a high, fierce voice, his gauntleted hand clutching his sword-hilt.

Ignoring him, Raphael murmured to his herald.

"The Divine Lord Pachacuti offers you the honor of death by his own hand!" the herald announced.

The *Sapa Inca* was silent a moment. "If I consent to this, will you accept the surrender of my people?" he inquired. "Will you spare them further bloodshed and horror?"

This time, Raphael deigned to reply on his own. "If they will acknowledge me the *Sapa Inca*, I will do so."

The ruler of Tawantinsuyo gave a single curt nod. "Then it shall be so." He turned to the throng behind him. "Such is my final act. When I am slain, you will kneel and swear loyalty to Lord Pachacuti. I order it so!"

There were a few cries of protest, and the two warriors at his side, whom I guessed to be two of his other sons, argued bitterly against it, but the vast majority of Qusqu's army, trapped between the heavily guarded moat and the seething mass of ants, simply looked stunned and relieved.

Waving all protests into silence, the *Sapa Inca* Yupanqui called for a ladder to be brought forth from the fortress and laid across the moat. His own sons lowered it in place, their copper-skinned faces expressionless save for the tears that streaked them. As the *Sapa Inca* made his careful way across the rungs, I found myself weeping, too.

Upon reaching the ground, he paused before me, reaching out with one finger to touch my tears.

"So such strange eyes can weep," he murmured. "It is good to know."

"I am sorry!" I whispered. "So very sorry."

An expression of profound regret touched his features. "That is good to know, too." Turning to Raphael, the *Sapa Inca* removed his headdress with dignity, holding it forth with steady hands. "Lord Pachacuti. This is yours now."

Raphael's hands trembled a bit as he received it, and he exhaled a long, shaking breath. "Lord Yupanqui, I thank you." Although I could sense he was itching to don it, he passed it instead to his herald, who accepted it with a reverent bow. "But I shall not wear it before the priests ordain me."

The older man gave an impassive nod. "That is wise. It is always wise to honor the gods. It seems it is their will that you prevail here." Sinking to his knees, he bowed his head, exposing his neck. "If you would show mercy, strike swiftly."

"I shall," Raphael promised, calling for a sword. "Bring me your best blades!"

His D'Angeline-armed warriors, the odious Prince Manco included, hastened to proffer their hilts. Ignoring the hilts, Raphael examined their blades instead and selected Temilotzin's. Unlike the others, the steel blade wielded by the Jaguar Knight had sustained no nicks or scratches, and the edge remained keen.

"You fought well today," Raphael said to Temilotzin. "You fought with wisdom and cunning."

The spotted warrior shrugged. "It is what I do, Lord Pachacuti. Your Quechua do not understand edged weapons."

Testing the heft of the sword, Raphael cut the air, making it sing, a bright, keening sound. "Now!"

Beneath the shadow of the blade, the *Sapa Inca* shuddered.

The blade fell.

It was a clean blow. Like all D'Angeline noblemen, Raphael knew how to wield a sword, and with his physician's knowledge of anatomy, he'd struck true, severing the *Sapa Inca's* neck. His head rolled free and his body slumped to the ground, blood spilling from the trunk of his neck. I swallowed against a surge of sorrow and nausea, thinking to myself that if I never saw another beheading in this lifetime, it would be too soon.

But the deed was done.

To a man, the warriors of the army of Qusqu knelt in homage to their new ruler.

Raphael de Mereliot was now the *Sapa Inca* of Tawantinsuyo. All that was left was the coronation ceremony.

SIXTY-NINE

—⸻✦⸻—

After consulting with the priests, Raphael declared that there should be a day of mourning before his coronation.

I had a day to make a plan.

One day.

I cursed myself for telling Raphael to make haste. It was true, our food stores were dwindling at an alarming rate. If the ants had not feasted on the Quechua dead in and around the fortress, the situation would swiftly become dire. But a few days of hunger would have been a few more days in which to plan.

Gods be thanked, the old high priestess Iniquill was a step ahead of me. On the eve of Raphael's triumph, she summoned a council that included Ocllo, Cusi, Machasu, several other maidens I did not know by name, and me.

"I have spoken with many of you these past days," Iniquill announced. "And it is my belief that the time of the ancestors is upon us. The sacrifice must be offered."

Cusi nodded gravely, her pretty face luminous.

"So we must find a way for the twice-born to take the place of the high priest Villac Umu," the old priestess continued. "This I propose. The ceremony is to be held at dawn. I will inform Lord Pachacuti that the Maidens of the Sun will ensure the sacrifice is in place. At nightfall, a dozen of your men including the twice-born will escort the holy sacrifice Cusi to pass the night in prayer in the temple. I will send my maidens to the temple quarters with many bowls of *chicha*, so that the priests may celebrate." She glanced at Machasu, then me. "I am told you possess a drug that will not harm them?"

"Aye, my lady," I said.

"Then an hour before dawn, your men will escort the sacrifice Cusi into the priests' quarters. There they will administer the drug, and the twice-born will take Villac Umu's place."

I frowned. "Will the priests not be suspicious? Raphael . . . Lord Pachacuti . . . keeps his countrymen as prisoners."

"The priests do not know this," Iniquill said in a tranquil tone. "But I am told that the Nahuatl who fights among silver-clad warriors is an ally of yours. If he accompanies them, there will be no suspicion. Will he do so?"

"I think so."

Her eyes glinted beneath wrinkled lids. "You must make it so!"

I took a deep breath. "Then I shall."

"Good." Iniquill gave an approving nod. "The Maidens of the Sun weave the wool of the *vicuña* for the garments of nobles. Tomorrow, we will provide you with fine clothing so that the priests do not doubt your men are in Lord Pachacuti's favor."

"What of the ants that keep watch over my companions?" I asked. "They may not allow them to leave."

"I do not think they do so any longer, lady," Machasu offered. "Lord Pachacuti has greater purposes for his black river now. They guard him and they keep anyone from leaving the city, but not from moving about within it."

"You're right," I said. "They do, don't they? That was clever of you to notice."

Machasu flushed with pleasure. "Thank you, lady."

"So it is decided?" the high priestess Iniquill inquired.

My palms were sweating, and I rubbed them on my knees. "It is a great deal to arrange in one day, my lady."

Her dark gaze was implacable. "I can give you no more aid than I have offered. If you are right, if we are all right and have read the signs correctly, it shall be as the ancestors willed it. I suggest you make an offering to them tomorrow. If we are wrong…" Her age-hunched shoulders rose and fell. "I fear we shall pay the price, every last one of us." Her gaze settled on Cusi, softening with compassion. "And for some, it will be terrible."

It was not exactly comforting.

In the chamber I shared with Machasu and a handful of other maidens, I drifted in and out of another night of restless sleep, my mind sifting through the myriad details I must accomplish on the morrow. I tossed and turned on my narrow pallet, shifting my body this way and that in a quest for comfort, avoiding the thought that troubled me most.

My oaths.

In all this time, I had still not found a way to resolve that conflict—and I was fast running out of time.

"You must gather stones from the river, Moirin," Jehanne's sweet, lilting voice informed me.

I opened my eyes. "What?"

She was perched on the edge of my pallet, her legs tucked beneath her. "Is that not how you discovered it was done? Warding a place within your twilight?"

I glanced around wildly. "Jehanne!"

"Hush." Jehanne touched my cheek. "I am here. Did I not tell you I would be here at the end?"

"Aye, but—"

"Aye, aye, aye," she mocked me, leaning forward to kiss my lips. "Do not be alarmed, my beautiful girl. I am here, but you do but dream yet. It will not wake the others. You must gather stones from the river and anoint them with your blood, placing them in Raphael's quarters so that you might invoke your magic. It is the only way I may come through and speak to him."

My eyes stung. "Can you turn him from his course?"

"I can but try," Jehanne said gravely. "I fear it may be too late. But at the least, I mean to free you from his oath. Call my name. It is all you need do." She kissed me again. "Trust me."

"*Jehanne!*"

I startled awake. I could still feel Jehanne's kiss lingering on my lips, the scent of her perfume in the air.

For the first time in many long days, hope stirred in my breast. Jehanne had saved me from Raphael's ambition before. If anyone could do it again, it was her.

Although it was not yet dawn, I rose and dressed. Summoning the twilight, I slipped forth from my quarters, taking with me the satchel that contained the *wurari* poison and the thorns wrapped in a length of fabric.

Following the pull of Bao's *diadh-anam*, I walked unseen through the streets of Qusqu. As the course through the city was not so straightforward as the bond between Bao and me, it took me several false turns and sojourns into blind alleys before I found the humble dwellings on the outskirts of the city where Bao and the others were lodged. The sun was rising in the east. In the twilight, it painted the snow-capped mountains beyond Qusqu with a mantle of pale silvery flame.

I stepped over the threshold of the dwelling that held Bao and a dozen others. Fast asleep, he had not sensed my approach. His face was serene and beautiful in sleep, but I could see the bright shadow that limned him, the shadow of death that Cusi had seen.

Releasing the twilight, I whispered his name. "Bao!"

He woke swiftly, reaching for a staff that wasn't there, and then yawned, his eyes crinkling. "Moirin."

The others stirred, waking more slowly. "Lady Moirin," Prince Thierry greeted me, his voice raspy with sleep. "I understand Raphael is to be coronated on the morrow. Tell me you come bearing welcome news."

"Whether or not it is welcome, I cannot say," I said. "But I come bearing a plan."

I told them.

I showed them the stoppered jar of *wurari*, explaining its usage and the timing of its effects. I unrolled the fabric-wrapped thorns, warning them that they must be very, very careful not to prick them-selves.

"This will be a tricky business to coordinate," Thierry murmured. "How do we avoid rousing Raphael's suspicions?"

"Raphael has well nigh forgotten your existence for the moment, your highness," I said to him. "The priestess Iniquill will assure him the Maidens of the Sun will see that the sacrifice is in place. I do not think he will take notice. And if the dead speak true..." I took a deep breath. "He will be otherwise distracted."

"Thinking on his forthcoming deification, no doubt," Balthasar Shahrizai muttered. "The mad bastard."

Bao gazed fixedly at me. "That's not what you meant, is it?"

I shook my head. "No. My lady Jehanne..." I took another deep breath, my chest feeling tight. My sense of hope faded. Giving voice to my dream, it sounded as wild and unlikely as all the rest of our plan. "She means for me to summon her. She means to convince Raphael to free me from the oath I swore."

"Is such a thing possible?" Bao asked in a steady tone. "Can you summon her?"

Hot tears slid from my eyes. "Stone and sea, I don't *know*! But we have placed our faith in the dead, and it is too late to turn back now."

"Moirin—"

"No." Prince Thierry raised one hand for silence, and there was command in the gesture. "Lady Moirin speaks the truth. We have made our choice. *I* have made my choice. I will not falter." He paused. "A dozen men, you say?"

Wiping my eyes, I nodded. "Assuming he is willing, I will send Eyahue to bring you suitable garb. And if all goes according to plan, Temilotzin will come to fetch you before nightfall."

"We will be ready," Thierry said firmly. "That I promise you." He glanced sidelong at Bao. "Messire Bao, when it comes to it, the moment in the temple...do you know what needs to be done?"

Bao was quiet.

"Do you?" I asked him.

"Yes, Moirin." Bao met my gaze, one hand dropping to finger the hilt of the bronze knife shoved into the waistband of his breeches. He smiled sadly. "Your handmaiden Cusi told me what was needful. I only wish it was not."

"So do I," I whispered.

Summoning the twilight once more, I took my leave of them. The sun had cleared the mountain range, and the city of Qusqu was stirring to life.

I needed stones.

I waded in the canals to gather them, my skirts hiked and wrapped around my knees. It took longer than I would have reckoned, but at last I collected four smooth, fist-sized stones, rattling along the walls of the canals, carried by the current. These, I stowed carefully in the bottom of my satchel.

By the time I had finished, it was noon, and the sun stood high overhead. I had to release the twilight and inquire of passersby to find Eyahue. As ever, the wily old *pochteca* had landed on his feet. Within a few days' time, he had established himself in Qusqu as a force for trade, and I found him talking with other traders in the marketplace.

"Do you see these animals, lady?" he demanded, indicating several shaggy beasts with haughty, long-nosed faces. "The Quechua use them to bear burdens." He sucked at his teeth, rocking back on his heels. "Pity they're bred for the mountains. No one's ever managed to get a breeding pair alive through the jungles."

I touched his cheek. "Eyahue, I am here to honor a promise, and I have a favor to ask you," I said in Nahuatl. "Gods willing, it will be the last one."

His gaze sharpened. "It is time you told me what you intend to do with the *wurari*, is it not?"

Nodding, I told him.

"So that's the secret of the ancestors," he mused. "You put a great deal of faith in dreams and portents, lady. I'll not risk my neck to aid you in this madness."

"I am not asking you to risk your neck," I said. "But if you would collect the clothing from the women's temple and deliver it to our men, it would be a kindness."

Eyahue cackled and rubbed his hands together. "Easily done! I'm always glad to pay a visit to the Maidens of the Sun."

That left Temilotzin.

He was not so hard to find. Lord Pachacuti's most trusted warriors were housed in the palace—and the Jaguar Knight was more trusted than most. I found Temilotzin and asked him what I must. For a mercy, I found him alone, and did not need to dissemble for the sake of onlookers.

He laughed deep in his chest. "You wish me to fetch your fellows to the temple? That is all?"

"Aye." I hesitated, mindful of the fact that I *was* asking Temilotzin to risk his neck. "It's a dangerous favor to grant. If we fail on the morrow, Raphael . . . Lord Pachacuti . . . will learn that you betrayed him."

"Little warrior," Temilotzin said fondly, laying one hand on my shoulder. "I will do as you ask. If you fail, I will do my best to kill Lord Pachacuti myself before he learns of my betrayal."

"Thank you," I whispered.

He shrugged. "Prince Manco and the Quechua who place their faith in him are fools. No man should possess such power. Lord Pachacuti will not be content with Tawantinsuyo. Sooner or later, if he is not stopped, his gaze will turn to the Nahuatl Empire."

"You're a wise man, Temilotzin," I said.

The Jaguar Knight smiled wryly. "Unlike the Quechua, the Nahuatl have had years to learn to distrust the ambitions of the strangers from across the sea. It is a pity, for this Raphael was not like the others, those men of Aragonia. He taught our *ticitls* how to stave off the spotted sickness that kills." He touched a finger to his temple. "But I think since then he has become sick himself, and there is no cure for it but death."

"I fear you're right," I murmured.

Temilotzin nodded. "I will pray for you."

Taking my leave of him, I made my way to the Temple of the Ancestors. Outside the edifice, there were vendors selling flowers. Many of them were unfamiliar to me, but I was pleased to see garlands of orange and gold marigolds. It seemed a hopeful omen, reminding me of the field I'd caused to blossom in Bhaktipur.

Whether through careless magnanimity or simple carelessness, save for my bow and quiver, Raphael had not taken my personal possessions from me. The value of those few items I had to trade was vastly in excess of the value of the flowers, but there was no point in being stingy at such a time.

The Quechua vendor stared in disbelief when I asked to trade a gold armband that had been one of Emperor Achcuatli's gifts for his stock of marigold garlands, but he swiftly agreed before the foolish foreign woman could change her mind. He and his assistant helped me carry them into the temple.

My chest tightened again as I entered the place in which Cusi intended to offer up her life.

It was an imposing, somber space. On one wall was the familiar sun-disk emblem depicting the god Inti. Before it stood an altar on which the headdress of the *Sapa Inca* rested, waiting for Raphael to lay claim to it. But it was the other end of the temple that made my breath catch in my throat.

The preserved remains of eight previous Quechua emperors were seated in a gallery. The bodies themselves were tightly wrapped in dingy cerements that clung to their ancient bones, the flesh beneath long since wasted away, but they had been lovingly dressed in fine garments of brightly dyed wool and adorned with gold jewelry and headpieces, feather mantles laid over their shoulders. War-clubs inlaid with precious stones rested in the crooks of their arms, and flowers were heaped at their feet, in their laps, around their necks.

It was terrible... and strangely beautiful.

There were other Quechua making offerings, although not as many as I might have expected. I wondered if it was because the *Sapa Inca* Yupanqui had not yet been embalmed and joined the ranks of the ancestors, or because Lord Pachacuti the Earth-Shaker had over-turned the order of their world.

Following their lead, I gathered an armload of garlands and ascended the stairway that bisected the gallery. I could not help but avert my gaze from the apex of the stairs, the highest place in the temple. If all went according to plan, that was where it was to be done.

Instead, I made myself gaze at the faces of the ancestors themselves as I turned into the gallery. They were sunken and featureless beneath their wrappings, but for all of that, they possessed a strange dignity. The walls behind them were carved with elaborate depictions of Quechua deities.

One by one, I greeted the ancestors, laying garlands around their necks, piling them in their laps.

"Forgive me, my lords," I whispered. "I am one who has brought this scourge to your people. Although I have no right to ask, I beg you to aid them in their time of need. For their sake, and the sake of the world."

Over and over, I repeated my offering and my prayer until my arms were empty.

The dead kept their silence.

SEVENTY

A day; one day.

Ah, gods! It passed all too swiftly. By the time I had finished making my offerings to the ancestors, the sun was already low on the horizon.

I hastened back to the women's Temple of the Sun, seeking out Ocllo. "I fear I cannot pass the night here, my lady," I apologized breathlessly to her. "There is a thing I must do that requires time I do not have to explain. But I have done everything Iniquill asked of me, and I will be in the temple on the morrow. Is all in readiness?"

Ocllo frowned at me. "The *chicha* is brewed, the maidens are prepared. Your old scoundrel of a trader has come to pester the maidens and gather the attire for your men. Beyond that, I cannot say. Lord Pachacuti has sent for you several times."

I took a deep breath. "It is to him I go. But before I do, I would see Cusi one last time."

She hesitated. "The holy sacrifice rests in seclusion, preparing for a long night of prayer."

Helpless, I spread my hands. "Might you ask if she will see me? It would ease my heart."

Ocllo relented. "I will ask."

As it transpired, Cusi received me gladly, glancing up with a dimpled smile as I entered her chamber. "I am happy you came, my sister," she said in a cheerful tone. "I was hoping to say farewell."

The knot in my chest tightened, and tears stung my eyes. "Cusi—"

She patted at my face. "Do not weep, lady! There is no need to weep. I am not afraid anymore. Tell me, did you offer prayers to the ancestors?"

I took another deep breath. "I did."

Cusi's smile deepened. "Did you find them splendid?"

"Aye," I said honestly. "I did."

"Then all is well." Rising on her toes, she kissed my cheek. "All is as it must be, my sister. Go, and do not trouble yourself with further thoughts of me. You have your own duties."

Wordless, I nodded and held out my hand.

Cusi clasped it firmly, the memory of shared blood pulsing between our joined palms. "Go," she repeated softly.

I went.

To steal into the palace, it was necessary to summon the twilight again. This, I did. Unseen, I found my way past the ants and sentries to Raphael's quarters, where I released the twilight and set my wards. Four stones, smoothed by the river. I pricked my hand with the dragon-hilted dagger that had been a gift from my Ch'in princess Snow Tiger what seemed so long ago, reopening the wound Cusi had given me.

I smeared my blood on the rocks, planting them in the four quadrants of the compass along the verges of Raphael de Mereliot's bedchamber.

There, I waited.

When he came, he was querulous, complaining to his companions. "No, no, it is not the most important thing," Raphael said irritably. "But I am telling you I *need* her." He checked at the sight of me. "Moirin."

"Raphael."

He frowned. "Why did you not come when I sent for you?"

I clasped my hands together. "I am here now."

"How did you get in—" He sighed. "No, never mind. I know full well how you got in here." Turning, he dismissed his companions. "You may go. I need to speak with her alone." Once they had left, he closed the door firmly behind them and turned back to me. "Now, about tomorrow—"

I summoned the twilight, and the anchor-stones flared to life, holding the cloak of the twilight in place within their compass.

Raphael startled, then glared at me. "What do you mean by this, Moirin? I've seen your magic at work, and I do not fear it."

"I know," I said. "It was one of the things that first drew me to you, my lord. When everyone else in Terre d'Ange found the magic of the Maghuin Dhonn strange and fearful, it delighted you. Would that I had known why, and where it would lead us."

He sighed again. "Moirin, now is not the time—"

I raised my voice. "*Jehanne!*"

"I told you not to say—" Breaking off, Raphael stared at me.

Moonlight.

That was what it felt like as Jehanne's spirit filled me—like being filled with moonlight, cool and silver and shimmering. I drew a breath to speak, and found I could not. My tongue was no longer my own.

Forgive me, my beautiful girl. Jehanne's light voice flowed through my thoughts. *I could not explain it before.*

I blinked, seeing double for a moment, as though I looked through two sets of eyes. I blinked again and my vision settled. Standing opposite me, Raphael de Mereliot looked stricken.

Jehanne unclasped my hands and raised them, and they were no longer *my* hands. They were the pampered hands of one who had been raised as a courtesan, lily-fair skin, translucent, polished nails.

She gazed at Raphael, and I gazed through her eyes.

"No!" He recoiled from her, his face twisting in fury. "I know this trick! Do you think my knowledge of arcane history lacking, Moirin? You've taken something of hers, you've taken on her semblance!"

"It's not a trick, Raphael." Jehanne's voice emerged from my lips, filled with sorrow. "Moirin's magic creates a doorway. You know that, too. Here before the end, I was allowed to pass through it."

"You're dead!" he shouted in anguish. "Name of Elua, Jehanne! *I watched you die!*"

"I know," she said softly. "And since that time, I have not been able to move onward because I needed to be here. Here, with you, today. I am your last chance, Raphael. I come to beg you not to do this thing."

Raphael was shaking. "I cannot believe it. I will not believe it!"

"But you do." Jehanne approached him. Lifting one hand, she touched his cheek, cupped the back of his neck. "You know me, Raphael de Mereliot. You know my touch." Stretching upward, she kissed his lips. "You know me."

With a groan, Raphael sank to his knees, wrapping his arms around her waist and pressing his face against her. "Why, Jehanne?" he asked in a muffled voice. "Ah, gods! Why here, why now? Why did you leave me? *Why?*"

"Hush." She stroked his hair. "You know why I am here. I told you. And I never stopped loving you."

"You *died!*"

"Yes." Jehanne's hand, my hand, went still for a moment. "Believe me, it is not the fate I would have chosen. We cannot always choose our fates. But *you* can. Here, today."

"No." Raphael shook his head. Wrenching himself away from her, he staggered to his feet, wild-eyed. "Moirin, stop it! This is some trick of yours. I swear to Elua, I'll feed your precious husband to the ants if you do not cease!"

"Moirin can banish me if she wills it," Jehanne said steadily. "All she has to do is release her magic, and I will be gone from your presence forever. Is that what *you* will?"

He was silent.

Jehanne went to him again. "Raphael, our deeds have repercussions. If not in this life, in the next." She gestured at herself. "Or in a limbo betwixt the two. I beg you to heed me, and turn aside from this course."

Raphael searched her face. "Will you stay if I do?"

She shook her head. "I cannot."

His expression hardened. "Then you have nothing to offer me. I will take my chances with the gods. What can they take from me that has not already been taken?"

"You would not ask that question if you had children," Jehanne murmured. "It is my life's greatest regret that I was taken from mine."

"Daniel's daughter!" Raphael shouted at her. "Must you throw it in my face?"

"*My* daughter." Her voice was unwavering. "Of whom you spoke great folly. How could you even think it for an instant, Raphael?"

He gave a broken laugh. "Why not, Jehanne? Mayhap it *was* meant to be. She could give me the one thing you could not. Her whole heart."

"Because you molded her thusly?" She raised her brows, my brows. "It is a profoundly wrong notion that violates the very essence of Blessed Elua's precept. Did I not pity you so, I should despise you for it. But I tell you, Raphael de Mereliot, you would never love her if you did. We may have fought and quarreled, you and I, but it was always born of the passion that lay between us. You cannot separate one from the other. It was part and parcel of what bound us together."

"Why wasn't it enough?" Raphael demanded, tears of frustration and pain in his eyes. "Why did you choose Daniel over me? Don't tell me the same passion lay between you! Was it mere ambition?"

It was Jehanne's turn to laugh, and her laughter was as hollow as his. "Oh, Raphael! Would you stand here on the cusp of seeking godhood and chastise me for ambition? It's true, in the history of Terre d'Ange, no Servant of Naamah had ever risen to the throne. I wanted to be the first. But I loved Daniel, too." She paused. "He was a good and kind man who loved deeply. But there was such sorrow in him, such grief. And I was able to take it away, at least for a time. When I did..." She drew a deep breath into her lungs. My lungs. "When I did, I truly understood Naamah's blessing."

"How can you possibly think telling me such a thing will sway me?" Raphael whispered hoarsely.

If I could have looked away from the pain in his face, I would have; but I was a passenger in my own body, and Jehanne did not look away. "I don't. I am telling you the truth. It is all I have to offer you."

He turned his back on her. "It is not enough."

She smiled with regret. "Then I will ask you a lesser boon. Raphael, you must release Moirin from her oath."

"No."

"Moirin will lose her magic the moment she honors it," Jehanne said simply. "And you will fail."

Raphael turned back to her with a scowl. "What new lie is this?"

"No lie." She shook her head. "I am not able to lie anymore. The oath Moirin swore to you is in conflict with another. She is Desirée's oath-sworn protector. While you mean to take my daughter to wife and mold her spirit, Moirin cannot honor both oaths. Her *diadh-anam* will be extinguished."

He raised his own brows. "And why, pray tell, would Moirin not tell me such a thing if it were true?"

With unrelenting honesty, Jehanne exposed my plan of last resort. "Because she is willing to make that sacrifice to prevent you from succeeding."

Ah, gods! I would not have consented to this if I had known it was what she meant to do. I thought of banishing the twilight, but the damage was done.

Peace, Moirin. Jehanne's voice poured through my thoughts once more. *It is not finished.*

Raphael frowned in thought. "You came here to sway me from my course, Jehanne. It makes no sense at all for you to warn me of such a pitfall."

"I came here to offer you the truth," she said calmly. "It is what I was meant to do. More than that, I cannot know."

For a long moment, they gazed at one another, and a faint hope flickered in me that somehow, against all odds, Jehanne's words had reached him. It died when Raphael shook his head. "No," he said. "I do not trust Moirin to keep her word without her oath; and I do not entirely trust that this is not some trick of hers."

"In your heart, you know better," Jehanne murmured.

A muscle in his jaw twitched. "There is another way. Desirée, your daughter . . . what is the nature of the oath Moirin swore?"

"The Montrèvan Oath," she said. "Moirin mac Fainche is sworn to regard Desirée's interests as her own, to seek to defend her from every danger, and hold her happiness as a matter of sacred trust."

"Elua have mercy! How did *that* come about?" Raphael muttered. "I can't imagine the realm would approve."

"Daniel willed it so," she said. "He saw that Moirin was able to love the spark of my spirit that lived on in our daughter, as he himself was unable to do. Daniel trusted her to care for Desirée's happiness. And in that, I do believe he chose wisely. Moirin has gone to great lengths in her effort to protect my daughter."

Raphael bowed his head. Locks of tawny hair touched with silver in the twilight spilled over his brow, obscuring his gaze. "It's why she came here, isn't it? Searching for Thierry?"

"Yes."

When he lifted his head, his eyes were wide and clear. "I will not do as you ask. I will not turn away from my course here, Jehanne. And I will not release Moirin from her oath. But . . ." His chest rose and fell as he took a deep breath. "I loved you, Jehanne. More than you knew. For the sake of all that has passed between us, I will do my best to love your daughter." His mouth twisted. "Not as I threatened. Not as a bridegroom, but as one who might have been her father had matters been otherwise."

Jehanne was silent.

"I will have the power to protect her," Raphael said softly. "Gifts such as Moirin never dared dream of possessing, political power such as Thierry could never have hoped to wield. I will hold your daughter Desirée's happiness as a matter of sacred trust. Everything I can do on her behalf, I will. I give you *my* oath. Does that not suffice to resolve the conflict?"

It did.

Raphael de Mereliot might turn the rest of the world upside down, raze empires in Terra Nova, but so long as he was pledged to protect Desirée's happiness, my oath to do the same was no longer in conflict with my oath to aid him.

"Yes," Jehanne whispered. "Ah, gods! Raphael..."

He closed the distance between them in a few swift steps, cupping her face and kissing her, kissing *me*, with fierce, starved ardor. Jehanne clung to him, her fingers digging into his shoulders as she returned his kiss with the same tempestuous passion; and I was caught between them, even as I had been when my lady was alive.

It was Jehanne who pulled away, genuine anguish in her voice. "Raphael, I cannot stay!"

His hands fell to his sides, turning to fists. "You break my heart," he said in a low tone. "Over and over."

"We break each other's hearts," Jehanne said quietly. "But we mend them, too. And someday, we may all understand Naamah's blessing. Now I must go."

"*Don't—*"

Now, Moirin. Jehanne's thoughts spilled through mine, still tinged with anguish. *Please!*

I released the twilight.

Just like that, Jehanne's presence was gone, extinguished like a candle. I dropped to one knee at the suddenness of it, drawing a ragged breath, my head hanging low. My lungs were my own again. My hands, splayed on the floor of Raphael's bedchamber, were mine—shapely enough, but scratched and callused with the ordeals of travel, my skin golden-brown once more.

"Moirin."

I looked up at Raphael.

His face was stony, and I knew without another word spoken

that he hated me more than ever for having borne witness to this encounter.

"I will keep my oath," he said. "As I expect you to keep yours. Will you be in the Temple of the Ancestors at dawn on the morrow?"

I nodded.

"Good. Now get out of my sight."

SEVENTY-ONE

⁂

Outside the palace, it was later than I had reckoned. Time moved differently in the spirit world, and it seemed the presence of Jehanne's spirit had altered the flow of time in the twilight, too.

I returned to the temple of the Maidens of the Sun, thinking to take a moment to collect my thoughts before the sacred fire. A lone figure knelt before the firepit, tending to the coals. She glanced up at my approach.

"Machasu," I said in greeting. "You do not sleep?"

She shook her head. "I was thinking of Cusi. I, too, wanted to spend the night in prayer." In a graceful, reverent gesture, she stirred the coals. Low flames flickered. "I did not think you were coming here tonight, lady."

I knelt beside her. "Nor did I."

"Is all well?" she asked.

My *diadh-anam* burned steadily in my breast, calling to Bao's in the distance, no longer in danger of being extinguished on the morrow. Jehanne had kept her promise. She had found a way to free me from my conflicting oaths. Whatever else happened come dawn, I would not be cast out of the presence of the Maghuin Dhonn Herself for eternity because I honored one oath, and broke another. Bao would not die because there was no way out of the oaths that bound me.

For that, I was grateful.

And yet it did not remove the burden of choice from me. It only altered it. Now I could obey Raphael without losing my *diadh-anam*.

But I could still refuse him and be forsworn if it were the only way to keep him from attaining his goal.

"Lady?" Machasu prompted me.

"I do not know," I said honestly. "But before I went to see Lord Pachacuti, Cusi told me all was well. She is closer to the matter than anyone. If anyone would know, it is her."

"I think so, too." Machasu stirred the coals again, then fed them a few sticks of firewood. "Do you think she is frightened?"

"A little, maybe," I said. "But she has great faith."

"Do you think it will hurt?" she asked.

I clenched my hand on the newly reopened wound. It hurt, but it had hurt a great deal more when Cusi had cut me with the dull-edged bronze dagger. And although I wanted to utter a soothing lie, it felt like blasphemy in this holy place. "Yes," I said quietly. "I think it will hurt."

"I think so, too," Machasu repeated. "But it will be swift. And then the ancestors will welcome her into the highest heaven."

I nodded. "So we pray."

"Yes."

My handmaiden fell silent, tending the fire. I gazed into the shifting embers and breathed the Five Styles, praying to the Maghuin Dhonn Herself to guide me. The great magician Berlik had broken his oath and been forgiven in the end, finding atonement in the distant Vralian wilderness.

But in the end, Berlik had given his life in penance. It was part of the bargain. What penance had I to give if I broke my oath? It was not the same, not at all. There would be no one to claim my life as a right of justice.

Trust me.

The words echoed throughout the temple, spoken in a voice as deep as oceans and as vast as mountains. I jerked my head upright, my chin having sunk to my chest. The sacred fire flared and crackled as Machasu fed it an especially dry branch, throwing a massive shadow on the wall—a shadow with an imposing silhouette filled with bulk and grace that I'd seen but once in my life, but would never forget. A bear, but a bear far, far greater than any mortal bear. As the flames danced it appeared to move, pacing with profound and solemn grandeur, and then shrank and dwindled as the fire subsided from its first eager blaze.

"Did you hear that?" I asked, my voice trembling. I pointed at the wall. "Did you *see* it?"

Machasu gave me an odd look. "Lady, you slept for a time. I did not wake you, for I thought you must need it."

My ears still rang with the words. *Trust me.* Jehanne had spoken the same words to me.

Mayhap it was why I had dreamed of them.

Or mayhap I had not dreamed. The scent that lingered in my nostrils was not Jehanne's perfume, but somewhat older and more savage—earthen and musky, tinged with the scent of wild berries.

Trust me.

I pressed the heels of my hands to my eyes. "I don't know what that means!" I cried aloud. "Trust, and keep my oath? Or break it, and trust to Your forgiveness?"

There was no answer.

My *diadh-anam* gave no guidance.

"Lady?" Sounding worried, Machasu tugged at my arms. "I am sorry your dreams were troubled, but dawn is near. I should have awakened you sooner. It is time to go and make ready."

I lowered my hands, summoning a reassuring smile. "You're right. Forgive me. It is as you said, I am short on sleep. Let us go."

A short time later, we assembled in the Temple of the Ancestors.

The first light of dawn gilded the snow-capped peaks of the mountains that lay west of Qusqu.

Streams of ants scuttled throughout the streets of the city, accompanying us in an informal manner. I walked in procession with the high priestess Iniquill, Ocllo, and a half-dozen Maidens of the Sun including Machasu, all of us clad in garments of fine-combed *vicuña* wool. Theirs were dyed a saffron hue while mine was blue, trimmed with red and saffron embroidery.

The temple was already crowded, filled with Prince Manco's Quechua warriors in D'Angeline armor, and other Quechua of high standing. I recognized the *Sapa Inca's* elder sons among the latter. Everywhere, ants crawled.

The ancestors in their gallery watched silently, blank, sunken faces wrapped in cerements, their laps filled with flowers.

Raphael de Mereliot stood behind the altar. He wore a long robe of scarlet wool, belted with gold, a great emerald-studded collar around his neck. His head was bare, awaiting the crown, and his face was stern and beautiful. Last night had been his final crossroads, and he had made his choice. There was no trace of the tormented mortal man who had loved so deeply and endured such a bitter loss. Somewhere in the small hours of the night, he had put the past behind him. Raphael was ready for the mantle of godhood.

At a gesture from him, his knights made way for me. Temilotzin caught my eye as I passed and gave an infinitesimal nod, his expression more grave than I'd ever seen it.

It should have reassured me, but it didn't. All he knew was that Cusi and the men had been safely delivered to the temple last night. My stomach was in knots, and I felt ill. Ah gods! I'd taken so much on trust. Now it seemed the gods asked me to take a further leap of faith, and I didn't even know in which direction.

"Moirin." Raphael acknowledged me in a flat tone. "Are you prepared?"

"Aye, my lord," I murmured, wishing it were true.

He gazed at the sea of copper-colored faces regarding him with superstitious awe, at the impassive figures of the ancestors, at the winding lines of ants. "Today will be a glorious day," he said, more to himself than to me, drinking it all in. "Today will be a day that lives forever in history."

I said nothing.

Raphael glanced at me. "You should be honored to witness it, Moirin. You should be honored that the gods have chosen you for this. But you have never, ever valued the gifts you have been given."

I met his gaze. "And you have never, ever understood them, my lord. I was not put on this earth to serve your ambition."

"You are mistaken," he said simply. "Your presence here is proof."

And then we spoke no more, for somewhere in the hidden chambers beyond the stairs at the rear of the temple, a drum began to beat. Silence settled over the Temple of the Ancestors. Even the restless ants stilled. The Quechua watched Raphael with fascination, awaiting the coronation of this second Lord Pachacuti the Earth-Shaker who had overturned the order of the world. Raphael fixed his own gaze at the apex of the stairs, awaiting the arrival of the head priest and the willing victim who was to be sacrificed on the altar before him, the terrible, worshipful offering he believed would give him the power to contain the fallen spirit Focalor.

Atop the stairs, Cusi appeared.

She stood alone for a moment, clad in a long shift of unadorned white wool, her black hair loose and gleaming over her shoulders, and ah, stone and sea, she looked so *young*! She gave a faint, tremulous smile, one cheek dimpling, and I knew that despite everything, she had to be afraid. Raphael stared hungrily at her, his breathing quickening.

I closed my eyes for the space of a few heartbeats.

When I opened them, the high priest had emerged to stand behind Cusi, and although his face was obscured by a gilded mask depicting the sun god and gold bands hid the tattoos on his forearms, I knew by the flare of my *diadh-anam* that it was Bao.

His head was averted, the hilt of the bronze knife clasped in his right hand. And I thought in a panic that this was wrong, all wrong. There was no way Bao could commit this dreadful deed, no way that he could take an innocent girl's life in cold blood in the service of the unknown dead and foreign gods.

Even as Raphael began to frown, wondering why they did not descend the stairs in procession, a line of priests behind them, a cry of protest rose in my throat.

But before I could give voice to it, Cusi spoke. "Brothers and sisters!" she cried. "The hour of our need is upon us!"

Beneath the shadow of the ancestors' gallery, the assembled Quechua turned, staring up at her in wonder.

Beside me, Raphael swore savagely, gripping my shoulder and shaking me. "What the hell trick is this, Moirin?"

I bit the inside of my cheek until it bled, wishing I could turn back time, wishing it were yesterday again and this was not happening.

Atop the stairs, Cusi sank to her knees. She lifted her chin, her pretty face luminous. Now that she had begun the invocation, there was no more fear in her. "Great ancestors, hear me!" she called, her voice clear and strong. "I call upon you to save us in our hour of need! In your names, I offer myself as willing sacrifice!"

"*No!*"

Raphael shouted the word, and I whispered it, but it was already too late. Bao's hand trembled only slightly as he laid the bronze blade against Cusi's slender throat. He did not hesitate. With one powerful slash, using all his strength to compensate for the dullness of the blade, he slit open the girl's throat.

A river of blood spilled from Cusi's throat, soaking the white wool of her garment and turning it crimson. Her eyes rolled up in her head, and she fell forward, catching herself briefly on her hands, her hair trailing in her own blood.

Blood spilled over the top stair; more blood than it seemed one small body should hold. It poured into channels etched into the carvings behind the gallery of the ancestors, limning them in scarlet.

There was shouting and pandemonium in the temple, the Quechua jostling and shoving and yelling amongst themselves, Raphael attempting in vain to regain control of the situation.

It was old Iniquill's voice that rose above the fray, high and fierce and quavering. "Let the ancestors speak!" she cried, pointing. "It is as the great Mamacoya foretold!"

The Quechua fell silent.

Atop the stairs, Cusi lay crumpled and still. Bao stood motionless, the knife yet in his blood-stained hand, his face yet hidden behind the sun god's mask. Runnels of blood made their way through the carved channels, made their way toward the seated figures of the ancestors. Drop by drop, blood fell to darken their ancient cerements.

Bones creaking, the ancestors stirred.

I stared, as transfixed as everyone, my heart in my throat.

"No," Raphael muttered frantically. "No, no, no! This is wrong, all wrong." Pacing, he grabbed Prince Manco's arm and pointed toward the head of the stairs. "Seize him! Seize the false priest!"

The prince hesitated.

Standing atop the stairs, Bao dropped the bronze knife and removed the high priest's golden mask. Behind it, his face was streaked with tears, but his voice was steady. "There is no falsehood here save yours, Lord Pachacuti!" he called. "You are no god, only a man misguided. I have bridged the worlds between life and death, and today I pay the price for it."

In the ancestors' gallery, eight seated figures slowly began to rise, their brittle, blood-stained cerements crackling. Flowers spilled from their withered laps, desiccated fingers gripped bejeweled weapons. And still the blood continued to fall, drop by drop.

Abandoning Prince Manco, Raphael returned to pluck the *Sapa Inca's* crown from the altar, placing it on his own head.

"It is done," he said wildly. "So be it." Lightning flared in his eyes as he rounded on me. "It is *done*! I rule in Tawantinsuyo; I, and I alone! I am worshipped here! Moirin, call your magic! Now!"

Trust me.

There was no time left to think.

Placing my faith in the Maghuin Dhonn Herself, in the words of my lady Jehanne, in the dead and the living and every god I knew, I obeyed.

I summoned the twilight.

"*Focalor!*" Raphael shouted, flinging his arms wide. "Come to me!"

In the temple, a doorway onto a raging maelstrom opened. The fallen spirit was there in inchoate form, answering the call of the spark of its essence that remained in Raphael de Mereliot. Raphael laughed aloud in triumph, and then stiffened. A thunderclap broke with a sound like boulders splitting and lightning-shot darkness poured through the doorway, poured into him, entering his open mouth. He cried aloud, his body convulsing in agony. Without a true sacrifice in his honor, he was not strong enough to contain it.

Mayhap he never would have been, but of a surety, he wasn't now. The storm that was Focalor's essence was consuming him.

And I felt the strength draining from me.

Bedecked with flowers, clad in finery, the ancestors continued their slow descent from the gallery, bony limbs clicking and creaking. The black tide of ants gathered and rallied, swarming them to no avail.

They could not stop the dead.

The tempest raged in the doorway, raged through Raphael's mortal flesh. Half the folk in the temple cried aloud in fear, pushing their way toward the doorway; half gazed in dumbstruck awe at the awakened ancestors. Ignoring the futile onslaught of ants, the Quechua ancestral dead continued their inexorable assault, ancient faces blank beneath their wrappings, war-clubs raised by crumbling fingers, petals falling all around them.

It rained marigolds, garlands severed and petals shredded by the relentless mandibles of the ants. Yellow and orange and gold and bronze, the latter a deep hue like blood drying, like Cusi's blood beginning to congeal on the stairway. I had fallen to my knees. Bits of cerement fell, and I caught glimpses of aged bone gleaming beneath tattered wrappings, bones gnawed in vain by Raphael's unnatural army.

I could not turn back the dead, either. But the storm that held Focalor's essence was another matter.

Lifting my head, I met Raphael's eyes.

In our different ways, we had loved and hated in equal measure, Raphael and I. Each other, Jehanne. My magic. Between his ambition and my youthful folly, we had left a trail of dead between us, beginning with poor, doomed Claire Fourcay and ending with my sweet, innocent handmaiden Cusi. Now he was drowning in Focalor's essence; drowning, and unable to save himself.

He grimaced, seeing his failure reflected in my gaze. There was enough of him left to recognize me. It was too late for Cusi, too late to halt the dead. It was not too late to banish Focalor. I prayed Raphael would hear me, for if he did not, the fallen spirit would be loosed unfettered on the world, and I did not think even the dead could stand against it.

"Raphael," I whispered. "Please…"

He shut his eyes, his throat straining as he fought to force the words out past the influx of Focalor's essence. "Close the doorway, Moirin," he gasped, his chest heaving. "I was wrong. I erred. Forgive me if you can. Just…do it."

I did.

It took strength, a great deal of strength. But I was not the foolish young woman I had been so long ago. Gathering every ounce of resolve that I possessed, I rose from my knees and faced the maelstrom I had unleashed. I was a child of the Maghuin Dhonn Herself, and no one's useful tool. The memory of Her acceptance lent me strength. Although thunder crashed, lightning crackled, and the wind howled in protest, I poured myself into the effort. I beat Focalor's essence back into the spirit world and closed the doorway, releasing the twilight at last with a sigh.

Shuffling across the temple floor on bony feet, the dead converged on Raphael, weapons raised. One by one, their weapons fell, bludgeoning him.

There was blood, darkness, and flowers.

And I shut *my* eyes.

I didn't want to see the end.

SEVENTY-TWO

In the aftermath, there was silence, broken only by the sound of a thousand indrawn breaths.

I opened my eyes.

Raphael de Mereliot's body lay sprawled on the floor of the temple. The crown of the *Sapa Inca* had fallen from his head, and blood clotted his tawny locks. The desiccated figures of the Quechua ancestors swayed around him. One by one, they dropped their weapons and crumpled into motionless heaps of rag-wrapped bones bedecked with gold, feathers, wool, and half-eaten garlands of flowers.

The ants fled, pouring through the temple door in an endless stream, joining throngs of their fellows in the streets. It was a considerable exodus.

Atop the stair, Bao stooped and gathered Cusi's body tenderly in his arms. He supported her head as carefully as though she were a newborn babe, so the gash that had opened her throat didn't gape. Everyone in the temple watched, silent and wordless. There were no words for what had transpired here.

Step by step, he descended. Cusi's hair trailed over his arms. Despite the blood that stained her white garment, her face looked peaceful, a faint, impossible smile curving her lips. With tears of grief drying on his face, Bao laid her body on the altar, arranging her limbs with dignity.

"Now it is done," he said quietly. "No more."

I opened my mouth to agree, but it seemed the temple tilted sideways. I heard Bao's voice calling my name—and then I knew no more.

I slept; and did not know how long I slept. I dreamed of doorways and blood and flowers, of darkness and storms. I dreamed of jungles and mountains and bones and maidens, and of the Maghuin Dhonn Herself lowering Her mighty head to breathe on me in approval.

I did not want to wake.

But in time, I did.

I awoke to sunlight and unfamiliar surroundings. I felt as empty and hollow as a scraped gourd. It took all the strength I had to drag myself to sit upright, and my *diadh-anam* guttered low in my breast.

Sitting cross-legged on the floor beside my pallet, Balthasar Shahrizai startled. "Moirin!" He ran his hands through his hair and yawned. "Forgive me, I fear I dozed for a minute."

Alarm surged through me. "Where's Bao?" I touched my chest, but my *diadh-anam* was so faint, I could not sense his. I feared that mayhap he had been punished for sacrilege—or worse, punished himself. "Is he—?"

"He's fine," Balthasar said in a soothing tone. "As well as can be expected under the circumstances." Turning his head, he called into the next chamber. "Machasu! Lady Moirin awakes. Will you send for Messire Bao?"

Machasu peered around the door, her solemn expression lightening with relief at the sight of me. "It is true! I will summon the twice-born."

I ran my hands over my face. "How long did I sleep?"

"Three days." Balthasar rose and poured a cup of water from an earthenware jug, handing it to me. "Bao was at your side most of the time, sick with worry. I finally convinced him to let me take over for a spell a few hours ago that he might sleep."

I had to use both hands to hold the cup steady, but the water tasted good. Until I drank it, I hadn't realized how parched my throat was, or how empty my belly. I drained the cup, and Balthasar refilled it.

"So." Glancing around, I determined we were in a chamber in the palace. I even saw my yew-wood bow and battered quiver propped in a corner. "I take it we're not in disgrace?"

"No." Balthasar perched on the edge of my pallet, holding the jug at the ready while I drank. "We are the honored guests of the *Sapa Inca* Huayna."

"Huayna?" I repeated.

"The eldest son of the *Sapa Inca* Yupanqui," he clarified. "He was coronated two days ago. We're not in disgrace, Moirin. We're heroes. There was some confusion for a time, but the Maidens of the Sun explained everything. In light of what happened, the priests had no choice but to forgive us." His mouth twisted wryly. "Would that I'd witnessed the scene in the temple! The aftermath alone was terrible and wondrous beyond belief."

I held out my cup, and Balthasar refilled it obligingly. "Is all well now?" I asked, uncertain. "As well as can be?"

He hesitated.

My empty belly rumbled in complaint. I drank more water, pressing my fist against my belly. "Forgive me, I'm famished. What is it? What's wrong?"

"I fear you've touched on it." Balthasar's face was grave. "The black river is gone, but it left precious little in its wake. Raphael's commands kept their appetite in check."

"The Quechua folk?" I whispered. "But I saw the ants flee the temple!"

He shook his head. "Not the Quechua. After Raphael's death, his ants didn't deign to take on large prey. But they stripped the fields, and devoured all manner of small livestock. They ravaged the land, Moirin." His lips tightened. "I daresay everything between Qusqu and Vilcabamba is a wasteland."

I felt sick. "The Quechua have stores..."

"Not enough," Balthasar said simply. "We raided all that lie to the north on our march here. The new *Sapa Inca* has sent out runners to the south ordering the storehouses emptied, and he's called for the

slaughter of pack-animals. No one thinks it will be enough to prevent starvation on a considerable scale. And for a surety, there are not
enough stores to supply our return journey."

I could have wept at the futility of it all, but at that moment, Bao
entered the chamber, the familiar length of his bamboo staff once
more strapped across his back. Both my heart and my *diadh-anam*
flared as his dark gaze met mine. With no memory of having risen, I
found myself in his arms, my face pressed against his shoulder as he
held me close.

"Balthasar told you, didn't he?" Bao murmured. "I saw it in your
face."

I nodded against his shoulder.

"Moirin." He stroked my hair. "The high priestesses Iniquill and
Ocllo have an idea you may be able to help."

A profound wave of weariness sapped me. "Oh, Bao!" I laughed in
despair. "Do they imagine I can quicken the crops of an entire city?"

"The crops would need to be planted anew," he said. "And yes."

"No." Pulling away from him, I shook my head. Thinking on
the leagues and leagues of stripped and barren fields that would
need to be replanted, the thousands upon thousands of plants that
would need to be quickened from mere seeds, the enormity of the task
seemed daunting and impossible. Never, ever had I even entertained
the thought of attempting somewhat on that scale. Hot tears burned
my eyes. "It's too much! It was difficult enough to coax a single field of
marigolds to bloom out of season in Bhaktipur, and I wasn't drained
to the dregs as I am now! Stone and sea, there's not enough *left* of me!
I cannot do it."

Bao was silent. The shadow of Cusi's death lay behind his eyes. He
had done the unthinkable.

I'd thought that banishing Focalor and closing the doorway was
the hardest task I faced; but I was wrong.

That was merely reparation for my own folly.

Trust me.

I had been spared the loss of my *diadh-anam* for a reason. The gift of life, Iniquill had called it. The Maidens of the Sun had wagered on my gift, pitting it against the black tide of death Raphael had brought. Cusi had offered herself as a sacrifice to save her people, and the ancestors had answered her.

I could not dishonor her memory. I could not let her people starve—and my own alongside them.

I bowed my head. "Do they at least have seeds to plant?"

"They do." It was Balthasar who answered, standing off to the side, his voice unwontedly soft. "Seed grains and potatoes. The *Sapa Inca's* set a guard on their stores. They're the staples of life here in Tawantin-suyo. And we've had ample experience in planting them, my lady," he added, striving gallantly for levity, rubbing his work-hardened hands together. "Thierry bids me tell you he will wield a digging-stick one last time if you think his efforts might bear fruit."

Lifting my head, I drew a long, trembling breath, placing one hand on Bao's chest. "Do you truly believe I can do this thing?"

"I do." Bao covered my hand with his own. "Can you look me in the eye and love me still, Moirin? Knowing what *I* have done?"

"Aye." Twining my fingers with his, I raised his hand to my lips, kissing his knuckles. "You did what was needful."

He shuddered. "It was awful."

"I know," I whispered. "I was there. And I am here."

Exactly when Balthasar Shahrizai made his discreet withdrawal, I could not say. Only that he did.

Lying entwined on the pallet, Bao and I held each other, taking solace in silence. I rested my head on his chest and listened to the slow, steady beat of his heart. I felt the spark of my *diadh-anam* grow stronger, the presence of his nurturing it. We were alive. We had survived. Focalor had been banished. Raphael, Lord Pachacuti with his army of ravenous ants, was no more. The starved ants, poor things, would return to their rightful habitats in the distant jungles.

The future I had seen in which the great empires of Terra Nova were crushed and eradicated would not come to pass. Cusi's sacrifice had ensured it. And so, ironically, had Raphael's actions. The physician with the healing hands I'd once thought I'd loved had taught the Nahuatl to stave off the killing pox.

"Mayhap there is a purpose in all this after all," I murmured. "Mayhap the gods have their reasons after all."

Bao's arms tightened around me. "I believe it must be so," he said, his warm breath stirring my hair. "But I hope they are done with us soon."

I raised my head to kiss him. "So do I, my magpie. So do I."

SEVENTY-THREE

I spent the day at rest, breaking my fast with a bowl of thin stew that Machasu brought. It was mostly water, but there were bits of potato and stringy meat in it. I ate it slowly, trying to make it last.

Various visitors came and went. When Prince Thierry arrived, I heard the whole tale of the nerve-racking night he and his hand-picked dozen men had spent in the temple, and the struggle to subdue the priests with *wurari* poison. There had been a number of scuffles while they waited for the poison to take effect, but no one had been harmed.

"It wasn't easy," Thierry said wearily. "A few of them fought like mad once they realized what we were about."

"But you kept your head, your highness," Bao said with quiet respect. "And you saw to it that the others kept theirs. It was well done."

"It was done," Thierry said. "And that is all that matters." They exchanged a glance, and I saw that the respect between them was mutual. "Moirin, I am sorry to have doubted you."

"Don't be," I said. "I doubted myself."

I did not add that if I could have stayed Bao's hand there at the end, I would have. He did not need to know that, ever.

On the morrow, we met with the *Sapa Inca* Huayna and went to view the devastation the ants had wrought.

At that, I did weep. All the terraced fields were stripped bare, the earth churned and barren. In their hunger, the ants had laid bare every stalk, burrowed the length of every furrow. Women and children scavenged the fields, sifting through the dirt with their fingers in the hope of finding an overlooked tuber.

But the ants had been thorough. Their passage had cut a swath a league wide across the land, a broad trail of lifeless brown leading eastward as far as the eye could see. Everywhere the land was cultivated, it had been ravaged.

"Ah, gods!" I whispered to the newly crowned *Sapa Inca*. "I'm so sorry."

Huayna gave a stoic shrug. "You did not bring the plague of ants upon us, lady. Lord Pachacuti did, with my foolish youngest brother's help." His expression softened. "I do not forget that you wept for my father's death, too." He held out one hand. Three kernels of *maize* lay in his palm. "In the past, we would seek to appease the gods with sacrifices were such a tragedy to occur. But the Maidens of the Sun say you possess a gift of life, and it is to life we must now trust. Is it so?"

I took a deep breath. "I pray it is."

He lowered himself to one knee, poking the kernels into the earth and making a mound. "Show me."

I knelt, pressing my hands into the soil. Summoning the twilight, I breathed softly over the mound. I felt the kernels awake and quicken, sending out green shoots that pierced the mound.

The *Sapa Inca* Huayna's eyes widened. "Can you do this for all?" He gestured across the devastated landscape. "*All* of this?"

"I don't know," I said honestly, brushing dirt from my hands. "Not like this, I think. Not all at once. But if you will set every man, woman, and child to replanting your fields, I will do my best to quicken them."

"It is a risk," he said slowly. "Many claim it would be better to eat the seeds we have in store, for there is no time for crops to ripen. Better to consume what we have, and send for new seed in the spring."

Trust me.

I echoed the words aloud. "Trust me."

His black gaze weighed me, and after a moment, he nodded. "We will attempt this thing."

It was a prodigious undertaking. True to his word, Prince Thierry lent his own hand to the endeavor, ordering our entire company to do the same. Under the direction of the Quechua farmers, D'Angeline noblemen burnt brown by the sun worked side by side with the denizens of Qusqu, digging and stooping in endless rows, planting multicolored kernels of *maize* and sprouting chunks of seed potatoes.

Day after day, I walked the fields where they labored, my feet bare that I might feel the soil beneath them, coaxing a thousand hidden sparks of life to quicken. Betimes it felt as though I walked amidst constellations of earth-bound stars. I breathed the Breath of Earth's Pulse and the Breath of Trees Growing. When the fields were irrigated, I breathed the Breath of Ocean's Rolling Waves.

At night, I slept like the dead, drained and dreamless. But I was using my gift as it was intended, and every morning, I found the strength to rise.

Without the system of distribution that even Raphael had found worthy of praise, I daresay we would have starved. But even as the last meager hoard of stores had been distributed and the last pack-animal shorn and slaughtered, supplies began trickling in from distant quarters.

Not enough to survive the winter without crops, but enough to keep going. I tightened the woolen cord knotted around my waist and ignored the hunger pangs in my belly.

I prayed to the Maghuin Dhonn Herself, and to Blessed Elua and all of his Companions, most especially to Anael, the Good Steward—the man with the seedling cupped in his hand, I had called him since childhood.

When green seedlings emerged from the earth, unfurling leaves and tendrils, I breathed the Breath of Wind's Sigh and the Breath of Embers Glowing, welcoming them to the open sky and the sun's warm kiss.

I do not know how many days it lasted, or how many leagues I walked amidst the fields, following furrow after furrow. I felt weight-less and insubstantial, suspended between sky and earth.

There was day and night, the fields and seedlings, and nothing-ness. But the crops grew. They quickened. The Quechua farmers tended them assiduously, weeding the fields and nurturing the grow-ing plants.

Betimes the Maidens of the Sun walked the fields with me, add-ing their prayers to the gods of Tawantinsuyo. In the palace, Machasu fussed over me, insisting that I ate every night before I slept. Betimes I suspected her of giving me her share of whatever food there was, but she denied it indignantly, and I was too tired and hungry to argue.

Always, I had Bao at my side, a constant and reassuring presence, his *diadh-anam* burning steadily when mine guttered low. Others accompanied us in shifts: Thierry and Balthasar and Septimus Rousse, and Jean Grenville and Brice de Bretel, who sang L'Agnacite hymns I found soothing. The Jaguar Knight Temilotzin, who watched me like a worried hawk, as quick as Bao to lend a shoulder when I faltered.

And the crops grew.

Seedlings thickened into stalks, sprouting arching plumes of leaves. Knee-high, then waist-high, then taller than my head. I walked between row after row, letting my trailing hands touch the leaves. The stalks sprouted buds of tasseled flowers that grew, thickening and lengthen-ing. In the potato fields, the tendrils turned to vines and issued broad leaves, then white and lavender blossoms.

I summoned the twilight and breathed life into them. The flowers expended themselves, withering and dying on the vine.

I thought of the skulls in the *tzompantli* in the city of Tenochtitlan, and the poem the Nahuatl Emperor had recited to me.

I thought of Cusi, and petals falling like rain.

And the crops grew and grew.

Until the day when I rose at dawn and walked out to the fields as I had done so many times before, and found them thronged with Quechua workers, hundreds upon hundreds of them, busy hands plucking and digging. All I could do was blink, uncomprehending.

"What are they doing?" My voice sounded hoarse with disuse. I tried to remember the last time I'd spoken, and couldn't. It had been days.

"They're harvesting," Bao said in wonder. Loosing a victorious shout, he turned to me with a fierce grin, a grin I'd feared I might never see again. "They're *harvesting*, Moirin!" Laying his hands on my shoulders, he gave me a little shake. "You did it!"

I felt bewildered. "I did?"

Bao cupped my face in his hands and gave me a resounding kiss. "Aye, Moirin. You did."

"He is right, little warrior," Temilotzin added. "You have won this battle."

I looked.

It was true. Even as I looked, a woman with a friendly, careworn face, some Quechua farmer's wife, approached us, a pair of young children following in her wake as she traversed the field. She held an ear of *maize* in her hands, cradling it like an offering.

"See," she said reverently, peeling back the limp silken tassels and the coarse, pale green leaves to reveal rows of healthy kernels. "It is ripe!"

My knees gave way, so swiftly neither Bao nor Temilotzin caught me before I sank to the earth. "Oh...!"

The Quechua woman smiled. "This is for you, lady." She pressed the ear of *maize* into my hands, patting them gently. In the manner of children everywhere, her toddlers peered at me around her skirt, their eyes wide and bright with a mixture of wariness and curiosity. "You have caused this to happen, and I come to give it to you. It is the first fruit of the harvest, and you should have it."

"*Sulpayki,*" I whispered, clutching her offering. "Thank you."

Her smile broadened, revealing unexpected dimples that tugged at my heart. "*Imamanta,*" she replied. "You are welcome."

Now it was truly done.

SEVENTY-FOUR

⬩──◦──⬩

Qusqu would survive.

There was a feast that evening, and it was a joyous thing to see the streets of the splendid city filled with folk celebrating the harvest. Exhausted as I was, the sight gladdened my heart, and I felt stronger for it.

A good deal of negotiating had transpired while I walked the fields in a waking daze. Counting on my success, Prince Thierry had engaged Eyahue to negotiate for the supplies everyone prayed were forthcoming for our return journey, and various live specimens and samples of Quechua workmanship. He was determined not to return to Terre d'Ange empty-handed after all his travail.

I would not have thought we had aught left with which to trade, but the *Sapa Inca* Huayna had acted with strict integrity to restore the arms and armor that Raphael had confiscated from our company. Thierry had declined to trade the swords, brigandines, and helmets, but in exchange for the bulkier pieces of plate armor, he was able to secure all he wanted.

"We've spoken of establishing further trade in the years to come," Thierry told me, a faraway look in his eye. "Captain Rousse is interested in returning with an expedition of mapmakers and engineers to dredge a river passage across the isthmus. It could open up Terra Nova in a manner the Aragonians never even dreamed of."

"You have duties at home, my lord," I reminded him, a bit alarmed. "Terre d'Ange needs you far more than Terra Nova does."

"I know." Thierry sobered, his gaze returning from the distance. "Believe me, Moirin, my adventuring is done. But if I am fortunate enough to survive this and take possession of the throne, I will have the means to back such an endeavor."

"Ambition can be a dangerous thing," I murmured.

"Yes, I know." He met my eyes steadily. "I watched Raphael de Mereliot descend into madness because of it. But men must have dreams, Moirin. And I watched Terre d'Ange descend into idle frivolity because my father didn't encourage the best and brightest among us to dream boldly." He smiled with sorrow. "He was a good man, and a fair and just ruler. But I do not wish to repeat his mistakes."

To that, I had no reply.

"I suspect it could not be done in a single lifetime," Septimus Rousse added. "But who better than us to attempt a beginning?" He nodded at the *Sapa Inca*, who was drinking freshly brewed *chicha* from a golden bowl. "We have a strong ally in this Quechua Emperor, and a foundation of trust on which to build. Both our nations stand to benefit." He paused. "Denis de Toluard and I spoke often during our journey of how such a thing might be accomplished," he added in a softer tone. "It helped pass the time and occupy our minds. I would undertake it in his memory."

I had no reply to that, either. I lifted my own bowl of *chicha*. "To Denis, then, and all our fallen comrades."

Bao's expression was shuttered as he drank, and I knew he thought of Cusi. But when I touched his arm, he summoned a quiet smile for me. "Do you harbor any ambitions I should know about?" I asked him.

His smile widened, turning genuine. "Just the one."

I raised my brows. "Fat babies?"

"Round as dumplings," Bao affirmed. "Just wait."

Balthasar Shahrizai snorted into his *chicha*. "Now that, I'd like to see."

I would, too.

That night, I slept and dreamed for the first time since the night of the sacrifice. Unsurprisingly, I dreamed of walking the fields, my bare feet sinking into the loose soil, the tall stalks of *maize* swaying around me. In my dream, I walked alone and unattended, breathing slowly and deeply, extending my arms to brush the leaves. And in my dream, it did not surprise me when I rounded a furrow and saw my lady Jehanne awaiting me beneath the green shadows of the arching leaves, her slender figure clad incongruously in the white satin garb of her Snow Queen costume, an ermine-trimmed cloak flowing from her shoulders and brushing the earth, diamonds glittering in her fair hair.

Her head tilted a little. "Moirin."

I smiled at her. "Aye, my lady."

She drew nearer, the expression on her exquisite face earnest. "You know why I've come?"

I nodded. "To say farewell."

"It ends here." Jehanne's shoulders rose and fell as she took a sharp breath. "You'll tell my daughter I loved her?"

Again, I nodded. "Does that mean I return safely?"

She shook her head. "That, I cannot know." Her blue-grey eyes searched mine. "I was only ever allowed to know what was needed. You do know that, don't you?"

"Aye," I said. "I do."

"Aye." Jehanne echoed the word with a smile. "Oh, Moirin!" She gestured all around her. "The world grows and changes, but a gift such as yours should not be allowed to pass from it. The world needs its ambitious dreamers, men who would shape it to their own ends. But it needs those who would keep them in check, too. The world needs its courtesans." She touched my cheek. "And the world needs its bear-witches, my lovely savage. You won't withdraw from it like the rest of your folk, will you?"

"No," I said. "I have an oath to keep. Assuming we *do* return safely, I will divide my time between Alba and Terre d'Ange, but I will remain a part of Desirée's life, I promise."

"I'm glad." Jehanne took my arm. In unspoken accord, we strolled along between the rows of tall stalks. She gave me a sparkling side-long glance. "To think I set out to seduce you out of spite all those years ago!"

I laughed. "To think I knew, and let you."

"Oh, please!" She squeezed my arm. "You never had a chance. Naamah's gift runs far, far too strong in you."

"In both of us," I said.

"You put it to better use." Jehanne's lips quirked. "Though it shames me to admit it, it's true."

I shook my head. "You have no cause for shame."

She walked a few paces in silence. "Would that it were true," she said at length. "But I made choices I regret. I spent far too much time being foolish and petty, indulging my every whim and desire. I abetted Terre d'Ange's descent into...what did Thierry call it? Idle frivolity."

"You were young," I murmured.

Jehanne shot me a look at once fond and wry. "I was your age now when first we met, Moirin. Look at what you've done."

"Aye, and I am here because of the foolish choices I made when I was even younger," I said mildly. "You never unleashed a fallen spirit on the world, my lady."

She tilted her head again. "How is it you always know the right thing to say to comfort me?"

"I come from a long line of royal companions," I said.

"True. Naamah chose wisely when she sent your father to your mother." Jehanne paused to stroke a *maize* leaf. Her tone shifted as she glanced at me, the expression on her lovely face turning vulnerable. "Moirin, I'm scared."

I halted and took her hands. "Of what?"

"Of what comes next." Tears shone in her starry eyes. "It's absurd, I know. For so long...has it been a long time? It's so hard to tell here, but it feels like it. I've been trapped *between,* waiting for this moment to come, and it's been so lonely, so very lonely. But now that it's finally here, I'm frightened." Freeing one hand, she wiped her eyes. "I don't imagine I'll be passing through the bright gate into Terre d'Ange-that-lies-beyond. What if I'm reborn into the world forgetting all I've learned? What if Daniel and Raphael are waiting for me to make the same mistakes all over again?"

"You won't." I pressed her hand between mine. "Jehanne, you answered your own question."

"I did?"

"Aye," I said. "You told Raphael we break each other's hearts, but we mend them, too. Trust yourself." I smiled. "You were always a great deal kinder and wiser than you pretended."

There was sorrow in her smile. "So you always said."

"Because it's true."

"My beautiful girl." Jehanne touched my cheek again. "Once more, you find the right thing to say."

"I quoted *you*," I reminded her.

"So you did." Leaning forward, she brushed my lips with a kiss. "You are the one love I have no cause to regret, Moirin. But for all that Naamah has blessed you, you'll not be taking the same journey when the time comes, will you? Your final destiny lies with your bear-goddess."

"Aye," I said. "But I would not be so sure it is the *final* destiny, my lady. Master Lo Feng said that all ways lead to the Way, and he was the wisest man I've ever met." I nodded at the rustling rows of *maize*. "Were it not for his teaching, I would not have had the strength to do this thing." Taking a deep breath, I continued. "And I believe it is possible that there is somewhat that lies beyond even the Terre d'Ange-that-lies-beyond, beyond the presence of the Maghuin Dhonn Herself, a vastness beyond men and gods and heavens, wherein all of us are part of a greater whole."

"It's a lovely notion," Jehanne murmured. "Do you suppose it's true?"

"I don't know," I said. "I hope so."

"I shall choose to believe it," she said firmly. "Because it is prefer-able to believing in a world in which our paths never cross again, Moirin mac Fainche." Unexpectedly, a dazzling smile lit her face. "Thank you. I had need of your gentle counsel one last time. But I think I am ready now."

It was my turn to be dismayed. "So soon?"

"It is long past time." Jehanne wound her soft, slender arms around my neck, gazing intently into my eyes. The intoxicating scent of her perfume mingled with the odor of fresh-turned soil and the green scent of thriving plants. "Be well," she whispered against my lips. "Be happy. I wish you every joy, Moirin. Do not forget to tell Desirée that I loved her. Do not forget to tell your own plump babes and your reformed ruffian of a husband. He loves you very, very much, and that will see you through every darkness."

My eyes stung. "Jehanne—"

"Naamah's blessing on you, my beautiful girl." She kissed me, her lips soft and tender, lingering; and I felt Naamah's blessing break over us like a wave, like a warm, golden embrace, an enduring affirmation of the power of love and desire.

I wrapped my arms around Jehanne, holding her close.

For a moment, my lady Jehanne was *there*, warm and living and present in my arms. And then there was only empty sunlight sparkling in my embrace, the stalks of *maize* waving their blameless tassels.

I awoke with a start.

On the pallet beside me, Bao roused sleepily to prop himself on one elbow, reading my expression. "You dreamed of the White Queen?"

I nodded. "She is gone now."

"I'm sorry." His sympathy was sincere. "It must be hard to lose her twice."

"It was." I found myself smiling through tears. "But it was time. As it is ours, too. Time to go home."

SEVENTY-FIVE

— ✦ —

There was one last matter to be dealt with ere we could depart the empire of Tawantinsuyo. Because he had worn the crown of the *Sapa Inca*, no matter how briefly, the Quechua had preserved Raphael de Mereliot's body.

"Whatever else is true, he commanded great magic," the *Sapa Inca* Huayna said soberly. "There can be no place for him among our ancestors, but we did not wish to offend whatever gods he served. Do you wish to return him to your own temple?"

"We are not lugging that maniac's carcass across the entire continent of Terra Nova," Balthasar muttered.

Prince Thierry silenced him with a scowl, then turned to me. "Moirin, you understand these matters better than most. What are your thoughts?"

I gazed at Raphael's face. Even beneath the cerements, one could see that he had been a beautiful man. I thought of the fallen spirit Focalor forcing his essence into him, and of the spark of lightning that had lingered in Raphael's eyes, haunting my thoughts for so many years. What if a spark lingered even now? Having seen the dead rise and walk, I did not wish to take any chances.

"I would build a funeral pyre," I said slowly. "Let the fire cleanse him and release any trace of the spirit that remains. Let his ashes be scattered to fertilize the fields."

"It seems a fitting end," the *Sapa Inca* Huayna said in quiet approval.

So it was done.

The Quechua built a pine-wood pyre in the temple square. There, Raphael de Mereliot's body was cremated, his cloth-wrapped limbs twisting and blackening in flames that burned so hot they were nearly invisible in the sunlight. Now and again, a burst of sparks rose into the sky.

I thought of Focalor and wondered.

Despite everything, I did not believe the fallen spirit was *evil*. It was a force of destruction that had been constrained for long centuries if the legends were true, and unleashed on the world, it would have wreaked havoc. So had the ants Raphael commanded done; and yet, within their rightful habitat, they had a role to play. Mayhap the fallen spirits had a role to play, too.

If the spirit Marbas had not given me the gift of finding hidden things, my Ch'in princess would have drowned in the reflecting lake atop White Jade Mountain, the dragon would have ceased to be, and the weapons of the Divine Thunder would have been loosed on the world, altering it forever.

Mayhap even my youthful folly had a purpose. The gods use their chosen hard, but reveal little to them.

When the pyre had burned down to a few restless embers, the Quechua gathered the ashes in earthenware bowls, transporting them to the fields where they were distributed with care, churned into the soil to nourish it.

I gazed at the waving rows of *maize*, praying silently that Raphael's bitter, tormented heart would find healing.

And then there was nothing left to do but say our farewells. Our supplies were gathered, our caravan in readiness. The long journey awaited us.

It was time.

"Good-bye, my sister," I whispered in Machasu's ear as I hugged her. "Thank you for your strength and courage, and thank you for sharing your food with me when I needed it most."

She gave an indignant sniff. "I did no such thing, lady!"

I smiled. "As you will."

The high priestess Iniquill acknowledged me with a grave bow of her silver-haired head, and I returned it with dignity.

Ocllo surprised me by seizing me in a fierce embrace, pressing me to her stalwart bosom, then releasing me just as abruptly. "On behalf of the ancestors, I thank you," she said in a formal tone. "And on behalf of my granddaughter..." Her voice broke. "Please thank the twice-born for making it swift and merciful."

I stared at her. "Cusi was your granddaughter? You did not tell me!"

Tears glinted in her eyes, but did not fall. "No, I did not. But it is true. And young as she was, I do believe the gods chose wisely when they guided Lord Pachacuti's hand in sending her to you."

I kissed her lined cheek. "Her courage shames us all. I will never forget her, I promise."

Ocllo blinked. "I should hope not."

One day after Raphael's cremation, we departed the city of Qusqu at dawn. Behind us, the slanting rays of the rising sun kindled the snowy mantles of the western mountains, turning them gold. The air was dry and crisp, and I breathed it deep into my lungs. I had my yew-wood bow and quiver slung over one shoulder, my battered satchel with a few wordly goods and a fair share of supplies over the other.

A long journey faced us. A long, long journey.

We would serve as our own porters. Every man among us, Prince Thierry included, carried a woven basket on his back, tump-lines of corded wool stretched across their brows. They carried baskets laden with stores, with samples and specimens, bits and pieces of gilded, jade-studded Quechua workmanship tucked amidst potatoes and *maize*, sacks of powdered *cinchona* bark, nuts and seeds from myriad plants, and the stores of herbs Eyahue had assiduously gathered.

Bao sighed, shifting his shoulders. His bamboo staff rode high atop his back, thrust through the handles of his basket.

"Home," I reminded him.

He echoed the word, his voice wistful. "Home. I am not sure what it means, but I like the sound of it, Moirin."

"So do I," I murmured.

SEVENTY-SIX

It was a long journey indeed.

It was a very, very long journey. We followed well-kept footroads in the empire of Tawantinsuyo, curving along the crests of mountains, camping in the arid open beneath a sky filled with countless stars. We crossed hanging bridges that swayed above rushing torrents, and we forded broad rivers that had never been bridged, picking our way with care.

We descended from the mountains and fought our way through jungles. We crossed vast savannahs. We marched until the light began to fade, and rose every day at dawn to resume our journey.

Those of us who could hunt, did. When we encountered villages, we bartered what we could.

Betimes we were hungry, but we did not starve. We were tired and footsore, but by this time all of us had long since grown inured to the hardships of travel. Even Balthasar kept his grumbling to a minimum.

After enduring the misery of the barren swamplands, we gained the isthmus and wound our way along the sloping spine of the long mountain range that divided it, catching glimpses of the sea. Septimus Rousse muttered to himself, scratching notes and maps on a piece of crude parchment he'd obtained in Qusqu.

The whole of the journey does not bear telling. I leave it to mapmakers like Captain Rousse to chronicle in exhausting detail the landscape we spent so many months traversing on our return. Suffice it to say that it was long and arduous, but at the end of it, the majority of our company reached the lands of the Nahuatl Empire alive.

Alas, not all.

There were losses suffered. One of the men from my original company, Bernard de Vouges, perished when he lost his footing during a difficult river-crossing. The swift current carried him downriver, dashing his head against a boulder and splitting open his skull, ribbons of blood staining the water.

At least we were able to retrieve his body and bury it with honor.

Two of Prince Thierry's men, Féderic Bardou and Perrin de Fleury, died in the mountains in a sudden rockslide—or so we were forced to presume. On Thierry's orders, we spent the better part of the day digging frantically amidst the rubble to no avail. Only the ominous creaking sounds from the slopes above us and Eyahue's urgent warnings persuaded Thierry to abandon the effort.

We mourned them and continued, entering the territory of the Cloud People, where we posted multiple sentries every night. We passed through without incident, those of us who remembered Pochotl's betrayal breathing a sigh of relief, and crossed the invisible boundary that marked the southern verge of the Nahuatl Empire.

There, we were greeted with astonishment. Eyahue and Temilotzin were hailed as returning heroes. And I began to believe that mayhap this seemingly endless journey had an end after all.

Without the burden of plate armor slowing the men, our pace was quicker than it had been at the outset. Still, rumor ran ahead of us.

We were some two weeks away from the city of Tenochtitlan when a startling sight greeted us—a company of mounted Aragonian soldiers in full armor, trailing a long line of pack- and saddle-horses, Commander Diego Ortiz y Ramos riding at their head.

Our own company halted, uncertain.

"Drop your packs," Thierry murmured, suiting actions to words. He laid one hand on his sword-hilt. "And be ready for anything."

My throat tightened, and I prayed silently that the Aragonians had not grown ascendant in our absence.

Commander Diego Ortiz y Ramos drew rein, his gaze sweeping over our weary, footsore crew and settling on Thierry.

"Your highness." He bowed from the saddle. "I am pleased to see that the rumors of your return are true, and that you are well. With the blessing of Emperor Achcuatli, my men and I are here to escort you and your people to the city of Tenochtitlan." His lips thinned above his pointed beard. "I hope that you will speak kindly of us when you return to Terre d'Ange and lay claim to its throne."

I felt like cheering. Clearly, the fellow had not forgotten that Balthasar had threatened to report that the commander had deliberately withheld information that would have assisted the Dauphin of Terre d'Ange.

Beside me, Bao chuckled.

Thierry de la Courcel gazed up at the Aragonian commander, a slow smile spreading across his lean, sunburned face. "Ah, the demands of diplomacy!" He gave a gracious nod. "By all means, Commander. We would be grateful for your aid."

In remarkably short order, our remaining goods were redistributed among the pack-horses and our company mounted.

After travelling so many leagues on foot, it felt strange to sit a horse. We travelled at a steady jog. I had to stifle a laugh at the sight of Eyahue jouncing in the saddle, his skinny legs dangling and his scrawny elbows akimbo as he sawed ineffectively at the reins, his mount sidling sideways and tossing its head in protest.

"Hold tight with your thighs," I advised him. "And use a gentle hand on the reins."

The old *pochteca* glared at me. "I'd sooner a woman's thighs gripped me, lady! I've a gentle enough hand with *them*."

I smiled. "So I hear."

Eyahue snorted.

"It puts me in mind of the first time Tortoise tried to ride a horse," Bao said, eyeing him. "Remember, Moirin? Only Eyahue sits more like a bag of sticks than a sack of cabbages."

"I remember."

Our eyes met. We had so very many shared memories between us, Bao and I. Some were wondrous, and some were terrible.

Some were both.

"Poor Tortoise," Bao said softly.

The remainder of the journey passed swiftly. After so long away, even returning to Tenochtitlan with its splendid, bloodstained temples and its mighty causeways felt like somewhat of a homecoming. I'd thought that the commander would wish us to lodge in the Aragonian stronghold, but it seemed that under the terms of his agreement, he was to escort us directly to Emperor Achcuatli.

Indeed, our approach had been noted, and a reception awaited us in the temple square beneath the rows and rows of hollow-eyed grinning skulls in the *tzompantli*. I could not help but steal a glance at them, and breathe a sigh of relief to find no fresh offerings among their ranks.

The Emperor himself was seated atop a gilded dais beneath a feather canopy, clad in the full regalia of his office, golden sandals and all. A faint smile touched his lips at the sight of me, and I felt myself flush.

At an order from one of the Emperor's attendants, we dismounted and approached on foot, the Aragonians remaining behind.

Beneath his feathered canopy, Emperor Achcuatli inclined his head ever so slightly. "Prince of Terre d'Ange," he said to Thierry. "I am pleased that the gods have spared you. I welcome you back to our city."

Like Diego Ortiz y Ramos, Achcuatli had withheld information that would have benefited Thierry, but there was no hint of apology in his voice. Unlike the Aragonian commander, the Nahuatl Emperor could not be dismissed for creating a potential diplomatic incident with an ally nation of long standing.

And I daresay Thierry understood it, for he bowed deeply in reply. "Your majesty, I thank you for your hospitality and for your generous aid." He gestured at Eyahue and Temilotzin. "Without your clever *pochteca* and your brave and loyal warrior, my countrymen would never have found us."

"I am pleased." The Emperor took stock of our meager baggage and our ragged, threadbare condition. "I fear your long journey met with little success. Have you aught left to trade?"

"No, your majesty," Thierry said candidly. "We have a few goods with which to return to Terre d'Ange. But we have gained knowledge, and that is more valuable than gold. And we have . . . that is, most of us have . . . returned with our lives, on which no price can be set."

"Your people place a great value on life," Achcuatli observed.

"I do not value my life above any other man's," Thierry said. "But I have a duty. I would live to see it done. I owe it to my people."

"That is spoken like a true ruler," the Nahuatl Emperor said in approval. "For as long as you wish, you will be my guests. You will rest and refresh yourselves in the palace of Tenochtitlan." He jerked his chin at Diego Ortiz y Ramos, hovering in the background. "When you are ready, the men of Aragonia may have the honor of escorting you on your journey to the city by the sea that they have built."

Thierry bowed again. "Thank you, your majesty."

Emperor Achcuatli rose and descended the steps of the dais, attendants sweeping the path before him with handheld brooms. His gold-plated sandals clanked with every step, but he managed the descent with practiced dignity. He paused before me, his obsidian eyes glinting. "It has been over a year since you departed," he remarked. "And yet I found myself thinking of you and dreaming of flowers, thousands upon thousands of them. And so I ordered the offerings of flower and honey to Xochiquetzal, goddess of desire, to be continued in your name. I do believe they pleased her, for here you are."

Again, I flushed. "You honor me, your majesty."

Once more, he inclined his head ever so slightly before stepping into the litter that awaited him. "We will speak later."

When the Emperor's litter was receding across the square, Bao raised his brows at me.

I raised mine back at him. "I did not ask for this."

"No," he said. "And yet it seems to find you anyway, Moirin."

SEVENTY-SEVEN

E mperor Achcuatli was generous.

Our entire company was lodged within the vast walls of the palace. Attendants brought us all the food we might have desired. They stoked the fires of the *temazcallis* that we might sweat the grime of our long journey from our pores, and brought clean attire to don afterward. Rendered indolent by luxury, we spent three days there.

On the second day, the Emperor sent for me.

"You don't have to go, Moirin." Bao wore his shuttered expression, his face unreadable. "You could refuse to meet with him."

"Is that what you want?" I asked him. He didn't answer. "If it is, I will," I added. "Only tell me."

Bao sighed. "No. He's given you no cause to refuse." He rumpled his unruly hair. "Just..."

"I won't," I promised.

He frowned at me.

"Stupid boy," I said fondly. "Whatever lies behind this, it's not Naamah's prompting, at least not on my end of the matter. That means I am free to choose." Sinking my hands into Bao's thick, springing hair, I pulled him toward me and kissed him, feeling our *diadh-anams* intertwine. "And I choose to be faithful to you, my husband."

His expression eased. "Oh, aye?"

I kissed him again. "Aye."

As it transpired, the decision was not entirely as easy as I reckoned it would be.

Summoned by Lord Cuixtli, I met the Emperor Achcuatli in the gardens. As we had done before, we strolled them together, gazing at the blooming flowers and the birds in the aviary, familiar strangers trailed by a horde of attendants. The Emperor kept his silence and I kept mine, waiting for him to break it.

It took some time.

"Since we were together, I have been unable to stop thinking of you," Achcuatli said at length, his tone formal.

"I am honored," I replied truthfully.

He turned toward me and laid his hands on my shoulders. "I ask but one more night before you go. Your husband may have his pick of my wives this time since the last one did not please him. And I will give your Prince of Terre d'Ange what he desires. The prince came here seeking glory. What he salvaged from Tawantinsuyo is a pittance. He seeks trade rights on equal footing with those I have granted to the men of Aragonia, does he not?" He gave a sharp nod, gazing intently at me. "I will see to it that his ship rides low in the water beneath the weight of Nahuatl gold and *chocolatl* beans. Whatever you desire. I will take it on trust that the favor will be returned. Only say yes."

Ah, gods!

If Thierry were to return from his ill-fated expedition with a full hold of trade goods from Terra Nova, he would win considerable glory.

I wanted that for him. I did. I wanted it for all of us. A triumphant return would be validation beyond reproach. And it was not as though I found Achcuatli unappealing; in fact, it was quite the opposite.

But I loved Bao, and I had made a promise to him. Given his pragmatic streak, he would forgive me sooner or later. I was not sure I would be able to forgive myself.

I looked away. "You flatter me, my lord," I murmured. "You flatter me, and you tempt me, too. But I must say no."

Achcuatli's hands fell away. "You're sure?"

I nodded. "I am."

To my surprise, he smiled. "So it is not true, what the men of Aragonia say of your people. You are not willing to sell yourself at any price. That is good to know. I was uncertain."

I scowled at him. "You were *testing* me?"

"Peace." The Emperor held up one hand. "Either answer would have pleased me for different reasons. I have already decided that I wish to engage in trade with your nation. The balance of power has shifted since first your prince came to our shores. Now that our people are no longer falling by the thousands to the spotted sickness, we are able to stand stronger against the men of Aragonia." He paused. "I note that the one who taught our *ticitls* is no longer among you."

"No," I murmured. "He perished in Tawantinsuyo."

"It is a pity." Achcuatli resumed his stroll, and I kept pace with him. "We owe him a great debt."

Since it was true, I said nothing to gainsay it. My heart ached a bit for the man Raphael de Mereliot could have been. "If you had already decided, why did you wish to test me, my lord?" I asked instead.

"I wished to learn more of the nature of your people," he said. "As your prince said, knowledge is more valuable than gold."

"There are those who would have taken the offer," I said. "Would you have thought less of me if I had?"

Achcuatli shook his head. "As I said, it would have pleased me for different reasons."

"Would you have told me that you intended to open trade with Terre d'Ange regardless of my answer?" I asked.

He gave me a sidelong glance, a glimmer of amusement in his eyes. "Of course not. I would have let your people believe that your women are irresistible to the men of the Nahuatl Empire."

At that, I had to smile. "You are a clever man, my lord."

Emperor Achcuatli gazed into the distance. "Since the coming of the strangers from beyond the sea, I have had to learn to rule in a new and different way. The world has changed, and we must change with it. The old ways are not always the best ways." He walked in silence for a time. "I have spoken with the priests regarding the words you spoke to me before. It is their belief that the goddess Xochiquetzal spoke through you. Do you suppose such a thing is possible?"

"I suppose a great many things are possible," I said. "It is hard to know the will of the gods."

He nodded in agreement. "This is true. But I believe that they need their people to remain strong. Strong in spirit and strong in numbers, no longer fighting amongst ourselves for glory and sacrifice, but standing strong together. To that end, I have made new allies amongst former enemies." He glanced at me again. "That should please you, I think."

"It does," I said. "But what you told me was true, too. When the gods thirst, sometimes blood *is* the only sacrifice." I swallowed involuntarily, reliving the memory of Cusi's blood spilling over the stair. "I wish it were not so."

"Perhaps it will not always be so," Achcuatli said gently. Reaching out with one hand, he ran a few strands of my hair through his fingers, then leaned down to kiss my lips. "Now go, and return to your husband."

I went.

Following the pull of my *diadh-anam*, I found Bao in a palace courtyard, sparring with Temilotzin. Both men were stripped to the waist, sweating in the sunlight, Temilotzin wielding a new obsidian-studded club and grunting with frustration as he tried in vain to either get inside Bao's reach or splinter his elusive bamboo staff. I held my tongue, fearing that if I interrupted them, there would be bloodshed.

"I cannot believe I am having such difficulty defeating a man with a *stick*," the Jaguar Knight complained, and then he caught sight of me and stayed his hand, lowering his club. "Ah! Hello, my little warrior."

I smiled at him. "Hello, Temilotzin."

Bao turned. "Moirin."

Mayhap it was petty of me, but the studied neutrality of his tone galled me a bit. "Emperor Achcuatli made me a considerable offer," I informed him. "One we did not expect. In exchange for a single night with me, he is willing to grant trade-rights to Terre d'Ange. You may have your pick of his wives, since the last one did not please you. As a token of his trust, he will fill the hold of our ship with gold and *choco-latl* until it wallows in the water under the weight of its cargo."

Bao's expression darkened. "At least you command a worthy price."

"I said no."

He stared at me, blinking.

Temilotzin chuckled. "Do not be concerned," he said in a helpful manner. "The Emperor does but toy with you. He has already made his choice, and he wishes to trade with your nation. Eyahue and I have agreed to sail with you if you will have us. We would learn more of this world across the sea."

It was my turn to blink. "You do? You are?"

The Jaguar Knight shrugged. "The old *pochteca* can't stand being idle, and his family is angry at him for his nephew's death, even though the idiot deserved it. As for me..." His voice trailed off. "You're not listening, are you?"

"Stupid girl," Bao breathed, crossing the courtyard in a few swift strides. His hands rose to cup my face, and he kissed me hard. "You knew the Emperor had already chosen. You were just trying to torment me, weren't you?"

"A little," I admitted. "I made you a promise, Bao. You might have trusted me to keep it."

He gave me a wry look. "When it comes to matters of fidelity, history is not on your side, Moirin."

I returned his kiss. "Nor yours, my magpie. *I* did not wed the Great Khan's daughter, or bed the Spider Queen Jagrati."

Bao's hands slid to my waist. "Jagrati does not count," he whispered against my lips. "I thought you were dead, not cavorting in the wilderness with some strapping milk-sop of a Vralian lad. And you would have done whatever Jagrati asked of you, were it not for the Rani Amrita." He kissed me again. "Which is another story, isn't it?"

I pressed a finger against his lips. "And you know why. I will not have you speak a word against our lady Amrita."

He narrowed his eyes at me. "Shall we speak of your dreams instead? Dreams held on the very eve of our wedding?"

"No." I twined my arms around his neck and kissed him. "If you don't mind, I'd sooner we don't speak at all."

Bao smiled. "I don't mind."

"You are a *very* strange people," Temilotzin commented, slinging his club over one shoulder. "Truly."

SEVENTY-EIGHT

---◆---

Two days later, we departed the city of Tenochtitlan escorted by a mounted company of Aragonians and trailed by a long line of Nahuatl porters carrying laden baskets.

Diego Ortiz y Ramos was none too happy about the turn of developments, but there wasn't much he could do about it. Emperor Achcuatli had made it clear we were in his favor, and the new allegiances he had formed within the Nahuatl Empire were strong enough that the Aragonians no longer dreamed of outright conquest, but worried about maintaining such favor as they had acquired.

Once more, we passed beneath the shadow of the White Mountain of Iztactepetl, eyeing its plume of smoke warily; but once more, the volcano remained quiet. I prayed it would do so for a good hundred years, and that the Nahuatl might have no cause to placate their gods with blood sacrifice.

The Maghuin Dhonn are not a folk who relish change, but it comes nonetheless; and that is not always a bad thing. Emperor Achcuatli spoke the truth. The world changes, and we change with it.

Without change, there can be no growth; and without growth, we stagnate and die.

The Aragonian port city of Orgullo del Sol had become larger and more refined in our absence, but after the splendors of the great cities of Terra Nova, it still looked crude and rough-hewn to my eyes. Septimus Rousse had had the presence of mind to suggest sending a-few members of our company ahead to alert the crew that they might make ready to sail, but by their reactions, I daresay they hadn't let themselves believe until they saw us.

Alaric Dumont, the first mate, wept openly as he embraced his captain in the city square.

"Sorry, sir," he muttered, dashing his forearm over his eyes. "I fear we'd been running short of hope for far too long." Turning to Thierry, he proffered a deep bow. "Your highness, I cannot tell you how much it gladdens my heart to see you alive and well. And I speak for all of us when I say it would be my very greatest honor to escort you home and see the rightful heir to Terre d'Ange restored to the throne."

Prince Thierry smiled quietly, laying a hand on the fellow's shoulder. "And I do believe I speak for all of us when I say I would like nothing better."

Someone raised a cheer, and it was taken up by scores of voices, ragged and heartfelt. Men pressed close to clasp Thierry's hand or clap his back. He accepted their acknowledgments with dignity.

Thierry de la Courcel had also grown and changed.

Amidst the joyous cacophony, there were a few discordant notes. There was Porfirio Reyes, the mayor of Orgullo del Sol, presiding unhappily over our reception in the port.

"So you succeeded after all, Lady Moirin," he murmured to me after the initial exchange of greetings. "Your missing Dauphin's unfortunate tale has a glad ending. I confess, I did not believe it possible."

"I know," I said. "You made it quite clear, my lord mayor."

Porfirio Reyes gave me a shrewd glance beneath his drooping eyelids. "Yes, and I was wrong. But as I recall, you also made it clear that it was not your intention to upset the balance of power in Terra Nova. And yet it has happened."

I spread my hands. "The world changes, and we must change with it. You were also wrong in saying I would find little to love in the Nahuatl. There is more to them than stone hearts and stone faces."

His voice hardened. "I have not found it to be so."

"I have," I said. "Mayhap you are not trying hard enough."

To that, the mayor of Orgullo del Sol had no answer.

There was also the matter of Alain Guillard and his fellow mutineers, who had rebelled and abandoned our company after the battle with the Cloud People.

"Your highness." The Azzallese lordling addressed Thierry in clipped tones, his proud face hot with shame. His co-conspirators wore hangdog looks. "I freely confess myself guilty of desertion and welcome whatever punishment you see fit to administer." The other two nodded in abashed agreement.

Thierry studied them a moment. "I do not by any means condone your disloyalty," he said presently. "But as this was a voluntary expedition, I do not think you can be considered formally guilty of desertion. I believe Lady Moirin charged you with escorting two men too grievously injured to continue to safety here, did she not?"

"She did," Alain Guillard said stiffly.

"Did you succeed?"

"Yes."

"Then I will consider your service fulfilled." Thierry paused. "As far as punishment goes, I suspect that the knowledge you will have to live with an act of cowardice and disloyalty on your consciences will suffice."

Alain Guillard's face reddened further, but he made no protest, nor did either of his comrades.

And lastly there was the matter of Edouard Durel, the sailor who had attempted to steal Captain Rousse's logbook and sabotage our voyage.

Thierry had heard the tale, of course. We'd had long months to share the details of our journeys with one another. He ordered the fellow brought to him. There in the square of Orgullo del Sol, Edouard Durel dropped to his knees, tears streaming down his face.

"I'm so sorry, your highness," he said in a broken whisper. "I was so sure you were dead, and this venture nothing but a vengeful woman's folly. I'd have never done it otherwise, I swear."

Prince Thierry drummed his fingers on his sword-belt. "Under ordinary circumstances, what would his punishment be, my lord captain?" he asked Septimus Rousse.

"Death," the latter said promptly. "The *Naamah's Dove* was sailing under a royal charter. It would be considered an act of treason, one that could well have resulted in the loss of the ship and all hands aboard. And at sea, the captain's word is law."

"And yet you chose to spare him."

Septimus Rousse nudged the fellow with the toe of one boot. "He's the only one who can testify that Claudine de Barthelme and her despicable sprat of a lad put him up to this. Under those circumstances, I didn't think you'd want him dead, your highness."

"No." Thierry bent his gaze toward Edouard Durel. "You *are* willing to testify, I trust?"

Durel nodded, still weeping.

"I promised him aboard the ship that his wife and daughter will be cared for no matter what his sentence afterward," Balthasar murmured discreetly. "I believe I mentioned it to you, my lord?"

"You did, and I am in accord." Thierry de la Courcel glanced around at our assembled company. "I do not blame any man here for harboring fears and doubts. We set forth on a journey of outlandish risk. If I had the choice to make over..." His voice trailed off briefly. "Let me say that I would never have caused my father such anguish. And you, my rescuers!" His voice grew stronger. "I would never have said my life was worth the cost of so many lost in the effort to save it. And yet, here on the far side of the world, we have witnessed wonders. Great and terrible wonders, beyond comprehending."

I found myself nodding in agreement.

Thierry cleared his throat. "Since Captain Rousse has held his hand, it falls to the court of law to pass judgment on this man. For now, I would see the slate wiped clean ere we set sail. Let there be no further recriminations. What is done, is done. We are all victims of our own ambitions, our own follies, our own weaknesses. Let us set them aside, and venture forth joined in one single goal. Let us return to Terre d'Ange and reclaim her throne!"

More cheers arose, and this time, there was a sound of unison in them. Thierry stooped, taking Edouard Durel's chin in his hand.

"Are you prepared to help convey me home, sailor?" he asked.

Still on his knees, the fellow lifted his damp gaze, his eyes shining with tears and gratitude. "Aye, your highness!"

"Good." Thierry let him go. "Let's be about it, then."

SEVENTY-NINE

The same day, the *Naamah's Dove* set sail.

Her hold was laden with trade goods: nuts and kernels and seedlings from Tawantinsuyo and the Nahuatl Empire alike. Samples of *maize* and a dozen different varieties of potatoes. *Tomati* plants reckoned in error to be deadly, hot peppers that seared the tongue. Sack upon sack of *chocolatl* beans, and the fragrant seed-pods called *tlilxochitl*, or "black flower." A few lengths of *vicuña* wool, fine-spun, light and airy.

Feathers; glimmering feathers, wrought into capes and tapestries.

Gold.

It was true, Terra Nova was rich in gold. Our ship did not quite wallow beneath its weight, but we carried a great deal of it, samples of Nahuatl workmanship along with raw, unprocessed ore.

I stood in the stern of the ship with Bao and Eyahue and Temilotzin, watching the shores of Terra Nova fall away behind us and the vast sea open up to swallow us, rendering us infinitesimal.

"It's big," Temilotzin said in a subdued voice. "Very, very big."

"No bigger than your courage," I assured him. "Do not fear, Captain Rousse will see us to safety."

Temilotzin glanced at me out of the corner of his eye. "I hope you are right, lady."

I did, too.

Days, weeks, months . . . it is hard to measure the passage of time on a journey. What matters is the distance between the starting point and the destination. League by league, wave by wave, we whittled it down, while Captain Rousse studied the skies and took complicated measurements with his instruments, marking our progress on his charts.

I wondered how it was that the folk of Terra Nova, who were cunning engineers, had never ventured out to sea. Of a surety, they were comfortable on lakes and rivers. Mayhap it was because the vastness was so very daunting that unlike our explorers, they had no cause to suspect there was aught on the far side of the enormous oceans. And I wondered, too, how much that would change in ages to come.

I hoped that we might learn from one another, sharing the best our disparate cultures had to offer.

I hoped that dreams might outweigh ambitions.

Prince Thierry was introspective on the journey, and I daresay many of the same matters occupied his thoughts—not to mention the conflict to come. From time to time, he summoned me to speak with him, plying me for details of House Barthelme's machinations. I told him everything I knew, including my own futile efforts to thwart them, and how it had divided the realm.

"I'm not surprised," he said. "Or rather, I'm surprised you found as many adherents as you did."

"Because I was born to the Maghuin Dhonn?" I asked.

"That, and the chaos and scandal you left in your wake." Thierry smiled wryly. "For all your uncanny ways, you were so young and naïve! I thought you were a fool for letting Raphael, and then Jehanne, turn your head."

"You were right about Raphael," I said. "Not Jehanne."

"No, I suppose not," he mused. "She changed, you know. Even after you left. It wasn't just a matter of being more pleasant to those around her. I do believe she began to take her role as Queen seriously." His face took on its faraway look. "I should have known how deeply her death wounded my father."

"You couldn't have known how deep the wound cut," I murmured. "It is not the sort of thing a parent shares with a child."

Returning from the distance, Thierry glanced at me. "What's *she* like? My sister, Desirée. She was scarce more than a babe when I left."

"High-spirited and willful, and filled with a yearning for love." I smiled with sorrow. "Or at least she was when I left. She's the image of Jehanne, and she has her mother's temper. They'll seek to use it against her, to convince her that she's unlovable because of it. That she bears a burden of guilt for every loss House Courcel has suffered. She's vulnerable to it."

"You seem very sure of this," he said.

I nodded. "I am."

Thierry propped his arms on the ship's railing, gazing out at the endless sea. "I'd like to see it for myself," he said. "I'd like to see House Barthelme tip their hand before I reveal mine. If we arrive covered in glory, they'll have time to prepare their lies, and if my sister was mistreated, it will be a child's word against theirs."

"Denis de Toluard managed to keep word of your presumed death silent until he reached the City of Elua," I said. "He honored his promise to you, that your father might hear it firsthand and not through cruel rumor. It can be done."

"I want somewhat more." Thierry gave me another glance. "I want to see for myself how they treat Desirée in my absence without allowing them the chance to dissemble. Your magic could accomplish that, couldn't it?"

I gazed at him, seeing the lines of maturity etched on his face, lending it a strength of purpose he'd never had before. "You'd have them believe you dead?"

"I would." His voice was grim.

I looked away. "Aye, I can conceal us in the twilight. Beneath its cloak, you could walk unseen into the Palace itself. But it will cause a great deal of unnecessary pain, especially to the child."

"Only for a short time." Reaching out, Thierry covered my hand with his on the railing. "If I can see the damage that was done to her, I will know better how to undo it," he said, his tone turning gentle. "Moirin, I do not think you would have become Desirée's oath-sworn protector if you had not come to love her. I hear it in your voice when you speak of her. I would wish to do the same, and give her the love for which she yearns."

"Do you believe you can?" I asked him, summoning an uncertain smile. "You and Jehanne had a... prickly relationship."

Thierry laughed. "So we did, for many reasons. But that had changed, too. I came to accept that in her own way, she did love my father—and he her. She made him happy, and he was seldom a happy man." His expression sobered. "I told you, I will not repeat his mistakes, Moirin. We are orphans alike, my sister and I. I will learn to love her."

I sighed. "I will do as you ask."

He squeezed my hand. "Thank you." He smiled ruefully. "I suspect I could spend the rest of my life thanking you, and it would not begin to be enough."

I shook my head. "If I had not let Raphael de Mereliot turn my head all those years ago, none of this would have happened."

Thierry gazed at the skyline. "We would have starved in the jungle without Raphael and his bedamned ants. They foraged for us. It's why none of us dared raise a hand against him on the journey, why we could not turn back."

"I know," I said.

"I gave up hope," he said, more to himself than me. "I'll not let that happen again, ever. The memory of Balthasar Shahrizai wielding a digging-stick in the far reaches of Terra Nova will suffice to remind me that anything is possible."

It made me laugh. "Balthasar, and not me?"

Thierry gave me a quick, fond glance. "For all your youth and naivete, you did always have an air of destiny about you, Moirin. I must confess, your presence did not surprise me as much as Balthasar's." He squeezed my hand again. "Do you remember, a long time ago, I said you and I had become family in a very odd manner?"

"I remember."

It had been on the Longest Night when Thierry had served as my escort, clad in the attire of a Cassiline Brother.

My lady Jehanne had worn the costume of the Snow Queen. I remembered the taste of *joie* lingering on her lips, her blue-grey eyes sparkling at me with delight. It was the same costume she had worn when she said farewell to me in my final dream, the satin edge of her ermine-trimmed cape brushing the freshly turned soil between the tall rows of *maize* swaying overhead, waving their tassels.

My eyes stung.

Staring at the surging waves once more, Thierry did not notice. "I'm glad," he said. "I'm glad I named you so."

Blinking away tears, I turned my hand beneath his on the railing, giving it an answering squeeze. "Do you forget, my lord?" I asked him lightly. "I am a descendant of House Courcel by way of Alais the Wise. You showed me her likeness in the Hall of Portraits when first we met. We were always kin, you and I."

"Forgive me, Moirin. I did forget." Thierry gave me a self-deprecating smile, and there was a hint of his old easygoing charm in it. "But kin is not the same as family." Raising my hand to his lips, he kissed it. "Rogier Courcel, Duc de Barthelme, is kin to me. *You* are family."

The ship bobbed beneath us, riding the waves. Up a crest, down a trough. Every inch carried us closer to home.

"And you," I whispered to Thierry. "And you. And the gods willing we make safe harbor, Desirée, too."

EIGHTY

After months at sea, we gained the harbor of Pellasus and began making our way up the Aviline River.

It felt strange knowing we were retracing the voyage poor, doomed Denis de Toluard had taken, practicing his deceit in reverse. He had withheld the knowledge of Thierry de la Courcel's death from Terre d'Ange.

We withheld the knowledge of his survival.

The crew of the *Naamah's Dove* and the men of our company obeyed unquestioning, united in common accord. No one gossiped, no one dropped so much as a hint of a rumor.

Of course, their very silence engendered rumors, and a bow-wave of gossip raced ahead of us.

Eyahue and Temilotzin strolled the decks clad in Nahuatl finery, fanning the flames of rumor. I thought they both rather relished the task, especially our reprehensible old *pochteca*. Someone had told them tales of the Night Court that had Eyahue cackling in anticipatory glee, and the Jaguar Knight slapping his thighs and laughing uproariously at the exploits the former had planned.

I didn't begrudge them, and I hoped they would find a warm welcome among the Thirteen Houses.

Whenever we approached a river port city, Bao and Thierry and I remained belowdeck, hidden from sight. I had argued against including Bao in the deception. Knowing Desirée's fondness for him,

I feared it would pain her twice over to believe that both Bao and I had perished in a futile effort to rescue her brother. But Bao had refused.

"I cannot look that child in the eye and lie to her, letting her believe you are gone, Moirin," he said. "Do not ask it of me. I have done one hard thing too many on this journey."

And so I did not press him.

As the leader of the expedition that had set out to find Prince Thierry, Balthasar Shahrizai was to be in charge of the delegation that would meet with the Regent, and I had every confidence in his ability to handle the situation. It was odd to think how I had once rather disliked him, reckoning him nothing more than an idle courtier with a sharp tongue and an even sharper-edged gift. Now I knew that there was a steely core of courage and loyalty beneath his facile surface, and his barbed wit concealed clear-sighted judgment and a generous and compassionate heart. I would gladly trust him with my life.

It was a warm spring day with a light drizzle falling when we at last reached the City of Elua and docked at the quay. Summoning the twilight, I ventured abovedeck and saw that a considerable crowd awaited us, keeping a respectful distance from the official reception party, which consisted of Duc Rogier de Barthelme, his sons Tristan and Aristide, and a score of royal guardsmen.

I caught sight of my father among the throng of ordinary citizens, his crimson robes an unrecognizable color in the twilight, his normally serene face strained with worry—and the sight nearly startled me into losing my grip on my magic.

Ah, gods! Of course he would be there. Caught up in my concern for Desirée, I hadn't even thought of it.

For a moment, my resolve wavered. Mayhap this was nothing but a cruel prank.

I made myself look at Duc Rogier instead. *His* face was calm and composed. He had heard the rumors, and he was anticipating the news of our failure. No doubt he had a speech of earnest condolences already prepared, spiced with just a dash of sanctimoniousness for having been right all along about the folly of our mission. I could almost see him rehearsing it in his thoughts.

At his side, his sons looked appropriately somber. Pretty golden-haired Tristan the Sun Prince was a young man now, taller and broader than the stripling I remembered. The younger lad, Aristide, took after his father. Him, I had met too briefly to form an opinion.

Duc Rogier wore a modest gold circlet with low points around his dark hair, the metal silvery in the twilight. It wasn't quite a crown, but it was a definitive step in the direction of one. The Regent of Terre d'Ange thought to solidify his hold on the throne today.

In my mind's eye, I saw Cusi's blood spilling over the stairs once more, and Raphael de Mereliot reaching for the *Sapa Inca's* crown.

My resolve hardened once more. I would have the full measure of House Barthelme's overreaching ambition exposed. My father would forgive me the temporary pain our ruse caused him.

I ducked belowdeck where Bao and Thierry were awaiting me, and released the twilight. "The Duc brought his sons and a contingent of guards," I reported. "There's no sign of the rest of the royal household."

"Balthasar knows what to do." Thierry's face was pale, but there was a fierce light in his eyes. "Are you ready?"

"Aye." I hesitated. "My father is there."

Thierry paled further, thinking of how his own father had taken the news. "You don't think he would—"

"No," Bao said firmly. "Brother Phanuel is not one to succumb to grief in such a manner. And the truth will soon be out."

I nodded. "Let's be done with it."

And so I summoned the twilight once more, wrapping Bao and Thierry in its cloak. Thierry drew a soft breath. "It's beautiful," he murmured. "I never realized." He smiled at me. "I am pleased to have a chance to see the world through your eyes, Moirin. Somehow, I feel I understand you better for it."

It made me feel better, too. A kind word at the right time can be bracing; and I thought once more that Thierry had the makings of a good ruler.

Abovedeck, Rousse's sailors worked to secure the final moorings and lower the gangplank. Balthasar had assembled his delegation, which consisted of a half-dozen men from our expedition as well as Eyahue and Temilotzin, representatives of Emperor Achcuatli. They had been careful to leave room for us, and we made our way to Balthasar's side.

"He will hear you if you will it," I reminded Thierry.

"Balthasar," he whispered. "We are ready."

Balthasar lifted one finger on his right hand, our agreed-upon sign to indicate that he'd heard.

It felt strange all over again to relive a familiar moment from the other side. I'd held Desirée's hand in mine as we watched Denis de Toluard walk slowly down the gangplank to deliver his terrible news. Now I walked it myself, unseen by the hundreds of watching eyes. I was glad Desirée wasn't there. I wasn't sure I could have borne it.

Duc Rogier wore a grave expression as he watched the delegation approach. Already, there were folk keening with grief in the crowd behind him, expecting to hear the sorrowful news a second time.

Upon reaching the Regent, Balthasar Shahrizai bowed, precise and correct. "Your excellence," he said. "We have returned from Terra Nova."

The Duc inclined his not-quite-crowned head. "I beseech you, my lord Shahrizai, to deliver your news."

"My news pertains to House Courcel," Balthasar said in a clear, carrying voice. "I would deliver it to the Dauphine myself. No ears should hear it before hers."

It wasn't what Rogier de Barthelme had expected to hear, and it took him aback, his mask of composure slipping as he blinked in surprise. "You cannot...she's a child, my lord!" Regrouping, he took on a tone of calm reason. "By your reticence, I trust you have not come to deliver happy news. Desirée should never have been allowed to hear word of her brother's death in such a public manner the first time. Let those of us who know and care for her deliver it to her now, and spare her the brunt of it."

"I will tell her myself," Tristan added with dignity. "She is my betrothed, you know."

Balthasar fixed him with an unreadable stare. "Yes. I know."

The lad flushed as though he'd been slapped, and for a few seconds, his mouth took on a petulant cast. His younger brother looked uncomfortable, and I liked him better for it.

"Desirée de la Courcel is the heir to the throne," Balthasar said simply. "I will deliver my news to her, or not at all." Pausing, he indicated Eyahue and Temilotzin. "As you can see, our mission was not entirely unsuccessful. Relations with the Nahuatl Empire have been established. Despite her tender years, a future monarch must be prepared to contend with such news. I note you have brought your own sons here today."

The tentative keening stopped, giving way to murmurs of curiosity and uncertainty. I avoided looking in the direction of my father.

Duc Rogier de Barthelme frowned. "My sons are young men, not little girls. It is an unnecessary cruelty."

Balthasar declined to reply and waited him out with implacable patience, the steely core of his will on full display.

"As you will, my lord," the Duc said at length, his voice hard. "She is a fragile child. On your head be her grief."

With a tight smile, Balthasar bowed. "I accept it."

We proceeded on foot through the streets of the City of Elua, following the royal carriage and its attendant guards. Hundreds upon hundreds of D'Angeline citizens trailed in our wake, the crowd growing with every block, amassing outside the Palace and waiting there as we passed beneath its doors.

Inside the Palace walls, Duc Rogier issued several crisp commands. Servants scuttled in various directions to carry out his orders.

"He acts as though he rules here, does he not?" Thierry murmured to me.

"He does," I said. "For now."

Rumors and gossip ran down the marble corridors, spreading throughout the labyrinthine Palace. By the time we arrived at the throne-room, a number of lords and ladies were demanding to attend the audience, several of them members of Parliament. With obvious reluctance, the Duc acceded to their demands.

We assembled in the throne-room, and waited. The throne sat empty. Rogier de Barthelme had more sense than to lay claim to it in this moment.

The cool and calculating Duchese Claudine de Barthelme arrived to take her place at the side of her husband and sons. She, too, wore a modest gold circlet atop her golden hair, hers adorned with pearls. I wondered if she was afraid her treasonous gambit with Edouard Durel had been uncovered. If she was, it didn't show. Mayhap she assumed he had failed to carry out her orders. No fear showed on the lad Tristan's face, either; but I didn't think he knew enough to be afraid yet. He was young, and life had dealt him no grievous setbacks, lending him confidence in the machinations to which he had been a party.

That was about to change.

We waited.

I breathed the Five Styles, holding the twilight in place, keeping Bao and Thierry and me unseen.

At last, Desirée arrived. Her eyes were downcast and her gait tentative. Sister Gemma, the Eisandine priestess whom I had appointed to serve as her nursemaid, was nowhere in sight. Instead, it was Desirée's grandmother who accompanied the child in her capacity as the Royal Governess; the Comtesse de Maillet, her mouth pinched and triumphant.

Beside me, Thierry drew a sharp breath. "I remember her!"

"Jehanne's mother," I murmured. "I told you as much."

"You did," he said. "But until I saw her, I'd forgotten how much Jehanne despised the woman."

Bao glowered, dark shadows arising around him. "I suspect it was with reason."

I gazed at Desirée, my heart aching. At six years of age, she was a girl now. She was thin and wan, all her mother's scintillating beauty faded to a pallid colorlessness. The Comtesse de Maillet steered her charge alongside her betrothed, Tristan de Barthelme. Desirée went willingly enough, but she kept her hands clasped firmly before her, refusing to take his hand in hers.

There was a sharp, whispered exchange. Desirée shook her head stubbornly, clinging to whatever it was she held clutched tight in her hands.

"Your highness!" Claudine de Barthelme addressed her. A hint of impatience surfaced in her tone, quickly smoothed away. "This is a matter of state, my dear. Toys are to be left in the nursery. You know better."

Desirée lifted her head, a spark of defiance in her eyes. "It's not a toy! Moirin said—"

Claudine interrupted her. "I could not possibly care less what that delusional half-breed of a bear-witch said, and it is long past time you ceased to care, too," she spat under her breath. "She did you no favors filling your head with fanciful tales of magic and dragons. Tristan, will you please talk sense to the child?"

"Come, ducky," he said in a coaxing tone, holding out one hand. "Give me the toy, and take my hand."

There was a mutinous set to her chin. "It's not a toy!"

He glanced at his mother. "You don't want to make a scene, do you, sweetheart? Come, give it over."

Desirée shook her head again. "No!"

Tristan stooped, lowering his voice. "Don't act the baby!" he hissed, prying ruthlessly at her hands. "Give it to me, now!"

A crystal bottle fell to the marble floor and shattered, a few drops of perfume scattered amidst the gleaming shards. An intoxicating scent, heady and ephemeral, rose to fill the throne-room.

Jehanne's perfume.

"It was my mother's," Desirée whispered, tears filling her eyes. "Moirin gave it to me."

I'd given it to her that she might remember that she was loved—by her mother and by me. I'd told her to keep it safe, that its scent might comfort her when she was feeling frightened and lonely. Like now.

"Thierry, please," I murmured. "Haven't you seen enough?"

"Wait," he said to me. "Just a little longer." He repeated the word to Balthasar, willing him to hear. "Wait."

"Enough." Duc Rogier took command of the proceedings, his voice firm. "Your highness, you may remember Lord Balthasar Shahrizai, who led the second expedition to Terra Nova. And I fear he brings unhappy tidings." A note of disapproval edged into his voice. "Tidings he insisted you hear yourself, tidings that concern the sad fate of Moirin mac Fainche, and I suspect a number of others, too." Gazing around the throne-room, he squared his shoulders. "My lords and ladies, I beg you to remember I advised against this."

Murmurs of agreement ran throughout the throne-room.

"Is it true?" Desirée lifted her gaze to meet Balthasar's, tears spilling over her pale cheeks. "Moirin is dead? And Bao, too?"

He hesitated, glancing around.

"Go ahead, my lord Shahrizai." Duc Rogier fixed him with a stony look. "You insisted on this moment. Break the child's heart."

"Now, Balthasar!" Thierry called from the twilight.

Balthasar Shahrizai lifted one finger in acknowledgment. "No, your highness," he said with improbable gentleness, sinking to one knee before the girl. "It's not true at all. And I am so very, very happy to have the honor of telling you so."

The blood drained from Desirée's face. "They're not—?"

He shook his head. "No."

I should have waited for Prince Thierry's command, but I couldn't. I couldn't wait a second longer. Taking a deep breath, I released the twilight and it fled in a rush, unveiling all three of us.

It was without a doubt one of the most satisfying moments of my life.

EIGHTY-ONE

In the stunned silence that followed our appearance, Desirée stared
at us, her face as white as a sheet. And then all at once, the color
rushed back into it, flushing her cheeks with a healthy pink. "Moirin?" she whispered.

"Aye, dear heart." My voice shook a little. "I'm so very sorry to
have frightened you. I didn't mean to."

With a stifled cry, Desirée flung herself toward me, shards of crystal crunching beneath her slippered feet. I stooped and caught her up,
and she wound her thin arms around my neck, clinging to me, her
entire body shaking with sobs. Over the top of her head, I gazed at the
assembled representatives of House Barthelme.

Like almost everyone in the room, Duc Rogier looked thunderstruck. Pretty, golden-haired Tristan looked stunned in a different
way, as though he were watching a play that had taken an unscripted
turn, a turn he couldn't yet fathom, the first inkling that his plans
had gone very, very awry only beginning to manifest. Aristide, the
younger lad, wore an alert look, as though his life had finally become
interesting.

And now, although she hid it well, Claudine de Barthelme was
afraid.

Before the rush of gossip and speculation could fill the silence,
Prince Thierry raised one hand. "My lords and ladies, I apologize for
the deception. My kinswoman Moirin was concerned that the young

Dauphine was treated unkindly in my absence." He leveled a flat stare at the Regent and his family. "If this is how you treat my sister in a public audience, I suspect Moirin's fears were well founded."

"Your highness..." The Duc's throat worked as he searched for words, spreading his hands in an impotent plea. "We are overjoyed to see you safe! I swear to you, no one harmed the child."

"One need not strike a child to harm her," Thierry said in an implacable tone. "But we will speak more of this later. Guards!" He beckoned sharply to the royal guardsmen. "Take the Duchese de Barthelme and her eldest son into custody." When they hesitated, overwhelmed and unsure, he raised his voice. *"Now!"*

"Have you lost your wits?" Duc Rogier asked in bewilderment. "My wife? My son? Your highness, what is the meaning of this?"

"Ask your wife," Thierry said curtly. "Ask her if the name Edouard Durel means aught to her. He's alive," he added to Claudine de Barthelme. "Unfortunately for you, he was caught in the act of committing sabotage aboard the ship. He has made a full confession and is prepared to testify against you and your son Tristan."

"Claudine?" Rogier turned toward her. "What in the name of Blessed Elua is he talking about?"

Even as the guards approached, her head was held high and her eyes blazed. Whatever else one could say of the woman, she didn't lack for courage. "I did it for you, Rogier! For all of us!" She gestured impatiently in my direction. "This is the very outcome I sought to prevent."

"A moment ago, I was but a delusional half-breed of a bear-witch, my lady," I said softly. "It seems you put more stock in me than you care to admit."

Claudine's lips thinned. "The stakes were high. I sought to leave nothing to chance." She shook off the hand of the guard who seized her arm. "Do not lay hands on me! I have given you no cause."

"Mother?" Tristan asked uncertainly as a pair of guardsmen flanked him. "Must...must I go with them?"

For the first time, I almost pitied the lad.

And until that moment, I do not think Claudine de Barthelme

fully realized how deeply she had implicated her son in her treachery.
Visible fear flickered in her eyes as she addressed Prince Thierry. "He's
just a boy, your highness," she said, trying to keep the despair from
her voice. "It was all a game to him, a game of wits and crowns. *I* drew
him into it! He didn't understand what was at stake were we to fail.
How could he? I beg you, whatever you do, have mercy on the lad."

I felt Desirée stir in my arms, no longer sobbing. "Do you want me
to put you down, dear heart?" I whispered to her.

She nodded against my shoulder. "Yes, please."

I lowered her gently. Desirée clutched my hand in hers, reaching
out blindly toward Bao. He took her other hand in his, closing his
fingers around hers.

Thierry looked over at us, his expression softening. "All will be taken
into account, my lady," he said to Claudine. "All will be conducted
according to the law. You shall have your chance to plead your case, and
your son's case, too. For the moment, I ask you to go peaceably."

They were escorted from the throne-room by the royal guardsmen, Claudine de Barthelme with her not-quite-crowned head held
high, and her eldest son casting uncertain glances over his shoulder.

"Your highness, I cannot expect you to believe it, but I knew nothing of this." Duc Rogier spoke in a stiff, formal tone. Beneath the circlet
he wore, there were beads of sweat forming on his brow, trickling down
his temples. "I swear to you, I would never have condoned it. Never."

Narrowing his eyes, Thierry considered him.

Once upon a time, it would have been nothing to be subjected to
the scrutiny of Thierry de la Courcel.

That time had passed.

"I do believe you," he said at length. "I believe you are guilty of
nothing but naked opportunism. To be honest, I am not sure which I
despise more. And so for the moment, I will ask you to remove yourself from my sight, cousin." He tilted his head. "Go."

Duc Rogier Courcel de Barthelme went, his shoulders slumped
and heavy, taking his younger son Aristide with him. Like his brother,
the lad glanced over his shoulder. Unlike his brother, Aristide gave

Desirée a brave smile, waving his fingers at her. Glancing down, I saw her offer a tremulous smile in reply, and I thought mayhap there was hope for House Barthelme after all.

"You may also go," Thierry said to the Comtesse de Maillet. "My stepmother Jehanne and I may have disagreed on many issues, but on this, I suspect we would be in perfect accord. Consider yourself dismissed from the service of House Courcel."

Jehanne's mother departed with an audible sniff, her delicate nostrils flaring; but she went.

I wondered, briefly, where her husband was.

And then I forgot, along with the rest of the realm, as Thierry took a knee and knelt before his little half-sister in an unconscious echo of the pose Balthasar had taken, hands braced on bended knee.

"Hello," he said to her. "I don't expect you remember me, do you?"

"No," she said gravely. "But I know who you are. I was very, very little when you went away, wasn't I?"

Thierry nodded. "Very little, yes. And I am sorry to have been gone for so long, little sister. But now that I have come back, do you suppose we might be friends, you and I? It would please me greatly."

Desirée glanced up at me.

I nodded.

Bao extricated his hand from hers. "You are fortunate to have such a brother, young highness," he said to her. "It was not easy to rescue him! He has many, many tales to tell you."

"I would like that very much," she said solemnly, extending her hand to Thierry, who clasped it with equal solemnity.

It was a private moment in a public setting, and I felt my throat tighten at the sight of them, the twice-orphaned survivors of House Courcel; and I daresay everyone in the throne-room felt the same way, for there were audible sighs.

"I have a great deal to do to set matters right here, little sister," Thierry said to her. "And I fear I will be busy for a time. But I will always have time for you, I promise. We are family, you and I."

Desirée hesitated. "You won't hurt them, will you?"

"The Duc and his family?" he asked. She nodded. Thierry considered his reply. "It is not for me to decide. Those who have broken laws will be judged in a court of law, and if they are found guilty, there will be a price to pay. Not even the King is above the rule of law. But if you wish to plead clemency for them, you may—and nothing will be done today." He squeezed her hand. "We will talk more about this later, all right? I promise, nothing will be done without your knowledge."

She nodded again.

Gently releasing her hand, Thierry straightened and placed himself before the throne, turning to address the assembly once more.

"My lords and ladies, I am blessed among men to stand before you today," he said to them. "I owe my safe return to the brave D'Angelines who accompanied me on my initial voyage. I owe it to my kinsman Balthasar Shahrizai and the valiant men who undertook this second journey. Many members of both parties perished in these efforts, and I honor their memories. I am in the debt of Emperor Achcuatli of the Nahuatl, and his representatives whom you see before you, the venerable guide Eyahue and the fearless Jaguar Knight Temilotzin."

Hearing their names spoken, both the Nahuatl inclined their heads and flicked their fingers toward their chests and brows.

"I owe my safe return to the Maidens of the Sun in faraway Tawantinsuyo," Thierry said softly. "And most especially to one who made a great sacrifice on behalf of her people; and to Messire Bao of Ch'in, who made a sacrifice that must have been equally difficult in its own way."

It was so quiet in the throne-room, you could have heard a pin drop, the peers of the realm hanging on every word.

Thierry took a deep breath. "Above all, I owe my safe return to my kinswoman Moirin mac Fainche, who had the courage to have faith in her visions." Turning toward me, he offered a courtly bow. "Never again let the name of the Maghuin Dhonn be spoken in fear and superstition, but with honor and profound respect."

It touched me, soothing an ache so deep I hadn't known it was there, bringing tears to my eyes.

"I know many of you did not support Moirin's mission," Thierry continued, overriding murmurs of protest. "Have no fear. I will hold no man nor woman to blame in this matter. It was well nigh an impossible quest, and I may well have counseled against it myself." He gazed into the distance. "But I am not the man I was. I have *seen* the impossible. I have seen great and terrible wonders, and I tell you, the world is a vaster and stranger place than ever I had reckoned."

Lost in his memories, he was silent for a moment, and then his gaze returned from the distance.

"Upon hearing the losses we suffered, you may wonder if this quest was worthwhile," Thierry said. "I stand before you to say that it was. Not because *I* was rescued." He shook his head. "I would not set such a price on my life. And not because the hold of the *Naamah's Dove* is filled with trade goods from Terra Nova, exotic spices and seedlings and gold ore—although it is."

At that, there were gasps of excitement.

Thierry permitted himself a slight smile. "But I fear the full telling of this impossible tale will have to wait, for it is too long and strange to relate here. For now, let it suffice to say that I am very, very grateful to be home."

It was Balthasar Shahrizai who gave the first cheer, an uncharacteristically boyish whoop of triumph.

"All hail his highness Prince Thierry!" he shouted. "Long live his majesty King Thierry de la Courcel!"

Other voices took up the cheer, chanting and clapping, laughing and weeping with sheer release until the marble halls of the throne-room echoed with the sound; and if it was no less joyous and heartfelt than the reunion in Orgullo del Sol, it was better and bigger, for this time we were home, truly home, and Desirée stood at my side, still clinging to my hand, her face alight with hope.

For my part, I shouted Thierry's name until my throat was raw, my heart filled with gladness.

At last, the hall quieted.

In the silence, Thierry took his seat on the empty throne of Terre d'Ange. He beckoned to his young sister, who went willingly to stand beside him.

Despite his lack of a crown, he looked very much like a king.

Glancing at Desirée, Thierry smiled at her. She returned his smile, her blue-grey eyes shining at him, the very picture of her mother in miniature.

I will own, I could not help but feel a faint pang of jealousy. Looking sidelong at Bao, I saw the same emotion reflected on his face. He squared his shoulders and we exchanged shrugs of rueful understanding.

All was right.

All was as it should be.

And for the first time since I'd passed through the stone doorway some seven years gone by, my *diadh-anam* was quiet within my breast, a steady, contented flicker assuring me of the enduring love of the Maghuin Dhonn Herself. For the first time since I could remember, the only destiny that called me and the only sea that beckoned me further was the narrow Strait between Terre d'Ange and Alba, and for a mercy, there was no urgency in it.

Seated on the throne, Thierry laid one hand on Desirée's head in a brief, gentle caress filled with all the brotherly tenderness I could have wished for her.

"Let the word go forth," he announced. "Let the realm of Terre d'Ange know that I have returned to claim my rightful role!"

And it was so.

EIGHTY-TWO

Outside the walls of the Palace, I was reunited with my father. The crowds that filled the courtyard made way for him as we emerged, creating a respectful space around Brother Phanuel.

A light drizzle continued to fall, but the smile on my father's face was as bright as sunlight, all the strain of worry erased from his features. I found myself laughing through tears as I embraced him.

"You did it," he murmured in my ear. "I should never have doubted you, my strange daughter."

"Oh . . ." I wiped away my tears. "I don't know about that."

"Messire Bao." My father turned to Bao, clasping his hand. The two of them grinned at one another. "Well done."

"Were you able to find my mother in Alba?" I asked anxiously. "Were you able to deliver my letter to her?"

My father nodded. "I read it to her myself. She said to tell you that she loves you, and that when you come home in your own time, to call her name on the western winds and bid her meet you wherever you are bound, and she will hear." He looked a bit bemused. "Do you suppose she meant it?"

I laughed. "It's quite possible. I suspect there's a lot I have yet to learn about my own people."

"You'll not go just yet, will you?" he asked.

"No," I promised. "Not yet. At the least, we'll stay for the official coronation ceremony."

Bao wrinkled his nose. "I'm not going *anywhere* without a hot bath first."

"Spoken like a true D'Angeline." My father smiled. "I'll leave you to rest and refresh yourselves, and trouble you for your tale on the morrow. 'Tis enough to know for now that you're alive and well."

A royal carriage arrived to convey us to the little house on the outskirts of town that had once belonged to House Shahrizai's most infamous scion, a house that Balthasar had assured us aboard the ship would be deeded to Bao and me in perpetuity upon our return. It seemed like it was a lifetime ago that he first proposed over a frothing goblet of *chocolatl* that we might benefit from the mutual alignment of our interests.

Our progress through the City of Elua was slow, hampered by the throngs of people spilling into the streets, pressing close to the carriage to call out grateful blessings. The news had spread swiftly. They must have stripped the stalls of every flower vendor in the city, for spring blossoms showered down upon us, filling the moist air with fragrance.

It was beautiful and wonderful, but I could not help but think of the blossoms piled in the laps of the Quechua ancestors, too. Catching my eye, Bao smiled quietly, and I knew he shared my thoughts.

There were shadows that would ever be with us.

If it seemed a lifetime ago that we had first taken up residence in the Shahrizai domicile, as far as the impeccable household staff was concerned, it might have been yesterday. After all the emotion and high drama, I was grateful for the steward Guillaume Norbert's calm, dignified greeting.

"Lady Moirin, Messire Bao." He proffered a deep bow, only a hint of a gleam in his eye betraying his pride and gladness at our return. "Welcome home."

I summoned a weary smile. "My thanks, Messire Norbert."

Home.

It had become true; not the whole truth, but true nonetheless. I was Naamah's child as surely as I was a child of the Maghuin Dhonn, and the City of Elua was home to me. A part of my heart would always abide here. Here in the city where I had found my lovely father, where I had committed the worst of my youthful folly, and stumbled unwittingly through my first steps toward patience and wisdom, finding the beginnings of the profound grace that existed in Naamah's blessing.

A faint sigh escaped me.

Bao touched my arm. "Moirin?"

"Aye," I said to him. "All's well. I'm bone-tired, that's all. It's been a long, long journey."

His mouth quirked. "You have a considerable gift for understatement, my wife. But I think we can rest now. At least until tomorrow," he added.

Bao was right.

Bathed and fed and pampered by the discreet household staff, both of us fell into the great bed with its crisp, clean linens scented with lavender-water and slept like the dead for long hours.

We awoke restored and refreshed to the dawn of a new era in Terre d'Ange. There were dozens of calling cards for us, as well as a summons from Prince Thierry to an audience in the Salon of Eisheth's Harp, and a message from my father that he would meet us there.

We went early to the Palace that we might pay a visit to Desirée, whom we found in high spirits.

"My brother Thierry came to visit me before I went to sleep last night!" she announced, her eyes wide with wonder and disbelief. "He sang me a song he said his own mother used to sing to him at night." A furtive shadow crossed her face. "You don't think that's too babyish, do you?"

I hugged her. "No, dear heart. Not at all."

"Song and music are sacred to Eisheth, young highness." Sister Gemma, restored to her position, offered the comment in a tranquil, reassuring tone, folding her hands in the sleeves of her flowing sea-blue robes. "There is never, ever any shame in taking comfort in them. To accept the gifts of the gods is to honor them."

Desirée cast a grateful look at her. "That's what I thought. His mother died, too, you know."

"I know," I murmured.

"But now you and your brother have found each other at last," Bao added. "And you are a family once more."

She cocked her silver-gilt head at him. "When will *you* start a family, Bao? You and Moirin? I would so like to have little baby cousins with funny eyes like yours."

Bao raised his brows at me.

"Soon," I said.

Sister Gemma cleared her throat. "In fact, I took the liberty of bringing a gift for you, Lady Moirin." Reaching into the folds of her sleeve, she withdrew a slender wax taper. "If you would care to make the invocation at the Temple of Eisheth here in the city, or to visit the Sanctuary of the Womb, of course, we would be delighted." Her gaze was soft and gentle. "But it matters only that you invoke Eisheth with a willing heart, wherever you may be, and light a candle to her. This one was wrought of wax gathered from our own beehives, and it carries our blessings."

I took it from her. The beeswax taper held the warmth of her body, and it smelled sweet and good, holding all the promises of hearth and home.

"Thank you," I whispered.

Eisheth's priestess inclined her head, her blue eyes glimmering. "When the time is right, you will know."

A short while later, we took our leave to answer Thierry's summons. There were a good many people crowded into the Salon of Eisheth's Harp, peers and comrades and loved ones alike, all anxious to hear the tale told, even those who had lived through it. And we learned that Sister Gemma was not the only member of the royal household to be restored to her position.

"My Lady Moirin, Messire Bao." Balthasar Shahrizai slung his arms around us both with casual affection. "Pray tell, have you met the new King's Poet, formerly the old King's Poet? Of course, Thierry's not been coronated yet, but that's only a formality."

"Moirin." Lianne Tremaine's voice was unsteady. Tears shone in her amber eyes. "It seems there's an epic tale to be told here. I should have found the courage to go with you after all, shouldn't I?"

I shook my head. "No, my lady poetess. 'Tis better, far better that you did not. He would have killed you, too."

Her gaze sharpened. "He?"

"Raphael," I said simply.

"Raphael de Mereliot?" She blinked. "Do you jest?"

"No," I said. "Not at all, I fear." Before I could begin to explain, the royal steward called the audience to order, and an attendant came to escort us to be seated in a semicircle of ornate padded chairs facing the crowd. There were shuffling and scraping sounds as everyone else took a seat, and then an expectant hush.

Prince Thierry surveyed the room. "There are many backdrops to this tale," he began. "One of which bears citing. Although my father did his best to keep the incident quiet, rumors abounded nonetheless. Many of you will remember the scandal surrounding the Circle of Shalomon some seven years gone by."

Lianne Tremaine paled. "Focalor?" she whispered to me.

I nodded.

"You will note that I have reinstated Mademoiselle Lianne Tremaine to the post from which she was dismissed after that incident," Thierry continued. "After what I have witnessed, and after the suffering my own youthful ambition engendered, I think it is only fitting that she be forgiven. And I think it is fitting that she among poets be given the task of transcribing this tale. The Circle of Shalomon attempted to summon spirits, fallen spirits, did they not, my lady?"

She met his gaze without flinching. "Yes, your highness. We did."

"Did you succeed?" he asked her.

"Yes." Her cheeks flushed slightly. "With Lady Moirin's aid, we did. But she did not give it willingly."

"I gave it nonetheless," I murmured.

"I do not seek to cast blame," Thierry said in a gentle tone. "Only to establish the chain of events. One of these spirits gave each of you a gift, I believe. Can you tell us what form that gift took?"

Lianne lifted one hand unconsciously to rub at her nose. "The spirit Caim taught us the language of ants."

A faint titter of laughter ran through the salon.

Thierry waited for it to subside. "I would laugh, too, if I knew only the ants of Terre d'Ange," he said mildly. "And not the black rivers of ravenous death that inhabit the jungles of Terra Nova. But I am getting ahead of the tale. It is also true that one of the fallen spirits, a powerful one, freed himself from your binding and sought to take possession of Raphael de Mereliot, is it not?"

"Yes, your highness," Lianne said. "Focalor, a Grand Duke of the Fallen." She glanced sidelong at me. "But Moirin, along with Messire Bao and his mentor, succeeded in banishing him."

"Not entirely, it seems." Thierry took a deep breath. "That is the backdrop to the tale I would have you hear today."

It took hours to spin out the tale in its entirety, hours in which our audience sat entranced and horrified, journeying with Thierry and his companions to the blood-soaked and disease-racked Nahuatl Empire where Raphael de Mereliot intervened with his physician's skills, and then deep into the wilds of Terra Nova in search of the empire of Tawantinsuyo, where Raphael fell prey to madness and learned to summon and control the black river.

When it came time for our second expedition to pick up the thread of the tale, Balthasar spoke on our behalf, his voice unwontedly candid and matter-of-fact as he chronicled our journey following in the footsteps of Thierry's party, all the way from the betrayal aboard the *Naamah's Dove* to the Emperor's patronage to the shock of our arrival in Vilcabamba, and Raphael's cold-blooded murder of Denis de Toluard.

Lianne Tremaine, scribbling notes to aid her prodigious memory, shuddered. "I take your meaning," she said to me in a low tone.

It was impossible to convey the profound strangeness of our captivity in that jungle city, surrounded by Raphael's army of ants and hostage to his mad ambitions, but Balthasar and Thierry between them did their best. Still, there were parts of the tale they could not tell.

"Moirin, will you tell of the Maidens of the Sun and the prophecy they guarded?" Thierry asked me.

I glanced at Bao.

His face was shuttered and unreadable, and I thought that his role in this story was one that no one who had not lived through it could ever possibly understand.

"Aye, your highness," I said to Thierry. "As much as I understand it myself, and deem fitting to tell."

A look of understanding crossed Thierry's features. "Of course."

And so I told the tale of the Quechua's prophecy of the ancestors; but I left out Bao's role, telling only of my quickening the fruit tree and the liana vine as the signs that convinced the Maidens of the Sun that the time of prophecy was upon them, and of how the maiden Cusi knew herself chosen for the sacrifice.

At that, there were many soft, indrawn breaths of horror.

"And you agreed to this?" Lianne Tremaine asked in shock, her pen poised forgotten in her hand. "*All* of you?"

"I thought as you did, my lady poetess," Thierry answered her gravely. "We all did, every one of us. But with the fate of the entire Quechua folk hanging in the balance, it was not our place to gainsay their faith. And I tell you this. I was one of a dozen men who escorted the maiden Cusi to the Temple of the Ancestors in the conquered city of Qusqu the night before Raphael's coronation. There is no doubt in my mind, not even the slightest, that she *knew* herself to be chosen for this fate, and went to it gladly."

"Nor mine," Bao murmured.

"Nor mine," Balthasar echoed. "She looked...sanctified. Holy." He nodded to himself. "Yes, holy."

I rubbed the faint scar on my palm. "She was."

There was a moment of utter silence in the salon before Lianne gathered herself with a shiver, dipping her pen in the inkwell. "You have gotten ahead of yourself again, your highness. Tell us of the conquest of Qusqu."

Prince Thierry obliged, for which I was grateful; but he could not relate the events that had transpired in the Temple of the Ancestors, only those that led up to them. Alone among our company, only Bao and I had actually witnessed Cusi's sacrifice, the resurrection of the Quechua ancestors, the near-summoning of Focalor. The others had seen only the aftermath.

So it fell to me once more, and I told it as one might tell a vivid tale remembered from a poem.

The stone temple, the stairway and the bronze knife, the gold-masked priest who wielded it.

I did not tell them it was Bao.

Blood spilling over the stair, running in the carved channels.

Focalor manifesting in a storm raging in the doorway I opened onto the spirit world, and Raphael drowning in his essence.

Ancient skeletons wrapped in cerements, stirring beneath feathers and flowers and fine-spun wool, descending from the gallery.

The black river of ants swarming the ancestors in vain, rendered impotent in the face of death's advance.

I told them of how Raphael found the courage and the strength to release me from my oath before the end, freeing me to banish Focalor a second time and close the doorway onto the spirit world. And closing my eyes, I told them how the Quechua ancestors had descended on him, slowly, so slowly, slow and inexorable, their rag-wrapped skulls blank-faced and impersonal, shredded marigold petals falling all around them, ornamental war-clubs raised in their bony, crumbling hands.

"I didn't watch," I said. "I couldn't."

No one spoke.

In the audience, I saw my father with tears streaking his face, and he was not alone in weeping. Beside me, Lianne Tremaine laid her pen down quietly.

"It is the end of a tale that began with the Circle of Shalomon," Prince Thierry said into the silence, fixing his gaze on me. "But it is not the end of *ours*. Still..." He gave a faint smile. "Although it is very nearly finished, I think mayhap it is enough for today. As you can see, we are here to continue the telling of it, and that is cause enough for gladness." He rose. "My thanks for listening."

One by one, folk filed out of the salon, their faces somber and wondering. Thierry paused beside my chair to lay a hand on my shoulder, peering down at Lianne's scribbled notes.

"Well, King's Poet? Did you record the account in full?" he asked her.

"I did, your highness." She stoppered her inkwell, then tapped her temple with one finger. "Pay no heed to my scratchings. Most of it is here. And believe me when I tell you I am very, very grateful for this opportunity." Her voice took on a familiar note, wry and rueful, as she asked a question equally familiar to me. "May I ask how much of it was true?"

"All of it," Thierry and I said at the same time.

"All save the parts left untold," Bao said quietly, glancing at the poetess, who returned his regard with keen interest. "Another day, I will tell them to you. And you may decide whether or not they make for a tale fit for the poets to tell."

"Bao…" I whispered. "You needn't do it."

He gave me a look, his dark eyes glinting. "One should not lie to poets, Moirin," he said. "After all, that's *their* job."

And despite everything, I had to laugh.

EIGHTY-THREE

Matters in Terre d'Ange proceeded apace.

A date was set for Prince Thierry's official coronation, but before it was to take place, Parliament decreed that the issue of House Barthelme's perfidy should be addressed in the court of law.

I attended the trial and testified to what I knew, although I took no pleasure in it.

For my father's sake, I was grateful that Rogier Courcel, the Duc de Barthelme, was found innocent of any legal wrongdoing, guilty only of the naked opportunism of which Thierry had accused him.

For Desirée's sake, I was grateful that his younger son Aristide was found innocent and blameless in the whole affair. She seemed fond of the lad, and he of her.

Claudine de Barthelme and her eldest son Tristan were another matter.

They were found guilty of the charge of suborning treason. Influenced by a heartfelt plea from the young Dauphine, who harbored conflicted feelings for what had been her foster-family for a good two years, the court did not accord them the sentence of death they deserved, or even the lesser sentence of exile, but merely sentenced them to a stay of ten years in imprisonment and stripped them of their titles and holdings.

The Duchese de Barthelme heard her sentence read aloud with unbowed pride, her chin held high.

Her pretty young son Tristan looked stricken throughout, and I could not help but pity him a little.

Only a little.

I had not forgotten how skillfully he manipulated Desirée's affections, nor how cunning he was in seeking to exploit the poor chambermaid when I had spied upon him. He had done his mother's bidding, abetting her in her schemes. He may have been too young to fully grasp the magnitude of his treason at the time, but he was old enough to know better now—and he had kept his mother's secrets.

Thanks to Prince Thierry's inclination toward clemency, the sailor Edouard Durel, who had confessed to treason, was not sentenced to death, either. He, too, was given a prison sentence, and barred from ever sailing again under a royal charter. True to his word, Balthasar Shahrizai discreetly saw to it that his wife and daughter would be cared for, with Thierry's tacit approval.

It was a relief to have it done.

I kept the candle that Sister Gemma had given me, but I did not light it. After all his years of unsubtle hints, it was Bao who now proved reluctant, suggesting that we wait until journeying to Alba.

"Are you reconsidering?" I asked him.

He gave me a puzzled look. "Reconsidering what?"

"Us," I said softly. With the city buzzing with gossip over the annulment of the betrothal between Desirée and Tristan, and the Duc de Barthelme initiating proceedings to annul his own marriage, I couldn't help but think of it. "Me. The entire notion of building a family together."

"No!" Bao's puzzled look turned to shock. "Gods, no, Moirin! It's just…." He groped for words. "I've been dreaming of it again. Of the stone doorway, and…and bears. Or a bear. A very, very large one. And I think…." He took a deep breath. "I think I would like to know that your bear-goddess accepts me before we do this."

"What happens if She doesn't?" I asked.

Bao was quiet a moment. "I don't know," he said at length. "But I think…" He pressed one hand to his chest. "I think her spark inside me would die. That's what would have happened to you, isn't it?"

"Aye." I hadn't thought it through before, and I felt a little sick. "And if it did…"

"I would die, too," Bao said quietly. "So I would rather wait, and be sure that if I must leave you a widow, it is not a pregnant one."

My eyes stung. "At least it would leave me a part of you!"

"One I'm not sure I could bear to lose." He brushed my hair back with one hand. "Do me this kindness, Moirin, and wait."

I eyed him. "You're sure you need to go there?"

"You need to ask?" Bao gave me a wry smile. "Yes, Moirin. It is your own *diadh-anam* that tells me so, and I suspect if I fail to heed it, it will gutter and die all the same." His smile faded. "I only wish I felt more surely that I am someone a foreign god would wish to claim."

"You are!" I said.

Bao shrugged. "We will see."

Before the date of his coronation, Prince Thierry summoned another audience to conclude the tale of our sojourn in Terra Nova. He told the tale himself, relating how Raphael's army of ants had laid waste to the crops of the Quechua as they fled back to their native jungle, leaving an immense swath of barren land in their wake. And he told the audience how I spent every waking hour in the newly replanted fields, walking the endless rows, causing the plants to quicken and grow an entire season's worth in a matter of weeks.

When he had finished, an attendant entered the salon carrying a specimen from the glass pavilion wherein all manner of exotic plants were grown, this one a small Aragonian orange tree in a large pot, hard little green fruits clustered on its branches.

"Cousin, I owe you an apology for failing to consult you in this matter," Thierry said to me. "I know others have sought to exploit your gift. And I know it was given to you by your Maghuin Dhonn, and it was meant to be used freely or not at all." He gestured at the audience. "But these good people have heard tales of magic and wonder, and I would take it as a personal favor if you would show them a simple taste of it."

I rose. "For you, my highness, of course."

There were murmurs in the audience, and some muttering about theatrics and parlor tricks. I did not sense any real malice in it, only a reactionary disbelief. I did not blame them. It is one thing to listen to tales of wonder from a distant land, and another to be told one is about to witness *magic* wrought in a familiar, urbane setting.

A blonde woman I recognized as the Marquise de Perigord raised an inquiring hand. "Is it permitted to inspect the tree, your highness? I do not mean to be contentious, but..." She gave a delicate shrug. "Lady Moirin and her husband have collaborated with Eglantine House to show us clever illusions before. One wishes to be sure."

Thierry beckoned to her. "Of course."

The Marquise and several other peers came forward to inspect the tree to their satisfaction, riffling through the leaves and poking their fingers into the soil to make sure nothing was hidden there, one lord even going so far as to pluck an unripe fruit and gouge it with his thumbnail, making a face as he sucked the sour juices. At last, they were forced to own that the tree was nothing more than it seemed.

I stroked its leaves. "His highness spoke an untruth unwittingly," I announced. "It is the gift of the Maghuin Dhonn Herself that allows me to open pathways others cannot, but the path onto which this opens is a gift of my father's bloodline." Finding him in the audience, I met his eyes and smiled. "I have seen them in my thoughts since I was small. The gods of Terre d'Ange. Always and ever, Naamah, the bright lady. And Anael the Good Steward, the man with a seedling cupped in his palm. Desire and fruition, the things that sustain life and love."

Summoning the twilight, I blew softly over the tree.

It grew several inches, stretching its slender trunk, extending its leaves. The bright green globes nestled in its branches swelled, their rinds turning slowly from green to vibrant orange as they ripened.

A soft sigh ran through the salon. Now they believed.

Thierry bowed to me. "Thank you, Moirin."

The remainder of the tale was told without theatrics; the tale of our return, the losses suffered along the way. Magic and wonder gave way to politics, intrigue, and trade-rights, augmented by the presence of Eyahue and Temilotzin, representing the interests of Emperor Ach-cuatli.

As soon as discretion permitted, Bao and I made a polite escape, and paid another visit to Desirée.

The day before Thierry's coronation, Bao had scheduled an appointment with Lianne Tremaine to tell the King's Poet the whole truth of what had transpired in the Temple of the Ancestors in Qusqu.

Since he wished to go alone, I spent the day with my father, walking the streets of the City of Elua with him, marveling once more at the simple, easy grace he dispensed with his mere presence, offering his benediction to any who asked for it.

Bao was late returning to our house, and silent and introspective when he did. The shadows were thick around him that evening.

"Do you wish to speak of it?" I asked him.

He shook his head. "No."

Trusting to my instincts, I let him be. We slept side by side in the great bed in the master chamber without touching, beneath the high rafters where an iron hook had once dangled from a great chain.

I awoke to wind and rain.

Sleep-addled, for a moment I thought myself back in the Temple of the Ancestors with Focalor's storm raging through the doorway I had opened. But no; it was a warm wind, and a benign spring tempest that spilled through the unlatched tall doors opening onto a courtyard outside the master bedchamber. Feeling at the sheets beside me, I found them cool. I wrapped a silk dressing-robe around myself and went to peer through the doors.

Beneath the restless flickers of lightning in the sky above me, I could make out the figure of Bao, sitting cross-legged and still on the terrace, clad only in a pair of loose drawstring breeches, his hands resting on his knees palm-upward in the downpour.

I went to him.

Pelting rain soaked my thin robe, plastering it to my body. I pushed the wet hair out of my eyes. Bao tilted his head and peered up at me as I sank to sit opposite him, raindrops clinging to his lashes. "Forgive me, I didn't mean to wake you. You don't need to be here, Moirin."

I breathed the first of the Five Styles, settling my hands on my knees. "Aye, I do."

Overhead, blue-white lightning crackled, illuminating the looming rain-clouds, thunderous and dark and towering.

I breathed and waited.

"It was warm," Bao whispered at length, lifting his hands to the cleansing rain, letting it run down his arms. "Cusi's blood. Hot and thick. Alive. I didn't expect it to be so...warm." He shuddered. "I can't help remembering. And the knife was so very, very dull. I did my best. I tried to make it swift, as swift as I possibly could. I tried...I tried to make it *right* for her. Does that sound terrible?"

"No," I said. "And you did."

Bao turned his hands this way and that, examining them. "Did I?"

"Aye." I caught his hands in mine, capturing them firmly. Naamah's gift stirred in me, lending me a sense of surety. I slid my hands up his lean-muscled forearms, marked with the stark zig-zag tattoos that showed the path to Kurugiri; and higher, sliding my hands up his wiry biceps, his skin slick with rain, his muscles shifting and twitching beneath my touch. "You did, Bao."

Lowering my head, I kissed him.

After a few heartbeats, he returned my kiss like a man drowning, desperate and fervent, and I felt Naamah's blessing wash over us, desire rising in a fierce spiral.

I wound my arms around his neck and pressed myself against him, aching nipples taut beneath my soaked robe. It was a blessed relief when his hands found my breasts, caressing and kneading them.

We tumbled over onto the rain-washed terrace, my soaked hair curtaining both our faces. Even the rain felt like a blessing.

"Moirin..." Whatever Bao wanted to say, he couldn't find the words. It didn't matter. The look in his eyes was eloquent enough.

"I know," I said, reaching for him. "I do. And it's all right. Everything is going to be all right."

Everything was.

EIGHTY-FOUR

The day of Thierry de la Courcel's coronation dawned clear and sunny, the world made bright and new by the cleansing rain. Bao and I awoke entangled in damp, disheveled linens, having made love both outdoors and in bed.

Bao rolled onto his back, folded his arms behind his head, and smiled sleepily at me. Although his hair was sticking up in a dozen different directions, his face was calm and peaceful. "You look very beautiful this morning."

I leaned over to kiss him. "And you look... messy. Come, time to prepare. We're escorting Desirée; you don't want to be late."

"They'll wait for us. We're heroes of the realm, Moirin." He yawned, then grinned. "Not bad for a peasant-boy and a girl who grew up in a cave, huh?"

"No." I kissed him again, then sat back on my heels. "Not bad at all, my magpie. Are you feeling better today?"

"Much better." Bao met my gaze, his expression softening. "Thank you."

Rising, I yanked the linens off him. "You're welcome. And you can thank me by not making us late."

Within an hour's time, we presented ourselves at Court, where the mood was glad but harried. Having passed the night in vigil, Thierry was already at the Temple of Elua where the coronation was to take place, but an ill-considered breakfast of honey-drizzled oatcakes had resulted in a sticky smear on Desirée's gown and delayed her departure. She stood wide-eyed and fearful, clad in a thin silk shift, while Sister Gemma scrubbed at the stain.

"I didn't mean to, Moirin!" Desirée said anxiously. "I'm sorry, I was *trying* to be careful. Have I ruined everything?"

"No, of course not." I glanced at Sister Gemma, now blowing assiduously on the damp spot. The priestess gave me a quick shake of her head, assuring me it wasn't she who had fed the child's fears. That was a legacy courtesy of Claudine de Barthelme and Jehanne's despised mother. "A hot iron will dry it in a trice."

"Of course it will," Sister Gemma murmured half to herself. "A hot iron. Forgive me, my lady, I wasn't thinking."

"It's a big day," Bao said cheerfully, perching on a child-sized chair beside Desirée's miniature desk. "Come, young highness, and give me a lesson to refresh my memory. I fear I've forgotten my D'Angeline letters. Don't worry," he added to Desirée in a confidential tone. "They'll wait for us. We're heroes of the realm, you know."

A quicksilver smile graced her exquisite face, a hint of mischief in it evoking a memory of her mother. "I *know!*"

I watched them with their heads bent together over a slate, Bao's half-tamed shock of black hair contrasting with Desirée's white-gold curls as she solemnly traced the letters of the alphabet and repeated them to him, the fellow student turned teacher.

"A pretty picture," Sister Gemma said quietly, applying a warm iron to the damp stain on the child's white satin gown.

I smiled. "Aye."

"Have you—?"

I shook my head. "No. But soon. In Alba, I hope."

She plied her iron. "That seems fitting."

In short order, the gown was rendered suitable for wearing. Desirée suffered herself to be dressed with a dignified patience that was new to her, and a coronet of white rose-buds was woven into her hair.

There was an escort of royal guardsmen awaiting us under the command of Brice de Bretel. I had always liked the steady-natured young L'Agnacite lord, who had been a loyal and reliable companion on our journey. I was pleased by his appointment, and pleased to see the unassuming deference with which he treated the little Dauphine.

Jehanne would have been pleased, too, I thought.

We rode through the streets of the City of Elua in a royal carriage, surrounded by a score of outriders, Brice de Bretel and his men clad in the livery of House Courcel. Folks lined the streets, watching the spectacle.

There was a hunger in their gazes; and a sense of waiting, too.

I understood it.

Stone and sea! So much sorrow had plagued House Courcel in recent generations. It was time and more for a measure of joy.

And we received it that day in the Temple of Elua. Only a formality, Balthasar had called the coronation. In a sense, it was true. Thierry de la Courcel was the rightful heir. From the moment he had sat in the throne and claimed it for his own, he had been the undisputed ruler of the realm. But this was Terre d'Ange, and formalities mattered.

It had been Thierry's choice to hold the coronation in the Temple rather than the Palace, to give thanks to Blessed Elua and his Companions for sparing him, and to ask their blessing on his reign.

We stood barefoot and bare-headed beneath the sun, the grass damp underfoot and the wind rustling through the oak trees while the Priest of Elua gave the invocation. I gazed at the tall marble effigy of Elua in his roofless altar, flanked by marble columns. He smiled his enigmatic smile, one hand extended in offering, the other hand, the hand he had scored with Camael's dagger, cupped.

Blessed Elua had shed his own blood in answer to the One God's messenger, summoning all the ancient power of the Earth, the very womb in which he was nurtured. I understood better the gravity of that gesture now. It symbolized his willingness to die for his people.

But Elua was not mortal and he had not died. He had passed *beyond*, taking his Companions with him to the Terre d'Ange-that-lies-beyond.

I could not help but think of my final conversation with Jehanne, and wonder what lay beyond the beyond.

First and always, I was a child of the Maghuin Dhonn Herself. I had passed through the stone doorway, and I had seen Her in all Her majesty. Once I would have been content with an eternity in Her presence.

Now I was not so sure. I had seen so very much of the world, and I had come to love so many people in it. I prayed that the tale I'd spun Jehanne was a true one, and there was a final *beyond* far greater than our comprehension, one in which everyone and everything was a part of a greater whole.

Bao nudged me. "Moirin."

I startled. "Hmm?"

"You looked like you were a thousand leagues away," he murmured.

"I was."

Prince Thierry was kneeling before the altar. One by one, a priest or priestess of each of the Orders of the Companions came forward to offer their blessing, laying their hands on his shoulders, leaning down to offer him a kiss. Although he was not the most senior in the priesthood, my father had been chosen to represent Naamah's Order, and it made my throat tighten with pride and love to see it.

Each of their blessings, Thierry accepted with grace and humility. And then the Priest of Elua approached him, carrying a golden crown with points wrought in the shape of oak-leaves.

"Thierry de la Courcel," the priest said in a resonant voice. "Rightwise-born heir to the throne of Terre d'Ange, do you accept the trust of ruling this nation? Do you pledge yourself to uphold her laws and the sacred tenets each and every one of us hold dear? Do you swear to honor the precept of Blessed Elua in all that you do?"

Thierry lifted his head. "I do."

The priest met his gaze. "Then in the name of Blessed Elua and his Companions, it is my honor to acknowledge you the rightfully crowned King of Terre d'Ange." He set the golden oak-leaf crown on

Thierry's head, the weight of it pinning his dark locks in place. "May Blessed Elua hold and keep you."

Thierry rose.

It was heavy, that crown. I could see it in the careful way he carried the unfamiliar weight, his neck and shoulders tensing as he began the process of learning how to bear the burden of a lifetime.

I could see the resolve settling into his bones.

A soft sigh of gratitude and relief escaped from Desirée. Glancing down at her, I squeezed her hand.

"Your majesty," Elua's priest murmured, bowing to him. All of us followed suit, bowing low.

"Thank you," Thierry said simply. "I will do my best to be worthy of this honor." There were tears streaking his cheeks, and he let them fall unheeded. "Today is a day for remembering, and a day for rejoicing, too." He summoned a grin, a hint of the feckless prince he had once been in it. "To that end, I've arranged for a *progressus* throughout the City of Elua, and declared a holiday for all! Today, let us remember who we are, and celebrate like D'Angelines!"

At last, as though permission had been granted, cheers arose, loud and deafening within the temple.

Desirée tugged at my hand, glancing up inquisitively at me. "Moirin, what is a *progressus*?"

"I don't know," I admitted.

"A fête," Bao said. "A travelling fête, young highness."

So it was.

Caught up in my own affairs, I'd paid scant heed to the preparations for the coronation ceremony and its aftermath. As it transpired, Balthasar Shahrizai had arranged for a surprise of his own. Upon donning our stockings and shoes in the vestibule, we emerged from the temple to find that he and a score of our companions had slipped out ahead of us. They had worked in secret with Temilotzin and Eyahue to have a gilded palanquin with a feathered canopy constructed, and Jaguar Knight costumes made for all of them, complete with dyed pelts, wooden shields, *macahuitl* clubs studded with shards of black glass, and tall feather headdresses.

Prince Thierry's—King Thierry's—grin broadened at the sight. "Do you actually intend me to ride in that thing, my lord Shahrizai?"

"Absolutely!" Balthasar's white teeth flashed in an answering grin as he swept a low, courtly bow, his headdress wobbling. "You and the young Dauphine, your majesty. It will be my honor to serve as one of your bearers."

Thierry laid a hand on his shoulder. "You've already carried me far enough, cousin," he said softly.

Balthasar shrugged with careless grace. "What's a few blocks farther?" He smiled at Desirée. "Would you like to ride in a Nahuatl palanquin, your highness?"

Her face glowed. "Oh, yes!"

So it was decided, and much to the delight of the crowds along the street and the peers pouring out of the temple, Thierry and his sister climbed into the palanquin. Raising his own genuine *maca-huitl*, Temilotzin roared a sharp command in Nahuatl, and Balthasar and seven others manning the long, gilded poles hoisted them to their shoulders. The palanquin swayed, then steadied. Beneath the bright, iridescent canopy, Desirée loosed an irresistible peal of laughter, her eyes sparkling with joy.

It was a glorious day.

Oh, aye, there were shadows that would ever be with us. There was sorrow and loss and sacrifice, the memory of brittle bones wrapped in cerements and yellowing beneath garlands of flowers a reminder of death's presence. There was the history of House Courcel, glorious and tragic.

But today was a new day, and a new beginning. The sun shone bright in the blue sky as we made our way through the streets of the City of Elua, trailing an ever-growing retinue of revelers.

Through the dense warrens of Night's Doorstep, where innkeepers emerged to press tankards of ale and flagons of wine into our hands . . .

Up the long slope of Mont Nuit, where adepts of each of the Thirteen Houses came forth to join our train, and *joie* and brandy began to flow freely . . .

On the descent back into the city, our progress slowed to a near-halt, but no one cared. As we inched our way down, tumblers from Eglantine House staged impromptu performances, musicians played, and singers sang serenades. The palanquin-bearers feigned exhaustion, pretending to stagger, drawing giddy shrieks from Desirée and cheerful shouts of imprecation from the newly crowned King of Terre d'Ange as the palanquin lurched in an alarming fashion. Sharp-eyed bookmakers from Bryony House plied the crowd for wagers, giving odds on whether or not the bearers would cause an ignominious spill.

They didn't, of course.

At last, we reached the foot of Mont Nuit once more, and made our way into Elua's Square.

Long tables adorned with pristine white linens were arrayed around the base of Elua's Oak, and a feast had been laid forth upon them.

I was hungry, but it could wait.

Descending from the carriage, I made my way to Elua's Oak. Seven years ago, I had arrived in the City of Elua by stagecoach and paid homage to the ancient tree, leaning my brow against the rough bark and sensing its long, slow thoughts. Seven years ago, a street-urchin had stolen my purse. I had summoned the twilight and chased him, and Raphael de Mereliot's carriage had run me down unseen in the street. Denis de Toluard had been with him that day. And later, it was Raphael who had presented me at Court, introducing me to my lady Jehanne and setting us on an unlikely path of love and redemption, a journey that would end far across the ocean in the distant fields of Terra Nova. I had travelled farther and grown more in those years than I ever could have believed possible.

It had all begun here.

Laying one hand on Elua's Oak, I breathed the Breath of Trees Growing, and remembered.

To the oak-tree, it had happened an eye-blink of time ago.

"Moirin?"

I turned toward Bao. "Aye?"

He gave me a quick, crooked smile. "You're a thousand leagues away again." Bao nodded toward the long tables, and the places held empty and waiting. "It's time."

Beneath his heavy crown, Thierry wore an expression of amused tolerance. At his side, Desirée looked happy and anxious, wanting everything to be perfect on this of all days, seeking assurance that it was.

And there were others who had become dear to me, even Eyahue and Temilotzin, reveling in their roles as honored ambassadors, no trace of the infamous Nahuatl stone faces and hearts on display here. Lianne Tremaine, an unlikely friend, committing every moment of the day to memory. Balthasar Shahrizai amidst his always slightly disreputable clan, tilting his head and regarding me with a predatory fondness I'd come to find reassuring. And there at a table lined with members of the various priesthoods was my father, his green eyes lit with quiet pride, the grace of Naamah's blessing shining forth from him.

A wave of love and gratitude overcame me. I was glad, so glad, I was here among these people on this day.

"They're waiting for us," Bao said. "For *you*."

I took a deep breath. "I am here."

EIGHTY-FIVE

A month later, we departed the City of Elua.

We would have gone sooner, but we stayed for Desirée's sake. After so much disruption and upheaval in her life, she was loath to see us go, fearful that this time we might not return. As her oath-sworn protector, I had sworn on my *diadh-anam* to hold her happiness as a sacred trust.

And so we stayed until Thierry's tactful intervention freed us to go.

"Do you miss your mother, Moirin?" Desirée asked me one day when we were paying a visit to her.

"Aye," I said in surprise. "Of course."

Bowing her head, she fidgeted with a bit of embroidery in her lap. "I think...I think she must miss you, too. That's what mothers do, isn't it?"

"Aye," I said softly. "It is."

"Thierry said so, too." Desirée lifted her head, screwing up her delicate features in fierce concentration. "*I* think you should go to see her. If *I* had a mother, I would not want to make her unhappy."

I opened my mouth to say somewhat soothing, to tell her for the hundredth or thousandth time that she did have a mother, one who had loved her very much and regretted leaving her more than anything; but Bao forestalled me.

"You know it would mean we will be gone for a time, young highness?" he asked her. "Away in Alba, all the way across the Straits?"

She scowled at him. "I know where Alba is!"

Bao smiled back at her. "Well, then."

"Are you sure?" I asked. "Bao and I will stay as long as you wish."

After a moment of silence, Desirée nodded. "Yes," she said with a child's dignity. "I'm sure. You should go see your mother, Moirin." She paused, her voice breaking a little. "But you will come back, won't you? Both of you?"

I hugged her, gathering her against me. "Always," I whispered against her silken hair. "Always and always, dear heart."

And so we left.

There were farewells aplenty, but they were small and private. When we left, we left without fanfare. Thierry begged us to accept an escort, but we declined. Terre d'Ange was at peace, and I didn't reckon we'd encounter any dangers. Eschewing the offer of a royal coach, we rode beneath the open skies, crossing the land that had become a second home to me since first I set foot on it.

Seven years.

When all was said and done, it was a short length of time in which to have lived so very much, and gone so very, very far from home. With Bao at my side, I retraced my passage across the breadth of Terre d'Ange, remembering how terribly young and incredibly naïve I had once been.

I breathed in the scent of lavender blooming under the hot sun. I savored once more the sharp, piney taste of rosemary flavoring a roasted capon, remembering my first taste of it, and how oddly the woman at the inn had looked at me when I'd inquired after the name of it.

Now it was all different. Herbs such as rosemary and basil were old, familiar friends, and the bear-witch from the back of beyond had served as a companion to Queens and Emperors alike.

Betimes we stayed at inns, and often we were recognized there from the tales that had begun to spread across the realm. But more often than not, Bao and I made camp in a stretch of wilderness or a fallow field, passing across the land like a rumor. When I could, I posted ward-stones and summoned the twilight to conceal us.

The closer we drew to the Straits, the more I felt the pull of my *diadh-anam* beckoning me home. By the time we reached the port city of Bourdes, it was a bright flame in my breast; not a blaze, but a steady beacon, like a lamp burning in a distant window, summoning a weary traveller homeward.

Which was a piece of irony, since the Maghuin Dhonn did not dwell in houses with windows.

Exactly where and how Bao and I were to live in Alba, I didn't know. I reckoned there would be time and more to worry about it after Bao had endured the trial of the stone doorway, assuming he survived as I fervently prayed he would. In the meantime, there were vast reaches of *taisgaidh* land where the Maghuin Dhonn were allowed to dwell undisturbed.

Bao was less sanguine regarding the matter.

"It is good to know that the Cruarch of Alba respects the ways of your ancestors, Moirin, but I am not raising my children in a cave," he said to me in our chamber at an inn in Bourdes where we had lodged for the night after booking passage across the Straits. "You're not thinking of it, are you?"

I toyed with one of the gold hoops in his ears, giving it a tug. "I had a joyful childhood, Bao. Can you say the same?"

"No." He kissed me. "But do you not think you have grown too civilized for caves?"

I smiled. "Actually, I hope not."

Bao eyed me. "We will see."

I returned his kiss. "Aye, we will."

We set sail from Bourdes the following morning, travelling a day and a night across the choppy grey water of the Straits. I could feel my *diadh-anam* quicken further, and I knew Bao felt it, too. And my heart... my heart soared at the first sight of Alba's shores, of the green and lovely isle where I had been born, the sanctuary to which the Maghuin Dhonn Herself had led Her children thousands and thousands of years ago, when the world was covered with ice. A wild energy coursed through my veins.

"Do you not feel it?" I asked Bao.

He was silent a moment. "Aye," he said at length. "I do."

When we made port in Bryn Gorrydum, a part of me wanted to leap and shout for gladness, to announce to the world that I was *home*, truly home, at last. But I was mindful that whatever Bao might feel, he was a very long way from the land of his birth, and that he had given up any life he might have had there to be with me.

And so I restrained myself, which was all to the good as shortly after disembarking, while we waited for our mounts and goods to be unloaded, we were greeted by a representative of the Cruarch of Alba.

He was a dark, wiry fellow with the elaborate woad-markings of a warrior on his face, half a dozen men attending him, one of them carrying a standard flying the Black Boar of the Cullach Gorrym. His dark gaze skated over us, taking in my green eyes and half-D'Angeline features, Bao at my side with his staff lashed across his back.

"Lady Moirin mac Fainche?" he inquired in Alban.

I smiled at him for the sheer pleasure of being addressed in my mother-tongue. "Aye, indeed."

The fellow bowed. "On behalf of his majesty Faolan mab Sibeal, allow me to welcome you home, and invite you to partake of his hospitality." He grinned, teeth white in his woad-marked face. "He is eager to meet with this distant kinswoman who has garnered such a name for herself and hear firsthand of your adventures." He accorded Bao a second salute. "And to learn more of your esteemed husband and his distant homeland."

I hesitated.

Courtesy dictated that I accept the invitation, and under ordinary circumstances, I would have been pleased to do so. We shared a common ancestress in Alais the Wise. Faolan mab Sibeal had a name for being a strong, just ruler, and I had not forgotten that he had sent a generous message of support and appreciation to King Daniel when he named me Desirée's oath-sworn protector.

But it would mean delaying my journey, like as not for days if the laws of hospitality governing the Cruarch's table were honored. It would mean celebrating my homecoming and sharing my tale with strangers, when all I yearned for was my mother's presence. I didn't know how to extricate myself politely. All at once, I felt out of my element, and scarce older than the seventeen-year-old girl who had left these shores years ago.

The Cruarch's man saw my hesitation. "It is an invitation," he said gently. "Not a command."

"His majesty would not take it amiss if I decline?" I asked.

He shook his head. "The invitation stands. You are welcome in the halls of Bryn Gorrydum at any time."

I smiled again, this time with relief. "Tell his majesty I am most grateful, and we will surely avail ourselves of his hospitality when next we return to his city." My *diadh-anam* flickered within me in a silent reminder, and I glanced sidelong at Bao. "But I fear we have pressing business among the Maghuin Dhonn at this time."

He bowed again, beckoning to his retinue. "I will do so, my lady."

"Do you reckon I was right to refuse his offer?" I asked Bao when the fellow and his men had departed.

Bao gave me a wry look. "I barely understood a word out of the man's mouth, Moirin. It's going to take me a while to master the Alban tongue. It's a tricky one."

"Ah, gods!" I said in chagrin, reminded all over again at how much he'd given up for me. We'd been practicing on the journey, but in my excitement on reaching Alban soil, I'd forgotten it wasn't his mother-tongue, too. "I'm sorry."

"Don't be." Bao touched my cheek, eyes glinting with affection. "No matter what happens, I have no regrets."

It heartened me. "No?"

"None," Bao affirmed. "I swear it."

The sailors finished the task of unloading our horses and baggage, and the ship's captain wished us good passage. We were left undisturbed in the harbor while we set about the task of saddling our mounts and arranging our gear on the pack-horses.

It was a fine day, the sky a pale blue overhead, streaked with thin, scudding clouds. A light breeze skirled around us, capricious and whim-sical, now carrying the tang of saltwater and spray from the ocean, now the odors of hewn stone, horse-dung, and the press of humanity from the streets of Bryn Gorrydum.

And then it switched again as I swung myself astride my mount, coming from the west and carrying a hint of deep green forests and sun-lit meadows to my nostrils. A familiar scent, the scent of my childhood.

Lifting my head, I inhaled deeply.

My heart beat faster.

"Mother?" I said softly. The teasing wind caressed my skin, tugged at my hair. Feeling only a little bit foolish, I cleared my throat and called her name aloud, speaking it to the wind. "Fainche mac Eithne! Your daughter has returned, and is bound for the hollow hill and the stone doorway. There, I will meet you."

The wind spun away, carrying my words with it. Bao and I exchanged a single wordless glance.

We rode.

EIGHTY-SIX

When first I had ventured to the hollow hill, it had seemed such a very long journey. Of course, I had been half out of my mind with grief, Cillian's death fresh on my mind, travelling on foot.

This journey passed swiftly.

Our long-legged mounts ate up the leagues with swift strides, rendering the green isle of Alba smaller than I remembered it. And indeed, after the vast tracts of land I had traversed, it was a small realm.

Even so, the wild spaces were a joy to me. Following the ancient markers, we travelled over hill and dale, through forest and meadow, keeping to *taisgaidh* paths and summoning the twilight to avoid the notice of fellow travellers. I hunted and foraged, sharing my earliest learning with Bao, showing him what greens, roots, mushrooms, and berries were edible, and which were to be left alone.

With every league that passed, my *diadh-anam* burned brighter inside me, beckoning me homeward, ever homeward.

I did not count the days, but as we drew nearer to the hollow hill, all my senses were keen and alert.

The forests through which we passed were not so deep and dense as the jungles of Terra Nova, but they were wild and untamed nonetheless. Leading our pack-horses with care, Bao and I picked our way along a burbling stream that flowed cold and clear over smooth, speckled rocks. Beech trees clustered thick, the slanting sunlight filtering gold through their green leaves. Maiden's-hair ferns grew along the banks, and there were deadfalls angling across the stream, thick green moss growing on their bark.

It was in the hush of mid-day that I sensed the presence of others. This deep in the wilderness, it was unlikely to be ordinary travellers. There was a hint of wood-smoke in the air, and when I strained my ears, I could make out the faint sound of piping notes carried on the breeze.

My throat tightened inexplicably. "Bao?" I whispered.

He drew rein, wiping his brow with one forearm. "Aye?"

I swallowed. "I think they're here."

Bao unslung his waterskin and took a long drink, then recorked it. "Well, then. Let's go meet them, shall we?"

Here was a clearing in a copse of hazel trees, where there was a campfire burning and several figures arrayed around it. One was my uncle Mabon, lounging idly and playing a tune on a silver pipe. One was Oengus, squatting on his haunches and poking at the fire with a long stick.

The last…

I loosed a joyous shout.

The last was my mother, *my mother*, her dark eyes shining, her face familiar and beloved as she rose to her feet.

I fairly flung myself out of the saddle, taking several swift steps across the clearing, and then she was there, slender and stalwart, her arms encircling me in a hard embrace. "Ah, Moirin mine!" Her voice was husky in my ear, her hands rising to cup my face. "Let me have a look at you."

Blinking back tears, I drew back so my mother could look at me.

"It's as I thought." There were tears in her eyes, too, but she was smiling. "You've grown into a rare beauty, my heart."

"The child was ever a rare beauty, Fainche," Oengus said mildly, rising. "No one ever denied it."

My mother laughed. "Oh, hush, you!"

Oengus grinned and embraced me. "Welcome home, child."

I turned to find Mabon assisting Bao with tethering the mount and pack-horse I had precipitously abandoned. My uncle jerked his chin toward us with a laugh. "Go and meet your wife's mother, lad!"

For all his insolence, Bao was Ch'in, and respect for family was ingrained in him. He greeted my mother with a deep bow when I introduced them. "It is an honor, Lady Fainche," he said in careful Alban.

My mother looked him up and down, her face unreadable, long enough that Bao flushed slightly under her regard. "So you would face the stone doorway and seek out the Maghuin Dhonn Herself for my daughter's sake?"

Bao raised his brows. "Do you speak against it?"

"No." She laid one hand on his chest. "There's pride in you, aye, and stubbornness, too. That much I can see. I pray it will be enough."

My skin prickled. "Do you doubt it?"

My mother turned toward me, her expression grave. "Ah, Moirin mine! You've done a thing no one has ever done before, sharing your *diadh-anam* with the lad and calling him into life out of death. We hope, aye." She shook her head. "But no one can say what the Great Bear Herself will make of it, not even Old Nemed, who remembers more than most of us have forgotten."

I glanced around. "Is she here?"

"No." There was a troubled furrow between my mother's brows. "Nemed will meet us at the hollow hill on the morrow."

"But tomorrow is tomorrow," my uncle Mabon said easily, coming over to offer me a warm embrace. "Today and tonight are for celebrating." He nodded toward the campfire. "There's a brace of coneys skinned and ready for roasting, carrots and tubers gathered and waiting for the embers, and a stolen cask of *uisghe* begging to be breached. So let's make merry, shall we?"

Oengus gave a decisive nod. "Indeed."

It was a strange and wonderful thing, that reunion there in the Alban forest. We ate food cooked beneath the skies, scalding our fingers on roasted rabbit-meat. We drank Mabon's stolen *uisghe*, the strong, fiery liquid burning a golden trail down our throats and warming our bellies.

We told stories, or fragments of stories, voices tumbling over one another, trying to cram seven years' of absence into a single day.

Bao watched with a dazed look, overwhelmed by the strangeness of it all. "It is very hard to follow, Moirin. Tell me again how Oengus is related to you?"

"I'm not sure," I admitted. "But he is family."

With the sunlight angling low through the hazelwood copse, my uncle Mabon issued a drunken challenge to Bao, wrestling a convenient branch loose and taking a defensive stance. With a fierce answering smile, Bao unslung his bamboo staff and went on offense. Back and forth across the clearing they sparred, their feet churning the loam, until a weary truce was declared.

"You did not tell me your uncle was a stick-fighter, Moirin," Bao said cheerfully, dropping to sit cross-legged beside me, sweat glistening on his skin. "He's quite good, you know."

I eyed Mabon. "I did not know. But he has a way with wood."

Mabon returned my gaze with a serene smile, hoisting the cask of *uisghe* to his lips. "Did the bow I made you serve you well, niece?"

"Aye," I said. "It did."

His smile deepened. "I thought it would."

It occurred to me that there was truly a great deal I had yet to learn about the folk of the Maghuin Dhonn.

Sunset gave way to twilight, dusk falling over the copse. Fireflies emerged in the undergrowth, golden lights flickering on and off in an elaborate dance of courtship. Oengus slumped sideways and began to snore. Mabon passed the cask to Bao and followed suit, arranging himself comfortably.

Bao nodded where he sat, his head hanging low, his hands cradling the cask of *uisghe* in a protective manner.

I glanced at my mother.

She smiled at me. "I like him."

"Do you?" I asked.

Lifting one hand, she stroked my hair. "I do, Moirin mine. He has a good, strong spirit, and I think he loves you very much, for all that he does not wear it on his sleeve." She paused, leaning forward to stir the embers of the campfire. "Cillian wanted you to be somcone you were not. This one doesn't, does he?"

"No," I said. "He doesn't."

My mother nodded, adding another branch to the fire and banking the ashes around it. In the low glow, she looked no older than I remembered, her face yet unlined, her black hair untouched by silver. "It makes all the difference in the world."

"What about tomorrow?" I asked.

She sighed. "Tomorrow is tomorrow, my heart. I do but pray you both return from the ordeal."

"Both?"

"Ah, Moirin mine!" Her gaze was deep and dark and sorrowful. "You and your husband share a *diadh-anam*, child. Did you not think you would have to pass through the stone doorway together?"

"No," I said honestly. "I hadn't thought on it."

"Tomorrow is tomorrow," my mother repeated. "But tonight is tonight." She stroked my hair again, pressed a kiss against my brow. "And come what may on the morrow, tonight is precious to me. Sleep, and be my little girl one last time."

Laying my head in her lap, I slept.

EIGHTY-SEVEN

On the morrow, the mood in our camp was markedly more sober. Since we were less than an hour's journey from the hollow hill, Bao and I began our ritual fast. At sunset, we would venture through the stone doorway.

Bao turned pale on learning I must accompany him. "But why? Your Maghuin Dhonn has already acknowledged you."

"That was before I gave away half my *diadh-anam*," I murmured.

"You didn't know!" he protested.

"I should have," I said. "And in some deep part of me, I must have known. I told Master Lo I was willing to give anything to restore your life."

For the rest of the journey, Bao was quiet. I daresay all of us were, not knowing what the day might hold.

When we reached the foot of the hollow hill, there was a man awaiting us. He gave me a shy, uncertain smile, and I recognized him as the young man Breidh who had been attendant on my first initiation.

"Old Nemed is waiting for you," he announced. "With your permission, I'll take your horses to her place and tend to them ere I return for the rite. She lives near."

It surprised me. "She has a *stable*?"

Breidh shrugged. "No, but there is a lean-to that will shelter them at need. There is a meadow where they may graze, and a stream where they may drink. Is there aught you need from your packs?"

I glanced at Bao, who shook his head. "No."

Once we had dismounted, Breidh blew softly into the nostrils of Bao's horse, then took the reins and led it silently into the forest. My mount trailed obediently behind him, the pack-horses following, all with ears pricked gladly.

Bao watched them go. "Your folk have a way with animals, Moirin."

"Aye."

This time, I knew the way. At a quiet nod from my mother, I began ascending the slope of the mountain, making for an ancient, gnarled pine-tree that jutted forth from the tall hill at a sharp angle. I wondered how long it had stood there, marking and concealing the path. When I reached it, I laid a hand on its trunk, sensing its age. It had stood for a long time, although not so long as Elua's Oak; but it was not the first to stand sentinel here. I brushed a green pinecone with one fingertip, wondering who would take its place.

Behind the pine-tree, a series of rough promontories led to a narrow crevice that led to an even narrower canal. I squeezed through it, my shoulders scraping, feeling the walls with my fingertips and edging my way through the darkness toward a faint, distant light.

"Gods!" Bao whispered. "It's like being born!"

Oengus' low chuckle sounded behind us. "Exactly right, lad."

When the passage into the hollow hill opened, it opened all at once. I stumbled out of constriction into emptiness.

Ah, stone and sea! It was beautiful, more beautiful than I remembered, more beautiful than any man-made temple. Light came from an opening somewhere far, far overhead, illuminating everything. Tall, tapering columns rose from the cavern floor, descended from the vaulted ceiling. The stone was smooth and milky-pale, hints of blues and greens flowing through its veins, patches of pink and rust blossoming here and there.

"Moirin..." Bao's voice was filled with awe. "Is this real?"

I smiled. "Aye, I think so."

One by one, the others emerged behind us, taking a moment to revel in the beauty of the place.

At length, my uncle Mabon stirred. "Do you remember the way, child?"

I pointed to a waterfall of frozen stone. "I do."

He nodded. "Lead on."

There were false passages where one could lose oneself; that, I remembered. We passed them by, climbing the slick frozen fall, passing in and out of shafts of light, past sparkling crystalline structures. With careful steps, we crossed the narrow, rocky bridge over a gorge where dark water spilled over a lip of stone to gurgle and flow far beneath us.

At last, we came to the final shaft that led to the uppermost cavern, hand- and foot-holds worn smooth by many hands carved into its steep walls. This time, I wondered who had carved the holds, and how many of the Maghuin Dhonn had made this ascent over the centuries.

Everything was as I remembered, the shaft emerging onto a spacious cavern of ordinary, rugged granite, the far end open onto sunlight and a vast swath of blue sky, smoke from a cooking-fire trickling upward into a natural chimney duct.

But if Old Nemed had been old before, she was ancient now, a wizened figure huddled in blankets beside the fire, tended by a young woman. The years that sat lightly on my mother weighed heavily on Old Nemed.

"Fainche's daughter!" Her voice was a thin wheeze in her chest. She freed one crabbed hand from the folds of her blanket and beckoned to me. "Come here." I went to kneel before her. Nemed's rheumy eyes had gone as milky as the walls of the hollow hill, filmed with cataracts. She lifted her gnarled fingers to touch my face. "So you've been out and about, eh? Overturning the order of the world, eh?"

"I've done my best to do Her will," I said humbly.

She patted my cheek. "Oh, sometimes you have to overturn things to restore them to rights. I trust you've learned that much, child." Craning her neck, she peered past me into whatever dim fog her vision afforded her. "Come, let's have a look at this young man who thinks to importune the Maghuin Dhonn Herself."

Brushing off dust from the walls of the shaft, Bao came forward to kneel beside me. "Greetings, old mother," he said in a respectful tone.

Freeing her other hand, Nemed felt at his arms and shoulders and chest, loosing an unexpected cackle. "You picked a nice specimen, anyway! Lean and firm, just the way I like them." Her laughter gave way to a rattling cough.

Leaning down, the young woman dabbed at her lips with a length of cloth, and I realized I recognized her from the previous time, too.

Old Nemed waved her away impatiently. "Wish I could get a better look at you, lad," she said in a wistful voice. "Reminds me of my younger days. You understand what we're about here today?"

"I think so," Bao said, concentrating hard on comprehending her words.

Nemed turned her head. "What do you say, daughter of Eithne?"

My mother made her way across the floor, Oengus and Mabon following her. "He understands, Nemed. Both the children know what is at stake."

"I am..." Bao hesitated. "Forgive me," he said, picking his words with care. "But how is it that all of *you* know?" He glanced at me. "I'm sorry, but I do not remember you putting all this in a letter, Moirin."

I shook my head. "I didn't. Did my father tell you?" I asked my mother.

"Not this, no." She said no more.

"There are more mysteries in the world than you know, child," Nemed said. "The Maghuin Dhonn Herself grant it, you may learn them yet." Her wrinkled eyelids flickered closed, then snapped open. "But we will speak of this later, if there is a later. Leave me in peace for now."

For the rest of the day, Old Nemed dozed, attended by the young woman I had recognized—Camlan was her name. The young man Breidh returned, assuring us in a soft murmur that the horses were fine.

There were a dozen questions crowding my thoughts, but I understood without being told that now was not the time to voice them.

Later . . . if there was a later.

Bao sat cross-legged in the cavern opening, gazing out at the stone doorway looming in the glade below us. It was as I remembered, two standing stones twice a man's height, a single slab laid across them. Its shadow moved across the glade, marking the hours like a vast sundial.

"It's as I've seen in my dreams," Bao said in a hushed voice. "And yet it seems such a simple thing."

I nodded. "It is and it isn't."

When the shadow began stretching eastward toward the cavern, Old Nemed roused herself. Reaching for a cooking-pot on the fire, she dipped a finger into it and stuck it in her mouth, tasting it with a slurp. "It's time," she announced in a surprisingly strong voice. "Let us begin."

All at once, it seemed all too soon.

I wanted . . . ah, gods! I wanted to slow the progress of the sun, I wanted another day with my mother—another week, a month.

I wanted to ask Oengus how exactly we were related, and what magic Mabon had imparted to my yew-wood bow, and how he would know I would need it one day. I wanted to know why Camlan and Breidh were attending the rite when tradition held it should be the last two to have passed through the stone doorway, and I wanted to know how many of the folk of the Maghuin Dhonn had done so since last I did seven years ago.

I wanted to tell Bao one last time that I was sorry for binding him to me without his knowledge or permission, sorry for forcing on him a fate in which his very existence was dependent on the acceptance of a foreign god.

But when I glanced at him, his face was calm with resolve. Bao had made his peace with this. He had told me he had no regrets. He had died once, and he did not fear the prospect.

And so I held my tongue and said nothing, and the rite began. Together, Camlan and Breidh dipped their fingers in a jar of salve, anointing first my eyelids, and then Bao's.

"May you see Her true," they chorused in unison.

Old Nemed ladled out two bowls of mushroom tea from the pot that had been simmering on the fire. We drank it down, both of us refraining from wincing at the bitter, acrid taste of it.

The slanting sunlight seemed to thicken like honey in the cavern as Camlan and Breidh helped us to the far opening where my mother and Mabon and Oengus stood waiting. Beyond them, the rocky slope fell away at a steep angle. Below was the verdant bowl of the glade, an immense cupped hand holding a sparkling lake, a scattering of pine-trees and the stone doorway, its shadow long and stark on the green grass.

"Do you remember what I said to you the first time, Moirin mine?" my mother murmured to me.

I nodded. "It gave me courage more times than I can count," I whispered. "I have never, ever doubted your love."

She gave me a hard, fierce embrace, then turned away, averting her face.

Oengus clapped a hand on Bao's shoulder. "Come back to us as one of our own, eh, lad?" he said in a rough voice. "Like to get to know you better."

Bao took a deep breath. "I pray it is so."

My uncle Mabon said nothing, only raising his pipe to his lips, then lowering it in silence.

No one knew what would happen.

Without a further word spoken, Bao lowered himself from the ledge, dropping to the slope below. Turning back, he held out his hand to me, helping me down. Loose pebbles skidded under our bare feet. Bao unslung his staff, bracing himself on it and lending me his arm as we made the long, precarious descent, both of us dizzy from Nemed's brew, gauging depths and distances with difficulty as we placed our feet with care.

At last we gained the bottom. As I had before, I turned back once to see six figures silhouetted in the opening.

As before, my mother raised her hand.

I raised mine in reply.

Soft blue twilight seemed to rise from the bowl of the glade, only a few streaks of gold lingering in the sky overhead. Bao and I walked toward the stone doorway, looking neither to the left nor the right. The doorway seemed to grow taller and taller as we neared it. We passed beneath its shadow and stood before it. Beyond it, the lake awaited us, shimmering in the dusk, lovely, but ordinary.

"So this is it," Bao said without looking at me.

"Aye."

He reached out his hand, and I took it. Together, we passed through the stone doorway, and the world changed.

Dusk turned to night, all at once pitch-black and brighter than day. Stars burst like pinwheels in the sky overhead. Every blade of grass was visible, every needle on every pine-tree, everything near and far at once. Everything was filled with splendid and terrible purpose, and ah, gods!

Knowing what to expect made no difference, no difference at all. It was so beautiful, so unspeakably beautiful.

"Oh, gods!" Bao whispered, tears in his voice. "Oh, Moirin!"

"I know," I said. "I know."

Dazed and stumbling, hand in hand, we made our way to the shores of the lake, silvery and shining, stars reflected in its depths.

There, we waited.

We sat cross-legged opposite one another, Master Lo's last pupils, and breathed. It seemed a fitting tribute in that place. We breathed the Breath of Earth's Pulse, grounding ourselves and listening to the heartbeat of the world. We breathed the Breath of Trees Growing, sensing the deep network of roots lacing the soil around us. We breathed the Breath of Ocean's Rolling Waves, aware of distant seas ringing the island, waves breaking on its shores. We breathed the Breath of Wind's Sigh, sensing the infinite vault of sky rising above us, and the Breath of Embers Glowing, fiery stars whirling before our eyes, heat pulsing in our veins.

There was no telling how long we waited. Time moved differently on the far side of the stone doorway.

A long time.

Long enough for hunger pangs to come and go. Long enough for weariness to settle into our bones, long enough for our heads to begin to nod, so that we must wake ourselves with a jerk, time and time again.

Long enough for fear, and the first inklings of despair.

I rubbed the faint scar on my right hand—not the scar of sisterhood on my palm that Cusi's knife had inflicted, but the one on the web of my thumb I didn't remember acquiring. Seven years ago, I had asked Old Nemed to demonstrate her gift, and she had taken that memory from me.

If we failed, she would take this memory away. All of it. The hollow hill and the glade, the world of beauty beyond the stone doorway. My *diadh-anam* would gutter and die within me, and I would no longer be myself.

And Bao would no longer *be*.

It came to seem that was what would come to pass.

In the blazing darkness, unshed tears glittered in his eyes. "I'm sorry, Moirin." His voice was hoarse from long disuse. "I didn't want to leave you."

"Don't say it!" My voice shook. I clambered to my feet, my legs unsteady. "Please!" I cried into the darkness. "Oh, *please*! I did all that I thought You wished! I know I made mistakes, but I tried, I tried so hard! We both did! Over and over again, we tried our best!" Sorrow stabbed me like a knife, but in its wake came anger. A futile mix of fury and despair seared my veins. "I beg You, do not do this to us!" I shouted in a ringing voice. "Does love mean nothing to You?"

Bao drew a short, shocked breath.

For a moment, it seemed as though the entire world stood still. No breeze stirred the pine-needles. The surface of the lake went as smooth as a mirror. Even the stars overhead seemed to pause in their ordered dance.

A low rumble shook the glade, making the ground tremble beneath us, a rumble rising to a growl, rising and rising to a deep, deafening roar that rattled my teeth and bones within me, a roar that rattled the very heavens. I clapped my hands over my mouth as if to take back my words, then clapped them over my ears to block out the deafening sound.

A massive shape rounded the lake and blotted out the stars, coming toward us, a mountain on the move. Beside me, Bao leapt to his feet, his staff in his hands. He shot me a single wild glance filled with rueful affection.

She came.

The Maghuin Dhonn Herself came, unhurried and roaring. More than a mortal bear, aye; but a bear, nonetheless. Her muzzle was parted, dagger-sharp white teeth glinting in the starlight.

Helpless and awed, I lowered my hands.

Bao lowered his staff.

Pace by terrible pace, She came toward us, brown fur silvered by moonlight, dwindling from a scale that was unthinkable to one that was merely terrifying. And stone and sea, She was so beautiful, I knew I would gladly die at a single swipe of Her immense paw. Still roaring, the Maghuin Dhonn Herself loomed over us, rising up on Her hind legs, the bulk of Her filling the sky.

"I'm so sorry," I whispered. "Forgive me."

The roaring ceased.

My ears rang in the silence that followed. The Maghuin Dhonn Herself dropped to all fours with a thud that shook the earth. With a barking huff that sounded for all the world like amusement, She lowered Her majestic head toward us.

And I understood all at once that I was forgiven, that I had always been forgiven, that I was Her child, and loved.

"Ohhh...!" Bao whispered.

I felt Her breath warm on my face, saw Her dark, luminous eyes filled with wisdom and compassion, love and forgiveness, amusement and apology, and a thousand, thousand things. I saw in their depths Blessed Elua crowned with vines, and Blessed Elua with his hand extended, dripping blood onto the earth. I saw the bright lady Naa-

mah lie down with kings and peasants alike, her face bright and holy.
I saw the good steward Anael walking the fields, touching the crops
and singing. One by one, I saw all of the Companions.

I saw Yeshua ben Yosef stooping to write a word in the dust, and
that word was *love*. I saw Yeshua suffering and dying on the cross, and
his eyes were the eyes of the Maghuin Dhonn Herself.

I saw Sakyamuni meditating beneath a tree, lifting his head,
enlightenment illuminating his face.

I saw the dragon rising from White Jade Mountain in all his glory
and splendor, summoning the rain and lightning as he coiled through
the sky.

I saw the elephant-headed god Ganesha laughing, his trunk
upraised in joy. I saw dark-skinned Kali dancing, terrible and beautiful, her tongue outthrust, a necklace of skulls adorning her neck.

I saw Xochiquetzal trailing a cloud of birds and butterflies in her
wake, and I saw the flower-garlanded ancestors of the Quechua rising
with dignity.

I saw a glimpse, a fleeting glimpse, of the beyond that lay *beyond*.

All one.

All part of a whole.

And then I blinked, and it was gone. Here on the far side of the
stone doorway, there was only the starlit glade, me, Bao, and the Great
Bear Herself. She gave another soft, whuffling cough, Her breath stirring our hair. I laid my hands on Her coarse, wiry fur, running my
fingers through it, feeling Her warm, living presence.

I wanted to thank Her, but there were no words.

She knew anyway.

Turning away, She left us, Her slow tread shaking the earth as She
dwindled into the distance and vanished.

EIGHTY-EIGHT

⬩

Did you...?" I asked, unable to frame the question.

Bao drew a long shuddering breath. "Aye," he said simply. "I saw."

"Well," I said in a display of profound inadequacy, still at a loss for words. "Well, then."

He glanced around, wonder and regret in his face. "We can't stay here, can we, Moirin? Not yet anyway."

I shook my head. "No."

"It's enough to know." Bao squared his shoulders, his expression turning to one of resolve. "More than enough for anyone's lifetime. Shall we go?"

I nodded. "Aye."

We turned as one toward the stone doorway, both of us pausing in surprise at the sight of a figure standing silhouetted in it. It was a young woman of the Maghuin Dhonn, a cloak of starlight seeming to cling to her. Even as I stared, she came toward us, her bare feet gliding over the silvered grass, her face unfamiliar and amused.

"Do you not know me, daughter of Fainche?" she asked; and if her face was strange to me, there was somewhat in her voice I knew.

"Lady Nemed," Bao said in a low tone beside me.

She laughed. "Death can't fool this one, can it?" Her eyes shone in the starlight, dark and clear. "It's good to get a look at you, lad."

I swallowed. "You're...?"

"I'm here, aren't I?" The mirth left Nemed's face, leaving it solemn. "The task falls to you now, Moirin mac Fainche. You've passed the final test. And now that I've passed through the stone doorway, you'll be its keeper."

I gazed at her in disbelief. "Me? But my lady, I can't! I don't know...gods have mercy, anything!"

"Hush." Nemed laid a hand on my cheek, and her touch was as soothing as my mother's. "You'll have teachers a-plenty, child. I've seen to it. But it was to you that my gift passed, and it is to you that the role falls."

"I *can't*," I repeated, feeling foolish. "My lady, I've obligations in Terre d'Ange, and an oath to keep!"

Nemed clicked her tongue. "Do you think the Great Bear Herself does not know this? She chose you."

"But..."

Her gaze deepened. "You bridge two worlds, Moirin mac Fainche, even as your husband has bridged the worlds between life and death. It is not a bad thing at all to let the mortal world know that it has need of the Maghuin Dhonn, nor to remind the folk of the Maghuin Dhonn that our time has not yet passed. You will find a way to honor your oath while making the rite your own. It need not be held every season." Nemed smiled a little. "A place in the hollow hills has been prepared for you, but you are not bound to it every waking moment, Fainche's daughter."

There was a suspicious glint in Bao's eyes. "A place?"

Nemed laughed again. "It is more than a mere cave, Yingtai's son. I do not think you will be displeased."

His eyes widened. "How do you know my mother's name?"

She patted his cheek without answering the question. "It is well that fate has appointed Moirin such a strong protector. But I fear you cannot linger here. A long life and joy to both of you."

"But—" I said again.

Old Nemed, no longer old, but young and lovely, made a shooing gesture at us. "Go on with you! The world is waiting."

We went.

We went with slow, uncertain steps. The stone doorway loomed above us, its shadow black on the starlit grass. I glanced back to see Nemed watching us, starlight sparkling all around her. With an expression of profound amusement and deep affection, she shook her head at me and pointed at the stone doorway.

Without a word, Bao reached out his hand to me. I took it, and we passed through the stone doorway as we had entered it, hand in hand.

In the space of a single heartbeat, starlight gave way to the bright, ordinary light of day. The sky was a bright, cheerful blue overhead, and the grass beneath our feet was green. There were birds singing and a faint scent of wood-smoke on the breeze.

I let out a breath I hadn't known I was holding.

"It seems our long journey has come to an end, Moirin," Bao murmured. "Truly and at last."

I squeezed his hand. "Aye."

When we reached the cavern, there was no need to explain. They knew. The mood was one of subdued sorrow and muted joy. Old Nemed's body lay swaddled in blankets, a makeshift litter waiting to transport her.

I stooped to touch it, then rose, tears in my eyes. "Mother..."

My mother wrapped her arms around me and pressed her lips close to my ear, sighing with relief, her warm breath stirring my hair. "Moirin mine. Ah, child! Don't grieve for her. She knew her time was nigh. This was the ending she hoped would come to pass."

"Did you?" I asked.

She kissed my brow. "I dared hope only for your safe return."

"I'm scared," I admitted. "And I don't know what I'm meant to do."

She smiled. "I know."

"You will learn in time." It was the young woman Camlan who spoke, clearing her throat in an apologetic manner. "It need not come

all at once. We are here to help, all of us. Nemed did her best to prepare us for this day, and we will do our best to teach you." She paused.
"The last thing she said before she passed...Is it true you made the
Maghuin Dhonn Herself *laugh*?"

I flushed. "Oh..."

Bao grinned. "Aye, Moirin did."

They absorbed that in silence, save for my uncle Mabon, who
played a merry, irreverent melody on his silver pipe. "Will you come
and see the place that awaits you?" he inquired, lowering his pipe and
winking at the young man Breidh, who gave him a shy, complicit
smile. "I've helped labor myself to make it ready."

We nodded.

The place was only a short walk away, less than an hour's time. It
was a cave, but as Old Nemed had promised, it was no mere cave. It
was part and parcel of the hollow hills themselves.

There were honeycombed passages, the walls themselves as smooth
and sleek and golden as honey. Light slanted in to illuminate it from
odd angles, openings covered with slatted shades that could be drawn
closed or opened. The main living space was vast and airy, and there
were a dozen other chambers suitable for lodging, and a deep, cool
cavern at the back that served as a larder, stocked with all manner of
supplies.

There was wooden furniture so smooth it gleamed, looking almost
as though it had been grown rather than crafted. There were pallets
stuffed with sweet, fragrant dried grass and herbs. Outside, there was
a stream a stone's throw from the cavern, a meadow where the horses
grazed contentedly, and forest beyond.

It was beautiful.

It felt like *home*.

"We'll stay with you for a time," Oengus announced. "We'll help
you learn all the ways of our folk there wasn't time to teach you after
your first initiation. Do you think you can abide here?"

I glanced at Bao.

He grinned back at me. "As caves go, this is something of a palace, Moirin. I could raise a family here."

"I would like that," my mother said quietly.

I hugged her. "So would I."

That evening, we laid Old Nemed to rest in a green mound in the meadow. It was a somber, peaceful affair. I watched Bao working side by side with Oengus, Mabon, and Breidh, laying thick green rolls of turf they had cut earlier, tamping them carefully back into place. His *diadh-anam* burned bright within him, still attuned to mine, but his own now that the Maghuin Dhonn Herself had claimed him.

Afterward, Mabon played his silver pipe, and Camlan sang in a clear, pure voice that melded with his song, notes rising up into the gilded sky.

And then we returned to the cavern, where there were lamps kindled against the gathering dusk, making the honeyed walls glow warm and amber. We ate and drank, sharing the last of Mabon's cask of *uisghe*, sharing memories and tales of Old Nemed's life and the folk of the Maghuin Dhonn.

Mostly, Bao and I listened.

There would be time and more to tell our own tales in full. For now, I was content to listen and learn, to feel myself well and truly home at last. And I was grateful, so very grateful, to see the same contentment reflected in Bao's face. Grace was not always found where one expected it. My restless magpie Bao had found it here in Alba, in the *beyond* of the fathomless eyes of the Great Bear Herself, in the Way to which all ways lead.

At last it was time to retire. It was quiet and hushed in the pleasant sleeping-chamber allotted to us, a faint summer breeze stirring through a hidden aperture. I set the lamp I carried in a smooth niche in the wall that might have been made for that very purpose. It burned with a clear, bright light, setting the shadows to dancing on the honey-colored walls of the cavern. My gaze fell on the pack that contained the candle Sister Gemma had given me.

"Now is likely not the time for lovemaking and thoughts of plump babes, is it?" I said, feeling suddenly and unaccountably shy.

"Moirin." Bao laid his hands on my shoulders. His dark, angled eyes glinted at me with fond humor. Lamplight glistened on the gold hoops in his ears, flickered along the stark zig-zag tattoos marking his corded forearms, and the hint of a smile curved his lips. "The choice is yours. But as one who has bridged the worlds between death and life, I think there can be no greater tribute than to celebrate the latter."

"Are you sure?" I asked him.

He kissed me. "Very."

It was a good kiss, gentle enough to be reassuring, firm enough to assert his desire, with enough passion in it to leave me a bit breathless.

Rummaging in my pack, I found the candle. Such a simple thing, a slender beeswax taper, sweet and fragrant.

All it required was an earnest prayer and a willing heart, Sister Gemma had told me. Kneeling before the lamp, I gazed at the homely flame.

I saw the future unfurl before me. Like the eyes of the Maghuin Dhonn Herself, the flame contained worlds, worlds of ordinary pleasure and ordinary pain. There was the pleasure of lovemaking and the grace inherent in Naamah's blessing, the bright lady's smile. There was the pain of childbirth, and the multitude of joys and terrors attendant on mother-hood; the first words, the first steps, injuries and illnesses. There was all the immense pride and delight, and all the helplessness and horror.

There was the terrifying prospect of further destinies that might claim my own children, sending them across unknown seas; and there was the peaceful prospect of a quiet hearth and home. There were quarrels fought and forgiveness rendered. There were hearts broken and mended, there were tears and laughter. There were children and grandchildren, and the wisdom and infirmities of old age.

There was life, in all its mortal, messy splendor. And always and always, there was love.

"Moirin?" Bao said behind me.

I blinked, and the flame was only a flame once more. "Aye," I murmured. "I am here." Lifting the wax taper, I took a long, slow breath and uttered the prayer. "Eisheth, I beseech you, open the gates of my womb."

And with that, I lit the candle.

Acknowledgments

As another D'Angeline adventure draws to a close, I'd like to thank my friends and family for cheering along the way. Thanks to my agent, Jane Dystel, and everyone at Dystel & Goderich for their support. Thanks to everyone at Grand Central, and especially to my editor, Jaime Levine.

And as always, thanks to my readers!